2

James Pattinson is a full-time author who, after travelling the world, now lives in the remote Norfolk village where he grew up. He has written articles for magazines, short stories and radio features.

THE UNKNOWN

Mrs Craydon was taken with the idea of digging up the history of the family. And once started she became more enchanted by the project. Even her husband George, having once seen the ancient photograph of a most attractive girl, long since dead, developed an interest in the family genealogy. The only snag was that even Great-Aunt Maud, the owner of the photograph, had no idea what had happened to the beautiful girl named Isabella. Apparently she had completely vanished and to the rest of the family had simply become The Unknown. Would the mystery ever be solved?

JAMES PATTINSON

◆

THE UNKNOWN

Complete and Unabridged

ULVERSCROFT
Leicester

First published in Great Britain in 2008 by
Robert Hale Limited
London

First Large Print Edition
published 2009
by arrangement with
Robert Hale Limited
London

British Library CIP Data

Pattinson, James, *1915 –*
    The unknown
    1. Missing persons- -Fiction. 2. Genealogy- -Fiction.
    3. Family secrets- -Fiction. 4. Large type books.
    I. Title
    823.9'14–dc22

    ISBN 978–1–84782–633–6

Published by
F. A. Thorpe (Publishing)
Anstey, Leicestershire

Set by Words & Graphics Ltd.
Anstey, Leicestershire
Printed and bound in Great Britain by
T. J. International Ltd., Padstow, Cornwall

CONTENTS

1

PROJECT

George Craydon had never been keen on the idea right from the start. He had been more or less dragged into taking part in the project by his wife. It might be all very fine, he said, for people who had notable characters back there in the family archives, but who ever heard of a Craydon doing anything worth writing home about?

'We're nonentities, that's what we are. Always in the rank and file. Menials, that's us.'

'I'm not a menial,' Joyce said. 'What's more, I wasn't even a Craydon until I married you. I was a Tate, remember?'

'Oh, I remember. But what has a Tate ever done? Tell me that. Apart from selling sugar, that is.'

'There's a Tate Gallery, isn't there? And there's probably a lot more stuff if we only knew. That's the kind of thing we might find out. And there'll be other names too, lots of them. The further back you go, the more you find. It's a tree, you see. It has loads of branches. It's going to be fun.'

George, forty-five years old, going bald and developing a paunch, worked in a bank and looked forward to the day when he would retire on a pension and no longer have to do a job that bored him. Joyce, two years younger and still not unattractive, helped part-time in a charity shop. They had a son and daughter who were both grown up and had flown the nest some time ago. They lived in a three-bedroom, semi-detached house in a quiet cul-de-sac in Ilford, with a little garden at the front and a rather larger one at the back. The mortgage had been paid off several years ago and they had no debts worth speaking of.

Taking one thing with another, George would sometimes reflect, they had little to grumble about. Not, of course, that this prevented a bit of grumbling at times.

'Everybody's doing it,' Joyce said.

'Even if that were true, which of course it isn't, it wouldn't be any good reason why we should.'

'Well, the Ropers are at it. Molly told me they'd found a great uncle who was a captain in the infantry in World War One.'

George sneered. 'A captain, eh? Big deal.'

'Well, it's something.'

The Ropers lived in the house next door,

from which they were separated by no more than the thickness of a shared wall. Tom was a travelling salesman, but the Craydons had never been able to discover what it was that he sold. He was away from home for much of the time, but this did not appear to bother Molly. He was over fifty and she was fifteen years younger. They had no children and appeared to have no desire for any. George said this was just as well, because who would want parents like them? Joyce said he ought not to say things like that even if it was true. Which maybe it was. Though she quite liked Molly and could never understand why she had got herself hooked up to a pig like Tom.

She was quiet for a while. Then: 'I think we should go and see Aunt Maud.'

'What on earth for?'

'Well, she's donkey's years old and if anyone can give us some information about our ancestors she'd be the one.'

'Your ancestors,' George said. 'She's not my aunt.'

'Now don't be pernickety. We can do your lot later.'

'It wouldn't bother me if we didn't do them at all. Anyway, where's this Aunt Maud of yours living? If she is still living.'

'Of course she is. We'd have heard if she

wasn't. She's got a cottage out in the backwoods.'

'What backwoods would they be?'

'Suffolk actually. A village called Long Seaton.'

'How do you know all this?'

'I write to her sometimes.'

George stared at her in disbelief. 'Are you telling me you actually write letters in this age of the internet and the e-mail?'

'She doesn't go in for things like that. She's over ninety, you know, and she's never caught up with modern technology.'

'And at that age I don't suppose she ever will. So you write to her, do you?'

'Well, when I say write I mean I send her a card at Christmas and on her birthday.'

'And does she respond?'

'My God!' Joyce said. 'Don't you notice anything? Of course she does.'

'And now you're proposing we should go and pick her brains. Is that it?'

'Why not? It'll be a nice outing. Perhaps the week after next. Or maybe the one after that, to give her time to reply to my letter.'

'Which you're proposing to write straight-away?'

'Yes.'

★　★　★

It was a fine September day when they started on the journey to the backwoods, and from the house in Ilford it was not much more than thirty miles.

'Maybe we should have called on the old girl before,' George said. 'She's probably lonely.'

'So now you're feeling guilty, are you?'

'Aren't you?'

'Maybe I am. A little. I've thought about suggesting it now and then but never got round to it.'

'Until you want to make use of her.'

'That's not a nice way of putting it. But yes, I suppose it is the truth.'

Molly Roper had been in her front garden when they set off. She came out on to the pavement and spoke to Joyce as she got into the car.

'We've found another one. Name of Bridges. Lived up north. Darlington. Had a bakery. Nineteenth century.'

'Good for you,' George said. 'A baker! That really is something.'

Joyce smacked him on the arm. 'Don't be snotty.' She turned to the other woman. 'Take no notice of him. He thinks it's all a waste of time. As a matter of fact we're off ancestor-hunting ourselves. An aged aunt may have memories.'

'If she isn't gaga,' George said.

'There's no reason to suppose she is. Not all old people are, you know. Some of them have sharper brains than others half their age.'

'Well, anyway,' Molly said, 'I wish you luck. And at least you've got a nice day for an outing even if you don't strike gold.'

★ ★ ★

They stopped at an inn for lunch. It turned out to be a remarkably good one and they did not hurry over it. They reached Long Seaton at around three o'clock in the afternoon. It was a rather larger village than they had expected. It even had a post office and a couple of shops as well as two public houses and a church.

'I understood villages were dying,' George said. 'Everybody moving into towns. But it seems that some are hanging on to life.'

'And a good thing too. I've always had a feeling I'd like to live in a village.'

George scoffed. 'You wouldn't, you know. You'd be bored stiff. Nothing going on.'

'How do you know nothing goes on? Maybe there's quite a lot of social activity. Perhaps more than there is where we live.'

'You could be right at that.'

They stopped and asked a passer-by whether he could direct them to Willow Cottage.

The man, who was wearing a rather frayed cloth cap and a tweed jacket that came down almost to his knees, seemed happy to oblige.

'Willow Cottage. That'd be where Miss Waters lives.'

'That's right. Can you tell us how to get there?'

He could and he did, in great detail. They thanked him and headed for journey's end, which turned out to be some way down a narrow, potholed lane with unkempt hedges on each side.

Willow Cottage stood well back from the road, and there was a front garden that had a rather neglected appearance. The cottage itself was obviously old and the brickwork was very much weathered where it was not covered with ivy. The roof was thatched and the straw looked quite new, as though it had been renewed fairly recently. The tops of some willow trees were visible in the rear, and these had no doubt given the cottage its name; or were perhaps descendants of those that had.

George parked the Volkswagen on the overgrown grass verge and they sat for a few moments gazing at the cottage.

'Pretty little place,' he said. 'What you might call picturesque. Fetch quite a bit on the open market, I shouldn't wonder. The sort of place rich people buy for a weekend retreat. Far from the madding crowd and all that jazz.'

'Possibly. But it doesn't happen to be on the open market.'

'No. There'd be an estate agent's signboard sticking up if it was. Well, let's go and see the old dear.'

An iron gate squealed for lack of oil on the hinges as they pushed it open, the bottom dragging on some weedy gravel of the path leading up to the front door.

There was a knocker shaped like a laurel wreath, but before they could use it the door was opened by a very old lady in a black dress.

'Ah!' she said, 'There you are, my dears. I've been keeping watch from the window and I saw you arrive. Do you know yours is the first car to come down here for at least half an hour. Not many people live on this lane and it leads nowhere, you see.'

She was not at all what George had expected. For no reason at all he had imagined a large, rather domineering woman with a loud voice. Aunt Maud was not a bit like that. She was diminutive and her voice was hardly above a whisper. Her face was round and wrinkled, like an apple that had remained on the shelf all winter, and she wore a pair of glasses with steel frames.

'Now do come inside. Joyce, you're a naughty girl. You should have come to see me ages ago.'

'I know. And I've always been meaning to. But you know how it is. Things get put off.'

Aunt Maud gave her hand a little pat. 'Of course. Young people have so much to occupy their time. But let's not stand here. Come into the sitting-room.'

Joyce noticed that she did not call it a lounge. If the house had been larger she would probably have referred to it as a drawing-room. It was small and much of the space was taken up by a sofa and two armchairs with loose covers. There was a fireplace with a screen in front of it and a mantelpiece above crowded with small ornaments and a clock in a glass dome with a revolving pendulum going first one way and then the other. A portable television set on a table in one corner seemed to be the only modern feature in the room.

'So,' Aunt Maud said when they were all seated, 'you've caught this craze for ancestor hunting.'

Which showed, Joyce reflected, that old as

her aunt might be she was not unaware of what was going on in the world. In fact she gave every indication of being a pretty spry old lady who might be a trifle deaf but had all her wits about her.

'George hasn't,' Joyce said. 'He's only here on sufferance. But I think it's fun. You never know what you might find until you start looking.'

'Could be some black sheep, my dear. Have you thought of that?'

'Oh, I hope there are. It would make it more exciting. Do you know of any?'

'Only Uncle Thomas. My uncle, that is. Died years ago. You haven't heard of him?'

'No. What did he do?'

'It seems he was treasurer of some charity. Ran off with the funds and lost it all on the roulette tables in Monte Carlo.'

'Oh dear! Did he go to prison?'

'No. Committed suicide. Threw himself in front of a train. I was a child at the time and I didn't hear about it until years later. I have a vague memory of him as a smartly-dressed man with black hair and a moustache and side whiskers.'

George was sitting up and taking notice now. 'Well, well! A skeleton in the cupboard.'

'Not your cupboard,' Joyce said.

'Of course not. The Craydons have always

been an honest lot.'

'As far as you know.'

'Now, now,' Aunt Maud said. 'No bickering, please. I've got some photographs which I think might interest you.'

She went to a cupboard on one side of the fireplace, opened it and took a large cardboard box from a shelf inside. This she carried to a table by the window. Joyce stood up and joined her, but George remained sitting. Aunt Maud removed the lid of the box to reveal that it contained a jumble of photographs of varying sizes and no kind of order.

'I've always meant to put them in an album but never got round to it.'

She upended the box and the photographs fell in a heap on the table. Most were the usual kind of amateur snapshots, some with dates and names on the back but many with no identification mark at all. Fortunately Aunt Maud had a remarkably good memory and was able to name members of the family whom Joyce had never met; many having been dead long before she was born. There was even one of the miscreant Thomas in a stiff white collar and with his hair parted in the middle.

'He looks quite honest.' Joyce said.

Aunt Maud gave a shake of the head. 'You

never can tell by their looks, my dear. Who would have thought Crippen was a murderer?'

'Who was Crippen?' George asked; suddenly showing interest.

'Before your time, young man. Before mine too as a matter of fact. Poisoned his wife and ran off with a floozie named La Neve or some such. They caught him on a ship going to America. She was dressed as a boy.'

'Well, well! The things they got up to in those days.'

'Now here,' Aunt Maud said, 'are some that might really interest you.'

The photographs she had picked out were quite small, about two and a half inches by three, but they were professional jobs; very old but still in perfect condition. One of them had printed on the back. Edwin T. Watson, The Studio, Haymarket, Norwich. It had a number on it: 628. There was also the information that further copies could be had on application. Written on it very lightly in pencil one could read: Uncle William. Aged 75, 1870.

The picture was of a white-haired man sitting on a Victorian armchair, probably with horsehair upholstery. He had a small beard and was wearing a dark suit and a bowtie. One hand was resting on a small table beside the chair and the other was on his knee.

'Even I don't remember him,' Aunt Maud said, 'but I believe he was a solicitor.'

'An honest one, let's hope,' George said.

'It would hardly make any difference now whether he was or not. But let's give him the benefit of the doubt.'

They continued sorting out the old photographs and came to one of a young girl, possibly sixteen or seventeen years old.

'Oh, she's pretty,' Joyce said.

George got up to take a look and he too was impressed. 'She certainly is. A real beauty. Who is she?'

Joyce turned the card over and read: Isabella. Age 16½. There was no date. She was standing and looking straight at the camera with a faint smile which might have had a trace of mockery in it. Her hair hung down in ringlets on each side of her face and she was wearing a white frock, taken in at the waist. She had white stockings and black shoes with silver buckles. She had obviously been dressed for the occasion and was maybe making something of a joke of it.

'Ah!' Aunt Maud said. 'That's Bella. One of the Fosters.'

The way she said it made Joyce look up. 'You knew her?'

'Oh dear me no. She was gone before I was born.'

'Gone? You mean she was dead?'

'Almost certainly. But also gone away. There was some mystery about her, and as a child I was never told anything to do with her. In fact her name was hardly ever mentioned in my hearing. It was as if there was some dreadful secret regarding her that mustn't be mentioned in front of the children. Later I lost interest, so I really don't know what happened to her.'

'What a pity. Sounds as if it might be worth hearing. Obviously she didn't have any children or you'd have known about them.'

'Oh yes. It's rather a wonder really that this photograph should have survived.'

'Are there any others? When she was older perhaps.'

'None at all. At least not in my collection. I doubt whether any exist. You can keep that one if you like. In fact you may as well take the lot. I don't really want to keep them.'

'You're sure?'

'Quite sure. This is the first time I've looked at them for years, and if they're of any interest to you you're welcome to them.'

'Well, thank you very much. And if we discover any interesting items of family history we'll come and let you know.'

'Is that a promise?'

'Yes, it's a promise.'

'Well mind you keep it.'

★　★　★

She insisted on providing them with some refreshment before they left: tea and cakes. These were brought in by a plump middle-aged woman whom she introduced as Mrs Biggs. She was a home-help, and Aunt Maud admitted that she had no idea how she would have managed without this competent and good-natured woman.

'I should have had to go into an old people's home.' She gave a little shiver. 'Perish the thought.'

'That won't happen while I'm around,' Mrs Biggs said. 'You can be sure of that.'

★　★　★

On the way home George remarked that the old girl appeared to be quite contented.

'How's she situated financially?'

'She was a teacher. Finished as headmistress of a primary school, so she'll have a decent pension, index-linked. She may have quite a bit put away.'

'I hope she's made a will. With us in it.'

15

'Don't be so mercenary.'

'Well, better us than a cats' home.'

Joyce smacked his arm. But the thought had been in her mind too, even though she did not admit it.

After a while George said musingly: 'That Isabella; I wouldn't be surprised if she was the most interesting one of all your lot. She was a real charmer, judging by that photograph. I'd really like to know what happened to her. The others must have known something.'

'Well, whatever they may or may not have known, they were obviously not passing the information on to Aunt Maud, and she's the only one who comes anywhere close to being a contemporary. So if she knows nothing it's dead certain nobody else in the family will have a clue. I'm afraid we shall just have to write dear Bella off as an unsolved mystery.'

2

EXECUTION

She had told herself that she would not go to the execution, that nothing in the world could persuade her to be a witness to that gruesome event. It would be too horrifying. It would live with her for the rest of her life. It would haunt her. It would be in her dreams, her nightmares for ever. There was every reason she could think of for not going. Strong reasons. Indeed, the strongest.

And yet she had come.

It was not as though she were not involved, that she could attend simply as one of these hundreds of others who had come to enjoy the spectacle. Here they all were, gathered shoulder to shoulder on the ground or gazing from the windows of private houses and the hotels that must have been doing excellent business that day. No doubt rooms overlooking the square had been reserved for days, if not weeks, ahead. Many of those who were here had, she imagined, been early enough to observe the erection of that grim instrument which had been specifically designed for the

17

efficient severing of a human head from the body to which until that moment it had been for a lifetime attached.

It was an instrument that had taken its name from Dr Guillotin, who had proposed its use as a more humane method of execution than the axe. It had acquired its evil reputation in the Reign of Terror when aristocrats and others were taken to it in tumbrels while the citizens looked on and cheered. Even Robespierre was forced to submit his neck to it in the end. Now, although the victims of Madame la Guillotine came to her only singly the crowds still gathered to watch an execution.

And she was there with them, unrecognised by all those pressing around her but the only one among those hundreds who had so intimate an interest in what was soon to happen.

By dint of much perseverance she had forced her way almost to the front of the crowd where she was so close to that dread instrument that she could see its every details. A man, whom she took to be the executioner, had tested it by drawing the massive triangular blade to the top of the frame and then releasing it, as though to make quite sure that it would perform its duty satisfactorily when the time arrived.

As if there could really be any doubt of that!

It had made her shudder, anticipating in her mind the fearful moment when a human neck would be there to provide some slight resistance to the final inches of the blade's descent.

She was living that moment already, though she knew that it might not come for another hour or possibly more. She felt a weakness in her legs and wondered whether they would continue to support her throughout the ordeal. Suppose she were to collapse and be trampled underfoot by the crowd. She caught snatches of conversation, ribald comments, laughter even, and she resented it. To these oafs it was nothing but an entertainment, almost as if it had been arranged simply for their benefit.

To her it was all so different. She felt as though she herself were a participant in the performance, not a mere member of the audience. And in a way she was; for had she not been involved in much that had led to this final scene of the drama? Or, to be more precise, the tragedy.

As time passed she had a feeling that the crowd was becoming impatient. Many of them had been there since early morning. Some of the more provident had brought food and drink with them. Those in the hotels were no doubt being well supplied. Some she could see had spyglasses in order to get a better sight of the proceeding. Nobody wanted to miss a moment of performance.

Those with the best positions were the first to catch sight of the main players in the drama but the news quickly spread to the rest and a hush fell on the gathering.

It was the priest whom she saw first. He had a book in his hand from which he appeared to be reading, although she could not hear his voice. He was walking backwards, facing the condemned man, as though to hide from his sight the dread instrument that must end his life.

Then she saw the man. It was the first time in weeks. She might have visited him in prison but she had not been able to bring herself to do it. What would there have been to say?

She thought he looked ill. His hands were manacled behind his back and there were chains on his ankles so that he could not run away. As if that would have been possible anyway.

At first he seemed to be looking at the ground, but then he lifted his head and appeared to be searching for someone in the crowd. She knew who that someone was, but she doubted whether he would see her. It might have been possible to catch his attention by raising her arm and waving, but she did not.

Nevertheless, as he drew level with the place where she was standing she thought that for a moment he might have caught a glimpse of her and that the faintest of smiles touched his lips. It was so momentary that she could not be certain that she had not imagined it. Then the chanting priest, a large fat man with a tonsured head, had gone by with the prisoner following.

He stumbled just before he reached the guillotine. They had to help him into the correct position, lying face downward, so that he was the only one there who could not see the blade that was to end his life. The crowd was silent now, as if for a moment it had lost its corporate voice.

She heard the rattle of the blade descending, but she did not see it reach the victim, for she had turned her head away. She heard a sound go up from the crowd; it was like the baying of some pack of wild beasts, inhuman. But she heard nothing more and saw nothing more. The entire scene had vanished from her consciousness.

She had fainted.

3

BELLA

Her name was Isabella Foster. To friends and relations she had always been known as Bella. There could not have been a more fitting name, for she was indeed beautiful. No one could have disputed the fact, and no one attempted to do so.

She had two younger sisters, quite pretty girls but not exceptional. She was.

Mr Foster was an ironmonger, and a prosperous one. A lean, hatchet-faced man who seldom smiled, he had a shop in a village a few miles south of Norwich and a large house adjoining it. To the rear of the shop was a range of outbuildings in which could be found a stock of hardware goods so comprehensive that few customers ever went away having failed to discover exactly what they required. From galvanised iron rainwater tanks of every size and shape to garden rakes and from scythes to table knives, all were there if you were prepared to seek them out. You could also have your horse shod if need be, for there was a smithy in an open-fronted shed nearby. Naturally Mr Foster himself did no such manual labour; he employed a smith named Arthur Hodges and a pimply apprentice who probably had a name but was always referred to as 'the boy'.

Henry Foster, having accumulated and invested a considerable amount of wealth, and with the prospect of gaining more every day, had certain aspirations towards raising himself and his family in the social scale. In this endeavour he was encouraged by his wife, Miriam, who had always felt that she had married rather beneath her when she agreed, after much hesitation, to become the wife of a village ironmonger.

Not that any unbiased person would have considered it much of a descent in the social pecking order for the daughter of a struggling tenant farmer with no more than a hundred acres of rather poor soil from which to scratch a living. But there it was; and if Mrs Foster had not brought much of a dowry with her she did at least possess certain physical attributes to pass on to her daughters, especially the eldest.

The girls themselves benefited by being sent as weekly boarders to a rather expensive private school run by a maiden lady of impeccable parentage but slender means. This school was some three miles east of

Norwich and at weekends Foster himself would drive a pony and trap to bring the pupils home for the weekend.

At some extra charge Miss Lowther could arrange for any of her girls — there were no boys — to take dancing lessons from a master of the art named Gerald Hardacre, who came up by train from London twice a week for that purpose.

This gentleman, if such he could be called, was possibly thirty-five years old and had a certain raffish air about him. He had oiled black hair, side whiskers and a small moustache. There were rumours that he was related, whether closely or distantly could not be determined, to Miss Lowther. But if this were so, neither of them ever gave any indication that it was.

Another rumour had it that Hardacre was connected in some way with the stage. And this might have been true, though nobody could advance any hard evidence for it. When the weather was fine he would walk from Norwich to the school, stick in hand and hat tilted at a jaunty angle, the very picture of a debonair man-about-town. One thing about Gerald Hardacre that could not be denied was that he was an excellent dancing-master. And another thing was that Isabella Foster was his star pupil.

'You,' he once told her, 'have it in you. All I have to do is bring it out. And that is not in the least difficult.'

It helped, of course, that she loved dancing. With her it amounted almost to an obsession.

She was sixteen when he first hinted at the possibility of a career on the stage. It had never occurred to her before, but now that he had put the idea into her head she could not help being fascinated by such a prospect. If only it could come true!

Yet she kept such thoughts to herself. She felt sure that her parents, especially her father, would never approve of such a thing. The stage! A dancer! It was unthinkable.

Moreover, after that initial hint Hardacre himself appeared to forget about it for a time. Certainly he did not mention it again and might perhaps have forgotten it; though she had not.

★ ★ ★

Months passed. It came into her mind now and then to broach the subject herself; to ask him whether he had been serious when he made that suggestion regarding a career on the stage. But she feared he might laugh and say that he had only been joking. So she said nothing.

Almost a year went by. She was seventeen now and would soon be leaving Miss Lowther's establishment. What she would do then was a question that had never been discussed. What did young ladies in her position do? Help their mothers with household duties; go to balls and parties while waiting for a suitable young man to make an offer of marriage? It all seemed so vague.

Then, quite out of the blue, Gerald Hardacre said: 'Well? Have you thought about it?'

She knew at once what he was referring to, though all those months had passed and there had not been so much as a hint that it was still in his mind. Now she realised that, far from forgetting the suggestion he had made, he had simply been biding his time, letting the idea take root, as it were, in her mind until the moment seemed right to repeat it.

Adroitly now he had managed matters so that they were alone together, and he spoke with some urgency.

'Of course you have. And it's what you want, isn't it? Don't deny it. I can see it in your eyes. And I can arrange everything. All you need to say is yes.'

But still she hesitated. It was such a big

step to take; leaving home and putting her trust in a man about whom she really knew so little. So for a time she resisted his blandishments even though her inclination was to give in and follow the dream.

Oddly enough it was her father himself who caused her to make the fateful decision. They had an argument over some trivial matter which she could never afterwards remember, even though it was to prove of such consequence to her future existence. The man had lost his patience and in a fit of temper had slapped her on the cheek.

It was no gentle slap; it really stung and brought tears to her eyes. Moreover, it was so unexpected, for he was not a man who habitually resorted to physical violence. Indeed, he regretted it at once and felt an urge to apologise, perhaps even to beg for her forgiveness, but he hesitated, and then it was too late.

'Beast!' she said. And the look she gave him was of such bitterness that it quite took him aback.

Then she turned and ran from the room. In that moment, though he did not realise it at the time, and indeed could not have guessed such a thing, he had lost a daughter.

★　★　★

For the rest of the weekend relations between the two of them were strained. Though neither of them made any reference to the incident, neither of them had forgotten it. Mrs Foster could not help noticing that something was amiss, but she refrained from making any remark. If either husband or daughter felt inclined to confide in her she was willing to listen to what they had to say, but it was up to them to make the approach; and as neither appeared inclined to do so she said nothing.

Then on the Monday morning the girls went back to school, and on his appointed day Gerald Hardacre came up from London to instruct the young ladies in the art of dancing. For Isabella Foster it was to be a visit that would have the most profound effect, for good or bad, on the future course of her life.

If anyone noticed that she and the dancing master had a rather lengthy discussion with each other when the lesson was over, no one mentioned it. Perhaps it was not even remarked, for Hardacre and Miss Foster had become adept at avoiding observation when they had their tête-à-tête discussions, and on this occasion, although the business might have taken rather longer than usual, it was, if observed at all, probably regarded as no more than some exchange of views concerning the dance routine that had just been completed. Certainly no one could have guessed that some much more serious matter was being discussed, and indeed that certain plans were being laid that for one at least of the pair would effect the most complete change to her way of life that could be imagined.

'So,' the man said, putting a hand on the girl's arm, 'you are quite sure this is what you want to do?'

It was almost as if, now that she had at last agreed to do what he had for so long urged upon her, he was himself having doubts regarding the wisdom of the move. Perhaps some trace of better nature, a touch of conscience, had hinted to him that he was taking advantage of the inexperience of an innocent young girl and maybe ruining her prospects in life.

But then she answered: 'Yes. Oh, yes. Of course it is.' And he suppressed those slight feelings of guilt and even convinced himself that what he was doing was for her benefit rather than his own. For was he not putting her on the path to a glittering career in the sphere that she yearned to enter? What could possibly be wrong with that?

So it was settled.

'You will never regret this,' he said.

And hoped that it might be true.

4

DEPARTURE

It happened at the weekend. To be more precise, it was the Sunday; eleven p.m. or a little later.

The Foster household was not in the habit of staying up late. After all, what was there to stay up for? It was simply a waste of fuel now that the autumn weather was becoming daily more like winter. So at eleven o'clock all were in bed and almost certainly sound asleep.

All, that is, with one exception: Isabella.

She was certainly not asleep. She was not even in bed, but was fully clothed and required no more than an overcoat and a hat to be ready to leave the house. Moreover, there was beside the bed a kind of trunk which consisted of two basketwork halves, one fitting into the other and secured by straps. This trunk appeared to be extended to its maximum capacity and it would certainly not have been possible to squeeze anything more into it.

Isabella, as the oldest girl in the Foster family, had a bedroom to herself; the two younger sisters sharing another. This was fortunate, since otherwise the operation planned for that night would not have been possible. Even as it was she waited on tenterhooks, fearing that something might go wrong. Suppose one of those sisters should wake and hear a suspicious noise. She knew it was most unlikely, for girls of that age slept like logs and took a deal of waking; but there was nonetheless a faint possibility that it might happen.

Fortunately too, her parents' bedroom was some distance away on the opposite side of the landing from which the stairs descended to the entrance hall. There was yet another bedroom in which the housemaid or skivvy slept, but this was an attic and it was unlikely that anything would wake that young person before the alarm-clock went off at the appointed hour of six a.m., when she would rise and start on her daily round of labour.

Isabella shivered. It was chilly in the bedroom. The flame of the candle which was the sole illumination flickered, revealing that there was a draught somewhere, and it threw dancing shadows on the flowery wallpaper. A cheap tin clock on the dressing-table ticked away the seconds, and she kept glancing at it and thinking how slowly time was passing.

Suppose, she thought, he did not come.

Suppose he had changed his mind or had never intended going through with the scheme. Suppose he had simply been playing a game with her; making a fool of her while all the time he had been laughing up his sleeve.

She almost came to believe this as she watched the guttering candle drip winding-sheets down its steadily diminishing length. Little pools of molten wax formed and hardened in the candlestick and the clock ticked on.

And then she heard it: a faint brushing sound coming from the window, possibly made by a small branch that had been plucked from a bush or garden hedge and was now being moved from side to side on the glass.

It galvanised her at once. She picked up the candlestick, carried it to the window and pulled one of the curtains aside to allow a sliver of light to escape for a moment before returning it to its former position.

Wasting no time now, she put on her hat and coat, took the candle to the door and opened it with great care to make as little sound as possible. With the candlestick still in her hand she tiptoed to the head of the stairs and set it down in such a position that it shed some light on the staircase.

There was now very little light in her bedroom, but she knew exactly where the trunk was, and she picked it up and carried it out of the room. She set it down for a moment so that she could close the bedroom door, then picked it up and carried it to the head of the stairs. It would have saved time if she could have carried both candlestick and trunk down the stairs together, but this was not possible. So she took the candlestick first, set it down near the front door and then returned for the trunk.

The door was a stout one, made of oak, and there were iron bolts at the top and bottom as well as a lock with a massive key which was hanging on a nail in the wall on the right.

Having set down the trunk, Isabella proceeded to draw back the bolts, and since they had not been greased for some time this was an operation that could not be completed without a certain amount of noise. To the girl, whose nerves were already somewhat jangled, it sounded loud enough to rouse all the sleepers in the house, and her hand shook as she reached for the key.

She had never before had any reason to lock or unlock the door and she was surprised to discover how difficult an operation it was. She tried first with one hand but could not move the key; it was as though it were solidly imbedded in the lock, and the sickening thought came to her that, after all the meticulous preparation she had made, all might yet be brought to nothing by so small a thing as the failure to turn a key.

In desperation she grasped the key with both hands and tried again. Still it resisted. She was almost weeping with frustration, but she gave a last twist to the key, and it hurt her fingers but the key gave way with an unpleasant grinding sound and turned in the lock. She lifted the latch and pulled the door open.

Immediately a gust of cold air came in and blew the candle out.

She heard a man's voice. 'So there you are. I thought you were never coming.'

There was a trace of peevishness in the tone, as though he resented having been kept waiting.

She could see him only as a shadowy figure, for there was no moon and none of the houses in the street was showing any light. A few stars were visible through breaks in the clouds but that was all.

'I had trouble with the lock,' she said. 'It was so stiff.'

'Well you're here now. Have you got your luggage?'

'Yes, it's here.'

She picked up the trunk and carried it over the doorstep.

'Give me that,' he said, taking it from her. 'Shut the door.'

She did so as silently as she could, though still the sound of it seemed to her loud enough to rouse everyone in the house.

'Now,' Hardacre said, 'let's be on our way.'

He set off up the street with the trunk on his shoulder and she followed, trotting to keep up with him, her heart beating like a wild thing now that she was breaking away from all that life had previously held for her and was heading into the unknown like a mariner sailing into uncharted seas.

The horse and gig were at the end of the street, and she caught the scent of the driver's pipe before she could see him. The gig had lamps with candles in them which would give warning to any other road users at that time of night that the gig was there but revealed little of the road ahead to the driver.

The man with the pipe had a hat pulled down over his ears and a muffler round his neck, so that, even if there had been more light, it would have been difficult to make out much of his face. It was obvious that there had to be a pipe stuck in his mouth, but only the occasional faint glow from this gave evidence of its whereabouts. He said nothing when Hardacre arrived with the girl, though he might have thought a lot. He was probably being well paid for his services so late at night and had been told as little regarding the true nature of what was afoot as was essential. Possibly he did not wish to know more.

Hardacre stowed the trunk in the gig and helped Isabella to follow it in, using the step on the near side. Then he followed, guided her to a seat and sat down beside her. Having done so he gave a word to the driver to be on his way.

The man cracked his whip and the horse responded, the iron-bound wheels grating on the stones in the road.

Isabella shivered, not only from the chill in the air but also from the thought that this really was a step which could not be retracted. It was all so different, this nocturnal ride in a gig which had almost certainly been previously used for the transport of pigs, from those other rides in the pony-trap driven by her father.

The thought came to her that she might never again see the ironmonger's shop and the smithy and Ben, the blacksmith with his massive arms and ready smile; and again she gave a shiver.

'Cold?' Hardacre asked.

'A little.'

'Well, it won't be long now.'

He did not say what would not be long and she did not ask.

5

HOME

They reached the station at Norwich in less than half an hour. Hardacre paid the driver of the gig and without a word he turned it in the forecourt and drove away. Isabella had caught no more than a glimpse of his face in the gloom and she doubted whether she would recognise him if she ever saw him again.

'Come along then,' Hardacre said.

He was carrying the trunk and led the way through the entrance to the station. This was a poorly lit and depressing kind of place at that time of night and there was not a great deal of activity in evidence. There was a waiting-room lit by one gas-lamp and some cinders in a fireplace gave evidence that a fire had been burning in it earlier. Now that it had gone out the room was decidedly chilly. The furniture comprised of some bare wooden benches and a table.

'Hardly luxurious,' Hardacre said. 'But at least we've got it to ourselves and we must make the best of it for a while, I'm afraid.'

He dumped the trunk on a seat and guided

Isabella with a hand on her arm. She sat down and he took his place beside her. He took a watch from his pocket and consulted it.

'By my reckoning,' he said, 'we have possibly six hours to wait. We could have gone to an inn or hotel, but that might have made us conspicuous. Don't want to draw attention to ourselves, do we?'

'You mean we are to wait in here until morning?'

'That's it. You don't object to some slight hardship for a start, do you? It's in a good cause.'

He had not mentioned this when he had sketched his plan for her and she had never questioned him closely. She had put her trust in him. He was a man of the world and surely knew the best course to take. Besides, what did a little initial discomfort matter if it was to lead to something so desirable?

'No,' she said, 'I don't mind.'

She did not think she could possibly sleep in such conditions, but in the event she did. She woke to find the man's arms around her and her head resting on his chest. She drew away from him almost violently.

He gave a chuckle. 'Ah, I see you're awake. I hope you've had a good refreshing sleep.'

'How long — ' she said, and stopped.

'How long have you been asleep? Oh, a few hours. I didn't like to wake you. After all, it's passed the time, hasn't it? For you at least.'

There was still no daylight, and it seemed to be even colder in the waiting-room.

'Our train leaves at six o'clock. That will give us time for an early breakfast.'

'Breakfast?'

'You sound surprised. My dear Miss Foster, surely you didn't imagine I would be so improvident as to neglect our bodily needs. Never.'

There was a haversack lying on the seat. She had noticed he was carrying it when they set out but had not remarked on it. Now he took from it some slices of bread and cheese wrapped in paper. There were also two bottles with screw stoppers.

'Beer for me,' he said, 'and lemonade for the lady. No tea or coffee, I'm afraid, but one cannot have everything in circumstances such as these.'

Although it was much earlier than her normal breakfast time she discovered that she was quite hungry. She would have preferred a hot drink to the cold lemonade, but there was no way the man could have brought a teapot or a pot of steaming coffee with him.

'What time is it now?' she asked after they had finished their meal.

He again fished up the watch on its chain from his waistcoat pocket and consulted it.

'It's a quarter past five,' he said. 'We haven't very much longer to wait. How are you feeling on this bright and shining morning.'

Rather to her own surprise she felt remarkably well after her brief sleep and the makeshift breakfast. Even the chill in the bleak waiting-room did not bother her. She was wearing a winter coat which reached down to her laced-up boots, and really she did not feel uncomfortably cold.

She wondered what was happening in the house she had left so secretly. She felt quite sure her absence would not yet have been discovered. Even the skivvy would not be up and about to begin her daily chores just yet; and even when she did there was no likelihood of her discovering the absence of Miss Isabella from her bedroom. She would probably be the first to notice the candlestick in the hall and then catch sight of the bolts on the front door and the key in the lock. But that would not be for some time yet, and when the discovery was made she and Gerald would already be on their way to London.

London! At the thought of it excitement bubbled up in her. That famous city was where her future lay. That was where she would make her name and fortune. She was sure of it. She had to be.

★ ★ ★

At the start of the journey they had a compartment to themselves, and the train had scarcely left the station when Isabella had a surprise: Hardacre flung his arms round her and kissed her on the lips.

It was utterly unexpected and also such a new experience. Hitherto the only kisses she had received had been little pecks from parents and aunts and the occasional pouting touch from some shy boy at a birthday or Christmas party. This kiss from Gerald Hardacre was of a different character altogether, and her initial reaction was one of shock. She made an effort to draw away from him, but this was difficult, if not completely impossible, since she was sitting at one end of the seat and was trapped between the man and the window of the compartment. She said nothing. Indeed, it would hardly have been possible to utter a word with the man's mouth glued to hers as if with some strong adhesive. Moreover, after the initial shock of this totally unexpected embrace had passed she discovered that she did not altogether dislike the experience and that it was really quite enjoyable.

Then he released her and remarked, as though the kiss had been of no consequence and was not worth mentioning: 'These carriages are very cold, don't you think? I suppose some day they'll find a way of heating them.'

'Yes,' she said, 'I suppose they will.' And though she tried to speak naturally she could not quite manage it. There was a slight tremor in her voice which betrayed the fact that she was still feeling the effect of that sudden embrace.

★ ★ ★

The train was a slow one. It stopped at all the small stations along the line and at several of them large churns of milk were put on board. At each station more passengers joined the train and long before they reached their journey's end the compartment was full.

Isabella could tell when they were nearing the Metropolis because there were more buildings on each side; some of them houses, rows and rows of them, and others which she took to be factories with tall chimneys belching out smoke. The train slowed; now and then it came to a halt for some reason

43

before going on again. None of the other passengers appeared to be at all concerned about this stopping and starting, so she concluded that it was normal procedure. They passed under some bridges and she could see from the window that there were several other railway lines. Then the train slowed even more and finally came to a halt under a high glazed roof.

'Well,' Hardacre said, 'here we are. London town.'

Someone had opened the door on the side where the platform was and people were leaving the compartment. Hardacre allowed them all to go before taking the girl's trunk from the luggage rack.

'Now let's go.'

Her first impression was of noise and activity. There was also a rather acrid odour which might have come from the engine, a mixture of steam and smoke. There were porters here and there with trolleys, others carrying hand luggage. One of these offered his services to Hardacre but was repulsed.

'I think,' he said, 'we should get something to eat. It's a long time since we had breakfast. Are you hungry?'

In fact she was feeling too excited to be aware of hunger, but she allowed him to guide her to a refreshment room where they had coffee and buttered rolls.

'And now,' Hardacre said after they had finished this light meal, 'we may as well go home.'

Home! Perhaps it was this word that fully impressed upon her the inescapable reality of the step she had taken. In the past home had meant nothing else but the house adjoining the ironmonger's shop and the smithy. Now it signified something else altogether; a place she had not yet set eyes on.

It was not a great way from Liverpool Street station. They could have walked it if it had not been for the girl's trunk. As it was, they took a cab and came very soon to a cul-de-sac with a row of houses on each side, the front doors of which opened directly on to the pavement.

Hardacre paid off the cabbie and carried the trunk to one of these doors, where he set it down and took a key from his jacket pocket. He unlocked the door, opened it and invited the girl to go inside. She did so and found herself, not in any entrance hall but in what was evidently the front room of the house. It was small and the well-worn sofa and two armchairs that constituted the main furniture occupied most of the space. There was a threadbare carpet on the floor, a fireplace with some dead cinders in it, a junk-loaded mantelpiece and a cracked mirror above. The dingy wallpaper was peeling away in places and some of the plaster had fallen from the ceiling.

The sight of this room came as an unpleasant shock to the girl. She could not have said precisely what she had been expecting, but certainly it had been nothing like this. She would never have imagined that a man as debonair as Gerald Hardacre would be living in a place like this. It would have been inconceivable.

He must have guessed what was in her mind; must have been aware of the unpleasant impression the sight of this room had made on her; for he said quickly:

'This is only rented, you know. Just a pied-à-terre until I find something more suitable. And you'll find it's quite cosy when we get the fire going.'

'Yes,' she said, 'I'm sure it will.'

But there was doubt in her mind.

He made haste to show her the rest of the house, as if to get the whole unpleasant business over and done with as quickly as possible. There was a kitchen with a washhouse adjoining it and a backyard with walls on each side to separate it from the neighbours. A rather narrow staircase led to a small landing and two bedrooms, the larger of which was furnished with a double bed and the smaller with a single bed.

Hardacre carried the girl's luggage up the stairs and into the smaller bedroom.

'There's some bed-linen in the cupboard,' he said. 'We can air it when I've lit the fires.'

He set about this task at once. There was coal and kindling in an outhouse, and he soon had fires going in the kitchen and the front room. She was surprised to see how adept he was at these tasks, but she supposed that, living alone, he had to do things for himself. There was no skivvy in this house. Soon there were sheets and blankets draped over chairs in front of both fires and the house was beginning to feel much warmer.

'There's a corner shop down the road,' he said. 'We can get provisions there. And there's a bakery not far off. Are you any good at cooking?'

'I've done a bit,' she said. 'My mother taught me. At weekends.'

'Well, that's fine.' He gave a grin. 'I can see that we're not going to starve.'

She noticed that he had made no mention yet of the stage, but of course there would be time for that later. No doubt he would tell what his plans were as soon as he had worked things out. She decided not to press him on that subject yet. It was enough for the present that she had broken the ties that had bound her to the family and all the petty restrictions of her former way of life. Now she was free to follow her own inclination without restraint or criticism.

Yes, without doubt she had done the right thing.

And if she had not it was too late to turn back.

6

CONFRONTATION

Two weeks passed and the main change that had taken place in the domestic arrangements was that she was sleeping with Gerald Hardacre.

She supposed that some people, indeed possibly most people, might have said that a man of the world had seduced a young and inexperienced girl. But the fact was that she had been only too willing, even eager, to be seduced.

She was in love with him; or imagined she was. Perhaps really she was in love with love. And no one could deny that Hardacre was a charming and handsome man; the kind that anyone might fall for. Moreover, sharing a comfortable double bed was certainly preferable to sleeping alone on an iron single bed with a hard mattress and springs that gave a metallic twang whenever one moved.

'I've told the neighbours you're my sister come to keep house for me,' Hardacre said. 'Don't want to set tongues wagging, do we? People do so love to pass scandal around. Not that I mind for myself, of course. They can say what they like about me. Water off a duck's back and all that. But we don't want a lot of tittle-tattle about you, my dear, do we?'

He had started putting out feelers, so he said. By which she understood that he was approaching theatre managements, though he did not say as much. She wondered why he did not take her with him; but perhaps that would come later. As he remarked, Rome was not built in a day.

It was one of those days when he had left her alone in the house that there came a knock at the front door. This was unusual; in fact it was unique. In the couple of weeks she had spent in the house no one at all had called. The postman had pushed one or two letters through the letterbox, but these had been for Hardacre and were of no importance, at least, so he had assured her. But until now no one had knocked on the door, and she wondered who it could be. It could hardly be someone calling to see her, since no one except the neighbours knew she was living there.

At first she made no move to the door and rather hoped that the unseen caller would conclude that there was no one at home and go away.

But this was not to be. Another knock

sounded rather louder than the first, as though the person outside were determined not to be put off.

Isabella decided to see who it was. She unlocked the door and pulled it open. There was a man standing on the doorstep and he spoke rather testily.

'So there you are at last. I was beginning to think you'd decided to keep me out.'

She saw with a sinking heart that it was her father; and she also saw that he was not in the best of tempers.

'Well,' he said, 'now that you've condescended to open the door aren't you going to invite me in?'

She guessed that he needed no invitation. The only way she could have kept him out would have been to slam the door in his face, and she could not bring herself to do that.

So she said: 'Well, I suppose now that you're here you'd better come inside.'

'Hardly the most gracious of invitations,' he said, 'but I'll accept it.'

He walked past her and she closed the door, wondering as she did so how he had discovered the address. He had taken off his hat and was casting a glance round the room with an expression of distaste, but he made no comment on it.

'Where's that scoundrel?' he demanded.

She answered with some asperity: 'If you mean Mr Hardacre he's not at home. And he's not a scoundrel.'

'That's a matter of opinion. But perhaps it's as well he's not here. I might have given him a sound thrashing.'

He had a walking-stick with him and he made a few passes with it as if to demonstrate what he might have done to the scoundrel if the fellow had been within reach.

'Now Pa,' she said, 'do calm down. Let me make you a cup of tea.'

'Tea!' He made it sound as if she had offered him a draught of prussic acid, but he did calm down enough to let her take his hat and coat and persuade him to sit down in one of the much-used armchairs.

'How did you find me?' she asked.

'Ah!' he said. 'Wouldn't you like to know?'

But he did not tell her, and she wondered just why it had taken so long.

7

SHOCK FOR MISS LOWTHER

The fact of the matter was that on the Monday morning after her departure the first intimation that anything was amiss in the ironmonger's household was given by the skivvy. She had been up and about for some time, raking out grates and lighting fires and attending to other duties, before she noticed the candlestick on the floor by the front door. It had puzzled her, but even when she had also observed that the bolts on the door had been slid back and that the key had been turned in the lock the full import of these facts did not strike her immediately. It was not until Mr Foster got up and she reported this odd fact to him that suspicions that something was very much amiss began to be aroused.

Still, however, it did not occur to the good man that one of his daughters might have made a nocturnal flight from the family home. What possible reason could there have been for any one of them to escape from a house where they had everything that a young lady could desire? It was unthinkable.

Not until the absence of Isabella from the breakfast table did the suspicion that all was not well in the Foster ménage begin to be entertained.

Then, of course, it took no more than a hasty visit to that young person's bedroom to confirm their worst suspicions.

There was a note left on the dressing-table. It was brief and to the point.

'When you read this I shall be far away. Do not try to follow me. I shall not come back. Love, Bella.'

Mr Foster was enraged. Mrs Foster was distraught. The two younger daughters were thrilled. The skivvy was envious.

★ ★ ★

When they had recovered from the initial shock Mr and Mrs Foster had a discussion regarding what had better be done. The girls were not initially consulted.

'There must be some man involved in this,' Foster said. 'She wouldn't run away by herself.'

'But she doesn't know any men, does she?'

'Not to our knowledge.'

'Where on earth can she have gone?'

'Goodness knows.'

'Do you think we ought to go to the police?'

'The police!' Mr Foster was aghast. 'Do you want everyone to know that our daughter has run away? Think of the gossip that would cause.'

'But what are we to tell people? Miss Lowther for instance when you take the other girls to school.'

Foster had to admit that this was a problem. 'I shall tell her that she is indisposed.'

'But Jenny and Paula know she's run away. Won't they talk about it to the other girls?'

'We must give them strict instructions not to mention it to anyone.'

Mrs Foster looked doubtful. She was not at all sure her younger daughters could be relied on to keep such a secret to themselves when they were with their friends at school, but she could think of no reasonable alternative. The maidservant of course would be ordered not to breathe a word regarding the matter to anyone, and she could be relied on to keep a still tongue in her head because there was a threat of instant dismissal if she did not.

★ ★ ★

So a week passed. Mr Foster went to fetch his daughters from school and assured Miss

Lowther that Isabella was progressing as well as could be expected, but they might send her to stay with an aunt in Brighton to recuperate.

'The sea air should be good for her.'

Miss Lowther said she hoped it would have the desired effect; but Mr Foster thought she had a rather worried look, as though there was something on her mind; but he supposed the running of a private boarding school for young ladies was bound to be a somewhat worrying business. It did not occur to him that Miss Lowther's worries could have any connection with his own, but at that time he had no reason to suppose they had.

* * *

Another week passed and the two Foster girls were home again for the weekend. Nothing had been heard from Isabella and they still had no idea where she had gone. Then, quite unexpectedly there came a breakthrough, or at least the possibility of one. The Foster family had just finished their midday meal when Jenny said:

'Paula and I think we know who Bell's run off with.'

Both parents stared at her.

'Are you serious?' Mr Foster demanded.

'Dead serious.'

'Then who do you think it is?'

'Mr Hardacre.'

'The dancing-master?'

'She's always been sweet on him,' Paula said. 'Talking to him in corners when they thought nobody saw them and all that.'

'And now,' Jenny said, 'he's stopped coming.'

'What do you mean — stopped coming?'

'Hasn't been seen these last two weeks. Dancing classes cancelled. Miss L says Mr H is indisposed, like Bella. But we don't believe that either. You can see she's bothered. He's her nephew, you know.'

'Who told you that?'

'Oh, it's common knowledge among the girls, though she's never admitted it.'

* * *

It was the end of his day of rest for Mr Foster. He put on his hat and coat, harnessed the pony to the trap and set off at once to pay a call on Miss Lowther.

He could tell by the expression on her face that she had guessed the purpose of his visit as soon as she saw him. She took him into her private room and closed the door.

'Pray sit down, Mr Foster. Perhaps you would care for a cup of tea?'

He sat down. 'No tea, thank you, Miss Lowther. The fact is I have had some information that rather disturbs me.'

'Information, Mr Foster?'

'Concerning my daughter Isabella.'

'Isabella? But is she not in Brighton?'

'Brighton? Oh, no. I don't think we need keep up that pretence any longer. I think we both know she never went to Brighton, don't we?'

Miss Lowther said nothing. She waited for her visitor to continue, and after a brief pause he did so.

'She has run away.'

'Run away, Mr Foster?'

'Run away, Miss Lowther. Run away with, so I am led to believe, your dancing-master.'

Miss Lowther raised her hands in horror. 'My dancing-master! Surely not. I cannot believe such a thing. No. It is quite impossible.'

'I only wish it was,' Foster said. 'Nothing would please me more than to be assured that such a thing was impossible. But tell me, Miss Lowther, when was the man last here to give instruction to the young ladies?'

Miss Lowther made no immediate reply. She seemed to be trying hard to think of some answer that might not be a lie and yet might also not be an admission that Gerald Hardacre had not been seen by her for the past fortnight. And as there was no way of doing this she remained silent.

Mr Foster prompted her again. 'This man. What is his name?'

Miss Lowther found her tongue, though with some apparent reluctance, as if she were aware that she was allowing a breach to be made in her defences.

'Gerald Hardacre.'

Mr Foster repeated the name with some apparent distaste. 'Gerald Hardacre. And would I be correct in suggesting that he is a relation of yours?'

Miss Lowther, having conceded one point, apparently could see no alternative but to concede another, even if it did appear to stick in her throat.

'He is my nephew.'

And at this moment she was sincerely wishing she had never obliged the young man by offering him employment when he was resting, as it was termed in the profession to which he belonged. She had even paid him a good deal more than she would have had to pay any other dancing-master simply out of the kindness of her heart in dealing with a near relation. And this was how her generosity had been rewarded. He had brought shame on the school, and if word of the sorry business came to the ears of her pupils' parents, as it inevitably would, there was no telling how many of them might decide to remove their little darlings from such undesirable influences as were apparently present in that establishment.

Miss Lowther saw ruin staring her in the face and her only hope was that Mr Foster would be just as keen as she was to repress the scandal. Of course she had always known that Gerald was a young man with a certain, not altogether desirable reputation, and she might have been warned by this that it would be unwise to place him in the company of a number of impressionable young ladies. But who would have imagined that he would have run off with one of them? And she no more than seventeen years old.

'Ah!' Mr Foster said. 'Your nephew, is he? And are you going to tell me that you had no knowledge of what kind of character he had?'

Miss Lowther made no reply to this.

'A nice sort of person, I must say, to let loose among a company of defenceless young girls.'

Mr Foster made it sound like a wolf being wilfully introduced to a flock of sheep. Which was perhaps how he regarded it.

'I shall require his address, of course. I assume you have it.'

Miss Lowther thought for a moment of

denying that she had such knowledge. But she knew that he would not believe her. And how would it have helped anyway? So she went to her davenport desk, opened it and wrote on a slip of paper which she then handed to her visitor.

'What do you intend to do?'

'Intend to do! What do you think? I shall do my duty as a responsible parent. I shall go and bring my daughter home. By force if necessary.'

He did not explain just what he meant by force. Perhaps he himself did not know precisely. Miss Lowther had visions of him putting a rope round the girl's neck and dragging her through the streets. She wondered just how Gerald would react. Would it come to a bout of fisticuffs between him and the irate father? Foster was a well-built man and perhaps would use a walking-stick on Gerald's shoulders. A good thing if he did perhaps. It might teach the young fellow a lesson. Though much good that would do now.

When he went back to his pony-trap Foster left Miss Lowther a very troubled woman, uncertain of what the future might hold for her and her school. But there was nothing she could do to change matters. She could only wait and hope for the best while fearing the worst.

8

WASTED JOURNEY

Sitting in the sagging armchair, Mr Foster made an examination of the room, his expression one of distaste.

'I hardly expected a daughter of mine,' he said, 'to exchange the drawing-room in my house for a place like this. Doesn't it sicken you?'

'Not at all,' she said. 'And of course it's only temporary. We'll soon be moving into somewhere much better.'

She had no grounds for this assertion apart from Hardacre's statement that this was merely a pied-à-terre until he found something more suitable. But two weeks had passed since then and he had said nothing more on that subject.

She was not sure what he did when he went out alone, sometimes for nearly the whole of the day. He said he was still making inquiries and doing some groundwork, whatever that was. Only to herself did she admit to a feeling of some uneasiness. When urging her to come away with him he had given the impression that there was a career on the stage just waiting for her in London and that he had influence in the right quarters to get things moving. But it had all seemed rather vague, and to date nothing had moved as far as she could see.

Then there was the question of money. She was not sure how much he had, but she doubted whether it was enough to last for long. She herself had none, and living on air was no more feasible in the Metropolis than it was in the country; perhaps even less so. The air was certainly more polluted.

Her father had finally accepted a cup of tea and some biscuits. She wondered when he had last had a meal. Perhaps he was really hungry.

She asked him again how he had discovered where she was living, and this time he told her the whole story. So it had been her dear little sisters who had given the game away. She supposed that was only to be expected. They would have been delighted to do so.

'Miss Lowther is most upset,' Foster said.

'I don't see why she should be.'

'You don't see? Why, isn't it obvious that if the story gets handed round it could harm the reputation of her school? And it will get round. These things always do. Of course she's regretting now that she ever employed her nephew as a dancing-master.'

'Her nephew? Are you saying Gerald is Miss Lowther's nephew?'

'Certainly. Didn't you know?'

She had not known. He had never mentioned the relationship. But perhaps he had assumed that she was already aware of the fact. Not that it made any difference to the situation of course.

Mr Foster took another sip of tea and looked at his erring daughter over the rim of the cup. She looked back at him and noticed how much grey there was in his hair. She had never taken much note of it before, and the thought occurred to her that perhaps he would blame her for turning his hair grey by the worry that her conduct had caused him. The idea made her smile. It was so ludicrous.

He noticed the smile and reacted at once.

'I suppose you think this is very funny.'

'No, Pa, not at all. And I'm sorry to have put you to the bother of making such a long journey for nothing.'

'You think it's been for nothing?'

'Well, hasn't it?'

'Not at all. I came to take you back to where you belong. And that's what I intend to do. You'd better start packing your things at once.'

'No, Pa.'

'What do you mean? No, Pa. Are you defying me?'

'Yes, I suppose I am.'

Mr Foster put down his teacup and moved forward to the edge of the chair. 'Now see here, my girl, you are in no position to disobey me. You are still a minor and subject to my authority. I have the law on my side, and though I should be reluctant to have recourse to it, if there is no alternative I may have to.'

'My goodness, Pa. Are you threatening to fetch a policeman and take me away in handcuffs?'

Mr Foster went quite red in the face. 'Oh, you may think it's all a joke, but I assure you it's not. And as for that young man, he could find himself in jail, you know. Abducting a minor is a criminal offence, and so he would very soon find out.'

Isabella stared at him. 'You would never do it.'

'Oh, indeed! And why wouldn't I?'

'You've been talking about the scandal, but what scandal could be worse than that? My goodness, there would be some tongue-wagging then, wouldn't there? And how they'd all love it.'

And suddenly he broke down. He buried

his face in his hands and she could see his shoulders quivering. Strange little sounds were coming from him and she realised that he was weeping.

She was shocked. It was so unlike him. She would never have suspected any such weakness in him. She put a hand on his shoulder.

'Don't, Pa, don't.'

Without looking up he started mumbling: 'You were always my favourite, you know.'

She did not know. As far as she could remember he had never shown any affection for any of his children. He had been kind but strict. Perhaps he had been reluctant to show any emotion. Well, he was showing it now.

He lifted his head and she could see the tears in his eyes. It embarrassed her and she could think of nothing to say.

'My lovely Bella,' he said. 'You are so beautiful, and now it seems I've lost you.'

It was an admission of defeat. He knew that when he left the house he would go alone. And a little later he took his leave.

He had to come back a moment later because he had forgotten his walking-stick. Even as an anticlimax it was hardly one of the best.

★ ★ ★

It was two hours later when Hardacre walked in. Isabella told him at once:

'Pa has been.'

'Your father! Here! What did he want?'

'What do you think he wanted? To take me back with him, of course.'

'And of course you refused.'

'Well, I'm still here, aren't I?'

'How did he find out where you were living?'

'Miss Lowther told him.'

'But I don't understand. Why did he go to her?'

'Because my dear little sisters told him I'd run away with you.'

'Ah!'

'You didn't tell me she was your aunt.'

'Miss Lowther? Didn't I?'

'You know you didn't.'

'Well, maybe not. But it makes no difference, does it?'

'I suppose not. There's another thing, though. Pa said that if he called the police in you could be arrested and sent to jail for abducting a minor.'

Hardacre looked concerned at this. 'He wouldn't do it, would he?'

She could see that the possibility that her father might resort to such drastic measures to get his daughter back had scared him.

Perhaps it had never entered his head when he was persuading her to go away with him that he might be committing a felony. Now the possible consequences of his action must have struck him for the first time, and he had turned quite pale.

Isabella mischievously allowed him to contemplate the awful possibility of arrest and imprisonment for a few moments before easing his mind.

Then she gave a laugh. 'Of course he wouldn't. Think of all the publicity there'd be. His name in the papers and everybody talking about it. He wouldn't want that. No, you can be sure he won't bring in the law to get me back. In fact he's given up trying. It's depressed him awfully. Said I'd always been his favourite daughter, which was news to me. In the end he really broke down. I never dreamed he'd be quite so upset about it. I felt more than a little sorry for him.'

'But it didn't make you change your mind.'

'Certainly not. For better or worse I've thrown in my lot with you, and nothing can alter that now. And you needn't worry about that threat of his. He won't do anything.'

Hardacre looked relieved, and she guessed that for a while he had imagined a policeman's hand on his shoulder and the sound of a key turning in a lock.

Then, as if casting all such gloomy thoughts aside, he said more cheerfully: 'I've news for you. Tomorrow morning we go to see a man named Walter Gage. So put on your best bib and tucker because we've got to impress him.'

'Who's Walter Gage?'

'Walter,' Hardacre said, 'is a man who could be the one to put us on the road to riches. Or, if not quite riches, at least to a decent income.'

Which did not tell her much. But he refused to say more. However, she had a feeling that something might be about to happen at last.

9

GATEWAY TO SUCCESS

It was the first time Miss Foster had ever entered a theatre by way of the stage door. Indeed, she had seldom been inside a theatre at all. When she had it was to see a pantomime in Norwich in the Christmas holiday. This was quite a different experience. The stage door was in a rather dingy side-street, and when Hardacre pushed it open and led the way inside they went into a kind of lobby with what appeared to be a small office on the right where a man in shirt-sleeves was doing some clerical work.

Hardacre appeared to know the man and spoke to him through a hatch in a glass window.

'Good morning, Alf. The guv'nor in?'

'Couldn't say, Mr Hardacre. You better go and see for yourself. You know the way.'

'I should.' Hardacre said. 'Come along, Bella.'

He led the way and she followed, her heart beating faster than usual with the realisation that she was in that part of a theatre which an audience never saw. They went past some dressing-rooms, the doors all shut, where a lingering suggestion of perfume and powder and bodily secretions hung on the still air as if waiting to greet the returning artistes later in the day.

They went up a stairway, a bare brick wall on one side, and found themselves at last in the wings of the stage. The curtain was up, and when they came out of the wings Isabella could see the dimly lit auditorium with the galleries and boxes higher up.

There were two men on the stage that appeared to be in conference. They were a complete contrast to each other. One was fat, squat and bald-headed, with a face that by its fiery appearance and its bulbous red nose gave evidence of a certain love of the bottle. The other was lean and lanky, with prominent cheekbones and a long, thin neck. He had a gloomy expression, as though he found nothing much in life to give him any pleasure.

Hardacre addressed the fat man. 'Good morning, Mr Gage.'

Gage turned and said in a husky voice which gave the impression that his words had been dredged up from somewhere deep in his throat: 'Ah, there you are, Mr Haitch. Brought the young lady, I see. Morning, Miss.'

He was giving her a very keen look and she felt slightly uncomfortable under the gaze. It was, she thought, as if he were seeing clean through her clothes and examining the naked body underneath. Which was quite ridiculous of course, but it made her blush nevertheless, and she was relieved when he turned again to Hardacre.

'Well,' he said, 'she's got the looks all right. But you and me, we both know as it takes more than that, don't we?'

'Of course,' Hardacre said. 'But I assure you she has far more than that.'

'Maybe. So let's see a bit of action. Fred, give us a tinkle on the ivories.'

The other man glanced at Hardacre. 'What you want. A waltz?'

'A waltz will do,' Hardacre said.

The thin man went down into the orchestra pit and started playing a piano. Hardacre took Isabella into the dance while Gage looked on. Very soon he called a halt.

'Nice,' he said. 'Very nice. But it'll take more than a bit of ballroom dancing, you know.'

'Of course,' Hardacre said. 'But we can work up an act. There's talent here.'

'Maybe there is and maybe there ain't. Remains to be seen.' He turned his gaze on the girl. 'Legs.'

She glanced at Hardacre, questioning.

'He wants to see your legs,' Hardacre explained. 'Lift your skirt.'

Somewhat reluctantly she stooped, took hold of the hem of her skirt and raised it slightly.

'Higher,' Gage said. 'Don't be shy, girlie. You wanta be on the stage you gotta forget all that.'

She looked again at Hardacre and he gave her an encouraging smile and said: 'It's all right.'

She gave a shrug, bent down again, grasped the skirt with both hands and pulled it up with the petticoat beneath to the level of her thighs.

'Nice,' Gage said. 'Very nice indeed. Nothing to be ashamed of there, young lady. As fine a pair of pins as ever I see.'

★　★　★

Before they left Hardacre told Isabella to wait in the wings while he had a little talk with Gage. The little talk lasted for at least a quarter of an hour and she was rather tired of waiting when he rejoined her. He looked quite pleased with himself, so she concluded that the little talk had been satisfactory. But all he said was:

'Sorry to have kept you waiting. Now we'll be on our way.'

It was not until they reached home that he said anything at all about the outcome of the talk with Gage, though he must have known she was dying to be told. Even then he said nothing but just hummed a little tune. She could see that he was teasing her, so finally she lost patience and cried:

'Well? How did it go?'

'How did what go, my dear?'

'You know what. Your talk with that man.'

'Gage? Oh, pretty well, pretty well.'

'And what does that mean?'

'It means that he likes the look of you and if we can work up a good dance routine we might just find ourselves taken on. The fact is he's looking for some new blood and we may have come just at the right time. What did you think of him?'

'Well,' she said. And then she stopped, hardly knowing what to say.

Hardacre laughed. 'Bit of a rough diamond, eh? Used to be a stand-up comic at one time.'

'Stand-up comic?'

'A man who gets up on the stage, usually in funny clothes, and tells jokes, often involving his fictitious mother-in-law. Maybe he'll do a little dance and end up with a song. It can be

74

a killer. If the audience don't like you they give you the bird.'

She looked puzzled. 'The bird?'

'That's stage slang. It means you get hissed. If they really dislike you they may start throwing things such as over-ripe tomatoes, rotten fruit, even bad eggs.'

'Did they ever do that to him?'

'I wouldn't be surprised. Anyway, he decided that the management side was more desirable. Let somebody else get up there on the stage and take the knocks.'

He must have noticed a slightly worried expression on her face and he hastened to reassure her. 'Don't let it bother you. They won't throw anything when you're up there, except maybe a bouquet. They'll love you. Take my word for it. You'll have them eating out of your hand.'

She wondered whether he himself had ever experienced that kind of thing. She still knew so little about him. Could it have been a lack of success on the boards that had persuaded him to take the post of dancing-master at Miss Lowther's establishment? Perhaps she had taken him on as a special favour and had been ill repaid for her generosity.

She cast the thought from her mind. In this world you had to look out for yourself, didn't you?

'That man — ' she said.

'Walter Gage?'

'Yes. Why did he call you Mr Haitch?'

Hardacre laughed. 'He's a cockney. Born within the sound of Bow Bells. What he meant was Mr H. First letter of my name. As he might call you Miss F.'

'Oh, I see.'

'I think fate may be favouring us. He's aiming to put some new acts in his programme and we may have come along at just the right time.'

She hoped he was right, because if he was not what did the future hold for them? They had both burnt their bridges and could not go back.

He saw her expression and gave a laugh. 'Don't worry, dear girl. We're going to be winners. See if we aren't. Walter Gage is our gateway to success.'

It seemed to her a curious gateway, but she had to believe him.

10

DRESS REHEARSAL

They went to the theatre every morning and worked on the routine. She enjoyed it, for dancing was in her blood. The skinny man named Fred played the piano and Walter Gage watched and made suggestions. They worked at it for a week and they went to a theatrical outfitters and bought costumes.

Isabella wondered where Hardacre was finding the money to buy the gear, and she came to the conclusion that Walter Gage was financing him. It would be an advance on their wages and he would be repaid by their services.

'Walter is taking a gamble on us,' Hardacre said. 'Though really it's not much of a risk. He's a shrewd judge of an act and he can see he's backing a winner in you and me.'

She hoped he was right, but she was nervous and perhaps just a little bit scared. Suppose the audience did not like them. Suppose they were given the bird.

Hardacre told her not to worry about that. He was confident that all would be well.

'They'll love us. Especially you.'

He told her that Gage was getting an entirely new set of acts together. He also told her that it was not really a theatre; it was a music hall.

'They never put plays on in this kind of place, and I doubt whether the audience would appreciate it if they did. It's all variety, a succession of acts. Nobody's on the stage for long.'

She began to meet some of the other performers when rehearsals began. She was sharing a dressing-room with some other girls; only the favoured few had rooms to themselves; you had to earn the privilege.

A young and attractive woman sitting next to her introduced herself as Laura Peart and added the information that she was the conjuror's assistant. In the act she wore tights which showed off her long slim legs to perfection. Gerald Hardacre said all conjurors' assistants were like that because it took the audience's attention off what the man was doing. Isabella doubted this, since it would be only the male section of the audience that was distracted in this way. She thought that for someone who regularly got sawn in half, had swords thrust through her while enclosed in a sealed box and suffered other indignities on stage Miss Peart looked remarkably well.

'Who are you with, dear?' she asked.

Isabella told her, and she looked surprised.

'So what happened to Rita?'

'Rita?'

'Oh, dear!' Miss Peart said. 'Have I said the wrong thing? Forget it, love.'

★ ★ ★

That evening when they were having supper Isabella repeated the question that Laura Peart had declined to answer.

'Who's Rita?'

Hardacre looked startled and somewhat annoyed. The question had obviously taken him off guard.

'Who told you about her?'

'Miss Peart.'

'Oh, did she? Well, I suppose someone was bound to. So what exactly did she tell you?'

'Nothing really. She just asked what happened to her. And when she realised I knew nothing she shut up.'

'Well, I suppose you may as well know. Somebody's bound to make it their business to tell you eventually. Stage people are no different from anyone else in that respect; they like a bit of gossip, especially if it puts somebody else in a poor light. So the fact is this; Rita Ling used to be my partner. Then she walked out on me and that killed the act.'

'I see,' Isabella said. And it occurred to her that this might have been why he had taken the job of instructing young ladies at Miss Lowther's establishment in the art of dancing. Perhaps it had been his lifeline. And then he had thrown it away for the chance he had seen of resurrecting the act with a new partner. Suppose he had failed. Suppose Walter Gage had turned him down. It hardly bore thinking about.

'Why did she do that?'

'Because a rich swine came along and offered her the chance of leading a life of ease and comfort without having to dance her legs off to keep the wolf from the door. If she's really smart she'll get the wedding ring on her finger before she loses her looks and he gets tired of her.'

He sounded bitter. And perhaps he had reason to be, since it appeared that the defection of Miss Ling had put him out of work, for a dancing partnership is no longer viable when one of the partners decides to call it a day. So when he got himself employed by Miss Lowther he had been on the lookout for a new partner to give his stage career a fresh start. And there he had recognised in her the very one who might fill the bill.

It had been a risk. He had seen her dancing only in the innocent manner that was expected of Miss Lowther's pupils. This was no proof that she could make the leap from drawing-room to stage. It might all have ended in failure. And of course it still might, for the proof could only come when the two of them performed before a critical audience which had no vested interest in their success.

'Were you and Rita a good partnership?' she asked.

He grinned at her. 'Not nearly as good as you and I will be.'

The trouble was that she could not be sure he was not saying this merely to encourage her.

In consultation with Walter Gage they had decided to call themselves Gerald and Bella.

'Could have been Pedro and Carmen,' Gage said. 'Just to give it the Spanish touch. But why bother? It's the performance as counts.'

So on the handbills they became 'Gerald and Bella. Dance of Delight.'

There was an act called Winthrop and Charlie. Winthrop was the comedian and Charlie was the straight man, or what Hardacre called the feed. He fed the material to Winthrop for him to make the laughs.

Winthrop was a tubby man with a rubbery

face which he could contort into all manner of grotesque shapes.

'People think he's the clever one because he makes them laugh. But he's not, you know.' Hardacre said.

'No?' Isabella said.

'No. It's Charlie who writes the stuff. Winthrop just puts it across. And Charlie's the nice one. Everybody likes him but they hate Winthrop. He's vain and boastful and he treats Charlie like dirt.'

'So why does he stick with him?'

'That's what everybody wonders. Perhaps because he knows Winthrop can put the stuff across and he might not find anyone else who could.'

There was an act called 'Professor van Osler and his Performing Dogs'.

'Professor indeed!' Hardacre said. 'People think maybe he's Dutch, and he puts on the accent to fool them. But the fact is he comes from Bootle and his real name is Dredge.'

Hardacre hated animal acts, especially dogs. 'Samuel Johnson had it about right, though he was talking about women parsons. 'A woman's preaching', he said, 'is like a dog's walking on its hind legs. It is not done well and the wonder is that it is done at all.' Or something like that. Damn brutes make a mess in the dressing-room. Need to be fumigated after they been in it.'

Isabella suspected that he was exaggerating. It was just that he disliked dogs. She herself thought they were sweet. She hoped that Gerald would not alienate a fellow performer by being rude to him. But she soon discovered that she need have no fears on this point when she saw him slap Dredge on the back and address him as Professor in the friendliest of manners.

When she taxed him with this he laughed and told her it was advisable never to make enemies in show business because you never knew when they might be in a position to injure you.

'Keep on good terms with everybody, that's the best policy, even if you can't bear the sight of them.'

★　★　★

She was nervous when they first rehearsed with an orchestra, but it was really much better than just the piano. She was even more nervous when they came to the dress rehearsal. They were dressed as gypsies tended to be on stage and probably never were in real life. Hardacre had a red and white spotted handkerchief on his head and a voluminous white shirt open at the neck with floppy sleeves buttoned at the wrist. The trousers were black, narrow in the leg and flared at the ankle. All the way down each outer seam was a row of pearly buttons ending at the highly polished black shoes. Brass rings dangling from his ears gave him quite a piratical look.

Isabella, the gypsy maiden, had the feminine equivalent: a pleated blouse and a black skirt that reached down to a few inches below her knees and was wide enough to provide a view of her legs to the top of her thighs whenever she whirled around in the course of the dance. Her hair was swept back from her forehead and tied in a pony-tail with a red ribbon. On one side of her head was an artificial red rose and her earrings matched the bangles on her wrists.

The sight of her might well have been enough to make any young man dream of giving up life in the smoke of the city and going off to live in a caravan and spend his evenings by a campfire.

The dress rehearsal did not go particularly well. Her nervousness did not help, and when the rose fell out of her hair and she trampled it underfoot this made things worse. She almost stopped then, but Hardacre hissed at her to keep going and somehow she got through the routine without further mishap.

Not all the other acts were free from hitches either, and there were some harsh words handed out. But Gerald told her this was quite normal and not to let it bother her.

'There's a saying: 'Bad dress rehearsal, good first night'. Things will be fine tomorrow. You'll see.'

She had doubts about that, but she did not say so.

11

DEBUT

The day which was to see the first performance of the pair of dancers calling themselves
Gerald and Bella could hardly have been more
depressing. It was cold, wet and windy. The
wind came in gusts, flinging the rain into the
faces of those unfortunate pedestrians who
were heading into it. The streets of London
were slimy and stank of wet horse droppings.
There were umbrellas everywhere, some of
them blown inside out by the gusting wind.

Isabella wondered whether people would
be kept away from the music hall by the
inclement weather. Hardacre said it might,
and if the seats were not all filled it would be
a poor start to their stage career. It was
unusual for him to take such a gloomy view
of things and it did nothing to suppress the
nervousness she was feeling as the hour of
their debut approached.

He must have realised this and hastened to
reassure her.

'It'll be all right, though. Even if the house
isn't quite full there's bound to be enough to

make a go of things. And they're going to like you. I'd stake my life on that.'

She hoped he was right, but still she could not help being nervous. Suppose all did not go well. Suppose she made a hash of things. Suppose they got the bird.

At midday it was still raining, but the wind had dropped. And early in the afternoon the rain ceased. There was still no hint of the sun, but at least they would be able to get to the music hall without being soaked.

'It's a good omen,' Hardacre said. His spirits had obviously risen with the improvement in the weather. 'I take it as an omen that we shall be a great success. Tomorrow everybody will be singing our praises.' He gave a laugh. 'We'll put Professor van Osler and his canine academy in the shade, see if we don't.'

*   *   *

When they got to the music hall Isabella was already feeling quite sick with apprehension. In the dressing-room Miss Peart, the conjuror's assistant, was kind enough to give her encouragement.

'This is your first time before an audience, isn't it, dear?'

Isabella admitted that it was.

'And you'll be nervous, I dare say.'

Isabella did not deny that she was.

Miss Peart put a hand on her arm. 'No need to be. I've watched your act from the wings and you're good. No doubt about it. They'll love you.'

'That's what Gerald says.'

'And he's right. You're better than that Rita ever was. Not that she wasn't good. She was. But there's a difference between just good and top-notch.'

'You think that's what I am?'

'No doubt about it, dearie.'

Isabella had a feeling that the other girl was, in a good-natured way, just trying to encourage her. Which was nice of her and was perhaps more than could have been expected.

But she was nervous nevertheless.

★   ★   ★

Her mouth was dry and her hands were shaking as she waited with Gerald in the wings, listening to the applause for the preceding act.

'If only,' she thought, 'it was the end of our act and the applause was for us.'

But there was no sense in having thoughts like that, and a little later they were on the stage in the glare of the foot-lights and the curtain was up.

She had caught a glimpse of the first few rows of the audience as they skipped on hand-in-hand and knew that hundreds of eyes were watching them. But she did not think of them because she and Gerald were in the dance and her nervousness had gone. She was dancing her heart out and not giving a thought to those people watching. It was as if she were being swept away out of this world into a dreamland where there was nothing but the sound of the music and the tapping of their feet.

As they took their bow the applause almost drowned the sound of Gerald's voice in her ear: 'I told you so. They love you.'

There were shouts that sounded to her like 'Core! Core!'

'They want an encore,' Gerald said. 'They haven't had enough of us.'

So they danced the rehearsed encore as the orchestra struck up again. Then there was more applause until finally they got off the stage for the last time after taking a curtain call.

★　★　★

She remembered it always. There were even better nights later, but this was the one that stayed in her mind because it was the first and there could never be another quite like it.

There was a backstage celebration after the show. The whole company was there, including Professor van Osler's dogs, each with a bone to gnaw. There had been a full house despite the weather and Walter Gage was pleased. Even Fred looked less gloomy than usual with a glass of milk stout in one hand and a ham sandwich in the other.

Laura Peart, the conjuror's assistant, said she was so pleased it all went well for Isabella.

'But I knew it would. You've got it in you. Wish I had your talent. All I'm good for is to show my legs and hand things to The Great Martello, as he calls himself.'

'Did you ever try dancing?'

'Oh, I tried. I wasn't all that bad, but I never really made the grade. It has to be born in you, I suppose. Anyway, not to grumble. Mine's a nice steady job and it doesn't tax the brain.'

Isabella liked Miss Peart. She was entirely without guile. With her there was none of the backbiting that some others in the profession were apt to indulge in.

Hardacre said it was because she was too simple-minded. 'If she was more intelligent she'd be doing something more rewarding than acting as assistant to a third-rate magician.'

She wondered why he called The Great Martello third-rate. To her he seemed very good, and she still could not see how the tricks were done. No doubt Laura could have told her why the swords thrust through the box in which she was contained drew no blood, though it should have been streaming out in floods. But it would have been as much as her job was worth to reveal any secrets of The Great Martello's trade.

'It's all done by mirrors,' Hardacre said.

Which was complete nonsense, of course. It just meant that he had no more idea than she had regarding the mechanics of the conjuror's art.

★ ★ ★

She was not so nervous on the second night, and the reception was not quite as rapturous. She wondered why this was. As far as she could tell they were performing just as well as on the opening night.

Gerald told her not to let it bother her. 'It's one of the mysteries of the stage. Take a comedy for instance. One night they're laughing their heads off and the next night there's scarcely a giggle. The night after that it's different again. In this business you have to take the rough with the smooth and just hope they don't start throwing things.'

Well, they were not doing that and she just hoped they never would, because that would be just too awful for words. But she didn't think it was at all likely. Not with their act. Gerald and Bella were good; everyone said so. She felt that she had the world at her feet.

The fact was that though the man was certainly a first rate performer, it was the girl who caught the eye. There was magic in her, every movement she made a delight to watch. He, with the eye of an expert, had probably detected it from the outset and had singled her out to replace the errant Rita.

Sometimes she wondered whether her family knew that she was performing on the stage and earning a living from dancing. She had told her father that this was what she intended doing, but she doubted whether he had believed that it would ever be anything more than a dream.

But just suppose they did find out and decided to come and see her perform. Suppose she were to take them back-stage and introduce them to people like Winthrop and Charlie, Professor van Osler, The Great Martello and the rest of the performers. What an experience it would be for them.

Now that the nervousness she had felt at first had almost entirely disappeared she found that she enjoyed appearing before an audience. It excited her, gave her a sense of achievement, even of power over all these people.

'Any regrets?' Hardacre asked.

'None at all.'

'Never feel you made a mistake throwing in your lot with me?'

'Oh, no.'

If she had not taken that step she might never have stepped on to the boards of a stage, might never have known the feeling of exhilaration that a wildly applauding audience could arouse.

'I love you, Bella,' he said.

'I love you too.'

But did she? She liked him certainly. She enjoyed being in bed with him. But she had had no experience to tell her what it was like to be really head-over-heels in love with a man. She had had her dreams of course, but in them the Prince Charming had been young and handsome. Gerald was good-looking; that could not be denied; and had charm of a mature kind. But could a girl as young as she was, truly be in love with a man of his age? Which of course brought up the question of what age he really was. He had never told her and she would not have presumed to ask.

But did it matter anyway? Surely what was really important was that their act should be a success on stage. And of that there could be no possible doubt. The evidence was there each night in the reaction of the audience. Everything was going better than she could ever have hoped for; so why should she bother her head with questions to which she could give no answer?

'You're frowning,' Gerald said. 'Is anything worrying you?'

'Worrying me? No, nothing at all. Everything is going fine, isn't it?'

'It certainly is. We've fallen on our feet, you and I. Fallen on our feet.'

She laughed. He could hardly have chosen a more apt expression.

12

MONSIEUR DUPIN

A year passed. The dance partnership, Gerald and Bella, became well known in the business. They had gained more prominence on the handbills. They had also added singing to the act. Hardacre had a rather fine baritone voice and Isabella was a soprano. They blended very well and, as Hardacre said, it was another string to their bow.

'It's an insurance too. One of us could break a leg.'

She was superstitious and thought it was tempting fate to speak of anything as disastrous as that.

They had done some touring; appearing in places like Nottingham, Manchester and Liverpool, staying in lodgings with landladies who catered for that kind of business. They had long since moved out of the rented house, to which Hardacre had originally taken her and had better quarters whenever they were in London.

Isabella had only a hazy idea of how much they were earning, but she guessed it was enough for a comfortable living. She left it to Gerald to take care of the financial side of things, but whenever she requested money for clothes or anything else he never raised any objection and she was content with this arrangement.

She had never been pregnant and had come to the conclusion that she was not meant to be a mother. She was not sorry. A child would have been a handicap in their line of business, especially when they went on tour.

In one of their London seasons they appeared on the same programme as Marie Lloyd who was at the summit of her career at that time. She had made her name with such songs as 'The Boy I Love Sits Up In The Gallery' and 'My Old Man Said Follow The Van'.

Hardacre maintained that she was not so very wonderful and he could never understand what made her so popular; but Isabella put this down to envy on his part. She herself thought Marie Lloyd was a first-rate performer who deserved her success. She had talked to her and had found her a very pleasant person. But she did not tell Gerald this.

★ ★ ★

It was at this time that a Frenchman named Henri Dupin appeared on the scene. He was a dapper little man, very smartly dressed, black-haired and sharp-featured, with a trim moustache and a Vandyke beard. He had a remarkably fine set of teeth, and when he spoke the whiteness contrasted sharply with the jet-black of his moustache and beard.

It transpired, after he had introduced himself, that he was in London on a mission, and this mission was to find talent in the entertainment line which might be tempted to make the crossing of the English Channel and appear on the stage in Paris. The stage in question was apparently at a theatre called Le Moulin Rouge.

Isabella, who had studied the French language at the educational establishment of Miss Lowther, had no difficulty in translating this as The Red Mill, which seemed an odd sort of name for a theatre or even a music hall, but she did not remark on this.

Apparently Monsieur Dupin, having seen Gerald and Bella on stage had no doubt whatever that this act would be eminently suitable for the Moulin Rouge. He suggested to Hardacre that they might earn rather more in Paris and at worst it would be a new experience for them.

Isabella was amazed and a trifle shocked at

the curtness with which Hardacre rejected the suggestion. He said nothing would induce him to leave England where he had been born and bred. He did not even consult his partner. Apparently she was to have no voice in the matter.

Monsieur Dupin looked surprised and possibly a little put out by the vehemence of the rejection. He glanced at Isabella.

'And you, Madame? Would you not wish to see Paris?'

Before she could reply Hardacre broke in: 'It is immaterial whether she would or not. The decision is for me to make, and I have made it.'

With that he turned and walked away.

Dupin gave a very Gallic shrug of the shoulders and a faintly regretful grimace.

'Monsieur Hardacre appears to have a strong dislike of my country. I hope you are not of the same persuasion.'

She hastened to assure him that she was not and to beg him not to take offence at Gerald's rather brusque rejection of his offer.

'If it were up to me, I'd be more than happy to go to Paris. It might be fun.'

'But of course you would not do so without Monsieur?'

'No. That would be quite impossible. We are a pair.'

'Naturally. But if there should ever come a time when you are no longer a pair?'

'Then things would be quite different of course. But I cannot foresee that happening.'

'No, perhaps not. But' — Monsieur Dupin stroked his beard and looked at her thoughtfully — 'if there should ever come a time when the unexpected were to happen and you were no longer linked with Monsieur Hardacre perhaps you would then consider such a move not entirely out of the question.'

He thrust a hand into an inner pocket of his jacket and pulled out a wallet from which he extracted a small pasteboard card which he held out to her.

'That is my address. If you should ever wish to get in touch with me a letter sent there would find me.'

She hesitated to accept the card. What would Gerald say? But then it occurred to her that there was no reason why he should even know. She felt sure she would never have occasion to write to Henri Dupin, but there could be no harm in taking his card, could there?

So she took it.

After that the dapper little Frenchman smiled, kissed her hand and took his leave.

13

CLIMAX

It was some time later when Isabella learned the true reason why Hardacre had such an aversion to the idea of trying his luck in Paris. It was a little shamefacedly that he told her. Apparently, as a young man he had taken a short sea-trip with some other people in a rowing-boat at Brighton, the oars being plied by a weather-beaten old salt in a knitted jersey.

It was a day when the sea, though not absolutely calm, had no more than a lazy swell to impart an up-and-down movement to the boat. Yet this was enough to have a most unpleasant effect on young Mr Hardacre. In fact, to the heartless amusement of the other holidaymakers in the boat, who were not in the least affected by the gentle motion, he was violently seasick.

The experience was so unpleasant that he had vowed never again to venture out to sea in any kind of vessel, large or small. Since it was impossible to get to France without crossing a treacherous stretch of water called by the English 'The English Channel' and by the French 'La Manche', he saw no possibility of accepting Henri Dupin's offer of employment at Le Moulin Rouge.

'Until they build a bridge over that nasty piece of water or dig a tunnel under it I'm staying in England.'

'But surely,' Isabella said, 'seasickness can't be so terribly bad.'

Gerald gave her a sour look. 'Have you ever been seasick?'

Having never been to sea, she had to admit that she had not.

'Then you can have no idea what it's like. So let me tell you, it's absolutely hellish, and it'll take more than Dupin and his damned Moulin Rouge to get me on the briny again.'

She thought he was exaggerating, but there was no point in arguing about it, so she said no more.

★　★　★

It was not long after this that she began to realise that Gerald was developing a drink problem. At first he took pains to hide it from her, and she was so inexperienced in such matters that she did not understand what was making him less than perfect in his dancing. She hesitated to remark on this; it would have

101

seemed too much like criticism and he would most certainly have resented it.

Eventually, however, she felt compelled to ask him whether he was feeling quite well. His reaction to this innocent inquiry was quite startling. He almost snarled at her.

'Well, of course I'm well. What the devil do you mean? Do I look ill?'

'No, but — '

'But what?'

'It's just that sometimes in the dance you seem — '

'Seem? Well, out with it. What do I seem?'

She felt intimidated by his angry reaction to what had been a perfectly harmless question regarding his health. He appeared to be taking it almost as an insult. So it was with some hesitation that she replied.

'It's as if just occasionally you lose something in the dance.'

'Ah!' he said. 'Now we have it. What you're accusing me of is being too intoxicated to keep the step. In plain language that I'm drunk. Is that it?'

She was completely taken aback by this question. It had never entered her head to suspect that his occasional loss of touch might be the result of slight intoxication. She had never had any experience of the effects of drunkenness even in its mildest form. The

Fosters had been practically teetotal, with just a bottle of port at Christmas, of which the girls were allowed no more than the merest sip. So this suggestion of Gerald's that she was accusing him of being drunk on stage came as a most unpleasant shock. Moreover, it then occurred to her that the faint odour she had detected on his breath now and then, and which had rather puzzled her, might have been produced by alcoholic liquor of some sort.

'My God!' Gerald said, as though now that the subject had been broached he were unwilling to let it go. 'It's a fine thing if a man can't swallow a drop or two of brandy without having it thrown in his teeth. It's not a crime, you know.'

She tried to protest that she had not been accusing him of anything. But he was not listening. He went on pouring out his grievances.

'This is one hell of a life. It'd drive a man crazy if he didn't take a drop or two now and then.'

She was surprised to hear this. She had always imagined he enjoyed being an entertainer; that he loved the limelight and the applause which to her were so delightful. Now it seemed that he hated it all; that he could endure the life only with the aid of alcohol. But perhaps he was using that simply as an excuse for his tippling.

Whatever the reason, however, it was doing no good at all to the act of Gerald and Bella.

And it got worse. After this revelation it was as if he no longer felt any need to conceal or put a check on his habit. The result was inevitable: their reputation suffered, and soon they could get only the poorest provincial engagements.

The climax came in, of all places, Aberdeen. The act they were following at the theatre in the Granite City was a pretty girl playing a concertina. She was good, but it should have been an easy act to follow. As it might have been if the male half of Gerald and Bella had not been absent and she had no idea where he was.

She was distraught, but there was nothing she could do but go on stage and do the best she could to improvise a solo performance. It did not go well. How could it? She knew then what it was like to get the bird. It was humiliating. It was also the end of Gerald and Bella as a partnership.

★ ★ ★

There had been a time when she might have wept. But the years that had passed since her

104

flight to London with Gerald Hardacre had toughened her, mentally as well as physically. She was twenty-one now and she saw that it was time to cut herself adrift from this man who was no longer anything but a burden to her.

He did not come back to their lodgings that night, but in the morning a policeman arrived to inform her that her partner was in a cell, having been arrested the previous evening for being drunk and disorderly.

She visited him at the police station and informed him bluntly that she never wished to see him again. He was abject; stone cold sober now, he pleaded with her not to abandon him; promised to mend his ways and never touch another drop of liquor if only she would stay with him.

But she was adamant. She could see that if she did not break away from him things would only get worse, and she had no intention of sacrificing her own future for the sake of a drunkard.

He did what she had not done. He wept. The sight of his tears disgusted her. It was scarcely believable now that there had been a time when she had been completely under his influence to such a degree that he had been able to persuade her to run away from home and defy her father when he tried to take her back. But four years made a difference. She had been a girl then; now she was a young woman with a future before her in which there was no place for this man.

She went back to the lodgings, packed her bags, paid the landlady and caught the next train that was going south. She had money, for she had for some time been accumulating a fund from the allowance that Gerald gave her in the expectation that she might have need of it some day.

Now that day had come.

14

DUPIN AGAIN

As soon as she arrived in London she wrote a brief letter to Monsieur Henri Dupin and sent it to the address on the card he had given her.

It was as if the man had been waiting expectantly for just such a letter. Three days later he arrived in London and met her at the hotel where she was staying so that Gerald would not be able to find her when he returned to the house, which had been their rented dwelling in the capital.

Monsieur Dupin was delighted to meet her again. He had, so he said, been waiting with hopes that she would write ever since their previous meeting.

'It has been too long, dear lady, far too long. But no matter. The time has come.'

He did not ask about Gerald Hardacre. She told him briefly that they had split up, but gave no reason why. She left it to him to figure that one out for himself.

It was spring, and Dupin made the suggestion that they should spend a few days in London seeing the sights and so on before leaving for France. He had anyway some little pieces of business, as he put it, to attend to, and she would have to get a British passport.

The few days stretched to a week, and Isabella found the company of Henri Dupin a refreshing change from that of Gerald Hardacre in that period when he had been going so rapidly downhill as an alcoholic. Dupin was polite, charming and all that could have been desired in a male escort. So pleasant were those few days when the two of them enjoyed the diversions of London that she was quite sorry when they came to an end. But of course it had to be.

The crossing from Dover to Calais was made on a day when the Channel was so calm that she doubted whether even Gerald would have been seasick had he been with her. But of course he was not and never would be again. That part of her life was finished; another phase was beginning, and what that might hold for her she could only imagine. She could not avoid being more than a little apprehensive, for she was venturing on a new path just as much as she had been when she had run away from her childhood home.

Monsieur Dupin appeared to guess what was going through her mind, for he said: 'You are not afraid, are you?'

'A little,' she confessed.

He gave a smile. 'It is natural. You cannot tell what the future holds and I can only tell you that I am confident all will be well. You have beauty and you have talent. Such a combination makes success inevitable.'

He put a hand on her arm and gave it a little squeeze, as if to impress upon her the truth of his words, and she tried to be as confident as he apparently was. But still the doubts were there at the back of her mind and it was not easy to dismiss them.

★ ★ ★

From Calais they took the train to Paris. Dupin bought the tickets, having already paid her fare for the Channel crossing. He appeared to be taking it as natural that he should deal with all expenses, and Isabella was content to let him do so, since her own resources were so limited.

It was evening when they reached Paris and Dupin said it was too late to transact any business that day, so the best thing to do would be to get a room for her at a modest hotel where he would call for her in the morning and take her to the Moulin Rouge.

Having found the modest hotel Dupin

suggested that as it was some time since they had had a decent meal she might be agreeable to sharing a meal with him at a nearby restaurant. She was hungry and could see no objection to this. Indeed, she was very glad he had made the suggestion.

It was a small restaurant where the patron was also the chef, but the meal was excellent, and she said so.

Dupin smiled. 'Ah,' he said, 'we do some things better in France, as I think you will agree. And when you have lived here for a while you may find much else to admire. I trust so.'

Before taking leave of her at the hotel to return to his home he agreed to call for her at ten o'clock in the morning.

'Sleep well and do not worry about a thing. Tomorrow you start on a new career and I am certain it will be a successful one.'

15

SETTLING IN

The dapper little Frenchman was waiting in the foyer of the hotel when she went down in the morning. The time was precisely ten o'clock.

'Ah!' he said, 'I see we are both creatures of punctuality. I trust you slept well.'

'Very well, thank you.'

It was not wholly the truth. In fact she had slept fitfully and had dreams in which she tried to dance but her feet would not move because of the lead weights attached to them. People were pointing at her and laughing and she wished to run away but could not. However, she thought it inadvisable to tell Dupin this.

'Good. Very good,' he said. 'Now let us be on our way.'

There was a cab waiting outside. The cabbie opened the door for them and Dupin assisted Isabella to get in before following her. The cabbie closed the door, climbed up to his seat, gave a flick of the reins and they were on their way.

It was not far, through streets that appeared to be as busy and muddy as those in London. The cab came to a halt, Dupin got out and helped the girl to follow. She stepped down on to the pavement and Dupin made a gesture with a sweep of the arm.

'Voilà!'

And there it was, Le Moulin Rouge, the Red Mill.

Once, she supposed, there had been a real windmill on that site, grinding corn for the citizens of Paris. Had it been red in those days? Possibly. And then an expanding city had grown up round it and now it was no longer a mill but a place of entertainment.

'This way,' Dupin said.

He conducted her to the stage door and they went inside. It was not so much unlike an English theatre backstage that she felt a strangeness in her surroundings. She was, after all, a professional. It was with this thought that she reassured herself.

They were greeted by a large, heavily-built woman whose height was enhanced by a small mountain of ginger hair piled on top of her head like the coils of a sleeping serpent. She had a prominent bust which served as support for the strings of gaudy beads which encircled her neck, and her dress was as colourful as an artist's palette.

She greeted them with effusion and, as was natural, in French.

'Ah! You have arrived. I have been waiting for you. And this is the young lady.' She gave Isabella a keen appraising look as if seeking any defects there might have been in her appearance; and then, apparently having discovered none, gave her verdict. 'Charming. Quite charming.'

'As I told you,' Dupin said.

'As you told me, Monsieur. But beauty is not everything. Has she talent? That is the question.'

'And the answer to that is: most certainly yes, she has. As you will discover.'

Isabella might have been less embarrassed listening to this exchange if she had not been able to understand what was being said. But the fact was that she could. The teaching of French at Miss Lowther's school had been done by a Frenchwoman who was married to an English engineer. Isabella Foster had been her favourite pupil because she had shown such an aptitude for the subject. Dupin had been pleasantly surprised when she had first spoken to him in his own language.

'That,' he said, 'is one handicap removed from your path when you go to France. Had you been able to speak only English it might have made things difficult.'

Isabella gathered that the large lady, whose name was Madame Cochet, was the one whose approval she had to gain. However, she was later to learn that it was Henri Dupin who wielded much of the power. Apparently he was a very wealthy man and had capital invested in a variety of enterprises; the Moulin Rouge being only one of them. It seemed to please him to search around for new talent to put on the stage, and as he was a shrewd judge in such matters he was allowed to have his way.

As things turned out Isabella was to see him only very occasionally in the future. Having discovered her in London and brought her to Paris it was as if he felt that as far as he was concerned the job was done. She was now in the ample hands of Madame Cochet, and as it turned out her future at the Moulin Rouge was assured.

It was arranged that she should have lodgings with a young dancer named Juliette LeBlanc, a slim blonde girl with a doll-like face and a voice that was seldom raised much above a whisper. The lodgings were in the Montmartre district and had formerly been occupied by a young artist who had decided to end a futile struggle for recognition by throwing himself in the Seine.

Miss LeBlanc had formerly shared her

two-bedroom apartment with another dancer, but that young lady had fallen for a handsome suitor with plenty of money and had departed with the avowed intention of never setting foot on a stage again.

'Her heart wasn't in it,' Miss LeBlanc said, and sighed.

Isabella was to discover that she did quite a lot of sighing.

As well as the two bedrooms there was a small sitting-room and an even smaller kitchen where they cooked late-night suppers with ingredients bought at a nearby market. Juliette had scarcely ever been out of Paris and was an enchanted listener when Isabella described some of the attractions of London.

She sighed. 'How I should like to go there some day.'

'And why not? Maybe we could go together. I would be your guide.'

The girl clapped her hands with delight. 'Oh, wouldn't that be splendid. Just the two of us.' Then she sighed again. 'But of course it will never happen. It's just a dream.'

Isabella reflected that she might be right at that. She had hardly got to know Miss LeBlanc and here she was suggesting a trip to London. What could be more unlikely?

Now and then she paused to wonder what Gerald was doing now that she had left him.

But she had no regrets; life with him had become impossible and she had taken the only course open to her. From this time forward her life was set on a new course and there was no profit in looking back.

16

L'ANGLAISE

It was quite remarkable how quickly she became an integral part of the programme at the Moulin Rouge. It was as though there had been a vacancy simply waiting for her to fill it.

Madame Cochet said she was not surprised for she knew she could rely on the judgement of Monsieur Dupin.

'He is never wrong. It is quite amazing. He has the eye, as one might say, and we are fortunate to benefit from it.'

Isabella could only feel glad that not only did Henri Dupin have the eye but that this eye should have discovered her. For there could be no doubt that, if she was good for the Moulin Rouge, the Moulin Rouge was certainly good for her. She had both figuratively and literally fallen on her feet, and those feet were her fortune.

Soon she was a favourite with audiences. She became known as L'Anglaise, adored by the clientèle and liked by her fellow artistes for her complete lack of pretension. She knew that as an alien she might be regarded by the other performers as something of an intruder, so for her own sake she decided to tread warily, even though she could detect no evidence of anglophobia in any of those with whom she worked.

She asked Juliette LeBlanc whether she had heard any nasty remarks made about her behind her back because she was English.

Miss LeBlanc seemed astonished that she should suspect any such thing.

'Why should anyone do that? Everybody loves you.'

Isabella suspected that this was perhaps an overstatement from an observer who might be more than a little biased; but it could have been close enough to the truth if you substituted 'like' for 'love'.

'You really are a sweet girl, Juliette,' she said, and was surprised to see the sweet girl go quite pink in the face.

★   ★   ★

She had not been working at the Moulin Rouge long before making the acquaintance of a man who had such short legs that he was little taller than a dwarf. The girls all seemed to be on good terms with him and addressed him as Toulouse, which seemed odd to her, since Toulouse was surely a town in the south of France. Then she heard that his name was Toulouse-Lautrec, that he came from an upper class family and was regarded by them with some disapproval because of the dissolute kind of life he led and the low company he kept.

She also learned that the reason why his legs were so short was that as a child he had fallen off a horse and damaged them so badly that they had ceased to grow any longer. As a result he was condemned to go through life when he grew older with a man's body mounted on a boy's legs. How much truth there was in this explanation, which sounded rather unlikely to her, it was impossible to say. But certain it was that his torso and shoulders were bulky enough, as well as his head with its black hair and prominent nose supporting a pair of spectacles through which he possibly took a rather jaundiced view of a life that had made him something of a freak.

That he was a gifted freak there could be no doubt. He was an artist and painted pictures of the Moulin Rouge performers for posters advertising the show. He painted one of Isabella, but she was not greatly pleased with it. She thought it was more of a caricature than a portrait. It was certainly not flattering.

What was perhaps more flattering was the artist's attempt to seduce her. She could not imagine making love with such a grotesque. She told Juliette about this experience and was informed that it was not by any means unique.

'He has something of a reputation in that respect.'

'You mean he has tried it with others?'

'Yes. And with some success.' She gave a giggle. 'I've heard that he is quite a remarkable lover.'

Isabella stared at her. 'You have heard?'

Miss LeBlanc smiled. 'Oh, I do not speak from experience. I don't think he has ever been attracted to me. I am one of those he has not painted.'

Isabella thought this might have been because the other girl was no great beauty, though she was far from plain. The blonde hair was almost golden in colour and her eyes were a deep blue, the nose small and retroussé and the lips slightly pouting. She was good-natured and one might have had a far less pleasant colleague with whom to share one's lodgings.

Then one night, six months since she had moved in, another side to Miss LeBlanc's character was revealed to Isabella.

She was not sure how long she had been

120

asleep but she woke to find that she was not alone in her bed. Someone else had crept in beside her, and this someone was caressing her. It took her no more than a moment to realise that it had to be Juliette and her immediate reaction was one of shock and an instinctive movement away from the caressing hand. But there was little room in the bed for any such movement and the realisation came to her that she rather enjoyed the caresses, the fingers that were moving gently over her body.

She said nothing, and the other girl said nothing either. After a while she dropped off to sleep again.

When she woke in the morning she was alone in the bed and she began to wonder whether it had been nothing but a dream.

At breakfast neither of them said anything regarding what might or might not have occurred in the night. They spoke of other things and Isabella came to the conclusion that she must after all have dreamed that she had had a visitor to her bed and that the incident had never occurred in fact.

Which would have been a perfectly believable conclusion if the experience had not been repeated the following night. She had scarcely got into bed and blown out the candle when someone came into the room and got in beside her. This was certainly no dream; and though she said nothing, Juliette began fondling her as on the previous night.

Still neither of them said anything, but this time Juliette stayed until morning before leaving. Soon it had become the regular thing for them to sleep together and the fondling was a mutual thing. In the warmer weather they slept naked. Their fingers probed each other's body, and rather to her own surprise Isabella discovered that there was much enjoyment in this.

Things went on in this way for almost a year. And they might well have continued if something had not occurred to bring this happy state of affairs to an abrupt conclusion.

Isabella fell in love.

And not with Juliette.

17

OTTO

Otto Axter-Mandel was a German, and since it was only a few years since a German army had been besieging Paris it might have been expected that he would not have been at all popular at the Moulin Rouge. But Otto had two great advantages: he was young and he was very very rich. He was also handsome and spoke perfect French with only the merest suggestion of a German accent.

Moreover, the Germans, although they had caused some discomfort to the besieged Parisians, had never actually entered the city. It was true that the French and the Germans had been historically opposed to one another on the field of battle, but those Germans had usually been Prussians and Otto was not a Prussian, he was a Bavarian. Also he was a well-mannered young man and his possession of considerable wealth was common knowledge.

He had an elder brother, Carl, who was a count and had a vast estate which would be handed down to Otto if his brother died first, since Carl was unmarried and had no son to inherit the title and land.

Taking all this into account, it was hardly surprising that Otto should be made welcome at the Moulin Rouge and that he should be taken backstage when he made a request to meet some of the performers. Moreover, when he said some of the performers it turned out that in fact, he meant one of them in particular: Isabella Foster, known as L'Anglaise.

It was thus that Otto Axter-Mandel met Isabella Foster, and if it was not for both of them love at first sight it was certainly something very close to it. And this was hardly remarkable, since Isabella was undoubtedly very beautiful and Otto was a handsome young man, six feet tall, well-built, with fair hair and sea-blue eyes. He also had delightful manners. What more could any woman demand?

He took her out to lunch the next day at a fashionable restaurant and described in glowing terms the estate to which he would shortly return. When he took her out to lunch a second time he asked her to go with him. He also told her that he loved her, that he was mad about her and would be devastated if she refused.

Had she been more sophisticated she might

not have accepted the invitation as readily as she did. She might have pretended not to believe he was serious. She might also have said that it was quite impossible, that she could not leave the Moulin Rouge where she was engaged as a performer.

She said none of these things.

She said: 'I shall have to break my contract.'

'And that bothers you?'

'A little.'

'But you will do it?'

'Yes.'

★　★　★

Madame Cochet was not pleased.

'You are going away just like that?'

'I am sorry.'

'Don't you think you are being a trifle foolish?'

'Perhaps.'

'But it makes no difference?'

'No.'

'You imagine, of course, that you are in love with this man?'

'I know I am.'

'After so short a time? What is it? Two days? Three?'

'Time makes no difference.'

'On the contrary. It makes all the difference in the world. As you will see, I fear. And of course he is in love with you?'

'I believe so.'

'He has told you he is, no doubt.'

'Yes.'

'Phoey!' Madame Cochet gave a snap of the fingers. 'Men will say anything, promise anything, to serve their own ends. So off you go to this estate somewhere in Germany and maybe for a time all is well. Two turtledoves. Then he tires of you. Maybe you tire of him. And what then? You come back to Paris expecting to have your old job back. But somebody else has taken it. What then?'

'It will not be like that,' Isabella said.

But she knew that it could be. She knew that Madame Cochet was telling the truth. Madame was a woman with experience and knew the way of the world.

Isabella felt a twinge of conscience. This woman had been very good to her, and now it was as if she were letting her down by quitting the Moulin Rouge just when she had become a favourite with the patrons. Nevertheless, she had no intention of changing her mind.

'You don't imagine, I suppose, that he will marry you?'

Isabella was silent. Neither she nor Otto

had made any mention of the possibility of marriage. She doubted whether the thought had even entered his mind. In her mind it had been no more than a passing thought; something perhaps to be brought up later, but certainly not imminent.

'No, of course not,' Madame Cochet said. 'He is a nobleman even if he is a German. He would not be expected to marry a dancer from a Paris theatre. When he does marry, as I have no doubt he will in the course of time, it will be to one of his own kind, not an entertainer from the Moulin Rouge, popular as she may be.'

All of which Isabella had to admit to herself was probably true. But it made no difference to the decision she had made. Come what may in the unforeseeable future, she was not going to change her mind.

Madame Cochet accepted the fact and gave a shrug of her shoulders.

'Very well then. So be it. And in spite of everything I wish you well. I sincerely hope that you will never come to regret taking this step.'

And then Madame Cochet did a most remarkable thing; she flung her arms round Isabella and hugged her to her ample bosom. There was even a hint when she released her of a tear or two in her eye. But this might have been merely imagined by the younger woman, since her own vision was certainly rather blurred at the time.

★ ★ ★

There could be no doubt regarding the tears in Juliette LeBlanc's eyes when the news was broken to her. She wept unashamedly.

'You are leaving Paris? You are going to Germany with that man?'

'Yes.'

'And I shall never see you again?'

'But of course you will,' Isabella assured her. 'There will be visits to Paris.'

'With him?'

'Well, yes.'

'So it will not be the same. Never again.'

Which was true, of course. And could she be sure there would be any visits? All would depend on Otto. Perhaps he had had his fill of Paris and would have no desire to see the place again.

'Have you not been happy living with me?'

'Very happy.'

'Then why — ?'

'Because — ' But how could one explain the inexplicable? 'Because I have to. Don't cry. Soon you will forget me.'

'Never.'

'Ah, you think so now. But time changes everything.'

And that, she thought, was a platitude which gave no consolation.

'I will write to you,' she said.

And knew it was a lie.

18

CARL

They travelled the first part of the way by train. It was a two-day journey and the final part was made by coach. It was dark when they arrived but there were lights burning in the schloss and some outside, so that Isabella gained an impression of the great size of the place.

Otto had already explained to her that, though of course it all belonged to his brother Carl, the Count, as a bachelor, had no need of the whole building and allowed Otto to occupy one wing where he could do as he wished without bothering the older man.

'You will meet him of course, but not tonight. He goes to bed early.'

The coach had stopped on a broad forecourt and there were wide steps leading up to the front door. Servants had come to take their luggage and Otto gave orders in German which she could not understand. It brought home to her the fact that she was now in a foreign land. She had become so used to living in Paris and speaking French that she had come almost to regard France as her native country. She saw that it would be necessary now to learn a third language. Perhaps Otto would teach her. It might be fun.

They went through a wide doorway into a vast tiled entrance hall from which other doors opened from left and right and two staircases ascended to a balcony.

'Come,' Otto said. 'I will show which is my part of the house.'

★ ★ ★

They had supper in a dining-room in which the polished mahogany table would have accommodated a banquet for forty. Places had been set for them at opposite ends of the table, but Otto said this was ridiculous. They would have had to shout at each other to carry on a conversation. So they both sat at one end and were waited on by a butler and two assistants.

'Tomorrow,' Otto said, 'I will show you round the place and I hope you'll like it.'

'I'm sure I'll love it.'

'Well, we shall see. You will also meet my brother.'

This, if the truth were told, rather scared her. Suppose the Count took a dislike to her.

Suppose he disapproved of Otto's conduct in bringing her there. In her imagination Carl appeared as something of an ogre.

They retired to bed soon after supper. She was conducted to her bedroom by a young maidservant who was plain but smiled a lot and said very little; which was just as well, since whatever she did say was unintelligible to Isabella.

The bedroom was larger than any she had ever slept in. Someone had already unpacked her luggage and she felt somewhat ashamed of the scantiness of the clothing that was almost lost in the vast wardrobe which could easily have accommodated twenty times the amount.

The bed was commodious in proportion, and when she got in she felt engulfed in sheets which had been pleasantly heated by a warming-pan which the maid had brought with her.

She snuggled down and tried to sleep, but sleep was elusive. So much was running through her mind to keep her awake. And then, when she had almost dosed off, she was brought back to complete wakefulness by someone slipping into the bed beside her.

'Otto!'

She heard him laugh. 'Who else?'

She felt his hands on her, the fingers

caressing, searching. There was no more sleep after that; not for quite a while. It was her first night at the schloss and it was to be a memorable one.

★ ★ ★

The meeting with Carl, which she had been secretly dreading, took place late the next morning in his part of the building. It was the library, a room in which the walls were lined with shelves of books; so many, she thought, that it would have taken anyone a lifetime to read. To get to this room they had to pass through a long gallery where portraits of the family ancestors, both male and female, hung in gilded frames, most of which had become tarnished with the passage of time. A few of the men were in armour, and all, both men and women, exhibited the changing of fashion over the years and even centuries.

Otto dismissed them all with a flip of the hand and a mocking laugh. 'All dead and gone. A horrible lot, don't you think?'

She said nothing. She was not sure whether or not he was joking. Perhaps he was really rather proud of his distinguished ancestors. Some of the women in ruffs bore an odd resemblance, she thought, to pictures she had seen of Queen Elizabeth.

When they entered the library they discovered the elder brother sitting at a desk with a pen in his hand. He dropped the pen at once, pushed back his chair and stood up. There was a considerable gap of years between the two brothers and there was little resemblance in their features. It made her think that perhaps they had had different mothers. All she had been told by Otto was that the parents were dead, leaving Carl with the title and the estate.

He was a tall, rather stooping man with craggy features and sparse hair beginning to turn grey.

He began to speak in German, then stopped abruptly and started again in rather guttural French.

Suddenly she realised that he was as shy of her as she was of him. He was no master of the French language, as Otto was, but she gathered that what he was trying to say was that he was very pleased to meet her and he hoped that her stay at the schloss would be an enjoyable one.

She replied that she was sure it would be, and after that they very soon left him to carry on with whatever it was he was doing before they interrupted him.

'Some day,' Otto said, 'you must get him to show you his collections.'

'So he is a collector. And what does he collect?'

'Almost anything. You'll see. I'm sure he'll be delighted to show you. Not many people are interested.'

'Does that include you?'

Otto grinned. 'It's not really in my line. I think he's given up on me. As you may have noticed, Carl and I are not exactly twins, in looks or tastes. We get on very well with each other largely because we are so seldom together. You saw all those books in the library? I wouldn't be surprised if he's read every one of them.'

'And you?'

Again he grinned. 'Do I look like a bookworm?'

She was not sure what a bookworm looked like, or even if they had any distinguishing features, but she felt quite certain he was not one. It occurred to her that she could not remember when she herself had last had a book in her hands. Yet as a child she had loved reading. So why had she allowed such a pleasure to vanish from her life?

She was still turning this question over in her mind when Otto said: 'Come. Let's go outside.'

19

COLLECTIONS

Viewed in daylight from the outside the schloss reminded Isabella of one of the more magnificent English country mansions that she had seen in pictures. It was built on a gentle slope so that from the front entrance one descended by wide steps to the shingled forecourt. In the centre of this was a fountain in the form of a nymph holding in her hands a ewer from which a constant flow of water descended to the pool in which she stood.

Beyond the fountain she could see a great park on which deer were grazing. In the distance a lake was visible, glinting in the sunlight. There were clumps of trees here and there and the total effect was wholly pleasing to the eye.

'It's beautiful,' Isabella said.

Otto answered, as though this were an idea that had never occurred to him until she mentioned it: 'Yes, I suppose it is.'

'How far does it extend?'

'Quite a way. We must go riding to take a look.'

'But I don't ride. I have never been on a horse.'

'Then I must teach you. And on the lake we can go sailing. That I will teach you also. There is so much to do here. One need never be bored.'

'Oh,' she said, 'I am sure of that.'

For how could one be bored with Otto for a companion? And a lover.

He took her to look at the garden, which was immense. It was the kind that could only have been maintained by a small army of gardeners. Not for the first time she wondered just how rich the Axter-Mandels were and how they had come by their wealth. Perhaps ancestors had acquired it in the past by pillage or other dubious means and later generations had maintained it by shrewd investment so that now Carl could amuse himself with his hobbies and Otto could live the playboy life with no concern regarding the expense.

Anyway, it was no concern of hers. For her love was everything and she was living in the present with no concern for the future. She refused to contemplate the possibility, even the certainty that this way of life would not go on for ever; indeed, that it might be of only brief duration.

That first day they walked in the garden,

inhaled the heady scent of the flowers and sat in the sun.

'Tomorrow,' Otto said, 'your riding lessons begin.'

'I look forward to it,' she said, 'with pleasure.'

For would not any activity in his company be a delight?

★　★　★

The riding lessons began soon after breakfast the next day. Otto picked a docile mare from a number of horses in the stables at the rear of the house. She had no riding-habit but he said this did not matter for the present; she could get one later. A groom fixed a side-saddle and held the bridle while Otto helped her to mount. She found this easy. As a dancer she had a body that was strong and supple. Under Otto's tuition she had by the end of the morning mastered the basic skill of riding.

She had also acquired a sore bottom.

★　★　★

Three days later they rode out to the lake. It was an idyllic spot: limpid water ruffled by a light breeze, shingly beaches here and there, an island in the centre, the rustle of leaves in the trees as they shivered in that same faint movement of air which was affecting the lake.

For a while they just sat on their horses and admired the view.

'What do you think of it?' Otto asked.

'It's wonderful. And all this is part of your estate?'

'All this and much more. Though of course it's not mine; it's Carl's. I'm only the younger brother, you know.'

'And does he come out here?'

'Let's just say it's not a frequent event. Riding a horse is not one of his favourite relaxations. And that's an understatement. He seems to prefer the four walls of the library to any physical exercise in the open air.'

There was a boathouse on the shore. They tethered the horses and Otto led the way to it. Inside were two boats, one equipped with a mast and sail.

'Would you care for a trip to the island?' he asked.

Isabella was ready to agree to any suggestion on his part, and soon they were in the boat and out of the boathouse. Otto stepped the mast and hoisted the sail. Progress was slow in the light breeze, but they had all the time in the world and were in no hurry. When they reached the island they went ashore and explored that small domain. That done they just lay and basked in the sun and let time go by.

'And this,' she thought, 'is only the beginning.'

Before her in imagination stretched an endless succession of idle sunny days spent in the company of this man she loved to distraction.

★　★　★

Some days they would go for a ride in one of the coaches that were housed near the stables. In the villages people stopped what they were doing to watch them pass. Some of the roads were full of potholes that made the coach shake and rattle. Otto said that in winter the mud became so deep they were practically impassable, especially when it snowed.

The nearest town of any size was Ulm, which could be reached in less than an hour by coach with four horses providing the traction. Whenever they went to town Otto would buy a piece of jewellery such as a diamond brooch or bracelet or necklace for Isabella. It was always an expensive item and he would never look at anything cheaper.

Now and then her conscience would prompt her to protest that he was spending far too much on these gifts, but he brushed the suggestion aside.

'It's my pleasure to buy things for you. And besides, no woman can have too much jewellery.'

Much later she was to remember these words and wonder whether even then he was looking to the future when she might have need of such rich gifts. But it certainly did not occur to her at the time.

Occasionally they went to Berlin, but that was a long journey, first by road to Ulm and thence by rail. They would put up at a grand hotel for a week or two and go to the theatre and the opera.

Isabella had never seen an opera and was enchanted by Mozart's 'The Marriage of Figaro', the first that Otto took her to.

'You see now what you have been missing,' he said.

Later they were to see 'Don Giovanni' and Verdi's 'Rigoletto', both of which she loved.

She was rather surprised to find that Otto had this taste for grand opera, but there was much about him that she was to discover in those first few months of their relationship.

One thing that soon became apparent to her was that he had no intention of introducing her to any of the other landowning families with whom he was acquainted. The reason he gave was that they were all very dull and she would be bored to tears if she had to spend an evening with any of them.

It was a lame excuse and she did not accept it.

'I believe you are ashamed of me.'

He laughed at this, though the laughter sounded to her a trifle forced. 'Ashamed of you! Quite the opposite, my dear. If I introduced you to those people all the men would try to seduce you and all the women would hate you for being so much more attractive than they are. I am protecting you from that.'

She still did not believe him, but she let the subject drop.

★ ★ ★

Once when he had departed in full evening dress for one of these parties that, according to him, she would have found so deadly boring she decided to pay a visit to the elder brother. She did so with some trepidation, not knowing what kind of reception she would receive, yet encouraged by Otto's statement that Carl would be delighted to

142

have someone express an interest in his collections.

So she made the journey through the long picture gallery and came to the door of the library where she hoped to find him. Her first tentative rap on the door produced no result and she thought that perhaps he was not there. However, she tried again with a somewhat louder knock and after a few moments heard shuffling footsteps on the other side of the door before it was opened a little way and Carl peered out.

He appeared surprised to see her, but not, as she had feared, at all annoyed.

'Oh,' he said, 'it's you, Miss Foster.' And then he opened the door wider and invited her to come in.

She did so, and said diffidently: 'I hope I'm not disturbing you.'

'Oh, not at all, not at all. What can I do for you?'

'Otto tells me that you are a collector.'

'That is so.'

'He also said you would be pleased to show me your collections.'

It was remarkable how his craggy features seemed to light up when she said this.

'And you wish to see them?'

'If it is not too much trouble.'

'No trouble at all. I will show you the way.'

It was a room even bigger than the library, and the first things that caught her eye, in the light of the lamp that he had carried from the library, were the big glass-fronted cabinets in which were displayed a great range of stuffed birds. Birds of every size and description were there, from eagles and vultures and a solitary albatross to tiny wrens and robins. All were neatly ticketed with their scientific names as well as their common ones and were perched on twigs or larger branches and even rocks to lend realism to the display.

'It is not complete, I'm afraid,' Carl said. 'But what collection ever is? I continue to search. I have my contacts far and wide.'

He collected butterflies and moths, which she thought were very pretty. The stuffed animals were truly lifelike, including a polar bear standing on its hind legs and apparently about to grab anyone venturing near it with its paws.

There were books of postage stamps which must have come from every country in the world. And then there were the coins displayed on boards with the usual neat little tickets identifying them. She noticed the heads of Caesars on some of them; and these were not the oldest.

So absorbed had she become in all this great collection with the collector himself at her elbow eagerly describing and explaining how he had come by this thing and another, that the hours slipped away uncounted.

She thanked him before leaving. 'It has been so enjoyable.'

It was obvious that he was pleased. 'You must come again. Any time, any time. I am never too busy.'

20

A DEATH IN THE FAMILY

It became a regular practice when Otto was away. She would visit the elder brother and he would show her parts of his collections and tell her the history of this or that object.

She was picking up the German language in that quick way she had with foreign tongues, so that very soon it became almost as easy to converse in German as in the French which he mangled so badly.

He lent her books from the library, some of which were beautifully illustrated. She did not read them but returned them with thanks for the pleasure they had given her.

He said that it was his pleasure to lend them. And she believed him because he was not the kind of man to say things he did not mean.

Otto was amused. 'Be careful. He'll be falling in love with you.'

She told him not to talk nonsense. But to tell the truth she was not so sure it was nonsense. She remembered how his eyes seemed to light up when he opened the library door and saw who it was that had knocked. And how the colour mounted to his cheeks if their hands chanced to touch in the passing of a book from one to the other. So could there be anything in it? And if there was, what complications might it cause?

Meanwhile, as the months passed, her own love affair with Otto seemed to have entered a new phase. She supposed it was inevitable that that first ecstatic period when it seemed there could be no limit to their passion for each other must come to an end. The flame could not burn so fiercely for ever; that fact had to be faced.

They were, of course, still deeply in love; it would have been a kind of betrayal to doubt it. But it was love of a different order, and the love-making had become a kind of routine, a habit.

★   ★   ★

So things might have gone on indefinitely had it not been for one shocking event: the murder of Count Carl Axter-Mandel.

★   ★   ★

It happened one night in early summer and was not discovered until morning. Then a

147

servant came to Otto in great distress to report that the Count had been found in the room where the collections were kept. He was lying on the floor with a knife in his chest and a lot of blood on the body.

Everything pointed to the conclusion that he had surprised a thief in the act, since it could be seen that a window had been forced open and one of the Count's collections of ancient coins was scattered on the floor, apparently dropped by the thief in his haste to get away.

It seemed to Isabella that Otto was more angered than distressed by the crime. It was the audacity of someone daring to break into the schloss and kill his brother that apparently affected him more than the death of that brother.

She herself wept. She and Carl had never been lovers in the sense that she and Otto were, but now that he was gone she realised that she had loved this shy, rather inarticulate man. She realised too that things in that great house would never be the same again; that with this death a vital change had come about which might well mark another turning-point in her life.

★ ★ ★

It was very easy to catch the murderer. He himself must have realised that it was inevitable, for he made scarcely any attempt to avoid arrest.

They found him in his cottage on the estate with some of the coins he had stolen. He had been one of the outdoor employees until he had been fired for some petty misdemeanour. He had a wife and two young children, a boy and a girl, and no doubt he had been at his wits' end to provide for them now that no wages were coming in. So in desperation he had decided to rob his former employer. He must have heard about the collection of coins that the Count possessed and decided to steal them, although a moment's reflection should have warned him that, even if he succeeded in stealing the coins, he could not have used them to buy as much as a single loaf of bread. They would have had to be sold for what they were: collectors' items. And where could he have hoped to sell them?

It was possible that the act had been seen by him as a form of revenge for his dismissal. But if so, it was ironical that he had killed the wrong man. It was Otto who had dismissed him without even mentioning it to his brother, who would probably have been too soft-hearted to take away his livelihood.

So he was arrested without delay in front of

a weeping wife and two small children, who would no doubt be thrown out of their home to make way for a new employee.

'What will happen to them?' Isabella asked.

Otto shrugged. 'That is no concern of mine.'

She thought this was heartless of him, but she said nothing.

'The man of course will be tried. It should not take long. His guilt is obvious.'

'And then?'

'The axe.'

She shivered. How could he speak so coldly of the chopping off of a man's head? To her it seemed a terrible thing.

'Perhaps,' he said, 'you would like to watch the execution. It would be an interesting experience for you. I am told that quite often the headsman, either through lack of skill or nervousness, does his job so clumsily that two or even three cuts are necessary.'

Again she shuddered. 'Nothing would induce me to watch such a horrible spectacle.'

'Ah, you are too squeamish. And after all, the punishment is deserved, is it not?'

He left her then to ruminate on how one fell act had changed the entire situation in the schloss. Things now would never be the same again.

21

MARRIAGE PLANS

'I think it is time for me to get married and have a son,' Otto said.

Isabella said nothing. She waited for him to enlarge upon this statement. And after a while he did so.

'While Carl was alive there seemed to be no urgency, although strictly speaking the situation was no different from what it is now. He was unmarried and childless, so I was the heir presumptive. But there was always the remote possibility that he might marry and produce an heir. Now that possibility no longer exists. I am the Count and if I were to die the title and estate would pass to my cousin, Hermann.'

'Would that be such a bad thing?'

'It would be a disaster. I can think of no one less fit to be my heir. That must be avoided at all cost. Therefore, as I have said, I must marry.'

Isabella was silent. It was apparent that when he spoke of marriage he was not suggesting that she should be his wife. A dancer from the Moulin Rouge whom he had regarded as being unfit to be introduced to his friends and acquaintances was hardly likely to come into the reckoning as a possible spouse. Nor was it possible that she would be retained as a mistress when a newly wedded wife arrived on the scene. Indeed, she herself would never have accepted that role.

'So,' she said, 'what you are telling me is that I am no longer welcome here. Is that it?'

He gave a shrug. 'It was always inevitable. You yourself must have realised that things could not go on like this indefinitely. It has been good while it lasted, hasn't it?'

'Oh, very good.' She spoke with a trace of bitterness. 'I must have been a fool to imagine it might last. But I did. I suppose you did not.'

He shrugged again, but said nothing.

'When do you wish me to leave?'

'There is no immediate urgency.'

'Perhaps not. But now that the decision has been made I would prefer not to delay my departure.'

'I see that you are being sensible,' he said. 'And of course it is not as if you will be leaving empty-handed.'

She guessed that he was referring to the jewellery. Perhaps in addition he would hand her some money. It was rather degrading.

Now that her services were no longer required she was being paid off. But she was far too level-headed to throw the jewels at his feet in a fit of pique or even to refuse any cash that he might hand out. She was still young, but the future was uncertain.

★ ★ ★

She departed later in the week with more luggage than that with which she had arrived. Otto had indeed given her a generous amount in marks to go with the jewellery, so it could certainly not have been said that she was leaving empty-handed.

He accompanied her to the railway station at Ulm, riding in one of the estate coaches. He bought her ticket and saw her on to the train, wished her luck and kissed her goodbye. But the kiss was so different from those earlier kisses that she remembered. It was perfunctory, a mere peck, meaningless. Everything was so different from that journey from France a year ago. Then she had been eager and excited, with the man she loved beside her. Now the love had faded and she was travelling alone to an uncertain future. Moreover, on this journey she had to fend for herself with no one to see to everything for her.

It was a two-day journey and she arrived in Paris late in the morning, jaded and with a slight headache. She lost no time in converting her German marks into French francs, and then engaged a cab to take her to a hotel where she booked a room. Having left her luggage there, she took her jewels to a bank which she had used during her previous sojourn in the city and deposited all except one ring. This she wore as a reminder of better times.

It was too late now to pay a visit to the Moulin Rouge and she decided to leave it until the next day. She was not at all sure what kind of reception she would get from Madame Cochet when she went there, but she felt confident that Juliette LeBlanc would give her a rapturous welcome. She felt a twinge of conscience for not having carried out her promise to write to her former lodging partner. In fact thoughts of the girl had never entered her head until now; there had been too much else to think about. But now all that was in the past and her great hope was that she might start again where she had left off when she had departed with Otto Axter-Mandel; now Count Otto and lost to her for ever.

22

DARK SECRET

Madame Cochet did not say: 'I told you so', though she might have been tempted to do so. For had not events turned out very much as she had predicted?

What she did say was: 'You're looking very well, my dear. Is this merely a brief visit to Paris or are you here to stay?'

'I am here to stay.'

'Ah! And does that mean you are seeking employment?'

'I shall have to earn a living.'

Madame sighed gustily. 'That, I fear, is a necessity which most of us encounter when there is no one else to foot the bills for us.'

It was the only guarded reference she made to the man Isabella had departed with so many months ago.

Now she said: 'I imagine you will not have kept in practice during your absence.'

Isabella had to admit that she had not.

'So it will take a little time for you to get back into form. You have put on a little weight perhaps?'

'It is possible.'

'It is probable. Where are you staying?'

'In a hotel room for the present. I shall have to find some suitable accommodation.'

'Undoubtedly.'

'I thought perhaps, if no one has taken my place sharing lodgings with Juliette LeBlanc — '

Madame Cochet stared at her. 'You have not heard?'

Isabella sensed immediately that it was something bad she had not heard, and she simply shook her head.

'No, of course not. You have been in another country. The news would hardly have been important enough to cross the border. That poor girl.'

'Juliette?'

'Of course. Who else?'

'Tell me, Madame. What happened?'

'It was just after you left. The very next day. She threw herself into the Seine.'

'Oh my God! No.'

'Oh my God! Yes.'

'She killed herself?'

'That is usually what happens when people throw themselves into a river, is it not?'

'But why? Why?'

Madame Cochet shrugged expressively. 'Who knows?' She looked hard at Isabella.

'You have no suggestion?'

'I? No, none.'

And yet she was remembering how the girl had wept when told that her fellow lodger was going away with a man. She remembered too that a failed artist had taken a similar path to oblivion after living at that same apartment. Perhaps the example had influenced Juliette in her choice of an exit from this life.

'I am so sorry.'

'As we all were. Such a nice young girl. But now she is almost forgotten. It is the way of the world.'

★　★　★

So there was no going back to the old lodgings for Isabella. She looked around and found a rather better ground-floor apartment in a different part of Paris. Even if the other place had been available she would not have wished to return to it. It would have been haunted by the dead girl, just one of an unending succession of misfits swallowed by that ever-hungry, never-sated river.

★　★　★

She paid a second visit to the Moulin Rouge the next morning. Madame Cochet had agreed, none too eagerly, to give her the chance to re-establish herself as a favourite with the public.

'You will need some practice, as I have said. And exercise to get fit. We will see how it goes.'

It did not go too well at first. It was so long since she had danced, and no one could hope to start again at the point where they had left off. It was not only some of the skill that had been lost but the stamina also. She became tired very quickly; her legs ached and she became short of breath. But she persevered and gradually it came back; not perhaps quite all the old panache but sufficient for Madame Cochet to give her approval.

'You have worked hard and I think next week we may introduce you to an audience.'

So the posters went up: 'Return of L'Anglaise!' There was the Toulouse-Lautrec picture of her too; the one she so disliked.

'Let us hope,' Madame Cochet said, 'that they have not forgotten you. You were a favourite before you left, but a year is a long time. However, we shall see.'

★ ★ ★

She need have had no qualms. L'Anglaise had not been forgotten. It was as though the

158

patrons of the Moulin Rouge had been waiting expectantly for her return. They came and were charmed again.

Madame Cochet was delighted, though somewhat surprised.

'I hardly expected it. I imagined they would have forgotten you. But apparently not. I wonder what it is about you that draws them to you. It cannot be because you are English. So what is it?'

This was a question that Isabella herself could not answer. She just had to accept the fact that she pleased the audiences and thank her lucky stars that it was so.

It was hardly to be expected that her return would be welcomed by all the other performers. There were a few who resented the fact that she could go away and come back just when it suited her. One of these was a girl named Colette who was rather tall and not particularly attractive. She would make snide remarks about foreign intruders which were obviously aimed at one English performer. The fact that Isabella ignored all this and refused to be drawn into any retaliation merely added to the other girl's resentment. For the present, however, the antagonism remained verbal, and sotto voce at that. So no harm was done.

★ ★ ★

One day an old acquaintance of Isabella's turned up. It was Monsieur Henri Dupin, the man who had originally brought her to France. She had seen him fairly frequently during the first period of her engagement at the Moulin Rouge, but this was the first encounter with him since her return from Germany.

He was as dapper as ever and greeted her with effusion.

'So you are back. That is good. You have been sorely missed. It was very wicked of you to go off like that and leave us mourning. However, now you are here again and all is well.'

She told him she was pleased to be back. And she was, in a way. She loved performing before an audience and the applause was music to her ears. Though she had not really missed it in those early days and months with Otto she had always felt as though there were something that she had lost by running away with him.

'That man you were with in England,' Dupin said. 'What was his name? I have forgotten.'

'Gerald Hardacre.'

'Ah yes. Do you ever hear from him?'

160

'Never. We lost touch when I left England. I am not even sure whether he is still alive.'

'No? Well, perhaps it was best to make a clean break.'

'I think so.'

She seldom thought of Gerald now. Yet it was he who had set her on the road to her present occupation. How long ago it seemed now. She was only seventeen at the time when he persuaded her to run away with him, and people might say it had been an evil thing to do, since it was surely to serve his own ends, but she did not regret anything. Life for her might have been horribly dull if he had not appeared on the scene. And surely it was better to be dead than dull.

Dupin had never made any attempt to make their relationship anything but a purely business one. He had acted more like a father than a prospective lover, though a very different kind of father from the real one, that country business man who had tried to bring her back to the family home and had wept when she refused.

She thought of two others in the family — her sisters. They would be grown up now and married perhaps to dull husbands with dull jobs. Did they ever speak of her, any of them back there in England, or was she regarded as an outcast, even a sinner, not to be mentioned in respectable company? It rather amused her to think so. Of one thing she was certain: she had no desire to return to the bosom of her family. It would, she imagined, be a somewhat chilly bosom for a returning prodigal such as she.

Anyway, it would never happen. She was sure of that.

Monsieur Dupin had been watching her closely. He seemed to be reading her mind, for he said: 'Your family in England. Have you ever had any desire to return to them?'

'Never.'

'Would they, do you suppose, approve of what you are doing?'

'I doubt it. I ran away, you see. My sisters might envy me. They might even wish they had the courage to do the same. My father made every effort to persuade me to return home.'

'And of course you refused.'

'Yes.'

'Your father. What is he?'

She hesitated, debating in her mind whether to tell the truth or invent some distinguished profession. But truth prevailed.

'He is an ironmonger.'

Monsieur Dupin looked as if he wanted to laugh but was making a valiant effort to suppress the inclination.

'An ironmonger?'

'In a small village.'

'You amaze me.'

'Well, now you know my dark secret. But please don't spread it around.'

'I shall be an oyster,' Dupin promised.

23

ACCIDENT

It was the girl named Colette who was instrumental in bringing Isabella's present stint as a dancer at the Moulin Rouge to a halt. Whether it was by design or accident no one could be certain. She herself vehemently denied any premeditation, but of course she would be bound to do so, and bearing in mind her hostility to L'Anglaise, not everyone believed her.

It happened when both were hurrying to the head of a short stairway. They reached it almost together and collided with each other. The result was that Isabella went tumbling down the stairs while Colette managed to remain at the top. The sound of an ankle bone breaking was distinctly audible and even more so the cry of pain given by the victim.

Others were soon on the scene. She was lifted up but could stand only on one foot. Madame Cochet was summoned to the scene of the accident, if accident it was, and was devastated. Even a sprained ankle would have been bad enough, but if, as had to be feared, this was a broken one, it was a disaster.

The victim was taken without delay to a hospital where the worst fears were confirmed: the ankle was indeed broken.

It could not, Madame Cochet said, have happened at a more inconvenient time. Where was she to find a replacement at short notice for L'Anglaise? How long, moreover, would it take for the ankle to heal?

The surgeon was not hopeful. It would be a lengthy process at best. It was not a simple fracture; by no means so. It was multiple; he had seldom had to deal with a worse case. Pressed by Madame Cochet to give an estimate of just how long it would be before the victim was able to dance again, he shook his head.

'To dance? Not for many months.' He did not add 'if ever' but it was there to be read in his expression.

So, instead of appearing on stage at the Moulin Rouge Isabella lay in a hospital bed in a crowded ward, feeling the pain in her ankle and worrying about the future. Suddenly everything, from appearing to be as good as it could possibly be, had become horribly uncertain.

One cheerful note was struck by the appearance of Monsieur Henri Dupin. He came to offer his condolences.

'Such a misfortune. Who could have foreseen such a thing? However, I am sure you will soon be back on your feet. Both of them. And all will be well. Meanwhile, my dear, you are not to bother your head about expenses. I personally will see to all that.'

She thanked him. It took a weight off her mind; for obviously she would be earning nothing while she was out of action. She had the jewellery in the bank deposit of course, but she would have had to trust an agent to handle any of that, and this she did not wish to do.

Sometimes she wondered whether it had really been an accident, that collision with Colette. She knew that the girl disliked her; was perhaps jealous because of the interest taken in her and the publicity she received. So maybe she had engineered that collision at the top of the stairs with the intention of sending her rival tumbling down. She could not, of course, have foreseen the result of the fall and perhaps had never had in her mind anything quite so disastrous. It was noticeable, however, that she had not paid a visit to offer her condolences. But, one way or another, what difference did it make? The damage was done and only time could undo it.

After a day or two she had become quite a

celebrity in the ward. 'A dancer from the Moulin Rouge! Fancy that! And English too!'

The nurses treated her with the respect due to such a person and the surgeon paid her more attention than might have been normal. At least, so she believed. She was, after all, even lying in a hospital bed, very beautiful, and he was male and young enough to be susceptible to feminine charm.

When he examined her ankle it seemed to her that he uncovered more of her leg than was strictly necessary; but then again he was young and the leg was one of the shapeliest ever put on show at the Moulin Rouge.

As things turned out the fracture was less serious than the surgeon had initially suggested. Soon she was in a wheelchair and, since the weather was warm and fine, she was allowed to sit out in the hospital garden; which was far more pleasant than lying in bed in the ward. Here again Dr Madelin, as the young surgeon's name was, made it his business to visit her.

'You are doing very well,' he assured her. 'Soon we will have you walking. With crutches at first, of course. No dancing yet, I am afraid, but all in good time. Be patient. Rome was not built in a day, so I have been told.'

She had the impression that he was talking

for the sake of talking; reluctant to hurry away, though he must have had plenty of other patients to attend to.

She was pleased nevertheless to have him assure her that the ankle was progressing well. She was impatient to be walking on it as the preliminary to an eventual resumption of dancing. She missed the atmosphere of the theatre and the applause from a crowded house, the feeling that she had all these people in the palm of her hand, or perhaps more accurately, at her feet.

It appeared that the original somewhat depressing prognosis had been rather exaggerated. The fracture turned out to be far less serious than Dr Madelin had suggested, and his later and more encouraging words were nearer the truth. The patient was indeed soon walking with the aid of crutches, and from there she progressed to a stick.

When finally she was able to throw the stick away and stand, as it were, on her own two feet, it might have been imagined that she would be in a very short space of time back on stage delighting audiences with her truly magical dancing.

So it might have been, but for one thing: she had a limp.

'Perhaps it will wear off,' Madame Cochet suggested.

But of course it was not the kind of thing that would wear off. It was permanent.

For Isabella it was a disaster. It was the end of her career on the stage, for who ever heard of a professional dancer with a limp?

Madame Cochet was sympathetic. 'Such a tragedy for one so talented. Who would have imagined it? What will you do now?'

It was a question Isabella had asked herself and had found no answer. She had no profession but that of a dancer, and now that was finished.

'Would it not be possible for you to go back to England?'

The thought had occurred to her, but she had rejected it out of hand. How could she ever bring herself to go crawling back to the family like a prodigal daughter? It would be an admission of defeat, a confession that she had been a fool to run away. Any course of action would be preferable to that.

It was not as if she were destitute either. She had some money and there were the jewels that Otto had given her lying in a deposit box in a Paris bank. She had no idea how much they were worth but it had to be a considerable sum, for he had been quite profligate in those days and bought only the most expensive offerings for the woman he loved. So the future was not entirely bleak, and she might perhaps find employment of some kind, though she had no idea what. Unfortunately experience of any but that which was now out of the question.

Six months later she still had not found a job, but she was no longer alone. She was living with a man.

24

JACQUES MAURAT

Though it might have been more accurate to say that the man was living with her, since it was her apartment that was accommodating the two of them.

It was a chance meeting that had brought them together. She was sitting by herself at a small table in a bar where she had gone more for the sake of some human company than the glass of wine which she had in front of her and was very slowly consuming. She did not notice the man approaching, and he was almost at her elbow when she heard his voice.

'Would it be an intrusion if I were to share this table with Madame?'

He had one hand on the back of a vacant chair and a glass of what might have been brandy in the other. He was a man of medium height wearing a dark grey suit and a hat which he removed at once. His hair was black and receding slightly and he had side-whiskers and a neatly-trimmed moustache but no beard. A stiff white collar looked as if it had been specifically designed for the purpose of supporting his head, since it reached almost to his ears. In age he might have been somewhere between forty and forty-five. He was neither handsome nor ugly, but had the kind of face that might have been forgotten as soon as it disappeared from sight. He had a soft voice which gave the impression that he was imparting some confidential information.

Isabella gave a little nod of the head to indicate that he was free to use the chair. She was in fact rather glad to have someone sitting there, since it made her feel less conspicuous. She had been aware of some curious glances in her direction. A young woman as attractive as she was drinking alone in a bar could hardly avoid rousing some unwanted interest.

'It is,' the man said, 'a pleasant evening.'

Isabella agreed that it was.

The man took a sip of whatever it was in his glass, put the glass down and said: 'Pardon my asking, Madame, but haven't we met somewhere before?'

'No,' she said, 'I don't think so. In fact I am sure we have not.'

'And yet I feel I have seen you somewhere. If I may take the liberty of saying so, yours is not a face one could easily forget. So where can it have been?'

He appeared to be genuinely convinced that he had seen her before, and she believed he was not inventing a previous encounter as an opening gambit. So could he have seen her without her seeing him? The answer should have been obvious at once.

'The Moulin Rouge?'

He slapped his forehead with the flat of his hand. 'But of course. You are L'Anglaise. How could I not have realised it at once?'

'So you go to the Moulin Rouge?'

'Now and then. But I have not seen you there lately.'

'And you never will again.'

He looked surprised. 'No? Why is that?'

'I can no longer dance. An accident. My ankle was broken and it has never healed properly. The fact is, I limp.'

'Oh, what a misfortune. And to happen to someone like you who was so brilliant a performer. I am desolated. It is a tragedy.'

She thought he was reacting a shade too extravagantly, but he did seem genuinely concerned, which made her inclined to regard him with some favour. Having thus, as it were, broken the ice they became more communicative. He introduced himself as Jacques Maurat and told her that he was a financial consultant. He had, so he said, several important clients, though he did not name them.

After this they got on very well together. They had more drinks, which he paid for, and she told him her name was Isabella Foster. She also told him that she had lost all contact with her family and had never been back home since leaving. He thought this rather sad. He himself was an orphan and had never had any family to call his own.

Later in the evening when she said it was time to return to her apartment he insisted on escorting her there, since it was not safe for a single woman to be out on the streets at that time of night. He was at present living in a hotel, since he had recently sold his own house and was looking around for a suitable replacement.

When they reached her apartment, which was not far distant, she thought he might expect to be invited in; and she almost did so but decided against it. Nevertheless, he seemed unwilling, now that he had made her acquaintance, to leave it at that, and he suggested that perhaps they might meet again, since for him at least it had been such an enjoyable evening.

Alarm-bells started ringing in her head, but they were faint and she ignored them. She was too much alone now that she had left the Moulin Rouge, and she clutched at the chance of some relief from this isolation.

Moreover, Monsieur Jacques Maurat was undoubtedly quite a charming man and certainly not old. What harm then could there be in agreeing to meet him again? If on a second encounter she discovered that they really had nothing in common there need never be a third. Nothing would be lost.

So she said: 'Yes, I think that might be rather pleasant.'

And thus it was arranged. He said he could not meet her the next day because he had some important business to transact. But the day after that, if it was convenient for her?

She said it was. And that was that.

25

WHO ELSE?

In the company of Jacques Maurat Isabella got to see more of Paris than she had ever done before. He became her guide and, incidentally, her lover. It was really most convenient; at least for him, since, having sold his house and having not yet acquired a replacement, he had been forced to live in a hotel room while he looked around.

Apparently, after moving in with Isabella, he had stopped looking around, for he made no further mention to her of any such activity. It appeared also that his business as a financial consultant did not take up a great deal of his time, though he did now and then set out with a briefcase and return only late in the day. She assumed that this was when he went to see his clients, but she asked no questions.

He seemed to have sufficient money and made an offer to contribute to the running expenses of the apartment. This was soon after he moved in.

'We must come to some arrangement,' he

said. 'I must put my share in the pot.'

Oddly enough, he made no further mention of this, and she supposed it had slipped his mind. She hesitated to remind him of the promise, and after all, the expense was very little greater than when she had had the place to herself, so why bother? She noticed that his wardrobe was well stocked, for he brought with him two large portmanteaus and later a trunk was delivered.

He was really something of a dandy and had quite a variety of suits. But she supposed he needed to be well-dressed when he went to meet his clients, since they would hardly have been favourably impressed by a financial consultant who looked like a tramp.

There was one great advantage of having a profession that left him with so much free time. He was in consequence able to act as her guide to those parts of Paris that she had never previously visited. He was amazed that she had never set foot on the Île de la Cité.

'My dear lady, it is the very heart of Paris. So you have never seen the Cathedral of Notre Dame?'

She admitted with some shame that she had not.

'But you must have read Victor Hugo's novel in which the hunchback Quasimodo appears.'

She shook her head, feeling very ignorant. For though they had been taught French at Miss Lowther's school for young ladies they had been introduced to scarcely any French literature.

'Well, well! It seems there is much to show you in this fair city.'

This, in the weeks and months that followed, he proceeded to do, proving himself a knowledgeable guide. One day he even hired a boat and took her for a row on the Seine; demonstrating that he was no mean hand with the oars. Another day they hired an open landau and took a turn along the Avenue des Champs-Elysée. The sun shone and there were quite a number of horse-riders to be seen.

'It is amazing,' Maurat remarked, 'that one sunny day can discover so many citizens with no work to do.'

'Like us.'

He smiled. 'As you say. Like us.'

This period, she reflected, was the most enjoyable she had experienced since the breaking of her ankle. Sometimes she wondered quite how long it would last; for, looking back, it seemed that just when things appeared to be going well there would come some incident to bring the good time to an end. But since one could never see into the future there was really nothing one could do to avoid these sudden changes in fortune. Therefore there was no sense in bothering one's head about possible disasters waiting round the corner. If they happened, they happened, and that was all there was to it.

She wondered whether Jacques had had similar experiences. She knew nothing about his life before that first encounter in the bar. He had revealed nothing of importance to her, and she had asked no questions. If there were any dark secrets back there she did not wish to hear about them. There was much to be said for a policy of leaving well alone.

★ ★ ★

It was a policy he too appeared to be observing. He knew something of her past of course. He knew that she had been a dancer at the Moulin-Rouge, but he did not know how she, an English girl, had come to be there. Nor did he know anything of that year-long gap in her career when she had been with Otto in Germany. She felt no inclination to speak of that to anyone.

In the end, however, it was Jacques who broke the unstated rule and asked a personal question. He did so hesitantly, admitting that it was something that had bothered him a

179

little. It was, he said, apparent that since leaving the Moulin Rouge she had had no paid employment; yet it was also apparent that she had money. Otherwise how could she afford to rent an apartment in that part of the city and purchase the necessities of life?

She gave a laugh, though it sounded more than a little forced. 'Don't you think that is my business?'

'And none of mine? Yes, I admit it. And of course you are in no way obliged to tell me. But as one who is more than a little interested in your welfare and has much experience of financial matters, it occurs to me that I might be able to help in some way. If help is needed.'

'Ah, you think I am incapable of dealing efficiently with money matters and that you might be able to put me on the right track. Is that it?'

She thought he seemed a little put out by her reaction to his inquiry, for he frowned slightly. When he answered it was with a degree of acidity.

'You are bound to tell me nothing if you do not wish to do so. I am trying to be helpful, but of course if you need no help, so be it.'

She hastened to smooth out any ruffling of his feathers she might have caused; for the truth was that she could not be sure she was managing her finances in the most sensible way.

'Please,' she said, 'don't be offended. As a matter of fact I should be grateful for some advice from an expert.'

He assured her that he was not at all offended and he would be delighted to help her in any way he could.

'Very well then. You would like to know how I'm managing to exist now that I have no job. The answer is simple: I'm living on my jewels.'

He looked puzzled. 'Perhaps you had better give me a little more detail. I am not quite sure I understand.'

'As I said, it is quite simple. I have some jewellery deposited in a bank. When I need money I sell a piece. Actually so far I've only had to part with one — a bracelet. It will keep me going for a while yet. The jewels were given to me by a certain person who was very, very rich. And still is, I imagine. I can assure you that whatever he bought for me was certainly not trash.'

She suddenly became aware of the expression on Maurat's face. It could only be described as one of horror.

'So this is how you intend to live? By selling your jewellery, piece by piece.'

'What else can I do? I have no alternative.'

'And when you eventually come to the end of this source of income. What then?'

'Oh,' she said, 'that will not be for a long time yet.'

But he had touched a nerve. This was a kind of spectre that she tried to keep shut away, but which now and then broke out to haunt her. What would she do when the well ran dry?

'A long time,' he said. 'Yes, maybe. But how long? And how long will you live? It will be a race between the two: your life and the jewels. Which will have the more stamina?'

'I know, I know. You mustn't suppose I haven't thought about it. I have. But what can I do? Are you suggesting I should seek work? I have no training for anything except dancing. And that is no longer possible.'

He looked at her and gave a little shake of the head. 'My dear, my dear! How ignorant you must be of financial matters, and how fortunate that you have me to advise you. Don't you see that your jewels can be converted into a source of regular income that will last indefinitely?'

'No. Tell me how.'

'Why, all you have to do is sell them and invest the proceeds. You could put the lot on deposit in a bank and draw the interest at regular intervals.'

'Oh,' she said, 'how stupid of me. I never thought of that. And you think the interest would be enough to live on?'

'That of course would depend on how much you got for the jewels. But there is a more profitable way of investing the money.'

'Tell me.'

'You could buy shares in a company. Then you would be paid dividends which, if you chose the right company would amount to much more than your interest from any bank.'

'But I know nothing about that sort of business. I wouldn't know how to set about buying these things you call shares. I'm completely ignorant of all that.'

Maurat smiled. 'Of course you are, my dear. That is why you would need to have an adviser. Someone whose business it is to handle this kind of thing.'

She looked at him with raised eyebrows. 'You?'

'Who else?'

26

MONEY MATTERS

One of the first things he told her was that she had almost certainly been underpaid for the first piece of jewellery she had sold.

'You took it to a jeweller and accepted just what he offered for it?'

She admitted that she had. 'What else could I have done?'

'You should have haggled. He would have expected you to. He must have been agreeably surprised when you walked away with his opening bid with no attempt to get more.'

'You really think so?'

'I am sure of it.'

'And yet he seemed such a pleasant obliging man.'

'He would. All part of the game.'

She felt stupid and also annoyed to think that she had been duped. And the fact was that she doubted whether she could ever become an adept haggler. It was just not her line.

Maurat appeared to read her mind. 'You

don't think you can do it, do you?'

'No, I don't.'

'So would you like me to handle that part of the business as well?'

It seemed the obvious solution to the problem. She did not doubt for a moment that he would get a better price for her jewellery than she could ever have obtained herself. So she accepted his offer without hesitation, reflecting how fortunate it was that she should have someone with so much knowledge of financial matters to advise her. Left to herself she would gradually have sold all her pot of gold for far less than its true value and might in not so very many years have had to sell it all merely to survive.

★ ★ ★

Maurat was amazed when he saw how much there was after she had taken it from the bank. Back in the apartment she spread out the collection on a table where the diamonds glittered and the emeralds and sapphires shone in their golden settings. There were rings, brooches, necklaces and bracelets, all of the finest quality. Otto had undoubtedly been lavish with his gifts, never reckoning the cost.

'Well,' Maurat said, 'you are certainly not

destitute. I never imagined there would be so much.'

He suggested that the best plan would be to take each piece separately to a different jeweller. There was no lack of choice in a city the size of Paris. Isabella agreed. She was willing to follow his advice, since she had come to put her trust in his experience.

She did not love him. There had been only one man in her life whom she had truly loved, and he was probably now married to a princess. But Jacques was a pleasant companion and she would have felt lost without him.

When he went to a jeweller she accompanied him. They would spend a little time inspecting the jewellery on display in order to get some idea of the price being asked for pieces similar to the one they wished to sell. One had of course to allow for the jeweller's profit, but it was a way of determining some approximation to the value of their own offering.

As soon as the jeweller understood that they were selling rather than buying he would take them into a private room at the rear of the shop where he would examine the object very closely with the aid of an eyeglass and then make an offer, which Maurat would treat with contempt. The bargaining would then go on for some time, and Maurat might pretend to lose patience, pick up the bracelet or whatever it was and get as far as the door before being called back to receive a somewhat higher offer. It was all a game of wits which Isabella watched without ever uttering a word.

Maurat always insisted on payment in cash, and the amount of francs in high denomination notes that they had in the apartment grew steadily larger. They stowed the paper money in various hiding-places until one day they put all, but a certain quantity retained to cover living expenses for the next few months, in a canvas bag and set off in a cab for the Paris Bourse. Here in a rather dusty office the money was handed over and a rather bemused Isabella signed her name in various places and finally came away with a very official-looking document which Maurat assured her was as good as money in the bank.

'It means,' he said, 'that you are now a shareholder in a company which is one of the most successful to be found. From now on you are free of any financial worries and you can set your mind at rest in that regard.'

She was rather bemused by it all, but she had to take his word for this. And indeed it soon appeared that he had been speaking nothing but the truth, as from time to time there would arrive in the post a piece of paper with some figures and her name on it which she would take to the bank and exchange for cash.

She was grateful to Jacques for sorting matters out for her. Now she need have no more qualms concerning the future: she had a steady income, a comfortable apartment and a man to take care of her. It was regrettable that her career at the Moulin Rouge had come to an untimely end, but it could in any case not have gone on for ever, so why shed tears about it?

She still knew very little about Maurat. She asked no questions, but now and then he would let fall a snippet of information; like the fact that he was not a native Parisian. He had been born in a small town in Normandy and had come to Paris as a young man to seek his fortune.

'And have you found it?'

He smiled at this. 'I think now I have.'

He was still making no contribution to their living expenses, but she was not bothered about this and made no demands. Occasionally he would ask for a small loan to tide him over a sticky patch, and she concluded that one of his clients in the financial consultancy line had not paid up or perhaps had taken his custom elsewhere.

There could hardly have been many of them anyway; otherwise he would not have had so much time to be with her.

She rather doubted that story of his having sold a house. He had never told her where it was or anything else about it. And what had happened to all the money he received for it? There probably had never been a house but was just a harmless piece of fiction.

27

PARTING

Five years passed and she wondered just where they had gone. Nothing much seemed to have happened in the course of those years. She was still living with Jacques Maurat, or, again to be more precise, he was still living with her. At first he had frequently acted as a guide to Paris, and she had enjoyed these outings. There had been evenings at the theatre too, though never the Moulin Rouge. But these, like the outings, had gradually been given up and life had really become somewhat dull. Sometimes it occurred to her that they were like an old married couple between whom all passion had been spent and living was just a changeless routine.

When she looked in a mirror she thought she could detect the telltale signs of ageing: little wrinkles here and there, a thickening below the chin, maybe even a hint of grey hair. She hated it. Other people grew old. She had never faced the certainty that it must happen to her also.

Yet she was still scarcely thirty.

Jacques was of course a good deal older, though he had never revealed his exact age and she had never asked him to. And with men perhaps it did not matter so much.

What really did matter, and indeed was in the nature of a bombshell, was that one morning she found him packing a portmanteau. When she asked him why he was doing it he answered briefly without looking at her.

'I'm leaving.'

She could not believe he was serious. It had to be some ridiculous kind of joke, though it was difficult to detect the humour in it.

'What is this nonsense?' she demanded.

Again he did not look at her, but just went on with the packing, carefully folding the clothes and stowing them away.

'It's not nonsense. I've been living with you too long. I think we've both become tired of it. Isn't that so?'

'And so you suddenly decide to walk out on me? Is that it?'

'I've been thinking about it for some time.'

'So why did you never mention it to me? Did you think I wouldn't be interested? That it was no concern of mine?'

He made no answer to that. He had not once turned to look at her. She was talking to the back of his head. And suddenly she knew what he was not admitting; the true reason for this sudden decision to walk out on her. Perhaps it was not so very sudden after all. Perhaps it had been building up for quite a while and only now had he found the nerve to bring things to a head.

'It's another woman, isn't it?'

He did not reply at once, but his hands had stopped moving, as if the question had arrested them in the carrying out of some nefarious act.

She had to repeat the question before she could get an answer.

'Isn't it?'

Then suddenly he turned and looked at her and snapped the answer that she had been demanding.

'Yes, it is.'

Though she had guessed correctly, the confirmation when it came was still a shock. It was so unexpected. She had imagined he was perfectly contented living with her and that their relationship would continue indefinitely. Now, abruptly, it was ended. She would be alone again. Though she had never loved Jacques she had liked him well enough, and there had never been any friction between them. Theirs had been a relationship remarkably free from disputes of any serious nature. There had been no bickering, none of those heated arguments that so often marred the lives of married couples. So why did he have to look elsewhere?

It angered her. So much so that at that moment she felt a sudden urge to hit him and thus give vent to her resentment by physical means. But she resisted the impulse. It would serve no useful purpose to lose control of herself. Instead she just said bitterly:

'I suppose she is more attractive than me?'

His answer surprised her.

'No,' he said. 'How could she be?'

'Then why?'

He shrugged as only a Frenchman could. 'It is useless to try to explain.'

He closed the portmanteau and fastened it. He took his overcoat from the wardrobe and put it on; then picked up the bag.

'I shall take this with me. The trunk will be called for later. I have already packed it. There is nothing of yours in it.'

His coolness exasperated her. Again she had the urge to strike him and again resisted it. He seemed to guess what was in her mind and shrugged again.

'You may hit me if you wish. Perhaps I deserve it. But it would not alter the situation.'

'I would rather not dirty my hand.'

He gave a little laugh. 'So I am dirt now, am I? Well, that's the way it goes. You would not, I imagine, wish me to kiss you goodbye.'

'Go,' she said. 'I never wish to see you again.'

In the hallway he picked up his hat and his stick. He opened the door and was gone.

28

TROUBLE

It was like the time before she had met Maurat. It was like it and yet different, because now she was older and she had the memory of how much better it had been having someone with whom to share the apartment; a companion to talk to and ask for help when she needed it. Time passed so slowly, pointlessly. There seemed to be no purpose in living; it was just one empty day after another.

She thought of visiting the Moulin Rouge, but then thought better of it. She could not be sure that Madame Cochet was still there; and even if she was, whether she would wish to renew the acquaintance. What would they have to say to each other?

She could have visited the places to which Maurat had taken her when he had been widening her knowledge of Paris; but there would have been no pleasure in it now. One needed a companion, and she had none.

One day when she was out shopping she caught sight of him with a woman on his arm.

The woman, no doubt. She was wearing a wide-brimmed hat adorned with artificial roses, and when she turned her head it was possible to see that she was of a dark complexion and the pouting lips might have indicated a sulky nature. She was certainly young, but her figure was dumpy and it was difficult to see what had attracted Maurat to her, apart from her youth. But of course it was impossible to see with another person's eyes; especially when that other person was of a different sex.

Isabella had quickly withdrawn into the cover of a shop doorway and Maurat had not even glanced in her direction. He was talking to the girl and seemed to be suggesting something with which she was disagreeing. Isabella could see that the man had put a hand on her arm and that she pulled the arm away with a pettish gesture. She also said something which Isabella could not hear.

Then they were gone and she saw no more of them. Indeed, as things turned out she was never again to see the girl who had taken her place in Jacques Maurat's life.

★ ★ ★

There was one thing for which she had to thank Maurat: he had put her finances on a firm footing. She now had no worries about the future in that respect, since the little slips of printed paper continued to arrive at regular intervals and were changed at the bank for a pleasing amount of cash.

But she would have been happier if she had had a companion. First there had been Gerald Hardacre, then Juliette LeBlanc, then the best of all, Otto Axter-Mandel, and finally Jacques Maurat. Now there was no one.

She decided that what she needed was some activity to pass the time. She tried knitting, but gave it up almost immediately. Crochet lasted a little longer but then went the same way. She bought a tin of paints and some brushes and attempted water-colour painting but soon discovered that she had no talent whatever in this line. Her artistic gifts had all been in the dance, and that was now denied her.

She had no friends. She scarcely knew the people who lived next door and she had no desire to make their acquaintance. She did a lot of reading. She browsed through second-hand bookshops and open-air stalls and carried her purchases back home in a shopping-basket. She read in bed by the light of a candle and often fell asleep, to wake up hours later to find the candle burnt out and the room in darkness.

So the days passed, and the weeks and the months, with nothing to stir the blood or relieve the monotony. Sometimes she thought of the family in England she had left behind her all those years ago; but she felt no desire to return. It would be humiliating. She could imagine the things that would be said about her. At the height of her success on the stage she might have faced them all, but not now that this was all behind her. No; she would never go back.

★   ★   ★

There came a day when boredom was banished; though she would have been happier if the banishment had never been effected in such a way. A thousand times better any amount of boredom than this.

It was autumn; late in the evening. There had been rain earlier but now it had stopped, leaving a chill in the air, and she had lighted a fire in the sitting-room. She loved fires. You could sit by them, warming your feet and watching the coals burn. Sometimes there would be a hiss and a flame would shoot out like a demon that had been suddenly released from prison. You could picture all sorts of things in the glowing embers of an open fire; fanciful pictures coming and going. She was doing just this on that fateful evening. You could also fall asleep in an armchair; as she did too.

The knocking seemed at first merely to be part of a dream she was having, and it did not immediately awaken her. But then she came out of her dreamland and back to reality. Moreover, the reality was that someone was hammering as if in a frenzy on the front door.

She did not go at once to open it. It was as if she had a premonition that opening the door could mean letting in something evil.

The fire had burnt low and she felt cold. It was late now, so who could possibly be paying a call on her at that time of night?

The knocking continued with scarcely any abatement. Indeed, it seemed to become even more frenzied. She wondered who it could be and she could think of only one person who could be calling on her at that hour: Jacques.

But why? She had not seen him since that afternoon when he had been with the girl. So why, if indeed it were he, would he be coming to her now?

The knocking continued with more insistence. Summoning up her courage she went into the dimly lit hallway and unlocked the door.

As soon as she opened it the man rushed in

and slammed it shut behind him before turning the key in the lock.

She saw at once that it was indeed Jacques Maurat, but with neither hat nor coat. She began to say something, but he brushed past her and went into the room where she had been dozing by the fire.

There was an oil-lamp on the table and by its light she could now see him clearly and was shocked by what she saw.

There was a red stain on his hands and on his jacket; stain that she guessed had not been made by paint.

He had collapsed rather than sat down in the chair she had been sitting in; and now he buried his face in his hands so that some of the crimson stain was transferred to his cheeks. His shoulders were shaking as if with an ague, and he seemed to be weeping.

She could not move. She stood there looking down at him and wondering what had happened and what it was he had been running from. She did not dare to ask.

When he spoke the words were so faint as to be almost inaudible. They seemed to stick in his throat. But she heard them and wished she had not.

'I've killed her.'

She was stunned. For a few moments the words simply did not make sense to her. They were just words: meaningless. Then he repeated them.

'I've killed her.'

And this time the full import of them got through to her. He was talking about the girl she had seen him with in the street. It was her blood staining his hands, his clothing, his face.

But why? Why would he wish to kill her?

Then, as if in answer to the question she had not voiced, he said: 'She goaded me. She was always doing it. She never did anything I asked of her. She sneered at me; called me an old man, a dodderer. It went on and on, day after day. I lost my temper. There was this knife, a cook's knife. I picked it up and stabbed her with it. She screamed. I went on stabbing, and then she was on the floor, not screaming any more; not making a sound; not moving; just lying there.'

He was mumbling now. He seemed to have lost the thread of what he was saying. And then his shoulders began to shake and he was sobbing again.

She stood there, looking down at him, and the full import of what he had said gradually revealed itself to her. She began to realise just how this must affect her. The moment he stepped through that doorway into the hall he had brought trouble for her. She saw it so clearly now: he had involved her in this crime he had committed.

It was so unfair. He had walked out on her when it suited him to do so, throwing her over for someone younger who had caught his fancy; and now, when that relationship had ended in tragedy, he had come back here for refuge.

But she would not let him do this to her. Why should she? She owed him nothing. He had treated her as badly as any man could, and now in this extremity he had come to her to provide a refuge for him. But that she would not do.

'You must go,' she said. 'You cannot stay here.'

He turned his head and looked at her, his face smeared with the blood from his hands and streaked now with the tears he had shed.

'But where else can I go? You can't throw me out. There is nowhere but here. For pity's sake, Bella!'

When he called her that it touched a nerve, and she knew that she had lost. She knew that she could not get rid of him. He had brought his trouble to her and now it was her trouble too.

'Oh, God!' she said. 'Why did we ever have to meet?'

29

WAITING

The days passed. Nerve-tingling days when the least sound was like a portent, a thing of ill omen.

Maurat was a wreck. He seemed to be trembling all the time, and the least sound startled him. He had washed the blood from his hands and face, and they had tried to wash it out of his clothes but without success; the stain was still there. Isabella had to go out to buy food, though he begged her not to go. He was fearful of being left alone. But she wanted to get away from the confines of the apartment, if only for a short while.

'You will come back?' he said, tugging at her arm. 'You won't leave me?'

She broke away from him, repelled by his touch as by something unclean. 'Where would I go? This is my home.'

And she thought: 'It is a home contaminated by this thing, this murderer, who has involved me in his crime.'

★ ★ ★

In a shop she overheard two women talking. She caught snatches of their conversation.

'Such a young girl — '

'Blood everywhere, they say — '

'An older man — '

'Police haven't found him yet — '

'But they will. Murder will out — '

'Must be hiding somewhere — '

She did not need to be told what they were discussing. It would be in the papers, of course. She could have bought one and read about it. But what good would that do?

★ ★ ★

He was waiting impatiently for her when she entered the apartment, using her key in the lock of the front door.

'You've been a long time.' It was as though he were accusing her of wrong-doing. 'I was beginning to think you'd gone to them.'

He did not say whom he meant by 'them', but she knew. He was afraid she might have informed the police; told them where they could find the man they were seeking. Maybe she should have done just that, for her own sake. For was she not committing a crime by harbouring him?

'The body has been discovered,' she said.

'People are talking about it. You can't stay here, you know.'

'But where can I go?'

'Suppose you were to slip away after dark, leave Paris, get yourself out into the country, use a different name — '

She could tell that the mere suggestion frightened him. He was fearful of leaving the apartment which had become a kind of sanctuary for him.

'You want to get rid of me, don't you?'

She answered in exasperation: 'Well, of course I do. Don't you see you're a threat to me? You've involved me in a crime I didn't commit.'

'There was nowhere else to go.'

'There was everywhere else. But you had to bring this trouble on me. Why? Why?'

He had no answer to that.

30

INTERROGATION

They came early one morning, heralded by thunderous knocking on the front door.

Maurat clutched Isabella's arm. 'It's them. Don't let them in. Don't let them in.'

'You fool,' she said. 'If I don't open the door they'll break it down.'

She wrenched her arm away from him and walked into the hallway just as another spate of knocking shook the door. She turned the key and opened the door, and they came in at once, pushing her in front of them like a wave casting some piece of flotsam up on a beach.

There were four of them; two in plain clothes and two in uniform. One of the plain clothes officers showed her a card of some kind, but she had no time to read what was on it.

'Monsieur Maurat is here?' he said. But he did not wait for a reply. It was a statement rather than a question.

He brushed past her and the others followed, one of them closing the door behind him.

They found Maurat hiding under a bed. He must have been out of his senses to imagine he could avoid being discovered in that way.

They arrested Isabella also; as an accessory.

★　★　★

There was a horse-drawn van waiting in the street outside. It had little windows with bars on them. Isabella and Maurat were bundled into it while one of the plain clothes officers locked the door of the apartment and pocketed the key. She heard the driver of the van whip the horses and felt the vibration as the wheels rattled over the cobbles.

Maurat was huddled in a corner and shaking as if with a fever, an expression of terror on his face. He seemed already to be anticipating what the end of the procedure must inevitably be for him. He had been a smart, self-possessed man, very full of his own importance, but it was evident now that he lacked courage when it came to the point.

Isabella was frightened too; for who would not be in such a situation; but she refused to show it. Perhaps it was the anger in her that suppressed the terror; for she was certainly angry, and the object of her anger was that wretched being huddled in a corner. For if it had not been for him she would never have been in this situation. But for his uncontrolled temper, preceded by his lust for a girl less than half his age, neither of them would have been in this black-painted vehicle on their way to some place of incarceration and who could tell what forms of maltreatment.

★ ★ ★

It seemed a long journey. Perhaps imagination of what might be at the end made it appear longer than it was. It was possible to tell when they turned corners and when the horses struggled up hills, and now and then she heard the crack of the driver's whip.

The two plain clothes officers conversed in low tones, but Isabella could not hear what they were saying. They might have been discussing domestic matters that had nothing whatever to do with the job in hand. Such men, she supposed, must have private lives, but she found it hard to imagine them with wives and children.

At last they turned a sharp corner and rattled over more cobblestones and came to a halt. One of the policemen opened the door and got out. The one in plain clothes who seemed to be the highest ranking officer of the four ordered the two prisoners to follow him.

Isabella went first and discovered that they were in a large courtyard with high walls on three sides, in one of which was an iron gate giving access to a narrow lane outside. On the fourth side of the courtyard was a tall, bleak building, which made Isabella's heart sink by the mere sight of it.

All the windows in this building appeared to have bars in them, and a door in the middle of the wall was studded with the heads of iron bolts. The entire outer side of this structure exhibited such a gloomy and forbidding aspect that it seemed to be saying: 'Abandon hope all ye who enter here'.

The interior, when they came to it, did nothing to dispel this impression. There was a damp, fusty odour about it, which might have come from the walls or the floor, or possibly the human beings who inhabited it. Some of these could be heard shouting or even screaming, though they could not be seen as one entered.

What could be seen was a long desk or counter, behind which was a fat uniformed policeman who appeared to be of higher rank than those who had accompanied the plain clothes officers. This man had a bushy moustache and mutton-chop whiskers. His nose was large and bulbous and the face was dotted here and there with warts, as though someone had started decorating it but had lost heart and left the job unfinished. He had a cold and kept wiping his nose on his sleeve.

There was a thick ledger on the desk in front of him, and it was in this that he wrote down the names and other particulars of the two prisoners. Maurat went first, and when asked the address of his residence he gave that of Isabella's apartment, which was a lie, and she felt an urge to contradict it. But she could not have told them where he had been living until the last few days because she did not know, and he was hardly likely to reveal it himself, since that was where the murder had taken place.

When it was her turn and she came to give her name as Isabella Jane Foster the man looked puzzled and she felt compelled to explain that she was English.

'Ah!' he said. And she wondered whether this would count against her.

When these preliminaries had been completed she and Maurat were separated and she was led away to find herself in a kind of iron-barred cage in which there were already some eight or nine creatures of a kind with which she had never previously rubbed shoulders. Some of them might have been young, but they all looked like hags; Macbeth's weird sisters multiplied by three. Their clothes were dirty rags and they were dirty themselves; their hair matted and greasy.

As soon as she entered they crowded round her, as though she were a creature from another world suddenly thrust into their company. Hands like claws with filthy broken nails stretched out to tug at the fabric of her dress which contrasted so sharply with the clothes which they were wearing.

'What you in for, dearie?' one of them asked.

She made no answer, but merely looked at them askance and tried to draw away from them. They cackled with laughter at this.

'Don't you like the company?' another asked. 'Not good enough for you? Well, you shouldn't have done what you did, then they wouldn't have pulled you in. Been a bad girl, have you? Oh, dear!'

The stench of their bodies and their rags nauseated her. She felt as if she was going to faint and she had to fight against it. Fortunately, after a while they seemed to lose interest in her and she withdrew to a corner where she waited with resignation for the next development.

It came before long. A saturnine officer

unlocked the door of the cage and called her name. She answered immediately, thankful to be moved from that present company.

He relocked the door after she had joined him and conducted her down a corridor, round a corner and up a flight of stairs to a room with bare walls and one high window to let in the light. The furniture was spartan, consisting mainly of a deal table and two upright chairs.

There she was interrogated; she seated on one of the chairs and the interrogator, an officer in plain clothes, sitting on the other chair and facing her across the table. Meanwhile, the man who had escorted her to the room stood by the door looking bored by the whole proceeding.

The interrogator was a plump, middle-aged man with a bald head and a rather beaklike nose from which hairs protruded like little pieces of thin wire. There was something almost avuncular about him and he sighed now and then, as though he regretted the necessity of questioning such an attractive young woman on so distasteful a subject. But it had to be done.

'My name,' he said, 'is Vaudrin. Inspector Vaudrin.'

There was a pad of blotting-paper on the table in front of him, together with a notebook and an inkstand with a selection of pens in a rack. Now and then as he asked questions he dipped a pen in the ink and wrote somewhat laboriously in the notebook, apparently making a record of her replies.

'Why did you harbour a murderer in your apartment?'

'A murderer?'

'You did not know Monsieur Maurat had stabbed a young girl to death?'

'No.'

'But there was blood on his hands and his clothing, was there not?'

'Yes.'

'So how did you suppose it came there?'

'I didn't know.'

'You didn't ask him?'

'No.'

'Come, come,' Vaudrin said, giving a sadly admonishing shake of the head. 'That is really hard to believe. Now let us try to do better. I ask you again. How did he explain the blood?'

She hesitated, then said: 'I think he said he had cut himself accidentally.'

'But there were no cuts on him when he was arrested. They would have had to heal remarkably quickly, don't you think?'

She was silent.

'Now,' Vaudrin said, 'I am going to suggest that he really told you the truth concerning

213

the origin of that blood. It was not his but someone else's, was it not?'

Still she was silent. What could she say?

'There is something that puzzles me,' Inspector Vaudrin said. 'Why in this extremity did he run to you for refuge?'

'I don't know.'

'Oh, I think you do. He knew you, didn't he?'

It would have been futile to deny it.

'Yes, he did.'

'How was that?'

'He used to live with me.'

'You were lovers?'

'I suppose you might say that.'

'But he left you?'

'Yes.'

'For a young girl?'

'I don't know.'

'Come, come! No more lies, please. You did know, and it must have irked you. Yet when he came running to you with blood on his hands you took him in and shielded him. That was really most generous of you. Some people, I might say most people, would have slammed the door in his face. But not you. You welcomed him in with open arms.'

She was stung to rebuttal. 'I did not. I did not. I wanted him to leave, but he would not. What was I to do?'

'You could have come to us.'

She was silent again.

'Did that not occur to you?'

It had, more than once. But she had never been able to bring herself to do it. She saw now how she had brought trouble on herself by not taking such action. And in the end she had not saved Maurat by not betraying him. So what in the end had either of them gained by her self-sacrifice?

The interrogation went on for some time longer, and Vaudrin did some more scratching with his pen. She could not tell whether he was satisfied or not, but in the end he let her go.

The officer who had been standing all this time took her in charge and they left the room. She was afraid he was going to take her back to the cage with the harridans, but he did not. Instead, he conducted her to a cell and locked her in.

The only thing that could have been said in its favour was that it was not the other place and there was no one to harass her. It was small and there was a hard bed with one grey blanket. The sanitary arrangements were primitive and there was a tiny barred window so high up that it was impossible to see out of it.

The cell was chilly and she shivered.

It was to be her home for the next six days.

31

FREEDOM

There was no more interrogation. She might have imagined that she had been shut away and forgotten if meals had not been brought to her regularly. She tried to get information from the officer who brought the food, but he would tell her nothing. He might as well have been a mute.

She wondered what the penalty might be for giving aid to a murderer. A long prison sentence? She tried to imagine what even one year shut up in a cell like this would do to one. It would be mental as well as physical torture. It would drive her out of her mind.

But it did not come to that. After six days they gave her back the key to her apartment and let her go.

There was no explanation. It just seemed that they no longer wanted her. Perhaps they needed the cell for someone else. She was not going to question the decision; she was only too happy to be released.

An officer conducted her to the gateway by

which the black van had entered, and when she had passed through the gate clanged shut behind her. It was a cold day and it was raining and she had neither coat nor hat. Moreover, she was ignorant of the way home. It took her more than two hours. She might have engaged a cab if she had had any money, but she had none. She had to make the journey on her own two feet, and by the time she reached home her shoes were in a sorry state and she was drenched to the skin. Her hand was shaking as she put the key in the lock and she could hardly turn it; but she got the door open and went inside.

Indoors it was scarcely warmer than it had been outside. The fire in the sitting-room had long since burned out and the cinders in the grate had an unwelcoming appearance. She was shivering uncontrollably, and before attempting to rekindle it she went to the bedroom, stripped to the skin and dried herself with a rough towel before finding some dry clothes to put on. Her hair was still damp and bedraggled but she would deal with that later. The next task was to get the fire going again.

Fortunately there was a supply of kindling and newspaper and it did not take long to have these blazing away and igniting the coal.

She sank into the armchair and watched the flames, savouring the blessed feeling of being free again.

But still she could not understand why they had released her.

★ ★ ★

Some possible explanation came to her in the form of a newspaper which she bought the next day. It was an item of news which closely concerned her. There was a heading: 'MURDERER CONFESSES', and below it was a report that Jacques Maurat had confessed to the killing of Josephine Gautier with a kitchen knife.

So that was her name. It was odd that until that moment she had not known who the girl was that she had glimpsed only once in the street.

She read the report, but all she really needed to know was in the headline. He had confessed and it must have been decided that she had been punished enough.

She wondered what kind of pressure had been brought to bear on Maurat to persuade him to confess. Who could tell what went on in that forbidding building which she wanted never to enter again.

He would be executed of course. It would

218

be a public exhibition and crowds would gather. But she would not be there. Nothing in the world would induce her to witness those last moments of Jacques Maurat's life.

Yet, when it came to the point, she went.

32

NOTORIETY

She would always remember that picture of him walking towards the guillotine with the priest reading from his book and walking backwards in front of him, as if to hide from his sight that lethal machine. At times he seemed to stumble, as though his legs had lost their strength, and she felt that she could detect the terror in his eyes even at such a distance.

She knew he was not a brave man. Those last days with him in the apartment had been evidence of that. So did they give the condemned man something to steady his nerves? A last drink of brandy, perhaps? Come what might, it had to be a dreadful ordeal, knowing that these were the last few steps of one's life before that lethal blade severed head from body.

In the end she did not see the final act of the drama. Even as the shining steel began to descend she lost consciousness. Did the executioner lift the head by its hair and exhibit it to the crowd, or was that simply a fable? She would never know.

She was not sure how long it was before she regained consciousness. It must have been quite a while, for the crowd had largely dispersed when she came to, and the guillotine was being dismantled. A woman was bending over her and fanning her with a glove. She was a stout, middle-aged person with a rosy face, and there was a man standing behind her who could have been her husband.

'Ah!' the woman said, 'She's waking up, poor soul.'

She was obviously speaking to the man, but then she addressed Isabella: 'We were beginning to be quite concerned about you, dear. You've been out so long. Been all too much for you, has it? The excitement.'

Isabella sat up, feeling sick. She struggled to her feet, the woman and the man helping her. There was mud on her coat, for the ground was dirty. She gazed about her.

'It is over?'

'Oh, yes,' the woman said. 'All over and done with. They've taken the body away. And the head too, of course. Don't know where they bury them. Do you, Jean?'

The man shook his head. 'In quicklime, so I've heard.'

Isabella shuddered at the thought of Jacques' body burning in quicklime.

The woman noticed. 'You're feeling cold. Better go home. Is it far? If it is, perhaps we could get a cab.'

'Oh, no. I can walk. It's not very far.'

'Well, if you say so. But you look a bit groggy to me. Are you sure you can make it?'

'Yes, quite sure. Thank you for helping me. I'm very grateful. I'll be on my way now.'

She wanted to be rid of them, to be alone. She started walking and the man and woman watched her for a while as if fearing she might fall. But when she did not they turned and walked off in the opposite direction.

It was a relief when she reached the apartment. She lit a fire and drank some wine and sat watching the coals burn. She wondered whether she would ever forget that last picture of Jacques walking towards the dread machine with its shining deadly blade. In wars men died in their thousands in all manner of horrible ways, but of course she had never been close to a war and the multitude of deaths she had not seen affected her far less than this solitary one to which she had been so close and so intimately involved. It would be in her dreams for a long time to come, even though she had not seen the head fall into the basket when the fatal cut was made she could certainly imagine it. And imagination was enough.

★ ★ ★

One result of the murder case, and it was a result she would gladly have gone without, was that she had become notorious in the neighbourhood in which she lived.

When she went out people stared at her as if she were some kind of fairground monstrosity. She knew she was being talked about, though no one ever spoke to her, except a shop assistant here and there who could not avoid it.

But this phase was short-lived. Very soon the interest died down and she became as ignored as she had been before the murder. Again her existence was one of unrelieved boredom, a succession of days, weeks and months with scarcely anything to distinguish one from another.

She came to believe that it would go on like this indefinitely, and she became resigned to it. She was still far from old, but it was as if there was nothing left in life that was of any interest to her. Still, she supposed she was fortunate in having a comfortable home and a steady income. There were hundreds of poor wretches in Paris who were homeless and starving. She came across some of them now and then begging in the streets, and she gave them a coin or two to ease her conscience.

It did not occur to her then that she might ever become one of them.

* * *

The blow fell when one of those little slips of paper which she would take to the bank and exchange for cash failed to arrive on the date when it was due. She was not worried at first. It had been delayed, that was all. It would arrive later.

But it did not. Two weeks passed and still it had not come. She decided to make inquiries at the bank where she regularly cashed the cheques. She took with her the document that Maurat had handed to her to keep when the original deal had been made.

At the bank she showed this to one of the tellers whom she was familiar with and acquainted him with the situation.

'There should have been the regular payment two weeks ago, but it has not come.'

The teller, a middle-aged avuncular kind of man, looked at the document and shook his head sadly. It really seemed to grieve him to have to tell her the dismal truth.

'I fear, Madame, that there will be no more

payments. The company has gone into liquidation. It was a goldmining concern in Mexico, the kind of enterprise it is always risky to invest in. It appears the gold petered out and — ' He gave a most expressive shrug of the shoulders which said all there was to say.

She was stunned. This could only mean that she was ruined. She stumbled out of the bank scarcely aware of where she was going. Somehow she reached home, went inside and collapsed in a chair.

It was hardly believable that it could all be gone; that now there would be no more money coming to her. She had never been in such a situation before, and it frightened her.

She blamed Maurat of course. He should have known it was a risky investment. He was supposed to be a financial expert, wasn't he? That was how he made a living, advising people on money matters. But perhaps it was because he was not very good at it that he had had so few clients and so much spare time.

She had been a fool to trust him. She saw that now, when it was too late. But he had been so persuasive and she so inexperienced in financial matters. Well, he was gone now, and she could not go to him for advice on how to climb out of the pit into which he had plunged her. She had to rely on her efforts to do so. And she could see no way.

33

THE SEINE

She sold the ring first. It was the one piece of jewellery she had retained when the rest had gone. She tried to haggle as Maurat had done, but she was no good at it and the jeweller knew that she would not hold out. He came back to the price he had originally offered her and she had to accept it.

The ring money kept her going for a while, but not for long. She sold the books next; but it was remarkable how much less you received for a book that had been read no more than once than you had paid for it when new. Moreover, many of her books had been secondhand when she bought them and were worth very little now.

She sold cutlery and bed-linen and china for next to nothing. She could not sell the furniture because the apartment had been taken furnished. She moved into cheaper accommodation in a less pleasant part of the city where she had never been before. She rubbed shoulders with the poor and was now one of them. She sold her clothes until she had only what she stood up in, and eventually she was evicted from the wretched lodging she was now living in because she had failed to pay the rent.

She was now on the streets, destitute and hungry, lacking even the skill to beg. She thought of the home in England that she had left so many years ago; and she knew that even that refuge was out of her reach, since she had no means to pay the expenses of travelling there.

★　★　★

It was as if by a kind of homing instinct that she found herself by the river. It was midnight, a thin rain falling, cold. There was a bridge. There were so many bridges across the Seine that you could hardly avoid finding one. She stepped on to the bridge and started walking. The bridge was only dimly lighted and the rain was falling more heavily now. If there were any other people about she failed to see them. She came to the middle and leaned on the parapet, gazing down at the dark water rushing past below her. Into her mind came the thought of Juliette LeBlanc and the failed artist from the apartment she had first shared with the girl. They had taken this way out and she would follow them, since life had become unbearable.

She climbed on to the parapet with the aid of a stanchion that supported one of the lamps. She stood there and looked down and heard someone shouting. It was a man's voice and there was a patter of feet, and then there was a hand clutching at her dress.

But it was too late; she had already released her grip on the stanchion and the clutching fingers could not hold her. Her dress billowed out as she fell; and then she was in the frigid water and being carried away by the current.

34

THE MORGUE

There were three naked bodies lying on the marble slab behind the plate-glass screen. Two were men, the third a woman. They were the latest harvest from the Seine, and they would lie there in the Morgue waiting for someone to walk in and claim them. If no one did so in the next day or two, they would be classified as unknown and would be taken away for burial in unhallowed ground on the outskirts of the city. No headstone would be erected to mark such a grave and the occupant would soon be forgotten.

A man came into the Morgue, nodded to the keeper and walked to the plate-glass screen. He was smartly dressed and might have been well past middle age. He hardly looked at the male bodies but he did look long and keenly at that of the woman, in whose features there was still some evidence that she had once been beautiful.

After a time he shook his head and muttered: 'No, it cannot be. And yet — '

He stayed there a while longer, then shook his head again and walked away.

The keeper of the Morgue watched him go. The woman would remain unknown.

35

A PITY

'It's a pity,' George said, 'that Aunt Maud couldn't tell us more about Bella. I wouldn't be surprised if she was really the most interesting one of the lot. A girl as pretty as that.'

Joyce laughed. 'Why, George, I do believe you've quite fallen in love with her.'

'Too late for that, isn't it? But I bet somebody did years ago. Maybe that's how it all started.'

'How what started?'

'Whatever it was that nobody mentioned in front of the children.'

'Maybe she ran away with a band of raggle-taggle gypsies-oh.'

'More likely a man.'

'And never came back?'

'Maybe. That's a thing about this family tree business. You may find out who your ancestors were and possibly how they got their living, but you really know nothing about their private lives. Like what time they got up in the morning, what they had for

231

breakfast and what they talked about while they were eating it. Most of all, what did they do for amusement with no radio, no telly and all that. No telephones even to get in touch with one another.'

'And no washing-machines and no central heating. Must have been a tough life.'

'Possibly. But they wouldn't have been aware of it because it was all they'd ever been used to.'

'Now you're getting philosophical, George.'

'Maybe I am. But I'm thinking about this Bella.'

'Again?'

'Yes, again. Because we know absolutely nothing about her, except that when Aunt Maud was young nobody talked about her. So we just have this picture of her and nothing else. There's no record of her death, so we don't even know where she died. And now I suppose we shall never know that or anything more. It's so frustrating.'

'Well, that's the way it goes.'

'That's so. But it really is a pity.'

EPILOGUE

In World War Two a German shell landed on a piece of open ground on the outskirts of Paris. It left a deep crater and some mounds of loose earth in which were mingled fragments of human bones.

These fragments were all that was left of a woman who had once been a dancer at the Moulin Rouge. She had been known then by an adoring clientèle as L'Anglaise, but her real name was Isabella Foster and she was the daughter of an ironmonger in a small Norfolk village not many miles from the ancient city of Norwich.

FINAL RUN
THE WILD ONE
DEAD OF WINTER
SPECIAL DELIVERY
SKELETON ISLAND
BUSMAN'S HOLIDAY
A PASSAGE OF ARMS
ON DESPERATE SEAS
THE SPAYDE CONSPIRACY
CRANE
OLD PALS ACT
THE SILENT VOYAGE
THE ANGRY ISLAND
SOMETHING OF VALUE
THE GOLDEN REEF
BULLION
SEA FURY
THE SPANISH HAWK
OCEAN PRIZE
THE RODRIGUEZ AFFAIR

We do hope that you have enjoyed reading this large print book.

Did you know that all of our titles are available for purchase?

We publish a wide range of high quality large print books including:
Romances, Mysteries, Classics
General Fiction
Non Fiction and Westerns

Special interest titles available in large print are:
The Little Oxford Dictionary
Music Book
Song Book
Hymn Book
Service Book

Also available from us courtesy of Oxford University Press:
Young Readers' Dictionary
(large print edition)
Young Readers' Thesaurus
(large print edition)

For further information or a free brochure, please contact us at:
Ulverscroft Large Print Books Ltd.,
The Green, Bradgate Road, Anstey,
Leicester, LE7 7FU, England.
Tel: (00 44) **0116 236 4325**
Fax: (00 44) **0116 234 0205**

Other titles published by
The House of Ulverscroft:

BAVARIAN SUNSET

James Pattinson

Sam Grant had to trace the vendor of a painting that had come up for sale at a London auction room. By a German Jewish artist who had perished in a Nazi concentration camp, the painting had been stolen from a schloss in Lower Saxony in World War Two. Then it had apparently vanished, until surfacing fifty years later. So who had possessed it in those years? Grant had to find the answer for Gerda Hoffman, an attractive blonde. But the case turned out to have a fatal aspect.

THE RODRIGUEZ AFFAIR

James Pattinson

Harry Banner turns up in London one November evening. Just arrived from Venezuela, he visits Robert Cade, a man he'd known six years earlier in Buenos Aires. Banner wants Cade to keep a certain parcel until he returns for it. But the package remains uncollected: the next morning Banner is found dead in his hotel room, with a stab wound to the chest . . . Other people come looking for the parcel — and Cade departs for Venezuela, intending to investigate Harry's murder. However, in San Borja the climate can be very unhealthy for someone asking too many questions . . .

OCEAN PRIZE

James Pattinson

The S.S. *India Star*, a valuable cargo ship, is abandoned in the mid-Atlantic after suffering an engine room explosion. And Captain Barling of the S.S. *Hopeful Enterprise* has very special reasons for wishing to tow it into port. But is he justified in risking men's lives for the sake of his own desires? Shipmate Adam Loder thinks it is nothing but a wild goose chase, and chief engineer Jonah Madden is worried about his ailing engines; whilst crewman Charlie Wilson is hiding a deeper worry . . . Meanwhile, Barling has more than fearsome gales to contend with as a tenacious rival threatens his chances.

THE SPANISH HAWK

James Pattinson

There were five dead men in the cabin of the boat, lying under ten fathoms of Caribbean water. They had been shot through the head at close range . . . John Fletcher had gone down to photograph a sunken ship, but he took photographs of the boat and its cargo of dead men instead. Soon he is having trouble with the island police, some men from President Clayton Rodgers' private army of thugs and two CIA agents. Now Fletcher wishes he had followed his first impulse and said nothing to anyone . . .

Rationality in an Uncertain World

Rationality in an Uncertain World

Essays on the Cognitive Science of Human Reasoning

Mike Oaksford
University of Wales, Cardiff

Nick Chater
University of Warwick

Psychology Press
a member of the Taylor & Francis group

Psychology Press Ltd., Publishers
27 Church Road
Hove
East Sussex, BN3 2FA
UK

British Library Cataloguing in Publication Data

A catalogue record for this book is available from the British Library.

   ISBN 0-86377-534-9

Typeset by DP Photosetting, Aylesbury, Bucks.
Printed and bound in the United Kingdom by
Biddles Ltd., Guildford and King's Lynn

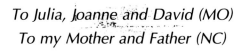

To Julia, Joanne and David (MO)
To my Mother and Father (NC)

Contents

Acknowledgements

We would like to thank the following people for their encouragement and inspiration: Alan Allport, John R. Anderson, Patrick Blackburn, Gordon D.A. Brown, Maggie Chalmers, Patricia Cheng, Robin Cooper, Martin Davies, Jonathan Evans, Gerd Gigerenzer, Vittorio Girotto, David Green, James Hampton, Keith Holyoak, Phil Johnson-Laird, Greg Jones, Brendan McGonigle, Mike Malloch, Ken Manktelow, Paulo Legrenzi, David Over, Ullin Place, Jerry Seligman, Steve Sloman, Neil Smith, Dan Sperber, Keith Stenning, Rosemary Stevenson, Peter Wason, and Norman Wetherick.

We would also like to acknowledge some of the works that have influenced us most: Nelson Goodman's *Fact, Fiction and Forecast*, Jerry Fodor's *The Language of Thought* and *Modularity of Mind*, Phil Johnson-Laird's *Mental Models*, and John R. Anderson's *The Adaptive Character of Thought*.

The authors acknowledge permission to use previously published material in this volume. The provenance of the essays is as follows.

Chapter 1 Mainly new material but some is taken from: Oaksford, M. (1997). Thinking and the rational analysis of human reasoning. *The Psychologist: Bulletin of The British Psychological Society*, *10*, 257–260. Reproduced with permission.

Chapter 2 Chater, N. & Oaksford, M. (1990). Autonomy, implementation and cognitive architecture: A reply to Fodor and Pylyshyn. *Cognition*, *34*, 93–107. Reprinted with kind permission from Elsevier Science – NL, Sara Burgerhartstraat 25, 1055 KU Amsterdam, The Netherlands.

Chapter 3 Oaksford, M., Chater, N. & Stenning, K. (1990). Connectionism, classical cognitive science and experimental psychology. *AI & Society*, *4*, 73–90. Reproduced with permission.

Chapters 4 and 5   Oaksford, M. & Chater, N. (1991) Against logicist cognitive science. *Mind & Language*, *6*, 1–38. Reproduced with permission.

Chapter 6   Oaksford, M., & Chater, N. (1993). Reasoning theories and bounded rationality. In K.I. Manktelow & D.E. Over (Eds.), *Rationality* (pp. 31–60). London: Routledge. Reproduced with permission.

Chapter 7   Oaksford, M. & Chater, N. (1992). Bounded rationality in taking risks and drawing inferences. *Theory & Psychology*, *2*, 225–230. Reprinted by permission of Sage Publications Ltd.

Chapter 8   Chater, N. & Oaksford, M. (1993). Logicism, mental models and everyday reasoning. *Mind & Language*, *8*, 72–89, and Oaksford, M., & Chater, N. (1995). Theories of reasoning and the computational explanation of everyday inference. *Thinking & Reasoning*, *1*, 121–152. Reproduced with permission.

Chapter 9   Chater, N. & Oaksford, M. (1996). The falsity of folk theories: Implications for psychology and philosophy. In W. O'Donohue & R. Kitchener (Eds.), *The Philosophy of Psychology* (pp. 244–256). London: Sage Publications. Reprinted by permission of Sage Publications Ltd.

Chapters 10 to 13   Oaksford, M. & Chater, N. (1994). A rational analysis of the selection task as optimal data selection. *Psychological Review*, *101*, 608–631. Copyright © 1994 by the American Psychological Association. Adapted with permission.

Chapter 14   Oaksford, M. & Chater, N. (1996). Rational explanation of the selection task. *Psychological Review*, *103*, 381–391. Copyright © 1996 by the American Psychological Association. Adapted with permission.

Chapter 15   Oaksford, M., & Chater, N. (1995). Information gain explains relevance which explains the selection task. *Cognition*, *57*, 97–108. Reprinted with kind permission from Elsevier Science – NL, Sara Burgerhartstraat 25, 1055 KU Amsterdam, The Netherlands.

Chapter 16   Mainly new material but some is taken from: Oaksford, M., Chater, N., Grainger, B., & Larkin, J. (1997). Optimal data selection in the reduced array selection task (RAST). *Journal of Experimental Psychology: Learning, Memory and Cognition*, *23*, 441–458. Copyright © 1997 by the American Psychological Association. Adapted with permission.

CHAPTER ONE

Introduction

Since Aristotle's claim that "man is the rational animal" the ability to reason has been regarded as one the hallmarks of the mental—organisms, like us, that can reason have minds, whereas organisms, like snails and pigeons, that could not reason do not have minds. For Descartes, animals were automata that simply responded to physical stimulation with no mediating processes of rational thought. Reasoning was not something that mere machines could do, but only non-physical souls.

Such dualism about the physical realm and the non-physical thinking mind is also implicit in our everyday way of explaining our behaviour using our "folk psychology". Suppose you see your neighbour arrive home; you see her pass the garage and look in to see that the car is gone. When she reaches the door instead of ringing the doorbell as she has done every night for the last 20 years, she takes out her key and opens the door. We can explain in an instant why your neighbour broke her habitual pattern of behaviour. The explanation will go something like this (Oaksford, 1997, p. 257):

> She saw that the car was gone, she therefore *inferred* that someone drove it away; because she *knows* that only her partner has the keys, she *infers* that her partner has driven it away; she further infers that if he is in the car she must *believe* that he is not in the house and hence he cannot open the door when she rings the bell, consequently she takes out her key and opens the door herself.

There are two important aspects of this mundane, everyday explanation. First, you attribute certain properties to your neighbour, "*knowing* that only her partner has the keys," and "*believing* that her partner is not in the house" and so on. These properties are quite unlike physical properties, like being tall, round, long or square, in so far as they can only be identified by what they are *about*. Second, this explanation suggests that you make inferences that somehow relate these properties to each other in a meaningful way, so that if your neighbour possesses one of these properties, "believing that her partner is in the car," then she must possess another, "believing that her partner is not in the house." Because it relates non-physical properties, inference too must be a facet of the non-physical mind. Consequently dualism about mind and body emerges not only from preconceived ideas about the existence of immortal souls but also from our commonsense folk psychological explanations of each other's behaviour.

The importance of cognitive psychology and the reason it supplanted behaviourism, is that it can say something scientific about these odd properties and the inferential relationships between them. The emergence of modern formal logic and the consequent development of computers was the key to being able to talk about these things in purely physical, scientific terms. Sentences of a language share the property with mental states like *beliefs* that they can be identified by what they are about. Moreover, and crucially, sentences can also be identified by their purely formal properties— literally the shapes of the letters and words that make them up. Computers manipulate symbols formally by virtue of the physical shapes of those symbols. The key to capturing inference is that modern, formal logic can also provide a systematic mapping between these formal operations and what the symbols are about. Consequently, inference can be mechanised and the result is something that for Descartes would have been a contradiction: *a rational mechanism*, i.e. a computer. As for Aristotle, in the cognitive revolution, reasoning is at the heart of having something to say about mind. The computer metaphor potentially provides a mechanistic theory of reasoning and for the cognitive psychologist "cognition is computation".

REASONING AND THE ADEQUACY OF COGNITIVE PSYCHOLOGY

A minimal adequacy condition on the cognitive "paradigm" would therefore appear to be that people reason logically. Over the last 40 years there has been a great deal of work in cognitive psychology on people's logical reasoning abilities (see Evans, Newstead, & Byrne, 1993, for a review). Researchers did not initially view this work as testing the adequacy of the cognitive paradigm but rather as testing the similar Piagetian assumption that the goal of cognitive development was to produce a logically competent adult (e.g. Wason, 1969). The conclusion of this work was that in many areas people seem unable to reason logically. For example, they do not appear to follow the logical advice (Popper, 1959) of seeking falsifying evidence when testing hypotheses (e.g. Wason, 1960, 1968). Moreover they do not apply the logical law of modus tollens in conditional inference (e.g., Taplin, 1971). Taking an example from our commonsense psychological explanation, modus tollens prescribes that if you believe that *if he is in the car* (*p*), *then he is not in the house* (*q*) and that *he is in the house* (*not-q*) then you ought to believe that *he is not in the car* (*not-p*); or formally: *if p then q*, and *not-q*, therefore *not-p*. In conditional inference people also erroneously endorse inferential fallacies such as denying the antecedent, e.g. inferring *he is in the house* on discovering *he is not in the car*; or formally: *if p then q*, and *not-p*, therefore *not-q*. People also do not always appreciate when statements involving logical terms, such as "if . . . then," are true and when they are false (e.g. Evans, 1972). The main conclusion of this work is that people's reasoning on tasks that have superficially obvious logical solutions seems prone to various systematic and non-logical biases.

One consequence of these results in the psychology of reasoning is that the solution apparently offered by cognitive psychology to the problem of placing the study of mind on solid, scientific ground may be illusory (see, for example, Stich, 1985, 1990). However, there are other possible responses to this problem (some are explored by Oaksford & Chater, 1991, in a related context, see Chapters 4 and 5). For example, one could question the ecological validity of these experimental tasks—perhaps using more realistic real-world materials would facilitate logical inference. Although this initially seemed a promising line of research (e.g. Wason & Shapiro, 1971) it became clear that the nature of the tasks had been altered so that researchers were simply not investigating the same logical problem (Manktelow & Over, 1987).

Other proposals have involved attempting to explain away the discrepancy between logic and behaviour. For example, mental logicians (e.g. Rips, 1994) argue that we implement logic formally but then miss out some of the rules. In contrast, advocates of mental models propose that we implement logic by manipulating mental tokens of what the premises of an argument are about (e.g. Johnson-Laird, 1983). Other accounts suggest that heuristic processes responsible for language comprehension produce reasoning errors but that otherwise people are generally logically competent (e.g. Evans, 1989). All these accounts attempt to preserve some degree of logical competence. (For completeness we should also mention Pragmatic Reasoning Schema theory [Cheng & Holyoak, 1985], which abandons the attempt to explain this behaviour in logical terms but which does not replace logic with any alternative account of which inferences a reasoner *should* make.)

A MORE RADICAL APPROACH

The papers in this book present a more radical approach. What if the real inferences people draw in their everyday lives are not actually logical *but* conform to the prescriptions of some other formal, mechanisable theory?

First, this possibility would suggest that people's behaviour in the reasoning laboratory may be the result of generalising their normal non-logical strategies to these unfamiliar logical problems. Second, it would suggest that accounts that attempt to preserve logic as central to human reasoning, like all those we have discussed, are misguided—being based on logic they will not be able to generalise from the laboratory to the real world. Finally, there would be no need to abandon the central insight behind the cognitive revolution's solution to placing the study of mind on a solid, physicalist footing.

Let us reconsider some of the everyday inferences you went through to explain your neighbour's behaviour. The first inference was:

> She saw that the car was gone, she therefore inferred that someone drove it away.

Logically this is an inference by *modus ponens: if the car is gone* (*p*), *then someone has driven it away* (*q*) and *the car is gone* (*p*), therefore *someone has driven it away* (*q*). However, a crucial aspect of this inference is that it is *uncertain*: it is possible that no one *drove* the car away even though it is gone, someone may have towed it away, a helicopter may have removed it, it may have spontaneously combusted, a trained chimp may have driven it away and so on. Any of these additional pieces of information would *defeat* this inference, which is consequently referred to as a *defeasible* inference. The problem with modelling such inferences logically is that classical logic is *monotonic*, i.e. no additional information, like that just outlined, can defeat a logical inference. Although this is a desirable property in mathematical reasoning it is almost antithetical to the kind of everyday reasoning that we use to explain our own and others' behaviour (Oaksford & Chater, 1991).

Could this behaviour be isolated just to this particular inference? Let us look at the rest of the inferences used to explain your neighbour's behaviour. The second inference was:

> Because she knows that only her partner has the keys, she infers that her partner has driven it away.

First, any of the aforementioned default defeaters would also defeat this inference. Second, her partner could have lent the keys to a friend; someone may have stolen them; someone could have hot-wired the car and so on. All these factors could defeat this inference. The third inference was:

> She further *infers* that if he is in the car she must *believe* that he is not in the house.

This is the first inference to have the feel of non-defeasibility—any defeater would appear to have to claim that it is causally possible to be in two places at once. However, he may have crashed the car into the house, or re-assembled it in the house in which case he can be in the car and in the house at the same time! In sum, it would appear that everyday commonsense inferences are defeasible, i.e. they are uncertain, plausible inferences, they are not certain, logical inferences.

One might argue that people regard these as logically certain inferences, and only question them when they fail and when consequently they must revise their beliefs about the situation (Rips, 1994). This strategy would involve questioning the literal truth of, for example, *if the car is gone, then someone has driven it away*. But this surely mischaracterises people's cognitive attitude towards this and the million other commonsense generalisations that people use to guide and explain their behaviour (Oaksford & Chater, 1995b). If in our commonsense descriptions of the world and of ourselves these are not candidates for truth then precious little else of what we call our commonsense knowledge of the world will be candidates for truth. We would then be in the paradoxical position of having to provide a system of human inference that is always based on false premises but which is nonetheless apparently capable of guiding successful action in the world! There are situations where false beliefs may be beneficial, e.g. being told falsely that the doctor thinks you will recover from some life-threatening disease may assist in your eventual and remarkable recovery. However, such situations certainly do not seem to be the norm.[1]

If real human reasoning is uncertain through and through then rather than model reasoning with standard logic, the calculus of certainty, perhaps we should use a calculus appropriate to uncertainty. In this introduction, which provides the background for the rest of the book, we look at two approaches to uncertainty. One is given by recent attempts to extend logic to account for uncertainty. The other, probability theory, which has a much longer history, models uncertainty directly, and has been characterised as the optimal calculus for uncertain reasoning. The tension between logic-based and probabilistic models of thought is the central theme of this book.

LOGICIST AND PROBABILISTIC APPROACHES TO UNCERTAINTY

The papers in this book consider the question of how cognitive science can account for people's reasoning abilities, given the uncertainty of everyday inferences. The book is in two parts. Part I considers standard "logicist" approaches to reasoning, which assume that human reasoning abilities (and other cognitive processes) are based on logic. Part II considers our alternative approach which sees reasoning as based on probability theory, rather than logic.

An initial, and crucial, question which frames our whole approach is: What is it for a theory of cognitive processes to be "based on" an abstract normative theory such as logic or probability theory? Although this seems to be widely recognised as a central question in the psychology of reasoning, it has received little detailed attention in the literature (although for exceptional examples see Baron, 1994; Johnson-Laird, 1983; Johnson-Laird & Byrne, 1991). In common with all other cognitive scientists, we are attempting to explain human reasoning in computational terms. Thus, our question becomes: What is it for a computational theory of cognitive processes to be "based on" an abstract normative theory? We answer this question by appeal to Marr's celebrated account of levels of computational explanation, which provides a specific, and indeed a crucial, role for normative theories.

Marr (1982) defined three levels of computational explanation. At the *computational* level (the level of Anderson's rational analysis which we discuss later on), *what* gets computed in performing some task is defined. For example, if we are designing a calculator we want to know that it computes arithmetic, so that if, for example, you input "2", " + ", and "2", the machine outputs "4". What goes on between input and output, i.e. *how* the calculator computes arithmetic, is specified at the *algorithmic* level. At this level the representations and algorithms that perform arithmetic are defined. So, for example, we may specify that the algorithm uses Arabic numerals and performs addition, say, by lining up columns, adding column-wise and then carrying. You can use many different algorithms to implement arithmetic, each having its own level of complexity. For example, another way of implementing addition would be to take 1 from the second number and add it to the first number until the second number is 0. Although this would take a lot longer than the first more familiar method, it still respects the rules of the computational level theory of arithmetic. Finally, at the *implementational* level, the physical structure of the device on which the algorithm runs is defined.

Most crucially for the present discussion, the computational level of explanation must have two roles. It must tell you what the device should compute—i.e. it must be normatively justified. Thus, the normative theory of arithmetic explains why the device is behaving appropriately in responding "4" to the query "2 + 2". But in application to human psychology, it is crucial that the normative theory adequately *describes* some aspect of human performance. The theory of arithmetic gives a good *description* of the behaviour of a calculator, but a poor description of a telephone. Thus, a computational-level theory must be both normatively justified, and descriptively adequate to explaining the behaviour of the device—in the context of psychology, this "device" is the human mind. We note in the introduction to Chapter 10 that the dual descriptive and normative function characteristic of computational-level explanation is also central to the notion of "rational analysis" introduced by Anderson (1990, 1991a), in terms of which we frame much of our positive discussion in Part II.

PART I: PROBLEMS WITH LOGICISM

With respect to proposals for dealing with uncertainty in the psychology of reasoning, computational explanation provides two adequacy criteria, which we exploit extensively throughout Part I. The first is that the computational-level theory must be descriptively adequate with respect to people's actual reasoning abilities. Here, empirical constraints come principally not from psychological experiments, but from intuitively clear-cut cases of uncertain inference. Logic-based theories have fundamental problems in accounting even for these basic intuitions. Moreover, we argue that the reasons why they have problems in accounting for these intuitions are also the reasons why they are inadequate in capturing the experimental data. We refer to the descriptive adequacy of a theory of reasoning as the criterion of completeness*. This is by analogy to the logical notion of completeness. A complete logical system is one in which all logical truths can be derived within that system. A (computational) system that is complete* is one in which all the intuitively correct inferences can be derived. We shall argue that logic-based accounts cannot meet this adequacy criterion, and that meeting completeness* requires a switch to probability theory as the starting point for computational-level explanation. We explore this alternative in Part II of the book.

A second adequacy criterion for computational explanation arises at Marr's algorithmic level. This criterion is that it must be possible for the algorithms postulated by a theory of reasoning to run in real-time in the brain. Minimally, this requires that these algorithms are computationally tractable, in the standard sense used in computer science. In Part I, we argue that the logicist programme in general fails to meet this criterion (Chapters 2, 3, 4, and 5). Moreover, we argue that logic-based theories in the psychology of reasoning fare no better, when generalised from the toy domains typically used in psychological experiments, to real-world uncertain inference (Chapters 6, 7, 8, and 9).

Strictly speaking, there is a third adequacy criterion, associated with Marr's implementational level—that it must be possible to implement the algorithms postulated by psychological theories in the neural hardware of the brain. We argue in Chapter 2 that this is, in principle, a powerful constraint on cognitive theories. Indeed, it is one of the plausible motivations for using neurally inspired computational architectures as the basis for cognitive science, most notably neural networks. When Chapter 2 was written, we had the hope that neural network models might inform solutions to problems at the algorithmic and computational level. With Anderson's (1990) extension of Marr's approach to high-level cognition, as embodied in rational analysis, we now believe that a more fruitful line of inquiry is to attempt to develop better computational-level explanations (although, as we argue in our concluding chapter, there may be important connections between the probabilistic approach we advocate and neurally inspired connectionist models).

Logicism and Uncertainty

We have noted that the uncertainty of everyday reasoning poses problems for logicist accounts of reasoning. In this introduction, we aim to connect our discussions in Part I with the broader philosophical, linguistic, logical and computational literatures on logic and uncertainty. Specifically, these literatures have converged on the view that standard first-order logic is inadequate to capture everyday reasoning about the real world. Although some psychologists are well aware of these literatures, we believe that their implications concerning the scope of first-order reasoning have not been fully recognised. Indeed, the very fact that the two leading formal psychological theories of reasoning, mental logic (e.g. Rips, 1994) and mental models (e.g. Johnson-Laird & Byrne, 1991) both retain the standard logical apparatus suggests that the inadequacies of first-order logic as a model for human reasoning are not universally accepted. Moreover, this discussion provides a background for the more detailed treatment of extensions of standard logic, which attempt to deal with uncertainty, and which we consider extensively throughout Part I.

In view of its fundamental importance in human reasoning, we focus on the conditional, if … then …, construction, which we used earlier to illustrate the uncertainty of human inference. We first sketch the standard logical treatment of the conditional, and then consider its problems and attempted solutions to these problems within a logical framework.

The standard approach within formal semantics of natural or logical languages is to provide a recursive definition of the truth of complex expressions in terms of their parts. The natural language phrase *if p then q* is standardly rendered as the material conditional of logic. The material conditional $p \supset q$ is true if and only if p is false or q is true (or both). This semantics licenses the valid rules of inference *modus ponens* and *modus tollens* introduced earlier in discussing our commonsense examples. There are certain well-known counter-intuitive properties of this semantics. For example, this semantics means that any conditional with a false antecedent is true—thus, the sentence "if the moon is striped, then Mars is spotted" is true according to the material conditional. But intuitively it is either false or nonsensical.

Further problems arise because the material conditional allows "strengthening of the antecedent". That is, given the premise *if p then q*, we can conclude that *if (p and r) then q* for any *r*. Strengthening of the antecedent seems appropriate in mathematical contexts. *If it is a triangle, it has three sides* does imply that, *if it is a triangle and it is blue, it has three sides.* Indeed, this is a crucial feature of axiomatic systems in mathematics— axiomatisation would be impossible if adding new axioms removed conclusions that followed from the old axioms. However, strengthening of the antecedent does not apply to most natural language conditionals, which as we have argued are uncertain. For example, *if it is a bird, then it flies* does not allow you to infer that *if it is a bird and it is an ostrich, then it flies.* That is, for natural language conditionals, conclusions can be lost by adding premises, i.e. strengthening of the antecedent does not hold. Further, note that whether some additional information *r* has this effect or not is content-dependent; for example, if you learn that this bird is a parrot, the conclusion that it can fly is not lost. The distinction between inference systems in which strengthening of the antecedent does or does not hold is of central importance to knowledge representation in artificial intelligence. Roughly, inference systems where strengthening of the antecedent holds are known as *monotonic* systems (continuously adding premises leads to continuously adding conclusions, without removing any); inference systems where strengthening of the antecedent does not hold are *non-monotonic*. In artificial intelligence, it is universally accepted that human everyday reasoning is uncertain and thus non-monotonic, and that developing systems for non-monotonic reasoning is a major challenge (Brachman & Levesque, 1985; Ginsberg, 1987).

Regarding our first problem with material implication, that a false antecedent guarantees the truth of a conditional, an intuitive diagnosis is that material implication fails to specify that there be any *connection* between the antecedent and consequent—they can simply be any two arbitrary propositions. Within the logical literature, there have been two general approaches to capturing this intuition—relevance logic and modal logic.

Relevance logic, as its name implies, demands that there is a relationship of "relevance" between antecedent and consequent, where this is defined in terms of the proof of the consequent involving the antecedent (Anderson & Belnap, 1975). From a logical point of view, systems of relevance logic are not well developed. For example, it has been very difficult to provide a semantics for relevance logics (Veltman, 1985) which means it is not clear quite *what* notion of relevance is being coded by the syntactic rules used in particular relevance logics. But in any case, the relation of relevance would not appear to be reducible to notions of proof, particularly not in everyday contexts, because the uncertain character of reasoning means that proofs are never possible. So relevance logics do not appear to be a useful direction for developing a notion of the conditional that applies to everyday reasoning (we consider relevance-based approaches in Chapter 5). However, in the psychology of reasoning, Braine (1978) has advanced a relevance-based account, arguing that people naturally only assert conditionals when the consequent is deducible from the antecedent.

The second approach to the conditional employs modal notions, such as necessity and possibility. Syntactic systems of modal logic and so-called strict implication based on them were first suggested by C.I. Lewis (1918). Semantic theories for modal logics were developed much later by Kripke (1963), which permitted an understanding of the notions of necessity and possibility that were being encoded in the syntactic rules. Specifically, Kripke provides a semantics in terms of "possible worlds". The idea is that different modal logics can be understood in terms of different relations of "accessibility" between possible worlds. In these terms, a proposition is necessary if it is true in all accessible possible worlds, and it is possible if it is true in some accessible possible worlds.

The most philosophically important account of conditionals is given by the Lewis–Stalnaker possible world semantics for the *counterfactual* conditional (D. Lewis, 1973; Stalnaker, 1968). A counterfactual conditional is one in which the antecedent is known to be false: "if the gun had gone off, he would have been killed". According to material implication, such claims are always true, simply because their antecedents are false. But clearly this cannot be correct—under most circumstances, the counterfactual "if he had stubbed his toe, he would have been killed" will be judged unequivocally false. Looking at the Lewis–Stalnaker semantics for such claims reveals all the problems that logical approaches to everyday reasoning must confront in philosophy and in artificial intelligence.

The intuitive idea behind the Lewis–Stalnaker semantics for a conditional such as "if the gun had gone off, he would have been killed" is based on the idea that in the world maximally similar to the actual world but in which the gun went off, he died. Clearly, the major issue here is what counts as the world maximally similar to the actual one. One important criterion is that the physical laws are the same, so that speeding bullets still tend to kill people, that the gun is pointing in the same direction, and so on—the only difference is that the gun went off in this world, whereas it did not in the actual world. But there is a vast range of specific problems with this account. For example, it is not at all clear how to construct a world where only a single fact differs from the actual world. This is problematic because for this to be true (assuming determinism) the difference in this crucial fact either implies a different causal history (the bullet was a dud, the gun was faulty etc.), or different causal laws (pulling triggers does not make guns go off in this possible world). Moreover, a different causal history or different causal laws will have different causal consequences, aside from the single fact under consideration. Thus, it appears inevitable that the so-called maximally similar world differs in many ways, rather than just in a single fact, from the actual world. So by changing one thing, we automatically change many things, and it is not at all clear what the inferential consequences of these changes should be. The problem of specifying the ramifications of a single change to a world (or in an agent's knowledge about its world) is immensely difficult—in artificial intelligence this problem has been called the frame problem (Pylyshyn, 1987) and it has bedevilled artificial intelligence research for the last 30 years (see Chapters 2 to 4). Hence a theory of conditionals that presupposes a solution to the frame problem is unlikely to prove satisfactory as a basis for a psychology of conditional reasoning.

These problems aside, this semantics for the counterfactual (i.e. where the antecedent—the gun going off—does not apply in the actual world) has also been applied to the indicative case (where the gun may or may not have gone off). Simplistically, the hypothetical element of an indicative statement such as "if the gun goes off, he is dead" seems to be captured by the same semantics—the only difference is that we do not know whether the actual world is one in which the gun goes off or not. Nonetheless, this kind of semantic account does avoid some of the absurdities of material implication. Thus, for example, sentences like "if the moon is striped, then Mars is spotted" are now clearly false—in worlds maximally similar to the actual world in which the moon is striped, Mars will still look red. Crucially, it is intuitively clear that strengthening the antecedent can no longer hold. For example, *if it is a bird, then it flies* does not allow you to infer that *if it is a bird and it is an ostrich, then it flies*. The worlds in which the antecedents are evaluated will clearly differ—the world most similar to the actual world in which something is a bird is not the same as the world most similar to the actual world in which something is an ostrich. In particular, in the first world, it will most likely fly (because most birds fly); but in the second world, it will not fly (because ostriches cannot fly). These examples suggest that the Lewis–Stalnaker semantics may provide a more descriptively adequate, or complete*, theory of conditionals than the material conditional.

For psychological purposes, however, we need an account of the formal processes that could implement this semantics. People do not have access to possible worlds—instead they have access to representations of the world, which they can productively recombine to produce different representations of the way the world might be or might not have been. The programme of attempting to mechanise reasoning about the way the world might be has been taken up by the study of knowledge representation in artificial intelligence. The starting point is the notion of a knowledge base, which contains representations of a cognitive agent's beliefs about the world. This approach involves formal representations and formal proof procedures that operate over these representations and that can be implemented computationally. However, it is far from clear that formal attempts in AI can adequately capture the Lewis–Stalnaker semantics and thereby provide a complete* theory of conditionals.

Let us reconsider strengthening the antecedent, and perhaps the most well-known approach to this problem within AI. Problems for strengthening the antecedent arise when the inferences that can be made from one antecedent intuitively conflict with the inferences that can be made from another. For example, knowing that Tweety is a sparrow leads to the conclusion that Tweety flies, whereas knowing that Tweety is one second old leads to the conclusion that Tweety cannot fly. This leads to the problem of what we infer when we learn that Tweety is a one-second-old sparrow, i.e. the problem of what we infer when the antecedent is strengthened. It is intuitively obvious that a one-second-old sparrow cannot fly: that when Tweety is one second old, the possible world in which Tweety cannot fly is more similar to the actual world than any other possible world where Tweety can fly. Although this is intuitively obvious, formally, it not obvious how to capture this conclusion. Formally we can regard these two pieces of information as two conditional rules, if something is a bird it can fly, and if something is one second old it cannot fly. Formal proposals in AI (e.g. Reiter, 1985) appear unable to break the symmetry between these rules and specify which of these conflicting conclusions we should accept. That is, these proposals are not complete* with respect to our intuitive understanding of how the Lewis–Stalnaker semantics should be applied. The point here is that in the example it is our knowledge of what the rules mean and how the world works that indicate that a one-second-old sparrow is not going to fly. More generally, it is not the *formal* properties of conditionals that determine the subsets of possible worlds in which they are evaluated in the Lewis–Stalnaker semantics. What matters is the *content* of the rules, to which the formal procedures for inference in logicist AI do not have access.

There have been a variety of alternative proposals within the AI literature to deal with the problem of strengthening the antecedent, or default reasoning. The best known are McCarthy's (1980) *circumscription*, McDermott and Doyle's (1980) *non-monotonic logic I*, McDermott's (1982) *non-monotonic logic II*, and Clark's (1978) *predicate completion*. However, the problems that we have described appear to apply equally to all of these approaches (Hanks & McDermott, 1985, 1986; Shoam, 1987, 1988) (see Chapter 4). Moreover, approaches based on formal logic within the psychology of reasoning, for example, mental logics (e.g. Rips, 1994) and mental models (e.g. Johnson-Laird & Byrne, 1991) also fail to address these issues, because the approach they adopt formalises the conditional using the standard logic of material implication. However, as we have seen, the material conditional completely fails to capture the use of conditionals in everyday inference (see Chapters 4, 7, and 8).

We have seen that conditional inference is of fundamental importance to cognitive science, as well as to artificial intelligence, logic, and philosophy. We have suggested that the difficulties that arise in capturing conditional inference indicate a very profound problem for the study of human reasoning and the study of cognition at large. This is that much of our reasoning with conditionals is *uncertain*, and may be overturned by future information; but logic-based approaches to inference are typically monotonic, and hence are unable to deal with this uncertainty. Moreover, to the extent that formal logical approaches embrace non-monotonicity, they appear to be unable to cope with the fact that it is the *content* of rules, rather than their logical form, which appears to determine the inferences that people draw. In Part I we explore these issues, and their implications for logic-based approaches to reasoning and cognition, and we note that the ramifications of these points are very general, applying to many psychological proposals that are not explicitly founded on logical principles. In Part II we take up the suggestion that perhaps by encoding more of the content of people's knowledge, using probability theory, we may more adequately capture the nature of everyday human inference. This seems to make intuitive sense, because the problems that we have identified concern how uncertainty is handled in human inference, and probability theory is the calculus of uncertainty.

PART II: THE PROBABILISTIC APPROACH AND RATIONAL ANALYSIS

In Part II we argue that if human reasoning is uncertain then rather than using the calculus of certainty, i.e. logic, to model such reasoning, we should use the calculus of uncertainty, i.e. probability theory. In our work we have adopted this approach and in the following section we briefly illustrate how it succeeds in accounting for the apparently irrational behaviour observed on Wason's selection task. Our probabilistic approach allows us to construct a "rational analysis" of reasoning as defined by Anderson (1990) which locates our account at a particular level of computational explanation. We first introduce some of the conceptual foundations of probability theory that are important to the subsequent chapters, and then outline the probabilistic methods that can be used to explain psychological phenomena using Anderson's (1990) rational analysis approach.

Probability Theory and Uncertain Inference

The elements of probability theory and statistics are familiar to researchers in cognitive psychology and the cognitive sciences generally. However, statistics are frequently encountered in their role as tools for data analysis, rather than in their broader context as methods for inference. It is in this latter context that statistical methods can plausibly be viewed as models of cognition (and we shall consider some aspects of the psychological tradition of statistical modelling, in relation to neural network models). Moreover, because of the dominance of a limited "data analysis" view of statistics in certain areas of the cognitive sciences, the claim that neural networks might be just statistical models is sometimes viewed with incredulity. Hence, we begin by sketching the broader view of statistics as very general mathematical methods for uncertain inference, within which statistical methods as used in data analysis in the cognitive sciences form only a small part.

Statistical inference is founded upon the mathematical theory of probability, and the distinct statistical traditions differ on how this theory is understood. The interpretation of probability theory has been controversial since its very beginnings. Nonetheless, the most usual early interpretation of probability theory was as a tool for formalising rational thought concerning uncertain situations, such as gambling, insurance, and the evaluation of court-room testimony (Gigerenzer et al., 1989). Indeed, the very choice of the word "probability", which referred to the degree to which a statement was supported by the evidence at hand, embodied this interpretation—that is, "probability" originally signified "rational degree of belief". Jakob Bernoulli explicitly endorsed this interpretation when he entitled his definitive book *Ars conjectandi*, or *The Art of Conjecture* (Bernoulli, 1713).

This "subjectivist" conception ran through the eighteenth and into the nineteenth centuries (Daston, 1988), frequently without clear distinctions being drawn between probability theory as a model of actual thought (or more usually, the thought of "rational", rather than common, people [Hacking, 1990]) or as a set of normative canons prescribing how uncertain reasoning should occur. In a sense, then, early probability theory itself was viewed as a model of mind.

As the distinction between normative and descriptive models of thought became more firmly established, probability theory was primarily seen as having normative force, as characterising rationality; whether or not people actually followed such normative dictates was seen as a secondary question. A wide variety of arguments that purport to show that individual degrees of beliefs should obey the laws of probability calculus have been developed, based on betting quotients and "Dutch book" arguments (de Finetti, 1937; Ramsey, 1931; Skyrms, 1977), theories of preferences (Savage, 1954), scoring rules (Lindley, 1982) and derivation from minimal axioms (Cox, 1961; Good, 1950; Lucas, 1970). Although each argument can be challenged individually, the fact that so many different lines of argument converge on the very same laws of probability has been taken as powerful evidence for the view that degrees of belief can be interpreted as probabilities (e.g. see Earman, 1992 and Howson & Urbach, 1989, for discussions). The suggestion that probability theory can be viewed as a normative theory of uncertain reasoning sets the bounds of probability theory much wider than the confines in which it is frequently encountered in introductory textbooks. According to this view, probability theory is not just concerned with reasoning about coins, dice, and accident rates, but is a calculus for rational thought.

Many inferential problems concern the relationship between models or hypotheses, and observation or data. Some of these problems are concerned with inferring the probability of various kinds of observation, given that the structure of the underlying model is known. So, for example, the model might be a fair coin, and the question of interest might be the probability that 50 heads or more will be obtained in 200 throws. Statistical inference, by contrast, applies in the opposite direction, using observed data to infer the structure of the underlying model. For example, given the observation of 50 heads in 200 throws, assessing whether the coin is unbiased, what its likely bias might be, and with what confidence the bias can be estimated, all involve statistical inference, because observed data are used to infer aspects of the underlying model.

The problem of inductive or statistical inference is very general, and arises, in different guises, in a variety of domains. In epistemology and the philosophy of science, the problem is that of choosing the hypothesis or theory that is best supported by a given body of empirical observations: this is the problem of induction. A particular approach to statistics, the Bayesian approach, is by far the most well-developed formal account of inductive reasoning (e.g. see Earman, 1992; Horwich, 1982; Howson & Urbach, 1989). In the context of psychology, cognitive science and artificial intelligence, machine learning, pattern recognition and the study of neural networks, statistical inference corresponds to the problem of learning underlying structure from experience. It is with this broad sense of the scope of statistics in view that the claim that the mind is an intuitive statistician (Gigerenzer & Murray 1987), or that cognitive processes can be viewed as statistical processes, can be understood. The claim is not merely that the mind performs t tests or ANOVAS (although this has been proposed [Kelley, 1967]). It is that the dictates of statistical theory concerning inductive inference are descriptive, not just prescriptive, regarding certain aspects of thought.

The project of characterising statistics is complicated by the variety of different statistical schools, many differences of which stem, as noted earlier, from different interpretations of the probability calculus. So far, we have considered the subjectivist interpretation, according to which probabilities are primarily interpreted as concerning rational updating of degrees of belief. This viewpoint sees no fundamental distinction between inference from beliefs about hypotheses to beliefs about data (the standard probabilistic case), and statistical inference in the reverse direction. Bayes (1763) showed that inference in the two directions can be related by a simple corollary of the axioms of probability:

$$P(H_j|D) = \frac{P(D|H_j)P(H_j)}{\sum_i P(D|H_i)P(H_i)}$$

This result is the foundation of Bayesian statistics, which allows the probability of a model or hypothesis H_j given data D to be estimated, given the probability of the data D given each possible model or hypothesis H_i, and the prior probability of each H_i. By the application of Bayes' theorem, the normal laws of probability can be used to infer how probable each of a range of hypotheses is, given a data set, simply by mechanical calculation. Notice that the denominator is the same whatever hypothesis is under consideration, and acts as a normalisation factor which ensures that the probabilities $P(H_i|D)$ sum to 1. It is often treated as a constant, and Bayes' theorem is then expressed, as above, by stating that $P(H_j|D)$ is proportional to $P(H_j|D)P(H_j)$

According to a subjectivist interpretation, the prior probability $P(H_j)$ can be interpreted as an initial degree of belief in the hypothesis H_j. But for alternative views of probability, such as the frequentist interpretation (according to which probabilities are the limits of relative frequencies of repeated events, e.g. Fisher, 1922; Von Mises, 1939) and objectivist interpretation (according to which probabilities are objective properties of the world [Mellor, 1971]), it is difficult to see how any sense can be made of such probability statements. For this reason, among others, various alternatives to Bayesian statistics have since been derived. The principal alternative schools are those of Fisher (1956, 1970) and Neyman and Pearson (e.g. Neyman 1950), and most standard statistical tests within the behavioural sciences (e.g. the f test, the ANOVA, χ^2 test) were developed by these schools (though the standard discussion of such tests in introductory statistical textbooks frequently blends incompatible elements of these approaches together—see Gigerenzer et al., 1989). We shall focus on Bayesian statistical methods henceforth, as it is these, and related methods, that most closely relate to neural network models. Furthermore, the subjectivist, Bayesian approach relates probability and statistics most directly to problems of belief updating, and hence has the most natural relation to cognitive processing.

At this level of generality, it should be clear that there is no limitation on the nature or complexity of the models (hypotheses, theories) that can be assessed using Bayesian statistics, aside from the fact that they must be well enough specified that the probability of each data outcome can be calculated given that the model holds. That is, hypotheses or theories must constitute probabilistic models. (In practice, of course, many hypotheses are not well enough specified for this to be possible, and additional assumptions must be made to fill out the hypothesis or theory into a full probabilistic model, but we shall not be concerned with this issue here.)

From a probabilistic point of view, the natural interpretation of conditionals is in terms of conditional probability. Thus, *birds fly* (or more longwindedly, *if something is a bird then it flies*) can be regarded as claiming that the conditional probability of something flying, given that it is a bird, is high. Probability theory naturally allows non-monotonicity. If all we know about a thing is that it is a bird, then the probability that it flies might be, say, 0.9 ($P[\text{flies}|\text{bird}] = 0.9$); but the probability of it flying given that it is both a bird and an ostrich is 0 or nearly 0 ($P[\text{flies}|\text{bird}, \text{ostrich}] = 0$). These statements are completely compatible from the point of view of probability theory. This approach to the meaning of conditional statements has been proposed in philosophy by Adams (1966, 1975), and has also been adopted in artificial intelligence (Pearl, 1988). Problems have been raised with this probabilistic interpretation of the conditional, essentially concerning the rather unnatural scenario in which conditionals are embedded—e.g. if (if P then Q) then R (Lewis, 1976)—although the relevance of these problems to the design of artificial intelligent systems and to human cognition is unclear (Pearl, 1988).

The application of probabilistic methods to inference is a vast topic. In Chapter 16, we consider some of the wider issues and problems for probabilistic approaches to inference, describing recent developments such the use of maximum entropy (Jaynes, 1989) and minimum description length (Rissanen, 1989). For the purposes of this book, the elementary treatment given earlier is sufficient to serve our goal of providing a "rational analysis" of human reasoning in the context of a particularly problematic experimental reasoning task, Wason's selection task, which will be the case study discussed in Part II.

Rational Analysis

Chapters 10 to 13 present our rational analysis of Wason's selection task. Chapter 14 defends the account against a variety of objections raised by Almor and Sloman (1996), Evans and Over (1996a), and Laming (1996). Chapter 15 applies the analysis to data obtained by Sperber, Cara, and Girotto (1995) and relates our rational analysis to their account based on relevance theory.

The essence of rational analysis (Anderson, 1990) is to view cognitive processes as approximating some normatively justified standard of correct performance. Thus, in the context of reasoning, *normative* theories such as logic and probability theory, can be used as the basis for a *description* of human reasoning behaviour (Oaksford & Chater, 1995b). The roots of rational analysis derive from the earliest attempts to build theories of rational thought, i.e. logic and probability. Probability theory was originally developed as a theory of how sensible people reason about uncertainty (Gigerenzer et al., 1989). Thus, the early literature on probability theory treated the subject both as a description of human psychology, and as a set of norms for how people ought to reason when dealing with uncertainty. Similarly, the earliest formalisations of logic (Boole, 1951/1854) viewed the principles as describing the laws governing thought, as well as providing a calculus for good reasoning. This early work in probability theory and logic is a precursor of rational analysis, because it aims both to describe how the mind works, and to explain why the mind is rational.

The twentieth century has, however, seen a move away from this "psychologism" (Frege, 1879, 1950/1884; Hilbert, 1925), and now mathematicians, philosophers, and psychologists sharply distinguish between normative theories, such as a probability theory and logic, which are about how people *should* reason, and descriptive theories of the psychological mechanisms by which people actually reason. Moreover, a major finding in psychology has been that the rules by which people *should* and *do* reason are not merely conceptually distinct; but they appear to be empirically very different (Kahneman & Tversky, 1973; Kahneman, Slovic, & Tversky, 1982; Wason, 1966; Wason & Johnson-Laird, 1972). Whereas very early research on probability theory and logic took their project as codifying how people think, the psychology of reasoning has suggested that probability theory and logic are profoundly at variance with how people think. If this viewpoint is correct, then the whole idea of rational models of cognition is misguided: cognition simply is not rational.

Rational analysis suggests a return to the earlier view of the relationship between descriptive and normative theory—i.e. that a single theory can, and should, do both jobs. A rational model of cognition can therefore explain both how the mind works and why it is successful. But why is rational analysis not just a return to the conceptual confusion of the past? It represents a psychological proposal for explaining cognition that recognises the conceptual distinction between normative and descriptive theories, but explicitly suggests that in explaining cognitive performance a single account that has both functions is required. Moreover, contemporary rational analyses are explicit scientific hypotheses framed in terms of the computer metaphor, which can be tested against experimental data. Consequently a rational model of cognition is an empirical hypothesis about the nature of the human cognitive system and not merely an a priori assumption.

The computational metaphor is important because it suggests that rational analyses should be described in terms of a scheme for computational explanation. Rational analysis provides a computational-level explanation of cognitive phenomena in the sense of Marr (1982) that we have already discussed. Moreover, rational analysis, unlike early developments of logic and probability, aims to model detailed experimental data on cognitive function—rational analyses must be descriptively adequate with respect to these data, as well as being normatively justified. Recent research on rational analysis spans a wide range of cognitive phenomena, including memory, categorisation, and search, as well as reasoning (see Oaksford & Chater, 1998a, for a survey of recent developments in rational analysis).

So far, we have considered rationality in the abstract—as consisting of reasoning according to sound principles. But the goals of an agent attempting to survive and prosper in its ecological niche are more concrete—it must decide how to act in order to achieves its goals. In the model we discuss in Part II we will make a very minimal but crucial assumption about the environment in which reasoners must act. We call this the "rarity" assumption, which is simply that most properties about which people reason apply to only a small proportion of the objects in the world. If this assumption holds then we can view people's behaviour as optimal with respect to some goal, e.g. maximising information gained, or maximising expected utility. This style of explanation is similar to optimality-based explanations that have been influential in other disciplines. In the study of animal behaviour (Kacelnik, 1998), foraging, diet selection, mate selection and so on, have all been viewed as problems, which animals solve more or less optimally. In economics, people and firms are viewed as more or less optimally making decisions in order to maximise utility or profit.

Models based on optimising, whether in psychology, animal behaviour, or economics, need not, and typically do not, assume that agents are able to find the perfectly optimised solutions to the problems that they face. Quite often, perfect optimisation is impossible even in principle, because the calculations involved in finding a perfect optimum are frequently computationally intractable (Simon, 1955, 1956), and, moreover, much crucial information is typically not available. The agent must still act, even in the absence of the ability to derive the optimal solution (Chater & Oaksford, 1996; Gigerenzer & Goldstein, 1996; Simon, 1956). Thus, there may be a tension between the theoretical goal of the rational analysis and the practical need for the agent to be able to decide how to act in real time, given the partial information available. This leads directly into the area of what Simon (1955, 1956) calls *bounded rationality*. Anderson's programme of rational analysis explicitly takes cognitive limitations into account—that is, the cognitive system is viewed is approximating a normative standard within the limits imposed by memory and processing restrictions.

In Part II we develop a rational analysis of a family of reasoning tasks formulated by Peter Wason (1966, 1968) which we now introduce.

Wason's Selection Task

In Wason's selection task, an experimenter presents participants with four cards, each with a number on one side and a letter on the other, and with a rule of the form *if p then q*. For example, *if there is a vowel on one side (p), then there is an even number on the other side (q)*. The four cards show an "A"(*p* card), a "K"(*not-p* card), a "2"(*q* card) and a "7"(*not-q* card). Participants have to select those cards that they must turn over to determine whether the rule is true or false. It has been standardly assumed that, logically, participants should select only the *p* and *not-q* cards. However, only 4% of participants make this response, other responses being far more common—*p* and *q* cards (46%); *p* card only (33%); *p*, *q*, and *not-q* cards (7%); *p* and *not-q* cards (4%) (Johnson-Laird & Wason, 1970a). These results appear to suggest that people are very poor at logical reasoning even on such a superficially simple task.

This is a very robust result that has been taken by many commentators as casting doubt on human rationality (Stich, 1985, 1990). Even popular-isations of human cognition cite the task as evidence of poor human reasoning performance, suggesting that similar errors occur outside the laboratory sometimes with tragic results (e.g. Sutherland, 1992). Indeed Wason's selection task has been taken as a benchmark against which to test theories of reasoning. For example, theories such as Evans' (1984, 1989) heuristic account, Cheng and Holyoak's (1985) pragmatic reasoning schemas, and Cosmides' (1989) Darwinian algorithms account were all introduced via their ability to predict effects in variants of the selection task.

The central importance of this task to the development of theories of human reasoning makes it a natural place to begin developing a probabil-istic approach to human inference. We argue that performance on this task is a reflection of people's everyday reasoning strategies which are adapted to the uncertainty of the real world. By switching to a probabilistic viewpoint we are able to develop a rational analysis of performance on a range of different versions of the selection task. According to our rational analysis, human performance, far from being in error, in fact displays an optimal adaptation to the environment. Consequently we are able to provide rational explanations for what had previously seemed a baffling and irra-tional pattern of experimental reasoning performance. So, rather than representing a blatant example of human irrationality, performance on this task can be viewed as an example of human *rationality*. Crucially, our account reconciles the paradox between the apparent irrationality of human performance on the selection task and the manifest success of human reasoning in the everyday, uncertain world.

SUMMARY

The closing chapter of this book has two sections. In the first we review the most recent evidence on our probabilistic account of the selection task and some new extensions to other reasoning tasks. This review reveals that the probabilistic approach to the selection task and to the psychology of reasoning in general is indeed proving fruitful. Moreover, the promise to provide detailed formal models of other reasoning tasks, thereby revealing the rational bases of participants' behaviour, is being fulfilled. In the second section we take up the challenge posed in Part I: Can a probabilistic approach resolve the problems for logicism that we have introduced here? Although we do not shy away from presenting the many problems confronting a probabilistic approach, we argue that it does provide a more descriptively adequate, or complete*, account of reasoning, i.e. it provides a far securer platform than logicism from which to build computational accounts of human reasoning.

NOTE

1. It may appear that Rips can appeal to the venerable distinction (Strawson, 1950) between statements (uses of sentences on particular occasions) and sentences. One could argue that using a rule to predict the world on a particular occasion involves "mentally asserting" that the rule holds in that particular context, even though the conditional sentence *if the car is gone, then someone has driven it away* is not invariably true, across all contexts. That is, you must state that the rule holds on a particular occasion in order to use it in inference. Of course, on this occasion, the rule may not hold, in which case the mental assertion is false. But then this means that Rips would have to make sense of a notion of truth in context (Levinson, 1983), which is precisely the project of devising schemes of uncertain reasoning, i.e. allowing that things that are true in one context can be false in extensions of that context or indeed in completely different contexts. That is, from a logical point of view, this way of attempting to maintain the idea that everyday conditional rules can be treated within standard logic, leads directly to the need to define a notion of truth in context. This move simply recreates all the problems of dealing with uncertainty, which notoriously cannot be handled in a standard logical framework.

PART I

Problems with Logicism

In Chapter 1, we introduced the problems of uncertainty in human reasoning, and the various proposals of the logicist approach to cognitive science for dealing with these problems. The papers collected together in Part I address these logicist proposals and their difficulties in detail. We suggest that the arguments put forward in these papers undermine the logicist approach to the psychology of human reasoning, and also the wider logicist programme in cognitive science as a whole.

CHAPTER TWO

Autonomy, Implementation, and Cognitive Architecture: A Reply to Fodor and Pylyshyn

INTRODUCTION

In Chapter 1, we noted that logicist cognitive science relies on the idea that logic can provide a way of solving the fundamental problem of understanding rational mechanisms. The idea is that logic provides a computational-level theory of human inference, and that formal, proof-theoretic operations can provide algorithms for logical inference. These algorithms are themselves assumed to be implemented somehow in the brain.

There are two criteria of adequacy that any computational-level theory of human inference must meet. The first is that it must adequately capture the pattern of real human inference. In Chapter 4, we express this constraint by saying that such a computational-level theory must be complete*, as defined in Chapter 1. The second is that it must be consistent with constraints from the algorithmic and implementational levels. That is, there must be tractable algorithms that at least approximate the computational-level theory, and it must be possible to implement these efficiently in the human brain.

This chapter deals with both challenges to logicism, starting with the question of compatibility between levels of analysis. Neuroscience has provided a wealth of information about the nature of the biological substrate of cognition. However, it is not immediately apparent how, or whether, this detailed information about implementation constrains the algorithmic and computational levels. Research on connectionism, which studies the computational properties of networks of neuron-like elements, has, however, begun to provide tentative suggestions about the form that such constraints might take. Some of these constraints, particularly concerning the slowness of neural hardware, and the comparative speed of cognitive operations, appear to be incompatible with many traditional accounts of cognition. Specifically, they appear incompatible with accounts using logic as a computational-level theory.

Fodor and Pylyshyn (1988) defended the logicist position against connectionist attack. They suggest that the fundamental dispute between connectionist and logicist cognitive science (which Fodor and Pylyshyn refer to as "classical" cognitive science) is that connectionists abandon *structured* representation. Structured representation is required to capture the systematicity of thought: that is, to differentiate the constituents of a relation, and the roles they play. For example, thinking that John loves Mary and thinking that Mary loves John appear to be systematically related—the same constituents occur, but related in different ways. The systematic relationship between the two thoughts is reflected in natural language by the fact that the interpretation of each sentence depends on its *syntactic structure*. Fodor and Pylyshyn argue that, in the same way, some internal system of *structured* representation is required to account for the relationship between the thoughts themselves. They claim that connectionist researchers deny that such structured representations are required by the cognitive system. Fodor and Pylyshyn therefore take the fundamental dispute between the logicist approach to cognitive science and connectionism to concern whether or not cognitive processes operate over structured representations.

In this chapter, we suggest that Fodor and Pylyshyn have misidentified the fundamental import of connectionist research for logicist cognitive science, and thus their attempted defence of the logicist position is not successful. We argue that connectionists and logicists alike agree on the importance of structured representations; connectionists are, however, concerned with how structured representations can be implemented in networks of simple computing elements, which are assumed to have some (rather abstract) relation to the neural machinery of the brain.

The substantive dispute between connectionism and logicism concerns whether or not the two adequacy criteria on logic as a computational-level theory of cognition can be met. First, connectionist research has suggested that properties of neural hardware may significantly constrain algorithmic and computational-level theories. Specifically, the classical symbolic architecture which provides the most natural implementation of logic appears unable to capture many properties of cognition, which connectionist systems capture successfully—Fodor and Pylyshyn refer to such properties as the "lures" of connectionism, and argue that they are spurious. Second, logic cannot model the patterns of human inference, because human inference is

defeasible, whereas logical inference is not—i.e. logic cannot be complete*
with respect to human inference. Attempts to extend logic to deal with
defeasibility appear to fail on both counts—they are not complete* and they
are computationally intractable, and therefore cannot be plausibly implemented on *any* computational architecture, including the human brain (we
deal with these problems with logical approaches to defeasible inference
extensively in later chapters). In this chapter, we suggest that some of the
"lures" of connectionism seem to provide just the properties required to
implement schemes for defeasible inference.

At one point, directly pursuing a connectionist theory of inference
appeared to us to be a promising direction for research. However, the
appearance of Anderson's work on "rational analysis", building on Marr's
levels of computational explanation, persuaded us that the project of providing an adequate computational-level theory, or rational analysis, of
human inference was a prerequisite before any other aspects of computational explanation could be developed. Therefore, we do not pursue connectionist approaches to inference in this book, but concentrate instead on
the question of completeness*—i.e. establishing the correct computational-
level theory of human inference. As we note in Part II of this book, probability theory may provide a more adequate computational-level theory of
human inference. In the final chapter, we discuss the compatibility of
probabilistic computational-level theories with connectionist implementations.

AUTONOMY, IMPLEMENTATION AND COGNITIVE ARCHITECTURE: A REPLY TO FODOR AND PYLYSHYN

Fodor and Pylyshyn's (1988) defence of the *classical symbolic paradigm*
against the emergent *connectionist paradigm* in cognitive science depends on
the assumption that connectionism eschews structured representation.
However, this assumption is belied by the numerous attempts of connectionists to implement structured representations in neural networks (Derthick, 1987; Hinton 1981; Rumelhart, Smolensky, McClelland, & Hinton,
1986; Touretzky & Hinton, 1985). Thus, the issue of structured representation cannot be the principal point of disagreement between classicist
and connectionist. We contend that although Fodor and Pylyshyn (1988)
are right to argue that connectionism is an *implementational theory*, this does
not detract from connectionism's relevance to psychological explanation.
Fodor and Pylyshyn's contention that implementational considerations are
irrelevant to psychological explanation only follows on the assumption that
cognitive and implementational levels are computationally and hence
explanatorily autonomous (Fodor & Pylyshyn, 1988, p. 66). We argue that

in attempting to account for the various alluring properties of connectionist systems, Fodor and Pylyshyn (1988) are systematically forced to abandon the autonomy assumption, thereby assuring the relevance of connectionism to psychological explanation.

The "Lure" of Connectionism

We now re-examine the various "lures" of connectionism. We argue that Fodor and Pylyshyn's objections stem directly from their stand on autonomy. There are two readings of the claim that the cognitive level is implementation-independent.

The first reading is that the cognitive level can be formally specified. This formal specification must be implementable, but is wholly independent of the particular implementation employed. We can understand the behaviour of a PROLOG program independently of the layers of software on which it runs, and the hardware realisation in the VAX. That such independence of higher levels is possible is a central result in computability theory. Establishing the notion of a Universal Programmable Machine demonstrates that hardware places almost no constraints on the class of implementable virtual machines. The second reading is that the implementational level cannot affect higher-level processes. Fodor and Pylyshyn are aware that this is an absurd position. Pylyshyn (1984) points out that implementation affects complexity profile, the effects of damage, reliability and so on. As the second reading is agreed to be absurd, the real nature of the dispute is whether the cognitive level can be formally specified in an implementation-independent way. The Classicist believes in formal autonomy; the Connectionist does not. Fodor and Pylyshyn take formal autonomy to imply that implementation is irrelevant to cognition. To explain the lures we will consistently urge that the cognitive level must *interact with* properties of the implementation, and so cognitive performance cannot be explained implementation-independently, *pace* formal autonomy. We will also argue that, in any case, implementational considerations severely constrain the class of cognitively plausible architectures, even if autonomy can somehow be preserved. Hence we will conclude that connectionism *is* relevant to cognition.

The "lure" of connectionism consists of a series of properties shared by connectionist devices and the human cognitive system. Fodor and Pylyshyn argue that the lures are consistent with an appropriately implemented formally autonomous classical architecture. By contrast the Connectionist is not convinced that this is possible. To resolve this issue we now discuss the lures in detail.

To begin, we must reclassify Fodor and Pylyshyn's breakdown of the lures as certain phenomena are cross-classified. They provide the following list:

1. Speed
2. Content addressability and pattern recognition
3. The blurring of rule-governed and rule-exceptional behaviour
4. Non-verbal or intuitive processes
5. Resistance to damage and noise
6. Active versus passive storage
7. All-or-none processing, including:
   a. Partial rule matching
   b. Non-determinism
   c. Graceful degradation
8. Brain-style modelling

Some of these issues cluster together. Connectionist approaches to massively parallel soft constraint satisfaction (6) purchase the alluring properties of graceful degradation (7c), content addressability (2), and a property Fodor and Pylyshyn do not mention, *automatic generalisation.* Fodor and Pylyshyn group noise and damage tolerance (5) together, but ignore the former. Noise tolerance and partial pattern recognition (7a) are special cases of graceful degradation. Damage tolerance and rule-governed and rule-exceptional behaviour (3) will be dealt with separately. We thus invoke five clusters:

1. Speed (Fodor and Pylyshyn's 1)
2. Tolerance of damage (Fodor and Pylyshyn's 5)
3. Massively parallel soft constraint satisfaction (Fodor and Pylyshyn's 2, 5, 7a, 7c)
4. The blurring of rule-governed and rule-exceptional behaviour (Fodor and Pylyshyn's 3)
5. Brain-style modelling (Fodor and Pylyshyn's 8)

Some of the issues that Fodor and Pylyshyn raise are peripheral to connectionism. The distinction between active and passive memory (6) concerns whether the control regime is completely distributed throughout the system (active, no CPU, no interpreter) or completely centralised (passive, CPU and interpreter). It is not about memories "doing" or "not doing" things. Thus, their discussion of Kosslyn and Hatfield (1984) is not germane (pp. 52–3). While many connectionist systems possess active memory in this sense, some do not (e.g. Derthick, 1987; Shastri, 1985).

Non-verbal and intuitive processing (4) are not addressed by Fodor and Pylyshyn, and so we will not discuss them further. We do not know the origin of the alleged "lure" of non-determinism (7b). The macroscopic non-determinism of human behaviour seems equally compatible with classicism or connectionism.

Speed

It has been argued that there is an upper bound of about 100 serial steps on any cognitive process lasting less than a second (Feldman & Ballard, 1982). The Connectionist claims that the Classicist cannot account for this fact. However, Fodor and Pylyshyn contend that "All [the 100-step constraint] rules out is the (absurd) hypothesis that cognitive architectures are implemented in the brain in the same way as they are implemented on electronic computers" (1988, p. 55). Yet the 100-step constraint *does* severely limit the class of cognitively plausible algorithms. For example, it rules out this algorithm for addition: subtract 1 from the second number and add 1 to the first until the second is 0; the sum is the final value of the first. We suspect that most people can add 1,000,000 and 1,000,000 in less than 1 second. However, our algorithm would require 1,000,000 steps. It is excluded by the 100-step constraint.

Fodor and Pylyshyn suggest that since "it is not even certain that the firing of neurons is invariably the relevant implementation property ... the 100 step 'constraint' excludes nothing" (p. 55). So, perhaps we can push up n (the number of steps that can be computed in less than a second). Connectionists themselves have suggested how this may be achieved by probabilistic coding (e.g. Hinton & Sejnowski, 1986) and have speculated that fast neuronal changes other than firing may be computationally important (Von der Malsburg & Bienenstock, 1986). Only by *doing connectionism* will we discover what neural properties are computationally relevant. At best Fodor and Pylyshyn may hope that n may be significantly greater than 100. However, even if n is higher by one or two orders of magnitude, the n-step constraint will still significantly restrict the class of cognitively plausible algorithms. The substantive practical issue is whether the Classicist can implement his favourite cognitive algorithms without violating the n-step constraint. As classicist algorithms typically require many millions of machine operations, the n-step constraint presents a non-trivial challenge to the Classicist.

Tolerance of Damage

The Connectionist claims that classical symbolic computation does not have the damage tolerance characteristic of human cognition. Connectionist systems achieve damage tolerance by using distributed representations. However, Fodor and Pylyshyn argue that "neural distribution of representations is just as compatible with classical architectures as it is with connectionist networks" (1988, p. 56). All the support they adduce for this claim is that "*all you need* [our italics] are memory registers that distribute their contents over physical space" (p. 56). However, distributed representations are damage tolerant not simply because they have spatially non-localised coding but because the internal structure of the symbol reflects its semantic properties, e.g. PEACH and APRICOT will have similar bit vectors. Arbitrary redundancy is like storing the same piece of information in many places. If all copies are damaged, however partially, there is a catastrophic loss of performance. In a non-arbitrary distributed scheme, similar objects are represented by similar bit vectors. Therefore, even if the representation is so damaged that PEACH cannot be reconstructed, a semantically related item will be selected, for example APRICOT (Hinton, McClelland, & Rumelhart, 1986, p. 102). This permits an understanding of graded semantically systematic error.

Massively Parallel Soft Constraint Satisfaction

This lure falls under four subheadings: (i) memory is content-addressable and pattern recognition easy; (ii) memory is noise resistant; (iii) rules can be partially satisfied giving (iv) graceful degradation. These issues are distinguished in Fodor and Pylyshyn, but are all direct consequences of the connectionist approach to massively parallel soft constraint satisfaction. Connectionists contend that standard symbolic computation does not have these properties. To maintain autonomy Fodor and Pylyshyn must believe that an appropriate implementation of a classical architecture can capture (i) to (iv).

In Fodor and Pylyshyn's reply to the lures, they say nothing about (i). So arguments that conventional methods such as "hash coding" are inadequate remain unchallenged (Hinton, McClelland, & Rumelhart, 1986).

Fodor and Pylyshyn identify the problem of noise (ii) to be tolerance of "spontaneous neural activity" (1988, p. 52). However, it is usually seen as the problem of achieving reliable computation with a degraded input. The input may be degraded for many reasons: e.g. noisy background conditions (in ordinary speech recognition); errorful memory retrieval cues (Hinton, McClelland, & Rumelhart, 1986); stimuli in peripheral vision; internal noise, whether generated by spontaneous neural activity or physical damage. The section "*Resistance to noise and physical damage*" does not mention noise but it *is* raised briefly in the discussion of "soft" constraints: "The soft or stochastic nature of [classical] rule-based processes arises from the *interaction* [our italics] of deterministic rules with real-valued properties of the implementation, or with noisy inputs or noisy information transmission" (1988, p. 58). This does not constitute an autonomous solution to the problem of noise, as interaction between implementation and cognitive architecture simply concedes autonomy.

Similarly, in discussing (iii), Fodor and Pylyshyn seem immediately to concede autonomy: "One can have a classical rule system in which the decision concerning which rule will fire resides in the functional architecture and depends on continuously varying magnitudes [thus abandoning autonomy]. Indeed, this is typically how it is done in practical 'expert systems' which, for example, use a Bayesian mechanism in their production-system rule-interpreter" (1988, p. 58). *Contra* Fodor and Pylyshyn the statistical processes of Bayesian inference in practical expert systems are defined at the level of cognitive architecture, not functional architecture (Charniak & McDermott, 1985, p. 460). So the traditional solution is an autonomous classical model. This approach seems unpromising in the light of complexity results for standard Bayesian techniques (Charniak & McDermott, 1985, Chapter 8). So the concession to non-autonomy is well motivated.

Autonomy is again apparently conceded in discussing (iv). Fodor and Pylyshyn argue that a classical rule system may capture graceful degradation: "rules could be activated in some measure depending on how close their conditions are to holding. Exactly what happens in these cases may depend on how the rule-system is *implemented*" [our italics] (1988, p. 58). To have the activation of a cognitive-level rule dependent on properties of the implementation completely abandons autonomy. Fodor and Pylyshyn suggest that it is possible *in principle* that some implementation of Newell's (1969) hierarchy of weak methods or Laird, Rosenbloom, and Newell's (1986) universal sub-goaling may capture graceful degradation. But the Connectionist doubts that it can be achieved *in practice* in an autonomous architecture. In contrast, many connectionist systems have been held to achieve graceful degradation quite naturally (McClelland, Rumelhart, & Hinton, 1986). Fodor and Pylyshyn deny this claim (1988, pp. 58–9) but in the absence of specific criticisms we must assume that the lure of graceful degradation stands.

Although Fodor and Pylyshyn separate the aforementioned points, they are all direct consequences of the fact that connectionist systems "provide an efficient way of using parallel hardware to implement best-fit searches ... Each active unit represents a 'microfeature' of an item, and the connection strengths stand for plausible 'microinferences' between microfeatures. Any particular pattern of activity of the units will satisfy some of the micro-inferences and violate others. A stable pattern of activity is one that violates the plausible microinferences less than any of the neighbouring patterns" (Hinton, McClelland, & Rumelhart, 1986, pp. 80–1). Given this intuitive picture we can see how the various lures emerge.

When an arbitrary sufficiently large fragment of a pattern is presented the microinferences produce the nearest possible completion (stable state). Hence, any sufficiently large part of the content of the memory will access the whole memory. That is, memory is content-addressable (i). If part of the presented fragment is wrong, the microinferences will still find the best available fit. Hence a degree of noise can be tolerated (ii).

This intuitive picture can be generalised from *within* layer interactions to *between* layer interactions generating (iii) and (iv). Consider a network trained to map each of a set of input patterns onto a corresponding output pattern. We may treat each input–output pair as a rule with a "condition" (input) and an "action" (output). Each bit of the output pattern is a function of *all* the elements of the input pattern. Thus the information about which output should be chosen is distributed throughout the input. Suppose that the input is a slight distortion of one of the learnt patterns. As the output is a function of the entire input, the loss of any particular part of the input does not lead to a catastrophic failure to produce any particular bit of the correct output. Rather it leads to a slight distortion of the whole output vector. Hence, as the fidelity of an input is smoothly reduced, the fidelity of the output smoothly reduces. This is *graceful degradation* (iv). This behaviour contrasts with that of conventional schemes, where either the input error is detected, corrected for, and the right output chosen, or the error is not detected, and a totally inappropriate output is produced (or none at all).

Suppose that the presented input pattern is a blend of the learnt input patterns (suppose we have learnt A $\Rightarrow$ X; B $\Rightarrow$ Y; etc.; a blend of A:1111100010 and B:1110000001 might be simply C:1111000011). What is the pattern Z that C is mapped onto? As the presented input pattern C is a slight distortion of A, the output it produces, Z, is a degraded form of the corresponding output X (by graceful degradation). However, similarly, Z will be close to the output corresponding to B. Thus if the input C is a blend of A and B, the output Z will be a blend of X and Y. Thus an input pattern may partially match several different rules, to a graded extent. This is *partial rule matching* (iii).

The Blurring of Rule-governed and Rule-exceptional Behaviour

Fodor and Pylyshyn claim that connectionists are committed to a common etiology for rule-governed and rule-exceptional behaviour (1988, p. 51). They appear to be adverting to Pinker and Prince's (1988) criticisms of Rumelhart and McClelland's (1986) Past Tense Learning Model which attempts to learn regular and irregular past tenses with a single mechanism. From a detailed consideration of the past tense system in English, Pinker and Prince argue that the model is unlikely to generalise. However, Fodor and Pylyshyn characterise the rule-governed versus rule-exceptional distinction in terms of the surely unrelated competence–performance distinction. The use of *went* as the past tense of *go* is to be attributed to linguistic competence yet it is rule-exceptional. The Connectionist may wish to blur the etiology of rule-governed and rule-exceptional behaviour while maintaining a sharp distinction between competence and performance.

Fodor and Pylyshyn further conflate the rule-governed–rule-exceptional distinction with the rule-implicit–rule-explicit distinction (1988, pp. 59–60). Although the issues surrounding the latter distinction are important and unresolved, we agree with Fodor and Pylyshyn that they do not *decide* between connectionist and classicist. As we advocate the implementation of high-level cognitive architectures in connectionist hardware we are committed to the need for explicit rules in the explanation of cognitive phenomena. However, with respect to particular behaviours, the Connectionist and Classicist may differ as to which sort of explanation is appropriate. If one retains autonomy, there are only two explanatory avenues open: rule-governed or errorful. Linguistic exceptions are either simply *mistakes* or are governed by *explicit* exceptional *rules*. It seems that all regularities must be encoded explicitly. Later on this fact will return to dog the Classicist's attempts to model human reasoning.

Brain-style Modelling

Fodor and Pylyshyn characterise this lure as the claim that connectionist models, in contrast to classical models, are constrained by the facts of neuroscience (1988, pp. 53–4). However, they claim that biology constrains cognitive architecture very little (p. 62) and further, that the biological plausibility of connectionist models is in any case problematic (p. 58). We argue that there are good reasons to work with connectionist models that do not map directly onto neural structures.

A given cognitive architecture running a particular algorithm will possess radically different real-time processing characteristics when implemented in different hardware. So although biological hardware cannot determine the high-level architecture, it severely constrains the class of possible cognitive architectures. It is hard to implement many features of standard architectures in connectionist systems (Touretzky & Hinton, 1985, for example). It is unclear whether tolerably efficient implementations of any standard symbolic architecture are possible. Adversion to Turing machine power is of no avail here, as we are concerned with real-time processing. We can only discover what cognitive architectures are compatible with biology by doing connectionist computer science.

Fodor and Pylyshyn hold that "brain-style" modellers expect biology to *specify properties* of the cognitive architecture and counter that "the structure of 'higher levels' of a system are rarely isomorphic, or even similar, to the structure of the 'lower levels' of a system" (1988, p. 63). This assumes that lower-level properties can only specify higher-level properties in virtue of an isomorphism. The relationship between atomic physics and chemistry seems to be an appropriate counter-example. In any case, the Connectionist need only claim that the facts of biology constrain rather than *specify* cognitive architecture.

The Lures: Concluding Remarks

Finally, we present some general remarks which argue against Fodor and Pylyshyn's response to the "lures" of connectionism. They argue that the Classicist can deal with the lures *in principle*. To satisfy the Connectionist, the Classicist will have to demonstrate this *in practice*.

The Classicist has Work to do! Fodor and Pylyshyn present no arguments to show that classical architectures are compatible in practice with (4.1) speed; (4.2) tolerance of damage; (4.3) massively parallel soft constraint satisfaction; or (4.5) brain-style modelling. The onus is on the Classicist to persuade us that a *single* classical architecture/implementation can have all these properties.

The Lures are Desirable in Standard Computer Science. If standard classical architectures can be implemented to use just 100 steps, to tolerate hardware failure, to implement rapid noise-resistant memory search and pattern matching, and to degrade gracefully under noisy conditions, then this is how they *should* be implemented. Such properties would be advantageous in everyday computational applications. If such implementations are possible, they cannot be obvious, or we would be running PROLOG on them!

Learning. The most persuasive lure is not mentioned by Fodor and Pylyshyn. This is that connectionist systems need not be hard wired, but can *learn*. Current learning methods such as back-propagation are not the last word in learning theory. However, the connectionist approach to learning gives some insight into how genuinely new structures can spontaneously emerge (Almeida, 1987; Hinton & Sejnowski, 1986; Rumelhart, Hinton, & Williams, 1986; Pineda, 1987; Rumelhart & Zipser, 1986; but see Minsky & Papert, 1988, for a general critique).

By contrast, standard learning models cannot develop new structures (see Fodor, 1975; Fodor, 1981), as classical learning is just hypothesis generation and confirmation. Everything that can be learnt must be representable innately. Such considerations lead to the conclusion that all concepts (e.g. PROTON) are innate (Fodor 1981; although see Chater, 1986). Connectionism promises a theory of learning that sidesteps these difficulties.

What was the Real Nature of the Dispute? Throughout their discussion of the lures, Fodor and Pylyshyn make no reference to structured representation or the systematicity of thought. Even for Fodor and Pylyshyn these issues do not bear on the dispute between classicist and connectionist approaches. The lures challenge the Classicist to implement some standard architecture which meets each lure. We will only know whether this is feasible by attempting to implement standard architectures in brain-style hardware. And this will involve doing connectionist computer science.

The connectionist hunch is that this project will prove impossible and that many computational properties should be directly purchased from the implementational level. The lures do not decide the issue, but we have independent grounds to suppose that the classicist project will prove unworkable. We argue that only by rejecting autonomy will we understand the computational characteristics of the mind.

Cognition as Proof Theory

Fodor and Pylyshyn argue that classical cognitive science amounts to "an extended attempt to apply the methods of proof theory to the modelling of thought" (1988, pp. 29–30). They seem to be proposing that we think in a high-level logic programming language (like PROLOG?) the domain of which is the everyday world. Proof theory guarantees truth-preserving inference. However, most everyday inferences are not guaranteed to preserve truth, i.e. they are *plausible* inferences. These have been discussed under the banners of inductive inference, abductive inference, and default inference.

Inductive Inference

Classical inductive reasoning involves hypothesis generation and confirmation (Fodor, 1975). Hence, classical inductive learning models, e.g. Winston (1977), can only learn new concepts by combining elements of an innate primitive basis. Fodor (1981) observes that the primitive basis may have to be as large as the lexicon of a natural language. Clearly the claim that, for example, PROLOG is innate is close to a *reductio ad absurdum* of the classicist theory of induction (but again, see Chater, 1986).

Abductive Inference

Fodor and Pylyshyn (1988, p. 58) observe that non-demonstrative inferences like abduction (inference to the best explanation) *may* be accommodated by supplementing proof theory with Bayesian inference techniques (cf. Charniak & McDermott, 1985). However, these are generally computationally intractable. In medical diagnosis, heuristic techniques are used to deal with multiple diseases (cf. *Caduceus*, in Charniak & McDermott, 1985, p. 474). These heuristics cannot be justified semantically within the formal system. For Fodor and Pylyshyn, the heuristics must be implementational details, e.g. the search strategy of the interpreter. This amounts to computational non-autonomy. This implementational detail *explains* Caduceus' ability to deal with multiple diseases. This amounts to explanatory non-autonomy.

Default Reasoning

Just about any everyday generalisation succumbs to indefinitely many counter-examples. If I see Fred going past my window at 9.00 a.m., I know he's about to buy his morning paper. But not if it's Christmas day, because there are no papers. And not if he's being mugged; or if he's already reading *The Times*. These possibilities override our generalisation that Fred buys a paper just after passing my window every morning. To preserve autonomy, we must encode the various conditions that might override our rules, and check that none of them applies in any specific case. This is the standard approach to default reasoning in knowledge representation. Unfortunately we have reason to suspect that it is unworkable.

Most standard logical schemes are monotonic. If on seeing Fred go past the window I infer he will buy a newspaper, then if I reason monotonically, no additional premise can invalidate my conclusion. In non-monotonic reasoning you can add premises and *lose* conclusions.

Reiter (1985) attempts to extend standard logic to incorporate non-monotonicity. McDermott (1986) notes that there are two problems with Reiter's approach. First, Reiter's logic is undecidable in principle and intractable in practice. Deciding whether a default rule applies involves consistency checking, which is an NP-hard problem. Second, the conclusions drawn are usually too weak. Although p is the conclusion desired, all that follows is $p \vee q$, where q is some arbitrary proposition.

This technical problem need not decide against autonomy in knowledge representation. However, there are more general difficulties for the classicist approach. We can invent indefinitely many conditions which override my inference about Fred buying his morning paper. For the Classicist, each possibility must be explicitly encoded in the appropriate rule. To avoid an infinite list of default clauses we must appeal to a finite taxonomy which captures the infinitude of specific cases. Perhaps Fred will not get his morning paper in distracting situations, dangerous situations and so on. However, what counts as a distracting situation is relative to what rule we are considering. A road accident might count as a distracting situation for Fred getting his paper, but not for him getting to work. So the categories in our taxonomy must be spelt out in detail in each rule. It is unlikely that such specifications will be forthcoming. This difficulty with the context-dependence of categories is endemic in concept combination (Lyon & Chater, 1990). The problem of defaults infects lexical inference as well as structural inference.

These problems with the classical account of knowledge representation and inference do not argue for a non-autonomous account unless we indicate how the implementation can help. Hinton, McClelland, and Rumelhart

(1986, p. 82) discuss an implementation of semantic nets in connectionist hardware (originally in Hinton, 1981):

> If ... you learn that chimpanzees like onions you will probably raise your estimate of the probability that gorillas like onions. In a network that uses distributed representations, this kind of generalization is automatic. The new knowledge about chimpanzees is incorporated by modifying some of the connection strengths so as to alter the causal effects of the distributed pattern of activity that represents chimpanzees. The modifications automatically change the causal effects of all similar activity patterns. So if the representation of gorillas is a similar activity pattern over the same set of units, its causal effects will be changed in a similar way.

The similarity metric used in automatic generalisation is induced by pattern similarity and need not be specified by the programmer, but is learnt by the network (Hinton, 1987). Gorilla has "likes onions" as a default which may be overridden by explicitly storing information to the contrary. The default may also be overridden if "gorilla" has a similar pattern to "orangutan" and orangutans do not like onions. The similarity metric gives us default rules for free, and the auto-associative mechanism finds the best fit to the soft constraints. Soft constraints, the very fabric of connectionist implementations, just *are default* rules. This is a paradigm case of the value of non-autonomous implementations of structured representations. This toy example is suggestive of how implementation may unburden the cognitive architecture of the problems created by non-demonstrative inference.

Psychology as Proof Theory

If the domain of psychology is a proof-theoretic cognitive level, then the following are apparently not psychology: Marr's (1982) models of low-level vision; J.R. Anderson's (1983) spreading activation models of semantic memory; any of the work on the capacity limitations of human memory (cf. Fodor, 1983); the whole of neurophysiology, neuropsychology, and physiological psychology; all the work on semantic priming; the trace model of speech perception (McClelland & Elman, 1986), etc. The only experimental work we know of that explicitly addresses the logical characteristics of the cognitive architecture is that on deductive reasoning (Evans, 1982, 1983; Wason & Johnson-Laird, 1972). On Fodor & Pylyshyn's demarcation principle, the domain of psychological concern is unexpectedly limited. What remains is also problematic for the Classicist, as no existing logical regime is capable of capturing more than an insignificant fraction of the experimentally observed inferences (Oaksford, 1989; Oaksford & Stenning, 1988).

CONCLUSIONS

On a representational theory of mind the central problem for psychology is providing a semantics for mental states and a mechanism the causal sequences of which are semantically coherent, i.e. cognition is computation (Fodor, 1975, 1980, 1983, 1987; Fodor, Bever, & Garrett, 1974; Pylyshyn, 1973, 1980, 1984). Fodor and Pylyshyn claim biological computations are autonomous, i.e. mental processes are simply an implemented formal system and cognitive science is proof theory. Fodor and Pylyshyn adduce evidence for structured representation and take this to decide against connectionism because of the autonomy assumption. We believe that this assumption is the real locus of the dispute between classicist and connectionist approaches. This diagnosis is borne out in the discussion of the lures, which provide empirical adequacy criteria on an autonomous architecture. It is unclear whether these criteria can be met without violating autonomy. Further, autonomous architectures may fail in principle to handle non-demonstrative inference. Admittedly, non-autonomous (Derthick, 1987) connectionist approaches are embryonic. However, to borrow a Fodorian phrase, they seem to be the only straw afloat. So we must take seriously the possibility that cognitive architecture is not autonomous from its implementation.

CHAPTER THREE

Connectionism, Classical Cognitive Science, and Experimental Psychology

INTRODUCTION

This chapter continues the theme of the relationship between connectionism and logicist, or "classical", cognitive science. In the last chapter, we examined the computational properties of symbolic systems, which are the most natural implementation of logic, and connectionist systems, which are loosely based on the structure of the brain. We argued that connectionist systems might be better at capturing important computational properties of the cognitive system—these were the "lures" of connectionism which have the potential to contribute to accounts of everyday, defeasible inference. These discussions focused on abstract computational issues. In this chapter, we turn to empirical evidence from the psychology of memory and inference, which, we argue, supports the conclusion that logicist cognitive science is not viable, and that connectionism holds the promise of providing a better alternative.

We argue that classical symbolic computational models of cognition are at variance with the empirical findings in the cognitive psychology of memory and inference. Standard symbolic computers are well suited to remembering arbitrary lists of symbols and performing logical inferences. In contrast, human performance on such tasks is extremely limited. Standard models do *not* easily capture content-addressable memory or context-sensitive defeasible inference, which are natural and effortless for people. We argue that connectionism provides a more natural framework in which to model this behaviour. In addition to capturing the gross human performance profile, connectionist systems seem well suited to accounting for the systematic patterns of errors observed in the human data. These arguments counter another aspect of Fodor and Pylyshyn's (1988) argument: that connectionism is, in principle, irrelevant to psychology.

CONNECTIONISM, CLASSICAL COGNITIVE SCIENCE, AND EXPERIMENTAL PSYCHOLOGY

There has been an enduring tension in modern cognitive psychology between the computational models available and the experimental data obtained. Standard computational models have assumed the symbolic paradigm: that it is constitutive of cognitive processes that they are mediated by the manipulation of symbolic structures. Such schemes easily handle formal inferences, and memory for arbitrary symbolic material. However, context-sensitive defeasible inference and content-addressable memory retrieval have remained problematic. By contrast, in the empirical data on human memory and inference, the opposite profile is observed. Everyday mundane reasoning is both context-dependent and defeasible, and yet is performed easily and naturally, whereas subjects are typically unable to perform the simplest formal reasoning task (Evans, 1982; Wason & Johnson-Laird, 1972). In memory, content-addressable access in knowledge rich domains seems natural and unproblematic for human subjects, whereas people can retain only very small quantities of arbitrary material. Despite this tension between experiment and theory, Fodor and Pylyshyn (1988) have recently reaffirmed what they term the "classical symbolic paradigm". That is, they argue that symbolic cognitive processes are autonomous from their implementation. Thus they question the relevance of connectionist theorising for psychology, and suggest that connectionism should be viewed as a theory of implementation for autonomous classical architectures. We have argued (Chater & Oaksford, 1990) that cognitive processes are not autonomous from their implementation, and that interaction between classical and connectionist models is required to explain much of cognition, on *computational* grounds. In this chapter, we review some *empirical* grounds for non-autonomous accounts of cognition. We raise problems for the classical (autonomous) approach, and suggest that connectionist (non-autonomous) models may have more explanatory power. Let us briefly summarise the main points of the debate between classicist and connectionist.

Classicism versus Connectionism

Fodor and Pylyshyn (1988) claim that connectionism eschews structured representations and thus amounts to an unwitting return to associationism.

They raise two problems which must be resolved by any cognitive theory. First, constituency: how do people keep track of symbols so that they can play the same role in different representations? Second, *inference*: how do mental states systematically track semantic relations? However, a large amount of connectionist theorising explicitly addresses the issue of implementing structured representations such as semantic networks (Hinton, 1981), frames and mental models (Rumelhart, Smolensky, McClelland, & Hinton, 1986) in PDP systems. So the issue of structured representations does not separate the connectionist and classicist approaches. Chater and Oaksford (1990) have argued that the real locus of the dispute concerns whether cognitive architecture is computationally and explanatorily independent of its implementation.

For Fodor and Pylyshyn (1988) psychology is the study of the symbolic structures and processes that define the cognitive level. They claim that as connectionist architectures are *non-symbolic*, connectionism is properly viewed as a putative implementational theory for a standard symbolic architecture. As they take the cognitive architecture to be independent of its implementation, they conclude that connectionism is irrelevant to psychology. It is this *autonomy* assumption that separates classicist and connectionist thinking (Chater & Oaksford, 1990). The Connectionist believes that (i) the primitives of the cognitive-level architecture depend on the implementational substrate (i.e. a neural network), and (ii) the cognitive processes that psychologists can postulate crucially depend on these primitives. So a psychological account of memory and inference should pay close attention to the properties of neural implementation, and PDP is a preliminary attempt to characterise these properties. Given any particular *psychological* phenomenon the Classicist must give an explanation at the cognitive level, i.e. in terms of purely symbolic processes. On the other hand, the Connectionist may freely advert to properties of both the cognitive (symbolic) level and the implementational (connectionist) level.

The autonomous symbol processing paradigm has an implicit theory of memory and inference. A memory for an individual is simply a stored atomic symbol denoting the individual, a property of that individual is simply another symbol or symbolic structure. That is, a memory is a proposition encoded in some logical language. Memory is just a repository for formulae of this language. Inference consists of formal operations defined over these formulae. On this view the psychology of memory delimits the capacity and retrieval operations of the database; the psychology of reasoning specifies the nature of the theorem prover. Both may set constraints on the nature of the data structures implemented in human memory (e.g. Collins & Quillian, 1969; Johnson-Laird & Steedman, 1978).

Prima facie this classicist model of cognition makes strong predictions for human memory and inference. Memory for individuals and their properties should be trivial; if the VAX can store and retrieve arbitrary lists of symbols, then humans should too. Inference should be trivial; any simple theorem prover can solve two-line propositional logic problems, so people should find them easy too. In this article, we will show that these predictions of standard computer models are in tension with the psychological data on memory and inference. We will argue that non-autonomous connectionist explanations, which advert to both implementational and cognitive levels, may be better able to model human performance. We now examine the psychological data on memory and inference.

The Psychological Data

The most obvious experimental approach is simply to have subjects learn arbitrary lists of properties and perform formal reasoning tasks. On the classicist position it seems that human performance on simple memory and reasoning tasks should be close to perfect. In the following sections we adduce evidence that appears to violate these predictions.

Memory

One principal empirical motivation for the development of connectionist systems has been the tension between the gross operating characteristics of human memory and those of standard symbolic devices. For example, human memory appears to be content-addressable, and display graceful degradation—human memory appears tolerant (within bounds) to degraded inputs and damage (Bobrow & Norman, 1975; Norman & Bobrow, 1975, 1976, 1979). In contrast, standard symbolic devices are not content-addressable and they will fail to retrieve a memory trace in the face of damage or degraded input. In this section we amplify on these criticisms of the classicist view of memory by considering (i) the abundant evidence on the limitations of the human memory system, and (ii) the specific way in which people bind together the properties of individuals in memory.

It has been a fundamental observation in the psychology of human memory that recall for arbitrary material is severely limited. Short-term memory tasks for arbitrary material reveal serious memory capacity limitations. To a first approximation, subjects can only recall 7 ± 2 "items" (Miller, 1956). Human memory performance for such material is also severely limited in long-term memory tasks (Baddeley, 1976; Lindsay & Norman, 1977). Typically, the only way of improving performance is by imposing a high-level organisation using mnemonic strategies (Lorayne & Lucas, 1974). Similarly, short-term memory performance is bounded by severe resource limitations which may, in part, be overcome by the use of high-level recoding strategies or "chunking" (Miller, 1956).

Performance is superior with normal structured material because subjects need only recognise a pre-existing organisation rather than impose their own (Bartlett, 1932). People seem to be remarkably good at exploiting redundancy in memory for large amounts of complex, structured material. For example, people have a reliable recognition memory for very large numbers of briefly presented photographed scenes (Shepard, 1967). In contrast, it is extremely hard to recall the layout of an impoverished visual stimulus, such as the fixed stars. However, people find it much easier to recall a much richer stimulus, such as a face. Faces are of course highly redundant, whereas the position of the stars is not. People attempt to remember such arbitrary material by imposing meaningful interpretations upon them. In the case of the stars, the naming of constellations attests to the utility of such a strategy. In general, the more coherent the subjects find the material to be, the better it is remembered (Bransford & Johnson, 1973; Craik & Lockhart, 1972).

These data reveal a mismatch in the gross organisation of human memory and classical computational models. We now turn to more recent experiments in which the fine detail of memory performance is examined. The MIT task (Stenning & Levy, 1988; Stenning, Shepherd, & Levy, 1988) requires subjects to recall the appropriate *bindings* of properties to individuals. It thus addresses the question of how people keep track of structured knowledge about individuals. Two individuals are described in a short paragraph of text, and on recall subjects select the properties that attach to each individual. If each individual has one of two professions, nationalities, temperaments, and statures there are 136 possible pairs of individuals. The task is to remember which of these pairs was presented.

Analysis of the pattern of errors reveals the organisation of the underlying representations. The average error rate is just half a property wrong per paragraph. Errors are clearly interdependent: there are more multiple property errors than would be expected if errors on each dimension were independent. A frequent error is assigning two different values (say tall and short) to the wrong individuals. What is difficult is *binding*, i.e. remembering whether it was a Polish bishop and a Swiss dentist or a Polish dentist and a Swiss bishop. It is easy to remember whether they were both Swiss or both Polish. Further, multiple errors are more common than would be predicted if each of the eight properties were represented independently. If the properties for each individual were stored in separate logical formulae such statistical dependence would not be expected. On a classical architecture binding is trivial and so it is unclear why there should be any interference between separate memory traces at all.

The patterns of performance revealed here seem wholly unexpected, on the classicist view. If the very basis of memory is the storing of formal symbolic structures, then encoding arbitrary lists should be trivial compared with storing complex material, where it is opaque how the stored memory (a face, or the gist of a passage) can even be represented in propositional form. If such material can be represented propositionally, then the structures required will surely be extremely elaborate. On a classical architecture, the property list should be easy to remember and the complex material hard to remember. Yet the data on human performance show precisely the reverse.

Adversion to the competence–performance distinction is to no avail here. If this distinction applies to the study of memory, then (i) content-addressability, (ii) graceful degradation, and (iii) capacity limitations provide the data that characterise the competence state requiring explanation. Similarly, grammaticality judgements in linguistics characterise the competence state captured by the competence grammar. Competence theories, moreover, must account for the majority of the evidence. Otherwise they cease to be falsifiable empirical theories. The classical model is at variance with findings (i) and (ii), can only account for (iii) via arbitrarily imposed ad hoc limitations, and moreover fails to explain subjects' *systematic* binding errors. Hence it could only be preserved as a model of human memory on the assumption that it is impervious to falsification. In this case the classical account is not a cognitive model but rather an a priori assumption concerning the nature of computation in the brain which could only be legitimised in the absence of a competitor. Connectionism may provide the competition that promotes the mismatch between the classical model and the empirical data to falsificatory status.

Inference

The Classicist has an implicit theory of memory and inference. The data we have surveyed on memory (Stenning & Levy, 1988) appear to violate the expectation that a declarative memory should easily keep track of simple property lists. In this section, we address similar difficulties with classicist predictions for inference. If symbol manipulation forms the very basis of cognition, then trivial deductive inferences should be trivial for human subjects. However, data on deductive reasoning appear to violate the Classicist's predictions.

The conditional *if . . . then* construction is central to formal attempts to characterise inferential processes in logic. However, relative to normative logical theories the human data present a problem. Human conditional reasoning appears beset by various non-logical biases apparently reflecting the influence of content (Evans, 1982; Wason & Johnson-Laird, 1972), memory (Griggs & Cox, 1982), and prior beliefs (Pollard & Evans, 1981). Thus, normative conceptions of rationality appear radically at odds with people's observed facility for logical thought. The most striking demonstrations of apparently non-logical performance occur in the Wason selection task (1966).

Wason's task concerns how people assess evidence relevant to the truth or falsity of a rule expressed by means of a conditional sentence, normally using the *if ... then* construction. Subjects are presented with four cards, each having a number on one side and a letter on the other. On being presented with a rule such as "if there is a vowel on one side, then there is an even number on the other" and four cards, showing, for example, an "A" (*p*), a "K" (*not-p*), a "2" (*q*), and a "7" (*not-q*), they would have to select those cards they *must* turn over to determine whether the rule is true or false.

The classicist expectation was that performance would depend on the *logical form* of the construction used to express the rule. Responses should be predictable from the truth tables which supply the meanings of the various logical terms. A conditional, $p \supset q$ is true just in case either p is false or q is true; conversely it is false just in case p is true and q is false. So, the rule is true if and only if each card has a consonant on one side or an even number on one side. Conversely, it is false if any card has a vowel on one side and an odd number on the other. Hence, only the "A" card and the "7" card must be turned over. If a subject is exhaustively trying to make the rule true then these are the only undecided cases. If a subject is trying to make the rule false then these are the only cases with the potential to do so.

Typical results were: p and q card only (46%); p card only selected (33%); p, q, and *not-q* card selected (7%) p and *not-q* card selected (4%); others (10%) (Johnson-Laird & Wason, 1970). The logical response was observed in only 4% of subjects' responses. Even more puzzling, on a proof-theoretic account, are the various manipulations that facilitate performance on this task.

The most significant manipulation to produce a marked facilitation of the logical response was in thematic variants of the task where realistic or contentful materials were used. Wason and Shapiro (1971) employed the following rule: "Every time I go to Manchester I travel by car". Presented with four cards indicating travel destinations on one side and modes of transport on the other, 63% of subjects made the logical response. It appears that the more sense subjects can make of the materials the more likely they are to perform logically. Yet on the classicist view this is puzzling, as logical reasoning depends only on the *form* not on the *content* of the materials.

Although subjects fail on deductive reasoning tasks that are trivial in symbolic architectures, human commonsense inference is far more sophisticated than that of any AI system. On the classical view, commonsense inference should involve very elaborate logical reasoning, defined over large sets of premises encoding the relevant world knowledge. According to this view, commonsense reasoning should be more difficult than simple deductive reasoning. Yet the data on human performance show precisely the reverse. Minsky's (1975/1977) frame theory was an attempt to capture the structure of the routinely performed defeasible inferences involved in the comprehension of even the simplest texts. It is unclear that such mundane reasoning can be constructed successfully in standard symbolic architectures (Chater & Oaksford, 1990; McDermott, 1986).

These data present a severe challenge to the classicist view of cognition as autonomous symbol manipulation. Reasoning appears to be crucially dependent on assimilating the task to world knowledge rather than extracting the formal structure of the task description. Subjects appear to be using *commonsense* knowledge-rich reasoning strategies, even when confronted by a formal task. Species of commonsense, non-demonstrative reasoning, like induction, abduction, and default inference are unlikely to be formalisable *in logic* (from an AI perspective: Israel, 1980; McDermott,1986; from the philosophy of logic: Harman, 1986; from the philosophy of science: Kuhn, 1970; Masterman, 1970; from cognitive science: Chater & Oaksford, 1990 and Oaksford & Chater, 1991). The Classicist attempts to explain commonsense reasoning in terms of logic, which may be impossible in principle. So, proof theory cannot be the basis of cognition. Rather, it seems that whatever (non-logical) processes underpin commonsense reasoning may also underpin performance on logical reasoning tasks. (For an account of the data that relies on commonsense principles of reasoning, see Oaksford, 1989 and Oaksford & Stenning, 1988.) As with memory, adversion to the competence–performance distinction is of no avail considering that up to 96% of the observed behaviour on Wason's task is beyond the scope of the competence model.

Theory

Prima facie in both memory and inference tasks, the richer the informational content of the materials used, the better performance seems to be. This seems mysterious on a classical account. To encode a richer stimulus should require more formulae to be stored in the declarative database, and so both storage and retrieval should become harder. On the classical view, resource limitations should become more acute with richer stimuli. However, the psychological evidence seems to indicate that in human memory, performance is not impaired but *enhanced* with richer stimuli. Turning to inference, on the classicist account of cognition, commonsense reasoning involves the construction of elaborate logical derivations. Commonsense reasoning should be very much harder for human subjects than proof-theoretically trivial logical deductions. Precisely the opposite performance profile is observed in the psychological data.

It seems that as the stimulus is made richer, the subjects' performance improves. Yet the stimulus must be enriched in an appropriate way. For example, a property list may be "enriched" by making it longer, making the properties more complex and so on. An inference task may be "enriched" by requiring that the subjects must use more premises, or must construct a more elaborate chain of deduction. Plainly such "enrichment" of the task will lead to worse rather than better performance. What sorts of "enrichment" lead to enhanced performance? We shall discuss this question in memory and inference in turn.

Memory

One simple suggestion is that the task will only become easier if the stimuli are made redundant. That is, each portion of the stimulus is not independent of the rest. Rather, there is organisation within the stimulus which allows each part (at least to some extent) to be predicted from the rest. Let us consider an example inspired by Miller and Selfridge (1950). It is very hard to remember a list of letters such as:

(1) D P H O J U J P O

However, it is far easier to remember a list of letters that are organised into some meaningful configuration.

(2) C O G N I T I O N

Remembering this sequence does not feel like remembering a sequence at all but rather is like remembering a single item, i.e. a word. In the case of (2) our lexical and morphological knowledge allows us to exploit the redundancy within the stimulus. This redundancy allows us to reconstruct the whole item from only a partial cue. Very simple-mindedly, if you recall that (2) begins COG ..., then you are highly likely to recall the whole word. On the other hand, recalling that (1) starts DPH ... seems to help not at all in reconstructing the rest of the list. However, apparently unpredictable sequences such as (1) can be seen as redundant *if* they can be assimilated to appropriate knowledge. And indeed a simple transformation (shifting each letter along one place in the alphabet) maps (1) on to (2). So once this is realised sequence (1) becomes as predictable as (2).

Quite generally, recall has been found to depend on the degree to which subjects impose an organisation on, or can make sense of the materials to be learnt. For example, in text comprehension, Bransford and Johnson (1973) had subjects read a passage with or without the title *Watching a peace march from the fortieth floor:*

"The view was breathtaking. From the window one could see the crowd below. Everything looked extremely small from such a distance but the colourful costumes could still be seen. Every one seemed to be moving in one direction in an orderly fashion and there seemed to be little children as well as adults. The landing was gentle and the atmosphere was such that no special suits had to be worn. At first there was a great deal of activity. Later, when the speeches started, the crowd quieted down. The man with the television camera took many shots of the setting and the crowd. Everyone was very friendly and seemed to be glad when the music started."

After hearing the passage Ss were asked to recall it. Most sentences were recalled well except for the one about the "landing." There was extremely low recall for this sentence, and Ss noted that there was one sentence (i.e. about the landing) that they could not understand. Even when presented with a "cue outline" (e.g. Luckily the landing—and the atmosphere—), Ss exhibited very low ability to remember what the sentence was about.

A second group of Ss heard the identical passage but with a different title: *A space trip to an inhabited planet*. These Ss showed much better free recall of the "landing" sentence than did the first group, as well as a greater ability to fill in the gaps in the cue outline presented above (see Bransford & Johnson, 1973). These results suggest that a sentence that would be comprehensible in isolation (i.e. "the landing" sentence) can become incomprehensible when viewed from an inappropriate context, and that such incomprehensibility has a marked effect on ability to recall. (Bransford & McCarrell, 1975)

In the present discussion the moral is as follows. If a particular item to be recalled fits with the context in which it occurs, then it is easier to recall. Given that the subjects know what the story is about, the contents of the sentences become predictable (i.e. redundant). The pattern of errors indicates that the principles that underlie normal successful recall relate to knowledge of the world. Given that subjects know the passage is about a space trip to another planet, the sentence about the landing is highly predictable. However, when the sentence violates the expectations of the subjects the sentence is no longer predictable and so a straightforward redundant coding is not possible. So it seems that recall is a matter of finding the item that *best fits* the residual memory trace given world knowledge. World knowledge provides a vast interlocking array of defeasible constraints encoding the predictable organisation of the world. Best-fit matching involves maximising the degree to which the vast number of contextually relevant constraints are satisfied. A memory that exploits these constraints will easily assimilate predictable material because, in as much as the novel stimuli cohere with existing constraints, only minimal adjustments will be required to lay down the memory trace. Much information may be left implicit, as it follows from world knowledge. If the material is unpredictable, world knowledge cannot be exploited, and so the information must be encoded explicitly.

Any such best-fit memory system will possess a variety of properties of human memories (Bobrow & Norman, 1975; Norman & Bobrow, 1975, 1976, 1979). Generally each part of a memory can function as the context of recall for the remainder of the memory. A best-fit memory will use predictability to reconstitute a whole memory from a sufficiently large arbitrary fragment (i.e. memory is *content-addressable*). Such a memory should be resistant to corruption, as a sufficiently large veridical fragment should be able to reconstitute the original trace (i.e. memory is *noise resistant*).

Unorganised material, like arbitrary property lists, is hard to remember because there are no constraints between the items in the list. Memory relies on the ability to impose organisation on the stimulus. So, the more deeply that a stimulus is processed (Craik & Lockhart, 1972) and the better it is understood, the better memory performance will be. Mnemonic strategies (Bower, 1970; Lorayne & Lucas, 1974; Young & Gibson, 1962) can be seen as enriching the stimulus so as to impose an organisation upon it. So, paradoxically, remembering more can allow you to remember better (cf. Stenning & Levy, 1988, on the "Mnemonic Paradox"). It is unclear whether classical accounts are capable of displaying these properties (Chater & Oaksford, 1990).

Inference

In inference it has been shown that facilitation is not simply determined by the use of contentful material (Griggs & Cox, 1982). Rather, subjects need to be *familiar* with the rule. Prior experience with a contentful rule was shown to facilitate reasoning, whereas contentful rules with which subjects had no prior experience were shown to be non-facilitatory. Specific experience of a rule means that it need not be assimilated afresh.

Yet in reasoning this cannot be the whole story. To suggest that successful reasoning with conditionals requires having reasoned with them before is altogether too restricting. It precludes people from generalising experience to novel domains, which is surely the sine qua non of human rationality and reasoning abilities.

More recent work (Cheng & Holyoak, 1985; Cheng et al., 1986) serves to indicate that what needs to be right about contentful material also involves the *relations* encoded by particular conditional sentences. When subjects were provided with a *rationale* explicitly characterising a permission relation, a significant facilitation was observed over their performances for both a thematic variant (no prior experience) and an abstract variant, neither of which was provided with a rationale. The facilitation to the logical response was explained in terms of the production rule set which constitutes a *permission schema*. This left open the possibility that other *pragmatic reasoning schemas* may drive inference when other relations, e.g. causation, are encoded, producing different patterns of inference. Assimilation of the task to *appropriate* world knowledge will facilitate response profiles that mirror logical performance, without invoking logical competence. In an abstract test, in which the materials cannot be assimilated to world knowledge, subjects cannot rely on pragmatic reasoning schemata, and may have to default to more general non-logical strategies. Since the rules by which we understand the world are typically defeasible, as we now show, it is not surprising that logical inference is so unnatural.

The data reviewed here suggested that the processes of inference are determined by world knowledge, however such processes may be implemented. Only by understanding the organisation of the world do you know that one thing follows from another. For example, you cannot infer that Fred is going to buy his morning paper from him passing your window at 9.00 a.m. if you do not know Fred's habits. On a proof-theoretic account this knowledge might be encoded in first-order predicate logic as a statement in some declarative data base, quantifying over events (e) and times (t):

1. $\forall e\ \forall t\ [\ (\text{Fred\_passes\_your\_window}(e,t)\ \&\ t\ =\ 9.00\text{a.m.})\ \supset$
    $\exists e'\ \exists t'[\ (\text{Fred\_buys\_his\_paper}(e',t')\ \&\ \text{just\_precedes}(t,t')]$

However, as we argued earlier, such a strategy cannot work in general, as all these commonsense generalisations about the organisation of the world succumb to indefinitely many counter-examples.

If I see Fred going past my window at 9.00 a.m., I know he's about to buy his morning paper. But not if it's Christmas day, as there are no papers. And not if he's been mugged; or if he's already reading *The Times*; or if he falls over and breaks a leg; or if his ferocious wife is with him wielding a shopping bag, etc. All of these possibilities override our generalisation that Fred buys a paper just after passing my window every morning. On a proof-theoretic account the various conditions that might override our rules must be explicitly encoded, and a check made that none of them applies in any specific case. This is the standard approach to defeasible commonsense inference which has been pursued in the logical/AI literature (de Kleer, 1986; McCarthy, 1980; Reiter, 1985). However, these approaches all involve consistency checking, which is an NP-hard problem. This means that such symbolic methods are computationally intractable (see Oaksford & Chater, 1991).

As we discussed in the last chapter (p. 37), although this technical problem does not decide the issue, there are a number of more general difficulties for symbolic accounts that strongly suggest that they will be unable to deal with defeasible inference.

Commonsense defeasible inferences, if derivable *at all* on a proof-theoretic account, must be extremely complex. For people, these inferences are just *common sense*. This mode of inference underlies comprehension, categorisation, perception, and action (Bransford & Johnson, 1972, 1973; Bransford, Barclay, & Franks, 1972; Bransford & McCarrell, 1975; Clark & Haviland, 1977; Minsky, 1975/1977; Murphy & Medin, 1985). It is the basis of all cognitive performance. People find this mode of inference easy. So, the computational architecture of the mind must be so constituted as to facilitate such inferences. But the classical proposal of an architecture based on symbol manipulation seems unpromising. So, perhaps the non-logical performance of tasks such as the selection task is not so surprising in view of these considerations. The strategies that subjects adopt when assimilation to world knowledge is impossible are nonetheless likely to reflect assumptions about the defeasible nature of the rules that we use to understand the world (Oaksford, 1989).

Modelling

The classical account of mind may be incapable of satisfying several well-established constraints on human cognition. Roughly, human memory should be able to implement large-scale best-fit searches by exploiting the organisation of the world; and the inferences people draw should be determined by their knowledge of the way the world is organised (rather than by deductive rules of inference). Next, we first outline how parallel distributed processing (PDP) captures many of these desirable properties. We then turn to a specific model of Stenning and Levy's (1988) data, which accounts for the observed dependencies between stored properties as revealed in the analysis of the error data (already discussed). We also briefly outline how such a memory system will give rise to automatic generalisation which begins to suggest an alternative account of the data on human inference by suggesting a possible mechanism for default inference.

Memory

Let us first recap on the desirable properties of human memory:

1. Human memory is content-addressable.
2. Human memory is noise-resistant.

These are both direct consequences of the parallel distributed processing approach to massively parallel soft constraint satisfaction or best-fit searches:

> One way of thinking about distributed memories is in terms of a very large set of plausible inference rules. Each active unit represents a "microfeature" of an item, and the connection strengths stand for plausible "microinferences"

between microfeatures. Any particular pattern of activity of the units will satisfy some of the microinferences and violate others. A stable pattern of activity is one that violates the plausible microinferences less then any of the neighbouring patterns. (Hinton, McClelland, & Rumelhart, 1986, pp. 80–81)

Given this intuitive picture it can be shown informally how the various properties emerge.

Content-addressability.   When an arbitrary sufficiently large fragment of the pattern is presented, the microinferences act so as to produce the nearest possible completion (stable state). Hence, any sufficiently large part of the content of the memory will address the whole memory.

Noise-resistance.   If part of the presented fragment is wrong (the fragment is inconsistent with any stored memory), the microinferences will still find the best available fit. Hence a degree of noise can be tolerated, because the correct part of the fragment will ensure that the best-fit pattern prevails.

In addition to being able to capture general properties of human memory, PDP models have also been used to model the fine structure of performance on particular memory tasks. For example, Stenning and Levy (1988) present a parallel distributed processing model of the MIT task, discussed earlier. The binary features derived in a multiple linear regression analysis are used to represent the pair of stored individuals. At retrieval time, the first and second individuals and their properties must be reconstituted from the complex distributed representation in terms of matched and mismatched properties and logical combinations of properties (roughly, these express that *someone* is, say, tall and Polish; they make no explicit references to the first or second individual mentioned). A three-layer network was used, where the binary input units stand for the features derived from the regression model. These input units are completely connected to a layer of 16 hidden units, which in turn are connected to two sets of four output units corresponding to the two individuals' properties. Just as the person can recall the individuals in either order, the network must be able to identify the individuals at either output location. The order of recall for the network is specified by an extra binary input.

The network learns the mapping from features to individuals by cycling through each logically possible input vector, each paired with its correct output (240 vectors in all). Learning reaches criterion after about 300 iterations of back-propagation. A good test of the adequacy of the representation postulated to underlie the human data is whether corrupting that representation generates similar error patterns to those found in the human data. The error patterns for the network were generated by coding the paragraphs human subjects saw into the input feature representations and then subjecting these representations to random noise. This involved flipping the values of the input features with a 3% probability. For comparison, the eight actual property descriptors were also directly subjected to a similar corruption with a 5% probability. This amounts to storing (and corrupting) each individual and their properties independently, as is most natural in a classical framework. The match of the corrupted inputs to the observed human error data is good, although not as good as that of the original regression model. Stenning and Levy (1988) note various specific similarities and discuss possible explanations for these. The direct corruption, on the other hand, leads to quite different error patterns. So the character of a distributed connectionist system may model the pattern of performance more closely than independent conventional symbolic architectures.

Inference

We have argued that an alternative must be found to classical symbolic accounts of commonsense reasoning. Current symbolic schemes fail to characterise the most frequently occurring inference patterns of subjects in deductive reasoning tasks, such as Wason's Four Card Problem. Our diagnosis has been that *commonsense* inference underlies performance on *deductive* reasoning tasks and not the other way round (Oaksford, 1989; Oaksford and Stenning, 1988). As we discussed in the last chapter (pp. 37–38), recent connectionist theorising suggests a promising avenue for research in capturing the defeasibilty of commonsense inference. Soft constraints, the very fabric of connectionist models, are just default rules. So, as suggested in Chapter 2 (p. 38), such models may be able to unburden the cognitive architecture of the problems created by commonsense inference.

Classical approaches to commonsense inference have proved to be computationally intractable due to their reliance on consistency checking. So, it may be the case that a PDP account is the only straw afloat in arriving at workable mechanisms for defeasible commonsense reasoning. Not only do symbolic approaches seem unable to capture commonsense inferences, the data on Wason's Four Card Problem reveal that human reasoning performance is radically at variance with classical expectations. Treating performance on deductive reasoning tasks such as Wason's Four Card Problem as mediated by commonsense inference can account for the most frequently occurring response patterns (Oaksford, 1989; Oaksford & Stenning, 1988). The possibility of PDP implementations provides the promise of models that can predict the *complete* response profile, *including* the errors. However, on a classical account, *all* error must be assigned to performance factors. This seems unsatisfactory when up to 96% of subjects' responses on a logically trivial task like the Wason Four Card Problem are beyond the scope of the competence theory.

CONCLUSIONS

Fodor and Pylyshyn (Fodor, 1975, 1980, 1983, 1987; Fodor, Bever, & Garrett, 1974; Fodor & Pylyshyn, 1988; Pylyshyn, 1973, 1984) have, over a number of years, defined the notion of computation as used in cognitive science. Cognition is computation. Computation is mechanised proof theory. So:

> It would not be unreasonable to describe classical cognitive science as an extended attempt to apply the methods of proof theory to the modelling of thought. (Fodor & Pylyshyn, 1988, pp. 29–30)

This view carries both theoretical and methodological significance. As we have seen, the theoretical implications for memory and inference seem not to accord with the empirical data. The implicit methodology fares little better.

On a classical symbolic model, errors in memory cannot be explained at the proof-theoretic, cognitive level, but rather must be seen as functions of the implementation. Similarly, apparent deviations from logical performance in conditional reasoning tasks must also be assigned to performance or implementational factors. According to the classicist account such error data can therefore only inform us about the character of the implementation of the cognitive architecture and not about the cognitive architecture itself. For the classicist, the study of psychology is the study of cognitive architecture independent of its implementation. In consequence, the vast bulk of the empirical considerations discussed in this chapter do *not* count as *psychological* considerations. On such a restricted view of the domain of psychology, there is little psychology left. If we exclude the study of errors, then almost all experimental memory, reasoning, and perceptual research is not psychology. Error methodology is a ubiquitous and powerful investigative tool in psychological practice.

For example, the pattern of errors in Stenning's MIT task gives insight into the normal function of human memory. The subjects appear to represent the individuals according to a complex task-specific set of features. For subjects to derive this encoding scheme means that they have extracted the particular organisation of the task. For example, as the dimensions are binary, a match–mismatch strategy is appropriate. The feature set of the multiple regression gives a redundant encoding of the individuals and their properties. However, *that* this encoding is redundant is dependent on the structure of the memory task. This illustrates the general point that subjects attempt to find organisation in the material to be remembered so that it may be encoded redundantly. The MIT task demonstrates the remarkable facility with which such encoding strategies are devised and implemented. Such redundant encodings may be directly tied to a PDP model of retrieval processes. The exploitation of systematic redundancy by PDP processes operating over distributed representations is responsible for many of the desirable computational properties of these systems—that is, Fodor and Pylyshyn's (1988) "lures" of connectionism; see Chapter 1 for discussion.

For Fodor and Pylyshyn, psychology is taken to be the study of an autonomous cognitive level, to which implementational considerations are held to be irrelevant. According to this view, psychologists should not be interested in connectionism (at best, they claim, a theory of implementation), just as they should not be interested in error. However, we have argued:

- Autonomous classical theories are radically at variance with human data on memory and inference. The limitations, patterns of errors and interference seem mysterious on the classical view.
- Contra classicist expectations, human performance in memory and inference improves as the stimulus becomes richer and can engage the vast interlocking array of defeasible constraints that encodes the predictable organisation of the world.
- Connectionist systems are able to exploit such redundancy and thereby emulate the observed characteristics of human memory, such as content-addressability and graceful degradation.
- Human performance on prima facie symbolic tasks is heavily influenced by the content of the materials, in the tasks we have discussed. So in so far as symbolic processes are implemented in the brain (and Fodor and Pylyshyn's arguments for structured representation are persuasive on this point) they crucially interact with the properties of the implementation. Content effects cannot be explained *proof theoretically*!
- This leads naturally to the conclusion that modern cognitive psychology has always been committed to the interaction of cognitive and implementational levels. So Fodor and Pylyshyn's advocacy of autonomy is a *revisionary* restriction of the appropriate domain of psychological concern. If psychologists adopt this novel stricture then they will not be interested in connectionism. However, accepting this restriction would deprive cognitive psychology of most of its subject matter and one of its most potent explanatory distinctions (i.e. architecture vs. implemementation). Thus, issues of the implementation of cognitive architecture will continue to be a major source of constraint in psychological theorising. Hence, connectionism may naturally be seen as providing new and important metaphors for thought, rather than as a psychologically irrelevant implementational theory.

Much of the data we have reviewed pre-date the emergence of the proof-theoretic view as the dominant meta-theory for cognitive science. The apparent incompatibility of data and meta-theory has been largely ignored. This is wholly legitimate while there is no competing computational paradigm that can address these data. Puzzling data only become falsifying data when an alternative explanation becomes available (Kuhn, 1970; Lakatos, 1970; Putnam, 1974). We believe that such an alternative computational and theoretical paradigm is now emerging in which much of this old data can be recast. However, we agree with the thrust of Fodor and Pylyshyn's (1988) argument that psychology must be concerned with structured representations, and structure-sensitive processes, which were the very stuff of the symbolic paradigm. We believe that PDP should attempt to capture structured representations while retaining the desirable computational properties we have outlined. In particular, we require that our models be able to deploy rich, context-sensitive world knowledge in a flexible and tractable way. Further, these models should be consistent with the empirical data, especially error data. Whether or not such a goal can be attained will ultimately decide whether PDP really does constitute a rival to the standard proof-theoretic orthodoxy. In any case, this reconsideration of the data provides a challenge to the proof theoretician: it is unclear that this challenge can be met.

CHAPTER FOUR

Against Logicist Cognitive Science I: The Core Argument

It would not be unreasonable to describe Classical Cognitive Science as an extended attempt to apply the methods of proof theory to the modelling of thought.

Fodor & Pylyshyn, 1988, pp. 29–30

INTRODUCTION

In Chapters 2 and 3 we concentrated on the potential of connectionism to tackle some of the computational and empirical discrepancies between logicism and some important properties of human cognition. We noted that there are problems for logicism, both at the computational, algorithmic, and implementational levels. In this pivotal chapter we move away from the implementational level and concentrate on the computational and algorithmic levels of explanation in considering the prospects for a logicist theory of everyday, defeasible inference. We focus on two issues. First, at the computational level, we assess the completeness* (see Chapter 1) of extensions of logic to capture defeasible inference. Second, at the algorithmic level, we look in detail at the computational tractability of these extensions of logic. These issues were raised in passing in Chapters 2 and 3, but here form the focus of discussion. We again take Fodor and Pylyshyn's characterisation (see our opening quote) as a paradigm of logicist cognitive science against which our arguments are explicitly directed. However, in this chapter we argue that these arguments apply more generally to a large class of theories in cognitive science. In the next chapter, we consider the generality of our arguments by examining a range of possible attempts to deal with the problems that we raise. We will argue that these are not successful, and conclude that the implications of our arguments are very general.

THE CORE ARGUMENT

In this chapter, we shall argue that the plausibility of classical, logicist cognitive science depends on its ability to provide a proof-theoretic account of the defeasible inferencing that is implicated in almost every area of cognitive activity. We shall show that such an account is unlikely to be forthcoming and hence cognition cannot be seen as mechanised proof theory.

A proof-theoretic account involves three components: the specification of (i) a formal language; (ii) a set of syntactic (ie. proof-theoretic) rules of inference; and (iii) a mechanistic implementation of (i) and (ii). That is, cognition is an implemented formal logic. This is the classical, *logicist* position in cognitive science and artificial intelligence (Fodor & Pylyshyn, 1988; Hayes, 1978, 1984a). *Defeasible* inferences are inferences that can be *defeated* by additional information. Inferences licensed by classical logic are *monotonic*: no additional premises can invalidate a previously derived conclusion. This contrasts with everyday, defeasible inference, which is *non-monotonic*: the addition of premises may invalidate a previously derived conclusion. In defeasible, non-monotonic inference it is possible to *add* premises and *lose* conclusions. Defeasible inference permeates every area of cognitive activity. Thus, at least prima facie, a logicist account of cognition must postulate proof-theoretic rules defined for some non-monotonic logic. We assess the practical attempt, in AI knowledge representation, to carry out this logicist programme using non-monotonic logics. We note that such logics are able to draw only unacceptably weak disjunctive conclusions; and that the theorem-proving algorithms over such logics are computationally intractable due to their reliance on solving the NP-complete problem of consistency checking. We suggest that the programme of logicist cognitive science is infeasible, and reply to a number of plausible objections to this conclusion.

The structure of the chapter is as follows. We first characterise the classical, logicist position, using the formulation of two of its most influential exponents, Jerry Fodor and Zenon Pylyshyn, and adduce various adequacy criteria on logicist explanations of cognitive phenomena. We then note that human inferential processes, in commonsense reasoning, and in a variety of specific cognitive domains, are quite generally knowledge-rich and defeasible. These difficulties infect logicist treatments invoking unconscious, implicit inferences in text comprehension, conceptual reasoning, problem solving, perception, and even in recent accounts of human performance on explicit deductive reasoning tasks. Further, to illustrate the nature of the problem, we then draw on a parallel between these difficulties and those experienced in the philosophy of science in attempting to provide a theory of confirmation, a parallel also noted by Fodor (1983) (see also Sperber & Wilson, 1986). A specific attempt to deal with defeasible inference using non-monotonic logics (Reiter, 1985), which has been proposed within the tradition of knowledge representation in AI, is then critically examined. We draw the general moral that non-monotonic logics license only unacceptably weak conclusions, and cannot be computationally implemented in real-time. There are a number of proposals that appear to circumvent these problems. However, in the next chapter we argue, case by case, that such proposed logicist solutions succumb to the difficulties that we raise, or amount to a retreat from the logicist position, and conclude that logicist cognitive science is ill founded.

Logicist Cognitive Science

Fodor and Pylyshyn (Fodor, 1975, 1980, 1983, 1987; Fodor, Bever & Garrett, 1974; Fodor & Pylyshyn, 1988; Pylyshyn, 1973, 1984) have, over a number of years, argued that folk-psychological explanation, in terms of the ascription of propositional attitudes such as beliefs and desires, must be reconstructed in any proper account of cognitive activity. According to this view, to have a propositional attitude is to stand in a certain relation (the relation of believing, desiring or whatever) to a mental representation, the content of which is the object of the propositional attitude. Because the contents of propositional attitudes are described in natural language, the interpretation of the corresponding mental representations must be at the level of everyday objects and relations. This is the substance of the representational theory of mind (see Fodor, 1980). Folk psychology explains behaviour in terms of inference over propositional attitudes. Hence, a representationalist reconstruction of folk psychology must provide mechanisms for drawing inferences over the representations that capture the content of the propositional attitudes. These mechanisms are typically taken to be formal operations over syntactically structured representations. That is, mental operations are taken to apply purely in virtue of the structural properties of the representations. These syntactic mental operations must be coherent with respect to the semantics of the representations being manipulated. This is the substance of the Computational Theory of Mind (Fodor, 1980). Currently, the only way in which the semantic coherence of formal structural manipulation may be guaranteed is by showing that each manipulation of the representations corresponds to a sound proof-theoretic derivation in some appropriately interpreted formal language. In other words, the language of mental representation constitutes a *logic*, in which mental representations correspond to well-formed formulae, and manipulations over them correspond to sound logical inferences. According to this view, a central task of cognitive science is to characterise the logical language of mental representation, the proof-theoretic rules defined over it, and the content of the representations employed in the production of particular behaviours.

For the logicist, this provides a complete *psychological* explanation of performance of those behaviours. This proof-theoretic psychological explanation is *autonomous* (Chater & Oaksford, 1990; Fodor & Pylyshyn, 1988, p.66) from the biological substrate underlying perception, memory, action, and so on. Lower-level biological explanations are taken to be independent from, and to fall outside the domain of, *psychological* explanation. This position may be elucidated by considering the three levels of explanation that David Marr (1982) took to constitute a complete account of the performance of a cognitive task. The claim that cognition is proof theory amounts to a restriction on the form of the level 1 (computational) theory. That is, a computational theory of some task must be specified (or at least must be *specifiable*) as a proof theory over some interpreted logical language, and particular representations used in the performance of the task. Further, the logicist position also places restrictions on the form of the level 2 (algorithmic) theory. That is, it must characterise the theorem-proving mechanism that animates the proof theory. This theorem-prover instantiates the control regime that determines which inferences are made when, in the performance of the task. This mechanism is defined over the formal properties of the logical expressions over which it is operating. It is these first two levels that the logicist takes to constitute *psychological* explanation. A level 3 (implementational) theory should constitute an account of how the theorem-prover specified at level 2 is instantiated in biological hardware. For the logicist this level is below, and largely independent of, the level of psychological explanation.

The classical cognitive science picture may be decomposed into four claims:

1. Cognition is computation.
2. Computation is formal.
3. Formal computation is mechanised proof theory.
4. The internal language over which the proof theory is defined is interpretable at the level of everyday objects and relations.

Within the framework of cognitive science, 1 must surely be taken as axiomatic. There is, however, substantial room for debate about the implications and status of 2, 3, and 4.

2. Computation is Formal.   That is, computational processes operate purely in terms of the *form*, syntax or shape of the symbolic structures over which they are defined. For example, consider the formal inferences of modus ponens (MP) and modus tollens (MT):

MP: $p \supset q, p$ $\therefore$ q
MT: $p \supset q, \neg q$ $\therefore$ $\neg p$

These may be computed without reference to the meanings of the propositions p, q or the meaning of the connective "$\supset$". The premise "$p \supset q$" is not treated as an atomic, unstructured lump, but as having syntactic structure: as having "p", "$\supset$", and "q" as constituents. From the point of view of formal computation, all that matters for the application of modus ponens is that the "p" in the second premise has the same shape as the "p" on the left-hand side of the first premise; and that the "q" of the conclusion has the same shape as the "q" on the right-hand side of the first premise. This applies, *mutatis mutandis*, for modus tollens. Formal processes need not, as in this case, involve logical inference. List manipulation, sorting algorithms, sequences of procedural instructions etc., all count as formal, as they are defined over the shape rather than the content of their inputs.

Given the wide range of processes and schemes that have been taken to be computational models of cognition, the claim that computation is formal is not strictly true. Or rather, the requirement that computation is formal is *prescriptive* of the way in which Fodor and Pylyshyn (1988) would like the term "computation" to be used, rather than *descriptive* of the way in which it is used in the range of literatures involved with mechanistic models of thought. For example, the mechanism of holographic memory, analogue computational methods, genetic learning algorithms, and connectionism are not syntactic—the representations over which they operate typically *have* no syntactic structure. A possible confusion may arise, as these computational mechanisms can be simulated to an arbitrary degree of accuracy (and in some cases, perfectly) by the formal operations of a digital computer. However, any system (formal or otherwise) can be represented by formulae in some formal language, and its behaviour modelled by structure-sensitive operations over those formulae. It is in virtue of this fact that the general-purpose digital computer is *general*-purpose.

3. Formal Computation is Mechanised Proof Theory.   Relevant information is represented as a set of formulae in a logical language, and computation proceeds by the operation of a theorem-prover for that language. The theorem-prover decides which proof-theoretic rule to apply and when. Prima facie, theorem proving is a very particular form of computation. Again a possible confusion arises, because any computation can be *simulated* by the operation of an appropriate theorem-prover. As any computation can be simulated on a Turing machine, for any computer program, there will be a corresponding Turing machine, with identical input–output behaviour. Any Turing machine can be axiomatised in first order logic (Boolos & Jeffrey, 1980), and hence any computation can be implemented on a theorem-prover for first order logic. Although any computation *can* be implemented in this way, almost invariably they are not.

   4. The Internal Language Over Which the Proof Theory is Defined is Interpretable at the Level of Everyday Objects and Relations.   The formulae over which the proof theory operates could, in principle, have an arbitrary semantics. As the logicist takes propositional attitudes to be relations to these formulae, the contents of (at least some of) these formulae must correspond to the objects of beliefs and desires. In particular, therefore, the semantics of these formulae will make make reference to everyday objects and properties—to tables, chairs, people, colours, feelings, and so on. It is hence unsurprising that the atomic terms of knowledge representation formalisms in artificial intelligence and cognitive psychology (such as semantic nets, schemas, production rules, and so on) stand in close correspondence with the lexical items of natural language. Indeed, for the sake of transparency, the atomic terms in AI knowledge representation are typically borrowed from the vocabulary of natural language. For example, a program that encodes knowledge about an average taxpayer might start as follows (Clocksin & Mellish, 1984, p. 87):

```
average_taxpayer(X):–
   not(foreigner(X)),
   not((spouse(X,Y), gross_income(Y,Inc),Inc > $3000)),
   > gross_income(X,Inc),  …
```

Of course, the logicist is not restricted to postulating representations defined at the level of tables and chairs. For the purposes of modelling specific cognitive processes, such as language understanding, perception and so on, the interpretations of the symbols may be phonetic, phonemic or syntactic categories, auditory and visual features, and the like.

   The conjunction of assumptions 2, 3, and 4 constitutes a strong hypothesis about the nature of mental representations and mental processes. Having characterised the logicist picture, we now discuss certain adequacy criteria to which such an account should, at least in principle, be able to conform.

Adequacy Criteria for Logicist Explanation

We shall outline two main adequacy criteria which the logicist programme must be able to meet. First, the proof-theoretic rules of inference defined over the postulated logical language (or languages) are capable of characterising the inferences implicated in human cognition. That is, the proof-theoretic rules must capture what we take pre-theoretically to be the semantically appropriate defeasible inferences. In Susan Haack's (1978) terminology, the logic(s) should be capable of respecting the appropriate *depraved* semantics (Haack, 1978, p. 188). So in the case of a non-monotonic logic for defeasible reasoning, the interpretation of the formalism must map appropriately onto our commonsense or *depraved* understanding of defeasible inference. Some suitable non-monotonic logic must therefore capture the range of inferences that common sense licenses or, in other words, it should be complete with respect to the depraved semantics. By loose analogy with the notion of completeness in classical logic with respect to a standard formal semantic interpretation, we shall call this the *completeness**
criterion. So a complete* logicist explanation in some domain must provide a logical language and set of inferential rules, which at least roughly capture our intuitions about inference in that domain.

Second, logicist explanation should, in principle, be able to provide a unified account of the cognitive processes within some domain, which covers each of Marr's (1982) explanatory levels. We shall call the constraint that such a unified explanation can be provided, the *coherence* criterion. A *coherent* logicist account would provide a specification of a logical language in which knowledge is represented, and a proof theory defined over that language (level 1); a theorem-prover for that proof theory (level 2); and an explication of how that theorem-prover is implemented in the brain (level 3).

A coherent logicist explanation must, among other things, be able to provide a level 2 algorithm appropriate to the level 1 proof theory, and to implement the level 2 algorithm in neural hardware. In practice the logicist is wont to insist that these relationships need not constrain theorising at each of the three levels. Indeed, one of the methodological appeals of the logicist view is that the implicit independence of each of the levels appears to license the pursuit of high-level cognitive theorising, while we remain in comparative ignorance of the operation of the brain. This tenet of the logicist view (Fodor & Pylyshyn, 1988) presumably depends upon the following reasoning. Neural hardware (level 3) is surely able to implement such a simple symbolic device as a Turing machine or equivalent. But as any computable algorithm can be computed by a Turing machine, neural hardware appears to place no constraint at all on the algorithms that are psychologically plausible. Moreover, as long as the level 1 theory of the task domain, specified in terms of a set of proof-theoretic axioms, is decidable, then there will be many level 2 algorithms for performing the task. By the previous argument, any such algorithm must be implementable at level 3, because any algorithm can be implemented in a Turing machine. So, according to the logicist, psychological explanations at levels 1 and 2 are relatively independent, that is they are *autonomous* (Chater & Oaksford, 1990) from the (level 3) biological substrate.

This line of reasoning may be taken to establish that almost any explanations postulated at each of the three levels are likely to be *in principle* compatible. To establish that logicist explanation is *coherent*, this weak, in principle, compatibility between explanatory levels must be supplemented by a strong compatibility in practice. That is, the level 1 proof theory must have a level 2 theorem proving algorithm which is not just computable but *computationally* tractable. Moreover, this level 2 algorithm must be able to run (level 3) on biological hardware with real-time characteristics compatible with the speed and effectiveness of observed behaviour. Indeed, only given a unified explanation of each of these levels can precise psychological predictions be made about the character of real-time performance.

The mere fact that we have a decidable set of proof-theoretic axioms (at level 1), guarantees only that there is a computable theorem-proving algorithm; it does not guarantee that any such algorithm is computationally tractable. *In principle* computability results are sadly no guide to practical computational feasibility. Moreover, although any computable algorithm can be implemented on a Turing machine, and although the biological substrate is able to implement an arbitrary Turing machine, the nature of the biological substrate and the way in which the algorithm is implemented in that substrate will crucially affect the run-time of the algorithm. Hence the nature of the hardware of the brain may considerably constrain the class of psychologically plausible algorithms.

Hence there are two species of doubt that may be raised concerning the coherence of the logicist programme. First, it may be doubted that it is possible to implement theorem-proving algorithms postulated by the logicist in biological hardware such that they satisfy the real-time processing characteristics of cognitive performance. Second, in many psychological tasks, it may be doubted that there exists a tractable level 2 theorem-proving algorithm that instantiates the postulated level 1 theory. We have argued elsewhere (Chater & Oaksford, 1990) that the first species of doubt, the constraint that level 2 algorithms must be biologically implemented, militates strongly against the feasibility of an autonomous logicist account. In this chapter, with regard to the *coherence* of the logicist position, we concentrate on the second of these concerns: tractability. We argue that there may be no tractable algorithms appropriate to the level 1 theory that the logicist is forced to postulate. Moreover, logicist explanation must be not only tractable but *complete**. That is, the level 1 theory must actually be able to account for human inferential processes. We shall argue that the logicist account is also inadequate in this regard: it seems unlikely that a proof-theoretic level 1 account of human inferential processes will be forthcoming.

As we are arguing against logicist approaches to cognition on the grounds that they may be unable to account for the defeasibility of human inference, it is incumbent upon us to show that human inference *is* defeasible, across a range of cognitive domains. It is to this task that we now turn.

The Defeasibility of Human Inference

Human knowledge is inherently revisable—expectations are routinely disconfirmed, norms violated, and what is certain today is discredited tomorrow. Human knowledge is also invariably partial and inferences must be drawn on the fly with incomplete knowledge of the relevant facts. The ability to reason and act appropriately in the face of overwhelming ignorance is one of human cognition's most remarkable and important achievements, and poses one of psychology's greatest challenges. In a mysterious and changing world, every conclusion is revisable and every premise open to question.

Consider, for example, the process of boiling an egg. Perhaps Egon has learnt from experience that if he puts an egg in boiling water then five minutes later the egg will be medium-boiled. Having put the egg in the water as usual, Egon infers that the egg will be ready for his breakfast in five minutes. Such inferences, however, are radically defeasible. After all, there might be a power failure or an earthquake, Egon's careless brother may upset the pan, there may be salt in the water, the egg may be at altitude in an Everest base-camp, and so on. In these situations, Egon's inference that the egg will be ready to eat in five minutes time will be defeated.

Such inference is difficult to capture within a proof-theoretic framework. It is a feature of most standard logics that if a conclusion follows from some set of premises, then it still follows when additional premises are added. Logics in which this property holds are *monotonic* logics. Such logics are, at least prima facie, inappropriate for modelling inference in examples such as the above. According to a monotonic system of inference, if Egon infers that his egg will be ready five minutes after putting it in the boiling water he will be unable to revise this conclusion. So, for example, he must necessarily continue to expect his egg to be medium-boiled even after his brother has knocked over the pan. In other words, if Egon were to reason according to a monotonic logic, then he would be unable to revise his tentative conclusions however strong the evidence to the contrary. This appears to imply that the proof theory that the logicist must postulate to deal with commonsense reasoning must be *non*-monotonic.

Non-monotonicity is required to model not just examples such as the above, but to capture non-demonstrative inference in general. Consider, for example, inductive reasoning, in which a general rule must be derived from a set of specific instances. This mode of reasoning is notoriously non-monotonic—however many premises of the form "Raven A is black", "Raven B is black", etc., are entertained, the inductive conclusion that "All ravens are black" may be defeated by a single additional premise "Raven N is white". The defeasibility of induction has led many to doubt that induction is a justifiable species of inference at all. Whether or not induction is philosophically justifiable, people manifestly induce general laws on which to base their reasoning and action, from specific observations. So, whether or not there is a *philosophical* theory of induction, there must be a *psychological* theory of induction. Moreover, for classical cognitive science the form of this theory must be proof-theoretic. That is, for the logicist, induction, and all other species of non-demonstrative inference, must be assimilated to deduction.

In philosophy, other forms of non-demonstrative inference are typically seen as derivative on induction (Peirce, 1931–1958). In the previous example, we assumed that Egon had induced the law that putting the egg in boiling water results in a medium-boiled egg five minutes later. Having put a particular egg in boiling water, he applies this law to make the specific prediction that the egg will be medium-boiled in five minutes. An inference from a particular occurrence of the antecedent of an inductive law, to a particular occurrence of the consequent of that law, is known as *eductive* inference. As we have already noted, eductive inference, like inductive inference, is non-monotonic. Similarly, Egon's brother, who has also induced this law, may infer that the egg was put in boiling water five minutes earlier, from the fact that Egon is about to eat a medium-boiled egg. Such an inference from a particular occurrence of the consequent of an inductive law, to a particular occurrence of the *antecedent* of that law, is known as *abductive* inference or inference to the best explanation. Abductive inference is again notoriously non-monotonic. That the egg is medium-boiled does not necessarily mean that it must have been in boiling water for five minutes—Egon may have boiled it for two minutes in the pressure cooker.

These non-monotonic modes of inference are implicated throughout almost every area of cognitive activity. The implicit inferences underlying text comprehension depend on the application of prior world knowledge to fill out and elaborate the information given in the text (Bransford, Barclay, & Franks, 1972; Bransford & Johnson, 1972, 1973; Bransford & McCarrell, 1975; Clark, 1977; Minsky, 1975/1977; Stenning & Oaksford, 1989). All such implicit inferences can be defeated by subsequent sentences contradicting our implicit conclusions. Theories of concepts that are concerned to capture the family resemblance or prototype structure of human categorisation implicitly recognise the defeasibility of semantic knowledge. So, although not all birds can fly, the prototypical bird is represented as flying, the majority of exemplar birds fly, the probability that a bird flies is high, depending on the theory that one considers (Medin & Schaffer, 1978; Nosofsky, 1986; Rosch, 1973, 1975). According to modern constructivist theories of perception, much of perceptual processing is taken to involve inference to the best explanation about the state of the environment, given perceptual evidence. The defeasibility of such inference is evidenced by the possibility of perceptual illusion and error (Fodor & Pylyshyn, 1981; Gregory, 1977; McArthur, 1982). Non-demonstrative modes of inference have even been argued to encroach upon apparently deductive tasks such as conditional reasoning (Byrne, 1989; Oaksford, 1989; Oaksford, Chater, & Stenning, 1990). Thus, the whole of cognitive performance depends upon non-monotonic inferential processes. If these cannot be elucidated within the logicist, proof-theoretic framework, then almost every interesting cognitive phenomenon will fall outside the scope of logicist psychological explanation.

Non-monotonicity and Confirmation in Science

Prima facie, the logicist programme is analogous to the Logical Positivist's attempts to provide a theory of confirmation for scientific theories (Carnap, 1923, 1950; Hempel, 1952, 1965). Roughly, it was hoped that such a theory could be axiomatised as an inductive logic, which has the form of deduction in reverse. The claim was that in induction a statement is confirmed by the truth of its deductive consequences, whereas in deduction the truth of a statement guarantees the truth of its deductive consequences. Unfortunately, the axioms of such putative inductive logics could not be made mutually consistent and generated many paradoxes. For example, from very minimal assumptions about the form of an inductive logic it is possible to prove that any hypothesis confirms any other hypothesis (Goodman, 1983, originally 1954). The proof is trivial, and exploits the fact that confirmation appears to flow in both directions between hypotheses and their consequences. Consider two arbitrary hypotheses H and H'. The conjunction H ∧ H' has H as a consequence, and hence, as confirmation is supposed to be deduction in reverse, H confirms H ∧ H'. If H ∧ H' is true then H' must be true—so according to any sensible confirmation theory surely H ∧ H' must confirm H'. Indeed presumably the strength of this confirmation should be the greatest possible as, if H ∧ H' is true, then H' is definitely true—i.e. maximally confirmed. We have concluded that H confirms H ∧ H' and

H ∧ H' confirms H'. Assuming transitivity, which again seems necessary for any inductive logic able to support the elaborate chains of confirmation in science, this means that H confirms H' (and, of course vice versa). As H and H' were chosen arbitrarily, we have the paradoxical conclusion that any two hypotheses confirm each other.

Further, Goodman's (1983) famous "grue" predicate $\forall x(x$ is grue at $t \leftrightarrow$ (x is green ∧ t < year 2050) ∨ (x is blue ∧ t ≥ year 2050))) showed that the problems of confirmation theory could not be resolved by purely formal considerations. Every emerald that has so far been observed is both grue and green. Yet the induction to *all* emeralds are green will continue to be true after the year 2050, whereas the induction to all emeralds are grue will clearly fail from the year 2050, after which no emeralds will be grue. In Goodman's terms, "green" is a projectible predicate where "grue" is not. The projectibility of predicates such as "green" and the non-projectibility of predicates such as "grue" could not inhere in their formal properties; the projectibility of a property could not be dependent on the shape of the predicate symbol used to denote it!

Fodor (1983) raises further problems for the procedures of inductive confirmation: such non-demonstrative fixation of belief is both *isotropic* and *Quinean*:

> By saying that confirmation is isotropic, I mean that the facts relevant to the confirmation of a scientific hypothesis may be drawn from anywhere in the field of previously established empirical (or, of course, demonstrative) truths. Crudely: everything that the scientist knows is, in principle, relevant to determining what else he ought to believe. (Fodor, 1983, p. 105)

> By saying that scientific confirmation is Quinean, I mean that the degree of confirmation assigned to any given hypothesis is sensitive to properties of the entire belief system. (Fodor, 1983, p. 107)

That confirmation is Quinean is indicated by criteria of theory preference which are based on global properties of a system of scientific beliefs. Properties such as simplicity, plausibility, conservatism, or projectibility are global properties in just this sense. Fodor (1983) argues that such global properties cannot be handled by any current theory of confirmation—and that, in consequence, there is no serious theory of scientific confirmation.

The failure of a logicist account of the science does not, of course, necessarily entail that a logicist account of mind will be similarly unsuccessful. However, there is reason to suppose that ordinary everyday commonsense inference may be relevantly analogous to confirmation in science, and hence that a logicist account of one may stand or fall with a logicist account of the other. Jerry Fodor (1983), although a staunch advocate of a proof-theoretic account of mind, argues for the analogy very eloquently. He notes that the problem of confirmation in science maps rather directly onto the everyday, commonsense reasoning problem of knowing how to update one's beliefs, given that one has performed some action—the notorious, and ubiquitous *frame problem* in AI. Fodor considers the predicament of an artificial robot acting on the world, and trying to revise its beliefs appropriately in consequence:

> How ... does the machine's program determine which beliefs the robot ought to reevaluate given that it has embarked upon some or other course of action? What makes the problem so hard is precisely that it seems unlikely that any *local* solution will do... The following truths seem to be self-evident: First, that there is no fixed set of beliefs ... that ... are the [only] ones that require reconsideration ... Second, new beliefs don't come docketed with information about which old beliefs they ought to affect ... Third, the set of beliefs apt for reconsideration cannot be determined by reference to the recency of their acquisition, or by reference to their generality, or by reference to merely semantic relations between the contents of the belief and the description under which the action is performed ... etc. Should any of these propositions seem *less* than self-evident, consider the special case of the frame problem where the robot is a mechanical scientist and the action performed is an experiment. Here the question "which of my beliefs ought I to reconsider given the possible consequences of my action" is transparently equivalent to the question "What, in general, is the optimal adjustment of my beliefs to my experiences?". This is, of course, exactly the question that a theory of confirmation is supposed to answer. (Fodor, 1983, p. 114)

The frame problem is simply a particular example of a problem in which defeasible, non-demonstrative inference must be performed in a knowledge-rich domain:

> as soon as we begin to look at ... processes ... of non-demonstrative fixation of belief we run into problems that have a quite characteristic property. They seem to involve isotropic and Quinean computations; computations that are ... sensitive to the whole belief system. This is exactly what one would expect on the assumption that non-demonstrative fixation of belief really is quite like scientific confirmation, and that scientific confirmation is itself characteristically Quinean and isotropic. (Fodor, 1983, pp. 114–115)

Of course, Fodor couches his discussion in terms of the fixation of *belief.* The same difficulties will arise for the management of any database over a knowledge-rich domain, whether or not the statements in that database may appropriately be interpreted as beliefs.[1]

Let us sum up the argument so far. Quite generally, it seems that in domains in which mental processes are held to be inferential, that inference will typically be non-demonstrative, defeasible inference. Hence the challenge of modelling non-demonstrative inference within a proof-theoretic framework is central to the feasibility of a logicist account. Yet the failure of logical positivism to assimilate non-demonstrative inference to a deductive framework, the failure to devise a successful inductive logic, the inability to account logically for scientific knowledge and theory change, and the like, raise the suspicion that the logicist programme in cognitive science and artificial intelligence may be unworkable. The analogy with the philosophy of science serves to indicate the magnitude of the problem confronting researchers who are attempting to develop non-monotonic logics.

Suggestive as such general theoretical considerations are, the proof of the logicist pudding is, of course, entirely in the eating. If the logicist framework does appear to provide a plausible account of defeasible inferential processes, then the general theoretical qualms that we have raised may be put aside. Moreover, profound and heretofore unrealised implications for the philosophy of science would result. In the following section we therefore examine the current state of the logicist attempt to account for defeasibility, as embodied in the field of knowledge representation in AI, and argue (i) that logicist accounts fail, and (ii) that they fail in principled ways.

First, the proof-theoretic rules for the non-monotonic logics that have been proposed to capture defeasibility do not adequately capture knowledge-rich human non-demonstrative inference—using the terminology that we introduced earlier, such logics are not *complete**. In particular, non-monotonic logic appears able to generate only unacceptably weak disjunctive conclusions. Second, such non-monotonic logics do not possess any tractable algorithms—that is, the computational resources required by theorem-provers for such logics increase explosively as the number of formulae over which we must reason increases. Prima facie, this appears to rule out a proof-theoretic view of cognition for domains in which a large amount of knowledge must be taken into account. In short, the proof-theoretic account of defeasibility does not give the right inferential behaviour, and is computationally intractable. Given the extent to which almost every cognitive task involves defeasible, non-demonstrative inference, the domain of the proof-theoretic account may perhaps be unexpectedly limited.

Artificial Intelligence and the Logicist Approach to Defeasible Inference

A central challenge of logicist cognitive science is to provide a proof theory and theorem-proving methods that capture non-monotonic inference. Workers in artificial intelligence have faced this challenge most directly, in attempting to build systems that can reason about real-world, commonsense domains, using mechanised proof theory (for a general introduction to this approach, see Charniak & McDermott, 1985). In this section, we discuss two difficulties with this approach. First, that non-monotonic inference licenses only unacceptably weak conclusions; and second, that theorem proving for such logics is computationally intractable.

In order to cope with the defeasibility of inferential rules in examples such as the one given earlier, it is necessary to devise a logical scheme in which defeasible rules may be encoded. A wide variety of superficially very different non-monotonic logics have been proposed. The best known are McCarthy's (1980) *circumscription*, Reiter's *default logic* (1980, 1985), McDermott and Doyle's (1980) *non-monotonic logic I*, McDermott's *non-monotonic logic II* (1982), and Clark's *predicate completion* (1978). The problems that we shall raise appear to apply equally to all of these approaches (Hanks & McDermott, 1985, 1986; Shoam, 1987, 1988).

Non-monotonic Logics and Weak Conclusions

For concreteness we shall consider a formalisation of defeasible inference which introduces a meta-theoretic **M** operator into the object language of a standard logic (Reiter, 1980, 1985). Defeasible rules (in AI terminology, default rules) are encoded as follows:

$$\phi \wedge \mathbf{M}\psi \rightarrow \psi$$

This formula reads: ψ can be inferred from ϕ as long as $\neg\psi$ is not provable, given the axioms of the system. So the intuitive interpretation of $\mathbf{M}\psi$ is that $\neg\psi$ cannot be proved given Γ (the set of logical axioms that govern the behaviour of the connectives) and Δ (the non-logical axioms that encode the domain-specific knowledge in the system). In other words, it is *consistent* to infer ψ from $\Gamma \wedge \Delta$ and ϕ. The **M** operator has the unusual property of introducing the meta-theoretic concept of deducibility $\vdash$ into the object language: i.e. $\mathbf{M}\psi$ is equivalent to $\Gamma \wedge \Delta \nvdash \neg\psi$. (This logically inelegant manoeuvre may be avoided by interpreting the **M** operator as a modal operator, and providing a possible worlds semantics for the resulting logic [McDermott & Doyle, 1980]. Which formulation is used makes no difference to the inferences that can be drawn, or to the theorem-proving algorithms employed.)

Returning to our example of Egon and the egg, suppose that Egon tells his brother that he has just put an egg in boiling water. Egon's brother's relevant prior knowledge may be encoded in axioms Δ of something like the following form—where the premises (4.3) and (4.4) simply encode the fact that an egg cannot be both hard-boiled and medium-boiled at the same time:

$\forall x \forall t [egg(x)$ & $(x$ in boiling water at $t)$ & $\mathbf{M}(x$ is medium-boiled at $t + 5$ minutes) $\supset (x$ is medium-boiled at $t + 5$ minutes)]   (4.1)

$\forall x \forall t \, [egg(x) \ \& \ x$ in pressure cooker at $t \ \& \ \mathbf{M}(x$ is hard-boiled at $t + 5$ minutes)
$\supset (x$ is hard-boiled at $t + 5$ minutes)] (4.2)

$\forall x \forall t \, [(x$ is medium-boiled at $t) \supset \neg \, (x$ is hard-boiled at $t)$ (4.3)

$\forall x \forall t \, [(x$ is hard-boiled at $t) \supset \neg (x$ is medium-boiled at $t)$ (4.4)

He now knows that a particular object a, which is an egg, is in boiling water at time t_1 and adds (4.5) to Δ:

$egg(a) \ \& \ (a$ in boiling water at $t_1)$ (4.5)

As (4.5) matches the first conjunct of the antecedent of (4.1) the possibility arises that a will be medium-boiled at $t_1 + 5$. As it is not possible to derive the negation of this conclusion from the propositions (4.1) to (4.5), then this conclusion is consistent with the database. That is, $\mathbf{M}(a$ is medium-boiled at $t_1 + 5$ minutes) holds. Therefore, the second conjunct of the antecedent of (4.1) is also satisfied. So, the consequence that this egg will be medium-boiled in five minutes may legitimately be inferred.

Egon's brother now walks into the kitchen, and observes that the egg must be in the pressure cooker (it is the only pan on the stove). In our formalism, this amounts to adding (4.6) to Δ:

$egg(a) \ \& \ (a$ in pressure cooker at $t_1)$ (4.6)

As (4.6) matches the first conjunct of the antecedent of (4.2) the possibility arises that a will be hard-boiled at $t_1 + 5$. As it is not possible to derive the negation of this proposition from Δ and (4.6), then this conclusion is consistent with the database. That is, $\mathbf{M}(a$ is hard-boiled at $t_1 + 5$ minutes) holds. Therefore, the second conjunct of the antecedent of (4.2) is also satisfied. So, the consequence that this egg will be hard-boiled in five minutes may legitimately be inferred.

Yet this situation may seem paradoxical. From Δ and (4.5), we have the conclusion that the egg is medium-boiled at $t_1 + 5$ (and hence, by (4.3), it is not hard-boiled). On the other hand, from Δ and (4.6) we have the conclusion that the egg is hard-boiled at $t_1 + 5$ (and hence by (4.4), it is not medium-boiled). This may seem counter-intuitive if we are used to monotonic logics. For in such a logic all the conclusions that follow from any subset of (4.1)–(4.6) must follow from the complete set. In particular, (4.1)–(4.6) would imply that egg is both hard-boiled and not hard-boiled—that is, the axioms are inconsistent. However, because the logic is non-monotonic, inconsistency does not follow.

The cases in which the egg is medium-boiled and hard-boiled are what are known as distinct *extensions* of Δ. Which extension is obtained depends on which default rule is used first. If rule (4.1) is used first to infer that the egg is medium-boiled, rule (4.3) can be used to infer that it is not hard-boiled. In this extension, it is inconsistent to assume that the egg is hard-boiled—that is, $M(a$ is hard-boiled at $t_1 + 5$ minutes) does not hold. Hence, the contrary default rule (4.2) is blocked, and hence no contradiction results. Similarly, we can consider the extension in which rule (4.2) is used first. In this case, the egg is inferred to be hard-boiled, and hence, by rule (4.2), it cannot be medium-boiled. Thus, rule (4.1) cannot apply, and no contradictory conclusion is derived. Given that there are two possible extensions of (4.1)–(4.6), what conclusions can be derived? The only valid conclusions are those that hold in *all* extensions—so rather than inferring any particular extension, we may infer only the disjunction of all extensions. In the present case, this is simply that:

a is medium-boiled at $t_1 + 5$ minutes $\lor$ a is hard-boiled at $t_1 + 5$ minutes

This disjunctive conclusion is not intuitively adequate. That default logics give only such weak conclusions amounts to what McDermott (1986) calls the "you don't want to know" problem. From the point of view of prediction and action, you don't want to know that the egg will be either medium- or hard-boiled—you want to know which! The performance of the system contrasts with human reasoning. If we know that the egg is in boiling water and that it is in the pressure cooker, then we will unambiguously infer that it will be hard-boiled at $t_1 + 5$. Whereas the system has no way of resolving conflicting default conclusions, at least in cases such as this, such resolution is an effortless feature of human cognition. Hence, to model human performance, the system must be able to determine how conflicting pieces of inconclusive evidence bear upon the inferences that may be drawn. In other words, the system must solve the problem of appropriately revising its beliefs in the face of incomplete and conflicting information. Yet this *is* the problem of non-demonstrative inference. So in trying to explain non-demonstrative inference, by invoking non-monotonic logics, we have succeeded only in raising it again. Given the failure of logical positivist attempts to reconstruct non-demonstrative inference proof-theoretically, perhaps the failure of AI to tackle the same problem is unsurprising.

Despite this worrying state of affairs, within the AI community there have been attempts to tackle the problem of resolving incomplete and conflicting evidence by using domain-specific heuristics. Such heuristics are intended to differentiate acceptable from unacceptable extensions of the logical system. In view of the generality of the problem that such heuristics are attempting to solve, it is not surprising that they have been criticised as inadequate (Hanks & McDermott, 1985; Israel, 1980). Moreover, in so far as cognitive processes are taken to be semantically justified—i.e. to correspond to valid derivations at the level of proof theory—the postulation of such heuristics in the control strategy of the theorem-prover constitutes a retreat from the logicist position. However, let us assume that the problem of resolving conflicting and incomplete information could be solved by some set of heuristics. Even given this (apparently counterfactual) assumption, the logicist proof-theoretic programme appears to be infeasible.

Non-monotonic Logics and Computational Complexity

To complete the programme of logicist cognitive science, it must be possible to construct tractable algorithms that embody the non-monotonic proof theory. In particular, the introduction of the **M** operator, or equivalent, requires the ability to check whether or not some premise is consistent with the current contents of the database $\Gamma \wedge \Delta$. Thus, *any* invocation of a default rule requires a complete consistency check over the whole database. However, as we shall see, consistency checking is computationally intractable.

Consistency checking constitutes a general class of problems in complexity theory called *satisfiability* problems. In this section, we note the intractability of such problems, and the consequent implausibility of the proof-theoretic account of non-demonstrative inference.

There are two approaches to computational complexity: a priori analysis and a posteriori analysis (Horowitz & Sahni, 1978). A posteriori analysis involves the observation of the run-time performance of an actual implementation of an algorithm, as the size of the input, n, is systematically varied. Such empirical observations can generate approximate values for best, worst, and typical case run-times. A more theoretically rigorous approach is to attempt to derive an expression that captures the rate at which the algorithm consumes computational resources, as a function of the size of n. The crucial aspect of this function is what is known in complexity theory as its *order of magnitude*, which reflects the rate at which resource demands increase with n. For present purposes, the relevant resource is the number of times the basic computational operations of the algorithm must be invoked. Orders of magnitude are expressed using the "O" notation

$$O(1) < O(\log n) < O(n) < O(n \log n) < O(n^2) < O(n^3) \ldots < O(n^i) \ldots$$
$$< O(2^n) \ldots$$

For example, $O(1)$ indicates that the number of times the basic operations are executed does not exceed some constant regardless of the length of the input. $O(n^2)$, $O(n^3)$, ..., $O(n^i)$ indicate that the number of times the basic operations are executed is some *polynomial* function of the input length, such algorithms are polynomial-time computable—strictly speaking this class includes all algorithms of order lower than some polynomial function, such as $O(\log n)$, $O(n \log n)$.

Within complexity theory an important distinction is drawn between polynomial-time computable algorithms ($O(n^i)$ for some i), and algorithms that require exponential time (for example, $O(2^n)$ ... or worse). As n increases, exponential time algorithms consume vastly greater resources than polynomial-time algorithms. This distinction is usually taken to mark the difference between tractable algorithms (polynomial-time) and intractable (exponential-time) algorithms. Applying these distinctions to *problems*, a problem is said to be polynomial-time computable if it can be solved by a polynomial-time algorithm. If all algorithms which solve the problem are exponential-time, then the problem itself is labelled "exponential-time computable".

An important class of problems the status of which is unclear relative to this distinction is the class of *NP-complete* problems. "NP" stands for *non-deterministic polynomial-time* algorithms. Problems that only possess polynomial-time algorithms which are non-deterministic are said to be "in NP". NP-complete problems form a subclass of NP-hard problems. A problem is NP-hard if satisfiability reduces to it (Cook, 1971).[2]

A problem is NP-complete if it is NP-hard *and* is in NP. There are problems that are NP-hard which are not in NP. For example, the halting problem is undecidable, hence there is no algorithm (of any complexity) that can solve it. However, satisfiability reduces to the halting problem which thus provides an instance of a problem that is NP-hard but not NP-complete. The class of NP-complete problems includes such classic families of problems as the travelling salesman problems—the prototypical example of which is the task of determining the shortest round-trip that a salesman can take in visiting a number of cities. It is not known whether any NP-complete problem is polynomial-time computable, but it is known that if any NP-complete problem is polynomial-time computable, then they all are (Cook, 1971). All known deterministic algorithms for NP-complete problems are exponential-time, and it is widely believed that no polynomial-time algorithms exist. In practice, the discovery that a problem is NP-complete is taken to rule out the possibility of a real-time tractable implementation.

Unfortunately for the proof-theoretic programme of logicist cognitive science, consistency checking, like all satisfiability problems, is NP-complete. Hence an instantiation of a non-monotonic logic, which invokes a consistency check over the whole database every time a default rule is used, appears to be a hopelessly unpromising account of real-time defeasible human inference which is invoked rapidly and effortlessly in almost every cognitive task.

Do We Need to Appeal to Non-monotonicity?

We have argued against the logicist approach to cognitive science by showing that human inference is defeasible, that proof theory must therefore be defined for a non-monotonic logic, and that theorem proving for such a logic is incomplete* and intractable. The opponent of the proof-theoretic programme may agree with these points but argue that the appeal to non-monotonicity is unnecessary to defeat the logicist programme. In particular, it may be argued that computational intractability bites equally for standard, monotonic logics. After all, in almost *any* logic the general problem of deciding whether a given finite set of premises logically implies a given conclusion is NP-complete (Cook, 1971), and, of course, checking the validity of arguments is equivalent to checking the consistency of sets of propositions. According to this line of thought, the considerations of defeasibility and non-monotonicity that we have stressed appear to be wholly beside the point. However, there is a crucial difference between the monotonic and non-monotonic cases. In monotonic logic, if a set of premises is consistent, any application of a rule of inference will maintain consistency. This contrasts with the non-monotonic case, where each time a rule is applied, a new consistency check must be performed. So, if consistency checking is a problem for monotonic logics, it is a far greater problem for non-monotonic logics. Hence models of thought based on proof theory are severely undermined by the defeasibility of human inference, and the consequent postulation that the logic of thought must be non-monotonic. For the logicist, proof theory is supposed to be the *basis* of all cognitive activity (in commonsense reasoning, language, perception). If the logic of that proof theory is non-monotonic, and hence rule application is intractable, then the logicist position is surely untenable.

NOTES

1. Fodor is concerned to outline an interesting and important distinction—between *central* processes of non-demonstrative belief fixation, which are Quinean and isotropic; and domain-specific processes, in which the inferential processes are not dependent on the whole belief system, but only on a prescribed set of information, relevant to that domain. Fodor takes the demarcation between the former *central* processes and the latter *informationally encapsulated* processes to distinguish areas in which cognitive science is likely to prove infeasible from areas in which progress may be made. Note that domain-specific systems may involve non-demonstrative inference, and that this inference may be Quinean and isotropic relative to all the knowledge encoded in the module. So the non-demonstrative defeasible inference that appears to be implicated in putatively domain-specific processes involved in language understanding and perception may be just as problematic as the central processes of commonsense inference. With regard to our concern in this paper, the key distinction is not between domain-specific and central processes but between processes that involve knowledge-rich defeasible inference and are at least prima facie problematic for a logicist account, and those that do not. Of course, it is

possible that this distinction is in practice rather trivial, all human inference being of the former kind.

2. The satisfiability problem is to determine whether a formula is true for some assignment of truth values to the variables, and "reduces" is a technical term of complexity theory (see Horowitz & Sahni, 1978, p. 511).

CHAPTER FIVE

Against Logicist Cognitive Science II: Objections and Replies

INTRODUCTION

In the previous chapter, we argued that an extreme version of the logicist view of cognitive science fails to provide a complete* account of real human reasoning, and that logic-based approaches to uncertain reasoning are computationally intractable. But how general are the implications of these claims? One way of assessing this is by considering various ways in which our arguments may be countered, and assessing how successful these are. Specifically, we claim that the scope of our arguments against logicist cognitive science includes relevance theory (Sperber & Wilson, 1986), semantic methods of proof such as mental models (Johnson-Laird, 1983), and heuristic methods of reasoning.

One possible counter to our arguments that we briefly consider involves using probability theory, rather than logic, as the computational-level theory. When we wrote the paper on which Chapters 4 and 5 are based (Oaksford & Chater, 1991), we could not see how probability theory could provide a more adequate computational-level theory of defeasible inference. In Part II of this book, we show how probability theory *can* provide a computational-level theory for explaining human inference, in the context of providing a theory of human performance on a particular psychological reasoning task, the Wason selection task. We will consider the degree to which the problems of defeasible inference that we raise in this chapter can at least partially be solved by probability theory in Part II of this book, and suggest that probability theory offers a much more promising starting point for providing an adequate theory of human reasoning. Nonetheless, as we shall see in Chapter 16, the problems of completeness* and tractability remain important challenges for probabilistic approaches to cognition.

At the end of the paper on which this chapter is based, we speculated that connectionism might provide a way forward in providing an adequate theory of human reasoning. As we noted in the Introduction to Chapter 2, our current position is less optimistic about the prospects for connectionist approaches to high-level cognitive processes. We would now suggest instead that the probabilistic approach, as exemplified in Part II of this book, is the most promising direction for future research. However, there are close connections between connectionist networks and probabilistic inference, as we discuss in Chapter 16—so connectionist networks may, nonetheless, prove to be part of the solution to the problems of completeness* and tractability.

OBJECTIONS AND REPLIES

Worst Case Versus Typical Case

The a priori intractability results that we have considered are worst-case analyses. In practice the possibility remains that in typical cases, non-monotonic reasoning may be effected without exhausting the available computational resources. The most direct way to test this hypothesis is to perform an a posteriori analysis of actual average-case run-times of implemented non-monotonic logics. However, to the best of our knowledge, no such implementations exist. Of course, in computer science, theory is often developed in advance of its implementation in real systems. Such a situation is healthy if there is some reason to believe that implementations may be forthcoming—this does not appear to be the case in current approaches to defeasibility in the knowledge representation literature. This is of particular concern for artificial intelligence and cognitive science in which successful implementation is taken as the benchmark of theoretical rigour and adequacy. It is not, of course, possible to distinguish reliably between progressive and degenerating research programmes, between temporary puzzles for, and outright falsifications of, some line of research (Lakatos, 1970). However, increasing theoretical elaboration and decreasing practical success is surely a straw in the wind.

Heuristics, Tractability, and Completeness*

Apart from the foregoing, there is another reason why a priori intractability results are not necessarily taken to rule out the possibility of practical computation. No algorithm—i.e. no procedure that is *guaranteed* to solve the computational problem—may be tractable, and yet there may be more or less reliable *heuristics* which often solve the problem, or at least provide something close enough to the solution to be useful. These heuristics need not necessarily be computationally intractable. Computational tractability may be bought at the price of the reliability of the procedures. Given that human inference is manifestly unreliable—we are always jumping to conclusions, forgetting to take into account important considerations, and so on—it may seem plausible that an appropriate set of heuristics may be the basis of human defeasible inference. In discussing heuristics as a method of solving a particular case of the problem of defeasible inference, the frame problem, Fodor says:

> The idea is that, while non-demonstrative confirmation (and hence, presumably the psychology of belief fixation) is isotropic and Quinean *in principle*, still, given a particular hypothesis, there are, in practice heuristic procedures for determining the range of effects its acceptance can have on the rest of one's beliefs. (Fodor, 1983, p. 115)

We noted earlier that such heuristics have been appealed to in the attempt to overcome the tendency of non-monotonic logics to give unavoidably weak disjunctive conclusions. Appropriate heuristics might, perhaps, systematically favour some possible extensions of knowledge-base over others—heuristics that take account of the structure of the world could, it may be hoped, show systematic bias in favour of what we intuitively consider to be the *right* extensions. Thus, the operation of the heuristics implicitly encodes knowledge about the world. This approach has indeed been pursued in the knowledge representation literature. Let us consider a famous problem in non-monotonic reasoning, the Yale shooting problem (Hanks & McDermott, 1985), and consider an heuristic designed to favour the "right" answers.

   A gun is loaded at some time, and fired at a person at some later time. The problem is to determine whether or not the person ceases to be alive. It is assumed that the firing of a loaded gun at a person is invariably fatal. Further, we assume two defeasible rules: that (i) if a gun is loaded at some time, then it will typically continue to be loaded at some later time; and (ii) if a person is alive at some time, that person will typically be alive at some later time. This scenario creates a problem analogous to the one we raised earlier with respect to Egon and the egg. For any non-monotonic or defeasible reasoning system, two contrary, albeit defeasible, conclusions are warranted: either the person is not alive at some later time or he is alive at some later time (Hanks & McDermott, 1986). Observe that this example is a specific application of non-monotonic logics to the frame problem (see Fodor's comments quoted above). The scenario creates the problem of how to revise one's beliefs appropriately concerning the person being alive or dead given that a shooting has taken place.

Specific proposals concerning how to resolve the problem of multiple inconsistent extensions of a non-monotonic theory all invoke some method of preferring one extension over another. Hanks & McDermott (1986) propose that if conclusions in two extensions are contraries, then an earlier defeasible conclusion should defeat later defeasible conclusions. Thus, in the Yale shooting problem, as rule (i) is invoked earlier than rule (ii) in the chain of reasoning, the intermediate defeasible conclusion that the gun is loaded when it is fired is to be preferred over the defeasible conclusion that the person is alive after the gun has been fired. This "solution" is justified on the basis of reflections on the nature of causality (Shoam, 1986). However, although this move resolves the problem in favour of the putatively desired defeasible conclusion—that the person is dead at the later time—such a preference for one extension over another is not legitimised within the logical system. It is an *heuristic* based on prior global knowledge concerning the nature of causality. Its heuristic status is further confirmed by Loui (1987), who observes that although this heuristic may accord with intuition in the Yale shooting problem, there are many other examples where intuitions are violated if the heuristic is applied across the board. Thus, although such a temporal precedence heuristic may usually allow the right conclusion (although even this is disputed, see Loui, 1987), it is not guaranteed to do so.

Other methods for preferring one extension over another (e.g. Loui, 1986; Nute, 1985, 1986; Poole, 1985) all involve explicitly "encoding the preference information" (Loui, 1987, p. 291). Thus the decision about what defeasible inferences are licensed is external to the inference regime, and reflects purely heuristic assumptions usually concerning the nature of causality. Relative to the isotropic nature of non-demonstrative inference it is doubtful whether any of these heuristic assumptions are of general applicability. Moreover, all of these assumptions are Quinean, they reflect global properties of our causal knowledge. However, in their implementation in non-monotonic logics they are imposed externally by the programmer. But to complete the proof-theoretic programme such properties need to be shown to emerge from the structure of our world knowledge and cannot be imposed by fiat. Hence all these "solutions" fail to be complete*.

It is important to note that the kind of heuristics proposed earlier to circumvent the incompleteness* of non-monotonic logics are distinct from the equally *non-logical* decisions enforced by any practical implementation of logic in for example PROLOG. Practical theorem proving requires various non-logical *control* decisions to be made in the search strategy of the theorem prover, for example, to employ backward chaining only, to use loop checkers and to employ the "cut" operator (Hogger, 1984). These decisions involve the control strategy of an implementation of logic and as such are wholly independent of the knowledge to be encoded in a particular database. However, the heuristics proposed earlier specifically involve the *very knowledge* that is to be encoded. As we stated earlier, this involves making heuristic assumptions about how beliefs are appropriately updated. But this is precisely the problem that, on the proof-theoretic logicist account, non-monotonic logics were invoked to resolve! McDermott (1986) proposes a retreat to *proceduralism* in which it is admitted that no semantic justification for the heuristics proposed will be forthcoming. We will discuss this option further later, but observe now that it directly contradicts Fodor and Pylyshyn's logicist account of cognitive science.

It seems that appeal to heuristics is unlikely to repair the incompleteness* of non-monotonic reasoning; and that, in any case, to the extent that world-knowledge is embodied in heuristics rather than represented in the logical language over which the proof theory is defined, the appeal to heuristics amounts to a rejection of the logicist account of inference. A further proposal, mentioned by Loui (1987), is to make reasoning *domain-specific*. If only information *relevant* to a specific domain is employed in a particular inference then certain desirable consequences may follow. First, if a formal account of relevance can be defined, then it may be possible to logically delimit the sets of premises over which reasoning takes place. This *may* satisfy the complete-ness* criterion. Second, by restricting the premises to the relevant ones, n may be suitably restricted to satisfy the tractability criterion. We now turn to two proposals concerning the concept of relevance.

Relevance

Relevance logic restricts the concept of deducibility so as to avoid the well-known paradoxes of material implication "⊃". For example, it seems bizarre that A ⊃ (B ⊃ A) follows from assumptions A and B, if "⊃" is held to capture an intuitive notion of implication. Anderson and Belnap (1975) define a notion of *relevant entailment* "⇒" which employs a system of indices that attach to assumptions. The indices guarantee that a logical relation of relevance exists between the antecedent and consequent of a conditional statement. Only assumptions B, which rely on assumptions A, will allow "⇒" (relevant entailment) to be introduced such that A ⇒ B. That is, A ⇒ B can only be concluded when A is part of the subproof of B. In this precise logical sense A is relevant to B. It has been proposed, for example, by Haack (1978), that this notion of relevant entailment could assist in avoiding the conclusion that confirmation is Quinean. Instead of the whole of scientific knowledge being the unit of confirmation, she suggests that it could just be the *relevant* subset in Anderson and Belnap's sense. Moreover, Levesque (1988) proposes that relevant entailment may be used to effect a *tractable* selection of relevant premises from a database for subsequent reasoning processes.

However, in reasoning in defeasible domains relevant entailment still violates both the completeness* and tractability criteria. Even supposing relevant entailment were employed, default rule application would still remain intractable (Levesque, 1988). There are also strong grounds to question whether relevant entailment is complete*. In introducing the complete* criterion we noted that formal concepts must respect the depraved semantics for the informal concepts they encode. However, it seems that the notion of deductive relevance captured in relevant entailment far from exhausts the ways in which one piece of knowledge may be relevant to another piece of knowledge. First, Fodor (1983) observes that in science, knowledge in one domain may be relevant to another domain analogically. Strictly, considerations of *analogical* reasoning move outside the domain of confirmation into the domain of scientific discovery. For example,

> what's known about the flow of water gets borrowed to model the flow of electricity, what's known about the structure of the solar system gets borrowed to model the structure of the atom. (Fodor, 1983, p. 107)

However, analogical reasoning processes are part of our non-demonstrative reasoning abilities and as such require explanation by the mechanisms that purport to account for those abilities.

Second, relevant entailment accounts for relevance between propositions—it is a purely structural notion. However, our intuitions about relevance appear to be crucially dependent on lexical rather than structural properties of statements. For example, the fact that Fred having a heart is relevant to Fred's having palpitations depends not on the structure of the two propositions, but on the meaning of "heart", "palpitation", and the causal structure of the world that putatively links the two. Further, it appears that relevance is not determined by the *extension* of the relevant properties. According to the well-worn philosophical example, having a heart and having kidneys are coextensive—so if Fred has either property he has them both. However, although Fred's having a heart may be relevant to his having palpitations, his having kidneys may not be.

This clearly suggests that "relevance" is an *intensional* concept and hence it might be expected that a well-defined concept of relevance would be forthcoming via an appropriate possible worlds semantics. However, the provision of a proper semantics for relevance logics is notoriously difficult:

> The relevance logicians run the risk of turning logical validity into a clumsy thing. The difficulties they have in providing their largely proof-theoretic theories with a proper semantics may be regarded as a symptom of this. The semantic theories which have thus far been put forward tend to lack the explanatory power which is to be expected from theories which purport to say what relevance means (Veltman, 1985, pp. 42–43).

In sum, it would appear that relevance logic fails to meet both our criteria. Default rule application remains intractable and there are grounds for considerable doubt over whether relevant entailment is sufficient to capture the numerous ways in which one piece of knowledge may be relevant to another piece of knowledge.

However, relevance logic does not exhaust attempts to define a notion of relevance that may be of more general applicability. *Relevance Theory* (Sperber & Wilson, 1986) is an attempt to account for how a person's beliefs may be appropriately updated which takes a less restricted view of relevance and also incorporates various processing requirements that bear on the issue of tractability. Sperber and Wilson (1986) first emphasise a disanalogy between their account of the spontaneous and almost instantaneous updating of beliefs that occurs in sentence comprehension and the reflective and time-consuming updating of beliefs that occurs in scientific theorising. It is the former that they are concerned to explicate. They suggest that the inferential processes underlying sentence comprehension must exploit only the accessible information. Sperber and Wilson (1986) then outline what we will term a *hybrid* inferential regime consisting of a restricted deductive mechanism and a non-logical component which is responsible for updating the *confirmation* strengths that attach to propositions stored in memory. The restricted logical component, which contains no introduction rules, is motivated primarily by issues of tractability but also represents a substantive claim about the nature of people's inferential processes in language comprehension. Sperber and Wilson (1986) are careful to emphasise that they do not intend their notion of confirmation strength to be conflated with the assignment of subjective probabilities to propositions that are explicitly manipulated in judging the relative strengths of those propositions. "Confirmation strength" is to be understood as a purely processing notion determined by a proposition's prior history of being accessed from memory. The concept of relevance is defined relative to a context C.

> *Extent condition 1:* an assumption is relevant in C to the extent that its contextual effects in C are large.
>
> *Extent condition 2:* an assumption is relevant in C to the extent that the effort required to process it in C is small.

Contextual *effects* and processing *effort* are defined in terms of the hybrid inferential regime introduced earlier. There is a trade-off between these two "extent conditions" in determining the relevance of an assumption.

The notion of relevance thus defined may not be helpful given our present concerns, as it appears to beg the very question we were hoping the concept of relevance would answer. That is, how do we choose from all we know the relevant items to update in response to new information? The foregoing definition is relativised to a context C, which is understood as the old information available from the immediately prior discourse and from memory for encyclopaedic or world knowledge. Sperber and Wilson (1986, pp. 132–137) argue convincingly that the whole of the latter may be included in C, although it is suggested that this would violate extent conditions 1 and 2 of the definition. However, as relevance is defined in terms of C, delimiting C's extent by appeal to relevance would be viciously circular. Thus, to avoid the charge of circularity, independent grounds are required to delimit C. Sperber and Wilson (1986, p. 138) appeal to the fact that in cognitive psychology and cognitive science knowledge is generally agreed to be compartmentalised in to "schemata", "frames", "scenarios", and "prototypes". However, it was precisely in search of principled grounds for this compartmentalisation that we embarked upon this discussion of relevance! "Schemata", "frames", "scenarios", and "prototypes" are precisely the names appropriated to the domain-specific units of knowledge that it was hoped that the concept of relevance would provide, thereby delimiting the isotropy of confirmation. It seems, therefore, that relevance theory, in order to define a restricted notion of relevance appropriate to sentence comprehension, must presuppose a solution to the more global problem of relevance, which is our present concern.

Apart from this, there are general problems for relevance theory. We will mention just two. First, Sperber and Wilson's (1986) account of their inferential mechanism seems to leave no room for *errors* of interpretation. These must be possible because the assumptions recruited from encyclopaedic memory in discourse are often of a defeasible elaborative form (Stenning & Oaksford, 1989). Such elaborative inferences can be defeated by subsequent discourse, and hence must be cancelled. This of course suggests that the logic of the inferential component is going to be non-monotonic even in sentence comprehension. Thus although introduction rules have been excluded to the benefit of the systems tractability, default rules will have to be included which, as we have seen, are unlikely to enhance the tractability of the system. Second, how the confirmation strengths are used and updated is currently opaque. The proposal is that as a proposition in memory is accessed more often so its ability to be accessed is enhanced. Thus its strength does not have to be explicitly represented. However, in a symbolic, deductive system, on the lines Sperber and Wilson (1986) propose, we can see no way of implementing this proposal. In a symbol system it matters not one jot how often an item is accessed, every time it is accessed it will be accessed in the order dictated by the programme—*unless* some parameter is attached to the item which is updated each time it is accessed so that the higher the value of the parameter the more likely it is to be accessed. But this is exactly the approach Sperber and Wilson eschew.

It appears that current notions of relevance are inadequate to the task of determining the relevant domains of knowledge which are updated in response to new information. Neither relevance logic nor relevance theory provide any grounds for believing that such an account is likely to be forthcoming.

Better Ontology

It might be thought that the locus of the problem for the logicist programme is the insistence that the rules encoding our commonsense knowledge adopt our everyday ontology of tables, chairs, and so on—i.e. the ontology implicit in folk-psychological propositional attitude ascriptions. Perhaps according to some more fine-grained ontology, what appear to be defeasible rules can be reconstructed as exceptionless generalisations, thus obviating the need for non-monotonic reasoning. A search for deterministic rules underlying apparently non-deterministic phenomena is analogous to Einstein's deterministic "hidden variable" interpretation of quantum mechanics. However, the very error-prone nature of most human perception, inference, and action appears to militate against the possibility that people actually employ such an ontology. Any explanation of cognition must surely account for making mistakes, changing our minds, reviewing our beliefs in the light of new information, etc. It appears necessary to explain the defeasibility of human inference, and impossible to *explain it away*.

Further, to retreat to the postulation of an alternative ontology, which does not correspond to everyday objects and relations, amounts to giving up point 4 in our characterisation of logicist cognitive science. This may not be a concern to many working on formalising commonsense knowledge. For example, Hayes (1984b) attempts to formalise our implicit understanding of the behaviour of liquids by postulating representational primitives which do not correspond one to one with the everyday concepts provided by pre-theoretic intuitions. Such primitives must be postulated in any case to handle inferential processes in specific cognitive domains: as we noted earlier, a variety of linguistic representations appear to be implicated in language understanding; a complex range of representations is computed in perceptual processes, and so on.

The rejection of everyday properties and relations as the basis for internal representation does, however, constitute a significant retreat for the logicist position of Fodor and Pylyshyn (1988). Fodor (e.g. 1987) and Pylyshyn (1984) argue that scientific cognitive explanation must be founded on folk-psychological explanation. Specifically, they advocate the Representational Theory of Mind according to which to have a propositional attitude is to stand in a certain relation (the relation of believing, desiring or whatever) to a mental representation. The content of this mental representation is the object of the propositional attitude. As the contents of propositional attitudes are described in natural language, the interpretation of the corresponding mental representations must be at the level of everyday objects and relations. No everyday properties and relations, no theory of propositional attitudes.

Domain-specificity

We have observed that as the size of the knowledge base increases, the complexity of consistency checking becomes unacceptable, and non-monotonic logics over that knowledge base becomes unfeasible. If, however, knowledge can be encoded in small, isolated sets of domain-specific axioms, perhaps the complexity of consistency checking may be kept within acceptable bounds. However, it is not sufficient to maintain consistency *within* domains; consistency must be maintained *between* domains, on the proof-theoretic story. As we noted earlier, Fodor (1983) is committed to the view that commonsense inference is precisely a domain that does not admit such modularisation. In particular, he notes that commonsense inference is *isotropic*. That is, any piece of knowledge may be made to bear on any other—there are no proscribed boundaries over which inferential processes cannot operate.

We have already seen that general principles like relevance fail to provide a basis for the compartmentalisation of knowledge into specific domains. Such general principles are required, as otherwise it is opaque as to how such compartmentalisation is achieved, other than by fiat, from the flux of information that an organism receives in interacting with its environment. However, let us suppose, counterfactually, that such compartmentalisation can be achieved. We now present an example that demonstrates the soundness of Fodor's intuition that domain-specificity cannot be the rule in knowledge-based systems (on the assumption that such demonstration may still be required).

On any reasonable principles of modularisation, seismographic knowledge is unlikely to be included in the domain-specific knowledge that allows Egon to predict that his egg will be medium-boiled in five minutes. However, suppose Egon is boiling his egg at the seismographic station monitoring the San Andreas fault. Egon notices the meter reading shoot off the scale. He infers that the building will be knocked flat in a few seconds and rushes out of the door. He subsequently realises that his egg will not be ready as usual, because the pan is unlikely to remain on the stove. So his knowledge of seismology seems to be implicated in explaining his expectations about eating eggs. It could reasonably be countered that Egon might not, in practice, make this inference in such a desperate situation. However, if knowledge were organised into completely isolated, domain-specific modules, he could not, *in principle*, make this inference, which seems counter-intuitive. In so far as inference *can* be based on premises from more than one knowledge domain, the axioms of each must be mutually consistent. So, as any knowledge domain *may* bear on any other, the global consistency of the entire knowledge base must be maintained, according to the proof-theoretic view. So appeals to domain-specificity cannot alleviate the problems of consistency checking for the proof-theoretic view of commonsense reasoning.

Explicit and Implicit Inference

One line of retreat for the Logicist is to grant that proof theory does not account for defeasible inference in commonsense reasoning, language processing, perception, and the like. Perhaps though, it *can* account for our explicit, conscious reasoning abilities. In explicit reasoning, only a very few premises can be entertained (Evans, 1982; Johnson-Laird, 1983; Wason & Johnson-Laird, 1972). As in these cases the input length *n* is small, the onset of the combinatorial explosion of consistency checking may be avoided. Indeed, some generally intractable exponential-time algorithms can outperform generally tractable polynomial-time algorithms for small *n*. The conjecture that this is so might be supported by the fact that, given more than about three premises, in an explicit reasoning task, reasoning performance degrades catastrophically (Johnson-Laird, 1983, pp. 44–45).

There are two reasons why even this retreat may be untenable. First, performance in explicit deductive reasoning tasks is extremely poor whatever the number of premises involved. This is, at least prima facie, puzzling if the basis of our inferential performance is proof theory (Oaksford, Chater, & Stenning, 1990). Second, performance even on explicit deductive reasoning tasks appears to be infected by the effects of stored world knowledge (Byrne, 1989; Cheng & Holyoak, 1985; Cheng, Holyoak, Nisbett, & Oliver, 1986; Cosmides, 1989; Evans, 1989; Oaksford, 1989). To model the interaction between the small number of explicitly given premises and the huge amount of implicit world knowledge appears to require (i) that *n* is, after all, very large; and (ii) that a non-monotonic logic may be required to model the influence of defeasible world knowledge on deductive reasoning performance.

Can Probabilities Help?

In discussing "relevance" we mentioned that Sperber and Wilson (1986) explicitly reject the idea of attaching subjective probabilities to propositions in memory. We now consider the possibility that so doing may go some way to resolving the problems we have raised. There seem to be two major ways in which probabilities may help. First, the defeasibility of rules that embody people's world knowledge need not be encoded as default rules, rather it could be conceded that all such rules are treated as probabilistic. This appears to satisfy the tractability criterion, as consistency checking over the whole database would no longer be required. However, we have also observed, in discussing non-monotonic logics and relevance, that defeasible inference regimes are required to solve the more general problem of which rules are to be updated in response to new information, i.e. the ubiquitous frame problem in AI. Treating all the rules that encode encyclopaedic world knowledge as probabilistic does not resolve the problem of *which* rules apply in a given context. Further problems, which relate to the completeness* criterion, also arise for this putative probabilistic solution.

Perhaps the most principled way of assigning probabilities to rules is given by Adams' (1966, 1975) *probability semantics*. Logically, rules are conditional statements, and hence concern centres on how probabilities should attach to conditionals. Adams suggests that the meaning of a conditional, "if ϕ, then ψ" is that the *conditional* probability of ψ given ϕ, $P(\psi|\phi)$, is high. However, this proposal is subject to a well known triviality result due to Lewis (1976), the upshot of which is that such an assignment of probabilities is only possible on the assumption that ϕ and ψ are not themselves logically complex conditional statements. This result seriously restricts the scope of Adams' theory in representing very simple reasoning problems (Veltman, 1985, p.40) and thus strongly suggests that such a proposal fails to meet the completeness* criterion.

Further grounds to believe that probabilistic rules will fail to be complete* are suggested by examples where probabilistic rules appear to act as blocks to further empirical inquiry. An example due to Alice ter Meulen (1986) can be adapted to illustrate the problem. She poses the question of what response is appropriate on encountering a complaisant donkey, given you believe that *all donkeys are stubborn*. The latter rule can be represented as a conditional statement and hence we may ask how it is to be revised in the light of this putative counter-example. Assuming that one such donkey is not taken to falsify the rule outright, the probabilistic suggestion would appear to be that a minor adjustment in the conditional probability assigned to the rule is required. Having made the adjustment, you can proceed on your way. However, surely it is at least possible that you want to *inquire* in to why this particular donkey does not conform to your aforementioned belief that all donkeys are stubborn. On so inquiring, you may discover that the animal was circus-trained, and hence you would be advised to encode the information that all donkeys are stubborn *except circus-trained donkeys*. Such an adjustment would surely better equip you to draw appropriate inferences on next encountering a donkey at the circus, than the minor adjustment to the conditional probabilities suggested by the probabilistic alternative. It would appear that *only if* no such default information could be found (i.e. no hidden variables can be discovered) would the probabilistic alternative be necessitated. Again it would appear necessary to explain the defeasibility of human inference, and impossible to explain it away.

A second proposal concerning how probabilities may help involves employing probabilities to determine which rules apply in which contexts. Thus rules are not soft and probabilistic but hard and logical. However, which rules apply is given by their probabilities of applying in a given context. This proposal is indistinguishable from Relevance Theory, except in the explicit use of probabilities which at least avoids the opaqueness of *confirmation strengths* in Sperber and Wilson (1986). If rules have probabilities assigned indicating their likelihood of applying in a given context, then at least two things are required: (i) a probability assignment to each rule *for each possible context*, (ii) a means of determining the current context. However, as with relevance theory, (ii) is just a restatement of the current problem. If the current context could be determined, then the problem we have invoked probabilities to resolve would not arise. Moreover, (i) requires that each rule has a probability assigned *for every possible context*. Not only is this an impossible requirement—the range of possible contexts is simply not known—but the spectre of intractability must again loom very large. In, for example, computational accounts of *abductive reasoning* in medical diagnosis, which employ Bayesian inference, the number of stored a priori and conditional probabilities increases explosively with the number of diseases and symptoms (Charniak & McDermott, 1985). Yet such a knowledge base must be regarded as trivial in comparison to the whole of world knowledge. In sum, there are strong grounds for believing that the probabilistic approach will be subject to intractability problems and for believing that such approaches violate the completeness* criterion.

Parallelism

From the discussion so far, it might be thought that the computational intractability of non-monotonic inference applies only to serial machines, in which computational operations must be executed one after the other. Perhaps an appeal to the parallelism of the brain may alleviate the problem of computational intractability. However, at best, appeals to parallelism can only reduce the time-complexity of a computationally explosive algorithm by a constant factor. All that this can do is slightly delay the onset of the computational infeasibility. Given that the proof-theoretic view of mind requires consistency checking over a database that encodes the whole of an individual's commonsense knowledge (so that n is, presumably, *very* large), the minor gains induced by appeal to parallelism are unlikely to be significant.

Semantic Methods of Proof

Within the psychology of reasoning, there is an important debate about whether or not human *deductive* reasoning is mediated by proof-theoretic methods (Braine, 1978; Henle, 1962; Piaget, 1953), or by semantic methods of proof, such as mental models (Johnson-Laird, 1983). Carrying this debate over to non-demonstrative inference, it might be thought that such semantic methods may provide an alternative to the standard proof-theoretic approach. However, such semantic methods of proof *work by* consistency checking. The validity of an inference from $A_1, A_2, \ldots, A_n$ to a conclusion C, is established by attempting to show that $A_1, A_2, \ldots, A_n \& \neg C$ is not consistent. The consistency check is performed by systematically attempting to find a model according to which each of $A_1, A_2, \ldots, A_n \& \neg C$ are true. Because consistency checking, *of whatever form*, is NP-complete, as the number of premises in the database increases the computation becomes intractable, and inferences cannot be made, even in a *monotonic* logic. Although semantic methods such as mental models may elegantly account for some explicit deductive reasoning tasks, they offer no prospect of providing more tractable mechanisms for reasoning in knowledge-rich domains.

Proceduralism

McDermott (1986) argues that the failure of proof-theoretic methods in AI to adequately account for non-monotonic reasoning requires that the attempt to provide a semantics for knowledge-representation formalisms must be abandoned. Yet this move amounts to abandoning the project of accounting for defeasible reasoning. If symbolic structures are assigned no semantics, then they have no representational content—that is, they are not *about* anything. Yet reasoning processes are defined in virtue of the content of the representations that they manipulate; to describe an inference as valid, justified, and legitimate is to appeal to the interpretation of the symbolic structures. For example, the inference from A and A $\supset$ B to B is *valid* because if A and A $\supset$ B are both *true*, then B must be *true*. Yet uninterpreted formulae, which are all that the proceduralist can countenance, cannot be true or false.

The only retreat is to appeal to some form of functional role semantics (see Block, 1986, for a review and references). That is, the idea that symbols can acquire meanings via their intrinsic relations to other symbols. This idea is usually illustrated (see, for example, Lloyd, 1989, pp. 24–25) by an analogy with learning the meaning of a term either in a foreign language or in an unfamiliar idiolect of a speaker's own language. A previously unencountered term may be acquired and used appropriately simply by observing its relations to other words, and its grammatical contexts of use. A speaker may finally become competent enough to use the term appropriately to utter truths *without ever having learned the precise denotation of the term*, i.e. without access to the full semantic content of the symbol. However, it is generally agreed that this story cannot work for all the terms of a language (Lloyd, 1989). At least some, more likely the majority, of the terms of a speaker's language must be such that the speaker has access to their full semantic content. Without such access no sense could be attached to talk of "using a term appropriately to utter truths". It is important to observe that Fodor himself does not believe a word of the functional role story (see Fodor, 1987). Although this view is easily conflated with Fodor's (1980) *methodological solipsism*, there is nothing *methodological* about it; this is *solipsism* pure, simple, and indefensible. Without appeal to full semantic content, cognitive science does not have a story to tell about its central explanatory concept, i.e. representation.

Quite generally, proceduralism abandons all notions of reasoning and inference, be they deductive, inductive, eductive, or abductive. *Very* generally, it is hard to imagine what a cognitive science (logicist or otherwise) could look like, without the notion of representation.

CONCLUSIONS

We have argued that the plausibility of logicist cognitive science depends on its ability to provide a proof-theoretic account of defeasible inference which is implicated in almost every area of cognitive activity. We assessed the practical attempt in AI to carry out this proof-theoretic programme using non-monotonic logics, and noted (1) that such logics are able to draw only unacceptably weak disjunctive conclusions; and (2) that the theorem-proving algorithms over such logics are computationally intractable due to their reliance on the NP-complete problem of consistency checking. We drew the conclusion that the programme of logicist cognitive science is infeasible, and replied to a number of plausible objections to this conclusion.

If logicist cognitive science constitutes an inappropriate framework in which to model cognition, the question arises of what alternative approach can be provided, which maintains both semantic interpretability and computational tractability. In discussing the central dogmas of logicist cognitive science, we repeatedly urged that the range of computational systems available is far from exhausted by the traditional symbolic approach. Nevertheless, it is beyond dispute that this is the approach that has been most thoroughly investigated, in part because of its early promise in providing a physicalist grounding for human cognitive processes. However, in virtue of this fact, it is the approach about which most is known relative to its abilities to handle cognitive phenomena. From the issues raised here concerning the defeasibility of human cognitive processes, it is clear that the conclusion of these investigations is that classical logicist cognitive science is inadequate. Therefore, it may well be time to explore the space of possible computational schemes for more adequate, albeit, as yet, less understood alternatives.

In this regard, recent work on distributed systems such as neural networks (e.g. McClelland & Rumelhart, 1986; Rumelhart & McClelland, 1986) and classifier systems (Holland, Holyoak, Nisbett, & Thagard, 1986), may perhaps constitute the beginnings of an alternative approach to mechanisms that deal with defeasible inference (Chater & Oaksford, 1990; Derthick, 1987; Shastri, 1985). Both Shastri (1985) and Derthick (1987, 1988) provide efficient implementations of algorithms for Bayesian inference and default reasoning respectively, which exploit connectionist systems. However, both implementations are hand-wired and thus do not exploit the principle advantage of connectionist systems, i.e. their ability to learn. Connectionist learning is notoriously slow, and thus our suggestion that such systems may aid in overcoming the objections to the logicist programme we raise in this paper may seem suspect. Complexity results for connectionist learning algorithms are as bad (in fact usually worse) than the non-monotonic systems we criticise. However, like is not being compared with like. In the case of non-monotonic systems the complexity of inference not learning was under discussion: these systems do not possess learning mechanisms. With regard to inference in connectionist systems, once a network has learned, it draws inferences as rapidly as it propagates activity from input to output. This pattern of complexity mirrors the human case whereas that of non-monotonic reasoning systems does not. Human learning is a slow process, but once some piece of knowledge is in place inference over it is effortless. Connectionist systems appear to display precisely the same complexity profile.

CHAPTER SIX

Reasoning Theories and Bounded Rationality

INTRODUCTION

In Chapters 4 and 5, we examined the consequences for logicist cognitive science of the defeasibility of everyday reasoning. We also considered a wide variety of potential solutions to the problem of defeasibility that have been proposed within the cognitive sciences, arguing that these were not successful. These included mental models theory, which forms one of a small set of highly influential theories that have been proposed within cognitive psychology to account for experimental evidence concerning human deductive reasoning. In this chapter, we consider more generally the extent to which psychological theories developed to account for human deductive reasoning can generalise to everyday defeasible reasoning. We argue that it is crucial that such theories do generalise to everyday defeasible inference, because, outside mathematical domains, deductive reasoning appears to find little application. This is because people need to reason about a world that is uncertain, and that does not admit of exceptionless generalisations, as argued in Chapter 4. So if psychological theories of reasoning apply only to deduction, then, as we remark in this chapter, they may be of no more interest than, say, the psychology of playing monopoly.

Deductive reasoning theorists, particularly from the mental logic (Rips, 1994) and mental models (Johnson-Laird & Byrne, 1991) viewpoints, explicitly view their theories as being involved in almost all aspects of reasoning and indeed of cognition more generally. In this chapter, we suggest that no accounts from the current psychology of reasoning can successfully "scale up" from constrained laboratory tasks to deal with the problems of everyday defeasible reasoning.

One of the lessons of artificial intelligence has been that algorithms that appear successful and tractable in "toy" domains, like the constrained laboratory tasks used in the psychology of reasoning, tend to fail completely when generalised to more realistic domains. One of the most notorious difficulties that artificial intelligence has faced in generalising to everyday domains is the cluster of problems known as the "frame problem" (McCarthy, 1977; McCarthy & Hayes, 1969). As we argue later, the frame problem appears to apply to psychological theories of reasoning, as well as proposals in artificial intelligence. This raises the concern that current theories in the psychology of reasoning may be successful only because they deal directly just with data from highly simplified laboratory tasks. In this chapter, we suggest that this concern is real, and that such theories are unlikely to generalise appropriately from the laboratory to everyday life. Another way of expressing this concern is that current theories of reasoning lack "ecological validity".

We focus largely on the algorithmic level of explanation, arguing that it is unlikely that existing psychological reasoning theories can "scale up" to deal with everyday defeasible inference without suffering from computational intractability. The problem of intractable theories of human thought and behaviour has a long history throughout the cognitive and social sciences. It was raised by Simon in the context of both economics (Simon, 1955) and psychology (Simon, 1956). Simon advanced the thesis that computationally intractable theories of "rational choice" must be replaced by theories of "bounded rationality"—i.e. theories of how the mind satisfactorily approximates optimal performance with limited cognitive resources (see Arrow, Colombatto, Perlman, & Schmidt, 1996; Gigerenzer, 1993; Gigerenzer & Goldstein, 1996). So, in these terms, the question that we address in this chapter is: Are psychological theories of reasoning, when generalised to everyday defeasible inference, compatible with bounded rationality? We argue that they are not, and that they do not generalise successfully beyond the laboratory.

REASONING THEORIES AND BOUNDED RATIONALITY

In this chapter we will argue that considerations of bounded rationality may fundamentally alter our present conception of the adequacy of psychological theories of reasoning. Since its inception, cognitive science has been concerned with the limitations on the cognitive system which inhere in virtue of the organisation of human memory and the need to act rapidly in real time (Kahneman, Slovic, & Tversky, 1982; Simon, 1969). Simon (quoted in Baars, 1986, pp. 363–364), for example, says that:

> cognitive limitations have been a central theme in almost all of the theorizing I've done ... They are ... very important limitations on human rationality, particularly if the rationality has to be exercised in a face-to-face real-time context.

Cognitive limitations mean that people may be incapable of living up to normative but computationally expensive accounts of their inferential behaviour,[1] i.e. human rationality is *bounded.*

The two most important limitative findings of cognitive science both affect human memory. The constraints imposed by people's limited short-term memory capacity have been mapped out in some detail (Baddeley, 1986; Miller, 1956) and have been appealed to in order explain certain biases in reasoning experiments (Evans, 1983a; Johnson-Laird, 1983). Perhaps a less well known limitative finding applies to retrieval from long-term memory.

In artificial intelligence this limitation has been labelled the "frame problem" (McCarthy & Hayes, 1969; see Pylyshyn, 1987 for overviews). This term tends to be used generically to describe a cluster of related problems, which as Glymour (1987, p. 65) observes, are all of the following form:

> Given an enormous amount of stuff, and some task to be done using some of the stuff, what is the *relevant stuff* for the task?

Some variant of the frame problem may arise for any task requiring the deployment of prior world knowledge. In this chapter we will trace out the consequences of the frame problem for theories of reasoning. We will argue that a bounded rationality assumption may have to be made in deductive reasoning research, just as in research into risky decision making (Kahneman, Slovic, & Tversky, 1982).

We begin by outlining the range of contemporary theoretical approaches to reasoning based on the taxonomy provided by Evans (1991) and suggest that bounded rationality provides an additional criterion of theory preference. We then introduce an important and implicit assumption, which motivates interest in these theories. This we have called the *generalisation assumption* (Oaksford & Chater, 1992). It states that theories of reasoning developed to account for explicit inference in laboratory reasoning tasks should generalise to provide accounts of other inferential processes. We will also offer a general characterisation of these inferential processes. We then outline more precisely how the limitations of the cognitive system may argue against certain process accounts by briefly introducing *computational complexity theory* (described more fully in Chapter 4). We will then show how complexity issues have raised problems for theories of perception and risky decision making and for theories of knowledge representation in artificial intelligence. We then argue that contemporary reasoning theories are all likely to fall foul of the same problems. We therefore conclude that these theories are unlikely to be psychologically real.

An important corollary to this argument is that because our reasoning abilities are bounded, empirically observed deviations from optimal rationality need raise few questions over our rationality in practice. The interesting questions are how rational the system needs to be to qualify as a cognitive system (Cherniak, 1986), and what kind of mechanism needs to be postulated to implement it (e.g. see Levesque, 1988). To end on a positive note, therefore, we will suggest that, following Rumelhart, Smolensky, McClelland, and Hinton (1986) and Rumelhart (1989), recent advances in neural computation may suggest mechanisms that more adequately address the issues we raise in this chapter. We will also suggest some ways in which reasoning research may profitably develop in the future to identify the kind of rational mechanism (Fodor, 1987) people actually are.

Theories of Reasoning

Evans (1991) offers a four-way classification of reasoning theories and a three-way characterisation of the questions they must try to answer. The questions that need to be addressed are: the competence question—the fact that human subjects often successfully solve deductive reasoning problems; the bias question—the fact that subjects also make many systematic errors; the content and context question—the fact that the content and context of a problem can radically alter subjects' responses. Evans (1991) argues that the four theories of reasoning tend to concentrate on one question or the other, but none provides a fully integrated account of all three. The first two theories address the competence question.

The *mental logic* approach argues for the existence of formal inference rules in the cognitive system (Braine, 1978; Henle, 1962; Inhelder & Piaget, 1958; Johnson-Laird, 1975; Osherson, 1975; Rips, 1983). These rules, for example modus ponens, i.e. given *if p, then q* and *p* you can infer *q*, rely only on the syntactic form of the sentences encoding the premises. Thus whatever sentences are substituted for *p* and *q* the same inferences apply. *Mental models* theory suggests that the semantic content of the sentences encoding a hypothesis is directly represented in the cognitive system (Johnson-Laird, 1983; Johnson-Laird & Byrne, 1991). It is these contents that are subsequently manipulated in reasoning. Hence the actual meaning of *p* and *q* may be important to the reasoning process.

Two further theories are directed at explaining content effects and the errors and biases that infect people's normal reasoning performance. *Pragmatic reasoning schema* theory proposes inference rules that are specific to particular domains to account for content effects. Cheng and Holyoak (1985), for example, invoke a permission schema to account for the facilitatory effects of thematic content. In these tasks contentful rules about permission relations were employed, e.g. *if you are drinking alcohol, you must be over 18 years of age.* Lastly the *heuristic approach* proposes that a variety of systematic errors and biases in human reasoning may be explained by the cognitive system employing a variety of short-cut processing strategies (Evans, 1983a, 1984, 1989).

Evans (1991) was concerned to get reasoning theorists to agree some common ground rules concerning the adequacy of their theories. He does so by providing criteria of theory preference—completeness, coherence, falsifiability, and parsimony—by which to judge reasoning theories, and seems to view mental models as scoring most highly on these criteria. We will argue that along with these general criteria—common to all scientific domains—limitations on long-term memory retrieval may also provide a valuable criterion by which to assess reasoning theories.

Cognitive limitations have been appealed to in order to account for the biases that occur in people's reasoning. For example, limitations on short-term memory capacity have been appealed to in order to motivate the heuristic approach (Evans, 1983b, 1989) and to explain error profiles in syllogistic reasoning (Johnson-Laird, 1983). Given the prominence of the frame problem in AI, why has it not also been taken as a potential source of constraint on theories of reasoning? We believe there are two reasons. First, no analysis has been provided of these process theories which might indicate that they are profligate with computational resources. Second, when accounting for laboratory tasks the demands of a generalisable theory of inference can be ignored. We now suggest that contemporary reasoning theories are intended to generalise appropriately to other inferential modes.

The Generalisation Assumption

Why has the psychology of deductive reasoning been so prominent within cognitive psychology/science? The principal reason appears to be the assumption that the principles of human inference discovered in the empirical investigation of explicit inference will *generalise* to provide accounts of most inferential processes. We call this the *generalisation assumption*. The generalisation assumption is, for example, implicit in the subtitle to Johnson-Laird's (1983) book *Mental Models: Towards a Cognitive Science of Language, Inference and Consciousness.* Little overt human activity involves deductive inference. Therefore, without the generalisation assumption the study of deductive reasoning would warrant little more interest than, say, the psychology of playing monopoly.

Within artificial intelligence knowledge representation, a similar generalisation assumption encountered the problem of *scaling up*. Quite often programs that worked well in *toy domains*, i.e. small well-behaved databases rather like the abstract domains employed in laboratory reasoning tasks, failed when scaled up to deal with larger more realistic databases. This was because the inference regimes in these AI programs were generally computationally intractable, but this was only apparent when they were scaled up to deal with more complex, real-world, inferential problems. Although a prominent issue in AI research (e.g. Levesque & Brachman, 1985; Levesque, 1988; McDermott, 1986), scaling up has not been an issue in the psychology of reasoning.

Theories of Reasoning and Bounded Rationality

We will deal with the four theories of reasoning in the order in which they were introduced: mental logics, mental models, pragmatic reasoning schemas, and the heuristic approach.

Mental Logics

The contemporary mental logic view explains explicit reasoning performance by appeal to various natural deduction systems (Gentzen, 1934) with (Braine, 1978) or without (Rips 1983) some specific assumptions concerning the processes that animate the inference rules.[2] From the perspective of computational complexity, mental logic accounts appear particularly unpromising. Even for standard monotonic logics, the general problem of deciding whether a given finite set of premises logically implies a particular conclusion is NP-complete (Cook, 1971).[3] Moreover, the a priori complexity results we have already discussed were derived from logical attempts to account for default reasoning in AI knowledge representation. In consequence it seems unlikely that the mental logic approach is going to satisfy the generalisation assumption. There would appear to be only two possible lines of retreat to avoid the conclusion that most inferential performance is beyond the scope of the mental logic approach.

Firstly, despite a priori arguments that most human reasoning is defeasible, people may employ a standard logic in much everyday reasoning. However, over the last 30 years or so it has been the failure to observe reasoning performance that accords well with standard, monotonic logic which has led to questions over human rationality. When as little as 4% of subjects' behaviour accords with standard logic in tasks where it is appropriate, it seems odd to generalise such an account to situations where it is not. Nevertheless, it must be conceded that this is an empirical issue. People *may* treat everyday defeasible claims as exceptionless generalisations. This possibility is, however, sufficiently remote for us to consider it no further.

Second, the generality of mental logics may be restricted to explicit reasoning and it may be denied that they are intended to cover implicit inferential processes involved in commonsense reasoning. Intractability is therefore not an issue because of the small premise sets involved. This proposal of course explicitly denies that mental logics can satisfy the generalisation assumption. Moreover, it may not save the mental logic account from intractability problems. We suggested earlier that it is highly unlikely that standard monotonic inference is generalised to everyday defeasible inference. We now argue that the converse is far more plausible: that explicit reasoning may be influenced by defeasible inferential processes. If this is the case, then explanations of human inferential behaviour, even on explicit reasoning tasks, will have to address the tractability problems we have raised.

The proposal that explicit reasoning may be influenced by defeasible inferential processes derives from recent empirical work on conditional reasoning. It would appear that even in laboratory tasks conditional sentences may be interpreted as default rules (Oaksford, Chater, & Stenning, 1990). Byrne (1989) and Cummins, Lubart, Alksnis, and Rist (1991) have shown that background information derived from stored world knowledge can affect inferential performance (see also Markovits, 1984, 1985). Specifically they have shown that the inferences that are permitted by a conditional statement are influenced by *additional antecedents*. For example:

(1)   If the key is turned the car starts.
(a)   Additional Antecedent: The points are welded.

(1) could be used to predict that the car will start if the key is turned. This is an inference by modus ponens. However, this inference can be *defeated* when information about an additional antecedent (a) is explicitly provided (Byrne, 1989). Moreover, confidence in this inference is reduced for rules that possess many alternative antecedents even when this information is left implicit (Cummins et al., 1991). In these studies additional antecedents were also found to affect inferences by modus tollens. If the car does not start, it could be inferred that the key was not turned, unless, of course, the points were welded. Modus tollens is *defeated* when information about an alternative antecedent is explicitly provided (Byrne, 1989) and confidence in it is reduced for rules that possess many alternative antecedents even when this information is left implicit (Cummins et al., 1991).

The rules employed in these laboratory tasks are being treated as default rules. Other evidence indicates that even abstract rules may be treated in this way. In conditional inference tasks (Taplin, 1971; Taplin & Staudenmayer, 1973) and Wason's (1966) selection task, subjects typically refrain from either drawing inferences that accord with modus tollens or from adopting the strategy of falsification that is sanctioned by modus tollens. This can be at least partially explained if it were a general default assumption that all rules are default rules. If this were the case, then modus tollens may be suppressed because the rules are treated as defeasible, just as in Byrne (1989) and Cummins et al. (1991).[4]

In sum, it seems likely that conditionals employed in explicit reasoning tasks are treated as default rules. Restricting the applicability of mental logic approaches to explicit reasoning does not, therefore, avoid the problems of computational intractability.

The influence of default rules on people's reasoning would appear to have been dismissed by mental logicians as interferring pragmatic or performance factors (Braine, Reiser, & Rumain, 1984; Rumain, Connell, & Braine, 1983). This is in marked contrast to the reaction of logicians and AI researchers. These researchers have almost uniformly abandoned restrictions on what is deducible to the monotonic case and have been exploring non-monotonic logics to capture just the phenomenon their mental counterparts dismiss (see, for example, the collection edited by Ginsberg, 1987). The intuition behind this reaction seems to be that unless logical methods can be applied to these cases then most interesting inferences may be beyond the scope of logical inquiry. Logical inquiry may proceed divorced from the requirement to provide computationally tractable inference regimes. Most AI applications and the cognitive science of human reasoning cannot, however, avoid these problems.

In conclusion, providing a viable theory of human inference must resolve the issue of intractability. Unfortunately a solution does not appear to be forthcoming from within the formal, logical approach. This is not incompatible with continued logical inquiry into systems that can handle default reasoning. Further, the possibility cannot be dismissed that some formal notation may be devised which allows for more tractable implementations. However, the lack of practical success in devising a tractable logic for default inference suggests that this may be what Lakatos (1970) referred to as a degenerative research programme (Oaksford & Chater, 1991). In consequence, it seems unlikely that the mental logic approach will satisfy the generalisation assumption.

Mental Models

The apparent failure of logical accounts to generalise appropriately to everyday commonsense inference appears to add further weight to the mental modeller's claim that "there is no mental logic". On the mental models view, the syntactic formalisms adopted by the mental logician should be abandoned in favour of semantic methods of proof (e.g. Johnson-

Laird 1983; Johnson-Laird & Byrne, 1991). Such methods do not possess formal, syntactic rules of inference like modus ponens or modus tollens. Rather the semantic content of premises are directly manipulated in order to assess whether they validly imply a conclusion.

In this section we will introduce two interpretations of mental models. One we refer to as "logical mental models" the other as "memory-based mental models".

Logical Mental Models.   In recent accounts of mental models the claim that "there is no mental logic" has been tempered. For example, "the [mental] model theory is in no way incompatible with logic: it merely gives up the formal approach (rules of inference) for a semantic approach (search for counter-examples)" (Johnson-Laird & Byrne, 1991, p. 212). So the dispute is not about *whether* there is a mental logic, but about *how* it is implemented. On this interpretation *logical* mental models may be seen as an attempt to provide the notation, to which we alluded earlier, which will allow a tractable implementation of logic.

Mental models contrast with some semantic approaches to searching for counter-examples but share similarities with others. Truth tables and semantic tableaux (e.g. Hodges, 1975), which are unquestionably logical,[5] contrast with mental models because they are defined over standard propositional representations. In this respect mental models are more related to graphical proof methods such as Euler's circles and Venn diagrams. In these semantic proof procedures the operations that correspond to the steps of a sound logical derivation are defined over graphical representations of the domains of the quantifiers.

As Evans (1991) observes, both the mental logic approach and mental models are attempting to account for human deductive competence. In assessing the mental models approach, it would be helpful, therefore, if answers could be found to the same *meta-theoretical* questions concerning computational tractability that we asked of the mental logic approach. Certainly, on the *logical* mental models interpretation, answers to these questions should be possible. However, none as yet would appear to be available. This makes it difficult to assess mental models by the same standards we have applied to mental logics. This is a general problem. Although mental models are supposed to do the same job as a mental logic, there are no *meta-theoretical* proofs that this is the case. Nonetheless, in the absence of the appropriate proofs, we can speculate about how the answers to these questions may turn out.

The first tractability question we looked at with mental logics was the standard case of monotonic inference where we found that the general problem of deciding validity was NP-complete. While this is generally the case, the situation is even worse with standard "semantic approach[es]". At this point we must head off a possible confusion. The semantic methods we mentioned earlier, truth tables and semantic tableaux, are formal *proof* methods (Hintikka, 1985). In contrast, the intention behind the "semantic approach" of mental models is to use *model theory* as a basis for inference. As Hintikka (1985) observes, model theory, per se, provides no inferential mechanisms. However, the models could be exhaustively checked. For example, the sentence "Gordon is in his room" (indexed to a particular space–time location, say *now*) will be true if and only if Gordon is in his room now, i.e. Gordon actually being in his room now provides *a* model for this sentence. Of course, this is a contingent claim and therefore there are many models in which it is false. Nevertheless you could check this sentence is true by looking at the arrangement of objects about which the claim is made. Could you check the validity of a putative logical truth in a similar way? Logical validity is defined relative to *all* models, which are potentially infinite in number. Moreover, many of them will be infinite in size. Attempting to prove the logical validity of statements in this way would be impossible, at least for the finite minds of human beings. In sum, basing a psychological theory of inference on model theory looks even less promising than using formal syntactic methods.

Mental models theorists are well aware of this problem (Johnson-Laird, 1983) and argue explicitly that mental models may provide a way in which model theory may be developed into a tractable proof procedure. Mental models only deal with small sets of objects which represent *arbitrary exemplars* of the domains described in the premises. This is analogous to Bishop Berkeley's claim that reasoning regarding, say triangles, proceeds with an arbitrary exemplar of a triangle, rather than the, in his view, obscure Lockean notion of an abstract general idea. Providing no assumptions are introduced which depend on the properties of this particular triangle, e.g. that it is scalene rather than equilateral, then general conclusions concerning *all* triangles may be arrived at.

The introduction of arbitrary exemplars highlights the lack of an appropriate meta-theory for mental models. There is no exposition of the rules that guarantee that no illegitimate assumptions are introduced in a proof. This does not mean that any particular derivation using mental models has made such assumptions. Nonetheless, guaranteeing the validity of an argument depends on ensuring that in a particular derivation one *could* not make such assumptions. Hence explicit procedures to prevent this happening need to be provided. In their absence there is no guarantee (i.e. no proof) that the procedures for manipulating mental models preserve validity. That is, it is not known whether, relative to the standard interpretation of predicate logic, mental models theory provides a *sound* logical system.[6]

While soundness is unresolved, there are strong reasons to suppose that mental models theory is not *complete* with respect to standard logic:

although all inferences licensed by mental models may be licensed by standard logic (soundness), the converse is not the case. Other *graphical* methods are restricted in their *expressiveness* due to physical limitations on the notation. Venn diagrams for example, can only be used to represent arguments employing four or fewer *monadic* predicates, i.e. predicates of only one variable (Quine, 1959).[7] They therefore only capture a small subset of logic. Although mental models have been used to represent relations, i.e. predicates of more than one variable, there is no reason to suppose that mental models will not be subject to analogous limitations. If so then mental models will not provide a general implementation of logic.[8]

The employment of arbitrary exemplars is central to providing a tractable model-based proof procedure. However, there are no complexity results for the algorithms that manipulate mental models. Such demonstrations may be felt unnecessary, if, as with the mental logic approach, mental models theory were restricted to the explicit inferences involved in laboratory tasks. However, mental models theory has been generalised to other inferential modes, including implicit inference in text comprehension (Johnson-Laird, 1983). These inferences are defeasible (as we have seen), as are most everyday inferences people make.[9] Further, in many laboratory reasoning tasks, conditional sentences would appear to be interpreted as default rules (as already discussed). So in order to provide a general theory of inference, mental models must account for defeasibility.

Proposals for incorporating default reasoning into mental models (Johnson-Laird & Byrne, 1991) rely on incorporating default assumptions into the initial mental model of a set of premises. These assumptions will be recruited from prior world knowledge and may be undone in the process of changing mental models. The problem of consistency checking can be avoided because no search for counter-examples to these default assumptions need be initiated. This proposal does not resolve the problem of default inference. A generalisable theory of reasoning must address the problem of which default assumption(s) to incorporate in an initial representation. For example, suppose you are told "Tweety is a bird", you may incorporate the default assumption that *Tweety can fly* in your mental model because most birds can fly. However, it would be perverse to incorporate this assumption if you also knew that *Tweety is an ostrich*. To rule out perverse or *irrelevant* default assumptions requires checking the whole of world knowledge to ensure that any default assumption is consistent with what you already know (or some relevant subset of what you already know). This will involve an exhaustive search over the whole of world knowledge for a counter-example to a default assumption.

It could be argued that the problem of searching for counter-examples for default assumptions is part of theory of memory retrieval which mental models, as a theory of inference, is not obliged to provide. Three arguments seem to argue against this suggestion. First, as we have seen, in AI at least, these memory retrieval processes are treated as *inferential* processes and therefore need to be explained by a theory of inference. Second, the memory retrieval processes involve the search for counter-examples. This indicates that *in its own terms* they are exactly the kind of *inferential* processes for which mental models theory should provide an account. Third, such an argument could only succeed if mental models theory itself did not already rely heavily on such processes to explain the results of reasoning tasks.

In recent accounts (e.g. Johnson-Laird & Byrne, 1991) the explanation of various phenomena depends on the way in which an initial mental model of the premises is "fleshed-out". "Fleshing-out", for example, determines whether a disjunction is interpreted as exclusive or inclusive *or* (Johnson-Laird & Byrne, 1991, p. 45); whether a conditional is interpreted as material implication or equivalence (Johnson-Laird & Byrne, 1991, pp. 48–50) which in turn determines whether inferences by modus tollens will be performed; whether non-standard interpretations of the conditional are adopted (Johnson-Laird & Byrne, 1991, p. 67), including content effects whereby the relation between antecedent and consequent affects the interpretation (Johnson-Laird & Byrne, 1991, pp. 72–73); confirmation bias in Wason's selection task (Johnson-Laird & Byrne, 1991, p.80); and the search for counter-examples in syllogistic reasoning (Johnson-Laird & Byrne, 1991, p. 119). Fleshing-out depends on accessing world knowledge. Moreover, the explanatory burden placed on fleshing-out demands that mental models theory account for the processes involved. In consequence it is reasonable to expect mental models theory to provide an account of how relevant defaults are also retrieved from world knowledge. As this issue is not addressed it seems unlikely that logical mental models can satisfy the generalisation assumption.

However, the processes of fleshing-out may suggest another interpretation of mental models which we briefly present before closing this section.

Memory-based Mental Models. The explanatory burden placed on fleshing-out suggests that the memory retrieval processes involved may be primarily responsible for mental model construction and manipulation. The representations that appear in, for example, Johnson-Laird and Byrne (1991) may be better regarded as the *products* of processes in which those representations are not explicitly involved. In other words they are the "appearance[s] before the footlights of consciousness" (James, 1890/1950) of processes that are not defined over those representations themselves. This contrasts with logical mental models where the processes that transform one model into another *are* defined over the representations that appear on the pages of, for example, Johnson-Laird and Byrne (1991).

Memory-based mental models appear to accord with an earlier thread in mental models theory:

> Like most everyday problems that call for reasoning, the explicit premises leave most of the relevant information unstated. Indeed, *the real business of reasoning in these cases is to determine the relevant factors and possibilities*, and it therefore depends on knowledge of the specific domain. Hence the construction of putative counterexamples calls for an active exercise of memory and interpretation rather than formal derivation of one expression from others. (Johnson-Laird, 1986, p. 45).

On a memory-based mental models position the "active exercise of memory and interpretation" would represent the heart of all inferential processes. Moreover, existing accounts of mental models could be interpreted as specifying the intended outputs of these processes given certain inputs. In this respect mental models theory could therefore be expected to provide a valuable source of constraint on a future memory-based theory of reasoning. We will return to this interpretation of mental models later on.

Summary.   Recent accounts of mental models theory appear to favour an interpretation in terms of a graphical, semantic proof procedure. On this interpretation, mental models provides an alternative notation for implementing logic in the mind. This invites a variety of *meta-theoretic* questions which need to be answered to assess the adequacy of *logical* mental models as a general, tractable, implementation of logic. Unfortunately answers to these questions are unavailable. Further, existing proposals for handling default inference are inadequate. Taken together these considerations argue for a Scots verdict of "not proven" on *logical* mental models. However, the processes of fleshing-out indicate that memory-based mental models, while less articulated, may act as a valuable source of constraint on a memory-based theory of inference.

Pragmatic Reasoning Schema Theory

Pragmatic reasoning schema theory emphasises the role of domain-specific knowledge in reasoning tasks (Cheng & Holyoak, 1985; Cosmides, 1989). Cheng and Holyoak (1985) suggest that people possess *pragmatic reasoning schemas*, which embody rules specific to various domains such as permissions, causation, and so on. Permission schema are invoked in explaining the results from some thematic versions of Wason's selection task where the rule determines whether or not some action may be taken. Cheng and Holyoak (1985) argue that the rules embodied in a permission schema match the inferences licensed by standard logic, thus explaining the facilitatory effect of these materials. Similarly, Cosmides (1989) appeals to domain-specific knowledge of "social contracts" to explain the same data (but see Cheng & Holyoak, 1989, for a critique). Although Cosmides' work on social contracts is important, it is only the postulation of data-structures specific to particular domains that will concern us.

We have frequently remarked that if the domains over which the search for counter-examples were suitably constrained, then exhaustive searches may be feasible. However, there are two reasons for suspecting that schema-theoretic or domain-specific approaches in general will not prove adequate.

First, default reasoning is about how beliefs are appropriately updated in response to new information (Harman, 1986). Within philosophy the processes involved have typically been discussed under the heading of confirmation theory (Fodor, 1983). In arguing that confirmation, and hence default reasoning, is subject to the frame problem, Fodor observes that confirmation is characteristically *isotropic*:

> By saying that confirmation is isotropic, I mean that the facts relevant to the confirmation of a scientific hypothesis may be drawn from anywhere in the field of previously established empirical (or, of course, demonstrative) truths. Crudely: everything that the scientist knows is, in principle, relevant to determining what else he ought to believe. (Fodor, 1983, p. 105)

Domain specificity can assist with intractability only if isotropy is abandoned. If default reasoning is isotropic, then placing rigorous boundaries on relevant information would be a move in exactly the wrong direction. A knowledge organisation that excluded the possibility of isotropy would be hopelessly inflexible. Although cross-referencing schemata is a possibility, as Fodor (1983, p.117) points out: "an issue in the logic of confirmation ... [becomes] ... an issue in the theory of executive control (a change which there is, by the way, no reason to assume is for the better)."

A second reason to suspect that domain-specific approaches are inadequate concerns the lack of any general principles concerning how an appropriate compartmentalisation of knowledge is to be achieved. Such general principles are required as otherwise how knowledge is organised into discrete compartments from the flux of information that an organism receives in interacting with its environment remains opaque (Oaksford & Chater, 1991). Although it may be legitimate to appeal to compartmentalisation, once appealed to, an account of how it is achieved must be supplied. Pragmatic reasoning schema theory does not explicitly address this issue. In consequence it is unlikely that this theory can satisfy the generalisation assumption.

Heuristic Approaches

The heuristic approach (Evans, 1983b, 1984, 1989) is that most concerned with the issue of cognitive limitations (Evans, 1983a). In computer science the use of heuristics may render a computationally intractable problem manageable. Tractable, approximate solutions may be found for many problem instances by employing the generally intractable algorithm with an heuristic (Horowitz & Sahni, 1978). Accuracy is traded for speed. In this section we will observe that the current heuristic approach does not address the intractability problems we have raised: the heuristics proposed are more often motivated by appeal to *pragmatic* rather than *processing* factors. We will suggest, however, that with some minor reinterpretation, one heuristic proposed by Evans (1983b) may address the intractability issue. None-theless, we will conclude that supplementing generally intractable algo-rithms with heuristics is unlikely to provide a general solution to the problem of intractability.

The *not*-heuristic (Evans, 1983b, 1984, 1989) is motivated by Wason's (1965) proposal that negations are typically used to deny presuppositions. For example "I did *not* go for a walk" denies the presupposition that you went for a walk. The topic of this sentence—what the sentence is about—is walking and not any of the things I could have done while not walking. On the basis of this example it was proposed that the language-understanding mechanism embodies a *not*-heuristic (Evans, 1983b). This heuristic treats information about, for example, what you did while *not* walking as irrele-vant. Attention is therefore focused only on the named values. More recently this heuristic has been regarded as a manifestation of a general bias towards positive information, i.e. information about what something is rather than what it is not (Evans, 1989; see also Oaksford & Stenning, 1992).

Such a general preference for positive information may be better moti-vated by processing rather than pragmatic considerations. A general posi-tivity bias may be one aspect of providing a tractable knowledge base. The frame problem was first noticed in reasoning about change. In a dynamic representation, the consequences of something changing had to include all the things that did *not* change. For example, along with the information that *if your coffee cup is knocked over your carpet gets wet*, all the information about what does not happen when your coffee cup is knocked over needs to be encoded. For example, that the window does not open, the lights do not switch off, and so on. There is a potentially infinite list of things that do not happen as a consequence of knocking your coffee cup to the floor, each of which would have to be explicitly represented. However, the *negation-as-failure* procedure obviates the need to represent all this information (Hogger, 1984).[10] If, from the current contents of the database, it cannot be proved that the window opens, then it is assumed that the window does not open. The upshot is that in a logic programme *no* negative information is stored (Hogger, 1984). This represents a prime case of positivity bias in the service of tractability.

So at least one aspect of the current heuristic approach could address the tractability issues we have discussed. However, as Evans (1991) says, the heuristic approach is *not* an approach to human reasoning in its own right. It needs to be married to a particular theory of competence. Such an approach is unlikely to prove adequate, however. The problem is that:

> The use of heuristics in an existing algorithm may enable it to quickly solve a large instance of a problem provided the heuristic "works" on that instance ... A heuristic, however, does not "work" equally effectively on all problem instances. Exponential time algorithms, even coupled with heuristics will still show exponential behaviour on some set of inputs. (Horowitz & Sahni, 1978)

There has been no attempt to articulate the sets of heuristics that would be needed to provide generally tractable inference regimes either within the heuristic approach or in AI knowledge representation. Hence, Evans (1991) may well be right that one way to proceed is to marry the heuristic approach to one or other of the theories that explicitly address the competence issue. However, it seems doubtful that an appropriate set of heuristics will be forthcoming to supplement these theories (Oaksford & Chater, 1991).

Default reasoning in particular presents new problems for the heuristic approach. Existing accounts of default reasoning fail to arrive at intuitively acceptable conclusions (McDermott, 1986). Quite often the only conclusion available is of the form $p \lor not\text{-}p$, i.e. a logical truth (Oaksford & Chater, 1991). This is particularly uninformative. It has been suggested that one way to resolve this problem is by appeal to various heuristics. These heuristics may also assist with tractability by cutting down the number of possibilities that need to be considered. The disjunction here is all that can often be concluded because each default rule may lead to a different possible conclusion. Logically the only conclusion that can be drawn therefore is their disjunction. However, if one default rule can be given preference, then all these possibilities need not be computed (see Oaksford & Chater, 1991).[11] Again, however, it is not at all clear that any of the heuristics proposed resolve this issue appropriately for all instances of a problem (Loui, 1987). In sum, it seems unlikely that an appropriate set of heuristics will be forthcoming to solve the problem of computational intractability. In consequence the heuristic approach is unlikely to satisfy the generalisation assumption.

Summary. In this section we have surveyed existing theories of reasoning with respect to their ability to appropriately generalise to everyday commonsense reasoning. The mental logic approach was perhaps the least promising in this respect. This is largely because it is sufficiently well articulated for the relevant meta-theoretic results to be available. This was in contrast to the logical mental models approach. Although there is a possibility that arbitrary exemplars may provide for a tractable model based inference regime, the absence of the relevant meta-theoretic results means that it is impossible to decide one way or the other. However, when it comes to default reasoning the mental models approach is demonstrably inadequate: the real problem is avoided. The possibility remains that memory-based mental models may nonetheless be explained as emergent properties of a theory of memory retrieval (this possibility is discussed later). The two theories perhaps most suited to addressing the tractability issue, pragmatic reasoning schema theory and the heuristic approach, were equally unpromising. Without an account of how compartmentalisation is achieved, schema-theoretic approaches *presuppose* a solution, they do not provide one. It moreover seems unlikely that an appropriate set of heuristics can be specified to resolve the intractability problem.

Discussion

There are two broad areas that require further discussion in the light of the arguments we have described. Both concern the issue of rationality. First, we will discuss philosophical implications for human rationality. Second, we will discuss the implications for psychological theories concerned to build rational mechanisms (Fodor, 1987).

Rationality

In this section we will discuss two issues, the implications of reasoning data for human rationality, and the possible charge that abandoning rule-based theories leads to relativism.

The intractability results we have reported indicate that a bounded rationality assumption should be made. This has the consequence that the empirically observed deviations from normative theories could not bring human rationality into question. The complexity results we have discussed indicate that people *could not* generally be using the normative strategy. It is only possible to condemn people as irrational for not using a particular strategy if they *could* use it. To think otherwise, would be like condemning us because we cannot breathe underwater even though we do not possess gills. It could be argued, however, that for laboratory tasks involving just a few premises, complexity issues are not a concern. We have partly replied to this response earlier where we observed that if just one rule is interpreted as a default rule a feasible real-time inference is doubtful. It also seems highly unlikely that people have been endowed with all the logical machinery to solve spontaneously just those tasks small enough not to tax their limited resources. If nothing else this is because the empirical data appear to indicate that they just so happen not to use that machinery! It seems far more parsimonious to suggest that the strategy that is used in everyday reasoning contexts is generalised to laboratory tasks.

It would be irrational to demand that people employ strategies that they are incapable of using. However, one attractive feature of rule-based theories is that they come with their own warrant of rationality as it were. Brown (1988, p. 17) argues that "[on] our classical conception of rationality ... the rationality of any conclusion is determined by whether it conforms to the appropriate rules." If rule-based theories are abandoned there may be no guarantee that the strategies that replace them are rational: as they will not be rule-based, they will not carry their own warrant of rationality. This, moreover, may be seen as the first step on the slippery slope towards *relativism*, i.e. the view that there are no universal principles of rationality.

Johnson-Laird and Byrne (1991) consider the same problem and conclude that rather than conformity to rules, the search for counter-examples provides a universal principle of rationality. However, this provides neither a necessary nor a sufficient condition for rational judgement. It is not necessary because it is not a principle universally adhered to in scientific practice which provides our paradigm case of rational activity (Brown, 1988). Within periods of normal science (Kuhn, 1962), scientists explicitly refuse to allow core theoretical principles to be subject to refutation. The search for counter-examples is also not a sufficient criterion for rational judgement. Continuing to search for counter-examples indefinitely is not rational when trying to reach a decision in real-time.

However, the idea that the search for counter-examples provides a universal criterion of rationality need not be wholly abandoned. It will, however, need to be supplemented by a theory of *judgement*: "Judgement is the ability to evaluate a situation, assess evidence, and come to a reasonable decision without following rules" (Brown, 1988, p. 137). It is a matter of judgement, for example, when and if counter-examples are allowed to falsify a core theoretical principle, or when the search for counter-examples has been sufficiently exhaustive. Quite frequently we appeal to experts, who have a wealth of experience and knowledge in order to make these judgements. A good example is the peer review system. There is no algorithm for determining whether an experimenter has made sufficient attempts to dismiss alternative explanations of a hypothesis. In consequence it is left to a researcher's peers to decide whether she/he has adequately dealt with the *relevant* possibilities. A further example is provided by the legal concept of *precedent*. In certain cases a defence lawyer will seek to find a case in which the facts are as similar as possible and where a not-guilty verdict was returned. Equally, the prosecution may seek a similar case where a guilty verdict was returned. Both defence and prosecution are searching for counter-examples to each other's arguments that on the basis of the evidence the defendant should (or should not) be convicted. Judgement enters into the decision process, in two ways. First, the judge of the present case must decide whether the cases are similar in the *relevant* respects. Second, the whole concept of precedent relies on allowing previous judgements to influence subsequent judgements.

In sum, the claim that we could not employ rule-based theories could lead to relativism. The search for counter-examples per se is an inadequate response to this charge. The examples we adduced indicate that the search for counter-examples must be supplemented by a theory of judgement before anything like a universal principle is available.

Rational Mechanisms

Rule-based systems operating over formal symbolic representations have the advantage that they possess a transparent semantics which allows us to see how mental representations can be causally efficacious in virtue of their meaning (Fodor, 1987). If we abandon rule-based theories do we also abandon the ability to provide causal, mechanistic explanations of the way representational mental states mediate behaviour? Part of an answer to this question has already been provided. If the concept of what it is to be rational changes, then the form that a theory of rational mechanism must take may also change. We now consider what kinds of mechanism may be consistent with our developing conception of rationality. We will first draw on an analogy with Kahneman and Tverksy's work on risky decision making, and then propose that connectionist systems may provide alternative rational mechanisms.

In response to similar complexity results for Bayesian inference, Tversky and Kahneman (1974) proposed a qualitatively different theory to explain risky decision making in which the normative theory was not retained in any form. The problem of deriving probability estimates was radically reconceived largely in terms of the processes of memory retrieval. Their *heuristic* approach can be contrasted with the heuristic approach in theories of reasoning. As we mentioned earlier, within reasoning theory, heuristics are regarded as supplements to a theory of competence (Evans, 1991). However, in Kahneman and Tversky's approach various memory-based heuristics are regarded as wholesale replacements for the competence theory. We suggest that, confronted with similar intractability problems, reasoning theorists should adopt the same response.

What could represent an analogous reconceptualisation of reasoning mechanisms? Levesque (1988) has suggested that connectionism may represent one strategy in the attempt to develop plausible cognitive mechanisms for inference. Rumelhart, Smolensky, McClelland, and Hinton (1986) and Rumelhart (1989) have also suggested that a predictive neural network may form the basis of people's reasoning abilities. What kind of reconceptualisation of reasoning does this involve?

Inference is the dynamics of cognition. In classical approaches (Chater & Oaksford, 1990; Fodor & Pylyshyn, 1988) inference takes static symbolic representations and turns them to useful work, predicting the environment, explaining an experiment, drawing up a plan of action, and so on. Formal inference over language-like representations has seemed the only way in which meaning and mechanism could combine (Fodor, 1987). Connectionism may offer a very different picture of how to achieve the marriage between mechanism and meaning. Logic provides a dynamics for representations of a particular type: atomic symbolic representations usually map one to one onto our commonsense classification of the world. Connectionism postulates distributed representations of a very different kind in which stable patterns of features represent items in that classification. The dynamics of the system, moreover, are defined at the featural level and owe more to statistical mechanics than to logic. Nevertheless it may be that these representations and the dynamics that transforms one such representation into another can form the basis of a theory of inference.

Let us consider the problem at a higher level of abstraction. Inference leads us from one interpreted mental state to another. The heart of the problem is how to get mental states to track states of the world systematically or, in other words, how to get the dynamics of cognition to "hook up" to the dynamics of the world (Churchland & Churchland, 1983). We see no reason, a priori, why connectionist systems cannot also perform this function.

While there are serious problems for a connectionist theory of inference, there may also be advantages. It may be compatible, for example, with the second interpretation of mental models we offered earlier (Rumelhart, 1989). Given a set of inputs, a network settles on an interpretation that least violates the constraints embodied in its weighted connections between units. These weighted connections embody the network's knowledge of a domain. One way of characterising such a relaxation search, is that prior to input clamping all the knowledge that is embodied in the network is potentially relevant to interpreting the input. However, as the net relaxes into an interpretation only those items most relevant will remain on. The stable state arrived at can be regarded as the initial "mental model" of the input. This model may embody default assumptions. For example, in the "on-line" schema model (Rumelhart et al., 1986), a constraint satisfaction network embodied information about prototypical rooms. If the bath unit was clamped on then units like toilet, toothbrush, and so on would come on as default values. In the search for counter-examples intermediate mental models may be generated by selectively clamping off units and allowing the net to settle into a new stable state (Rumelhart, 1989).

Further, this mode of operation seems to capture something of what it means to make a *judgement*. As we said earlier, determining whether relevant counter-examples have been exhausted is a matter of judgement based on what you know. In a simple connectionist system all that it knows (all its synaptic weights) contributes to determining what is relevant to interpreting current inputs. The example of precedent also indicates that counter-examples to *novel* situations may be sought by reference to *similar* situations. The partial pattern-matching capabilities of networks make them good candidates for implementing the processes responsible.[12]

The burden of complexity may also be located in the right place. Within connectionist systems learning is the computationally expensive process. Once learnt, however, an inference over the representations embodied in the network is effortless. In contrast, in classical systems inference is computationally expensive while learning is an issue rarely addressed. This may seem like just trading one complexity problem for another. However, the connectionist system at least mirrors the difficulty people actually appear to encounter with learning and inference.

There are serious problems, however. Current network dynamics are insufficiently articulated to provide an account of the productivity of language and thinking (Fodor & Pylyshyn, 1988). In particular, thinking is not a purely predictive process that is triggered by external events. Indeed, in thinking, people appear able to "un-hook" the dynamics of cognition from the dynamics of the world, enabling them to step out of real-time. This will require networks to have their own intrinsic dynamics to allow thoughts to chain together in the absence of provoking stimuli. While posing a serious problem there is, nonetheless, a great deal of work going on in this area (Chater, 1989; Elman, 1988; Jordan, 1986; Oaksford & Brown, 1994; Rohwer, 1990; Shastri & Ajjanagadde, 1993). We see no reason to be pessimistic about its outcome and the consequent prospects for a connectionist theory of inference.

CONCLUSIONS

We have argued that an adequate theory of reasoning must be able to "scale up" to deal with everyday defeasible inferences in real-time. We observed that no contemporary theory of reasoning provided a tractable account of everyday inference and that in consequence none of these theories was likely to be psychologically real. Concentration on limited laboratory tasks would appear to have led to the development of theories of dubious ecological validity. Further, it would appear more likely that people "scale down" their everyday strategies to deal with laboratory tasks and that this is the source of the systematic biases observed in human reasoning. Although these arguments do not bring human rationality into question, they do demand a reconceptualisation of appropriate mechanisms for inference. We suggested that connectionist systems may be appropriate, which appeared consistent with memory-based mental models and the requirements of a theory of judgement.

In conclusion, empirical research into human reasoning may need to be more ecologically valid. The boundaries of *real inference* need to be mapped out: how do people deal with defeasible knowledge, how do they make relevance judgements, and how does background information (Cummins et al., 1991; Byrne, 1989) interact with reasoning processes? Answers to these questions could be pursued on two fronts. First the complexification of the laboratory situation. Most reasoning tasks are still pencil-and-paper exercises (although, see Mynatt, Doherty, & Tweney, 1977, for example). In contrast the computer game may offer the prospect of engaging subjects in novel dynamic environments over which the experimenter has control. In such environments, context-sensitive rules, varying difficulties of obtaining information, and differing utilities for correct inference can be arranged and their consequences for behaviour mapped out. Second, more direct analyses of real inferential settings such as the court room and science itself need to be conducted (e.g. Tukey, 1986; Tweney, 1985). Explaining the inferential processes that obtain in such real-world settings must be the ultimate goal of a psychological theory of reasoning.

NOTES

1. It is important to be clear about whose inferential behaviour reasoning theorists are attempting to explain. Throughout this chapter it is assumed to be the spontaneous, unassisted, inferential performance of logically untutored subjects. By "spontaneous and unassisted" we mean that the subjects are not allowed to use aids such as pencil, paper, or computer to make calculations, nor are they able to consult with friends or experts. By "logically untutored" we mean that subjects should have no explicit formal logical training. In other words reasoning theorists are attempting to explain the reasoning abilities that people possess solely by virtue of genetic endowment and general education.

2. Natural deduction systems contain no axioms and all inferences are drawn by the application of various inference rule schemata, e.g. p OR q, not-p $\models$ q (where "$\models$" can be informally glossed as "therefore").

3. This applies equally well to semantic proof procedures, such as truth tables and semantic tableaux as to syntactic procedures such as axioms or natural deduction systems.

4. This would appear to predict that inferences by modus ponens should also be suppressed in these tasks, which is not the case.

5. We should also note that under standard interpretations, the search for counter-examples does not distinguish syntactic from semantic approaches. All proof procedures are regarded as "abortive counter-model constructions" (Beth, 1955; Hintikka, 1955; see also Hintikka, 1985).

6. There are *logical* systems that eliminate quantifiers, e.g. combinatory logic (see Curry & Feys, 1958) and Fine's (1985) theory of arbitrary objects. Perhaps a translation between these systems and mental models may provide the desired results.

7. This is simply due to the inability to draw more than four overlapping two-dimensional shapes such that all possible relationships between them are represented.

8. This is far less important than *soundness*. However, if mental models theory is to avoid the charge of ad hoc extension to deal with new phenomena, then some account of expressiveness must be provided. Otherwise there can be little confidence that the notation is sufficiently well understood to perform the functions demanded of it.

9. At the beginning of Johnson-Laird and Byrne (1991) the example of a classic piece of default reasoning by Sherlock Holmes is provided, which eloquently illustrates this point.

10. The cost is that logical negation is not fully implemented in such a database.

11. These possibilities are known as different *extensions* of a *default theory*. A default theory is simply a collection of axioms, including at least one default rule, which describes the behaviour of particular domain (see Chapter 4 for discussion).

12. It also suggests that sensible reasoning in novel domains does not demand an abstract inferential competence sensitive to the logical form of arguments. Just as with precedent, old judgements are brought to bear on new problems.

CHAPTER SEVEN

Bounded Rationality in Taking Risks and Drawing Inferences

INTRODUCTION

Chapter 6 concentrated on bounded rationality and theories of deductive reasoning. However, the issue of bounded rationality applies and has been influential in other reasoning domains. Specifically, Simon's ideas about bounded rationality have had a profound impact on the development of psychological theories of human probabilistic reasoning and decision making (although see Lopes, 1992, for arguments that Simon's influence on some of this work was limited). This chapter provides a discussion of the concept of "bounded rationality" as it applies to the theses advanced by two leading reasoning researchers in the inaugural issue of the journal *Theory and Psychology*. Lola Lopes works on human decision making, and Jonathan Evans works on human deductive inference.

This chapter generalises the arguments developed in Chapter 6 to apply both to probabilistic and deductive reasoning. We argue that Lopes' (1991) assessment of the irrationalist consequences of Tversky and Kahneman's (1974) work on heuristics and biases in probabilistic reasoning is premature because bounded rationality implies that people *could not* employ optimal strategies. Considerations of bounded rationality also provide additional criteria by which to judge the theories of deductive reasoning discussed by Evans (1991). Judged by this criterion, theories the goal of which is to explain logically competent performance are inadequate (Oaksford & Chater, 1991). Thus Evans' assessment of the state of current theories of reasoning requires revision.

BOUNDED RATIONALITY IN TAKING RISKS AND DRAWING INFERENCES

This commentary is on two articles that appeared in *Theory & Psychology*, volume 1(1), by Lola Lopes (1991) and Jonathan Evans (1991). Our reasons for offering a joint commentary is that in both papers an issue appears to be overlooked which has potentially serious consequences for the theses each author was concerned to advance. We begin with the article by Lopes.

Heuristics and Biases

Lopes (1991) criticises work in the "heuristics and biases" tradition because the rhetorical emphasis of the papers reporting this work has led to an overestimation of human irrationality. The original papers (Kahneman & Tversky, 1972, 1973; Tversky & Kahneman, 1971, 1973), Lopes argues, were about the *processes* involved in spontaneous judgements in risky decision making: were suboptimal heuristics being employed or were optimal algorithmic procedures being used? Lopes observes that in the summary article on this early work by Tversky and Kahneman (1974) in *Science*, the emphasis changes from process to cognitive *bias*. Rather than discuss the successes of the quick and dirty heuristics they discovered, Tversky and Kahneman (1974) dealt at length with the lapses from optimal rationality to which the use of such heuristics may lead. As Lopes observes, this emphasis set the tone for much subsequent discussion leading to possibly premature conclusions about the irrationality of human decision-making and reasoning processes.

Interpreting the influence of a body of work may often depend upon the perspective adopted. From the perspective of computational modelling there is an interpretation of the heuristics and biases literature which fails to lead to any particularly dire conclusions for human rationality. Kahneman and Tversky were working within the framework of "bounded rationality" which they attribute to Jerome Bruner and Herb Simon (see the Preface to Kahneman, Slovic & Tversky, 1982). The nature of these bounds can best be understood by taking into account the constraints placed on cognitive processes by the claim that they are computational processes. A major constraint is that these processes must be capable of utilisation within the time scale at which normal human judgements are made. In computer science these issues are discussed under the heading of *computational complexity theory* (see, for example, Garey & Johnson, 1979). Some computational processes are more complex than others requiring more computational resources in terms of memory capacity and operations performed. Measures of complexity are expressed as a mathematical function relating the length of an input (n)—very roughly the amount of information which the process must take into account—and the amount of computational resources consumed. Any process that requires exponentially increasing resources (i.e. increasing at a rate of 2^n, or worse) is regarded as computationally intractable. That is, for some n this process may not provide an answer in our lifetimes if at all.

Issues of computational complexity have cropped up quite frequently in the history of cognitive psychology and artificial intelligence, perhaps most notably in vision research. Early work on bottom-up object recognition of blocks worlds resulted in the notorious combinatorial explosion (see McArthur, 1982, for a review, and Tsotsos, 1990, for a more recent discussion of complexity issues in vision research). In the research into risky decision making, it was realised very early that complexity issues were relevant. Bayesian inference makes exponentially increasing demands on computational resources even for problems involving very moderate amounts of information. A salutary example is provided by the discussion of an application of Bayesian inference to medical diagnosis problems involving multiple symptoms in Charniak and McDermott's (1985) introduction to Artificial Intelligence. Diagnoses involving just two symptoms, together with some reasonable assumptions concerning the numbers of diseases and symptoms a physician may know about, require upwards of 10^9 numbers to be stored in memory. As typical diagnoses may work on upwards of 30 symptoms, even if every *connection* in the human brain were encoding a digit, its capacity would nonetheless be exceeded.

Spontaneous, real-world, risky decisions, even of moderate complexity are not being made using Bayesian inference processes because they *could not* be. As the mind–brain is a limited information processor the processes of risky decision making cannot be based upon optimal, algorithmic procedures. This means that the only rationality to which we can aspire, as individual decision makers, is one bounded by our limited computational resources. In consequence, the observation that we do not behave in accordance with Bayes' theorem could not impugn our rationality. Our rationality could only be questioned if we were capable of using the optimal strategy but failed to do so. Thinking otherwise is akin to condemning us because we do not fly even though we do not possess wings.

Three further issues deserve mention. First, Lopes and we are concerned only with individual decision making, without pencil, paper (computer) or friends as it were. The additional resources available in groups and societies means that decision making can transcend the limitations of the individual. The existence of Bayes' theorem is a testament to the collective rationality of a culture embodied in modern mathematics. Second, it could be argued that the laboratory tasks employed by Kahneman and Tversky would have permitted the use of the normative strategy because the amount of information (n) was kept well within manageable bounds. Thus the fact that the heuristics were still employed may have some negative implications for human rationality. However, with no schooling in statistics, the only strategy available is to generalise those strategies normally employed in more complex settings to the laboratory task. Restricting the information could only encourage the use of Bayes' theorem if it had been previously learned. Third, Lopes adduces evidence (Gigerenzer, Hell, & Blank, 1988) that when some problems are presented more realistically subjects do take account of prior probabilities in accordance with Bayes' theorem. From the perspective of bounded rationality, of course, it is such apparent displays of competence that create a problem as (i) they do not cohere immediately with the heuristic approach, and (ii) they *could not* be a product of a general, unlearned competence with Bayes' theorem.

In summary, considerations of bounded rationality temper the irrationalist consequences of the work on heuristics and biases. Only by ignoring bounded rationality could the rhetoric of Tversky and Kahneman (1974) be interpreted as leading to the dire conclusions drawn by Lopes in her article. Given the unjustifiable presumptions of normative rationality, which were rife in the psychological literature at the time, the rhetorical bias of Tversky and Kahneman's summary article may have set just the right balance to provide a much needed corrective.

The Fragmented State of Reasoning Theories

The deductive reasoning literature reviewed by Jonathan Evans raises directly analogous issues concerning human rationality to those we have seen in the area of decision making under uncertainty. Evans' paper discusses the way that research into deductive reasoning has fragmented of late with different theories answering different questions raised by the data. He observes that there are three questions that need to be answered: the competence question—the fact that human subjects often successfully solve deductive reasoning problems; the bias question—the fact that subjects also make many systematic errors; the content and context question—the fact that the content and context of a problem can radically alter subjects' responses. The major theories in this area—mental logics, mental models, schema theories, and heuristic approaches—all tend to concentrate upon one question or the other, none providing a fully integrated account of all three. Evans does, however, provide criteria of theory preference—completeness, coherence, falsifiability, and parsimony—by which to judge reasoning theories, and seems to view mental models as scoring most highly on these criteria. Evans' paper is an important and laudatory attempt to get reasoning theorists to agree some common ground rules concerning the adequacy of their theories. However, an additional criterion of theory choice may place a very different complexion on the adequacy of current theoretical proposals.

Bounded rationality is not an issue that is frequently discussed in the deductive reasoning literature. However, issues of computational complexity may serve as a valuable additional criterion for choosing between reasoning theories in addition to the general criteria proposed by Evans, which are common to all areas of scientific inquiry. To the extent that issues of resource limitation are mentioned in the reasoning literature they are restricted to discussion of how our limited short-term memory capacity may lead to systematic errors in explicit reasoning tasks (Johnson-Laird, 1983). However, one reason why the deductive reasoning literature has been so prominent within cognitive psychology/science, is the assumption that the principles of human inference discovered in the investigation of explicit inference will *generalise* to provide accounts of all inferential processes. This is important because *qua* computational process, *all* cognitive processes can be viewed as inferential (Boolos & Jeffrey, 1980). We will call this the *Generalisation Assumption*. The generalisation assumption is, for example, embodied in the subtitle to Johnson-Laird's (1983) book *Mental models: Towards a cognitive science of language, inference and consciousness*. Without the generalisation assumption the study of deductive reasoning would warrant little more interest than, say, the psychology of doing crosswords.

In artificial intelligence, studying theories of inference and knowledge representation usually begins by examining their capabilities in *toy* domains. Toy domains are specially contrived micro-worlds about which very little needs to be assumed. There is, however, a long-standing problem with this approach. Theories of inference that are adequate in such domains (e.g. the inference engine in SHRDLU (Winograd, 1972)), tend to fail disastrously when they are *scaled up* to deal with real-world inferential problems involving more information (higher n). This is because they are generally computationally intractable. A directly analogous issue arises for psychological theories of reasoning designed to account for laboratory tasks but with pretensions to satisfy the generalisation assumption. *All* the theories that attempt to answer Evans' competence question hit computational intractability problems when scaled up to deal with real-world inferential problems (Oaksford & Chater, 1991). It is, moreover, a recent realisation that even in explicit reasoning tasks the range of information (n) taken into account in drawing an inference transcends that explicitly provided in the task. As Evans observes, Johnson-Laird and Byrne's (1991) "fleshing out" strategy involves the incorporation of more information, derived from prior world knowledge, to supplement that explicitly provided, as does the addition of implicit premises in a mental logic account. Oaksford and Chater (1991) point out that logics based on syntactic proof procedures, like those proposed in mental logic accounts, are computationally intractable in everyday inferential contexts. Moreover, semantic proof procedures, like mental models, are known to be *worse* in complexity theoretic terms than syntactic procedures. Hence the two major contenders to answer the competence question may not only fail to satisfy the generalisation assumption, to the extent that explicit inference relies upon "fleshing out", they may also be poor contenders as theories of laboratory reasoning tasks.

In summary, a bounded rationality assumption may also need to be made in theories of deductive reasoning. On analogy with Bayes' theorem in decision making under uncertainty, our ability to perform in accordance with logical dictates cannot be taken as evidence that we possess a general unlearned logical competence—*if*, by logical competence, we mean that we employ a logical system in our reasoning, be it syntactically *or* semantically realised. Again, in the general case, this is because we *could not* be using such a system and again, therefore, that we occasionally deviate from logicality could not impugn our rationality. As mentioned earlier, this means that Evans' competence question is the problematic one. Again it is reasonable to assume that whatever quick and dirty mechanisms we have evolved in order to resolve the complex inferential problems of everyday reasoning will also be generalised to the laboratory tasks studied by reasoning theorists. However, apart from Evans' own proposals concerning the use of heuristics in the interpretation of premises, we appear to remain profoundly ignorant of the nature of these mechanisms.

CHAPTER EIGHT

Logicism and Everyday Reasoning: Mental Models and Mental Logic

INTRODUCTION

In Chapters 5 to 7 we have argued that the defeasibility of everyday reasoning creates problems for most cognitive scientific approaches and, in particular, for theories in the psychology of reasoning. In this chapter we turn to two of our responses to counter-arguments to our position. The first section of this chapter (Mental Models and Defeasibility) is based on our response (Chater & Oaksford, 1993) to a paper by Alan Garnham (1993) directly arguing against our position presented in Chapters 4 and 5 from the perspective of mental models theory. The second section (Mental Logics and Defeasibility) is drawn from Oaksford and Chater (1995b) and responds to arguments often made by mental logicians (e.g. Politzer & Braine, 1991; Rips, 1994) to the effect that the human reasoning may not be defeasible because default rules are always false. They therefore claim that the apparent defeasibility of human inference is not to be explained by a theory of inference, but by pragmatic or performance factors. We argue that neither of these defences against the problems that we raised for logicist cognitive science is successful.

MENTAL MODELS AND DEFEASIBILITY

Alan Garnham (1993) has provided a lucid and thoughtful challenge to our arguments against logicist cognitive science (Oaksford & Chater, 1991; Chapters 4 and 5 in the present volume). He considers that many of our arguments are misdirected or fallacious, and that we draw entirely the wrong moral from the comparison of human reasoners and logic-based artificial reasoning systems. Some of Garnham's objections are due to a misreading of our argument against logicism. We first reiterate the structure of that argument and then show that many of Garnham's points are best read as supportive of our conclusions though critical of our presentation. Garnham's central point, that mental models theory supplies a distinct, and distinctly more promising alternative to logicist cognitive science, requires a more substantial treatment, however. We argue that mental models theory provides no defence against the twin difficulties of intractability and incompleteness* that we raised for logicism.

The Structure of Our Argument

Our argument ran as follows. Firstly, we characterised logicist cognitive science, the theoretical view of the nature of cognitive science expounded by Fodor and Pylyshyn (e.g. Fodor, 1975; Fodor & Pylyshyn, 1988; Pylyshyn, 1984). Roughly, logicism is the view that cognitive processes are proof-theoretic operations over internal logical formulae which can be interpreted in terms of our everyday ontology of tables, chairs, and so on. We took this view as a definite target at which to aim our arguments, rather than as representative of cognitive scientists at large; the degree to which our arguments carry over to variants of logicism is deferred until later in the chapter.

Secondly, we considered how such explanation might fare as an account of cognitive processes which involve knowledge-rich defeasible inference (see, for example, Note 1 of Chapter 4). The central processes (Fodor 1983) involved in commonsense reasoning are paradigm examples of knowledge-rich processing. To the extent that aspects of perception, language processing, and so on are also knowledge-rich, the same problems should apply.

We noted that the central processes involved in what may variously be thought of as belief revision, commonsense inference or everyday reasoning are a species of inference to the best explanation (Fodor, 1983). That is, given certain information, the reasoner must infer what fits best with, what best explains, and is explained by, that information. Inference to the best explanation is notoriously difficult to capture within the framework of deductive logic. For one thing, standard deductive validity entails that if the premises of an argument are true, then the conclusion must certainly also be true. This means that standard deductive logic is *monotonic*: if a conclusion follows deductively from a set of premises, it will follow from the conjunction of that set of premises with any other additional information. Yet in inference to the best explanation a hypothesis that seems plausible in the light of partial evidence will often seem implausible in the light of a fuller picture. That is, such inference is invariably tentative rather than certain and will be *non-monotonic*.

This mismatch poses a serious problem for logicism: if cognitive processes are proof-theoretic, and proof theory standardly can only handle monotonic deductive reasoning, how can the non-demonstrative inferences which appear to be cognitively ubiquitous be explained? We noted that this dilemma had a historical correlate in the unsuccessful attempts of the logical positivists to cast inference to the best explanation in science in a deductive mould, and suggested that a logicist account of central processes would be likely to fare no better. The argument could have stopped here: to the extent that commonsense and scientific inference are analogous, it should be equally easy (or difficult) to model either by proof-theoretic methods. And it is universally acknowledged in the philosophy of science that scientific inference cannot be understood in this way (Goodman, 1983/1954; see also Holland et al., 1986; Thagard, 1988). Rather than rely solely on this argument by analogy, we turned to a practical test of the feasibility of logicism: the attempt to model everyday reasoning within artificial intelligence.

Third, then, we considered logicist work on building computational models of aspects of commonsense inference. The volume of such work is vast, and the range of techniques employed is also great (see, for example, the collection edited by Ginsberg, 1987). Rather than attempt a survey, we focused on a particular approach, which is closest to the spirit of logicism, is dominant within artificial intelligence, and to which other approaches are very intimately related (Hanks & McDermott, 1985, 1986; Shoam, 1987, 1988). This approach involves developing *non-monotonic* logics, in which the addition of premises can lead to the withdrawal of conclusions, to account for the revisability of everyday reasoning. Thus, in principle at least, proof theory over non-monotonic logics may be able to reconcile logicism with the defeasible character of inference in central processes. We then raised two serious and apparently fatal problems with the enterprise. Firstly, non-monotonic logics are generally not able to capture plausible but revisable everyday inferences. The conclusions licensed by such logics are, in general, irremediably weak, often to the point of total vacuity. Thus the attempt to model common sense using non-monotonic logics has not bridged the gap between proof-theoretic methods and inference to the best explanation, but simply illustrated how great that gap is. Secondly, even if non-monotonic logics were able to model everyday inferences in principle, they would still be unviable because proof methods for such logics are radically computationally intractable. In sum, the attempt to fit apparently non-deductive commonsense reasoning into a deductive framework fails because it does not specify the right answers, and in practice it is so intractable that it does not give any answers at all. We concluded that these considerations undermine the plausibility of logicism as a model of central cognitive processes.

The fourth step in our argument (Chapter 5) was to consider possible replies and objections. The thrust of many of the objections was that if the unnecessarily tight constraints of the logicist position are loosened, our arguments no longer apply. Variants that we considered included: using heuristics to supplement purely proof-theoretic operations, abandoning proof theory altogether and using entirely procedural symbolic methods, and denying that the internal language can be interpreted in terms of our commonsense ontology of tables and chairs. Thus, in this section, the question of how widely the arguments against the rather specific target of logicism apply to nearby positions in cognitive science was addressed. Among the neighbours of logicism that we considered was the use of semantic or model-based, rather than syntactic methods of proof. Garnham argues that this dismissal was not compelling, and that such methods do not succumb to our arguments. We shall discuss this proposal extensively in the present chapter. The upshot of our discussion was that the arguments against the specific target of logicism apply very much more widely; they hit equally forcefully at positions that respect the spirit, but not the letter, of logicism.

Have We Been Misconstrued?

In the light of this outline (and indeed, in the light of the original text, where this structure is perhaps less clearly highlighted), many of Garnham's points seem somewhat tangential to our argument. So, for example, Garnham suggests that Marr's work on vision provides an existence proof of the possibility of logicist cognitive science. Yet Marr's work is certainly not logicist: the operations that Marr discusses are not proof-theoretic and the internal representations Marr discusses cannot be interpreted in terms of our commonsense ontology. Moreover, Marr's work does not concern knowledge-rich processes—precisely those processes with which we are concerned. Indeed, Marr (e.g. 1982) is concerned to avoid knowledge-rich processes as far as possible, precisely because such processes are so little understood. So while we entirely agree with Garnham that Marr's work is an object lesson in cognitive science, we do not see this as bearing on the argument against logicism.

Similarly, Garnham provides a detailed analysis of each of the tenets of logicism, but these do not appear to be at variance with our position. In each case, Garnham suggests that these claims, while acceptable to Fodor and Pylyshyn, would not necessarily be common ground in the cognitive sciences more widely. The implication is that even if our arguments against logicist cognitive science (on the narrow Fodor and Pylyshyn reading) are valid, these arguments may not generalise to other accounts in the same spirit. Certainly, our arguments do not *necessarily* generalise. However, we argued extensively in the *Objections and Replies* section of our paper (reprinted in Chapter 5) that they would appear to generalise in fact: the numerous variations on logicism we considered appeared to do nothing to deflect these arguments.

The range of theoretical positions that deviate in one way or another from Fodor and Pylyshyn's position is, as Garnham amply illustrates, very broad indeed. Rather than attempt to set up an all-inclusive characterisation of accounts of central processes in cognitive science, we picked the most specific, best worked-out and most influential account as our primary target. We then considered piecemeal whether or not variations on the strict logicist position would be of any help. So while we agree with Garnham that the tenets of logicism are not by any means universally accepted, this point seems to be compatible with, rather than inimical to, the conclusions reached in Chapters 4 and 5.

Furthermore, Garnham suggests that, in replying to possible objections, we conflate the two problems we identify for non-monotonic logics: that they do not license inferences strong enough to capture everyday reasoning (the constraint that we called "completeness*" and that Garnham calls "adequacy") and tractability considerations. Probably, as Garnham suggests, it would have been helpful to label explicitly which of these problems each of the possible patches to logicism addressed.

Nonetheless, we are not sure that there is really much room for confusion between the tractability and completeness* issues in our original *Objections and Replies* section (Chapter 5 of this book). As each of these problems is dealt with in a separate section in the original argument, and as we stress that completeness* and tractability pose independent problems for logicist accounts, it is implicit that a successful objection to our arguments must show how *both* of these difficulties can be overcome. In practice, the objections that we consider can generally only handle one of these objections *at best*, and we were concerned to show that even such minimal inroads could not be sustained.

Garnham goes on to argue that our discussion of the tractability of non-monotonic logics is beside the point if adequacy criteria cannot be met. "There is no point in worrying about the computational properties of a system, if that system can be rejected as a model of everyday reasoning on the grounds that it is irredeemably inadequate" (Garnham, 1993, p. 55). "If nonmonotonic logics don't capture everyday reasoning, why try to draw conclusions about the nature of cognitive science on the assumption that its models of everyday reasoning will be based on nonmonotonic logic? The obvious tactic is to look elsewhere" (Garnham, 1993, p. 55).

It is difficult to disagree with these sentiments. We too suspect that meeting completeness* (adequacy) poses insuperable problems for logicist accounts; and hence that the conclusion stands even without the tractability considerations (actually Garnham thinks that our conclusions concerning tractability, particularly in relation to human inference, are wrongheaded in a rather different way, which we consider later). On the other hand, not all readers may be as convinced as Garnham by completeness* considerations, and some may find the second line of attack more compelling. Furthermore, the tractability problems of non-monotonic logics are an instructive illustration of the appalling computational tangle that results from trying to assimilate non-deductive reasoning to a deductive framework. In any case, it is clear that the only point of disagreement (if any) concerns economy of presentation and that none of these points rebuts our conclusions. Regarding Garnham's additional point, that given that non-monotonic logic violates completeness*, we should look elsewhere, again we agree. As we noted earlier, in the *Objections and Replies* section of our original paper (see Chapter 5), we devoted considerable space to a number of possible alternatives.

It seems likely that there is also no substantial disagreement over our discussion of heuristics, although the use of the term, borrowed from the literature on knowledge representation in artificial intelligence, may indeed have puzzled some readers (Garnham, 1993, pp. 56–58). Certainly, the term "heuristic" is generally used to refer to a quick but fallible computational trick to shortcut a computationally expensive algorithmic computation. Accordingly, there is no possibility that heuristics can give correct answers when the algorithm does not, only that they can arrive at an answer more quickly. In the present context, appeal to heuristics in this sense could indeed only address tractability and certainly not completeness*/adequacy. The sense of heuristic with which we were working, borrowed from the knowledge representation literature in artificial intelligence, *does*, however, place the onus on heuristics embodying constraints that allow a computational system to obtain the right (commonsense) inferences, when application of the proof-theoretic approach would not do so alone (see e.g. Hanks & McDermott, 1985, 1986; Loui, 1987). Thus Garnham is entirely right to note, "No wonder O & C conclude that explanatory power has been shifted from the logic to the heuristics: they are trying to make the heuristics get things *right* when the algorithmic procedure gets things wrong!" (Garnham, 1993, p. 57).

Quite generally, the thrust of Garnham's comments, while written as if they were hostile to our position, appears to be read better as a series of points concerning how our argument might have been made more briefly, less confusingly, and so on, and reveals no real points of disagreement. But in the later parts of his paper, Garnham counters our arguments directly.

While granting that logicist cognitive science, strictly characterised, may fall victim to the kind of arguments that we present, he suggests that semantic methods of proof, and in particular approaches to inference within the framework of mental models, may not succumb to this line of reasoning.

Semantic Methods of Proof

The discussion of semantic methods of proof, in our section *Objections and Replies* in the original paper (see Chapter 5), briefly considered whether or not semantic methods of proof could address the issue of tractability. Semantic methods of proof are based on the search for a model that provides a counter-example to the inference, i.e. a model in which the premises are true but the conclusion is false. If such a model can be found, the inference is not valid; if there is no such model, then the inference is valid. As the space of models which must be considered grows exponentially with the number of premises under consideration we concluded that semantic methods of proof are unpromising with respect to providing a solution to the tractability problem. Indeed, within the study of theorem proving in computer science, syntactic methods of proof are preferred as being more tractable than their semantic counterparts.

Garnham grants that semantic methods of proof are computationally intractable, but argues that when the nature of the human inferential performance is properly analysed, tractability is revealed to be a pseudo-problem. He also suggests that semantic methods, and in particular the mental models framework (Johnson-Laird, 1983) may be able to address the completeness* problem: that semantic methods of proof have the potential to account for everyday inferences. For appeal to semantic methods of proof to be effective, clearly both of these claims must be upheld. We shall argue that, on the contrary, neither of them can be defended.

Semantic Methods and Tractability. Garnham provides both general and specific arguments that complexity is not the problem that we take it to be. The general argument is: the fact that an algorithm is intractable does not necessarily mean that it cannot be successfully used in practice. First we "have no direct argument against the claim that proof procedures for adequate nonmonotonic logics (if there be such things) might run into problems only on problems that are never encountered in everyday life" (Garnham, 1993, p. 60). And second, our "arguments do not generalise to model-theoretic accounts that are not directly related to failed nonmonotonic logics."

With respect to the first point, it seems to us that the boot is securely on the other foot. It is up to the proponent of a computational scheme that is computationally intractable to explain why practical problems will not in fact arise. In the absence of any reason to suspect that this is true, there is surely every expectation that such a remarkably convenient state of affairs will not arise. As non-monotonic logics (and related schemes) require an (intractable) consistency check *every time a plausible inference is made*, and this consistency check is performed over the *entire knowledge base* (or at best over a very large fragment of this knowledge—see the discussion of domain specificity in the *Objections and Replies* [Chapter 5] section of our original paper), it seems extremely unlikely that tractability problems can be avoided. As we noted in the original paper, the fact that no reasoning system based on a non-monotonic logic has been implemented with more than a handful of premises testifies to the drastic limitations that the problem of intractability imposes.

It is difficult to know what underlies the second point: that our arguments do not generalise to semantic methods of proof. If semantic methods of proof offer no succour with respect to tractability, as Garnham admits, it seems that generalisation to semantic methods has already been granted.

The specific reasons why Garnham suspects that complexity is not a problem is that human reasoning is actually susceptible to complexity considerations. It is, after all, well known that, as the number of premises in a reasoning task increases beyond two or three, reasoning performance collapses catastrophically. So, Garnham argues, "if a semantically-based account of human reasoning predicts that the problems become intractable, and hence impossible to solve in a reasonable amount of time, as the number of premises increases, so much the better. To the extent that it does, it accurately models human performance" (Garnham, 1993, p. 60).

This argument seems to be entirely beside the point. What is under consideration is commonsense reasoning, rather than deductive reasoning. In deductive reasoning, to be sure, human performance is extraordinarily poor and brittle, and only very minute problems can be tackled (e.g. Johnson-Laird 1983, pp. 44–45). Yet this stands in direct contrast to the case of commonsense reasoning, where we appear to be able effortlessly to recruit vast amounts of knowledge in drawing plausible conclusions (indeed, the entire knowledge base may be in play, rather than two or three premises).

What conclusion should we draw from the drastic limitations on human deductive reasoning, in comparison to our facility at everyday reasoning? There are two broad answers, neither of which offers comfort to the logicist. One possibility is that these different species of reasoning are effected by entirely different processes, one of which is very poorly developed and inefficient, and the other of which is remarkably powerful and fast. If this is correct, then the complexity profile of human deductive reasoning is irrelevant to the question in hand (providing a tractable and adequate account of commonsense inference).

A second, perhaps more interesting possibility is that the same mechanism is responsible for both deductive reasoning and the inference to the best explanation involved in commonsense reasoning. If so, then the disparity in the levels of human performance between the two can best be explained by assuming that central processes are adapted to commonsense reasoning, and only co-opted into performing deductive reasoning (Oaksford & Chater, 1992, 1993; Oaksford, Chater, & Stenning, 1990; Oaksford & Stenning, 1992). Consider an analogy with human locomotion. The properties of the limbs are presumably highly adapted to walking and running, at which they are very successful. The limbs are also crucially involved in walking on one's hands, to which they are not adapted, and at which performance is very poor. Structures that originally have one function can, if necessary, be co-opted to perform some other function. So, one might imagine, the mental apparatus whose function is commonsense reasoning may be co-opted to attempt to solve deductive reasoning problems, although performance would be expected to be poor. If there is a single underlying mechanism subserving commonsense and deductive reasoning, then the study of a putative underlying mechanism should presumably focus on its operation in tasks to which it is adapted, rather than in tasks for which it is not primarily designed, just as the study of locomotion focuses on walking and running rather than on more arcane ways of moving about.

If this is right, theories that are primarily constructed to model deductive reasoning performance are prima facie unlikely to be good candidates as theories of commonsense reasoning, just as a theory of human locomotion that focused on hand-walking data and attempted to generalise to walking and running would be unlikely to be of value. This is, however, precisely the strategy that Garnham adopts. He considers the mental models account of deductive reasoning as a sound foundation for a model of the general case, commonsense reasoning, even though he considers that deductive and commonsense reasoning may well be carried out by the same mechanisms. Our locomotion analogy would be no more than a straw in the wind in the absence of independent grounds for believing that mental models are not an adequate account of commonsense reasoning. It does however illustrate why it may be an unreasonable, though not unusual (e.g. Johnson-Laird, 1983; Johnson-Laird & Byrne, 1991) expectation that mental models theory will generalise from deductive to non-deductive reasoning.

We have argued that tractability considerations are both severe and germane for theories according to which reasoning processes assume that the cognitive system employs semantic, rather than syntactic, methods of proof. Thus, with regard to complexity considerations there seems to be every reason to suppose that semantic methods of proof cannot be the basis of commonsense inference, over very large bodies of information, which people so rapidly and routinely perform. As we shall now see, semantic methods of proof are equally unable to address the problem of completeness* or adequacy. Just as with syntactic methods of proof, semantic methods would give the wrong answers, if they were computationally tractable enough to give any answers at all.

Semantic Methods and Completeness. Is it possible that semantic methods of proof can provide the extra "power" required to account for the strength of commonsense inferences, where syntactic methods can only license hopelessly weak conclusions? More specifically, what is the relationship between semantic methods of logical proof, which involves constructing models and searching for counter-examples, and standard syntactic proof-theoretic methods, where a syntactic consequence relation between formulae is defined, and shown to be sound (i.e. not to lead from true premises to false conclusions) with respect to the semantics of the logical formulae?

The answer is disappointing: these proof methods are equivalent in the conclusions they license. Generally while insisting on the distinction between the language in which the world is described (syntax) and the described world (semantics), with respect to proof theory, logicians do not regard the syntax/semantics distinction as an appropriate dimension of difference (Scott, 1971). As we have pointed out elsewhere (Oaksford & Chater, 1993), *all* proof methods are formal and syntactic and amount to "abortive counter-model constructions" (Hintikka, 1955, 1985). Thus, the axiomatic method, truth tables, semantic tableaux, natural deduction, and the sequent calculus are all formal proof methods which, if an argument is valid, represent abortive attempts to find a counter-model (example). Some confusion may arise, if proof theory and *model* theory are confounded, a problem we look at further in the following discussion. For the moment we note that these proof methods are equivalent with respect to the inferences they are capable of making (they may, however, differ in complexity) and hence appeal to different proof procedures appears to offer no advantage to the beleaguered Logicist.

The situation is more discouraging still in the context of everyday non-monotonic reasoning. As noted earlier, in deductive reasoning, showing that a conclusion follows from a set of premises involves checking that the conclusion is true in all possible models in which the premises are true. However, in the case of non-monotonic reasoning it will be possible, by definition, for the conclusion to be false while the premises are all true. After all, in such reasoning, inferences are provisional, and conclusions may have to be retracted in the light of further information. Thus an exhaustive search for counter-examples for any non-deductive inference will inevitably be successful and no inferences will be licensed. Accordingly, it appears that, far from being readily extendible to commonsense inference, semantic methods of proof are fundamentally incompatible with it (Garnham makes just this point, in a slightly different context—Garnham, 1993, p. 62).

It might be said that this argument is too swift. Perhaps semantic methods of proof are applicable to non-monotonic reasoning, if there are suitable restrictions on which models are entertained (and something of this sort seems to be implicit in Garnham's discussion). In particular, perhaps the appropriate method of proof in the non-monotonic case is not to search all possible models exhaustively, but to entertain only the most plausible models, perhaps even just the single most plausible model. Consider, for example, the default inference from learning that Fred ate a banana to assuming that Fred peeled it first. Certainly, there are many models in which the premise is true and the conclusion false—Fred may have had the banana peeled by a friend, eaten it whole, and so on. But these models are not, at least in the absence of additional information, plausible. Much more plausible is the model in which Fred peeled and ate the banana as normal. To reason successfully about these matters, it might be argued, what is required is just that a plausible, rather than an implausible model is constructed; if implausible models are constructed at all, they must be recognised as implausible and rejected.

This line of reasoning has, in Russell's phrase, all the virtues of theft over honest toil. The use of semantic methods of proof is bought at the expense of assuming as given a mechanism that can distinguish between plausible and implausible models—and, furthermore, come up with plausible models spontaneously. In other words, it presupposes a mechanism that is able to carry out inference to the best explanation—to devise and assess the plausibility of hypotheses to explain and be explained by known information. But, of course, inference to the best explanation is the very cognitive capacity for which logicism and its allies attempt to account by adverting to methods of proof, be they syntactic or semantic. An account in which the ability to construct just the right model (the best explanation) as a primitive operation is vacuous.

Semantic methods of proof seem, therefore, inevitably, to founder on either of these two difficulties. Without some notion of which models are plausible and which are not, it will invariably be possible to construct some (implausible) model, even for the most persuasive of commonsense inferences, and hence semantic methods will license no commonsense inferences at all. This is an even more extreme version of the problem of weak conclusions for syntactic methods of proof: the problem of *no* conclusion. On the other hand, if some notion of plausibility of a model is presupposed, then the solution to the problem of accounting for commonsense reasoning has simply been assumed rather than explained.

Garnham appears to veer towards the latter course in discussing how a model-based theory of non-monotonic reasoning might look. Rather than addressing the problem that building only a very small number of models requires some way of picking the most plausible models (that is, inferring the best explanation) Garnham argues that certain quite unexpected considerations may be sufficient to distinguish models that should and should not be considered in reasoning: "The *should* is more likely to be cashed out in terms of what people can be expected to do, given their cognitive capacities, in particular the processing and capacity limitations of short-term memory, working memory and the organisation and retrieval of information from long-term memory. Thus, people should consider revisions of their mental models that are required by a specific piece of information that has entered working memory, from long-term memory or elsewhere" (Garnham, 1993, p. 63). This does not, however, seem to provide any comfort for the advocate of semantic methods of proof. No doubt the organisation of human memory is importantly related to human reasoning abilities; indeed, it may very well be that memory is so organised that in some way plausible models can readily be accessed, and implausible models cannot, that relevant information is fed into a short-term store as required and that irrelevant information is suppressed, and so on. This is just to say that human commonsense reasoning processes may be profoundly bound up with human memory, a view with which most theorists would probably concur; it goes no way at all to providing an account of how such reasoning occurs, or suggesting how such an account (presumably somehow implemented within long-term memory itself) would look like a semantic method of proof.

Apart from appealing to memory, Garnham pursues a rather different line, adverting to simple strategies which can be used to guide the model-building process. So, for example, "revisions that falsify a conclusion consistent with the current model should not be considered, unless they are unavoidable" and "A conclusion can be accepted (tentatively, if it is defeasible) if there is some model of the premises that will accommodate it" (Garnham, 1993, p. 63).

Yet such proposals are entirely unable to distinguish between good and bad inferences, at least without covert assumptions concerning which models are plausible and which are not. With regard to the first principle, suppose that a reasoner who has learned that Fred ate a banana, created a model of the situation in which he peeled the banana before eating it. Suppose the reasoner then learns that Fred choked on the banana skin and had to be rushed to hospital. A natural reaction to this additional information is to overturn the tentative conclusion that Fred peeled the banana before eating it, and assume instead that he attempted to eat it all at once. This seems more plausible than alternative models in which Fred peels and eats his banana and then eats the skin too, or whatever it might be. However, Garnham's principle does not allow such a retraction to occur, because revision of the tentative conclusion is certainly not unavoidable—just rather unlikely. Unless there is some hidden appeal to plausibility, and, we would urge, to a prior solution to the problem of inference to the best explanation, Garnham's principle will not allow us to account for the obvious common-sense conclusion.

The second principle fares no better. If any proposition that can be accommodated by some model of the premises can be accepted (albeit tentatively) then inferential anarchy appears to follow immediately. So, for example, there will be a model in which Fred eats a banana and a pig is sitting on the roof of his house (assuming no information to the contrary). Thus Garnham's second principle then licenses this (bizarre) conclusion which is (tentatively) accepted. Of course, similar reasoning can also lead to the acceptance of the opposite conclusion (although, by the first principle, the first of these to be accepted will preclude the other from being accepted). There is, of course, a very large difference between models in which there is and is not a pig on the roof—the latter will, of course, be markedly less plausible, other things being equal. But we are arguing that plausibility is what is to be explained, and thus cannot itself be presupposed in explanation.

A natural move to dampen down the inferential chaos that Garnham's principles appear to license is to appeal to relevance—models that make specific assumptions which are entirely irrelevant to the given information (for example, models that specify the presence or absence of farmyard animals in the context of fruit-eating) should be ruled out. But appeal to relevance is just as circular as appeal to plausibility—only given the ability to infer successfully what explains what it is possible to know which facts are relevant to which other facts (see the discussion of relevance in the *Objections and Replies* section of the original paper, now Chapter 5).

Quite generally, the principles that Garnham invokes and others like them are inevitably doomed to fail, because they do not take into account what is being reasoned about, what it is plausible to assume, what is relevant to what, and so on; formal principles such as those we have just considered will fare no better than the rules of deductive logic in trying to account for the flexibility of commonsense inference. And of course appeals to content, plausibility, or relevance are not open to the advocate of semantic methods of proof as theories of reasoning, as they assume what is to be explained.

Overall, the difference between Garnham's position and ours is that we see the problem of finding the right model as simply a restatement of the original problem of performing inference to the best explanation, whereas he treats it as a relatively straightforward matter, to be explained in terms of memory limitations, relatively simple strategies and the like. We suspect that one of the most significant contributions of recent work on knowledge representation in artificial intelligence has been precisely that it has made clear, in painful detail, that simple formal proposals about how common-sense knowledge can be managed almost invariably rely on covert intuitions about what is and is not plausible; hence, as soon as such proposals are implemented computationally, or just formalised logically, their short-comings become all too readily apparent.

Mental Models and Mental Logics

Our discussion of semantic methods of proof has so far been quite general, and has not been targeted at any specific proposals concerning the semantic methods of proof putatively involved in reasoning. Furthermore, we have assumed that semantic methods of proof are, like more standard syntactic methods, defined over formulae of a logical language; psychologised, this means that semantic methods of proof are defined over an internal mental logic. Semantic methods of proof are simply an alternative way of passing from premises to conclusions.

Garnham stresses that mental models theory, which he proposes as a salvation for logicist cognitive science, is not a theory of mental logic, and wonders if it is this spurious identification that leads us to describe mental models theory as a semantic method of proof. Certainly, in the original paper, and in the preceding discussion, we have assumed that mental models theory is an alternative method of proving theorems of logic, rather than an alternative to logic itself. This is not to run together explanations of human reasoning based on mental models and those based on, say, natural deduction (e.g. Braine, 1978; Rips, 1983). The difference between these is precisely the difference between semantic and syntactic methods of proof (although as we have mentioned, for the logician this is not a coherent distinction amongst proof theories). But we are assuming that both of these explanations are fundamentally explanations in terms of logical proof, though of rather different sorts. Perhaps there is no substantive disagreement here: Garnham may be using "theory of mental logic" to apply only to syntactic proof-theoretic methods, whereas we would apply the phrase more broadly. However, it may be that the importance that Garnham attaches to this objection stems from the view that mental models theory should not be assimilated with proof-theoretic methods as it is very different in character, in ways that we have failed to appreciate. For example, he notes that our discussion "equivocates on the term 'logic'. Much of the time they write as if the only hypothesis worthy of consideration is that the system of operations underlying human reasoning corresponds to some established logical system (e.g. one of the standard nonmonotonic logics) ... [yet] there are many logics that cannot be reduced to first-order logic ... and which can be formalised model-theoretically. And although extended model theory has its primary application in mathematics, there are certainly aspects of everyday reasoning ... that call for formalisations which are model-theoretic and not proof-theoretic in nature" (Garnham, 1993, p. 63, note 14).

The thrust of this disagreement is perhaps not entirely clear. Initially, we are held to equivocate on the term "logic"; yet the follow-up point is that certain logics that may be important for understanding everyday reasoning cannot be formalised proof-theoretically. So it seems that the term "logic" is not in dispute after all; Garnham has just as wide a notion of logic in mind as we do. Presumably this means that the question of whether or not a model-based account is a theory of mental logic is similarly a red herring. The substantial claim appears to be that model-based accounts of reasoning are, in principle, more powerful than proof-theoretic methods.

As discussed earlier, this claim is not correct because the distinction between semantic and syntactic methods of proof is not one that can generally be enforced. As we also mentioned earlier, the reason that the opposite view can seem plausible is due to a conflation between model-theoretic semantics (which provides *truth conditions* for formulae of a logical language) and mental models theory (which provides an inference mechanism). Providing a semantics and providing an inference mechanism are, of course, very different things (see e.g. Hintikka, 1985), yet in Garnham's discussion the term model-theoretic is used to apply to both. When Garnham notes that many logics can only be formalised model-theoretically, what is meant is that while higher-order logics can be given a semantics in terms of abstract, set-theoretic structures, a syntactic proof theory that captures all and only the valid inferences licensed by that semantics cannot be provided. The standard semantic notion of validity, that all models in which the premises are true must also make the conclusion true, can be applied using such model structures, but the class of semantically valid inferences cannot be captured using proof-theoretic rules—there will, in particular, be semantically valid inferences that any proof theory will be unable to capture. Thus, it will not be possible to construct a mechanised proof theory that will capture all and only semantically valid inferences.

This by no means implies that mental models can fare any better, however. Indeed, for incomplete logics there is provably *no* mechanism, based on whatever principles, which will capture all and only valid inferences (Boolos & Jeffrey, 1980). In practice, semantic methods of proof become entirely unworkable as the logic becomes more complex, because the space of possible models becomes enormously large (for example, in second-order logic, involving each possible *set* of objects corresponding to a predicate; in modal logics, involving the interpretation of a term across *each possible world* may have to be considered). Thus, practical attempts to build reasoning systems using higher-order logics have generally attempted to implement incomplete syntactic proof theories rather than search for counter-examples through gigantic sets of possible models. In particular, this means that the mechanism of mental models theory appears, in general, *less* well suited than traditional syntactic proof theory to dealing with the kind of reasoning that Garnham notes is important in formalising everyday reasoning.

However, mental models theorists are well aware of these problems (Johnson-Laird, 1983) and argue explicitly that mental models may provide a way in which model theory may be developed into a tractable proof procedure. Mental models only deal with small sets of objects which represent *arbitrary exemplars* of the domains described in the premises. This is analogous to Bishop Berkeley's claim that reasoning regarding, say, triangles, proceeds with an arbitrary exemplar of a triangle, rather than, in his view, the obscure Lockean notion of an abstract general idea. Providing no assumptions are introduced that depend on the properties of this particular triangle, e.g. that it is scalene rather than equilateral, then general conclusions concerning *all* triangles may be arrived at.

The introduction of arbitrary exemplars highlights the lack of an appropriate meta-theory for mental models (Oaksford & Chater, 1993). Mental models theorists provide no exposition of the rules which guarantee that no illegitimate assumptions are introduced in a proof. This does not mean that any particular derivation using mental models has made such assumptions. Nonetheless, guaranteeing the validity of an argument depends on ensuring that in a particular derivation such an assumption *could* not be made. Hence, explicit procedures to prevent this happening need to be provided. In their absence there is no guarantee (i.e. no proof) that the procedures for manipulating mental models preserve validity. That is, it is not known whether, relative to the standard interpretation of predicate logic, mental models theory provides a *sound* logical system.

While soundness is unresolved, there are strong reasons to suppose that mental models theory is not *complete* with respect to standard logic, i.e. while all inferences licensed by mental models may be licensed by standard logic (soundness) the converse is not the case. Other *graphical* methods of proof, such as Venn diagrams or Euler's circles, are restricted in their *expressiveness* due to physical limitations on the notation. Venn diagrams, for example, can only be used to represent arguments employing four or fewer *monadic* predicates, i.e. predicates of only one variable (Quine, 1959). They therefore only capture a small subset of logic. Although mental models have been used to represent relations (predicates of more than one variable), there is no reason to suppose that mental models will not be subject to analogous limitations.

The employment of arbitrary exemplars is also central to providing a tractable model-based proof procedure (see Oaksford & Chater, 1993). However, in the absence of complexity results for the algorithms that manipulate mental models, a demonstration that mental models can avoid the intractability which bedevils the syntactic approach to non-monotonic reasoning remains wanting.

It is perhaps because of a conflation between set-theoretic and mental models, that mental models accounts do not generally attempt to define a semantics for their mental models notation. For example, the following, from the most recent text that Garnham cites (Johnson-Laird & Byrne, 1991), are the mental model representations of three possible interpretations of the conditional sentences employed in Wason's (1966) selection task.

```
[A]   2       [A]  [2]       [A]   2
 . . .         . . .              not-2
```

This is a complex notation, the precise meaning of which is only specified intuitively. Yet the notation of mental models theory stands as much in need of a semantics as the notation of standard logic. Without a well-defined semantics it is impossible to know whether or not rules postulated for manipulating such models are valid. In this sense, then it could perhaps be said that mental models theory, in its current incarnation, can be distinguished from logic, in being less fully formalised. It seems unlikely however that this distinction is one which mental models theory will find to its advantage.

Conclusions

In the paper that Garnham attacks (Chapters 4 and 5 in this volume), we argued that a logicist cognitive science of central processes cannot account for the commonsense inferences that people draw, and cannot be tractably implemented. We argued furthermore that positions closely related to logicism, including those, such as mental models theory, that use semantic rather than syntactic methods of proof, equally succumb to these problems. We have found no persuasive reason to alter this conclusion in the light of Garnham's discussion.

MENTAL LOGICS AND DEFEASIBILITY

Mental logicians appear to have dismissed the influence of default rules on reasoning as an interfering pragmatic or performance factor (Braine, Reiser, & Rumain, 1984; Rumain, Connell, & Braine, 1983). This is in marked contrast to the reaction of logicians and AI researchers. As we have seen in the preceding chapters, these researchers have almost uniformly abandoned restrictions on what is deducible to the monotonic case and have been driven to explore non-monotonic logics to capture just the phenomenon the mental logicians dismiss (see, for example, the collection edited by Ginsberg, 1987). Embracing the defeasibility of everyday inference, these researchers immediately confront unsolved problems at both the algorithmic and the computational levels. Mental logic researchers, by contrast, have attempted to avoid these difficulties by maintaining—at least with respect to the experimental data they consider—that reasoning is in fact monotonic.

Perhaps the best worked-out example is Politzer and Braine's (1991) attempt to deny that some data that we discussed in Chapter 6 from Byrne (1989) and Cummins et al. (1991) reflect defeasible inferential processes. We outline their position, and argue that it involves a fundamental misunderstanding of the nature of everyday, defeasible reasoning.

Politzer and Braine (1991) argue that Byrne's (1989) results do not show that additional information can defeat (or suppress) modus ponens because the premises result in an inconsistency.[1] Their argument is as follows. Byrne presented subjects with premises like,

If she has an essay to write then she will study late in the library   (8.1)

She has an essay to write   (8.2)

in response to which subjects spontaneously make the inference by modus ponens that she will study late in the library. However, adding a further premise,

If the library stays open then she will study late in the library   (8.3)

leads to a significant reduction in the number of subjects concluding that she will study late in the library. Subjects instead conclude that she may or may not study late in the library. Byrne (1989, p. 76) describes this effect as showing "that context can suppress ... valid ... inferences." Politzer and Braine (1991) argue that general knowledge of libraries means that (8.1)–(8.3) are likely to lead subjects to add:

If she studies late in the library then necessarily the library stays open   (8.4)

to their premise set because (8.3) "actually expresses a necessary condition", i.e.

If the library is closed, then she cannot study late in the library   (8.3′)

But now there is an inconsistency because (8.1) and (8.4) entail

If she has an essay to write then necessarily the library stays open   (8.5)

which subjects know to be false. Politzer and Braine argue that subjects therefore question the literal truth of (8.1) and hence fail to infer that she will study late. They also suggest that all putative cases of suppression of modus ponens are cases where one can question the literal truth of the premises.

Politzer and Braine's modal argument is not valid. But it is not necessary to delve into the technicalities (outlined in the appendix to this chapter) to appreciate that this line of reasoning cannot be sound. First, intuitively (8.1)–(8.3) do not seem to be mutually inconsistent. And Politzer and Braine's argument that they *are*, given appropriate world knowledge, is not compelling. The crucial conclusion (8.4) is intuitively and logically bizarre: it suggests that a contingent truth about whether somebody studies late in the library implies that it could be a necessary truth that the library stays open. But whether or not somebody works late cannot make it necessary (in a logical, physical, causal, or any other substantive sense of necessity) that the library stays open, because counter-examples abound: she might break into the library, be locked in accidentally, may have a key, be a friend of the librarian, and so on. As we show in the appendix, our intuition that this inference—that supposedly demonstrates the inconsistency in (8.1)–(8.3)—is invalid, is supported by the fact that it is also invalid in modal logic. Given that (8.4) does not follow, even if we grant that people may infer (8.3') from world knowledge, the rest of Politzer and Braine's (1991) argument collapses.

Treating these rules as default rules, however, leads to a far more natural interpretation of these experimental materials. The "inconsistent" conclusion that the library stays open if she has an essay to write only looks aberrant because Politzer and Braine explicitly add (8.4) and (8.5) as derived theorems. This presentation makes "the library stays open" seem like the consequence of a false rule (8.5). However, by treating (8.1) as a default rule, we can see "the library stays open" for what it is—a default assumption. Interpret (8.1) as above:

> If she has an essay to write and *there is no reason to suppose otherwise*, (8.1')
> then she will study late in the library.

Given (8.2) the second conjunct must be satisfied. This involves checking whether she will not study late in the library can be proved from (8.1), (8.2), and (8.3'). Assuming forward and backward chaining (Rips, 1983, 1994), (8.5') provides a match that yields the library is closed as a subgoal. This cannot be proved from (8.1), (8.2), and (8.3'). However, by the closed world assumption used by AI systems, as we have noted, (Hogger, 1984) *not*(the library is closed), i.e. the library is open, can be inferred.[2] Consequently, that she will not study late cannot be proved either, and hence it is safe to infer that she will study late in the library. Therefore (8.2) leads to the apparently undesirable assumption that the library is open. This assumption is innocuous, however. Informally, you infer that she will study late in the library because (i) she has an essay to write, and (ii) although you do not know whether the library is open or not, with no evidence to the contrary, you assume that it is. Subjects' willingness to endorse the conclusion that she has an essay to write is therefore dependent on their willingness to make this assumption and it is this assumption that experimenters manipulate in the task. Thus interpreting conditionals as default rules makes much better sense of the observed performance in conditional reasoning tasks than the attempt to maintain a logical interpretation.

Rips (1994) takes a rather different line to Politzer and Braine, conceding that "defeasible inferences must be extremely common in everyday thinking, and any general theory in AI or psychology must accommodate them" (Rips, 1994, p. 270). But he argues that default reasoning arises in the context of inductive inference and that although "Oaksford and Chater [1991] may be right that inductive inference will eventually be the downfall of these [classical logicist] approaches" (Rips, 1994, p. 411), this does not vitiate the mental logic approach. Rips argues that non-demonstrative belief fixation may come about "in other ways than making it the conclusion of an argument" (Rips, 1994, p. 411). But in addition to these "other ways," Rips assumes that people have considerable resources for deductive reasoning, and argues for a particular account of these in terms of natural deduction.

But if our arguments are correct, then this intermediate position is not tenable. The conclusion that people do not interpret natural language conditionals logically, but rather interpret them as default rules (Holyoak & Spellman, 1993; Oaksford & Chater, 1992, 1993) applies to almost any reasoning that mental logicians attempt to explain. For example, Rips offers the following example as a paradigmatic case of deductive inference:

If Calvin deposits 50 cents, he'll get a coke.   (8.6)

Calvin deposits 50 cents.

Therefore, Calvin will get a coke.

Rips treats this inference as deductive and hence modus ponens applies. But, in the light of previous discussion, the conditional premise is clearly about as good an example of a default rule as one could find. Calvin will not get the coke if the machine is broken, if the cokes have run out, if the power is turned off, and so on.

It is possible to reply, as seems implicit in Politzer and Braine (1991) and Rips (1994), that such additional circumstances do not show that the first premise is defeasible (and therefore that some non-monotonic inference regime must be invoked), but simply show that it is false, according to the standard, non-defeasible interpretation of the conditional. But if this is how people interpret conditionals, then the only conditionals that people believe true will be those that never admit of counter-examples. Because any everyday conditional, including (8.6), admits exceptions, then all such conditionals will be false. Clearly, people do not reject such conditionals, but freely assert them, argue about whether they are true, and use them to guide their behaviour. This makes perfect sense if people interpret conditionals as default rules; it makes no sense at all if they interpret conditionals logically.

In summary, mental logicians have on the whole attempted to marginalise defeasible reasoning. One argument is to deny (O'Brien, 1993; Politzer & Braine, 1991) that the empirical evidence supports the claim that people view the rules used in laboratory task as default rules (Holyoak & Spellman, 1993; Oaksford & Chater, 1992, 1993). We showed that these arguments are not valid. However, even if they were valid, the mental logician would still have to account for the many clear-cut cases of default inferences that occur in everyday life outside the laboratory. Rips (1994) attempts to avoid this problem by arguing that most default inferences are inductive and that such processes do not have to involve argument. However, we argue that even the paradigm examples that mental logicians do intend to explain are not logically valid, but involve defeasible inference. Given that standard logic cannot provide an appropriate computational-level model of defeasible, uncertain reasoning, one might expect that the mental *logician* would therefore embrace non-standard, *non-monotonic logics*. However, they are rightly cautious—such logics fail to characterise the intuitively correct inferences and hence could not provide an appropriate computational-level theory.

APPENDIX: THE VALIDITY OF POLITZER AND BRAINE'S (1991) MODAL ARGUMENT

We show that Politzer and Braine's argument is not valid and that it relies on inappropriately mixing modal and classical arguments. Politzer and Braine argue that (8.4) and (8.1) lead to (8.5) and that (8.4) is a necessary truth. On closer examination neither claim is sustainable. We note first that (8.4) does not follow from (8.3′), although a similar modal conclusion to (8.4) does follow on the assumption that the conditional in (8.3′) is interpreted as strict implication (*p could* not be true and *q* false) rather than the material conditional (*p is* not true and *q* false) (Haack, 1978). (A8.1) follows from *not-q*

$$L(p \supset q) \tag{A8.1}$$

which means (8.4) should read:

Necessarily, if she studies late in the library,   (A8.2)
then the library stays open.

This inference is valid in Brouwer's System T, and systems S4 and S5, which form the basis of most modal logics (Hughes & Cresswell, 1968). In none of these systems, or to our knowledge, in any modal logic, is the inference that Politzer and Braine's argument relies on $((\textit{not-q} \supset \textit{not-p}) \models (p \supset Lq))$, a valid inference. As Hughes and Cresswell (1968, p. 27 n.) observe $p \supset Lq$ (7) is "often confused [with (A8.1)] in ordinary discourse, sometimes with disastrous results." The result here is that (8.1) and (A8.2) do not entail (8.5), because (A8.1) is equivalent to $Lp \supset Lq$, but (8.1) and (8.2) do not lead to the conclusion that *necessarily* she will study late in the library. So, (8.1) and (A8.2) could not transitively entail (8.5). Consequently, Politzer and Braine's argument is not valid. Moreover, far from being a necessary truth (A8.2) is strictly false, as it is possible that she studies late in the library while the library remains shut—she could break in, get accidentally locked in and so on. Thus neither (8.4) nor (A8.2) expresses necessary truths as Politzer and Braine assert.

NOTES

1. We here ignore Byrne's (1991) response to Politzer and Braine (1991) because we concur with O'Brien (1993) that Byrne misrepresents Politzer and Braine's argument.

2. We use an AI interpretation of defaults here for illustration only. As we noted earlier, such interpretations of default rules are not in general adequate.

CHAPTER NINE

The Falsity of Folk Theories: Implications for Psychology and Philosophy

INTRODUCTION

In Chapters 2–8, we have concentrated on problems for the programme of logicist cognitive science at the implementational, algorithmic, and computational levels. We have focused, in particular, on the problems raised by the defeasible character of everyday inference. In this chapter, we consider some wider implications of the defeasible character of human reasoning for the cognitive sciences and for philosophy.

Notice that in previous chapters, we have drawn our examples of reasoning from everyday language—we have considered how people reason about whether birds fly, cars start, or eggs boil. We have noted that almost all generalisations of this kind are defeasible, and therefore they have counter-examples. This seems to be a feature of our everyday "folk" theories of the world. Most of human everyday knowledge is made up of default information, rather than strict, exceptionless generalisations, of the type dealt with by logic.

The question arises, as it did in discussing mental logics in the last chapter, whether the generalisations that folk theories postulate are true or not. To assess this, it seems appropriate to compare folk theories and the generalisations that they support with scientific theories and their generalisations. In science, we argue that theories that have been unequivocally rejected in the history of science—theories commonly thought of as false— typically have the same default structure as folk theories. For example, their generalisations typically have many exceptions. In contrast, in science, theories that are regarded as true, while admitting some defeasibility, aim to minimise this as much as possible—and the degree to which defeasibility can be eliminated is related to the degree of confidence that the theories are correct.

This means that the radical defeasibility of folk theories marks them as analogous to false scientific theories. Consequently the objects and relations that folk theories postulate are analogous to the objects and relations that are postulated by scientific theories that have been rejected as false. If this analogy is correct, then it suggests that we should regard "chair", "anger", and "molasses" as having the same status as "phlogiston", "animal spirits", and the "luminiferous aether".

At first sight this might appear to be an outlandish claim. There may be a crucial and obvious disanalogy between, say, "chairs" and "phlogiston": that chairs exist, and can be kicked, picked up, and sat in, whereas animal spirits do not exist, and cannot be interacted with, or even perceived. However, this is to confuse two kinds of question. The first kind concerns the existence of "particulars", and the second concerns "universals".

Suppose that you are sitting on a chair in front of a log fire. One question you may ask is: Is there anything that you are sitting upon? Similarly, you may ask: Is there any gaseous matter being given off by the fire? In both cases, the unequivocal evidence from the senses (e.g. tactile and visual cues) is that there is something that is being sat upon, and that there is something gaseous being emitted. To affirm this is merely to deny complete scepticism about the evidence that the senses provide about the existence of an external world. However, the *nature* of the objects that are supporting or warming you is not determined by the mere judgement that there *are* some objects which have this function. In philosophical terminology, this first type of question is about the existence of *particulars*, not the nature of the general categories, or *universals*, that apply to those particulars.

But having established that there is *something* supporting you is not to have established that you are supported by an instance of the putative universal *chair*. This *would* follow if the meaning of "chair" were anything that supported you. But clearly this is not correct—you can be supported by a rock, a table, a bench, or a car seat. It might also follow if the meaning of "chair" could be analysed as consisting of some necessary and sufficient set of visual and tactile properties. But it is now widely agreed that the logical positivist programme of attempting to define everyday categories in terms of sense data is unworkable. A standard alternative viewpoint is that the meaning of everyday terms, such as *chair*, is determined by their role in the "web of belief" in which they figure, in just the same way that terms of scientific theories, such as *phlogiston*, are frequently viewed as "implicitly defined" by their theoretical role. To deny that there is any such thing as phlogiston is not to deny that there is something given off from the fire, but rather that the set of beliefs in which phlogiston figures (specifically, the phlogiston theory of bleaching and burning) is false. Similarly, to deny that there are any such things as chairs is not to deny that there is something there when you sit down, but rather that the set of beliefs in which the concept "chair" figures (our folk theories of everyday objects) is false. So our claim that commonsense theories are false, and that commonsense categories are incoherent does not have any disturbing consequences.

In psychology, indeed, the idea that the categories into which we divide up the world do not correspond neatly to physical or other scientific descriptions of reality is familiar. For example, an "edge" from the point of view of the visual system does not correspond straightforwardly to any known physical property of images, and theorists do not assume that the environment consists of "edges" that the visual system is attempting to detect. Rather, the idea of an "edge" is a psychological notion, and it is the *product* of psychological processes. It is not possible to understand what an edge is without understanding the properties of the human visual system— edges do not fall under any physical description of the world. When the visual system labels a part of the visual field as containing an edge, it is not merely responding to a local physical regularity of some kind, but is inter- preting an entire visual image to make best sense of the visual scene. As perceptual theorists since Helmholtz have argued, this is a process of unconscious inference, where the interpretation arrived at must be as con- sistent as possible with the implicit theories that the visual system respects. Discovering the implicit theories respected by the visual system, and how it applies these theories in interpreting visual input, is a task for perceptual psychology. But the terms in which the visual system classifies the world are products of perceptual activity, not part of the world that is being classified. Put bluntly, *chairs* are more like *edges* than they are like protons.

This might suggest that because perceptual psychologists have made progress in making sense of what an edge is, and how edges are detected, it should be no more difficult for cognitive psychologists to make progress in making sense of what a chair is, and how chairs are detected. But there may be a crucial qualitative difference between the two cases. It seems at least possible that the principles according to which the visual system assigns edges are very simple and restricted, and crucially do not make reference to arbitrary world knowledge. So it seems plausible that these principles and their application may be relatively easy to specify. But everyday, commonsense categories are, by definition, embedded in general world knowledge. As we discussed in Chapter 4, the isotropic and Quinean properties of general knowledge raise extremely difficult problems for the attempt to provide a psychological theory of everyday objects. Firstly, because general knowledge is isotropic, to understand one commonsense category may involve understanding arbitrary aspects of a person's entire theory of the world, rather than some limited and restricted set of principles. Secondly, because general knowledge is Quinean, to understand how general knowledge is applied in classifying the world appears to require solving the problem of how a particular categorisation can be influenced by knowledge as a whole, rather than being influenced only by a restricted set of principles. So the problem of providing a psychological explanation of terms in our everyday theories of the world, such as *chair*, *ice creams*, or *umbrellas* will be, at the very least, much more difficult that providing an account of edges or colours. Indeed, this expectation has been amply borne out by the difficulties experienced within artificial intelligence in attempting to formalise such everyday concepts. Similar programmes of formalisation in philosophy, lexical semantics, and law have been equally unsuccessful.[1]

If we are right that our folk theories of the world are generally false, then why are such successful agents as human beings apparently afflicted with such radically inadequate systems of belief? This apparent puzzle rests on the misconception that it is possible that people could guide their actions by a true and complete theory of their world. But such a theory would have to await the successful completion of a whole science of human affairs, which remains elusive to say the least. Moreover, the way science proceeds is by picking and choosing the most tractable problems, a luxury that the human cognitive system cannot afford in guiding us through the complexities of the real world. So although by scientific standards commonsense theories are false, they are nonetheless useful in guiding our actions. Successful action for the wrong reasons is not unfamiliar. For example, if you held the phlogiston theory of bleaching and burning and decided to build a lighter-than-air craft, this theory would suggest filling a balloon with the phlogiston emitted from combustion. This would indeed be a successful strategy but it would succeed for the wrong reasons. But from the point of view of cognition, success is all that matters, not whether the reasons for that success are correct. We suggest that our commonsense theories are analogous to highly successful but false theories such as Newtonian mechanics, which has been superseded by general relativity and quantum mechanics, but is still fundamental to our ability to manipulate our world.

THE FALSITY OF FOLK THEORIES: IMPLICATIONS
FOR PSYCHOLOGY AND PHILOSOPHY

We assume that commonsense knowledge, including our commonsense understanding of human behaviour, is organised into theories. After considering certain difficulties in finding out more about these theories, we argue that folk theories are analogous to bad scientific theories, and that the ontology of common sense is on a par with epicycles or the *yin* and *yang*. That is, folk theories are false, and the entities that they postulate do not exist. We consider various possible replies to our arguments, and suggest that the underlying reason that folk theories are bad science is that common sense must deal with matters that do not yield to scientific analysis. We draw out some philosophical and psychological implications of our position.

Introduction

It has become increasingly popular to assume that everyday, commonsense knowledge is organised into theories. In philosophy, it has become standard to conceive of our commonsense beliefs about the mind as a theory: folk psychology (e.g. Fodor, 1987; Stich, 1983). In developmental psychology there has also been much discussion of the child's theory of mind (e.g. Leslie, 1987; Perner, 1991; Wellman, 1990), and more generally there has been an emphasis on children as theorisers (e.g. Carey, 1988; Karmiloff-Smith, 1988). In social psychology, there has been much study of "lay theories" of a wide variety of domains (e.g. Furnham, 1987), and everyday thought has been compared extensively to scientific theorising (Nisbett & Ross, 1980). The psychology of concepts has increasingly stressed that concepts are theoretically embedded (e.g. Medin & Wattenmaker, 1987; Murhpy & Medin, 1985). In artificial intelligence, commonsense ideas concerning the everyday world have been formalised as axiomatic theories, where inference is supported by formal logical methods, or some variant (Charniak & McDermott, 1985; McCarthy & Hayes, 1969).

Most researchers who view knowledge as organised into folk theories shy away from trying to give a precise account of exactly what a theory is. Viewing theories as made of knowledge does not amount to a precise and specific doctrine, it seems, but rather to an emphasis on an analogy between the structure of everyday knowledge and science, from which talk of theories is borrowed. We believe that this analogy is a valuable one, and that when taken seriously it yields significant conclusions for folk psychology and cognitive science.

The structure of the chapter is as follows. We first consider the problem of how folk theories can be known, stressing that natural language does not give direct access to them. Nonetheless, we suggest that it is possible to judge folk theories in broad terms by looking at the explanations to which they give rise, and we present a range of arguments to show that these explanations fare poorly when judged by the standards applied to explanation in science. We conclude that folk theories are false. We then consider the status of the ontologies of our putative folk theories and argue that, from the point of view of scientific inquiry, they should naturally be viewed as being on a par with terms of other false theories, such as phlogiston or epicycles. We conclude that the entities described by folk ontologies do not exist. Until this point, the discussion appears to take rather a dim view of folk theories, when compared to science; we attempt to correct this impression by stressing the differing roles of scientific and folk theorising. Finally, we briefly draw out some philosophical and psychological implications of our position.

What Do We Know About Folk Theories?

One of the most pressing and problematic points of difference between folk and scientific theories is that folk theories are not explicitly articulated for public consumption, but appear to be buried in the individual's cognitive innards. This means that the folk theories that guide thought and action must somehow be inferred from what agents do or say.

Naïvely, we might hope that speakers can simply tell us what their underlying theories are, so that if, for example, people tell us that they believe that people usually act in their own best interests, then this is likely to be part of their underlying folk theory of human behaviour.

A first difficulty with this naïve picture is that social psychologists have persistently found that people's reports of their underlying beliefs do not readily cohere into a single picture of the world, but often reflect a wide variety of conflicting points of view (e.g. Potter & Wethrall, 1987). This has led to the view that the ideas expressed in linguistic behaviour are better thought of as constructed for a specific purpose, dependent on the particular occasion, rather than as direct reflections of an underlying fund of knowledge.

A second difficulty is that it is not clear to what extent we are able to verbalise commonsense knowledge at all. This point has been stressed across a range of disciplines. For example, the psychology of memory has stressed the importance of implicit information, which cannot be verbalised (Schacter, 1987). Coming from a very different point of view, ethnomethodologists have stressed that shared commonsense assumptions tend to be inaccessible to individuals; ethnomethodological investigation attempts to discover such assumptions by training to violate them, rather than relying on introspective reports (Garfinkel, 1964; see Place, 1992, for discussion). A final example is given by philosophical inquiry, in which (among other things) intuitions concerning meaning, good and evil, or beauty, are taken as starting points for constructing theories in the philosophy of language, ethics, or aesthetics. The very fact that developing philosophical theories that capture such intuitions is so extraordinarily difficult is a testament to the fact that any folk theories underlying these intuitions are not readily available to the investigator.

These problems in articulating our folk theories of the world have been an important stumbling block for artificial intelligence. It has proved to be extremely difficult to specify the knowledge underlying the most mundane aspects of everyday thought. Specifying such knowledge is, of course, a prerequisite for putting such knowledge into a machine, according to standard artificial intelligence methodology. Attempts to formalise apparently constrained aspects of common sense, such as the naïve physics of the behaviour of fluids, have been instructive. First, it is not possible simply to take verbal descriptions of what people say as the relevant knowledge and embody this in logical axioms, which can be used as the basis for inference. Instead, it has been necessary to attempt to formulate extremely complex underlying theories of the ontology that people are implicitly using and to devise very complex and subtle principles concerning what people know about this ontology and how this knowledge can be used to reason successfully. Such sophistication is required even to begin to build systems that reason about such everyday matters as the spread of spilt coffee or the results of leaving a tap running (e.g. Hayes, 1978, 1984a, 1984b). Needless to say, the formalisation of folk psychology and other more complex domains has scarcely been attempted.

This work suggests that, in general, the terms of folk theories may not always have correlates in everyday natural language. But terms of folk theories will be little, if any, easier to understand even if they do happen to be expressed by the words of natural language. For the mere existence of a natural language label goes no way at all towards explaining the meaning of the term and its relation to the rest of the folk theory. After all, it took enormous theoretical effort to make sense of intuitive notions of "weight" or "set" (in the sense of collection), which do have natural language labels. Whether this effort should be thought of as making coherent previously incoherent ideas, or simply as making explicit what was really being talked about all along is a controversial question, to which we shall return briefly later. In any event, it is clear that even if we are able to identify people's concepts with words of natural language, this does not solve the problem of specifying what these concepts are. Thus, even though we have a natural language label for "chair", "elbow", and "jazz", and have an intuitive sense of what these labels are supposed to signify, it is notoriously difficult to define (Fodor, 1981) or characterise in any way what these terms mean. If knowledge is organised into theories, then explicating such terms involves specifying the particular folk theories in which they figure; and, as we have seen, this is extremely difficult to do.

The upshot of these considerations is that, if common sense consists of folk theories, then the nature of these theories is unknown and likely to be subtle, complex, and only indirectly related to explicit verbal behaviour. The problem of discovering the theories underlying commonsense thought seems, therefore, to be analogous to, for example, the problem of discovering the underlying knowledge of language that governs linguistic behaviour. Linguistics uses verbal behaviour (and grammaticality judgements, and the like) as the starting point for constructing theories of the underlying knowledge involved in language processing. The resulting linguistic theories are highly elaborate and sophisticated and are, of course, entirely inarticulable from the point of view of everyday speakers. It seems likely to be an equally difficult task to tease out the theories underlying commonsense thought; and the nature of such underlying theories is likely to be no more apparent to naïve intuition. In particular, the ontology of folk theories cannot be assumed to be limited to the vocabulary of natural language—indeed, restriction to the ontology of natural language appears to be entirely inadequate to formalise commonsense thought, which is what drives Hayes (1984a) to define notions such as "portal", "enclosure", "directed surface" in attempting to formalise the naïve physics of fluids. It seems likely, then, that much of the ontology of folk theories may be no more captured by everyday language than are phonemes, island constraints, or traces.

Are Folk Theories Good Science?

We have argued that folk theories must be inferred from verbal and other behaviour and are not directly accessible by, for example, verbal report. Although the details of such theories are hidden, however, it is nonetheless possible to use the verbal and other behaviour to which they give rise to assess how such theories fare when considered as scientific theories. We shall concentrate on assessing the quality of commonsense explanations and assume that the scientific respectability of these explanations is a reasonable reflection of the scientific status of the underlying folk theories. We outline two arguments why folk explanations are very poor by scientific lights. The first argument compares folk and scientific ideas in domains that are well understood by science; the second, more general argument declares that the ineliminably defeasible character of folk explanation is a hallmark of bad science. Given that the underlying folk theories giving rise to these explanations are hidden, it is just possible, of course, that these theories are actually consistent, coherent, well-confirmed and scientifically respectable accounts but that, for some reason, they give rise to verbal explanations that are confused, ad hoc, and readily succumb to counter-examples. This possibility is sufficiently bizarre, and lacking in any evidential support, that we shall not consider it further, and shall simply judge folk theories by folk explanations. Let us turn to our two lines of argument.

Where Common Sense and Science Compete

An obvious way to assess how folk theories compare with science is to consider domains that can be described in both folk and scientific terms. In such domains, it may be possible to assess the quality of commonsense thought by directly comparing it against the corresponding scientific account. We shall concentrate on the physical sciences in the examples that follow, leaving aside for the present, the more controversial case of folk psychological explanation.

The development of physics, chemistry, biology, medicine, and so on, no doubt originates in folk intuitions. However, in modern accounts of the phenomena of these areas, little or no vestige of this heritage remains. Rather than supplementing and regimenting folk intuitions about dynamics, reactions, the basis of life, and the cure of disease, modern theories have totally discredited and supplanted these accounts.

There are numerous illustrative examples of folk accounts that even had a measure of scientific respectability but which now appear completely unfounded. In physics, the motion of an artillery shell was commonly conceived of as consisting of a straight line motion along the line of sight of the gun barrel followed by a vertical descent. In chemistry, it was commonly believed that there are few constraints on the ability of substances to transmute from one form to another, which motivated the search for the "philosopher's stone", which would turn base metals into gold. Even after the development of scientific chemistry, our folk taxonomy of substances has little or nothing to do with the periodic table and molecular composition. In biology, the spontaneous generation of life from decaying substances was a prevalent view as recently as the seventeenth and eighteenth centuries. It was thought that flies arose spontaneously from faeces and even that signets emerged from rotting logs. Equally, folk accounts of medicine, some of which go under the banner of "alternative" medicine, do not provide a foundation for, but appear completely at variance with, modern western medicine. For example, the effectiveness of acupuncture is usually justified as bringing the life forces of the *yin* and the *yang* into balance.

These examples show that commonsense conceptions of the world, while they may provide a historically important starting point in scientific investigation, are typically superseded and, crucially, dismissed as false. In particular, the intuitive notions of "impulse" and "natural place" that underwrote naïve understandings of ballistics are no longer considered to make sense. Similarly, the philosopher's stone and the alchemical conception of transmutation are not thought to refer to any aspect of the real world. Equally, modern biology does not countenance the possibility of spontaneous generation. Modern western medicine claims that the postulates of "alternative" accounts, such as "life force", "yin", and "yang" do not exist. Notice that modern science does not simply contend that the categories of folk science happen to have no members. As the entire standpoint of folk theory is rejected, it becomes difficult or impossible to conceive of what it would be to encounter an example of such putative categories—the categories are simply rejected wholesale as completely nonsensical. (Of course, some of the vocabulary of false naïve theories may survive, for example, "impulse", but construed very differently.)

Backing up such historical considerations are experimental studies of folk beliefs about scientific matters. Modern students of physics are prone to reveal a bizarre conception of basic physical principles (McCloskey, 1983). For example, when asked to describe the trajectory along which a ball will travel after being released from constrained spiral motion, a common response is that it continues in a spiral motion, rather than travelling in a straight line (Kaiser, McCloskey, & Proffitt, 1986). Furthermore, such misconceptions are remarkably difficult to change by instruction (Carey, 1985, 1986; Gentner & Stevens, 1983; West & Pines, 1985; see Kuhn, 1989, for discussion). It is remarkable that we are able to navigate our way through a complex world so successfully, when our explicitly held beliefs about its structure seem to be consistently and dramatically off-target.

Now, if folk theories appear to be bad science in domains that are scientifically well understood, there seems little reason to suppose they will fare better in domains that are scientifically poorly understood. It seems reasonable to assume that domains that have resisted scientific analysis are likely to be especially complex; hence, in these domains, folk theories are even less likely to provide a scientifically respectable analysis. In particular, folk psychology, along with folk economics, folk sociology, and folk theories concerned with tables, cars, music, and shopping, are all likely to prove to be scientifically ill founded.

The Defeasibility of Commonsense Generalisations

In the previous section, we did not consider folk psychology directly, but drew morals from the firmer ground of explanation of physical phenomena. In this section, by contrast, we start by considering folk psychological explanation and extend our conclusions to folk theories in general. Consider this schematic folk psychological generalisation:

(9.1)   If you desire D and have the belief B that action A will lead to D, then you will perform action A.

This can be filled out, for example, as a useful rule for parents. "If a child desires ice cream and has the belief that tidying her room will lead to her being given ice cream, then she will tidy her room." However, bitter experience indicates that this, like other specific instances of the schema, admits of many counter-examples. For example, the generalisation will not hold if the child believes that ice cream will be forthcoming in any case, because her parents are weak willed. Equally, she may believe that the room is so untidy that it is not worth the effort, that there is a fierce dog in the room, that her big sister will take the ice cream anyway, or that there is an alternative, more desirable, action available, such as watching a favourite television programme, going swimming, and so on. For this specific instantiation of the generalisation, it is clear that there will be no way of ruling out all these possibilities one by one. There cannot be a clause ruling out the possibility of swimming, one for watching television, one for each of the possible dangers that might be encountered in the bedroom, and so on. The only hope of ruling out such possibilities without specifying an exhaustive and presumably indefinitely long list of exceptions is to attempt to save the folk psychological generalisation at the schematic level (Chater & Oaksford, 1990; Oaksford & Chater, 1991).

However, at the schematic level, too, it is hard to imagine how the appropriate modification can be achieved. One possibility, which takes account of the counter-examples just described, might be that the generalisation should read:

(9.2)   If you desire D and you have no other more pressing desire D′ and have the belief B that action A will lead to D, and that it will not lead to any unwelcome consequences, and that D will not be satisfied if A is not performed, and that you are able to exploit D if it occurs, then you will perform action A.

But this, of course, succumbs to further counter-examples. There may well be a less pressing desire D′, which can be achieved by action A′, which is less arduous than action A. In this case, it may be judged not worth going to the extra trouble of performing A, even though the desire D is the most pressing. Further, it must be possible to perform A, and the agent must believe that A can be performed (the child will not attempt to tidy the room if she believes that the door is locked and that she cannot get a key). Clearly, further elaboration of the generalisation by adding extra clauses of the same kind will not help because further counter-examples can always be generated.

The fact that folk psychological generalisations succumb so readily to counter-examples is recognised in that they are usually stated as holding "*ceteris paribus*" or "everything else being equal". That is, the situations in the counter-examples just described are viewed as situations in which all other things are not equal. Of course, the use of such a locution does not remove the problem of counter-examples, but simply changes the problem from one of adding conditions to refine the original generalisation so that it is always true, to one of specifying the conditions under which all other things are equal. This is, of course, simply the original problem in a different guise.

If it is impossible to reconstruct folk psychological generalisations so they are true, then surely folk psychology must be rejected as a false account of human behaviour. In consequence, the postulates of the theory—beliefs, desires, and their kin—should be treated as incoherent. Beliefs and desires will not figure in a scientific account of mind any more than the *yin* and *yang* figure in modern western medicine. Putting the point bluntly, folk psychology is false and beliefs and desires do not exist.

While this kind of argument is reasonably familiar with regard to folk psychology (see Fodor, 1991; Schiffer, 1987, 1991), which has been the centre of intense debate (e.g. Churchland, 1986; Fodor, 1987; Kitcher, 1984), parallel arguments appear to be equally persuasive with regard to other folk theories, to which much less philosophical attention has been devoted.

Consider the falsity of the following commonsense generalisations: "All chairs have legs"; "All birds can fly"; "If you turn the key, the car starts". Armchairs do not have legs, swivel chairs have a central column; ostriches, penguins, and injured birds cannot fly; if the battery is dead the car will not start. Perhaps these generalisations are false because they are formulated with insufficient precision—perhaps not *all* birds can fly, but all uninjured garden birds can fly. But what about very young birds, very old birds, birds tangled up in nets, birds in extremely cold weather or high winds, birds with clipped wings, and so on? Refining further, we may say that "all birds can fly" means that every bird will have or has had the ability to fly at some time in its life— according to this reading, very young, very old, and entangled birds count as flyers; and transient meteorological conditions may be ignored; and perhaps having clipped wings counts as an injury. What, then, of very young abandoned birds, destined to starve before they learn to fly; genetically abnormal birds; caged birds, and so on? The terms used in these attempts to refine the generalisation themselves equally require refinement in order to save the original generalisation from counter-examples. What counts as a garden bird—a turkey in a run at the end of garden? an ostrich in an African garden? There seems to be no end to this refinement—every term adduced in refining the original generalisation itself requires refinement.

This phenomenon has been given many different labels in different areas of cognitive theory, from cognitive psychology and philosophy to artificial intelligence. Folk theories are said to be context-sensitive (Barsalou, 1987); to hold only relative to some background conditions (Barwise & Perry, 1983); to be defeasible (Minsky, 1975/1977); to admit exceptions (Holland et al., 1986); to lack generality (Goodman, 1983); and to have intention-relative categories (Winograd & Flores, 1986). These are many ways of saying that every commonsense generalisation, just like the generalisations of folk psychology, succumb to endless counter-examples.

We have focused on the fact that folk generalisations have counter-examples. On the reasonably standard assumption that every good scientific law is without exceptions, this immediately implies that folk theories are bad science. But it has been argued that scientific laws are quite generally defeasible but not thereby false. An extreme version of this view has been advocated by Cartwright (1983), who argues that the "phenomenological" laws of science, which are defeasible, are the only candidates for truth and that "deep", putatively exceptionless laws should be rejected as false.

Even independently of the inference from counter-examples to falsehood, however, folk theories, when judged as scientific theories, are woefully inadequate—they correspond to bad science rather than good science. This inadequacy has a number of aspects, including the inchoate, poorly articulated nature of such theories, internal inconsistency, the ad hoc character of explanation, lack of predictive power, and so on. These properties are evident in the commonsense explanations we have considered here.

So our reaction to folk theories does not presuppose that the laws of a good scientific theory do not admit some exceptions. We merely require that there be some distinction between good and bad science and that common sense falls into the latter category. In view of this, the discussion could stop here. However, while our arguments do not hinge on the issue of defeasibility, we actually believe that it is central to a proper understanding of the distinction between good theory and bad theory. In particular, we view the abundance of exceptions to the laws of common sense as the diagnosis for its other ailments. An abundance of exceptions goes hand in hand with an abundance of predictive and explanatory failures, the invocation of ad hoc rules to account for these exceptions, and an ability to retain theoretical consistency in the face of endless counter-examples. Hence, although for the purposes of our argument we need not be committed to drawing a distinction between the defeasibility of commonsense generalisations and good scientific laws, we actually believe maintaining such a distinction to be very important.

In any case, the defeasibility of scientific laws does not offer a means of maintaining the truth of folk theories. Whether or not defeasibility can ever be entirely eliminated within scientific theories, it is uncontroversial that defeasibility should be minimised. The degree of defeasibility (in conjunction with other factors such as breadth of coverage and simplicity) is a crucial measure of theoretical adequacy. As we have already argued, the generalisations of folk theories are defeasible through and through. So on this score, folk theories will always be ranked at the bottom.

In this section, we have argued that folk theories are false. We now argue that this means that the entities of folk theories do not exist.

Folk Entities Do Not Exist

If common sense is organised into theories, then commonsense categories correspond to the meaning of theoretical terms. If folk theories are bad science, then, prima facie at least, it seems that their ontologies should also be rejected.

After all, because we assume that modern chemistry is true, we assume that "oxygen" is ontologically respectable—what it refers to is determined by chemistry. On the other hand, since we reject alchemy, we assume that "phlogiston" does not apply to anything; it is a term without reference. That is, terms of the internal theories underlying commonsense knowledge are analogous to phlogiston rather than to oxygen. In plain terms, the upshot may be stated: the referents of the terms of folk theories do not exist.

If this formulation seems shocking (and we have found in presentations that it certainly does!), we recommend an alternative: that folk ontologies cannot be used as the basis for scientific explanation. This leaves open the possibility of making sense of some notion of existence in some extra-scientific sense. Given the problems involved in making sense of just one kind of existence, the postulation that there are two or even more kinds does not strike us as attractive. We shall continue to use the shocking formulation in the following discussion.

The conclusion that folk entities do not exist (or its milder variant) appears to be too rapid, however. It may be objected that surely the adoption of a new scientific theory cannot automatically mean the wholesale rejection of the ontology of the previous theory. After all, the vocabulary of one theory is typically largely preserved in the new theory. For example, modern relativistic physics retains mass, momentum, and so on from Newtonian mechanics, although rejecting such constructs as the lumini-ferous aether (the medium through which light waves were supposed to travel). Or consider the stability of the term "electron" over the vagaries of the development of twentieth-century physics (Hacking, 1983). Such examples suggest that some terms of false theories may refer after all. It might be argued that "table" and "chair" may be more like "mass" and "momentum" than "epicycle" and "phlogiston". Therefore, it may seem entirely plausible that a significant fragment of folk ontology may exist despite the falsity of the folk theories in which they are embedded.

One version of this position is that a term may refer not because the theory in which it currently plays a role is true, but because some future theory in which it will one day figure is true. This line appears to be advocated by Putnam (1975), who argues that "gold" was a referential term even before the chemical composition of gold was known, and that this coherence is underwritten by the truth of modern chemistry. This suggestion presupposes that a theoretical term may continue to have the same reference when the theory in which it is embedded changes; this is a controversial thesis. Moreover, adversion to a future true theory is of no avail in attempting to maintain the coherence of folk categories, as it seems, to put it mildly, unlikely that "table", "chair", and "eating ice cream" will feature in any future scientific theory.

There is, however, a more radical way of retaining ontology and rejecting theory: by denying that the coherence of terms is dependent on the truth of a theory in which they may be embedded. This position, entity realism, views entities as prior to theories about them. If it is denied that ontology is determined by an embedding theory, some other account of how ontologies are fixed is required. Two possibilities have been advanced, one that applies specifically to *biological* categories and can offer a defence of folk ontologies if they can be treated in the same way; and one that applies more generally. Very roughly, the first approach individuates entities *historically* and the second individuates entities by their *effects*. We now consider these in turn and argue that they do not change our conclusion that, like phlogiston and epicycles, the entities of folk theories do not exist.

Individuation by History

Millikan (1986) aims to explain what makes biological categories coherent, without assuming that coherence must be guaranteed by embedding in a true theory, for the now familiar reason that biological generalisations, like folk generalisations, typically have counter-examples. She notes that generalisations about, for example, hearts, like the generalisations about birds, tables, and so on that we considered earlier, seem to admit of countless exceptions: "A heart ... may be large or small (elephant or mouse), three-chambered or four-chambered etc., and it may *also* be diseased or malformed or excised from the body that once contained it, hence unable to pump bloody" (Millikan, 1986).

For Millikan, counter-examples to biological generalisations pose no threat to the coherence of biological categories, since coherence is judged by other historical–functional standards to which we shall turn presently. If an appropriate alternative basis for ontological coherence can be found for biology, this might be applied to folk theories—indeed, Millikan suggests that folk psychological terms should be construed as biological categories.

Millikan's approach is complex, but can be illustrated by an example:

A heart ... falls in the category *heart*, first, because it was produced by mechanisms that have proliferated during their evolutionary history in part because they were producing items which managed to circulate blood efficiently in the species that contained them, thus aiding the proliferation of that species. It is a *heart*, second, because it was produced by such mechanisms in accordance with an explanation that approximated, to some underdefined degree, a Normal explanation for production of the majority of Normal hearts of that species. By a "Normal explanation" I mean the sort of explanation that historically accounted for production of the majority of Normal hearts of that species. And by a "Normal heart", I mean a heart that matches in the relevant respects the majority of hearts that, during the history of that species, managed to pump blood efficiently enough to aid survival and reproduction (Millikan, 1986, p. 51).

This approach turns out, however, to be extremely liberal. Suppose, for example, you are sceptical about the laws of Freudian psychoanalytic theory, and doubt the relationship between the failure to resolve certain conflicts that arise at specific psychosexual stages and consequent specific forms of neurosis. On the orthodox view, this would entail a similar scepticism with respect to the Freudian categories of, for example, the Oedipus complex, the id, the ego, and the superego. However, according to Millikan's account, these categories can be maintained in the face of scepticism concerning the laws in which they figure. Consider how the term *superego* may be grounded in the same way as Millikan grounds heart:

> A superego ... falls in the category *superego*, first, because it was produced by mechanisms that have proliferated during their evolutionary history in part because they were producing items which managed successfully to resolve psychosexual conflicts in the species that contained them, thus aiding the proliferation of that species. It is a *superego*, second, because it was produced by such mechanisms in accordance with an explanation that approximated, to some undefined degree, a Normal explanation for production of the majority of Normal superegos of that species. By a "Normal explanation" I mean the sort of explanation that historically accounted for production of the majority of Normal superegos of that species. And by a "Normal superego," I mean a superego that matches in the relevant respects the majority of superegos that, during the history of that species, managed to successfully resolve sufficient psychosexual conflicts to aid survival and reproduction.

For the Freudian theorist such a line of argument might seem to be extremely appealing. For it appears to establish the coherence of the fundamental categories of Freudian theory, even though the laws of Freudian theory may not hold; similar arguments appear to establish the *yin* and *yang* as respectable entities, the purpose of which is setting life forces in balance. This liberalisation of the criterion for ontological commitment appears to allow the grounding of the terms of false theories of all sorts, folk psychology and other folk theories perhaps included. But if the categories of folk theories exist only in the sense that the *yin* and the *yang* exist, this sense of existence is surely too weak to be of any interest.

It might seem, however, that there is a crucial difference between Millikan's grounding of *heart* and the apparently analogous grounding for *superego* or the *yin* and *yang*, however, the first explanation seems to be intuitively plausible and the second does not. For example, it seems entirely plausible that the heart has proliferated because of the survival-related benefits of pumping blood; it may seem far less plausible that the superego has proliferated because of the survival-related benefits of resolving psychosexual conflicts; and it seems entirely implausible that the *yin* and *yang* have proliferated because of the survival-related benefits of balancing the life forces.

In what, however, does the intuition that these cases are different consist? Why should the superego and the *yin* and the *yang* not proliferate because of their survival-related benefits? The most obvious reply is that this is because, unlike hearts, they do not exist. Yet existence is the very issue that the historical account is supposed to decide, so this appeal is illegitimate. A further suggestion may be that while "heart" is a biologically respectable category, the superego and the *yin* and the *yang* are not. But the historical account is intended to distinguish genuine biological categories from bogus biological categories, so this appeal too begs the question. Finally it could be suggested that "heart" plays a role in some true biological theory, whereas the superego plays a role in an at best highly controversial theory, and the *yin* and the *yang* are parts of a radically false folk theory of medicine. Yet the historical account is intended to provide an alternative to this appeal to the truth of the embedding theory and thus cannot rely upon it. In sum, it seems that the historical account is entirely neutral between purportedly genuine and presumably bogus categories. Hence it cannot be used to demonstrate that folk ontologies have a legitimate basis, despite the falsity of folk theories.

Individuation by Effects

Although Millikan's approach to individuating entities theory independently seems too liberal, an alternative approach, developed in the philosophy of science, is motivated by the stability of theoretical terms, such as electron, in the context of dramatically changing scientific theories. As mentioned earlier, in the last 100 years there have been a wide variety of very different scientific accounts of the electron. Nonetheless, it seems natural to view all of these accounts as theories *of the electron*. That is, while theories have come and gone, entities seem to have remained the same.

Hacking (1983) suggests that what is common between the same entity in different theories is its effects. For example, in theories as different as the plum pudding model of the atom and contemporary particle physics, the electron is held to propel a vane in a vacuum (the "electron wind"); to be sensitive to both electrical and magnetic fields (as evidenced, for example, in the Maltese cross experiment); to produce, on average, a three-centimetre track in a cloud chamber, and so on. That is, although theories about electrons have changed considerably, the set of effects that electrons have been taken to explain has remained relatively stable.

However, although in some cases the set of effects that a theoretical account attempts to explain has a real basis, in other cases more than one entity or property explains what was erroneously supposed to be a set of phenomena with a coherent basis. For example, the putative negative weight of phlogiston could be used to explain both the gain in mass of materials after burning (since phlogiston was released) and the fact that hot air balloons rise (by trapping phlogiston released from burning). However, these phenomena have very different origins. The first is explained by oxidisation during burning and the second is explained by the expansion of air when heated. Because the set of phenomena that phlogiston was postulated to explain turned out to *fractionate* in just this way, the preservation of the term "phlogiston" would have been rather confusing from the point of view of Priestley's account of bleaching and burning. Thus, a new term "oxygen" was used to refer to the postulated entity, which explained the gain in mass of materials after burning.

The criterion of individuation by effects appears to apply equally well to entities that are dismissed by modern science as to entities that are accepted. That is, it could explain the stability of the term "phlogiston" over hundreds of years of chemical theorising just as well as it explains the preservation of the term "electron" over the last 100 years. It is, therefore, entirely neutral with regard to the existence of the entities postulated. In particular, it will apply to folk terms whether they refer or not, and hence provides no defence of the coherence of folk entities.

In the previous section, we argued that folk theories are bad science: in this section, we have argued that the ontologies of folk theories are not scientifically respectable. These conclusions appear to cast common sense in a very poor light; the next section aims to correct this impression. Folk theories, while poor science, are remarkably successful at helping us to make sense of and to act in a world that is far too complex for scientific analysis to be tractable.

Differing Goals: The Art of the Solvable Versus Coping with Complexity

Despite the notional goal of explaining all aspects of the natural world, in practice, science is, to use Medawar's famous dictum, the art of the solvable. That is, scientists seek out and explore just those areas where theories can be built, tested, and applied; they shy away from areas that presently appear to be intractable to scientific methods. The ability to choose to focus on tractable matters and to ignore the intractable marks an important difference between science and common sense. Folk theories must allow us to make the best possible sense of our everyday world and guide our actions as successfully as possible; to do this they must face up to the full complexity of the everyday world, which, we suggest science rightly prefers to avoid.

Most aspects of our everyday world are simply too complex, and too downright messy, to be the basis of science; there simply is no clear-cut theory of the behaviour of everyday objects, of the changing patterns of food supply, of the nature and degree of various types of danger, or, most challenging of all, of human nature itself. From the point of view of science, each of the domains is criss-crossed by a myriad different causal paths, most of which are little understood by science; furthermore, the complexity of these causes, and their interactions, makes such matters inherently resistant to scientific analysis. Consider, for example, the problem of predicting the likely effects of falling down the stairs: the range of relevant biological and physical factors—exact layout of the stairs, shape of body, clothing worn, etc.—make scientific study quite impossible. The scientist may choose to pick apart these causes, studying gravitation, blood flow, bone strength, and so on, independently, without ever having to put all these factors back together to deal with a specific case of falling.

The agent faced with the problem of successfully coping with the baffling complexity of the everyday world has no such luxury. Folk theories must provide rough and ready advice—that here falling is dangerous and extreme care must be taken; that there it is not so dangerous and it is safe to hurry, and so on. Our folk understanding of mind provides another good example. Human behaviour appears to be generated by an extraordinarily complex mix of factors, both psychological and biological, upon which scientific psychology and biology have made only partial inroads. Yet folk theories allow us to make rough and ready assessments of how and why people behave; and when it comes to guiding action appropriately, such theories, for all their faults, are much better than nothing.

In general, then, folk theories must deal with aspects of the world that science avoids as intractable, i.e. it must deal with domains in which good science is more or less impossible, and rough and ready generalisation must suffice. Thus, the fact that folk explanations do not stand up to scientific scrutiny should not be viewed as a criticism of folk theories; it is an inevitable consequence of the fact that folk theories must venture where science cannot. If we are right, then the very domains that folk theories must cover, where scientific analysis is impossible, means that folk theories will inevitably be bad science; and that the ontology of common sense will not be scientifically respectable. We now turn to consider briefly some of the implications of this perspective for the study of mind.

CONSEQUENCES AND CONCLUSIONS

We have argued that folk theories are false and that the entities they postulate do not exist. If we are right in equating the objects and relations of common sense with the ontology of false scientific theories, then folk ontologies do not carve nature at the joints any more than Ptolemaic astronomy. Just as the theory of epicycles was a remarkable product of human attempts to make sense of the astronomical world, so our everyday categories "chair", "home", and "friend" represent remarkable *products* of human attempts to understand the everyday world of artifacts, dwellings, and human relationships. The character of common sense is perhaps obscured because we are so close to its objects; but just because we make friends, build homes, and manufacture chairs does not lessen the individual and social achievement of creating the folk theories in which these terms are embedded. This is the heart of the thesis of this chapter—common sense is an *explanandum*, not an *explanans*. A science of cognition must explain the basis of our folk theories and hence cannot use them as its foundation.

This view has significant consequences for the theory of meaning, whether for natural language or for mental states: it undercuts the project of devising a theory of reference for the terms of natural language, as this project is traditionally conceived. Typically, the problem is viewed as that of specifying some naturalistic relation between, for example, the symbol "chair" or "ice cream", and actual chairs and ice cream. There are a number of suggestions about how this "naturalisation" problem can be solved. The crudest suggestion is that the appropriate relation is that the tokening of symbols is caused by encounters with their referents, or that symbol-tokenings *correlate* with such encounters. Causal theories of reference (e.g. Kripke, 1972; Plantinga, 1974; Putnam, 1975) and informational semantics (Dretske, 1981; Fodor, 1987, 1990; Stampe, 1977) have devised extremely sophisticated versions of these views. But if commonsense categories are incoherent, then there are no chairs or ice cream. A fortiori, the tokening of the symbols "chair" and "ice cream" cannot be caused or correlated with instances of chairs and ice cream, because there are none. A causal/correlational story is no more appropriate for commonsense categories than it would be for explaining the meaning of "phlogiston" and "epicycle". Quite generally, any view that attempts to explain the meaning of commonsense terms as a relation to the corresponding category in the environment is simply not applicable—the naturalisation problem for everyday folk terms cannot, in principle, be solved.

As this argument applies just as much to mental states as to natural language, this view also poses problems for any representational theory of mind that specifies the content of mental representations in terms of commonsense, folk categories. For example, any theory that assumes that mental representations correspond to the contents of propositional attitudes is ruled out immediately, because there is no coherent folk ontology to which the contents of the attitudes can map. In particular, this constitutes a rather nonstandard attack on folk psychology as a basis for scientific psychology. Typically, folk psychology is attacked directly on the grounds that it postulates entities, beliefs, and desires that do not exist. According to our more general arguments to the falsity of folk theories, the contents of propositional attitudes are equally in doubt. Hence, if folk theories are put into doubt, folk psychology is doubly vulnerable: first, because the integrity of the contents of folk psychology presupposes the truth of other folk theories; and second, because folk psychology is itself a folk theory.

A practical consequence of this additional line of attack on folk psychology is that a putative scientific psychology cannot merely reject the attitudes while retaining their contents to act as the interpretations of the representations it postulates. So practical work in knowledge representation in cognitive science and artificial intelligence, which is typically neutral with respect to the nature of the attitudes, nevertheless must be rejected, because they retain the folk ontology of tables, chairs, and so on. Such considerations apply just as much to most connectionist approaches to knowledge representation, where states of networks are interpreted in terms of folk ontologies (e.g. see papers in McClelland & Rumelhart, 1986; Rumelhart & McClelland, 1986). Notice that this applies to "distributed" as well as "localist" connectionist representation. A distributed representation of an object in a connectionist network modelling commonsense inference still relies on a featural decomposition such that the feature nodes of the network correspond to the types of which the object represented is a token. The types that provide the interpretation of the feature nodes are typically the categories of our folk ontologies. Hence on the current position, interpreting features is as pressing a problem for connectionism as interpreting the predicate symbols of the knowledge representation language is for traditional AI (Christiansen & Chater, 1992, 1993).

In the light of these considerations it is perhaps not surprising that the areas of cognitive science and cognitive psychology in which most progress has been made are those that do not involve knowledge-rich inferential processes. That is, progress is only really apparent in those areas that, from a philosophical standpoint, as Davies (1992) has pointed out, are not really *cognitive* domains at all. Fodor (1983) captures the distinction very neatly. He divides the cognitive system into informationally encapsulated input (and output) "modules", on the one hand, and informationally unencapsulated central processes on the other. Central processes are explicitly identified as those involving knowledge-rich inferential processes of belief fixation and revision, i.e. precisely the processes for which our theories postulate inference over representations the content of which is given in terms of our folk ontology. Fodor argues that progress in the cognitive sciences has only been and is only likely to be forthcoming for the informationally encapsulated input and output modules.

One way of viewing this diagnosis of lack of progress is that cognitive science has failed to resolve the problems that beset behaviourism.

Behaviourists eschewed an introspectionist methodology and imposed rigorous strictures on psychological practice and theory. In particular, they demanded that stimulus and response be physically rather than intentionally characterised. However, as Fodor (1968), Chomsky (1959), and other pioneers of cognitive science have observed, in behaviourist theorising (e.g. Skinner, 1957), such physicalist characterisations were, in practice, supplanted by inadvertent use of intentional terminology—in particular, the stimulus and response were not described in the terms of physical (or other) science, but rather in terms of the experimenter's commonsense understanding of the task. Description of the conditioned stimulus as a pencil and the conditioned response as, say, the act of writing, is description in terms of folk theories rather than physics. The cognitivist response was to attempt to legitimise this nonphysicalist, intentional vocabulary. This presupposed that everyday vocabulary can be naturalistically grounded as a relation between mental representations and the world. As the domain of this intentional vocabulary is folk ontology and the objects of our folk ontology do not exist, naturalisation is impossible. The assumption that scientific psychology can be founded on the principal *product* of psychological processes—commonsense theories and commonsense ontologies—whether implicit, as in behaviourism, or explicit, as in contemporary cognitive science, is unsustainable.

NOTE

1. In philosophy, the logical positivist programme aimed to explain commonsense knowledge in terms of reductions to logical constructs out of data; they claimed that where this is not possible (e.g. in much of relegious and ethical discourse), the language of commonsense was meaningless. In lexical semantics, a similar approach has been followed with the aim to provide componential accounts of the meaning of lexical terms, using some set of underlying semantic primitives. In the law, there has been a vast programme of theoretical research aiming to give precise definitions of legal and everyday terms, in order to remove the interpretive quality of legal decision making. None of these projects has proved to be tractable.

PART II

The Probabilistic Approach

In Part II, we introduce our probabilistic alternative to the logicist approach to human reasoning. We argue that the uncertainty of human reasoning is best modelled probabilistically and that when this is done many of the apparent biases observed in human reasoning can be understood as reflecting people's normal reasoning strategies for dealing with their uncertain world. We concentrate on Wason's selection task which has been taken to raise more problems about human rationality than any other psychological task.

CHAPTER TEN

A Rational Analysis of the Selection Task I: Optimal Data Selection

INTRODUCTION

The next four chapters present our core illustrative example of how a probabilistic approach may resolve some of the fundamental problems in the study of reasoning. We provide an account of Wason's selection task, probably the most intensively studied task in the psychology of reasoning. In this task, people are asked to assess the relevance of possible classes of evidence to testing a hypothesis.

One of the reasons that this task has been intensively studied is that it seems to have a simple structure and an obvious "logical" solution, but people consistently fail to adopt this logical solution. This has been viewed as evidence of human irrationality by early investigators of the task (e.g. Wason & Johnson-Laird, 1972), and has raised issues of human rationality in philosophy, as we noted in the introduction. Our probabilistic rational analysis will show that people's performance of this task need not be viewed as irrational. In this chapter we re-introduce the task (which we also discussed briefly in Chapter 3) and present our rational analysis.

OPTIMAL DATA SELECTION

Over the last 30 years, results in the psychology of reasoning have raised doubts about human rationality. The assumption of human rationality has a long history. Aristotle took the capacity for rational thought to be the defining characteristic of human beings, the capacity that separated us from the animals. Descartes regarded the ability to use language and to reason as the hallmarks of the mental that separated it from the merely physical. Many contemporary philosophers of mind also appeal to a basic principle of rationality in accounting for everyday folk psychological explanation whereby we explain each other's behaviour in terms of our beliefs and desires (Cherniak, 1986; Cohen, 1981; Davidson, 1984; Dennett, 1987; also see Stich, 1990). These philosophers, both ancient and modern, share a common view of rationality—to be rational is to reason according to rules (Brown, 1988). Logic and mathematics provide the normative rules that tell us how we should reason. Rationality therefore seems to demand that the human cognitive system embodies the rules of logic and mathematics. However, results in the psychology of reasoning appear to show that people do not reason according to these rules. In both deductive reasoning (Evans, 1982, 1989; Johnson-Laird & Byrne, 1991; Wason & Johnson-Laird, 1972) and probabilistic reasoning (Tversky & Kahneman, 1974) people's performance appears biased when compared with the standards of logic and probability theory.

Recently, however, some psychologists and philosophers have offered a different account of what it is to be rational (Anderson, 1990; Evans, 1993; Stich, 1990). In particular Anderson (1990) argues that we must distinguish *normative* from *adaptive* rationality. An organism's behaviour is rational if it is optimally adapted to its environment, even if reasoning according to logical rules had no causal role in producing the behaviour. Such optimality assumptions have become widespread in contemporary social and behavioural science, from economics (Simon 1959) to optimal foraging theory (MacFarland, 1977; MacFarland & Houston, 1981). Moreover, Anderson has extended this approach to provide "rational analyses" of memory, categorisation, and problem solving (Anderson, 1990, 1991b; Anderson & Milson, 1989).

In this chapter we apply this approach to Wason's selection task, which has raised more doubts over human rationality than any other psychological task (Cohen, 1981; Manktelow & Over, 1993; Stich, 1985, 1990). As we have seen previously, in the selection task (Wason, 1966, 1968), an experimenter presents subjects with four cards, each with a number on one side and a letter on the other, and a rule of the form *if p then q*, for example *if there is a vowel on one side (p), then there is an even number on the other side (q)*. The four cards show an "A"(*p* card), a "K"(*not-p* card), a "2"(*q* card), and a "7"(*not-q* card) (see Fig. 10.1). Subjects have to select those cards that they must turn over to determine whether the rule is true or false. Logically subjects should select only the *p* and *not-q* cards. However, only 4% of subjects make this response, other responses being far more common: *p* and *q* cards (46%); *p* card only (33%), *p*, *q* and *not-q* cards (7%), *p* and *not-q* cards (4%) (Johnson-Laird & Wason, 1970a).

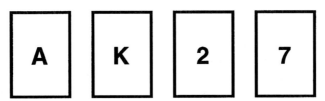

FIG. 10.1   The four cards in the abstract version of Wason's selection task.

The selection task is a laboratory version of the problem of choosing the best experiments to test scientific laws. Popper's (1959) method of falsification provides the standard normative account of this situation. Popper argues that, logically, experiments can only falsify general laws, they cannot confirm them. Hence, scientists should only conduct experiments that can falsify a general law. The selection task provides an opportunity to see whether people spontaneously adopt Popper's falsificationist strategy (Wason & Johnson-Laird, 1972). Logically, the only way to falsify the conditional rule *if p then q* in the selection task is to look for cards with *p* on one side and *not-q* on the other. Only two visible card faces are potentially of this type—the *p* card and the *not-q* card. Hence, according to falsification, subjects should choose only these two cards. However, in the selection task, as few as 4% of subjects make this card selection. This lack of fit between normative theory and behaviour is responsible for the widespread doubts over human rationality we have mentioned.

Contemporary philosophers of science have rejected falsificationism as unfaithful to the history of science (Kuhn, 1962; Lakatos, 1970) and to be in any case unworkable (Churchland, 1986; Duhem, 1954; Putnam, 1974; Quine, 1953). More recent accounts of scientific inference take a Bayesian probabilistic approach to confirmation (Earman, 1992; Horwich, 1982; Howson & Urbach, 1989). In particular, the Bayesian theory of optimal data selection (Federov, 1972; MacKay, 1992) offers a different account of how scientists should choose experiments, which does not place an exclusive emphasis on falsification. Using this theory to develop a rational analysis of the selection task fits well with other rational analyses (e.g. Anderson 1990) that also employ Bayesian methods. Our rational analysis will show that we can view behaviour in the selection task as optimising the expected amount of information gained by turning each card.

The purpose of a rational analysis is to show that behaviour is optimally adapted to the environment. Good fits between a rational analysis and behaviour indicate only that such an analysis provides an organising framework for describing the behaviour. Whether the behaviour is rational depends on whether the rational analysis adequately characterises the environment. Anderson (1990) uses diffuse Bayesian prior distributions to model the environment. Although we do not use such distributions we do make some assumptions about the environment that we will not justify until the discussion section. In particular we assume that the properties that figure in causal relations are rare in the environment. We call this the *rarity assumption*. We show that we can organise the data on the selection task on the assumption that subjects act as Bayesian optimal data selectors with rarity. In the discussion we argue that the environment respects rarity and hence we can view people's behaviour on the selection task as adaptively rational.

The organisation of this chapter is as follows. In the first section, we develop our rational analysis. In the following sections, we apply this analysis to a range of selection task data: the standard abstract results, the non-independence of card selections (e.g. Pollard, 1985), the negations paradigm (e.g. Evans & Lynch, 1973), tasks that vary the probabilities of so-called fictional outcomes (Kirby, 1994), the therapy experiments (e.g. Wason, 1969), the reduced array selection task (e.g. Johnson-Laird & Wason, 1970b), and the thematic selection tasks (e.g. Cheng & Holyoak, 1985). Finally, we discuss the assumptions and implications of our account.

RATIONAL ANALYSIS

In this section we first informally outline the problem of optimal data selection, and how it applies to the selection task. We then present the Bayesian approach to optimal data selection. We then apply this account to derive a rational analysis of the selection task. Finally, we explore some general properties of the model's behaviour.

Informal Outline

Optimal data selection involves choosing experiments to decide between rival hypotheses (Federov, 1972; Good, 1966; Hill & Hunter, 1969; Lindley, 1956; Luttrell, 1985; MacKay, 1992a). For example, suppose that a metallurgist has various competing hypotheses about the underlying relationship between temperature and tensile strength. To decide between these hypotheses the metallurgist must choose new temperatures at which to test a metal's tensile strength. Intuitively, the most informative temperatures will be those where the hypotheses make divergent predictions (Platt, 1964). The Bayesian theory of optimal data selection formalises these intuitions.

Everyday hypothesis testing also involves optimal data selection. Suppose that you are interested in the hypothesis that eating tripe makes people feel sick. In collecting evidence, should you ask known tripe-eaters or tripe-avoiders whether they feel sick? Should you ask people known to be, or not to be, sick whether they have eaten tripe? This case is analogous to the selection task. Logically, the hypothesis can be written as a conditional sentence: if you eat tripe (p) then you feel sick (q). The groups of people that you may investigate then correspond to the various visible card options, *p*, *not-p*, *q*, and *not-q*. In practice, who is available will influence decisions about who to investigate. The selection task abstracts from this practical detail by presenting one example of each potential source of data. In terms of our everyday example, it is like coming across four people, one known to have eaten tripe, one known not to have eaten tripe, one known to feel sick, and one known not to feel sick. You must then judge which of these people you should question about how they feel or what they have eaten.

Let us consider informally what seems to be a rational selection of data in this situation. First, asking a person who has eaten tripe (*p*) is likely to be informative. If this person feels sick, then the hypothesis gains some credence; if not, then this evidence falsifies the hypothesis. Second, asking whether a tripe-avoider (*not-p*) feels sick is futile, because the rule says nothing about how people feel if they have not eaten tripe. Third, asking whether a person who feels sick (*q*) has eaten tripe is worthwhile. The hypothesis will gain credence if they have eaten tripe, although if they have not, no conclusion appears to be forthcoming. Fourth, the person who is not feeling sick (*not-q*) is also worth questioning. If they have eaten tripe this evidence falsifies the hypothesis. If they have not, no conclusion appears to be forthcoming. In this example, it seems that the *p* card is certain to be informative, the *not-p* card certainly will not be, and the *q* and *not-q* cards may or may not be informative. We now introduce the Bayesian approach to optimal data selection and show how to justify and extend these intuitions.

The Bayesian Approach

We begin by characterising a participant's job in the selection task as selecting data to discriminate between two hypotheses representing possible states of the world. The first hypothesis represents the belief that there is no dependency between the antecedent *p* and the consequent *q* of a conditional rule, if *p* then *q*. Using our example in the last section, this is the hypothesis that there is no relationship between eating tripe and feeling sick. Each hypothesis is characterised probabilistically as a contingency table (see Table 10.1). We represent the hypothesis that there is no dependency between *p* and *q* by a contingency table in which *p* and *q* are statistically independent, i.e. $P(q \mid p) = P(q)$. We call this the "independence model" or M_I (see Table 10.1). This representation is reasonable because the purpose of scientific laws and everyday contingencies is to render the world more predictable. So, for example, if there is a relation between eating tripe and feeling sick then knowledge of whether someone has eaten tripe permits you to predict whether they will feel sick. If there is no relation between these two events then knowing whether someone ate tripe should give you no

TABLE 10.1

The contingency table of probabilities appropriate for the dependence model M_D[10.1(a)], where there is an exceptionless dependency between the p and q. 10.1(b) shows the equivalent table for the independence model M_I. a corresponds to the probability of p, $P(p)$, and b corresponds to the probability of q in the absence of p, $P(q|not\text{-}p)$

(a) M_D	q	$not\text{-}q$	(b) M_I	q	$not\text{-}q$
p	a	0	p	ab	$a(1-b)$
$not\text{-}p$	$(1-a)b$	$(1-a)(1-b)$	$not\text{-}p$	$(1-a)b$	$(1-a)(1-b)$

more ability to predict whether they feel sick than when you do not know whether they ate tripe. This latter situation is well characterised by statistical independence. In Table 10.1, in M_I the probability of p, $P(p)$, is given by the parameter a, and the probability of q, $P(q)$, is given by the parameter b. For M_I, calculating the joint probabilities in the various cells of the table is achieved by multiplying the corresponding marginals because these are the expected joint probabilities assuming independence. To represent a dependency between p and q we adopt the simplest strategy of making the minimal change to M_I so that the conditional probability of q given p is 1. So for example, this means that if tripe-eating and sickness are related then knowing someone has eaten tripe allows you to predict with certainty that they will be sick. That is, the probability of someone being sick given that they have eaten tripe is 1, i.e. $P(q|p) = 1$. This situation is represented in Fig. 10.1 by the dependence model M_D. In M_D the joint probability of p and q ($P(p,q)$) is set equal to $P(p)$ (i.e. a) and the joint probability of p and $not\text{-}q$ is set to 0, consequently $P(q|p) = P(p,q)/P(p) = a/a = 1$.

This minimal change strategy in setting up the dependence model has various consequences. First, across both models the parameter b now represents the probability of q given $not\text{-}p$, i.e. $P(q|not\text{-}p)$. This is obvious in M_I because assuming independence, $P(q|not\text{-}p) = P(q)$ and in M_I we set $b = P(q)$. In M_D, b also equals $P(q|not\text{-}p)$ because the values for the $not\text{-}p$ cells have not been changed and consequently in both models $P(q|not\text{-}p) = b(1 - a)/(b(1 - a) + (1 - b)(1 - a)) = b/(b + (1 - b)) = b$. Second, this change does mean, however, that although $b = P(q|not\text{-}p)$ in both models, b equals $P(q)$ only in M_I. In M_D, $P(q) = a + b(1 - a)$. This reflects the fact that, for example, if tripe does invariably make people sick, i.e. M_D truly describes the world, then there must be more sick people than tripe-eaters, i.e. $P(q)$ must be greater than a ($P(p)$). If this were not true then there would have to be some tripe-eaters who did not get sick, in which case M_D could not truly describe the world. Third, in most of the experiments that we will go on to model, although it is reasonable to assume values for $P(p)$ and $P(q)$ it is not reasonable to assume that people have estimates of $P(q|not\text{-}p)$. Consequently, to set up the models b is calculated from the following formula which is derived from rearranging the expression for the expected value of $P(q)$ calculated over both models:

$$b = \frac{P(q) - P(p)P(M_D)}{1 - P(p)P(M_D)} \quad (P(q) \geq P(p)P(M_D)) \tag{10.1}$$

In this equation $P(M_D)$ represents the probability with which the dependence model is believed true and $P(M_D) = 1 - P(M_I)$, where $P(M_I)$ is the probability with which the independence model is believed true. Equation (10.1) does not demand that $P(p) < P(q)$. However, we assume that people will not consider testing a hypothesis for which this constraint does not hold. This is reasonable because if this constraint does not hold then there is no reason to inquire into the truth or falsity of the hypothesis by consulting evidence, because it is already known that M_D could not truly describe the world. That is, the hypothesis is a no-hoper at the outset and so there is no need to work out what is the best evidence to select.

In order to calculate what is the best evidence to select we first calculate the uncertainty concerning which hypothesis is true before selecting any evidence. Our goal will be to select evidence that leads to the greatest expected reduction in this level of uncertainty. Initial uncertainty depends on the prior degree of belief in the two models, i.e. it depends on $P(M_I)$ (note that $P(M_D)$ $= 1 - P(M_I)$). We quantify uncertainty using Shannon–Wiener information:

$$I(M_i) = \sum_i P(M_i)\log_2\left(\frac{1}{P(M_i)}\right) \tag{10.2}$$

Shannon–Wiener information encodes the amount of uncertainty that is reduced by discovering which is the true hypothesis (note that this is not quite what we wish to encode, which is how far uncertainty is reduced by finding possibly inconclusive evidence). This quantity takes a maximum value when $P(M_I) = P(M_D) = 0.5$, i.e. it captures the idea that people are maximally uncertain when they believe that M_D and M_I are equally likely to be true (or false). Inserting these values into equation (10.1), yields a value of information of one bit, that is, if it is initially assumed that these hypotheses are equally likely, then finding out which one is true reduces uncertainty by one bit.

Having determined the uncertainty about which is the true hypothesis before any evidence is selected the uncertainty after seeing some evidence must be determined. This means we are now interested in $P(M_i|D)$, i.e. the probability that a hypothesis is true given some data. To calculate these values we use Bayes' Theorem:

$$P(M_i|D) = \frac{P(D|M_i)P(M_i)}{\sum_j P(D|M_j)P(M_j)} \qquad (10.3)$$

which specifies the posterior probability of a hypothesis M_i, given some data D, $P(M_i|D)$, in terms of the priors of each hypothesis, $P(M_j)$, and the likelihoods of D given each M_j, $P(D|M_j)$. We treat the values of the priors $P(M_I)$ (and consequently $P(M_D)$), as a free parameter, which we will usually set to 0.5, i.e. before the experiment we assume participants are maximally uncertain about which hypothesis is true. In order to calculate (10.3) the likelihoods therefore need to be calculated. We illustrate how we do this by our example. Consider someone who has eaten tripe (p). The data, D, is whether this person is sick or not (q or *not-q*). Let us assume that she is sick, then the probability that she is sick under each hypothesis must be determined, i.e. the probability that she is sick given she has eaten tripe under M_i ($P(q|p, M_i)$) and under M_D, ($P(q|p, M_D)$). These values are straightforwardly calculated from each contingency table in Table 10.1. Indeed we have already illustrated calculating $P(q|p, M_D)$, in M_D, $P(q|p, M_D) = a/a = 1$. In M_I, $P(q|p, M_I) = P(q) = ab/a = b$. Putting the values into (10.3) yields the following posterior probability that there is a dependency between eating tripe and being sick, i.e. the probability that M_D truly describes the world given these data:

$$P(M_D|sick) = \frac{1 \times 0.5}{1 \times 0.5 + b \times 0.5} = \frac{1}{1 + b}$$

and of course the probability that M_I truly describes the world, given these data, is simply 1 minus this value. To calculate the new uncertainty given the data, these posterior probabilities are simply put into equation (10.2):

$$I(M_i|D) = \sum_i P(M_i|D)\log_2\left(\frac{1}{P(M_i|D)}\right) \qquad (10.4)$$

How much this piece of data has reduced our initial uncertainty can now be calculated, it is simply the initial uncertainty minus new uncertainty:

$$I_g = I(M_i) - I(M_i|D) \qquad (10.5)$$

We call this quantity the *information gain* associated with this data point.

However, in the selection task participants never actually get to turn over the cards, i.e. they never actually get to see the data. Consequently, rather than actual information gains *expected* information gains must be calculated. So for example, if you look at a person who has eaten tripe you do not know whether they are sick or not sick; what we calculate, therefore, is the information you could expect to obtain given either possible outcome. This involves calculating $I(M_i|\text{sick})$ and $I(M_i|\text{not-sick})$. The latter is calculated in exactly the same way as we have already outlined. To calculate the expected value these new uncertainties must be weighted by the probability of finding each type of evidence given someone has eaten tripe. To calculate these probabilities we compute the expected value of each data type over both models. So for example, to calculate the probability that someone is sick, given they have eaten tripe $P(q|p)$ the expectation is calculated over both models:

$$P(q|p) = P(M_D)P(q|p, M_D) + P(M_1)P(q|p, M_I) \qquad (10.6)$$

The probability of the other possible data point, that having eaten tripe someone is not sick $P(\textit{not-q}|p)$, is calculated in the same way. The new *expected* uncertainty associated with examining someone who has eaten tripe $(EI(M_I|p))$ is then calculated by weighting the information gains associated with each possible data outcome by the probability of finding that data outcome:

$$EI(M_i|p) = [P(q|p)I_g(q|p) + P(\neg q|p)I_g(\neg q|p)] \qquad (10.7)$$

To calculate expected information gain and expressing the quantity in (10.7) more generally:

$$EI_g = I(M_i) - \sum_k P(D_k)I(M_i|D_k) \qquad (10.8)$$

This quantity encodes the reduction in uncertainty that can be expected from examining a card in the selection task. In all these calculations there are only three free parameters $P(M_I)$, $P(p)$, and $P(q)$. We now illustrate the calculation of expected information gain by assuming various values for the parameters in our example.

In the remainder of this paper we assume that the properties that figure in the antecedents and consequents of conditional hypotheses are rare. So in the general population the number of people who have eaten tripe or who are sick is small and so the probabilities $P(p)$ and $P(q)$ will be small. We also assume that $P(p) < P(q)$ for the reasons we outlined earlier. For the purpose of this illustration we assume $P(p) = 0.1$ and $P(q) = 0.2$. As we discussed earlier, we also assume that people are maximally uncertain about which hypothesis truly describes the world, so $P(M_I) = 0.5$. We calculate expected information gain on the assumption that you want to know the value of this quantity if you examine someone who has eaten tripe (p). We begin by constructing the relevant contingency tables. As we noted earlier, we assume that a given value of $P(q)$ is an estimate of the expected value calculated across both models. To fill out the relevant cell values we therefore first calculate b using equation (10.1):

$$b = \frac{0.2 - 0.1 \times 0.5}{1 - 0.1 \times 0.5} = 0.158$$

This value is then used to construct the contingency tables in Table 10.2. Notice that the expected value of $P(q) = 0.2$ (i.e. $0.5(0.1 + 0.142) + 0.5(0.016 + 0.142)$). We introduce a small value of 10^{-9} for $P(p, not\text{-}q)$ in M_I to prevent infinities produced by division by zero.

As we showed earlier, with $P(M_I) = 0.5$, initial uncertainty $I(M_i)$ is maximal at 1 bit. To calculate the posterior uncertainty for each possible data outcome we now calculate the relevant likelihoods. The probability of someone being sick, given they ate tripe in the dependence model ($P(q|p, M_D)$) is $0.1/0.1 = 1$. The probability of someone being sick, given they ate tripe in the independence model ($P(q|p, M_I)$) $= ab/a = b = 0.158$. Consequently,

$$P(M_D|sick) = \frac{1 \times 0.5}{1 \times 0.5 + 0.158 \times 0.5} = \frac{1}{1 + 0.158} = 0.864$$

Given that our tripe-eater is sick, we therefore arrive at a posterior uncertainty $I(M_i|sick)$ of:

$$I(M_i|sick) = 0.864 \log_2\left(\frac{1}{0.864}\right) + 0.136 \log_2\left(\frac{1}{0.136}\right) = 0.574$$

Suppose however that they are not sick. The probability of someone not being sick, given they ate tripe in the dependence model, $P(q|p, M_D) = 10^{-9}/$

TABLE 10.2
The contingency tables for the illustrative example of computing expected information gain

1(a) M_D	q	not-q	1(b) M_I	q	not-q
p	.1	10^{-9}	p	.016	.084
not-p	.142	.758	not-p	.142	.758

$0.1 = 10^{-8}$. The probability of someone not being sick, given they ate tripe in the independence model, $P(q|p, M_I) = a(1 - b)/a = 1 - b = 0.842$. Consequently,

$$P(M_D|\neg sick) = \frac{10^{-8}}{10^{-8} + 0.842} = 1.88 \times 10^{-8}$$

Given that our tripe-eater is not sick, we therefore arrive at a posterior uncertainty $I(M_i|not\text{-}sick)$ of:

$$I(M_i|\neg sick) = 1.88 \times 10^{-8} \log_2\left(\frac{1}{1.88 \times 10^{-8}}\right)$$

$$+(1 - 1.88 \times 10^{-8})\log_2\left(\frac{1}{(1 - 1.88 \times 10^{-8})}\right) = 5.096 \times 10^{-7}$$

We now need to calculate the expected value of these uncertainties. To do so we need to calculate the expected probabilities of the data, i.e. of finding that someone is sick given they have eaten tripe ($P(q|p)$) or that they are not sick given they have eaten tripe ($P(not\text{-}q|p)$):

$$P(q|p) = P(q|p, M_D)P(M_D) + P(q|p, M_I)P(M_I)$$
$$= 1 \times 0.5 + 0.16 \times 0.5 = 0.58$$
$$P(\neg q|p) = P(\neg q|p, M_D)P(M_D) + P(\neg q|p, M_I)P(M_I)$$
$$0 + 0.84 \times 0.5 = 0.42$$

The expected uncertainty after examining a tripe-eater is therefore:

$$EI(M_i|p) = [0.58 \times 0.574 + 0.42 \times 5.096 \times 10^{-7}] \approx 0.333$$

Consequently, the expected information that can be gained, or the expected reduction in uncertainty, from turning this card is:

$$EI_g = 1 - 0.333 = 0.667$$

Having illustrated the calculation of expected information gain we now look at the general behaviour of the model over the full range of parameter values.

Model Behaviour

We illustrate the behaviour of the model in Fig. 10.2. The three parameters, $P(p)$, $P(q)$, and $P(M_I)$ define a three-dimensional space. We calculated $E(I_g)$s for each card for five values (0.1, 0.3, 0.5, 0.7, 0.9) of each parameter. The not-p card does not appear in Fig. 10.2 because its $E(I_g)$ value is always zero.

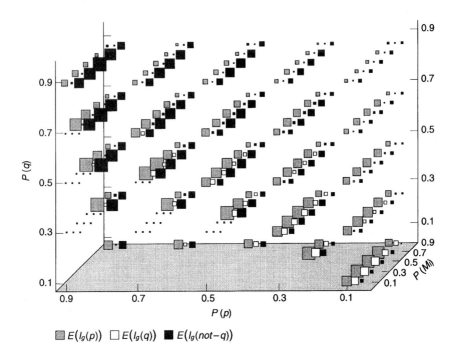

$\square E(I_g(p))$ $\square E(I_g(q))$ $\blacksquare E(I_g(not-q))$

FIG. 10.2   Model behaviour. At each $(P(p), P(q), P(M_I))$ co-ordinate the three boxes represent the $E(I_g)$ values for the three cards. The area of the box is proportional to the $E(I_g)$ for the corresponding card. Co-ordinates where there are three dots indicate regions where the inequality $P(q) \geq P(q)P(M_D)$ is violated, and hence the probability values are inconsistent.

At each co-ordinate the three boxes represent the $E(I_g)$ values for the three cards. The area of the box is proportional to the $E(I_g)$ for the corresponding card.[1] Co-ordinates where there are three dots indicate regions where the inequality $P(q) \geq P(q)P(M_D)$ is violated, and hence the probability values are inconsistent. Figure 10.2 reveals the following pattern of expected informativeness for the four cards.

P Card: Is informative in so far as $P(q)$ is low. It is largely independent of $P(p)$.[2]

Q Card: Is informative when $P(p)$ and $P(q)$ are both small.

Not-q Card: Is informative to the extent that $P(p)$ is large. It is independent of $P(q)$.

Not-p Card: Is not informative.

We highlight three aspects of the model's behaviour. First, variation in $P(M_I)$ rescales the $E(I_g)$ values but does not change their order for the four cards. In consequence the relative informational value of each card is insensitive to the priors (but see note 2). Second, $E(I_g(not\text{-}p))$ is always zero. This is consistent with the intuition that conditional rules make no assertions about what occurs if the antecedent is not satisfied. So, as we suggested earlier, consulting non-tripe-eaters cannot tell you whether eating tripe causes sickness. Third, when $P(p)$ and $P(q)$ are small (in the bottom right hand corner of Fig. 10.2), $E(I_g(q))$ is greater than $E(I_g(not\text{-}q))$. Figure 10.3 shows the entire region, R, (shown in black) where $E(I_g(q)) > E(I_g(not\text{-}q))$ in more detail. Here, as in all subsequent analyses (unless explicitly stated otherwise), $P(M_I)$ is set to 0.5.[3] At all other values of $P(p)$ and $P(q)$, either $E(I_g(not\text{-}q))$ is greater than $E(I_g(q))$, or these values are undefined.

In modelling experimental data we assume by default that $P(p)$ and $P(q)$ lie within R, i.e. subjects treat p and q as rare. We refer to this assumption as the "rarity assumption". Optimal data selection, together with the rarity assumption, will allow us to capture a wide range of experimental results. In Chapter 13 we consider whether the rarity assumption can itself be rationally justified. But first, in the next chapter, we use this framework to organise the data on the selection task.

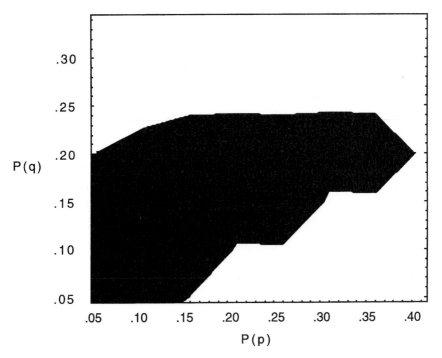

FIG. 10.3   Plot of $P(p)$ against $P(q)$ with $P(M_I) = 0.5$, showing the region R (in black) where $E(I_g(q)) > E(I_g(not\text{-}q))$.

NOTES

1. We thank Mike Malloch for suggesting this method of visualisation and for writing the software that generated this figure.

2. However, when $P(M_I)$ is low (i.e. $P(M_D)$ is high) equation (10.1) reveals that b can still be low. This leads to high values of $E(I_g(p))$ when $P(M_I)$ is low, and $P(p)$ and $P(q)$ are high. See the top left-hand corner of Fig. 10.2.

3. Much theoretical debate concerning the validity of Bayesian statistics centres on how to assign prior probabilities and there is a complex literature that considers how to do this (Earman, 1992; Jaynes, 1978; Skilling, 1989). When we have just two discrete hypotheses (that *if p then q* holds, and that p and q are completely independent), the most obvious prior, that each model has prior probability 0.5, is also the most theoretically justified (it corresponds to the maximum entropy prior, and to Bayes' own principle of indifference: Bayes, 1763). We shall assume this prior in all subsequent analyses except when it is explicitly varied.

CHAPTER ELEVEN

A Rational Analysis of the Selection Task II: Abstract Materials

INTRODUCTION

Having introduced our rational analysis of the selection task, we now show that it provides a descriptively adequate account of performance on the abstract, or "indicative" versions of the selection task. In these versions of the task, the task rule putatively describes the way the world is, e.g. ravens are black, birds fly, and so on. Typically these experiments have been conducted with abstract contents, e.g. if there is an A on one side of a card, then there is a 2 on the other side. For each version of the task, our strategy will be to introduce the data and then show how our model accounts for them.

THE ABSTRACT SELECTION TASK

Standard Abstract Results

Data

We described the standard abstract selection task in the last chapter. Abstract tasks use unfamiliar content and contrast with thematic tasks that employ familiar everyday contents. We discuss the thematic tasks in the next chapter.

We conducted a meta-analysis (Wolf, 1986) of the abstract data that revealed the following ordering in individual card selection frequencies $p > q > not\text{-}q > not\text{-}p$. Table 11.1 shows the results of the studies included in our meta-analysis.

TABLE 11.1

Studies where an affirmative abstract version of the selection task has been employed and individual card selection frequencies are reported or can be inferred from exhaustive reporting of card combinations. For all studies using Evans' negations paradigm (Evans & Lynch, 1973), only the data for the affirmative rule is included.

Study	Expt./Condition	Card selection frequencies				
		p	q	$\neg q$	$\neg p$	N
Wason (1968)	Expt. 1/Experimental	18	14	5	3	18
	/Control	16	11	2	1	16
	Expt. 2	26	13	3	3	26
Evans & Lynch (1973)	Single Expt.	21	12	8	2	24
Manktelow & Evans (1979)	Expt. 1/Abstract	23	15	8	3	24
	Expt. 2/Abstract	20	16	6	4	24
	Expt. 3/Abstract	14	9	6	6	16
	Expt. 4/Abstract	11	10	2	0	16
	Expt. 5/Abstract	14	13	1	2	16
Griggs & Cox (1982)	Expt. 1/Trial 1	16	9	1	1	16
	/Trial 2	16	11	1	1	16
	Expt. 3/Trial 1	14	14	8	6	20
	/Trial 2	13	15	6	6	20
Griggs (1984)	Expt./Non/mem./T-F	21	13	2	4	25
	/Non-mem./Vio.	23	19	4	4	25
Chrostowski & Griggs (1985)	Expt./Non/mem./Vio.	52	46	9	7	60
	/Non-mem./T-F	58	47	5	4	60
Hoch & Tschirgi (1985)*	Expt./Bachelor's	22	15	10	6	25
Valentine (1985)	Expt./AA	20	14	6	3	24
Yachanin (1986)	Expt. 2/Widgit/Vio.	20	16	4	3	20
	/Widgit/Test	19	14	6	4	20
Beattie & Baron (1988)	Expt. 1/4-card, +ve	17	10	1	1	18
	Expt. 2/4-card, +ve	16	10	8	1	16
	Expt. 3/4-card, +ve	16	10	2	0	16
Cosmides (1989)	Expts. 1 & 2	46	15	21	10	48
	Expts. 3 & 4	46	23	25	11	48
Girotto et al. (1992)	Expt. 1/Arbitrary Rule	20	14	6	4	24
	Expt. 2/Arbitrary Rule	23	13	8	7	24
	Expt. 3/Arbitrary Rule	19	10	13	7	24
	Expt. 4/Arbitrary Rule	16	12	5	2	20
Oaksford & Stenning (1992)	Expt. 2/Abstract	19	15	5	6	24
	Expt. 3/Coloured Shape	15	15	7	7	24
	/Vowel-Even	23	17	7	4	24
	/Control	21	12	4	4	24
TOTALS		754	522	215	137	845
Mean proportion cards selected		0.89	0.62	0.25	0.16	
SDs		0.15	0.12	0.14	0.09	

* Only the Bachelor's condition is included because the other two conditions (High School and Master's) were not comparable to the Ss used in the remaining studies.

We included all studies reporting individual card selection frequencies. We found 13 such studies reporting 34 standard abstract selection tasks, involving 845 subjects.[1] Table 11.1 shows the frequency of individual card selections for each of these tasks and the average across studies. We performed a one-way analysis of variance taking task-instance as the unit of analysis (see Glass, McGaw, & Smith, 1981, for rationale), card-type as the independent variable, and proportion of cards selected as the dependent variable.[2] This was highly significant ($F[3,99] = 271.01$, $p < 0.0001$). *Post hoc* Tukey HSD tests revealed that each pairwise comparison between cards was significant at least at the 0.05 level. This provides strong evidence for the $p > q > not\text{-}q > not\text{-}p$ ordering in card selection frequencies.

Model

To model this ordering, we assume that by default subjects are operating in region R of Fig. 10.3. For every such point in R the expected information gain is ordered such that $E(I_g(p)) > E(I_g(q)) > E(I_g(not\text{-}q)) > E(I_g(not\text{-}p))$. Average $E(I_g)$ values sampled across R were: $E(I_g(p)) = 0.76$; $E(I_g(q)) = 0.20$; $E(I_g(not\text{-}q)) = 0.09$; $E(I_g(not\text{-}p)) = 0$.[3] This order mirrors the $p > q > not\text{-}q > not\text{-}p$ ordering in card selection frequencies. Therefore card selection frequencies are monotonically related to expected information gain. This relationship suggests that subjects base their card selections on the expected information gain of each card. We tested the prediction that the cards are ordered in this way using Page's L-test for ordered alternatives (see Siegel & Castellan, 1988, pp. 184–188). As expected, this proved to be highly significant ($L(N = 34, k = 4) = 1007.5$, $z_L = 9.36$, $p < 0.00001$).

Non-independence of Card Selections

Data

Some studies have investigated whether card selections are statistically associated. In an analysis of just the q and $not\text{-}q$ cards, Evans (1977) found that selection of these two cards was statistically independent. However, in a more detailed meta-analysis of three experiments, Pollard (1985) found consistent associations between card selections. He found that similarly valenced cards, i.e. the p and q cards, and the $not\text{-}p$ and $not\text{-}q$ cards, are positively associated, whereas selections of dissimilarly valenced cards, i.e. p and $not\text{-}p$, p and $not\text{-}q$, q and $not\text{-}p$, and q and $not\text{-}q$, are negatively associated. Although these associations are not always statistically significant, their direction, positive or negative, is consistent across experiments.

We confirmed and extended these findings in a further meta-analysis. We took data from the studies analysed by Pollard (1985) and five further studies, three from Oaksford and Stenning (1992) (designated O & S2, O &

S4, and O & S5) and two further unpublished control experiments (O & S1, O & S3). All these experiments used task rules with negations varied in their antecedents and consequents, a manipulation that we discuss in the next section on "The Negations Paradigm Selection Task". Table 11.2 shows the results of our meta-analysis (see the rows labelled "AA" in Table 11.2). For the AA rule the following identities should be born in mind: TA = p card; FA = $not\text{-}p$ card; TC = q card; FC = $not\text{-}q$ card (we explain the TA, FA, TC and FC categories in the next section).

We performed the meta-analysis following Pollard (1985). We tested all six possible pairwise associations using Fisher's exact tests in the direction of the association present. We assigned a positive or negative z score to each result, setting z to 0 if the test yielded $p > 0.5$ in either direction (because this reveals a two-tailed probability of 1.0). We then calculated combined z estimates for each comparison and rule form using Stouffer's method (Wolf, 1986). Concentrating on the AA rule form, the combined estimates (see Table 11.2) were all significant (one-tailed) apart from the positive association between p (TA) and q (TC). The signs of the associations never reversed for any of the six pairs across all eight experiments. This was significant in one-tailed binomial tests (see Siegel & Castellan, 1988, pp. 38–44) for each of the six associations ($p < 0.005$).

Model

To model these associations we make three assumptions about how $E(I_g)$s map onto card selections. First, we assume that every card has some probability of being chosen because some subjects will simply not perform any, or an appropriate, analysis. In particular, subjects will sometimes choose the $not\text{-}p$ card, with $E(I_g (not\text{-}p)) = 0$. We account for this by adding a small fixed constant (0.1) to the $E(I_g)$s for each card. Second, because of the four cards present in the selection task, we assume that card choice is a competitive matter. A card should have a greater chance of being chosen if it is less distinguishable from alternatives. One way to ensure that this happens for all four cards, including the $not\text{-}p$ card, is to scale the $E(I_g)$s by the mean information available. We do this by dividing the derived score ($E(I_g) + 0.1$) for each card by the mean of this quantity for all four cards. We refer to this value as the "scaled expected information gain" ($SE(I_g)$). We assume that subjects choose cards as a monotonic function of their $SE(I_g)$ value. Third, a reasonable constraint on values for $P(p)$ and $P(q)$ is that $P(q) \geq P(p)$, otherwise the dependency model could not hold.

We sampled a variety of points corresponding to pairs of values for $P(p)$ and $P(q)$ at intervals of 0.025. The points satisfied the inequalities, $P(p) \leq 0.2$, $P(q) \leq 0.2$, $P(q) \geq P(p)$, $P(q) \leq P(p) + 0.025$. The first two inequalities enforce the rarity assumption. The third inequality ensures that the

TABLE 11.2

Meta-analysis of non-independence of card selections

Comparison	Rule form	Study from which z is derived								Comb. z	Overall comb. z
		E & L	M & E1	M & E2	O & S1	O & S2	O & S3	O & S4	O & S5		
TA vs. FA	AA	-0.70	-0.60	-1.84	-2.49	-1.55	-2.72	-1.55	-0.97	-4.39	-10.43
	NA	-2.50	-2.94	-2.69	-1.92	-2.38	-1.23	-4.00	-0.71	-6.49	
	AN	-1.38	0.00	-0.34	0.00	-0.98	-2.58	-2.52	-0.40	-2.90	
	NN	-2.06	-4.00	-4.00	-1.54	-2.72	-1.54	-4.00	-0.16	-7.08	
TA vs. TC	AA	0.00	0.00	0.87	0.37	0.00	0.00	0.00	0.43	0.59	1.32
	NA	0.00	-1.40	0.00	0.00	0.00	0.29	0.80	0.00	-0.11	
	AN	-2.68	-0.50	0.30	0.00	-1.27	-0.92	0.00	0.71	-1.54	
	NN	1.82	1.35	3.98	1.13	0.88	0.00	1.29	0.00	3.69	
TA vs. FC	AA	-0.67	-1.17	-2.28	-0.51	-0.16	0.00	-1.55	-0.55	-2.44	-2.42
	NA	0.89	1.59	1.67	-1.26	-0.88	0.00	1.13	0.00	1.11	
	AN	0.98	0.00	0.00	-1.55	0.05	0.00	-0.27	0.00	-0.28	
	NN	0.00	-2.46	-2.29	-0.61	-1.42	-0.67	-0.56	-1.13	-3.23	
FA vs. TC	AA	0.00	-0.12	-1.24	-2.29	0.00	0.00	-1.55	0.00	-1.84	-1.21
	NA	-0.15	2.09	0.32	-0.45	0.00	0.00	-1.29	-0.14	0.13	
	AN	0.89	1.59	1.67	2.58	0.00	0.16	-0.45	-0.71	2.03	
	NN	-0.89	-2.38	-2.91	0.00	0.00	0.00	-1.55	0.00	-2.73	
FA vs. FC	AA	1.27	0.87	2.66	2.19	1.20	0.00	0.00	1.56	3.45	2.55
	NA	-0.72	-1.17	1.01	-1.74	-2.01	0.00	1.34	1.61	-0.59	
	AN	-0.21	-0.65	-1.07	0.00	-0.05	0.00	0.00	0.00	-0.70	
	NN	0.00	2.41	2.65	1.56	0.00	0.00	0.00	1.73	2.95	
TC vs. FC	AA	-0.67	-1.17	-2.28	0.00	-1.29	-0.48	-0.37	-0.97	-2.56	-4.89
	NA	0.89	1.59	1.67	0.00	-0.82	0.00	-2.26	-2.10	-0.36	
	AN	0.98	0.00	0.00	-0.45	-2.05	0.00	-2.68	-1.85	-2.14	
	NN	0.00	-2.46	-2.29	-1.33	-2.85	0.00	-1.67	-2.75	-4.72	

Note. E & L = Evans and Lynch (1973); M & E1 and M & E2 = Manktelow and Evans (1979) Experiments 1 and 2; O & S2, O & S4, O & S5 correspond to Oaksford and Stenning's (1992) Experiment 3/control, Experiment 3/subject–predicate, and Experiment 3/vowel–even conditions, respectively; O & S1 and O & S3 are Oaksford and Stenning's two unpublished control experiments; Comb. = combined; TA = true antecedent; FA = false antecedent; TC = true consequent; FC = false consequent; AA = affirmative antecedent and affirmative consequent; NA = negative antecedent and affirmative consequent; AN = affirmative antecedent and negative consequent; NN = negative antecedent and negative consequent. z scores greater than 1.65 or less than –1.65 are significant at P < .05 (one-tailed).

191

dependency model can hold. The last inequality corresponds to the reasonable constraint that although the probability of q is greater than the probability of p, it is only marginally greater (Klayman & Ha, 1987). In Chapter 13 we discuss the justification of this constraint. We calculated $SE(I_g)$s for all four cards for each pair of $P(p)$ and $P(q)$ values (the z-scores of the computed $SE(I_g)$s for each card appear for the AA rule in Fig. 11.1). We then computed Spearman rank order correlation coefficients between the $SE(I_g)$s for all six card pairs. We used rank correlations because we assume only that card selection is a monotonic function of $SE(I_g)$. The results of these analyses appear in the AA column in Table 11.3. The $SE(I_g)$s for the similarly valenced cards are positively correlated whereas the $SE(I_g)$s for the four dissimilarly valenced card comparisons are negatively correlated. This pattern of correlations is the same as that observed experimentally. The agreement in the sign of the correlation between model and data was significant in a one-tailed binomial test ($p < 0.025$). This analysis applies only to the AA or purely affirmative rule. We now show how to extend this analysis to account for data from the negations paradigm selection task.

The Negations Paradigm Selection Task

Data

In the negations paradigm selection task (Evans & Lynch, 1973) the antecedent and consequent of a rule can contain negated constituents (*not-p*, *not-q*). There are four possible conditional rules, the original *if p, then q* (AA), together with *if p, then not q* (AN); *if not p, then q* (NA) and *if not p, then not q* (NN). Each subject performs a selection task for each of these four rule types.

We have so far described the cards in the selection task in terms of *p*, *q*, *not-p*, and *not-q*. In the negations paradigm cards are normally described in

TABLE 11.3

Spearman rank order correlation coefficients between $SE(I_g)$s for each card pair for each of the four rule-types in the negations paradigm selection task. Figures in brackets indicate the combined z-scores for each pairwise comparison taken from Table 11.2

Comparison	AA	AN	NA	NN
TA vs. TC	+0.11 (+0.59)	−0.47 (−1.54)	−0.85 (−0.11)	+0.99 (+3.69)
FA vs. FC	+0.79 (+3.45)	−0.70 (−0.09)	+0.67 (−0.59)	+0.92 (+2.95)
TA vs. FC	−0.69 (−2.44)	−0.94 (−0.28)	+0.54 (+1.11)	−0.99 (−3.23)
TA vs. FA	−0.21 (−4.39)	−0.22 (−2.90)	+0.97 (−6.49)	−0.92 (−7.08)
TC vs. FC	−0.64 (−2.56)	+0.59 (−2.14)	−0.88 (−0.36)	−0.99 (−4.72)
TC vs. FA	−0.92 (−1.84)	−0.53 (+2.03)	−0.93 (+0.13)	−0.94 (−2.73)

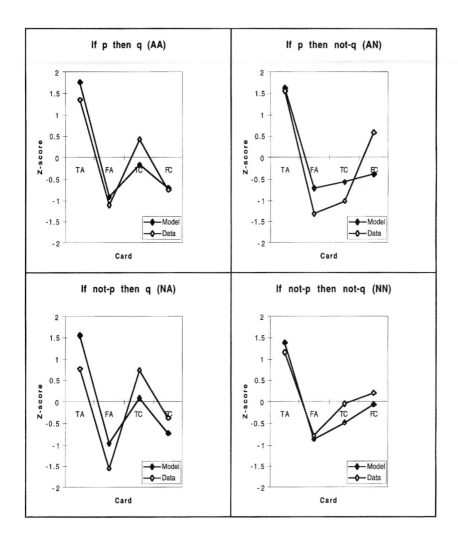

FIG. 11.1 Comparison of the average $SE(I_g)$s and the selection frequency for each card for each of the four rule-types in the negations paradigm selection task. For purposes of comparison the average $SE(I_g)$s and the selection frequencies have been converted to z-scores in order to normalise the scales. The data are taken from the eight studies mentioned in the text.

terms of whether they make the antecedent or consequent of the rule true or false. For example consider the rule "if there is *not* an A on one side, then there is *not* a 2 on the other side". For this rule the *p* card (A) and the *q* card (2) are the false antecedent (FA) and false consequent (FC) cases respectively. The *not-p* (K) and *not-q* (7) cards are the true antecedent (TA) and true consequent (TC) cases respectively. The TA, FA, TC, FC *logical cases* permit a uniform classification of the cards in the negations paradigm.

Using the negations paradigm, Evans and Lynch (1973) reported an effect that they called "matching bias". Subjects tend to select the cards that are named in the rules, ignoring the negations. For example, consider the rule "if there is not an A on one side, then there is not a 2 on the other side", and the four cards showing an "A", a "K", a "2", and a "7". Here the matching response is to select the A (FA) and the 2 (FC) cards. The confirmatory response is to select the K (TA) and 7 (TC) cards, and the falsificatory response is to select the K (TA) and 2 (FC) cards. More recently it has become clear that matching occurs mainly for the consequent cards (Manktelow & Evans, 1979; Evans, 1989), whereas antecedent card selections accord with logical case (subjects choose the TA card in preference to the FA card for all four rule forms).

Card Orderings.   As in the standard selection task, we can describe these data in terms of orderings over card selections. The ordering in card selection frequencies for affirmative consequent rules (*if p then q; if not-p then q*) is TA > TC > FC > FA. The ordering in card selection frequencies for negative consequent rules (*if p then not-q; if not-p then not-q*) is TA > TC > FC > FA. Both these orders are consistent with matching.

A meta-analysis confirmed these orderings. We analysed the studies used in our meta-analysis of non-independence of card selections, less O & S4 and O & S5. We omitted these studies because they included manipulations to counteract matching (as we shall see). We performed a one-way analysis of variance for each rule type (AA, AN, NA, NN) with card-type as the independent variable and number of cards selected as the dependent variable. For the affirmative consequent rules these analyses were significant (AA: $F[3, 15] = 111.81$, $MS_e = 2.75$, $p < 0.0001$; NA: $F[3, 15] = 21.19$, $MS_e = 6.78$, $p < .0001$). For both rules the order of mean number of cards selected reflected the TA > TC > FC > FA order. Each pairwise comparison between cards was significant at least at the 0.05 level in *post hoc* Neuman–Keuls tests except for the TA vs. TC and FA vs. FC comparisons for the NA rule. Similar analyses were also significant for the negated consequent rules (AN: $F[3, 15] = 100.64$, $MS_e = 4.45$, $p < 0.0001$; NN: $F[3, 15] = 11.64$, $MS_e = 13.69$, $p < 0.0005$). For both rules the order of mean number of cards selected reflected the TA > FC > TC > FA order. Each pairwise comparison between cards was significant at least at the 0.05

level in *post hoc* Neuman–Keuls tests except for the FA vs. FC comparison for the AN rule and the TC vs. FC comparison for the NN rule.

The z-scores of the mean frequencies of card selections for each rule type are shown in Fig. 11.1 (Data). This table reveals that the orderings in card selections are weaker for the negative antecedent rules, NA and NN. The NA rule also appears to cause comprehension problems. Subjects are significantly slower to comprehend this rule than each of the other three rule forms (Ormerod, Manktelow, & Jones, 1993). This result is unexpected because the standard finding has been that sentences containing negations are harder to comprehend (Fodor, Fodor, & Garrett, 1975). This would predict that a sentence with two negations should be harder to comprehend than similar sentences containing single negations. However, subjects comprehend the NA rule significantly more slowly than the NN and the AN rule.

Suppressing Matching. Two experimental manipulations suppress matching and re-establish the TA > TC > FC > FA order for all four rule types in the negations paradigm. First, although Manktelow and Evans (1979) initially found matching even with thematic material, Reich and Ruth (1982) and Griggs and Cox (1983) found that matching disappeared when they used more realistic thematic material. Second, Oaksford and Stenning (1992) found that matching also disappears when the linguistic framing of the rules is more appropriate. They argued that rules such as "if there is not an A on one side then there is a 2 on the other side" are ambiguous. The *not-A* card could be the K, *or* the 2, *or* the 7 cards. Oaksford and Stenning (1992) found that removing this ambiguity, suppressed matching and re-established the TA > TC > FC > FA order for all four rule types.

Non-independence of Card Selections. Pollard (1985) also investigated associations between card selections for the negations paradigm. His meta-analysis looked at associations between *card cases* (*p, not-p, q, not-q*). He found positive associations for similarly valenced cards and negative associations for dissimilarly valenced cards, not only for the standard affirmative rule (AA), but also for the remaining three rules (AN: *if p, then not-q*; NA: *if not-p, then q*; and NN: *if not-p, then not-q*).

Our extended meta-analysis, shown in Table 11.2 shows these associations in terms of *logical case*. The overall combined z-score (final column in Table 11.2) for each pairwise comparison, treats each rule in each study as a separate unit of analysis ($N = 32$). The final column of Table 11.2 shows that the signs of the combined z-scores are positive for similarly valenced cards (TA vs. TC and FA vs. FC) and negative for dissimilarly valenced cards (TA vs. FA, TA vs. FC, TC vs. FA, and TC vs. FC). These results follow the pattern for the standard selection task that we discussed earlier.

Although this finding is clear for the similarly valenced rules, AA and NN, the results for the dissimilarly valenced AN and NA rules are more ambiguous. We highlight this division in Table 11.3 where we summarise the combined z-scores for each rule separately (see figures in brackets).

Model

The key to understanding a variety of effects in the negations paradigm is the notion of a "contrast set" (Hampton, 1989; Oaksford & Stenning, 1992). Contrast sets provide the interpretations of negated constituents. For example, the interpretation of "Johnny didn't serve *tea*" (where the word in italics indicates the focus of a negation) is that he served a drink other than tea. In terms of set theory, the superordinate category "drinks" provides the universe of discourse. Contrast sets are plausible subsets of the complement in a universe of discourse. In our example, all other drinks less tea form the complement. When Johnny did not serve tea it is more likely he served soft drinks rather than, for instance, scotch on the rocks. Soft drinks is therefore the contrast set, i.e. a plausible subset of the complement. Background knowledge may restrict the membership of the intended contrast set even further. So, in our example, coffee is perhaps the most likely single contrast set member. This indicates that a negation rarely identifies the complement, i.e. the whole set consisting of the superordinate category less the named constituent, as the intended contrast set. More commonly the intention is to identify much more restricted contrast sets. We now apply this behaviour of contrast sets to the negations paradigm.

We have good reason to believe that $P(TA)$ or $P(TC)$ are greater when they are negated. This is because the class of things referred to by a constituent is generally smaller than the size of the contrast class defined by its negation. For example, there are many things Johnny could have drunk, when he did not drink tea.[4] However, the intended contrast set is unlikely to be all drinks other than tea. We made the reasonable assumption that the probability of a contrast class does not exceed 0.5.[5] We therefore set that the probabilities of un-negated constituents to vary between 0 and 0.2 as for the AA rule, and those of negated constituents to vary between 0.2 and 0.5.

Card Orderings.   We have already explained the AA rule. For the other three rule types we sampled points at 0.025 intervals as in the section *Non-independence of Card Selections.* As for the AA rule, we now outline our rationale for the region over which we sampled points for each rule form. For the AN rule, $P(TA)$ is low but $P(TC)$ is high. We therefore sampled points in the region that satisfied the inequalities: $P(p) \leq 0.2; 0.2\ P(q) \leq 0.5$. For the NA rule, $P(TA)$ is high but $P(TC)$ is low. This rule therefore violates the inequality that $P(TC) \geq P(TA)P(M_D)$—see equation (10.1)—i.e. this rule corresponds to the region of the parameter space in Fig. 10.3 where $E(I_g)$ is undefined. Informally, an NA rule is like the hypothesis that all black things are ravens. This rule must be false because there are more black things than ravens (i.e. the dependency model could not hold). So, to interpret an NA rule as having a chance of being true involves either revising $P(TA)$ down or revising $P(TC)$ up. Subjects appear to resolve the ambiguity by revising $P(TA)$ down. The NA rule then leads to low $P(TA)$ and $P(TC)$ values. However, it is reasonable to assume that $P(TA)$ is still greater than $P(TC)$ because the antecedent is negated. We therefore sampled points that satisfied the inequalities, $P(p) \leq 0.2$; $P(q) \leq 0.2$; $P(q) < P(p)$; $P(q) \geq P(p)$— 0.025. For the NN rule, both $P(TA)$ and $P(TC)$ are high. We modelled this rule by restricting the values of $P(q)$ and $P(p)$ to the range 0.2 to 0.5. We therefore sampled points from the region that satisfied the inequalities, $0.2 \leq P(p) \leq 0.5$; $0.2 \leq P(q) \leq 0.5$; $P(q) \geq P(p)$; $P(q) \geq P(p) + 0.025$.

The z-scores of the average $SE(I_g)$ values for points sampled across the four regions appear in Fig. 11.1. The z-scores of the mean number of cards selected in the eight studies used in our meta-analysis of the negations paradigm selection task are also shown. As can be seen, there was a good fit between data and model (Spearman's $rho(16) = 0.92$, $p < 0.0001$). Finally the need to resolve the ambiguity between revising $P(TA)$ down or $P(TC)$ up, accounts for why subjects are significantly slower to comprehend the NA rule than each of the other three rule forms (Ormerod et al., 1993).

Suppressing Matching.   "Realistic" thematic content restores the TA > TC > FC > FA ordering in card selection frequencies for all rule forms (Reich & Ruth, 1982). We argue that this is because prior world knowledge restricts contrast sets to the most plausible member(s). For example, if Johnny did not drink tea, then it is most likely that he drank coffee. In a context where drinking tea is a possibility, drinking scotch on the rocks, for example, probably is not. Relative to the class of drinks, tea and coffee are both rare (subject to the caveats in Note 5 at the end of this chapter). Such examples show that familiar thematic material reduces contrast set size, thereby re-establishing rarity. Unrealistic thematic content fails to restore the TA > TC > FC > FA ordering because it cannot engage prior knowledge to constrain contrast sets in this way (Manktelow & Evans, 1979).

The same reasoning explains the restoration of the TA > TC > FC > FA ordering for all rule forms in Oaksford and Stenning (1992). The intention in this task was for subjects to regard the *not*-A contrast set to consist of only the K card. However, the K, 2, and 7 cards are all potential members of the *not*-A contrast set. To restrict this contrast set the materials had to indicate unambiguously that only other letters are potential contrast set members. Oaksford and Stenning (1992) used the original vowels and even numbers material used by Wason (1968). "Vowels" and its complement set "consonants" only apply to letters. In the context of the task, where K is the only consonant, it should therefore be clear that K is the only possible member of the *not*-A contrast set. The antecedent is therefore unambiguously about the K card and so rarity again holds. This predicts the standard—TA > TC > FC > FA—ordering for all four rule forms as Oaksford and Stenning (1992) found.

Non-independence of Card Selections.   Even when negated constituents are used, similarly valenced cards show positive associations and dissimilarly valenced cards show negative associations. We modelled this behaviour in the same way as the AA which we discussed earlier. We calculated Spearman rank order correlation coefficients for each card pair for the same sets of points used to calculate average $SE(I_g)$ values in Table 11.3. These coefficients appear in Table 11.3 together with the combined z-scores taken from Table 11.2 (in brackets). We assessed the fit between data and model in terms of the direction ($+/-$) of association or correlation using the Phi coefficient (Siegel & Castellan, 1988, pp. 232–235) which showed a significant fit between data and model ($r_\phi = 0.64$, $p < 0.025$). The fit was perfect for the AA and NN rules. For the AN and NA rules the fit was less good, although the model does capture some of the interesting differences between the AA/NN rules and the AN/NA rules. The poorest fit was for the NA rule where subjects must revise $P(TA)$ down and where they experience comprehension problems. Such problems may lead to a residual matching tendency. The overall agreement between data and model was highly significant as assessed by a one-tailed binomial test (19 agreements vs. 5 disagreements: $p < 0.005$).

Probabilities of Fictional Outcomes

Data

Recently, Kirby (1994) explicitly manipulated $P(p)$ in a selection task. To understand the rationale behind Kirby's studies, it is necessary briefly to outline his theoretical account of the selection task. This account uses the vocabulary of subjective expected utility and signal detection theories. Kirby starts from the falsificationist assumption that a subject's goal is to find p and *not-q* instances, which he calls an "inconsistent outcome". He then assumes that two factors determine performance. The first factor concerns the probability of an inconsistent outcome arising from a visible card face (C). So like our model, Kirby's takes into account the probabilities of the fictional other sides of each card ("fictional" because the subjects never turn the cards). The second factor concerns the utilities associated with a card choice. There are four possibilities, which Kirby classifies using signal detection theory: a *hit*, i.e. choosing a card with a hidden face that is inconsistent with the rule; a *miss*, i.e. *not* choosing such a card; a *false alarm* (*FA*), i.e. choosing a card with a hidden face that is consistent with the rule; and a *correct rejection* (*CR*), i.e. *not* choosing such a card.

Kirby proposes that a subject should choose a card when the posterior odds of an inconsistent outcome exceeds a simple function of the utilities— see equation (11.1). In deriving predictions for his experiments 1–3, Kirby assumes that the utilities on the right hand side of equation (11.1) remain constant.

$$\frac{P(\text{inconsistent outcome present} \mid C)}{P(\text{inconsistent outcome absent} \mid C)} > \frac{U(CR) - U(FA)}{U(\text{Hit}) - U)\text{Miss})} \qquad (11.1)$$

On this analysis the *q* and *not-p* cards have probability 0 of yielding an inconsistent outcome. Therefore, as with other falsificationist accounts, Kirby's predicts that subjects should never turn these cards. The interest of his account therefore centres on the *p* and *not-q* cards.

Kirby notes that in Wason's (1968) original rule, *if a card has a vowel on one side then it has an even number on the other side*, the posterior odds of finding an inconsistent outcome with the *not-q* card are low, i.e. 5/21 (this analysis assumes that each letter is equally probable and that there are five vowels and 21 consonants). Kirby suggests that this might be why subjects do not select the *not-q* card. Equation (11.1) predicts that these odds will increase if $P(p)$ is larger, and hence that subjects should choose the *not-q* card more frequently. Equation (11.1) predicts no changes for the *p*, *not-q*, and *q* cards, however.

In Kirby's experiments 1–3 subjects checked whether a computer had made a mistake in generating cards with integers between 0 and a 1000 (or 0 and 100 in experiments 2 and 3) on one side and either a " + " or "–" on the other side. In experiment 1 subjects were told that the computer had an error rate of 0.01, and in experiment 2, 0.1. In experiment 1 the rules were: *if there is a 0 on one side, there is a + on the other side* (small P set condition), and *if there is a number between 1 and a 1000 on one side, there is a + on the other side* (large P set condition). If each number is equally probable, then when 0 is the antecedent $P(p)$ is 1/1001 and when any number between 1 and 1000 is the antecedent $P(p)$ is 1000/1001. In his experiments 2 and 3 Kirby used three values, so that $P(p) = 1/100$, 50/100 or 90/100.

As he predicted, Kirby found that selections of the *not-q* card increased as $P(p)$ increased (see the figures in brackets in Table 11.4). However, he also found unpredicted movements in the frequency of card selections for the other cards. As $P(p)$ increased selections of the *p* card and *q* card decreased and selections of the *not-p* card increased, although the finding for the *q* card was not robust. Kirby considers a variety of possible explanations for these

TABLE 11.4

$SE(I_g)$s for each card using the $P(p)$, $P(q)$ used by Kirby (1994) in his Experiments 1 to 3, with $P(M_l) = 0.01$. Figures in brackets shows the proportion of these cards selected in Kirby's experiments. Med. = medium

		Cards			
	$P(p)$ and $P(q)$	not-q	p	not-p	q
Experiment 1					
small P set	1/1001	0.746 (0.49)	1.311 (0.78)	0.745 (0.29)	1.198 (0.60)
large P set	1000/1001	1.372 (0.73)	0.911 (0.55)	0.858 (0.48)	0.858 (0.41)

Note: Spearman Rank Order Correlation Coefficient ($N = 8$) $= 0.87$ ($p < 0.01$).

Experiment 2					
small P set	1/100	0.745 (0.40)	1.332 (0.91)	0.740 (0.17)	1.182 (0.50)
med. P set	50/100	1.009 (0.53)	1.337 (0.80)	0.745 (0.27)	0.909 (0.57)
large P set	90/100	1.248 (0.61)	1.262 (0.80)	0.737 (0.38)	0.753 (0.56)

Note: Spearman Rank Order Correlation Coefficient ($N = 12$) $= 0.90$ ($p < 0.001$).

Experiment 3					
small P set	1/100	0.745 (0.26)	1.332 (0.88)	0.740 (0.11)	1.182 (0.39)
med. P set	50/100	1.009 (0.39)	1.337 (0.84)	0.745 (0.28)	0.909 (0.61)
large P set	90/100	1.248 (0.39)	1.262 (0.78)	0.737 (0.41)	0.753 (0.61)

Note: Spearman Rank Order Correlation Coefficient ($N = 12$) $= 0.69$ ($p < 0.025$).

effects that we now argue are direct consequences of our model of optimal data selection.

Model

From the perspective of optimal data selection, the failure of Kirby's model to predict the movements in card selections for the *p*, *not-p*, and *q* cards (indeed, the failure to predict that subjects should choose the *q* and *not-p* cards at all) is due to its exclusive focus on falsifying instances. By contrast, in our optimal data selection framework a card can still be informative even though it could not yield a falsification. This permits us to model these data straightforwardly.

Our model predicts that the *not-q* card is informational to the extent that $P(p)$ is large. Our model therefore predicts Kirby's principal finding. It moreover predicts the other changes in the frequency of card selections that he observed for the *p*, *not-p*, and *q* cards. The independent variables Kirby manipulated in his experiments 1 to 3 correspond closely to the parameters of our model. Kirby varied $P(p)$ directly. We assume that $P(q) = P(p)$. This assumption is reasonable because Kirby's materials are binary, i.e. the antecedent is either 0 or 1 to a 100 (or a 1000) and the consequent is a + or a –. Staudenmayer and Bourne (1978) interpreted the effect of such material as leading to a biconditional interpretation which is consistent with the assumption that $P(q) = P(p)$. Kirby provided specific information about the error rate, i.e. in experiment 1 it was 0.01 and in experiment 2 it was 0.1. We assume that subjects use the error rate as an estimate of the probability of the independence model. However, because an error rate of 0.1 is unreasonably high for a computer, we assume that subjects take $P(M_I)$ to be 0.01 for both experiments 1 and 2. Using these parameter values we calculated $SE(I_g)$s for all cards in each condition of Kirby's experiments 1 and 2. These appear in Table 11.4 together with the proportions of cards selected in Kirby's data (in brackets). In his experiment 3 Kirby provided no error rate information. Nonetheless it is reasonable to assume that subjects regard computers as having a low error rate. Hence we used the same parameter values to model experiment 3 as in experiment 2. As can be seen from Table 11.4 the fit between data and model is very good. The correlation for experiment 1 is 0.87 and for experiment 2 it is 0.9. The fit in experiment 3 is weaker (0.69) but nonetheless significant. This may be due to subjects assuming a broader range of $P(M_I)$ values.

The Therapy Experiments

Data

As their name suggests, these experiments (Wason, 1969; Wason & Golding, 1974; Wason & Johnson-Laird, 1970) involved therapeutic procedures to help subjects see where they were going "wrong", and to encourage them to adopt the falsificatory *p*, *not-q* selection. The experimenter engaged subjects in a dialogue concerning their task performance exposing them by degrees to inconsistencies "between their initial selections of cards and their subsequent independent evaluations of specific cards as falsifying or verifying the rule" (Wason & Johnson-Laird, 1972, p. 179). In Wason (1969), subjects performed an initial selection task, and were then given three increasingly direct therapies, weak hypothetical contradiction, strong hypothetical contradiction, and concrete contradiction. Each therapy was followed by a further selection task to assess whether it was successful. Subjects also performed a final selection task making five in all.

The therapies aimed to get agreement that a card with *p* and *not-q* faces falsified the rule. Three therapies laid an increasing emphasis on the *not-q* card. The weak hypothetical contradiction therapy focused on the *p* card. The strong hypothetical contradiction therapy focused on the *not-q* card. Hypothetical contradictions involved asking subjects what they thought could be on the hidden faces of the cards and getting them to agree that a *p* and *not-q* instance falsified the rule. In the concrete contradiction therapy, the experimenter turned over the *not-q* card to reveal a *p* on the hidden face.

These attempts at therapy were not wholly successful. By the final selection task only 42% adopted the falsificatory response. The steps by which these subjects moved to this response followed two main patterns (Wason, 1969), which later became the focus of various "insight" models (as we shall see). In the first, subjects begin with an initial *p* card only response, they then move to a *p, q, not-q* response and finally to a *p, not-q* response (i.e. *p → p, q, not-q → p, not-q*). Notice that therapy on the *not-q* card unexpectedly causes some subjects to choose the *q* card. In the second, subjects begin with an initial *p, q* response, they then move to a *p, q*, and *not-q* response and finally to a *p, not-q* response (i.e. *p* and *q → p, q, not-q → p* and *not-q*) (Wason, 1969). Subjects successfully completed the second sequence less often (just 23.1% of subjects who made the initial *p, q* selection, rather than 62.5% of subjects who made an initial *p* selection [Wason, 1969]).

Various "insight" models attempted to explain these transition sequences (Bree, 1973; Bree & Coppens, 1976; Goodwin & Wason, 1972; Johnson-Laird & Wason, 1970a; Moshman, 1978; Smalley, 1974). A common feature of these models is that they postulate three levels of "insight" into the task, which subjects pass through sequentially and which correspond to the stages in the transition sequences identified in the last paragraph. Thus, in a state of "no insight" the subjects turn the *p* card and possibly also the *q* card; in a state of "partial insight" they turn the *p, q*, and *not-q* cards; and in a state of "complete insight" they turn the *p* and *not-q* cards (Johnson-Laird & Wason, 1970a).

Model

We explain these findings by the way subjects use the ordering in $SE(I_g)$ values to determine which cards to select:

$$SE(I_g(p)) > SE(I_g(q)) > SE(I_g(not\text{-}q)) > SE(I_g(not\text{-}p))$$

Let us consider the first transition sequence, which is the most striking, because therapy concerning the *not-q* unexpectedly induces the selection of the *q* card. The subject initially chooses *p* only, and assumes that the $SE(I_g)$ values of the other cards are not high enough to warrant their being turned. The effect of therapy is to persuade the subject that the experimenter considers that the *not-q* is worth turning. If, as we have assumed, subjects consider card choice to be a monotonic function of $SE(I_g)$, then they should also turn the *q* card, because $SE(I_g(q)) > SE(I_g(not\text{-}q))$. Hence, subjects subsequently choose *p, q*, and *not-q*. Subjects require further therapy to persuade them to violate monotonicity concerning the informativeness ordering, and choose only *p* and *not-q*. We explain the second transition sequence in the same way, the only difference is that subjects' initial card selections are *p*, *q*. Thus we can account for the main transition sequences observed in the data.

Subjects are reluctant to make the falsificatory response, even when strongly prompted to do so (only 42% of subjects finally make the *p*, *not-q* selection), because falsification requires them to violate the informativeness ordering. Our model does not directly predict that the the first transition sequence should lead to more *p*, *not-q* responses. However, it does suggest a possible explanation. Subjects' reluctance to move to the *p*, *not-q* response stems from the tendency to want to turn the *q* card. It may, therefore, be difficult to persuade subjects not to turn the *q* card when they turned it initially. Hence, subjects who initially select *p*, *q* are less likely to complete the transition sequence than subjects who initially select *p* only.

The Reduced Array Selection Task

Data

In a reduced array selection task (RAST) subjects choose between the *q* and *not-q* options only (hence "reduced array") (Johnson-Laird & Wason, 1970b; Wason & Green, 1984). The stimuli in the original RAST consisted of 30 coloured shapes. The experimenter informs the subjects that there are 15 black shapes and 15 white shapes, each of which is a triangle or a circle. The shapes are in two boxes, one containing the white shapes and the other containing the black shapes. On being presented with a test sentence, e.g. *All the triangles are black*, subjects have to assess the truth or falsity of the sentence by asking to see the *minimum* number of black or white shapes. In Johnson-Laird and Wason (1970b), although all subjects chose some confirmatory black shapes (no subject chose more than 9), they all chose all 15 potentially falsificatory white shapes. Thus, where subjects in effect perform multiple selection tasks, they tend to show falsificatory behaviour.

Wason and Green (1984) report a variant on this task. In one condition the materials consist of cards coloured on one half and depicting a shape on the other half. In this condition the rule is *disjoint*, e.g. *All the cards which have a triangle on one half are red on the other half* (the *All the triangles are red* rule they describe as *unified*). In this condition, Wason and Green (1984) found that subjects predominantly select the *q* card. They also observe that their "experiments show relatively good performance in reasoning about conditional sentences using the RAST technique" (Wason & Green, 1984, p. 608). Even in the disjoint rule condition there was a falsificatory response rate of between 29% and 45%, compared to as low as 4% in the standard selection task.

Model

The RAST makes explicit that the rule applies to a limited domain of cards or shapes that the experimenter describes as being in a box or a bag (or, in Wason & Green, 1984, "under the bar"). The experimenter also informs subjects that in this limited domain there are equal numbers of q and *not-q* instances. It follows that $P(q) = 0.5$, violating the rarity assumption. At this value $E(I_g(not\text{-}q))$ is higher than $E(I_g(q))$ (Fig. 10.3), and hence our model predicts more *not-q* card selections than q card selections.

Our model does not directly predict that a disjoint rule reduces the facilitatory effect of the RAST (Wason & Green, 1984). It does suggest a possible explanation, however. The standard RAST rule specifies class inclusion, whereas the disjoint rule specifies a relationship between two distinct items. The latter suggests a causal relationship which cannot be restricted to the limited domain of cards "in the bag" or "in the box" (Goodman, 1954). Hence the default rarity assumption may again be made in the disjoint condition.

SUMMARY

In this chapter we have shown how the probabilistic model of optimal data selection we developed in Chapter 10 can be used to explain the detailed pattern of results observed on abstract versions of Wason's selection task. In the next chapter we turn to the thematic versions of this task where people most often make the p, *not-q* response which accords with what would be expected by logic. We will argue, however, that this response does not reflect an underlying logical competence but rather a sensitivity to the utilities available in the often very rich contexts set up in these task versions.

NOTES

1. By "affirmative" we mean that the task rule contained no negations. Later in this chapter we will look at Evans' "negations paradigm" where negations are included in the task rules.

2. While advocating the use of Bayesian statistics in our model, we continue to use standard statistical tests here.

3. We selected the points by laying a grid over Fig. 3 with a mesh size of 0.025 on both axes. We then took the average over all points that fell in R.

4. It is possible that the token frequencies of the constituent are so large that they might outweigh the token frequencies of all the other possible drinks (i.e. if tea is much the most common drink). But if this is true for tea, it cannot be true for any other drink. Hence, in the domain of drinks, negations will still most commonly identify highly probable contrast classes.

5. Note that this means that the probability of an event and its most plausible contrast class will rarely sum to 1, although the probability of an event and its complement must sum to 1.

CHAPTER TWELVE

A Rational Analysis of the Selection Task III: Thematic Materials

INTRODUCTION

In this chapter we discuss work on the selection task using thematic or contentful materials. The particular materials used and the difference they make to selection task performance is discussed in detail later. In general, however, the move to thematic materials marks a shift from indicative task rules to "deontic" task rules, i.e. rules that state how the world *ought* to be, such as, if you are drinking beer, you must be over 18. As Manktelow and Over (1987) pointed out, this marks a profound shift in the nature of the task and perhaps of the underlying cognitive processes involved. We argue in this chapter that while much of the machinery introduced in Chapter 10 is required, this shift in emphasis requires a move to a model where people are regarded as maximising the expected utility of turning a card rather than the amount of information that can be gained about its truth or falsity.

THE THEMATIC SELECTION TASK

Most recent work on the selection task has concentrated on how thematic content affects reasoning (e.g. Cheng & Holyoak, 1985, 1989; Cosmides, 1989; Evans, 1989; Gigerenzer & Hug, 1992; Girotto et al., 1992; Griggs & Cox, 1982; Jackson & Griggs, 1990; Johnson-Laird & Byrne, 1991, 1992; Manktelow & Over, 1987, 1990a, 1990b, 1991; Rumelhart, 1980). In the selection task, this work originated in the attempt to facilitate falsificatory reasoning (Johnson-Laird, Legrenzi, & Legrenzi, 1972; Wason & Shapiro, 1971). For example, subjects may have to imagine that they are an immigration official enforcing the rule that *If a passenger's form says "ENTERING" on one side, then the other side must include cholera* (Cheng & Holyoak, 1985; Cheng et al., 1986), or they may have to imagine that they are a tribal elder enforcing the rule that *If a man eats cassava root, then he must have a tattoo on his face* (Cosmides, 1989). Subjects are also given a *rationale* for enforcing the rule (the prevention of disease, and that cassava root is a rare aphrodisiac that only married men, who have their faces tattooed, are allowed to eat). These thematic rules have typically facilitated the selection of the *p* and *not-q* cards.

Researchers now generally accept that these versions of the task address people's abilities at *deontic* reasoning, that is, reasoning concerning what *ought* to be the case (Manktelow & Over, 1987, 1990a, 1990b, 1991). In the abstract tasks subjects "are asked to decide whether an indicative conditional is true or false, while in ... [the deontic tasks] ... they are asked whether a conditional obligation has or has not been violated. A conditional obligation, of course, is not falsified when it is violated" (Manktelow & Over, 1990b, p. 114). Thus a subject's task in the deontic versions is very different to that confronted in the abstract versions of the selection task. However, we argue that the same probabilistic framework we used for the abstract selection task also applies to these data.

We describe these findings following Gigerenzer and Hug's (1992) classification by rule type and perspective. We also discuss recent work by Kirby (1994a), who manipulated probabilities and utilities in a thematic task, in a separate section *Utilities and Probabilities of Fictional Outcomes*.

Rule Type and Perspective

Data

There are two dimensions on which the pattern of cards selected in the thematic selection task depends. The first is rule type. Cheng and Holyoak (1985) use rules like *If a passenger's form says "ENTERING" on one side, then the other side must include cholera*, which they describe as "permissions". However, as Manktelow and Over (1987, 1990a, 1990b, 1991), observe, these rules are actually of the form of an *obligation*, i.e. people who want to carry out the *action* described in the antecedent are obliged to satisfy the *condition* stipulated in the consequent. Obligations are of the form: *if action (p) then must condition (q)*. A corresponding *permission* would be *If a passenger's form includes cholera on one side, then they may enter the country*. Here people who have satisfied the condition described in the antecedent are permitted to perform the action described in the consequent. A permission is of the form: *if condition (p) then may action (q)*. Notice that in going from an obligation to a permission, *action* and *condition* switch their clausal positions between antecedent and consequent of the conditional sentence.

The second dimension on which the pattern of card selections depends is the *perspective* a subject must adopt. Using an obligation rule, Cheng and Holyoak (1985) had subjects adopt the role of *enforcers* of the rule, i.e. subjects had to imagine they were immigration officials checking immigration forms. They found that subjects were more likely to select the *p* and *not-q* card combination under these conditions. Cosmides (1989) replicates this finding (as do Gigerenzer & Hug, 1992), and shows that from the enforcer's perspective, a permission (what Cosmides calls a "switched social contract") led subjects to select the *not-p* and *q* cards. (Notice that both these responses still correspond to selection of the *action* and *not-condition* pair.) Using the obligation rule, Cosmides (1989) also asked subjects to adopt the role of *inquirers* into whether a deontic rule was in force. She found similar results to those found in the abstract selection task.

Manktelow and Over (1991) were the first to argue that social role or perspective was an important factor in the deontic selection task. They induced response shifts between the *p*, *not-q* selections and the *not-p*, *q* selections by asking subjects to adopt different perspectives. They used a permission rule and two perspectives: what we have been calling the *enforcer's* perspective, and what we shall refer to as the *actor's* perspective. For the enforcer's perspective Manktelow and Over (1991) found the same *not-p* and *q* card selections as Cosmides (1989, see also Gigerenzer & Hug, 1992), but for the actor's perspective they found that subjects predominantly chose the *p* and *not-q* cards. We illustrate the reason for this change using the permission form of the cholera rule. From the enforcer's perspective cheaters are people who try to enter the country without having been inoculated against cholera, i.e. relative to the permission rule the *not-p* and *q* instances. However, for an actor, i.e. someone trying to enter the country, the enforcer cheats if having had the inoculations the actor is still not let in to the country, i.e. again relative to the permission rule, the *p* and *not-q* instances. Gigerenzer and Hug (1992) show that the actor's perspective on an obligation led subjects to select the *not-p* and *q* cards, because an obligation reverses the clausal position of action and condition. Gigerenzer and Hug (1992) also manipulated the same rules systematically along both dimensions (except the inquirer's perspective) for the first time.

Model

The thematic selection task requires that we refocus our existing probabilistic model away from *rule testing* and onto *rule use*. In modelling rule testing we used our basic probability model defined by the dependence and independence matrices (Table 10.1) to calculate expected information gain.

In modelling rule use we use these probability models to calculate expected utilities and argue that subjects use the rules to maximise expected utility.

We assume that there is a small fixed cost for turning any card. This cost is implicit in the task, because the instructions say that subjects should only pick the cards which they "would have to" (Cheng & Holyoak, 1985), or "must" (Manktelow & Over 1991) turn. We further assume that subjects associate particular utilities with particular card combinations, dependent on the perspective they adopt and on the particular rule.

The enforcer's goal is to discover instances of rule violation, i.e. where the actor performs the action without satisfying the condition. We model this by assigning a positive utility to instances of rule violation that is larger than the cost of turning over a card (otherwise subjects would have no incentive to turn cards at all). Subjects in the enforcer's perspective associate no other cards with positive utility. In particular, this means that whether someone performs the action when they satisfy the condition is not the enforcer's concern. The actor's goal is to discover instances of unfairness, where the enforcer disallows the action even though the actor satisfies the condition. We model this by assigning a positive utility to uncovering instances of unfairness that is larger than the cost of turning over a card. Subjects in the actor's perspective associate no other cards with positive utility. In particular, this means that whether someone performs the action when they do not satisfy the condition is not the actor's concern. The inquirer's goal is to discover whether the rule holds, just as in the abstract tasks. The inquirer has no direct involvement in the situation and therefore has no relevant utilities concerning it. We adopted the inquirer's perspective in modelling the abstract task, and the same analysis applies to the inquirer's perspective in thematic tasks.

We summarise the utilities assigned to the enforcer's and the actor's perspective in Table 12.1. In this table we have adopted the convention that

TABLE 12.1

Utilities of card combinations for the enforcer and actor perspectives. We assigned a small negative utility (–0.1) to every combination of cards, which is derived from the assumption of a fixed cost for turning any card. For the enforcer's perspective, we assigned a large positive utility (+5) to finding cases where the *action* occurs but the *condition* is not satisfied (*not-condition*). For the actor's perspective, we assigned a large positive utility (+5) to finding cases where the *condition* is satisfied but the *action* is not performed (*not-action*). All that is important in the choice of these numerical values is that the positive utility is large in comparison to the fixed cost

Enforcer	action	not-action	Actor	action	not-action
condition	−0.1	−0.1	condition	−0.1	5−0.1
not-condition	5−0.1	−0.1	not-condition	−0.1	−0.1

p corresponds to the condition and q to the action, i.e. we assume a permission rule.[1]

We assume that subjects do not know whether the rule is being obeyed. For simplicity, we assign equal prior probabilities to the rule being obeyed and the rule being ignored, i.e. $P(M_I)$ and $P(M_D)$ are equal. The interpretation of the parameter $P(M_I)$ changes between the abstract and thematic tasks. In the abstract task it represented the probability that the independence model is true of the world. In the thematic task it represents the probability that an individual is disobeying the rule. With this modification, we model the task in exactly the same way as in the abstract selection task, except that we introduce utilities with respect to the model.

To model the card selections in the enforcer's and actor's perspective, we calculate expected utilities for each card as follows (we use the abbreviations "act" for action, and "con" for condition):

$$EU(con) = P(act|con)U(con,act) + P(\overline{act}|con)U(con,\overline{act}) \qquad (12.1)$$

$$EU(\overline{con}) = P(act|\overline{con})U(\overline{con},act) + P(\overline{act}|\overline{con})U(\overline{con},\overline{act}) \qquad (12.2)$$

$$EU(act) = P(con|act)U(con,act) + P(\overline{con}|act)U(\overline{con},act) \qquad (12.3)$$

$$EU(\overline{act}) = P(con|\overline{act})U(con,\overline{act}) + P(\overline{con}|\overline{act})U(\overline{con},\overline{act}) \qquad (12.4)$$

Where the conditional probabilities $P(x|y)$ are the expected values calculated with respect to the two models:

$$P(x|y) = P(x|y,M_I)P(M_I) + P(x|y,M_D)P(M_D) \qquad (12.5)$$

In equations (12.1) to (12.4) the expected utility of each card is calculated as the weighted sum of the probabilities of each possible outcome given the visible face of the card. The weights are the utilities ($U()$) of each outcome.

We derived expected utilities for each card by sampling points in the parameter space defined by $P(p)$ and $P(q)$ at intervals of 0.1 in the range 0.1 to 0.9, with the utilities specified earlier (–0.1 fixed cost, and +5 for the target). We sampled over a whole range of values for $P(p)$ and $P(q)$ because for deontic rules it is not reasonable to prejudge rarity. For example, in monitoring passengers, whether most or only some of the passengers are entering will depend on factors such as the particular flight. If Manila is the flight destination, then most passengers will be entering. However, if the passengers are on the long-haul flight from London to Sydney, then only some passengers may be entering, the rest will be in transit. We show the average expected utilities in Table 12.2 for the enforcer's perspective [12.2(i)] and for the actor's perspective [12.2(ii)].

The enforcer seeks the case where the actor performs the action but does not satisfy the condition. In the model, selecting the face that denotes the

TABLE 12.2
Average expected utilities for each card face (*action,
not-action, condition, not-condition*) for (i) the
enforcer's perspective, and (ii) the actor's perspective

Card Face	(i) Enforcer	(ii) Actor
action	+1.20	−0.10
not action	−0.10	+2.31
condition	−0.10	+2.23
not condition	+1.03	−0.10

action being performed and the face that denotes the condition not being satisfied maximises expected utility. Table 12.2(i) shows that only the cards showing the *action* and *not-condition* have positive expected utilities. Hence subjects should turn only these cards. For an obligation, *if p* (action) *then must q* (condition), this corresponds to selecting the *p* and *not-q* cards. For a permission, *if p* (condition) *then may q* (action), this corresponds to selecting the *not-p* and *q* cards.

The actor seeks the case where although the actor satisfies the condition the enforcer disallows the action. In the model, selecting the face that denotes the condition being satisfied and the face that denotes the action not being taken maximises expected utility. Table 12.2(ii) shows that only the cards showing the *not-action* and *condition* face have positive expected utilities. Hence subjects should turn only these cards. For an obligation, *if p* (action) *then must q* (condition), this corresponds to selecting *not-p* and *q* cards. For a permission, *if p* (condition) *then may q* (action), this corresponds to selecting the *p* and *not-q* cards.

In sum, our model makes the predictions for card selections in the deontic selection task shown in Table 12.3. These predictions agree perfectly with the results of the studies indicated. We also predict that a permission rule with an inquirer's perspective will lead to the standard abstract results because from the inquirer's perspective our standard abstract model should apply.

Utilities and Probabilities of Fictional Outcomes

Data

Kirby (1994) has recently demonstrated that the utilities and probabilities of outcomes affect card selections in the deontic selection task. Equation (11.1) again forms the basis of his analysis. In his experiment 4, Kirby used a drinking age deontic rule as used by Griggs and Cox (1982): *if a person is drinking beer, then the person must be over 21 years of age.* Kirby used the following cards: "drinking beer" (*p*), "drinking ginger-ale" (*not-p*), "22

TABLE 12.3
Patterns of card selections observed in the thematic selection task for different rule types (Obligation vs. Permission) and perspective (Enforcer, Actor, and Inquirer), indicating the studies reporting these results

	Perspective		
Rule	Enforcer	Actor	Inquirer
Obligation	p, not-q (Cheng & Holyoak 1985; Cosmides 1989; Gigerenzer & Hug 1992)	not-p, q (Gigerenzer & Hug 1992)	standard abstract result p > q > not-q > not-p (Cosmides 1989)
Permission	not-p, q (Cosmides 1989; Manktelow & Over 1991; Gigerenzer & Hug 1992)	p, not-q (Manktelow & Over 1991; Gigerenzer & Hug 1992)	standard abstract result p > q > not-q > not-p (prediction)

years of age" (*q*), "19 years of age" (*not-q*). This rule is an obligation rule and subjects must adopt the enforcer's perspective which predicts the *p* and *not-q* response. Kirby argued that the high frequency of *not-q* card selections found by Griggs and Cox (1982) may be due to the high probability of finding a 19-year-old drinking beer. He therefore provided two additional *not-q* cards that varied this probability, "12 years of age" and "4 years of age"—the younger the person the less likely they are to be drinking beer.

In the same experiment Kirby (1994) varied the utilities of making correct and incorrect decisions. In a DON'T CHECK condition, the instructions read: "However, keep in mind that your employer does not want you to offend innocent customers, and you could be fired if you check an innocent person". From equation (11.1) these instructions should increase the cost of a false alarm. Kirby therefore predicted an overall *decrease* in the number of cards selected. In a DON'T MISS condition, the instructions read: "However, keep in mind that your employer is very concerned about illegal drinking, and you could be fired if you miss a guilty person". From equation (11.1) these instructions should increase the cost of a miss. Kirby therefore predicted an overall *increase* in the number of cards selected. In a CHECK condition, the instructions read, "However, keep in mind that your employer is very concerned about illegal drinking, and you could receive a large bonus if you catch a guilty person". From equation (11.1) these instructions should increase the benefit of a hit. Kirby therefore predicted an overall *increase* in the number of cards selected. He compared these data to a baseline condition with no manipulation of these utilities.

In his experiment 4, consistent with prediction, Kirby observed a trend for fewer selections for *not-q* cards with a lower probability of an inconsistent outcome. Moreover, the DON'T CHECK condition led to fewer card selections than the baseline and the DON'T MISS condition led to more card selections than the baseline, as predicted. Similar effects were not observed for the CHECK condition. Kirby argues that this was because this condition involved a less extreme benefit, and subjects weight costs more than benefits (Kahneman & Tversky, 1979).

Model

Modelling Kirby's (1994) data is straightforward. First, in the abstract task we set the parameter M_I to the error rate in Kirby's experiments 1 to 3. For the thematic task this parameter reflects the probability that an individual is disobeying the rule. We therefore varied this parameter to model the effect of the various ages of potential violators (*not-q* cards). We set M_I to 0.4 for the 4-year-olds and then incremented by 0.1 for the 12-year-olds ($M_I = 0.5$) and the 19-year-olds ($M_I = 0.6$). These values seemed reasonable because even though 4-year-olds in general are unlikely to be drinking beer, the probability of 4-year-olds *in a bar* drinking is far higher. Certainly the subjects in Kirby's experiment 4 felt it necessary to check the 4-year-olds, the proportion of these cards being turned never dropping below 0.39.

To capture the effects of the different instructions we varied the utilities specified in Table 12.1 for the enforcer's perspective. The DON'T CHECK condition increases the cost of a false alarm. We model this directly by increasing the costs for all cells other than the *action, not-condition* cell, as any of the outcomes corresponding to these cells represents a false alarm. We cannot increase costs too much, however, otherwise they will outweigh the benefits for all possibilities and enforcers will carry out no checks at all. We therefore increased the costs from -0.1 to -0.5. We doubt whether subjects make the distinction between a cost for a miss and a benefit for a hit. It seems more reasonable to assume that the cognitive interpretation of costs for misses is benefits (failure to incur a cost) for hits. Therefore, the DON'T MISS condition is a more extreme version of the CHECK condition. We, therefore, model the DON'T MISS condition by increasing the utility of the *action, not-condition* cell in Table 12.1 for the enforcer's perspective from 5 to 7.

We illustrate the behaviour of the model with $P(p) = P(q) = 0.5$. (Any pair of values in the range 0.1 to 0.9 displays the same behaviour in response to variations in M_I and the utilities.) Figure 12.1 shows the z-scores of the expected utilities for each card for the BASELINE, the DON'T CHECK, and the DON'T MISS conditions compared to the z-scores of Kirby's observed frequencies of card selections. The fit between data and model was good with a correlation of 0.94 ($p < 0.0001$). As in the abstract task, our model captures effects that Kirby's model cannot explain. From equation

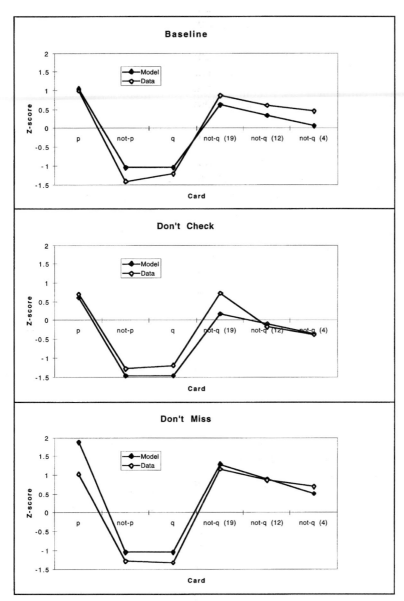

FIG. 12.1 Comparison of the average expected utilities and the selection frequency for each card in each condition in Kirby's (1994) experiment 4. For purposes of comparison the expected utilities and the selection frequencies have been converted to z-scores in order to normalise the scales.

(11.1) Kirby must predict increases and decreases in card selections *for all cards*. However, while there were overall increases and decreases according to equation (11.1) in Kirby's data (see Fig. 12.1 *not-q* cards), these effects were only in line with prediction for the *p* and *not-q* cards. There were no significant changes in the proportion of cards selected for the *not-p* or *q* cards, and where Kirby found differences they were counter to the predictions of equation (11.1). In contrast, our model predicts no changes for these cards in response to Kirby's manipulations, which is consistent with Kirby's results.

SUMMARY FOR THEMATIC TASKS

Our account of the thematic selection task is consistent with some recent proposals. It supplements our standard probability model with a maximum expected utility account of the role of perspectives. Following Manktelow and Over (1991, 1992) and Gigerenzer and Hug (1992) the notion of a perspective is the main explanatory concept. Moreover, we have built on Manktelow and Over's (1991) qualitative explanation of the influence of perspectives in terms of subjective utilities. Our emphasis on the distinction between rule testing and rule use is also consistent with Jackson and Griggs' (1990) finding that the checking (rule use) context is a more important factor in reasoning in these tasks than their deontic nature. Our proposals are also in the spirit of Gigerenzer and Hug's (1992, pp. 169) expectation that "the two fields [i.e. deductive and probabilistic reasoning] will converge in the next few years." In this light, perhaps the most important feature of our model is how well it accounts for Kirby's recent data (Kirby, 1994) where both probabilities and utilities are explicitly varied in a deontic task.

NOTE

1. We could have equally adopted an obligation rule and hence let *p* be the action and *q* the condition. However, this is only a convention and the expected utilities come out the same either way.

CHAPTER THIRTEEN

A Rational Analysis of the Selection Task IV: Implications

INTRODUCTION

The last three chapters have outlined a rational analysis of the selection task, modelling detailed patterns of data from both indicative and deontic versions of the task. In this chapter, we explain in detail how our account relates to Anderson's (1990) methodology for rational analysis. We compare our rational analysis to other accounts of the selection task and to other accounts of reasoning more generally. Finally, we consider the level of detail at which our rational analysis should be related to process-based accounts of reasoning performance, and we relate our work to the wider programme of understanding human behaviour as rational.

IMPLICATIONS

The detailed account of performance on the selection task that we have outlined in the last three chapters is complex, so before dealing with the implications of our account, a brief informal summary is in order. We have seen how the standard abstract selection task can be viewed as an inductive reasoning task: subjects must choose which card-turning experiments they expect to yield the most information about which of two hypotheses are true. One hypothesis is that a dependency of the form *if p then q* exists, the other is a foil hypothesis, that *p* and *q* are independent. We defined expected information gain as the expected decrease in information-theoretic uncertainty between these two hypotheses in response to some data. We formalised expected information gain, $E(I_g)$, using the theory of optimal data selection from statistics. We then assumed that card selection frequencies are a monotonic function of the expected information gain associated with each card.

The model of the standard selection task has only three free parameters: the prior probability of the independence model, $P(M_I)$, the probability of p, $P(p)$, and the probability of q, $P(q)$. We explain the majority of the effects on the abstract selection task by assuming that p and q are rare by default, and that experimental manipulations influence these parameters by moving them away from their default values. When parameters $P(p)$ and $P(q)$ are low the ordering in expected information gain corresponds to the standard pattern of card selection frequencies ($p > q > not$-$q > not$-p). With the standard results as a baseline we explained the associations between card selections by making two minimal assumptions about the nature of the decision process that translates expected information gains into card selections. These assumptions allowed us to compute scaled $E(I_g)$s that showed the same pattern of associations found in the empirical data. We accounted for the negations paradigm selection task, using the same assumptions and by allowing $P(p)$ and $P(q)$ to vary according to an account of contrast sets. Our account also captures all of Kirby's (1994) recent data where he explicitly varies $P(p)$. Further, our model accounts for unexpected selection transitions in the therapy experiments, and for the facilitation of the logical response in the reduced array selection task.

Following Manktelow and Over (1987, 1990a, 1991), we assume that the strikingly different results observed in many thematic selection tasks stem from the deontic nature of the rules used. Such rules are not hypotheses to be tested, but rules that must be obeyed. We model the thematic task using decision theory together with the same basic probability models used to model the abstract task. Subjects have utilities concerning various outcomes, which depend on their perspective towards the rule. We assume that they choose cards to maximise expected utility. The assumption that subjects follow this rational policy captures a broad range of data on the thematic selection task. In particular it captures the effects of perspective and rule type that have been much studied recently; it also captures Kirby's (1994) data where utilities and probabilities have been explicitly varied in a deontic selection task.

Relation to Rational Analysis

Our model provides a rational analysis of the selection task in the sense of Anderson (1990, 1991a, 1991b; Anderson & Milson, 1989). According to Anderson (1990) rational analysis involves six steps:

1. Specify precisely the goals of the cognitive system.
2. Develop a formal model of the environment to which the system is adapted.
3. Make minimal assumptions about computational limitations.
4. Derive the optimal behaviour function given 1–3 above.
5. Examine the empirical evidence to see whether the predictions of the behavioural function are confirmed.
6. Repeat, iteratively refining the theory.

We assume that the goals (1) involve selecting relevant data; that the structure of the environment (2) is given by the frequency of properties occurring in that environment, and that the costs (3) are incurred in looking at irrelevant data. We derived an optimal behavioural function using Bayesian optimal data selection (4) and compared this to the empirical evidence (5). In sum, our model demonstrates the utility of Anderson's (1990) approach by showing how it can organise data on human reasoning that has previously seemed the most recalcitrant to rational explanation.

Relations to Theories of Deductive Inference

We deal with the relation of our model to theories of deductive inference in two parts. First, we look at the relations between our model and theories of deductive inference taken to account for the same data. Next we look at some recent probabilistic approaches in reasoning research to which our account is more closely related.

Theories of Deductive Inference

Evans (1991) has proposed a taxonomy of deductive reasoning theories that divides the four principal approaches into two classes: those that deal with the issue of deductive competence, and those that do not. On the one hand, mental logic accounts (Braine, 1978; Rips, 1983, 1990) and mental models (Johnson-Laird, 1983; Johnson-Laird & Byrne, 1991) are theories of deductive competence. On the other hand, domain-specific approaches, such as pragmatic reasoning schemas (Cheng & Holyoak, 1985) and social contract theory (Cosmides, 1989), and heuristic or "relevance" approaches (Evans, 1983, 1984, 1989), account for the content effects and biases found in deductive reasoning tasks. We look first at the relations between our model and accounts of deductive competence.

Accounts of Deductive Competence

According to the mental logic approach (e.g. Braine, 1978; Rips, 1983, 1990) deductive reasoning involves an abstract logical competence implemented in something like the syntactic rules of a standard logical system.

This approach does not attempt to explain the selection task. Rips (1990) argues that the selection task is a "loose" probabilistic task, rather than a "tight" deductive task. We agree, and note that our theoretical account shows how the selection task can be modelled in probabilistic terms. Consequently, selection task data cannot be used as an argument against a mental logic and hence the case against a mental logic is weaker than perhaps it once was.

The mental models framework (e.g. Johnson-Laird, 1983; Johnson-Laird & Byrne, 1991) proposes that people do not reason by manipulating syntactic rules, but by manipulating representations of the semantic contents of an argument. Mental models has problems with accounting for the data on the selection task. For example, Johnson-Laird and Byrne (1991) claim that subjects who do not turn the *not-q* card do not represent it in their mental model. This suggests that when an experimental manipulation draws explicit attention towards this card subjects should select it. However, in the therapy experiments, where the experimenter focuses attention on the *not-q* card and its falsifying properties, the majority of subjects still do not select it.

Problems of predictive failure to one side, mental models has most difficulty in accounting for the influence of probabilities and utilities on reasoning performance. Johnson-Laird and Byrne (1992) argue that such factors only enter into the construction of appropriate mental models and hence they need not incorporate these factors in their framework. Garnham (1993) has attempted a similar argument in defending mental models theory from the criticism that it fails to account for everyday inference (Chater, 1993; Chater & Oaksford, 1993; Oaksford, 1993; Oaksford & Chater, 1991, 1992, 1993; Oaksford, Chater, & Stenning, 1990). In our view, theories of everyday inference (Galotti, 1989) will involve how factors such as probabilities and utilities interact with reasoning processes (see also Gigerenzer & Hug, 1992). Mental models theorists, on the other hand, appear to believe that they already have a theory of everyday inference (Garnham, 1993; Johnson-Laird & Byrne, 1991). However, this is only true if the mechanisms that construct just the right kinds of mental model are assumed as primitive. As Chater and Oaksford (1993, see also Kirby, 1994) observe, this line of argument has, in Russell's phrase, all the virtues of theft over honest toil— most interesting inferential processes are presupposed and not explained (Oaksford & Chater, 1993).

In closing we observe that, in contrast to Kirby's (1994) account, our model does not require an abstract logical competence. Kirby's signal detection theory analysis defines hits as revealing a logically inconsistent outcome, and hence presupposes an understanding of conditional logic. In our model we characterise the hypotheses probabilistically by the matrices in Table 10.1. Thus our account divorces selection task performance more completely from theories of deductive competence than Kirby's account.

Accounts of Biases and Content Effects

Our principle criticism of approaches put forward to account for biases and content effects is that they lack the generality of our model. Domain-specific approaches such as pragmatic reasoning schema theory (Cheng & Holyoak, 1985) and social contract theory (Cosmides, 1989) deal only with the data from the thematic task. Both these accounts assume domain-specific rules for checking for violators in deontic contexts. The main difference is that on pragmatic reasoning schema theory these rules are learned whereas on social contract theory they are innate. The emphasis on domain-specific information is compatible with our account (see also, Kirby, 1994). Specific domain knowledge may influence the parameters in our model, and the utilities subjects employ, as noted in the previous chapter.

The heuristic approach of Evans (1983, 1984, 1989) deals only with the data from the abstract task. Evans (1983, 1984, 1989) proposed that various heuristic processes involved in language understanding may explain the biases observed in the abstract selection task. In particular, Evans has applied this approach to matching bias, which we discussed in Chapter 11. However, Oaksford and Stenning (1992) have shown that the particular heuristics Evans proposes are unnecessary to account for these data.

Relation to Probabilistic Approaches

There have been some "loose" probabilistic approaches (Rips, 1990) to the selection task (Fischhoff & Beyth-Marom, 1983; Klayman & Ha, 1987; Rips, 1990) and to the related Wason [1960] 2–4–6 task [Hoenkamp, 1989]). Fischhoff and Beyth-Marom (1983) and Rips (1990) both adopted a Bayesian approach, but as part of more general frameworks for looking at hypothesis testing and loose reasoning tasks respectively. In consequence neither of these Bayesian approaches went beyond accounting for the standard p and q card selections which is perhaps why they have had little influence on selection task research. Similar comments apply to Klayman and Ha (1987, 1989) who generalised their "positive test strategy" from Wason's (1960) 2–4–6 task to the selection task. They based this strategy on a demonstration that the likelihood of finding disconfirming evidence was higher when using positive instances of a hypothesis than when using negative instances of a hypothesis (as in falsification). In sum, these earlier accounts pointed the way to our probabilistic treatment of the selection task but were never themselves sufficiently developed to account for the range of data reviewed here.

Only Kirby (1994) tries to explain both the abstract and the thematic tasks from a probabilistic or decision-theoretic perspective. The main failing of Kirby's otherwise excellent work is that his theory can explain so little of his important data. This is because his analysis requires that subjects concentrate solely on finding falsifying instances. In contrast our Bayesian analysis explains all of Kirby's data straightforwardly.

Interestingly our model bears close relation to probabilistic approaches to causal reasoning, an area that until now has been treated as unrelated to the selection task. Anderson (1990) also uses Bayesian model comparison in his model of causal estimation that provides a rational explanation of biases in the analysis of 2 × 2 contingency tables (e.g. Schustack & Sternberg, 1981). Cheng and Novick (1990, 1992) have also taken a probabilistic approach to both causal inference and to causal attribution (see e.g. McArthur, 1972) in their probabilistic contrast model. Cheng and Novick (1990, 1992) do not propose a full Bayesian treatment of these data. However, their emphasis on probabilistic contrasts is similar to our emphasis on information gain in deciding between hypotheses. In both cases subjects are assumed to concentrate on probabilistic differences. We may, moreover, be able to derive the probabilistic contrast model from our Bayesian framework. We can compare an independence model and a model (or family of models) in which a contingency holds (or parameterised family of models, each representing a different contingency reliability) not just for a single data point (as in the current analysis), but for an entire set of data. This could provide the basis for a normative analysis of experiments on contingency judgements, causal reasoning, and causal attribution. This opens up the exciting possibility of unified rational explanations of formerly disparate phenomena in the reasoning field.

Finally our model is consistent with a growing trend in accounting for putative biases in inferential behaviour using rational probabilistic models. Anderson's work is the most comprehensive of such approaches, applying Bayesian methods to a variety of cognitive phenomena (Anderson, 1990, 1991a, 1991b; Anderson & Milson, 1989). Gigerenzer (Gigerenzer, Hell, & Blank, 1989; Gigerenzer, Hoffrage, & Kleinbölting, 1991; Gigerenzer & Murray, 1987) has also applied probability theory to explaining biases in reasoning tasks and Cheng and Novick's (1990, 1992) work is also consistent with this trend.

Rationality

There are two issues about rationality that require discussion. The first concerns the actual parameter values that we have chosen in our analyses and whether we can provide them with a rational justification. The second concerns the normative status of our rational analysis.

Parameter Values

We have explained the data on the selection task by assuming that p and q are rare by default, and that experimental manipulations influence the parameters $P(p)$ and $P(q)$ by moving them away from their default values. An initial and important point is that our model organises a wide range of data in a single theoretical framework. This argues strongly that subjects behave as Bayesians with the rarity assumption. This in itself is an important discovery, even if we could not rationally justify the rarity assumption. Testing the validity of this assumption will require an environmental analysis of the type Anderson (1990) proposes. However, we argue that there is evidence to support the view that most lexicalised properties refer to objects and events that are rare in our environment. In consequence, subjects' behaviour in the selection task may be optimally adapted to that environment and hence rational.

First, note that no other parameter values are better justified. For example, the principle of indifference (Keynes, 1921) that $P(q) = P(p) = 0.5$ is only reasonable on the assumption of complete ignorance. However, subjects have extensive prior experience with other conditional rules. If these generally relate properties that respect rarity then it is reasonable for subjects to extrapolate from prior experience and assume that a novel task rule also respects rarity. Other possibilities are equally questionable. For example, Kirby (1994) argues that the probability of finding a vowel (p) on the back of an odd number (*not-q*) is low because there are 5 vowels but 21 consonants. However, the level of letter-*types* may not be the relevant level at which to assess these probabilities. It could equally be the level of letter-*tokens* in experience that is the determining factor.

The rarity assumption organises data from more than the selection task. We mentioned earlier that, in the 2–4–6 task, Klayman and Ha (1987) showed that positive tests were more likely to yield falsifying evidence than negative tests. This result also relies on a rarity assumption, or what Klayman and Ha call a "minority phenomenon" assumption. That is, the properties that figure in hypotheses about their causes are in the minority. For example, AIDS only has an incidence of about 10^{-4} to 10^{-5} in the population. A hypothesis of the form "if you have contracted HIV, then you will develop AIDS" will therefore respect the rarity assumption. This is because scientists are unlikely to put much stock in this hypothesis if $P(\text{HIV}) > P(\text{AIDS})$ [this is a further application of our constraint that $P(q) \geq P(p)$]. Further, Anderson's (1990) work on causal inference indicates that subjects make a rarity assumption in causal estimation from 2×2 contingency tables. In fitting parameters to Schustack and Sternberg's (1981) data, Anderson derived expected prior probabilities of an effect of 0.27 and of a cause of 0.25. Given a causal (*if cause then effect*) relation, these results confirm the rarity assumption and the reasonable constraint that while $P(q)$ is greater than $P(p)$ it can only be marginally greater. In sum, the rarity assumption appears capable of organising a great deal of data on human reasoning.

Normative Status

As we mentioned in the introduction, Anderson (1990) draws the distinction between normative and adaptive rationality (see also, Evans, 1993; Stich, 1990). Normative rationality concerns reasoning according to the rules of a formal logico-mathematical theory. Following such rules provides the standard account of rationality going back to Plato (see Brown, 1988). Adaptive rationality concerns whether behaviour is optimally adapted to the environment. We have shown that in the selection task subjects' behaviour can be regarded as rational in the second sense, i.e. as optimally adapted to an environment where the properties that enter into predictive relations are rare. Although we have used a normative mathematical theory to derive this rational analysis, there is no requirement that people achieve this optimal adaptation by following the rules of the normative theory. Hence while our account argues for the adaptive rationality of reasoning on the selection task it need not address the question of normative rationality.

However, although a rational analysis does not require that people make Bayesian calculations it does not preclude this either. A range of views is possible. At one extreme, we can view the calculations involved in deriving the rational analysis as specifying a set of mental operations carried out by the subject. This view attributes people with sophisticated, though not necessarily explicit (Reber, 1989), probabilistic reasoning abilities. It also corresponds to the view that people are not only adaptively rational but are also normatively rational. At the opposite extreme, as we have mentioned, a rational analysis may just specify which behaviour is optimal, and remain neutral about the mental operations underlying that behaviour. The reason that people conform to our analysis of the selection task, might be due to innate constraints or learning, rather than sophisticated probabilistic calculation. Between these two extremes, that all the calculations of the rational analysis are internally computed, and that none is, lies a smooth continuum of intermediate positions, which assume that some aspects of the analysis are calculated internally, and others are not.

The view taken towards rational analysis has behavioural and computational significance. In so far as people calculate optimal behaviour internally, subjects' knowledge of the specifics of the task can influence those calculations. For example, in the *Reduced Array Selection Task* we assume that the way in which the materials violate the rarity assumption influences subjects' behaviour. If subjects performed no calculation, but simply applied learned or innate strategies, then it is unlikely that such parameter changes would affect their performance. It is, of course, possible that subjects choose between various strategies that do not involve calculation depending on the specifics of the situation. Nonetheless, in general, the more flexible subjects' behaviour to relevant aspects of the task, the stronger the case for internal calculation, and the less plausible non-computational strategies. We will need to conduct further empirical work to assess which aspects of our rational analysis of the selection task people internally calculate, and which they have prestored.

In so far as people make internal calculations of our rational analysis, we must consider the computational feasibility of those calculations. The calculations of our analysis of the selection task are very simple. However, as we have argued elsewhere (Chater & Oaksford, 1990; Oaksford & Chater, 1991, 1992, 1993), plausible reasoning theories must "scale up" from laboratory reasoning tasks to everyday inferential processes. Simple Bayesian calculations rapidly lead to the notorious combinatorial explosion (e.g. Charniak & McDermott, 1985). Recently Pearl (1988) has proposed a novel and more tractable implementation of Bayesian inference using Bayesian networks. However, this method too does not scale well (Dagum & Luby, 1993). These problems are not specific to probabilistic inference, but apply equally to logical reasoning (Oaksford & Chater, 1991).

The problems of computational tractability suggest that a scaled-up rational analysis would have to pay considerably more attention to computational limitations (step 3 in Anderson's account of rational analysis), than is required for modelling laboratory tasks. In Simon's (1959) terms, this means that people should be modelled as having *bounded* rationality (see also Oaksford & Chater, 1992, 1993).

CONCLUSIONS

Chapters 10–13 have provided a rational analysis of the selection task, which accords closely with the empirical data, using a Bayesian account of hypothesis testing. This account contrasts sharply with the standard falsificationist model. The poor fit between this model and the empirical data has led to doubts about whether humans are rational. We suggest that people are rational, but that we must define rationality in terms of optimal performance in real-world, uncertain, inductive tasks, rather than purely in terms of deductive logic. Clarifying the detailed relationship between normative theory and observed behaviour suggests a programme of empirical investigation and theoretical generalisation to related tasks which we discuss in the closing chapter. In conclusion, our model establishes that subjects' behaviour while performing the selection task need have no negative implications for human rationality.

CHAPTER FOURTEEN

Rational Explanation of the Selection Task

INTRODUCTION

The last four chapters outlined a rational analysis of the selection task, which appears to reconcile human performance with rational, probabilistic norms. This model, originally presented in Oaksford and Chater (1994a), attracted three extended commentaries (Almor & Sloman, 1996; Evans & Over, 1996a; Laming, 1996). This chapter summarises these commentaries and replies to them.

Evans and Over (1996a) suggest that the expected information gain measure is inappropriate from a normative point of view, because information gain can be negative—it is possible to be *more* uncertain after conducting an experiment than before. This has a rather counter-intuitive flavour—because even in this case, the experiment has still provided useful information, even though it is associated with a negative information gain. We note that this query poses no problems for our account. First, our rational analysis assumes that cards are chosen in order to maximise *expected* information gain, which cannot be negative. Second, we can switch to a new measure, the Kullback–Liebler distance between the probabilities before and after the experiment (turning the card) is conducted, which is always positive. It turns out that using this measure requires no changes whatever to our rational analysis, because the expected value of Kullback–Liebler distance is mathematically identical to the expected value of information gain. Evans and Over also attempt to propose an alternative

225

account, which they label "epistemic utility". But the nature of this account is unclear. They provide desiderata, based on their distinction between rationality$_1$ and rationality$_2$, which we discuss in Chapter 16, to the effect that an account of the selection task based on epistemic utility should be based on the goals of the agent, criticising expected information gain for having no reference to such goals. But the alternative measure they appear to endorse, the expected absolute log-likelihood ratio, also has no reference to goals, and hence appears to fail by their own criteria as an appropriate measure of "epistemic utility". Moreover, the expected absolute log-likelihood ratio measure also fails from an empirical standpoint, because *infinite* log-likelihood ratios arise for cases of falsification. Hence the expected value of any experiment where there is a non-zero probability of falsification is also infinite. This means that the Evans and Over's proposal implies that people should prefer the *p* and *not-q* cards in the selection task, which have infinite expected log-likelihood ratios, to the *q* and *not-p* cards. Thus, Evans and Over's proposal collapses onto the standard "logical" account which provides such a poor fit with the empirical data. There are various ways in which Evans and Over's proposal could be modified to avoid this difficulty—but it is unclear whether any of them would fit the broad sweep of empirical data captured by the information gain account outlined earlier. It is also worth noting that a log-likelihood-based measure has the disadvantage of being limited to cases in which there are just two hypotheses to be compared—expected information gain applies however many hypotheses are involved. Presumably this additional generality may be important in providing a complete account of how people decide how to select information, outside the narrow confines of the selection task. Evans and Over also discuss some empirical data which they suggest may be difficult to account for using our rational analysis. Oaksford and Chater (1998b) provide an extended optimal data selection model that captures these data and a variety of other results.

Laming (1996) attacks the normative soundness of our account on statistical grounds. This is puzzling, because the approach to optimal data selection that we used, based on expected information gain, is well established in the Bayesian statistical literature (e.g. Lindley, 1956). The fundamental source of Laming's disagreement stems from his insistence that probabilities be interpreted in frequentist terms, rather than the subjective interpretation of probability that we explicitly adopt, and which is the starting point for Bayesian statistics (see Chapter 1 for a discussion of these different interpretations of probability). Thus, whereas it makes sense, from a Bayesian point of view, to speak of the probability that a hypothesis is true, or the probability that there is a 7 on the back of a card, this makes no sense at all for Laming. The hypothesis is either true or not; the card either has a 7 on the back or it does not—so for Laming, these probabilities must be 0 or 1. Having misconceived the interpretation of probability that we use, Laming is therefore unable to provide sensible interpretations for the formulae that we developed in our account. But once the appropriate interpretation of probability is adopted, Laming's concerns disappear. It might appear that there may be a genuine debate concerning the appropriate interpretation of probability in this context—after all, in mathematics and science there are substantive debates over the appropriate interpretation of probability. But in this psychological context the issue does not arise—because probabilities are used to represent states of knowledge or uncertainty for cognitive agents, the subjectivist conception is, inevitably, in play.

Laming also argues that our mathematical treatment implicitly allows at least five substantive psychological assumptions, which we do not justify. We argue that these assumptions make sense both from a normative point of view and in accounting for the empirical data. Further, Laming offers a "correct Bayesian" re-analysis of the selection task as a putative alternative to our account. But we show that this "correct Bayesian" analysis is not Bayesian at all.

Almor and Sloman (1996) provide some interesting new experimental data, which, they argue, are not readily accounted for by our rational analysis. They argue that the distinction between deontic and indicative tasks, which we model separately, is misleading. They show that they can set up tasks using standard indicative rules where participants predominantly select the *p* and *not-q* cards. In reply we argue that those tasks where Almor and Sloman find this response the materials that they use are either deontic, and so our model in Chapter 12 explains their results, or "analytic", i.e. true by definition. No one has used analytic rules in a selection task before, and no one makes predictions for what should happen when they are. Consequently, we conclude that Almor and Sloman's interesting data do not bear on the models we presented in Chapters 10 and 12.

RATIONAL EXPLANATION OF THE SELECTION TASK

Research on Wason's (1966, 1968) selection task brings human rationality into question because of the mismatch between subjects' performance and what is "logically correct". Recently, Oaksford and Chater (1994a) vindicate human rationality by providing a *rational analysis* (Anderson, 1990, 1991a) of the selection task. Oaksford and Chater observe that the selection task is an *inductive*, rather than a *deductive*, reasoning task—subjects must assess the truth or falsity of a general rule from specific instances. In particular, subjects face a problem of *optimal data selection* (Lindley, 1956): they must decide which of four cards (*p*, *not-p*, *q*, *not-q*) are likely to provide the most useful data to inductively assess a conditional rule, *if p then q*. The standard "logical" solution is to select just the *p* and the *not-q* cards. Oaksford and Chater argue that this solution presupposes a "falsifica-tionist" approach to inductive reasoning (Popper, 1959), which dictates that people should only collect data in order to disconfirm, not to confirm, hypotheses. In contrast, Oaksford and Chater's rational analysis uses a *Bayesian*, rather than a falsificationist, approach to inductive confirmation (Earman, 1992; Horwich, 1982; Howson & Urbach, 1989), and specifically to optimal data selection (Lindley, 1956; MacKay, 1992). According to this approach, people assess whether to select a card by the *expected information gain* $[E(I_g)]$ from turning that card.

Oaksford and Chater's account differs from most previous accounts of the selection task in three ways (a partial exception being Kirby, 1994a). First, it provides an explicit alternative to the "logical" view of what is rational behaviour in the task. Second, Oaksford and Chater specify their model formally, so that they could derive predictions mathematically, rather than by appeal to intuition. Third, it provides quantitative fits with the full range of empirical data.

EVANS AND OVER

Evans and Over (1996) argue that our model is inadequate on two counts. First, it is not normatively justified, because the $E(I_g)$ measure has some counter-intuitive properties. Second, it is descriptively inadequate, with respect to Kirby's (1994a) and Pollard and Evans's (1983) results. We respond to these points in turn, and then consider Evans and Over's resi-dual arguments.

Is Our Theory Normatively Justified?

Evans and Over suggest that "even as a normative proposal, [Oaksford and Chater's] approach has serious problems" (p. 7) because of cases of the following kind: the subject begins with $P(H) = 0.25$, and after turning the card, changes to $P(H) = 0.75$. As Evans and Over show, the amount of uncertainty is the same as before; and hence information gain (I_g) is 0. So I_g seems an inappropriate measure of the value of information, because the subject has clearly learned something important from turning the card. Evans and Over also note that turning a card can lead to *less* certainty about whether the rule is true—again, turning the card intuitively provides useful information, although I_g is negative. This is a relatively minor matter, because *expected* information gain, $E(I_g)$, is always positive (this result follows from the analysis in the appendix to this chapter), and all our cal-culations concern expected values. Nonetheless, Evans and Over do point out an unattractive feature of our $E(I_g)$ measure.

We can take Evans and Over's insight into account by choosing a different measure of the amount of information obtained by turning a card. Intuitively, Evans and Over's point is that a card is informative depending on the magnitude of the difference between your degree of belief in the rule before and after turning the card. If it turns out that you must revise your belief from certainty that the rule is true or false, to less certainty, then the card has still been informative.

How can we formalise this suggestion? We need to compare the probability distributions representing the new and old degrees of belief. These probability distributions contain just two values: $P(M_D)$, the probability that the conditional rule is true, and $P(M_I)$ the probability that antecedent and consequent are independent. To measure the difference between the new and old distributions we use the standard information-theoretic measure: the Kullback–Liebler distance, D, between the new and old probability distributions (Kullback & Liebler, 1951; see the appendix for details[1]). D is always positive, and is 0 only when the two distributions are identical (i.e. turning the card has not led to any revision of previous beliefs). Specifically, D is positive in the cases Evans and Over mention, where I_g is negative or 0.

Taking on board Evans and Over's point then, we can switch from I_g to D to assess the informativeness of a card. Remarkably, this requires no change whatever in the theoretical analysis in the original paper! It turns out that although the new and old measures are very different, their *expected value* is provably always the same (we prove this result in the appendix). Because we base all our predictions on *expected information gain*, this means that we can switch to *expected Kullback–Liebler distance* with no theoretical revision whatsoever (apart from expository differences). In somewhat different forms, this result is well known in the information-theoretic literature (see e.g. Cover & Thomas, 1991; MacKay, 1992).

Is Our Theory Descriptively Adequate?

Our model always assumes that participants interpret the four cards in the selection task as a sample from a larger population of cards, over which the conditional rule is defined. Evans and Over observe that this interpretation does not seem to apply to Kirby's or Pollard and Evans' experiments, where subjects know there are exceptions to the rule. Consequently they argue that the rule can only apply to the four cards. On this assumption they then generate predictions from our model that seem to conflict with the data. We make three points here. First, the occurrence of exceptions does not entail that an exceptionless rule must apply just to the four cards. For example, in Kirby's experiments the rule could apply to the cards the machine subsequently produces.[2] Second, we have argued elsewhere that everyday conditional rules are not interpreted as exceptionless (Chater, 1993; Chater & Oaksford, 1990, 1993; Oaksford, 1993; Oaksford & Chater, 1991, 1992, 1993, 1995b, see Chapters 2–9). It is straightforward to produce a more realistic model by incorporating an exceptions parameter. As Oaksford and Chater (1998b) show, when this is done the model's predictions seem to be unchanged and the fits appear comparable to the original model.[3] Third, to derive their predictions for Pollard and Evans' experiment, Evans and Over assume that participants estimate $P(p)$ and $P(q)$ from the data. However, Pollard and Evans' learning phase uses a prediction task that focuses attention on $P(q|p)$. $P(q|p)$ does not determine $P(p)$ and $P(q)$. Consequently, it is reasonable to argue that participants adopt default rarity values for $P(p)$ and $P(q)$ in computing information gain. As Oaksford and Chater (1998b) show, when this is done, the predictions of the optimal data selection model are in line with Pollard and Evans' data. Therefore Pollard and Evans' results are not inconsistent with optimal data selection.

Residual Arguments

Evans and Over make three residual points, that we briefly address. First, Evans and Over distinguish between

> $Rationality_1$: reasoning or acting in such a way as to achieve one's goals
> $Rationality_2$: reasoning or acting in conformity with a relevant normative system such as formal logic or probability theory. (p. 4)

and then note "it may ... appear that [Oaksford and Chater] have provided a rational₁ ... account of the problem. On reflection we fear that this is not so. They have in fact substituted one rational₂ analysis for another" (p. 5). This suggests that rational₂ analysis is not a good thing. However, because Evans and Over give no argument supporting this claim, there is nothing to which we can reply. Also, Evans and Over give no argument why our model is not a rational₁ account. In our model, the subjects' goal is to reduce their uncertainty in indicative selection tasks, and to maximise expected utility in deontic tasks. Consequently, our account is a rational₁ theory by Evans and Over's definition.[4]

Second, the title of Evans and Over's paper suggests that they have an alternative account, "epistemic utility", but they leave this concept undefined throughout the paper.[5] Evans and Over say that "intuitively, people's subjective epistemic utility is measured by the relevance of some data for them given their goals" (p. 7). Without an account of relevance or goals, this is uncontroversial—both Oaksford and Chater and Evans and Over believe that explaining the selection task involves specifying people's goals, and what relevance means. For Oaksford and Chater, a subject's goal is to reduce uncertainty, and relevance means expected reduction in uncertainty. Evans and Over offer no alternatives. Instead, they state that "it is not our purpose here to propose alternative formalisms to define normative standards for epistemic utility" (p. 8). They do however suggest the absolute value of log-likelihood ratios as a measure of epistemic utility. But this measure is insensitive to goals, and hence is not a measure of epistemic utility by their own criterion. In conclusion, Evans and Over, by their own admission, do not have a coherent notion of "epistemic utility" to compare with our account.

Third, Evans and Over say that we "provide no psychological theory to explain subjects' selection whatever" (p. 3). However, Evans and Over do not explain (i) what they mean by "psychological theory"; (ii) why being a psychological theory (in their sense) is a good thing; and (iii) why our theory is not psychological. It is therefore difficult to respond to this claim. Our model quantitatively fits data from a wide range of experiments, and hence appears to be a psychological model of sorts. Perhaps Evans and Over are using "psychological theory" to mean an algorithmic-level account, rather than a rational analysis. Following Anderson (1990, 1991a, 1994), we assume that a complete psychological theory requires both levels of explanation but that rational analysis is prior to the algorithmic level (Oaksford & Chater, 1995b). Having specified a rational analysis, two questions arise: (i) are there algorithmic-level accounts that implement the rational analysis?; and (ii) if there are many such accounts, how can these be distinguished empirically? Regarding (i), because our rational analysis involves simple mathematical relationships, we can provide many different algorithmic-level accounts. Regarding (ii), because our rational analysis already captures the bulk of the empirical data, any implementation would capture these data. Therefore, without additional data, speculation at the algorithmic level seems premature.

Summary

None of Evans and Over's criticisms of our account is persuasive. First, we accommodated their theoretical objections about information gain without change to the theory by using an alternative measure—expected Kullback–Liebler distance. Second, we have shown that Kirby's and Pollard and Evans' data support, rather than contradict, our account. Third, Evans and Over's account of "epistemic utility" contradicts their own criteria. Fourth, Evans and Over do not consistently apply their rational$_1$/rational$_2$ distinction. Finally, Evans and Over's claim that our theory is not "psychological" is unsupported.

We now turn to Laming's discussion of our paper and argue that it too provides no grounds to abandon the view that our model is the most compelling and comprehensive account of the selection task currently available.

LAMING

Laming (1996) argues that our optimal data selection model makes implausible psychological assumptions, and that a "correct" Bayesian analysis of the selection task makes the same predictions as the "logical" solution. We discuss Laming's arguments in the order they arise.

How to Construct a Psychological Theory

Here we address each point in Laming's section "Constructing psychological theories," which provides an overview of Laming's arguments.

First, Laming argues that the optimal data selection relies on arbitrary and psychologically implausible assumptions. These assumptions are not arbitrary, but were derived from the theory of optimal data selection (Chaloner & Verdinelli, 1994; Good, 1960; Lindley, 1956; Luttrell, 1985; MacKay, 1992a) and Bayesian epistemology (Earman, 1992; Horwich, 1982; Howson & Urbach, 1989; Mackie, 1963).[6] What is remarkable is that these assumptions, derived to solve normative problems in statistics and in epistemology, also make accurate predictions in the selection task. Further, as we will show, each of these assumptions has a psychological justification.

Second, Laming objects to the information measure (Shannon–Wiener) used in the optimal data selection model because "to be psychologically meaningful, the measure of information has to relate to *the question put to the subjects*" (Laming, 1996, p. 6, our italics). We argue that to be psychologically meaningful, an information measure has to relate to *the question that participants think they have been asked*. Experimenters cannot legislate for how people understand psychological tasks. The interpretation people adopt is an empirical matter which must be determined by fitting theoretical models to data. Because the optimal data selection model fits the data whereas Laming's model does not, it would seem that subjects may indeed interpret the problem as one of optimal data selection.

Third, Laming notes correctly that in deriving the optimal data selection model we use the subjective, rather than the "objective", interpretation of probability. He argues that the subjective/objective distinction is "irrelevant to the validity of the theory" (Laming, 1996, p. 6). We argue, on the contrary, that the subjective interpretation is crucial, and failure to realise this leads Laming to misunderstand our model, and to propose an inappropriate alternative. On the *frequentist* interpretation (Laming's "objective" interpretation), probabilities are limiting frequencies in a repeated experiment (e.g. Von Mises, 1939). Accordingly, probabilities can only be assigned to events that are repeatable, so that limiting frequencies are defined. The frequentist view underlies classical approaches to hypothesis testing (e.g.

Fisher, 1922; Neyman & Pearson, 1928). On the *subjective* interpretation, probabilities are degrees of belief (Keynes, 1921; Ramsey, 1931). Accordingly, probabilities can be assigned to *all* statements including those describing unrepeatable events. Consequently, the probability that, for example, Oswald shot Kennedy, is well defined, whereas on the frequentist interpretation it is not. The subjective interpretation underlies the Bayesian approach (Cox, 1946; de Finetti, 1937; Good, 1960; Lindley, 1971; Ramsey, 1931; Rosenkrantz, 1981).

Finally, Laming argues that our data fits are not impressive, assuming we set parameters arbitrarily. We show later that we did not set parameter values arbitrarily, but by reference to the literature on Bayesian epistemology. Moreover, we show that these parameter values, as with our other assumptions, are psychologically plausible. We now turn to Laming's specific points.

Optimal Data Selection and Testing Statistical Hypothesis

The role of Laming's tutorial section "Testing Statistical Hypotheses" seems to be twofold. First, it gives the impression that the optimal data selection account is suspect. Second, it provides the background for Laming's "correct" Bayesian analysis. We address these issues in turn.

First, our analysis is not suspect, but represents a straightforward application of a Bayesian measure of the information provided by an experiment, introduced by Lindley (1956), one of the world's leading Bayesian statisticians. Lindley (1956, p. 987) argues that "the measure of information [provided by an experiment] is given by Shannon's function [i.e. Shannon–Wiener information]" and that "prior probability distributions are ... basic to the study. It seems obvious to the author that prior distributions, though usually anathema to the statistician, are essential to the notion of experimental information. To take an extreme case, if the prior distribution is concentrated on a single parameter value [or a single hypothesis], that is if the state of nature is known, then no experiment can be informative."[7] Thus we have simply applied long-standing ideas from Bayesian statistics[8] and therefore Laming's suggestion that our information measure is suspect misses the mark.

Second, Laming states that the use of priors is the essence of Bayesian statistics. However, as we discuss below, this misrepresents the Bayesian approach, which actually depends on the subjective interpretation of probability (Howson & Urbach, 1989; Lindley, 1971). Further, Laming recommends estimating parameters using maximum likelihood, which has no Bayesian justification (Lindley, 1971). This is particularly inappropriate in the selection task, where no data are available on which to base such estimates. These problems lead Laming to his "correct" Bayesian analysis, which, as we shall see, is not really Bayesian.

Psychological Assumptions

We now come to the core of Laming's argument: that the optimal data selection model does not apply to the selection task and that it fits the data only by using arbitrary and psychologically implausible assumptions. He makes six specific points to which we reply individually. First, however, we outline two important issues bearing on Laming's arguments.

Rational Analysis and Task Interpretation

Laming states that the task set cannot be captured by our model. This presupposes that the purpose of rational analysis is to specify what people *should* do given the task description—rational analysis only has a *normative* function. However, as Oaksford and Chater (1995b) argue, the purpose of rational analysis is to characterise the task participants *think they have been set*. A rational analysis must be both normatively justified *and* descriptively adequate. In practice this means that we are concerned with modelling people's actual behaviour rather than deriving models of the experimenter's preconceived ideas about what the task investigates.

The distinction between the task set as viewed by experimenter and participant is familiar in the reasoning literature. For example, critiques of Piaget's reasoning studies (Bower, 1974; Bryant & Trabasso, 1978; Donaldson, 1978; Harris, 1975) argue that many tasks were not understood by children. When presented in a more child-centred way, reasoning previously absent would emerge. Another example is Smedslund's (1970; and see Evans, 1993) observation that you cannot assess whether people reason logically, independent of their task interpretation. A final example is the observation that "errors" in probabilistic reasoning may occur because the materials violate people's natural ways of representing probabilistic information (Birnbaum, 1983; Gigerenzer, Hell, & Blank, 1988; Gigerenzer & Murray, 1987), so that the task that the participants tackle is not the task that the experimenter intended.

In summary, rational analysis characterises both how participants interpret and solve a problem. Consequently, Laming's claim that we do not model the task people have been set is irrelevant because this was not our goal.

Bayesian Epistemology and Rarity

Laming argues that the data fits that the optimal data selection model reveals rely on setting parameters arbitrarily. We now show that our rarity assumption, which determines the parameter values we used, is not arbitrary but derives directly from the literature on Bayesian epistemology.

We now quote an influential Bayesian epistemologist (Horwich, 1982) discussing Mackie's (1963) solution to one of the paradoxes of confirmation theory (Goodman, 1983). The "ravens paradox" is that non-Bayesian confirmation theory entails that a non-black, non-raven, e.g. a pink flamingo, confirms the hypothesis that all ravens are black:

> The central idea of Bayesian accounts is that our background assumptions concerning the proportion of ravens and black objects in the universe affect the extent to which hypotheses are confirmed by various kinds of evidence. Suppose we believe that the proportion of things which are ravens is very small: call it x; and the proportion of black things y. Then our relevant background assumptions may be represented by the following table:

	R	not-R
B	xy	$(1 - x)y$
not-B	$x(1 - y)$	$(1 - x)(1 - y)$

> Thus we suppose that the subjective probability of observing a black raven $P(BR)$, is xy; and similarly, $P(BnotR) = (1 - x)y$, $P(notBR) = x(1 - y)$, and $P(notBnotR) = (1 - x)(1 - y)$.

Now consider the table which according to Mackie, would represent the further supposition—All ravens are black:

	R	not-R
B	x	$y - x$
not-B	0	$1 - y$

> If H is true, there are no non black ravens. (Horwich, 1982, p. 56)

Mackie's argument implies that although a non-black, non-raven "*will* tend to confirm 'All ravens are black,' it will do so only to a negligible degree and will not carry as much weight as the observation of a black raven" (Horwich, 1982, p. 57) as long as $x \approx 0$, i.e. if rarity holds. Thus, contrary to Laming, the parameters of our model were not set simply to fit the data. Our goal was to see whether Bayesian models that resolve conceptual problems in epistemology could also model human behaviour.

We now take the six specific assumptions that Laming identifies and show (i) that they are normatively justified, and (ii) that they make psychological sense.

1. Shannon–Wiener Information

Laming's criticism of our use of Shannon–Wiener information has several problems. First, as we have seen, it is standard in Bayesian optimal data selection (Good, 1960; Lindley, 1956, 1971; MacKay, 1992a). We suspect that Laming's objection derives from his view that optimal data selection does not apply to *the task that participants are set*. But as we have already noted, our goal was to model *the task that participants think they have been set*.

Second, Laming claims that using the information measure used in our model is statistically inappropriate. He algebraically transforms our $E(I_g)$ measure into his equation (10), which measures "the expected information from a single event in favour of the communication channel being functional (H_i and D_k related) and against the alternative that they are independent" (p. 27). Laming's equation (10) is expected Kullback–Liebler distance which is shown in our equation (A4), in the appendix to this chapter. Hence, Laming's analysis confirms our own. However, Laming argues that his interpretation using communication channels invalidates our model. This argument rests on the false assumption that if a formula has one interpretation, it cannot have another. Rather than invalidating our original interpretation, Laming has simply shown that the information measure we used has yet another interpretation.

Third, Laming objects that this measure does not discriminate between hypotheses. However, it does discriminate between hypotheses (Fedorov, 1972, Chapters 6 and 7). Discrimination depends on sequential sampling and recomputation of information gain to determine the optimal data to select next. This involves iteratively recomputing the priors at each stage in the standard Bayesian way. By selecting data using $E(I_g)$ the posteriors converge on the true hypothesis using the minimum number of observations. So the measure used in our model can discriminate between hypotheses. Of course the selection task is not a sequential sampling task— participants never see the data. Nevertheless, Bayesian hypothesis testers should use their prior beliefs to select data that will optimise discrimination between models in the long run.

Laming also argues that the optimal data selection model is paradoxical: participants must already possess the information they should derive from the data. The "paradox" arises because Laming uses a frequentist, whereas to derive the optimal data selection model we used a subjectivist, interpretation of probabilities. According to the frequentist interpretation, the probability of uncovering a particular number or letter having turned the card ($P(D_k|H_i)$) must be either 0 and 1 (as Laming notes later). This is because however many times you turn the card, it will give the same result, and hence the limiting frequencies can only take the values 0 (you never reveal the number or letter) or 1 (you always reveal the number or letter). However, in the selection task, participants do not know what is on the other side of the card, and hence cannot assign these probabilities (in the frequentist sense). But we use these probabilities in our calculations. Laming concludes, therefore, that our account assumes that participants must know what is on the back of the card, even before they have turned it.

Laming's difficulty is inevitable on his frequentist interpretation. But on the subjectivist interpretation, there is no difficulty. The $P(D_k|H_i)$ captures degrees of belief about what is on the back of the card, before it is turned. Because participants are not certain what is on the back of the card, these probabilities will take intermediate values, rather than being 0 or 1, depending on prior knowledge. This approach is standard in Bayesian statistics (e.g. Lindley, 1971). It also makes psychological sense, reflecting the psychologically reasonable assumption that prior knowledge will affect where we look for evidence.

In summary, the information measure we use makes both normative and psychological sense.

2. Rationality

Laming objects that our rational recommendations do not provide a *perfect* fit with the experimental data, e.g. only 89% of participants choose the *p*-card, which is the most informative card. But requiring a perfect fit between theory and data seems entirely unreasonable, and is not demanded of any other psychological theory.

Laming also states that "a rational Bayesian theory ought to look like this: calculation shows that some particular card offers the greatest expected gain of information, and that card is the universal first choice. Depending on what is discovered on the underside of the card, one or other of the remaining cards is chosen next because it offers the greatest expected gain of information of those remaining" (Laming, 1996, p. 25). That is, Laming is correct that a Bayesian analysis of the task assumes sequential sampling. But he is wrong to conclude that such an analysis is inappropriate to the selection task, where participants choose cards without turning them over. As mentioned in the last section, it is perfectly rational to select data to minimise the length of a sequential sample required to discriminate hypotheses, before that sample becomes available.

3. Bayesian Analysis

We are unclear about Laming's argument here. He appears to believe that, for the Bayesian, priors must be set from previous data, if they are not to reflect mere bias. Because, in the selection task, the participant sees no data, he assumes priors cannot meaningfully be set. But Bayesian analysis must always begin from some priors before data are observed, on pain of infinite regress. The question of how priors should be set to take account of general knowledge is a major issue in Bayesian statistics (Berger, 1985; Box & Tiao, 1973; Lindley, 1971). Moreover, we argue that people have a great deal of prior knowledge about conditionals (e.g. that rarity almost always holds), which is taken to be relevant to the task.

4. Characterisation of the Task

Here, Laming's objection seems to arise from his frequentist interpretation of the probabilities in our model. He imagines the situation in which there are many vowels, some with odd and some with even numbers on their undersides—in this context, the probability that a randomly chosen vowel has an even number on the back may lie between 0 and 1 (if you repeatedly choose a random card with a vowel uppermost many times, the limiting frequency will be in proportion to the number of vowels with odd and even numbers on their undersides). Laming argues that we are implicitly committed to this set-up, if our intermediate probability values are to make sense.

But, because our account is Bayesian, all probabilities are degrees of belief, and hence no fictitious repeated experiments need be imagined to make sense of the probability statements in our theory. Further, there is evidence that participants do interpret the cards as being drawn from a larger population when only confronted with four cards (Beattie & Baron, 1988). Moreover, when the experimenter draws the four cards from a larger pack in front of each subject before they perform the task (Evans & Lynch, 1973; Oaksford & Stenning, 1992) the results are the same as in the standard task.

Laming also argues that we do not consider the full range of possible hypotheses. In our model the rule is compared with a particular independence model, rather than a fully general "foil" model. This assumption was not introduced arbitrarily to fit the data. As the quote from Horwich reveals, Mackie used the same characterisation of people's background knowledge to resolve the ravens paradox. Moreover, although Laming downplays explaining the data, the fact that our simple model accurately captures the empirical results must be a virtue. Other researchers may propose alternative rational analyses, should these be necessary to capture further empirical data.

Laming also objects to our assumption that participants discriminate between two particular instances of M_D and M_I rather than comparing these models in the abstract. This is reasonable, because the values of a and b reflect particular degrees of belief in the antecedent being true, and in the consequent being true, when the antecedent is false. This assumption is psychologically innocuous. These values relate to people's degrees of belief about the proportions of various properties in their environments. It is *psychologically* reasonable to assume that people have access to this information. This assumption also makes *normative* sense—it resolves an important paradox in the logic of confirmation.

In sum, our choice of models makes both normative and psychological sense.

5. Identification of Model Parameters

Laming objects that we equate parameters a and b between models. As we saw in the quote from Horwich, Mackie (1963) makes a similar assumption, except that Mackie equates $P(p)$ and $P(q)$ between models, whereas we equate $P(p)$ (a) and $P(q|not\text{-}p)$ (b). Laming's objection is unclear because he endorses our rationale for equating these parameters, as we now see.

Equating a between models, as Laming notes, is equivalent to asserting that the antecedent (p) has the same probability in each. As we argued, if, by contrast, the probability of p were, say, higher in M_D than in M_I, this would mean that observing p and *not-p* instances alone (without being able to see both sides of the cards) would discriminate between models (by the application of Bayes' theorem). Laming's response is puzzling: "Not true ... [The conditional rule] says nothing about the relative frequencies of vowels [p cards] and consonants [*not-p* cards]" (p. 22). This is puzzling because Laming agrees that the conditional rule says nothing about the frequencies of p and *not-p* cards, which implies that it should not be possible to discriminate between models by observing one side of the cards. It is this intuition that requires equating the parameter a between models.

Similarly, we equated b, the probability of q in the absence of p, between models. Laming (1996, p. 21) argues that our "models are formulated the way they are in order to accommodate the relatively uncommon selection of the 'K'." He then proposes alternative models in which the "2" card receives zero information gain rather than the "K" card as in the optimal data selection model. The suggestion is that our decision to keep b constant between models was made solely to fit the data. However, this assumption was constrained both psychologically and normatively. Psychologically it reflects the finding that participants regard false antecedent instances, i.e.

the *not-p* cases, to be irrelevant to the truth or falsity of a conditional rule. This was established using an independent experimental paradigm—the truth-table task (Evans, 1972; Evans & Newstead, 1977; Johnson-Laird & Tagart, 1969). Further, normatively, Quine (1959) has suggested that conditional sentences do not assert a conditional, but rather assert the consequent, *q*, conditional on the antecedent, *p*. From this logical point of view, cases where the antecedent is false, *not-p* cases, are irrelevant to the truth or falsity of a conditional rule. No such evidence or normative proposals exist in support of the models Laming proposes in which the "2" card has zero information gain. Consequently, Laming's alternative model is irrelevant.

6. The Rarity Assumption

Laming objects to the rarity assumption—that $P(p)$ and $P(q)$ are low. He suggests that the rarity assumption has a bizarre consequence in the standard selection task. If the antecedent and consequent of the rule *if there is a vowel on one side of the card there is an even number on the other* are rare, then most cards must have consonants on one side and odd numbers on the other. However, the rarity assumption again makes perfect normative and psychological sense.

Normatively, the quotation from Horwich reveals that the rarity assumption is critical to Mackie's resolution of the ravens paradox. Moreover, Horwich's (1982) own analysis of this paradox assumes that $P(not\text{-}p \,\&\, not\text{-}q) \approx 1$. Consequently, the assumption that Laming appears to find bizarre is precisely the one that allows Bayesian confirmation theory to avoid paradox. Again we based our assumptions on Bayesian epistemology and did not introduce them simply to fit the data. What is remarkable is that an assumption derived for this normative purpose should prove so valuable in modelling empirical data.

Psychologically, we argued that people's everyday encounters with conditionals influence their behaviour in the selection task, and that in everyday contexts rarity almost invariably holds. Thus, everyday strategies for hypothesis testing may be adapted to an environment where rarity is the norm. Moreover, we assumed that these default strategies are a major influence on behaviour, even when participants do not know whether rarity holds. We (1994a, pp. 627–628) provided two lines of experimental support for this claim, that explaining results on Wason's (1960) 2–4–6 task (Klayman & Ha, 1987) and causal reasoning (Anderson, 1990) both require rarity. More generally, we have argued extensively that people transfer their reasoning strategies from the everyday world to the laboratory (Chater & Oaksford, 1990, 1993; Oaksford & Chater, 1991, 1992, 1995a, 1995b). In sum, contrary to Laming, the rarity assumption is normatively and psychologically reasonable.[9]

Data Coverage

Laming then argues that "all these assumptions [in our rational analysis] are invoked to match merely the rank order of the frequencies with which the different cards are selected for inspection [in the standard selection task] ... Moreover, if that rank order had been other than it is, it would simply have dictated different parameter values and assumptions. For that reason there is no need to examine Oaksford and Chater's treatment beyond the basic experimental paradigm" (p. 30). Laming's argument is wrong in two respects. First, we did not set our parameters arbitrarily. Consequently, according to his own reasoning, Laming must consider the other data that our model explains. Second, even if the parameters of our model were set in order to explain the rank order in the standard task, then the other data would provide a test of the model.

We showed good fits with data from most of the studies reported on the selection task since Wason's (1966, 1968) original papers. For example, the model captures the associations between card selections observed in abstract selection tasks (Pollard, 1985), data from the reduced array selection task (Johnson-Laird & Wason, 1970), the negations paradigm (e.g. Evans & Lynch, 1973; Manktelow & Evans, 1979), tasks with "fictional" outcomes (Kirby, 1994a), the therapy experiments (Wason, 1969; Wason & Johnson-Laird, 1970) and a range of thematic selection task results (e.g. Cheng & Holyoak, 1985; Cosmides, 1989; Gigerenzer & Hug, 1992; Manktelow & Over, 1991). These studies are not a homogeneous set, consisting of many near replications. On the contrary, they show that varying the nature of the task produces radically different results. Our rational analysis explains this variation. Further, no other account of the selection task attempts this breadth of data coverage.

We now turn to the second part of Laming's argument, that a "correct" Bayesian analysis confirms the standard "logical" solution.

Laming's "Correct" Bayesian Analysis

Laming gives a "correct" Bayesian analysis of the selection task. He assumes that the conditional probabilities of an odd or even number on the back of, say, the "A" must be one or zero, depending on whether the underside *actually* is odd or even. For Laming, that participants do not know whether the underside of the card is odd or even is not grounds for some intermediate probability because he does not interpret probabilities as degrees of belief. Laming argues that participants should turn only the "A" and "7" cards in the standard task, in line with the standard "logical" account.

Laming's "correct" Bayesian analysis is mathematically correct, but it is not Bayesian, because it begins by rejecting the fundamental principle of

Bayesian statistics, that probabilities are degrees of belief. Laming states that "the essence of Bayesian analysis is the inclusion of the priors, not that they be subjective" (Laming, 1996, p. 11). This is a common mis-understanding, against which Bayesians often warn (e.g. Howson & Urbach, 1989; Lindley, 1971). Contrasting the Bayesian approach with the fre-quentist view, Howson and Urbach (1993, p. 11) say, "The other strand of inductive probability treats the probabilities as a property of our attitude toward them; such probabilities are then interpreted, roughly speaking, as measuring degrees of belief. This is called the *subjectivist* or *personalist interpretation*. The scientific methodology based on this idea is usually referred to as the methodology of *Bayesianism*." Laming confuses the use of Bayes's theorem (an uncontroversial theorem of probability theory), and Bayesian statistics (a vigorous, though controversial, approach to statistical inference).

In summary, Laming's "correct" Bayesian account poses no problems for our rational analysis. Laming grants that his account does not fit the empirical data—for Laming, participants' behaviour is simply not rational. However, our rational analysis shows that behaviour can be viewed as rational. It does not, and could not, show that it is rational on any defen-sible view of rationality. Therefore, the fact that Laming's non-Bayesian account gives different prescriptions is irrelevant.

Summary

Laming misrepresents our rational analysis because he is concerned with the task set, rather than the task that participants think they have been set, and because he misinterprets the statistical basis of our theory. Rational analysis must be normatively justified and descriptively adequate. Our model is normatively justified because it is based on Bayesian optimal data selection. It is descriptively adequate because it provides fits to a wide range of data, without setting parameters arbitrarily.

ALMOR AND SLOMAN

Almor and Sloman (1996) argue that the optimal data selection model cannot account for data where *p* and *not-q* card responses are elicited without using deontic materials. Almor and Sloman use four rules that they claim are not deontic, and for which it is not clear whether the rarity assumption holds. However, the logical *p* and *not-q* card response pre-dominates for these rules. They conclude that we cannot explain these data. Moreover, Almor and Sloman argue that their results are not com-patible with any theory that uses the distinction between deontic and indi-cative tasks to explain so-called "facilitation" effects, i.e. choosing the *p* and *not-q* cards.[10]

Almor and Sloman raise the important issue of how to explain p and *not-q* responses in non-deontic selection tasks. Such results threaten any theory that rules out p and *not-q* responding for non-deontic tasks. They are less threatening to the optimal data selection model because it also allows p and *not-q* responses when the materials violate rarity. However, as Almor and Sloman argue, it is unclear whether their materials do violate rarity.

There have been other demonstrations of p and *not-q* responses in abstract tasks without violating rarity (Green, 1995; Green & Larking, 1995; Platt & Griggs, 1993, 1995). However, they are only problematic on a strong interpretation of our claims, that violating rarity is not only *sufficient* but is also *necessary* for the p and *not-q* response. Although Almor and Sloman and these other experiments suggest that rarity violation may not be a necessary condition for the p and *not-q* response they do not question that rarity violation is a sufficient condition. Moreover, there is evidence that rarity violation is indeed sufficient for the p and *not-q* response (Kirby, 1994a, 1994b; Oaksford & Chater, 1995b; Sperber, Cara, & Girotto, 1995). Consequently, inducing high p, *not-q* selections without violating rarity is consistent with our account.

However, we argue that Almor and Sloman obtain high p, *not-q* selections only by altering the task. Almor and Sloman's materials are either analytic, i.e. true by definition and so our model does not apply, or they are deontic and so our maximum expected utility model applies. We first contrast Almor and Sloman's experiments with other studies revealing the p and *not-q* response in the abstract task.

The p and *not-q* Response in the Abstract Task

Other experiments revealing high p, *not-q* selections use manipulations to force a logical interpretation of the rule (Green, 1995; Green & Larking, 1995; Platt & Griggs, 1993, 1995). For example, Platt and Griggs (1995) explicitly provide the logical interpretation, telling participants that "A card with an A on its letter side can only have a 4 on its number side, but a card with a B on its letter side can have either a 4 or an 5 on its number side." They also told participants to look for cards that violated this rule.[11] Green (1995) first told participants to imagine and write down all the different possible combinations of letters and numbers for each card. Participants then had to imagine which combinations could violate the rule. Finally they were asked to indicate which cards had such a combination. With this amount of coercion observing high p, *not-q* selections is not surprising. What is more surprising is how *few* participants gave the p and *not-q* response. In most of Green's (1995) experiments, in the full externalisation condition (that we have outlined already) more than 50% of participants still did not make the p and *not-q* response. Platt and Griggs (1993, 1995) and Green and Larking (1995) found similar results. It seems that participants' natural reasoning strategies are very resistant even to these quite extreme attempts to force a logical interpretation in the abstract selection task.[12]

Almor and Sloman's experiments contrast with these because Almor and Sloman do not use any additional instructions to force a logical interpretation but they achieve similar-sized effects. Therefore, Almor and Sloman's manipulations are of more theoretical interest.

Deontic and Analytic Rules

We argue that Almor and Sloman's rules are either deontic or analytic.[13] However, even in their "abstract" experiment Almor and Sloman cue participants into realistic settings that have plausible deontic interpretations. Consequently, we could argue that our maximum expected utility account of the deontic selection task explains all of Almor and Sloman's results. That model predicts the *p* and *not-q* response for obligation rules and an enforcer's perspective which could reasonably characterise Almor and Sloman's materials. However, as we noted earlier, we believe that the analytic nature of two of Almor and Sloman's rules affects their results.

We can contrast standard rules with each of Almor and Sloman's by asking what the reaction would be to a counter-example. Consider two standard rules:

> If A on one side then 2 on the other. (14.1)
> A3 implies that the rule is false.

> If it is a raven then it is black. (14.2)
> White raven implies that the rule is false.

(14.1) is a standard selection task rule. It represents a claim about the way the world is, like (14.2). The reaction to the counter-example, A3, is that the rule is false.[14] Contrast this with the reaction to a *p*, *not-q* instance of Almor and Sloman's rules:

> If a large object is stored then a large container must be used. (14.3)
> Large object in a small container implies a contradiction.

> If the weak force wins the strong force must have been weakened first. (14.4)
> Weak force wins, strong force not weakened implies a contradiction.

In both (14.3) and (14.4) the "counter-examples" seem to violate the meaning of "large object" and "strong force", e.g. large objects require large containers otherwise they would not be large. Similarly, strong forces overcome weak forces otherwise they would not be strong. This contrasts with the indicative rules in (14.1) and (14.2).

Another test is to append "It *must* be the case that" to each of (14.1) to (14.4). Although this results in true sentences for (14.3) and (14.4) it is nonsense for (14.2), i.e. it is simply not true that "It must be the case that if it is a raven then it is black" and similarly for (14.1). (14.1) and (14.2) make contingent claims about how the world *might* be. (14.3) and (14.4), in contrast make definitional or analytic claims about how the world *must* be for these terms to apply. Analyticity matters for our account because it is about how people optimally select data to determine the truth of a rule. But when a rule is analytically true $[P(M_D) = 1]$ there is no uncertainty, and so no data (no card selections) can reduce it. Consequently, optimal data selection does not apply to analytic materials. It is therefore not surprising that Almor and Sloman's results differed from results in standard selection tasks. *No* current theory of the selection task makes predictions when the conditional rule is analytic. Consequently, Almor and Sloman's experiments require a novel theoretical analysis from any point of view. Almor and Sloman's remaining rules have a different interpretation:

If a product gets a prestigious prize then it must have a distinctive   (14.5)
quality
Winning prize has no distinctive quality implies that the rule is still in force.

If the product breaks then it must have been used under abnormal   (14.6)
conditions.
Product breaks under normal conditions implies that the rule is still in force.

We argue that Almor and Sloman's contexts encourage participants to understand (14.5) and (14.6) deontically. For example, in (14.5), participants adopt the perspective of a journalist investigating prize-winning products. The criterion for winning the prize (having a distinctive quality) defines a norm, i.e. which products *ought* to win prizes. The rule is deontic. Specifically, the journalist is interested in whether these norms really determine which products win prizes (rather than, for example, prizes being awarded by corrupt means).

A final test is to append "It should be the case that" to (14.2) and (14.6). Although this makes sense for (14.5) and (14.6) it is nonsense for (14.2), i.e. "It should be the case that if it is a raven then it is black". It is equally nonsensical for (14.3) and (14.4), for example—it is not that you should store large objects in large containers, it is that you have to! Given the deontic interpretation of (14.5) and (14.6), we can explain these data using our maximum expected utility model.

All the rules that Almor and Sloman use differ from the rules normally used in the abstract selection task. For Almor and Sloman's rules it does not make sense to collect information to see whether they are true or false. Therefore, the optimal data selection model could not apply to any of them, and hence is not challenged by Almor and Sloman's results.

CONCLUSION

Evans and Over and Laming have given us the chance to elaborate the theoretical foundations and empirical consequences of our optimal data selection model. The information measure we used, to which Evans and Over and Laming object for different reasons, is standard in Bayesian optimal data selection, and can be reinterpreted to meet Evans and Over's concerns. Further, the assumptions to which Laming objects make sound normative sense, being derived from Bayesian epistemology. Our model also makes sound psychological sense, both because its assumptions are psychologically reasonable, and because it is consistent with further data that Evans and Over believe to be problematic. Further, Almor and Sloman's data showing that analytic rules also elicit high p, not-q selections do not question that the model provides a sufficient condition for the p and not-q response in the abstract task. Nor does it question the theoretical distinction many researchers in this area have drawn between abstract and deontic tasks. In sum, neither Evans and Over, Laming, nor Almor and Sloman provide grounds to question the view that the optimal data selection model provides the most compelling and comprehensive explanation of the selection task currently available.

NOTES

1. Note it is not a true distance—e.g. it is not symmetrical.

2. However, subjects could interpret the rule as exceptionless, but applying to some set of cards not including those that have been shown to include errors, such as cards that the computer will print in future. Intuitively, this is analogous to a person checking whether a machine is now working after observing a breakdown. Consequently our original model of Kirby's data could apply to participants' interpretation of the experimental set-up.

3. This may be unsurprising given that we have allowed ourselves the luxury of an extra parameter. However, as Oaksford and Chater (1998b) show, the model's predictions turn out to be insensitive to large variations of this parameter. Consequently, its function is to achieve a better mapping between task and model, not to achieve better data fits.

4. Discussions of the rational$_1$/rational$_2$ distinction (Evans, Over, & Manktelow, 1993; Evans, 1993) do not appear to be consistent. Evans (1993) identifies rationality$_1$ as rationality of purpose and rationality$_2$ as rationality of process and claims "the notion of maximizing utility is clearly a case of rationality$_1$," (p. 8). We use maximising utility to explain deontic selections tasks, but Evans and Over argue that this account is a rational$_2$ theory. It is also unclear why Evans and Over imply that rational$_2$ explanation is a bad thing, given that Evans (1993) states that rationality$_2$ explanation is often successful in psychology (he cites the example of learning theory).

5. Further, we could not find a formal account of epistemic utility to compare with $E(I_g)$, in any of the references Evans and Over cite.

6. In the original submission of our paper (Oaksford & Chater, 1994a) to *Psychological Review* we clearly outlined the origins of our assumptions. However, for reasons of journal space, the reviewers suggested, and we agreed, that this material should be left out. Consequently, Laming's critique was very welcome for the opportunity it afforded us to make the origins of our assumptions explicit.

7. We note that Lindley, somewhat confusingly, but for sound reasons (see Lindley, 1956, p. 989) introduces a sign reversal. We followed this convention, which caused some confusion which both Evans and Over and Laming pointed out. In our appendix, and elsewhere (Oaksford & Chater, 1995b, 1995c) we adopt the standard convention of not reversing the sign.

8. Laming, by contrast, recommends against using Shannon's measure and the use of prior distributions.

9. Klayman and Ha's minority phenomena assumption is somewhat less restrictive than our rarity assumption, specifying only that probabilities are less than 0.5.

10. Note that if we are right, the view underlying this terminology, that participants performance is "facilitated" from an initially irrational baseline, is wrong (see also Manktelow & Over, 1987). Almor and Sloman are careful to avoid this misleading terminology.

11. As Platt and Griggs (1995) observe the use of much modal terminology, i.e. "can", "can only", and the violation instruction may well have induced a deontic context that produced the facilitation.

12. Two of these studies, Green (1995) and Platt and Griggs (1995), claim to show that probabilistic manipulations fail to have the effects predicted either by Kirby (1994a) or by Oaksford and Chater (1994a). However, in both cases the experimenters have embedded the probabilistic manipulation in other manipulations, which we outlined in the text, designed to force a logical interpretation of the rule. Consequently, how these data bear on Oaksford and Chater's model is obscure—other factors so confound the data as to make them uninterpretable. Moreover, as Platt and Griggs (1995) concede, they cannot be sure that participants' subjective probabilities were appropriately calibrated to the letter and number frequencies used in these experiments. This is especially true because they make no distinction between type and token frequencies which Oaksford and Chater (1994a) argue may be an important factor. Green (1995) and Platt and Griggs (1995), assume that what matters to people's everyday hypothesis testing is that there are 5 vowels and 21 consonants, i.e. the frequencies of letter types. However, as Oaksford and Chater (1994a) argue, it is more likely that people's prior experience with particular letter and number tokens provide the priors they use in optimal data selection.

13. All Almor and Sloman's rules also use the modal "must" in the consequent. In contrast, the rules used in other studies eliciting *p* and *not-q* responses were explications of standard *abstract* rules. Almor and Sloman, however, used this modal in all rules in their experiments so this is unlikely to be a factor.

14. However participants may not interpret the occurrence of a falsifying instance, A3, immediately as meaning that the rule is false, as (14.2) reveals. It makes sense to seek evidence for the truth or falsity of this generalisation, however, observing a white raven would not necessarily lead you to reject (14.2) as a very useful rule. As Oaksford and Chater (1991, 1992, 1993, 1995b) have argued, most of the rules that make up our world knowledge admit some exceptions.

APPENDIX

Proof of the Equivalence of Expected Information Gain and Expected Kullback–Liebler Distance

Consider hypotheses, *h*, and data, *d*. The uncertainty associated with *h* before the data are collected is:

$$- \log_2(P(h)) \tag{A14.1}$$

This is sometimes known as the surprisal of h. The uncertainty associated with h after the data are collected is:

$$-\log_2(P(h|d))$$

(A14.2)

That is, the same as (A14.1), but with the appropriate revision of the probability. Information gain, I_g, is therefore:

$$\begin{aligned}&-\log_2(Ph)) - (-\log_2(Ph|d)))\\&= \log_2(P(h|d) - \log_2(P(h))\end{aligned}$$

(A14.3)

We are interested in the expectation of this quantity, with respect to the joint distribution of h and d. In symbols, expected information gain, $E(I_g)$ is:

$$EI_g =_{h,d} \left\langle \log_2(P(h|d)) - \log_2(P(h)) \right\rangle$$

$$= \left\langle \log_2\left(\frac{P(h|d)}{P(h)}\right)\right\rangle_{h,d}$$

$$= \sum_{h,d} P(h,d)\log_2\left(\frac{P(h|d)}{P(h)}\right)$$

(A14.4)

The calculations in (A14.4) simply write out the expectation explicitly.

Now let us turn to our new approach, based on the difference between new and old distributions. The Kullback–Liebler distance from a distribution $P'(x)$ and a distribution $P(x)$ is:

$$D(P',P) = \sum_{k} P'(x_k)\log_2\left(\frac{P'(x_k)}{P(x_k)}\right)$$

(A14.5)

The distribution of interest here is the distribution of belief in the available hypotheses, h. The new distribution is given by the $P(h|d)$ values, which take the data into account; the old distribution is given by the $P(h)$ values. Applying (A14.5), the Kullback–Liebler distance from the new to the old distribution is:

$$D(P^{new},P^{old}) = \sum_{h} P(h)\log_2\left(\frac{P(h|d)}{P(h)}\right)$$

(A14.6)

We are already summing over hypotheses, so we need take expectations only over data (taking expectations over the joint distribution of h and d produces the same result). The expected value of D, $E(D)$, is given by:

$$E(D) = \left\langle \sum_d \sum_h P(h|d)\log_2\left(\frac{P(h|d)}{P(h)}\right) \right\rangle$$

$$= \sum_d P(d) \sum_h P(h)\log_2\left(\frac{P(h|d)}{P(h)}\right)$$

$$= \sum_{h,d} P(h, d)\log_2\left(\frac{P(h|d)}{P(h)}\right) \tag{A14.7}$$

That is, expected information gain ($E(I_g)$) equals expected Kullback–Liebler distance ($E(D)$). As all the calculations in Oaksford and Chater (1994a) involve $E(I_g)$, we can adopt $E(D)$ without altering any substantive aspect of the original analysis. Further, D has none of the counter-intuitive properties that Evans and Over point out for I_g.

CHAPTER FIFTEEN

Information Gain Explains Relevance, Which Explains the Selection Task

INTRODUCTION

In this chapter we consider how the rational analysis of the selection task that we have discussed in the last five chapters relates to an alternative approach developed by Dan Sperber, Francisco Cara, and Vitorio Girotto (Sperber, Cara, & Girotto, 1995) in an article entitled *Relevance Explains the Selection Task*. They present a set of new experiments that they attempt to explain in terms of Sperber and Wilson's (1986) Relevance Theory, which we discussed in Chapter 5. In this chapter, we suggest that the notion of expected information gain that is central to our rational analysis can be thought of as giving a quantitative explanation of the meaning of "relevance" in the context of this task. Thus, we suggest that a relevance-based account of the selection task is not necessarily an alternative to our rational analysis, but can be viewed as entirely compatible with it. We therefore reconsider the experimental data that Sperber et al. argue favour their relevance account, and show that the data can be modelled successfully using information gain. Hence our conclusion, echoing the title of Sperber et al.'s article, that information gain explains relevance, which, in turn, explains the selection task.

INFORMATION GAIN EXPLAINS RELEVANCE, WHICH EXPLAINS THE SELECTION TASK

Sperber et al. (1995) argue that relevance theory (Sperber & Wilson, 1986) explains the selection task. The main tenet of relevance theory is that relevant information has the greatest cognitive effects for the least processing

251

effort. Sperber et al. construct experimental materials that they take to vary the cognitive effect and the processing effort required to solve the selection task. They argue that the results of their experiments conclusively support the relevance account, and discount other explanations of selection task performance. In particular, they suggest that their data and their approach are not compatible with our rational analysis (Anderson, 1990) of the selection task that uses "information gain" to determine card selection. By contrast, in this chapter, we argue that the information gain and relevance accounts are compatible, rather than in competition. Our notion of expected information gain provides a quantitative measure of relevance appropriate to the selection task. We demonstrate the validity of this interpretation by showing that the information gain account can explain the experimental results of Sperber et al. (1995).

Why do Sperber et al. (1995) conclude that information gain and relevance approaches are incompatible? First, they contend that the information gain approach does not explain important aspects of the data in the empirical literature, which, they argue, the relevance account can handle. In particular, they argue that the information gain account does not address the facilitation of the "logical" *p, not-q* response when the consequent of the task rule contains a negation (Evans & Lynch, 1973; Oaksford & Stenning, 1992). However, as we seen in earlier chapters, the rational analysis provides a detailed quantitative analysis of these experiments, including data from Evans and Lynch (1973), Griggs and Cox (1983), Manktelow and Evans (1979), Oaksford and Stenning (1992), Pollard (1985), and Reich and Ruth (1982). Overall, we have shown that theoretically derived expected information gains correlate highly, and significantly, with the observed data.

Second, Sperber et al. (1995) argue that their own data (experiment 2) are incompatible with the rational analysis account. Given the large range of experimental data for which our theory provides a quantitative explanation, it is not clear how to interpret a single anomaly, even if it was completely inexplicable in terms of the theory. Moreover, it is not clear that the relevance account is compatible with the range of data covered by the information gain approach (which provides a comprehensive, quantitative analysis of the majority of the past literature). The Bayesian approach that we adopt in our model of the selection task is in explicit opposition to falsificationism—you can always explain away a single inconsistent result (Duhem, 1914/1954; Quine, 1953). What is important is the ability of a theory to account for the broad pattern of replicable results. In any case, we shall argue that there is a plausible interpretation of experiment 2, which is compatible with the information gain account.

Third, along with almost all existing accounts of the selection task, they accuse the information gain account of falling "short of either predicting or ruling out good performance (more than 50% correct) on yet untested varieties of the task." Sperber et al. argue that their relevance account does provide predictions. We are at a loss to know what differentiates all these other views from the relevance account in relation to predictive power. In particular, we have made predictions from the information gain account, which we mention in Oaksford and Chater (1994a), and which have been tested experimentally (see Chapter 16 for discussion). Further, we note that Oaksford and Chater (1994a) formulated the information gain theory and submitted it for publication before Kirby's (1994a) results were available. Oaksford and Chater's (1994a) subsequent analysis showed that the information gain theory predicted Kirby's results.

We have suggested that the information gain account may be a way of making a relevance account of the selection task formally precise. We now show how to apply our rational analysis to model the experiments of Sperber et al.

Recall that Oaksford and Chater (1994a) (see Chapter 10) calculated $SE(I_g)$s for each card assuming that the properties described in p and q are rare. They motivate the "rarity assumption" from the observation that it seems to apply to the vast majority of everyday conditional sentences. They also cite support for this view from the literature on other reasoning tasks (Klayman & Ha, 1987; Anderson, 1990). Hence, Oaksford and Chater (1994a) argue that people's strategies for dealing with conditional rules will tend, by default, to be adapted to the case where rarity holds.

Adopting the rarity assumption, the order in $SE(I_g)$ is:

$$SE(I_g(p)) > SE(I_g(q)) > SE(I_g(not\text{-}q)) > SE(I_g(not\text{-}p))$$

This corresponds to the observed frequency of card selections in Wason's task: $n(p) > n(q) > n(not\text{-}q) > n(not\text{-}p)$, where $n(x)$ denotes the number of cards of type x selected. This account thus explains the predominance of p and q card selections as a rational inductive strategy. This ordering holds only when $P(p)$ and $P(q)$ are both low. We noted in Chapter 11 that task manipulations that suggest that this condition does not hold (at least one of $P(p)$ or $P(q)$ is high) leads to alternative orderings, predominantly that:

$$SE(I_g(p)) > SE(I_g(not\text{-}q)) > SE(I_g(q)) > SE(I_g(not\text{-}p))$$

This ordering is more consistent with Popperian falsificationism, where the p and $not\text{-}q$ instances are favoured. The effect of rarity and its violation will enable us to account for many of the results of Sperber et al.

Oaksford and Chater (1994a) also show how their model generalises to all the main patterns of results in the selection task. Specifically, it accounts for the non-independence of card selections (Pollard, 1985), the negations paradigm (e.g. Evans & Lynch, 1973), the therapy experiments (e.g. Wason,

1969), the reduced array selection task (Johnson-Laird & Wason, 1970b), work on so-called fictional outcomes (Kirby, 1994a) and deontic versions of the selection task (e.g. Cheng & Holyoak, 1985) including perspective and rule-type manipulations (e.g. Cosmides, 1989; Gigerenzer & Hug, 1992), and the manipulation of probabilities and utilities in deontic tasks (Kirby, 1994a).

Modelling the Results of Sperber et al.

We now apply the information gain account to Sperber et al.'s four experimental studies in turn, and argue that these studies confirm this account. The basic strategy of these experiments is to show that in a "relevance" condition, participants consistently select the p and $not\text{-}q$ cards, whereas these selections are much less frequently observed in an "irrelevance" condition, where the p, q card selection dominates. Our approach to modelling experiments 1–3 will be to show that in the relevance condition the materials violate rarity, whereas they adhere to rarity in the irrelevance cases. We provide a more quantitative analysis of the richer data obtained in Sperber et al.'s experiment 4.

Experiment 1

Sperber et al.'s experiment 1 contrasts a relevance condition concerning what they call the "virgin mothers" problem, with an irrelevance condition consisting of a standard abstract selection task. The irrelevance condition uses standard materials, and hence we assume that the default rarity assumption applies, giving the normal ordering: $n(p) > n(q) > n(not\text{-}q) > n(not\text{-}p)$. This is exactly the ordering found in Sperber et al.'s data: $n(p) = 25 > n(q) = 11 > n(not\text{-}q) = 8 > n(not\text{-}p) = 1$ ($N = 27$).

The "virgin mothers" problem employs the rule "if a woman has a child, she has had sex". In this rule, both the antecedent and the consequent violate the rarity assumption, because the majority of women have children, and the majority of women have had sex. Therefore, we would predict that $not\text{-}q$ card selections will exceed q card selections leading to the overall pattern: $n(p) > n(not\text{-}q) > n(q) > n(not\text{-}p)$. As before, this is exactly the ordering found in Sperber et al.'s data: $n(p) = 26 > n(not\text{-}q) = 23 > n(q) = 2 > n(not\text{-}p) = 1$ ($N = 27$).

Experiment 2

In experiment 2, both relevance and irrelevance conditions involve contentful materials, concerning the visit to Padua of a group of English schoolchildren. Volunteers are required to look after these children, and there is speculation over the sex and marital status of people who put themselves forward as volunteers. The relevance condition uses the rule: "if a volunteer is male, then he is married". The irrelevance condition uses the rule: "if a volunteer is male, then he is dark haired". Unlike experiments 1 and 3, it much less clear how to assign the probabilities in this experiment, because it depends on participants' assumptions about the people who are likely to put themselves forward in this type of situation. The uncertainty here is paralleled by the uncertainty in Sperber et al.'s account of the task. They assert that "if a volunteer is male, then he is married" is relevant on the ground that its counter-example is lexicalised (i.e. bachelor); and that "the most salient cognitive effect of the conditional statement is on the presence of bachelors among the volunteers." Although these are perhaps reasonable speculations concerning how participants represent the problem, these assertions do not follow from any well-specified theory of relevance. Therefore, if the information gain account can also provide a plausible interpretation, then it should be favoured as an account of the computation of relevance in this context.

We suggest that in the volunteering context, participants assume that male volunteers will be rare (the instructions for the relevance condition explicitly reflect this). So, we argue that rarity holds for the antecedent in both the relevance and the irrelevance conditions. In the irrelevance condition, the consequent is "dark-haired", which is presumably rare.[1] Therefore, we would predict that q card selections will exceed not-q card selections leading to the overall pattern: $n(p) > n(q) > n(not$-$q) > n(not$-$p)$. This is exactly the ordering found in Sperber et al.'s data: $n(p) = 16 > n(q) = 12 > n(not$-$q) = 7 > n(not$-$p) = 5$ ($N = 19$).

In the relevance condition, the consequent is "married". Because most people are married this violates the rarity assumption. Importantly on the information gain account if either $P(p)$ or $P(q)$ is high (or they are both high) then the expected information gain associated with the not-q card exceeds that associated with the q card. Therefore because $P(q)$ is high, i.e. the materials violate rarity for the consequent alone, the theory still predicts the ordering: $n(p) > n(not$-$q) > n(q) > n(not$-$p)$. As before, this is exactly the ordering found in Sperber et al.'s data: $n(p) = 15 > n(not$-$q) = 13 > n(q) = 5 > n(not$-$p) = 1$ ($N = 17$).

Experiment 3

Sperber et al.'s experiment 3 contrasts two problems about employment. In the irrelevance condition, the rule is: "if a person is older that 65, then this person is without a job". Because most people are younger than 65, and most people are in work, both antecedent and consequence adhere to the rarity assumption, and hence the theory predicts the standard ordering: $n(p) > n(q) > n(not$-$q) > n(not$-$p)$. This is exactly the ordering found in Sperber et al.'s data: $n(p) = 15 > n(q) = 10 > n(not-q) = 9 > n(not-p) = 5$ ($N = 20$).

In the relevance condition, the rule is: "if a person is of working age, then this person has a job". Because most people are of working age, and most people have a job, both antecedent and consequent violate the rarity assumption. Therefore, the theory predicts the ordering: $n(p) > n(not-q) > n(q) > n(not-p)$. As before, this is exactly the ordering found in Sperber et al.'s data: $n(p) = 19 > n(not-q) = 17 > n(q) = 6 > n(not-p) = 2$ ($N = 20$).

Experiment 4

Sperber et al. used four conditions in experiment 4 corresponding to all possible combinations of high and low cognitive effects (Ec+/Ec−) and high and low effort (Et+/Et−). The materials used were very similar to those used by Kirby (1994a) and involved a machine that is printing double-sided cards with letters on one side and numbers on the other side. The rule used was "if a card has a 6 on the front, it has an E on the back". We interpret all the conditions in this experiment as directly setting the parameters of the information gain account. In showing how we assume that participants interpret "numbers" as referring to the numerals (1, 2, ..., 8, 9).

In the high cognitive effects and low effort (Ec+/Et−) condition participants are told that the machine prints a 4 or a 6 on the front of a card at random, it then prints an E on the back if there is a 6 on the front, and an E or an A at random if there is a 4 on the front. p (6) and not-p (4) are therefore equiprobable and so $P(p) = 0.5$. When there is a 6 on the front there is always an E printed on the back, so the probability of p, q is 0.5. When there is a 4 on the front then whether an A or an E gets printed on the back is equiprobable, so the probability of not-p, q is 0.25. Therefore the probability of q, $P(q) = P(p, q) + P(not-p, q) = 0.75$.

In the high cognitive effects and high effort condition (Ec+/Et+), participants are told that the machine prints a number on the front of a card at random, it then prints an E on the back if there is a 6 on the front, and a letter at random if there is not a 6 on the front. p (6) is therefore $\frac{1}{9}$, and not-p (not 6) is $\frac{8}{9}$ and so $P(p) = \frac{1}{9}$. When there is a 6 on the front there is always an E printed on the back, so the probability of p, q is $\frac{1}{9}$. When there is another number on the front then a letter is printed at random on the back so the probability of not-p, q is $\frac{8}{9} \times \frac{1}{26} = \frac{8}{234}$. Therefore, the probability of q, $P(q) = P(p, q) + P(not-p, q) = \frac{17}{117}$.

In the low cognitive effects and low effort condition (Ec−/Et−), participants are told that the machine prints a 4 or a 6 on the front of card at random, it then prints an E or an A at random on the back. Therefore, p (6)

is 0.5, *not-p* (*not* 6) is 0.5, *q*(E) is 0.5, and *not-q*(*not* E) is 0.5. So $P(p) = P(q) = 0.5$.

In the low cognitive effects and high effort condition (Ec−/Et+), participants are told that the machine prints a number on the front of card at random, it then prints a letter at random on the back. Therefore p (6) is $\frac{1}{9}$, *not-p* (*not* 6) is $\frac{8}{9}$, q(E) is $\frac{1}{26}$, and *not-q*(*not* E) is $\frac{25}{26}$. So $P(p) = \frac{1}{9}$ and $P(q) = \frac{1}{26}$.

In the high cognitive effects conditions (Ec+/Et−, Ec+/Et+), participants are told that the machine has broken down but that Mr Bianchi has now fixed it. In the low cognitive effects conditions (Ec−/Et−, Ec−/Et+), participants are told that the machine has broken down and that Mr Bianchi thinks that the task rule is now in force (rather than the card faces being printed at random as they should be). In both cases an expert informs participants that the rule is in force. Participants should therefore assign a low value to the probability that the independence model holds, i.e. $P(M_I)$ should be low. We therefore set $P(M_I)$ to 0.1 and then used the parameter values derived earlier to compute scaled expected information gains for each card in each condition of Sperber et al.'s (1995) experiment 4. However, in our model, the values of $P(p) = \frac{1}{9}$ and $P(q) = \frac{1}{26}$ in the Ec−/Et+ condition are inconsistent. It is a constraint on our model that $P(q) > P(p)$, otherwise the dependence model cannot hold. A similar problem arises for rules with negated antecedents (see Oaksford & Chater, 1994a, pp. 617–618) and was resolved by arguing that participants must revise $P(p)$ down so that it is less than $P(q)$. Confronting the same situation, this is what we assume participants do here and so we reset $P(p)$ in the Ec−/Et+ condition to $\frac{1}{28}$.

Figure 15.1 shows the *z*-scores of (i) $SE(I_g)$s for each card in each condition of Sperber et al.'s experiment 4 and (ii) the individual card-selection frequencies they observed (as before this simply normalises the scores on the same scale, to give a beter feel for the fit between data and model). The fit between data and model is very good ($r(14) = 0.89, p < 0.0001$). This result indicates that information gain may well provide an excellent measure of relevance in this task.

Sperber et al. (1995) go on to apply their relevance approach to other versions of the selection task, in particular the recently much studied deontic versions (e.g. Cheng & Holyoak, 1985, 1989; Cosmides, 1989; Gigerenzer & Hug, 1992; Girotto et al., 1992; Griggs & Cox, 1982; Jackson & Griggs, 1990; Johnson-Laird & Byrne, 1991, 1992; Manktelow & Over, 1987, 1990b, 1991; Rumelhart, 1980). They argue that their approach is to be preferred because it generalises to these data. However, Oaksford and Chater (1994a, 1995a) also provide a further quantitative measure of relevance based on expected utilities that provides excellent fits to the data on the deontic selection task. So, again, Oaksford and Chater (1994a) provide a more compelling, formal account of relevance in this domain.

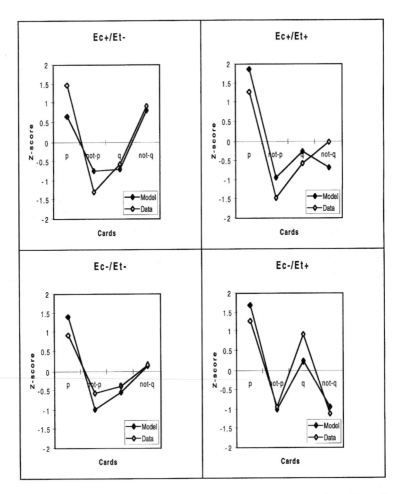

FIG. 15.1 Comparison of the $SE(I_g)$s and the selection frequency for each card in each condition of Sperber et al.'s (1995) Experiment 4. For purposes of comparison the $SE(I_g)$s and the selection frequencies have been converted to z-scores in order to normalise the scales. $r(14) = 0.89$ ($p < 0.0001$). Ec+/Et− = High effects and low effort condition; Ec+/Et+ = High effects and high effort condition; Ec−/Et− = low effects and low effort condition; Ec−/Et+ = Low effects and high effort condition.

CONCLUSIONS

This chapter has shown that information gain can provide a quantitative account of relevance in the selection task and that consequently Sperber et al.'s relevance approach and our information gain (and expected utility) approach are compatible rather than in competition. Evans (1989, 1993) has also advocated the view that participants select those cards in the selection task that they view as relevant or salient. Sperber et al. suggest that Evans fails to "develop an explicit notion [of relevance] of his own." However, recently Over and Evans (1994) have suggested that "epistemic utility" may provide a quantitative measure of relevance in the same way as information gain. It remains to be seen whether epistemic utility can be appropriately formalised and applied to the range of selection task results in the same way as Oaksford and Chater's information gain and expected utility measures. Nevertheless the goal of uncovering suitable relevance measures now seems firmly established.

Why are relevance measures needed? The principal reason concerns the computational intractability of current theories of reasoning (Chater & Oaksford, 1990, 1993; Oaksford & Chater, 1991, 1992, 1993, 1995b). All current theories tacitly assume that participants only represent the most relevant or plausible information from which to draw inferences. In artificial intelligence (AI) the problem of retrieving relevant information from memory in order to draw inferences is known as the frame problem (Glymour, 1987). This problem has bedevilled work in AI knowledge representation since the 1960s (McCarthy & Hayes, 1969). However, people do not seem to be prone to these problems—from the vast store of world knowledge people seem unerringly to access the most relevant and plausible information to solve a problem or to interpret a situation. As Sperber and Wilson (1986) identified, what linguistics and psychology requires is a well-defined theory of relevance. As Oaksford and Chater's (1994a) model reveals, developing formal relevance measures may also resolve many outstanding problems in the psychology of reasoning.

NOTE

1. One might object that the assumption of rarity for dark hair is not appropriate for the Italian participants who took part in this study. However, we suspect that the task instructions force an interpretation in which dark hair is relatively rare (i.e. a particularly strict standard of what counts as dark must be in play). This is because the task instructions state: "Mrs Bianchi, who has strong views on many things, says: 'Men with dark hair love children! I bet you, if a volunteer is male, then he is dark haired'." Conversational maxims suggest that utterances such as "Men with dark hair love children!" must be informative. For this utterance to be informative requires that most men have *not* got dark hair, otherwise, very little information will be conveyed because most men will be assumed to love children, irrespective of the statement. This line of thought suggests an interesting possible relationship between the pragmatic principles that relevance theory was designed to explain, and probabilistic measures of information. It may be that pragmatics affects reasoning via its impact on people's subjective probabilities.

CHAPTER SIXTEEN

Current Developments and Future Directions

In this chapter we consider current developments and future directions in reasoning research suggested by the approach we have been developing in this book. We first discuss recent empirical developments, including new areas of human reasoning that are susceptible to a probabilistic analysis. We also trace the relation between our research programme and recent empirical work on probabilisitic reasoning. Second, we look at wider theoretical issues relating to a probabilistic account. Specifically we consider the extent to which the probabilistic approach deals with the problems of completeness* and tractability that framed the discussion of logicist cognitive science in Part I. We also consider the relations between our approach and some influential recent proposals concerning human rationality.

EMPIRICAL EVIDENCE

In this section we describe the recent empirical evidence that is emerging in the literature on probabilistic approaches to reasoning and, in particular, to the selection task. We first look at two sets of experiments on the selection task where the probabilistic effects predicted by Oaksford and Chater (1994a, see Chapters, 10, 11, 12, and 13) are in evidence (Oaksford, Chater, Grainger, & Larkin, 1997; Oaksford, Chater, & Grainger, 1997). Some of these experiments revealed unpredicted effects of "sequential sampling", which is allowed in the reduced array version of this task that we discuss first. We therefore also show how the optimal data selection model may explain these effects (Oaksford & Chater, 1998b). We then look at some recent experiments confirming the prediction of the optimal data selection model that people treat negated categories in the rules in the selection task like high-probability categories (see Chapter 11). Perhaps one problem with our approach is the apparent assumption that while people are poor logicians they may be good probabilistic reasoners. This assumption seems to be belied by the work of Tversky and Kahneman (1974) showing that people are as error-prone in their probabilistic reasoning as in their logical reasoning. We argue that such a criticism assumes the wrong computational level of explanation and that anyway there is recent evidence that people are far better probabilistic reasoners than Tversky and Kahneman supposed. Finally, we turn to some recent extensions of the probabilistic approach to other modes of reasoning, specifically, syllogistic reasoning and conditional inference.

The Reduced Array Selection Task

Oaksford, Chater, Grainger, and Larkin (1997) have used the reduced array selection task ("RAST") to test the predictions of the optimal data selection model. In a reduced array selection task (RAST) participants choose between the q and not-q options only (hence "reduced array", Johnson-Laird & Wason, 1970; Wason & Green, 1984). The stimuli in the original RAST consisted of 30 coloured shapes. The experimenter informs the participants that there are 15 black shapes and 15 white shapes, each of which is a triangle or a circle. The shapes are in two boxes, one containing the white shapes, and the other containing the black shapes. On being presented with a test sentence, e.g. *All the triangles are black*, participants have to assess the truth or falsity of the sentence by asking to see the *least* number of black or white shapes. In Johnson-Laird and Wason (1970), although all participants chose some confirmatory black shapes (no participant chose more than nine), they all chose all 15 potentially falsificatory white shapes. Thus, where participants in effect perform multiple selection tasks, they tend to show falsificatory behaviour. Wason and Green (1984) report a variant on the RAST, and Girotto and Light and their colleagues (Girotto, 1988; Girotto, Light, & Colbourn, 1988; Girotto, Blaye, & Farioli, 1989; Light et al., 1989) have used it in developmental studies using thematic content.

In Chapter 11 we suggested the following explanation for the basic findings on the RAST. The RAST makes explicit that the rule applies to a limited domain of cards or shapes that the experimenter describes as being in a box or in a bag. The experimenter also informs participants that in this limited domain there are equal numbers of q and not-q instances. It follows that $P(q) = P(not$-$q) = 0.5$, violating the rarity assumption. If participants are sensitive to these experimentally given frequencies, then this leads to a value of $SE(I_g(not\text{-}q))$, which is higher than $SE(I_g(q))$. Consequently, optimal data selection predicts more *not-q* card selections than *q* card selections as is typically observed in the RAST.

Oaksford, Chater, Grainger, and Larkin (1997) tested this explanation of performance on the RAST by systematically varying $P(q)$. They used stacks of cards depicting coloured shapes on one side, rather than boxes of coloured shapes. The numbers of cards in each stack were varied to achieve the probability manipulation. By varying these probabilities they showed that the proportions of *q* and *not-q* cards selected varied in accordance with the optimal data selection model, i.e. as $P(q)$ falls, *q* card selections rose and *not-q* card selections fell.

Figure 16.1 shows the results of Oaksford, Chater, Grainger, and Larkin's (1997) Experiment 1. The principal prediction they made was that the discrimination between the $SE(I_g)$s for each card should determine the difference in the number of *q* ($n(q)$) and the number of *not-q* ($n(not\text{-}q)$) cards

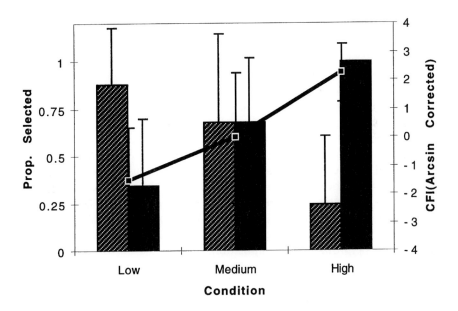

FIG. 16.1   The results of Oaksford, Chater, Grainger, and Larkin's (1997) Experiment 1. The cross-hatched bars indicate the proportion of *q* cards selected in each condition and the black bars indicate the proportion of *not-q* cards selected in each condition. The line connecting the filled squares shows the consequent falsification index (CFI) in each condition. The error bars show a single standard deviation.

selected, i.e. as $P(q)$ rises so should $n(not\text{-}q) - n(q)$. This difference measure, which Oaksford and Stenning (1992) called the consequent falsification index ("CFI"), is shown by the line in Fig. 16.1. As can be seen, it increased steadily and significantly as $P(q)$ rose. Moreover, individual trends for the q and the *not-q* cards were also observed in line with predictions of the optimal data selection model. As $P(q)$ rose, so there was a significant increase in the number of *not-q* cards selected and there was a significant decrease in the number of the q cards selected.

A possible alternative explanation for these effects is that participants were selecting cards from the smallest stack or were selecting cards at random. In the low $P(q)$ condition the smallest stack corresponded to the q card and in the high $P(q)$ the smallest stack corresponded to the *not-q* card. Consequently, a small stack bias could explain the pattern of selections in Oaksford, Chater, Grainger, and Larkin's (1997) experiment 1. However, they argue that if this were the case then participants should also select from the smallest stack if the stacks contained just the antecedent, p and *not-p*, cards. But the optimal data selection model predicts that participants should select the p card in preference to the *not-p* card in all conditions. In their experiment 2, Oaksford, Chater, Grainger, and Larkin (1997) therefore used just these cards with the same probability conditions as in experiment 1 but now varying $P(p)$. As predicted, participants selected the p card in preference to the *not-p* card in all conditions. However, every theory of the selection task predicts that the p card should be preferred to the *not-p* card. Although, as Oaksford, Chater, Grainger, and Larkin (1997) point out, all other theories only incorporate this preference *post hoc*. Only the optimal data selection model shows how this preference emerges as a consequence of a formal theory of the task. Nonetheless, to confirm further that a small stack bias or random selection was not responsible for the results of experiment 1, the experiment was repeated but this time having participants select cards from equal sized stacks of cards. This was achieved by having the experimenter deal 10 cards from different sized packs, so although the probability information was available the stack sizes were the same. The results of this experiment, Oaksford, Chater, Grainger, and Larkin's experiment 3, replicated their experiment 1 confirming that the effects were indeed due the probability manipulation.

There was one discrepancy between the results of experiments 1 and 3 and the predictions of the optimal data selection model. In the medium $P(q)$ condition, where $P(q) = 0.5$ and hence rarity is violated, participants tended to select marginally more q cards than *not-q* cards. As Oaksford, Chater, Grainger, and Larkin point out, one possible cause of this result could be a lack of sensitivity to probability manipulations at the lower end of the probability scale. However, another possibility is that sequential sampling influences participants' selections. One possible reason for this is that in the RAST when rarity is violated participants should only select *not-q* cards, which in these experiments always had a *not-p* on the other side. According to Bayesian updating, observing just such data, i.e. *not-p*, *not-q* instances, will allow participants to come to believe that the rule is true. However, this is counter-intuitive. It means, for example, that you could come to believe that "all ravens are black" simply by observing non-black, non-ravens, e.g. pink flamingos. This is the ravens paradox of standard confirmation theory (Goodman, 1954), which the rarity assumption resolves (see Chapter 14). However, when rarity is violated people may want to see at least one black raven before coming to the conclusion that "all ravens are black". If the effects observed for the medium $P(q)$ condition were the result of sequential sampling then they should disappear for the first card selected, i.e. participants should prefer the *not-q* card to the q card for the high and the medium $P(q)$ condition. Oaksford, Chater, Grainger, and Larkin (1997) tested this hypothesis in their experiment 4. Consistent with the optimal data selection model, participants made more initial *not-q* card selections than initial q card selections in the high *and* in the medium $P(q)$ conditions. Consequently the effects for the medium $P(q)$ condition seem to be the result of sequential sampling.

Oaksford, Chater, Grainger, and Larkin (1997) offered several possible explanations of the effects of the medium $P(q)$ condition. More recently Oaksford and Chater (1998b) have proposed that a principled solution can be derived within the optimal data selection framework. Oaksford, Chater, Grainger, and Larkin (1997) assumed that only prior beliefs, $P(M_I)$, in the two hypotheses (models) were revised trial-by-trial, i.e. they assumed that $P(p)$ and $P(q)$ are fixed at the beginning of the experiment and that they remain fixed throughout regardless of sequential sampling. The participants in their experiments were told the values of $P(p)$ and $P(q)$ in the form of frequency statements and, moreover, they also had stacks of cards in front of them that concretely reflected these frequencies. Although these procedures may successfully encourage participants to utilise these probabilities in their initial assessment of which card to select, it may not, and perhaps should not, prevent them from actively updating these probabilities when they begin to sample the actual cards. Oaksford, Chater, Grainger, and Larkin (1997) speculated that subjects may revise $P(p)$ and $P(q)$ trial-by-trial in the RAST and that this may explain the apparent failure of the optimal data selection model to predict the results for the medium $P(q)$ condition.

Oaksford and Chater (1998b) make two assumptions about how participants should update their beliefs about $P(M_I)$, $P(p)$ and $P(q)$. First, people are conservative in revising their beliefs. Consequently Oaksford and Chater (1998b) assume that participants revise their degree of belief in a hypothesis by only a half of what Bayes' theorem would recommend. So if Bayes recommended that your degree of belief in the independence hypothesis should be revised from 0.5 to 0.3, i.e. it should be decreased by 0.2, Oaksford and Chater (1998b) assume that you only revise your degree of belief by half this amount, i.e. from 0.5 to 0.4. More formally, on trial n your conservative degree of belief in the independence model, $\mathrm{Cons}P(M_I)_n$, is:

$$\mathrm{Cons}P(M_I)_n = P(M_I)_n + \tfrac{1}{2}(\mathrm{Cons}P(M_I)_{n-1} - P(M_I)_n) \tag{16.1}$$

Second, Oaksford and Chater (1998b) assume that if people revise their degrees of belief about $P(p)$ and $P(q)$, this is because they lack confidence in the values they have given. This lack of confidence is embodied by assuming that participants regard the values they are given for $P(p)$ and $P(q)$ as being based on a small sample size. This will influence the magnitude of the effects of sequential sampling on participants' estimates of $P(p)$ and $P(q)$ (Gigerenzer, 1994). For example, if you have seen 1000 things and 100 of them are black, then seeing one more black thing is not going to change your degree of belief very much, i.e. from 0.1 to 0.1009. But if you had seen ten things only one of which was black, then seeing one more black thing will almost double your degree of belief, i.e. from 0.1 to 0.182. So a small sample size is more susceptible to revision than a large sample size. Oaksford and Chater (1998b) assumed that participants base the initial values of $P(p)$ and $P(q)$ on an assumed sample size of six cards.

Figure 16.2 shows the predicted sequence of card selections for the Medium $P(q)$ condition in Oaksford, Chater, Grainger, and Larkin (1997). The filled diamonds show the learning curve as $P(M_I) \rightarrow 0$ after a card is selected at each trial. The open triangles show the cumulative frequency of *not-q* card selections and the open squares show the cumulative frequency of *q* card selections. These are the selections dictated by optimal data selection at each trial. As can be seen in this condition as a consequence of updating $P(p)$ and $P(q)$ on-line, a point is reached where the frequency of *q* card selections exceeds that of *not-q* selections. The reason for this behaviour is that as participants select *not-q* cards their estimates of $P(p)$ and $P(q)$ will go down because these are all *not-p*, *not-q* instances. Moreover, although in the normal range $P(M_I)$ has little effect on the ordering of $SE[I_g(\;)]$s, as $P(M_I) \rightarrow 0$, it would appear that rarity becomes relaxed, i.e. higher values of $P(q)$ can still lead to $SE[I_g(q)] > SE[I_g(\textit{not-q})]$. This factor is responsible for the prediction of long sequences of *q* card selections as $P(M_I)$ approaches the stopping criterion $(P(M_I) < 0.01)$. Figures 16.3 and 16.4 show similar graphs of the predicted trial-by-trial behaviour in the Low $P(p)$ and the High $P(p)$ conditions respectively.

In summary, a revised optimal data selection model that allows that during sequential sampling participants are learning both about which hypothesis is true and about the distribution of p and q cards seems able to model the Medium $P(q)$ condition in the RAST. Optimal data selection also captures the basic findings for the Low and Medium $P(q)$ conditions as well as predicting response alternations that Oaksford, Chater, Grainger, and

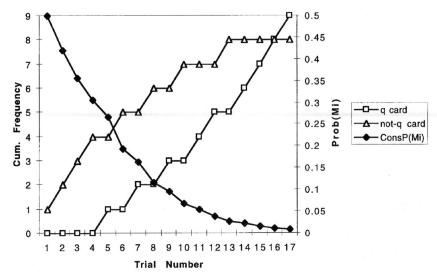

FIG. 16.2 Simulation results showing the predicted sequence of card selections for the Medium $P(q)$ condition in Oaksford, Chater, Grainger, and Larkin (1997). The filled diamonds show the learning curve as $P(M_I) \rightarrow 0$ after a card is selected at each trial. The open triangles show the cumulative frequency of *not-q* card selections and the open squares show the cumulative frequency of q card selections.

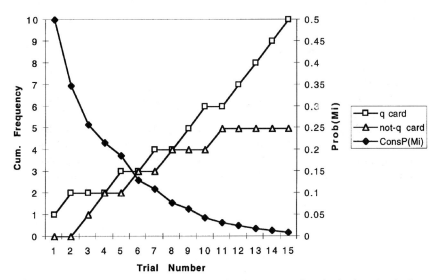

FIG. 16.3 Simulation results showing the predicted sequence of card selections for the Low $P(q)$ condition in Oaksford, Chater, Grainger, and Larkin (1997). The filled diamonds show the learning curve as $P(M_I) \rightarrow 0$ after a card is selected at each trial. The open triangles show the cumulative frequency of *not-q* card selections and the open squares show the cumulative frequency of q card selections.

267

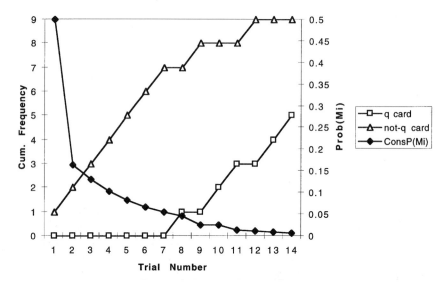

FIG. 16.4 Simulation results showing the predicted sequence of card selections for the High $P(q)$ condition in Oaksford, Chater, Grainger, and Larkin (1997). The filled diamonds show the learning curve as $P(M_i) \to 0$ after a card is selected at each trial. The open triangles show the cumulative frequency of *not-q* card selections and the open squares show the cumulative frequency of q card selections.

Larkin (1997) noticed in participants' card selections. This account relies heavily on the particular sequence of cards used in the RAST. Future research should concentrate on testing different models' predictions for trial-by-trial effects when the structure of sequential samples are systematically varied. In the next section we turn to some more recent evidence regarding the status of the optimal data selection model.

Contrast Sets and Probability Effects

Oaksford, Chater, Grainger, and Larkin's (1997) results establish that effects of probability manipulations predicted by the optimal data selection account are observed in the data on the selection task. The reduced array task has, however, been regarded as an anomaly in the literature since it was first introduced because it reveals conflicting results to the standard task. Consequently it is important that probabilistic manipulations can also be shown to have the predicted effects on the standard four card selection task. Recently Oaksford, Chater, and Grainger (1997) have tested the predictions of optimal data selection using a variety of probabilistic manipulations in this task version. They systematically varied $P(p)$ and $P(q)$ to produce four rule types: Low-$P(p)$, Low-$P(q)$ (henceforth "LL"); Low-$P(p)$, High-$P(q)$ ("LH"); High-$P(p)$, Low-$P(q)$ ("HL"); and High-$P(p)$, High-$P(q)$ ("HH"). This allowed Oaksford, Chater, and Grainger (1997) to test the predictions of Oaksford and Chater's (1994a) account of the negations paradigm selection task which relied on Oaksford and Stenning's (1992) "contrast set" account of processing negations and which we discussed in Chapter 11. In the negations paradigm selection task (e.g. Evans & Lynch, 1973) the antecedent and consequent of a rule can contain negated constituents (*not-p*, *not-q*). There are four possible conditional rules, the original *if p, then q* (AA), together with *if p, then not q* (AN); *if not p, then q* (NA) and *if not p, then not q* (NN). Each participant performs a selection task for each of these four rule types.

Recall from Chapter 11 that in the negations paradigm, the cards are normally described in terms of whether they make the antecedent or consequent of the rule true or false, i.e. using the TA (true antecedent); FA (false antecedent); true consequent (TC); and FC (false consequent) labelling. The principal finding was the existence of a matching effect whereby people select cards named in the rule and ignore the negations. This predicts the following ordering in card selection frequencies. For the affirmative consequent rules (*if p then q*; *if not-p then q*) the order is TA > TC > FC > FA. For the negative consequent rules (*if p then not-q*; *if not-p then not-q*) the order is TA > FC > TC > FA.

As we argued in Chapter 11, the key to understanding a variety of effects in the negations paradigm is the notion of a "contrast set" (Oaksford & Stenning, 1992). Contrast sets provide the interpretations of negated constituents. For example, the interpretation of "Johnny did not serve *tea*" (where the word in italics indicates the focus of a negation) is that he served a drink other than tea. In terms of set theory, the superordinate category "drinks" provides the universe of discourse. Contrast sets are plausible subsets of the complement in a universe of discourse. In our example, all other drinks less tea form the complement. When Johnny did not serve tea it is more likely he served soft drinks rather than, for instance, scotch on the rocks. "Soft drinks" is therefore the contrast set, i.e. a plausible subset of the complement. Background knowledge may restrict the membership of the intended contrast set even further. So, in our example, coffee is perhaps the most likely single contrast set member. This indicates that a negation rarely identifies the complement, i.e. the whole set consisting of the superordinate category less the named constituent, as the intended contrast set. More commonly the intention is to identify more restricted contrast sets. This behaviour of contrast sets may explain the negations paradigm.

There is good reason to believe that $P(TA)$ or $P(TC)$ are greater when they are negated. This is because the class of things referred to by a constituent is generally smaller than the size of the contrast set defined by its negation. For example, there are many things Johnny could have drunk, when he did not drink tea. This behaviour of contrast sets suggests that negated constituents can be regarded as defining high-probability categories. This suggests the following equivalences between the rules used in a negations paradigm and the rules Oaksford, Chater, and Grainger (1997) investigated: AA ⇔ LL; AN ⇔ LH; NA ⇔ HL; and NN ⇔ HH. In Chapter 11 we modelled negated constituents as high-probability categories and affirmative constituents as low-probability categories. We showed very close fits between the optimal data selection model and the data (see Fig. 11.1). In the present experiments optimal data selection predicts that varying high- and low-probability antecedents and consequents should produce analogous behaviour in the selection task to varying negated and unnegated antecedents and consequents respectively.

In Chapter 10 we argued that it is a constraint on the optimal data selection model that $P(q) > P(p)$, otherwise the dependence model cannot hold (Oaksford & Chater, 1994a, 1995a; Oaksford, Chater, Grainger, and Larkin , 1997). This constraint affects the HL rule, which is like asserting that "if something is black then it is a raven"—you do not need to look for evidence to know that this rule is false because you already know that there are many more black things than ravens! A similar problem arises for NA rules on the contrast set account of negations (Oaksford & Chater, 1994a; Oaksford & Stenning, 1992). In order to resolve the inconsistency in being asked to test a rule already known to be false, we argued in Chapter 11 that participants revise $P(p)$ down so that it is less than $P(q)$. This means that on the optimal data selection account an HL rule will be treated like an LL rule in the same way as we argued in Chapter 11 that NA rules are treated like AA rules. This aspect of the optimal data selection account has recently been confirmed by Green, Over, and Pyne (1997). Green et al. found that participants' estimates of the probability of finding a p card on the back of the *not-q* card, systematically underestimated $P(p)$ such that $P(p) < P(q)$, even though in the experimental materials $P(p) > P(q)$ and participants' estimates of $P(q)$ were accurate. As Oaksford (1998) points out, this finding is consistent with participants revising down $P(p)$ when $P(q) > P(p)$ as Oaksford and Chater (1994a) suggested happened under these circumstances.

Exploiting the correspondence between negated categories and high-probability categories allows the following predictions to be made. We would expect an ordering over card selections within rules analogous to that found in the negations paradigm. So for the low $P(q)$ rules (LL and HL) the order is $p > q > not-q > not-p$, and for the high $P(q)$ rules (LH and HH) the order is $p > not-q > q > not-p$. Within cards we would also expect more q card selections for the low $P(q)$ rules than the high $P(q)$ rules, and more *not-q* card selections for the high $P(q)$ rules than the low $P(q)$ rules. We use Oaksford, Chater, and Grainger's (1997) experiment 4 to illustrate their results in Fig. 16.5. In this experiment they used abstract material very like those used in Oaksford, Chater, Grainger, and Larkin (1997) in order to

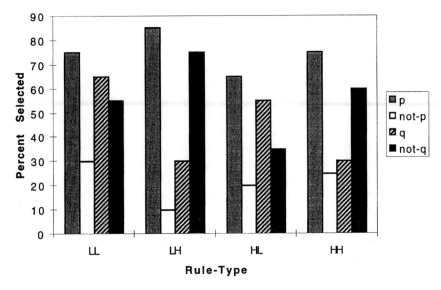

FIG. 16.5   Results of Oaksford, Chater, and Grainger's (1997) experiment 4 showing the frequency of card selections in each condition.

encourage participants to use the probability information. That is, they used stacks of cards (*p*, *not-p*, *q*, and *not-q*) to convey the frequency information and dealt one card off each stack to create the standard four card task. Figure 16.5 reveals all the effects of probability manipulations based on the predictions of the optimal data selection model.

Oaksford, Chater, and Grainger (1997) also used other materials that approximated the results of experiment 4 to varying degrees. Their experiment 1 used contentful rules the antecedents and consequents of which were pre-tested for probability of occurrence. Although the results for the consequent cards produced highly significant trends in the directions predicted by optimal data selection, the materials in experiment 1 did not lead to $n(q) < n(not\text{-}q)$ for the LH and HH rules. Oaksford, Chater, and Grainger (1997) argue that this was due to the naturalistic materials that allowed participants to redefine the reference classes against which they assessed probabilities. For example, with reference to all foods, the likelihood that you are consuming tea as opposed to any other food is low. However, with reference just to all drinks, the likelihood that you are consuming tea is far higher. In experiment 2, Oaksford, Chater, and Grainger (1997) ruled out the possibility of redefining reference classes by using the closed world provided by the voting behaviour of members of Parliament. The results of this experiment were consistent with optimal data selection—effects of both *P(p) and P(q)* on *not-q and q* card selections were again observed. Moreover, using the closed domain Oaksford, Chater, and Grainger (1997) now observed $n(q) < n(not\text{-}q)$. However, this occurred for the LH and HL rules, and not for the HH rule. This was consistent with participants' assessments of the relevant probabilities for the HL rules but not for the HH rules which participants appeared to treat like an LL rule. Oaksford, Chater, and Grainger suggest that these effects may be due to the particular materials they had used in this experiment and therefore in their last two experiments they moved to using abstract materials. In their experiment 3 they used the probability manipulations implicit in Sperber et al.'s (1995) experiment 4 and noted by Oaksford and Chater (1995c; see Chapter 15). They also used two levels of relevance: the factor identified by Sperber et al. as being responsible for leading to more responses that accord with logic in the selection task. Although there were significant probabilistic effects as predicted by optimal data selection, Oaksford, Chater, and Grainger (1997) also found effects of relevance. The final experiment in Oaksford, Chater, and Grainger (1997), as we have discussed (the results are shown in Figure 16.5), confirmed all the effects predicted by optimal data selection.

Contrast Sets and Matching

In their experiments, Oaksford, Chater, and Grainger (1997) have assumed that high-probability categories should behave like negated categories. As their experimental designs more closely resembled those normally used with the negations paradigm, i.e. abstract materials and completely within subjects, so their results more closely approximated a negations paradigm result. This is important as it suggests a rational explanation of the matching phenomenon that we described in Chapter 11. This phenomenon, whereby people apparently ignore the negations in a task rule and simply match the named item, has, perhaps more than any other effect, led to questions over human rationality. Although we should stress that its discoverer, Jonathan Evans (Evans, 1972; Evans & Lynch, 1973), has always sought a rational explanation of why people do this: as we shall see, Evans (e.g. 1984, 1989) concentrates on various interpretive heuristics. We have shown that similar effects are obtained using high-probability categories. However, showing that high-probability categories behave like negated categories does not demonstrate directly that people interpret negations in terms of contrast sets. In this section we argue that the current evidence supports the contrast set account and not the Evans heuristic account. First we argue that data on the interpretation of negations in discourse support the contrast set account and second we show that recent evidence apparently contradicting that account (Evans, Clibbens, & Rood, 1996) needs to be reinterpreted.

The fundamental prediction of Evans' relevance account is that a *not*-heuristic focuses participants' attention on the named item, ignoring the negation. This idea is based on Wason's (1965) suggestion that the normal discourse function of a negation is to deny a presupposition, e.g. "the train is not late" is used to deny the presupposition that it normally is late, i.e. the focus of attention is still on the lateness of the train. Consequently, the central prediction of Evans' presuppositional account is that people's attention remains focused on the named constituent in the scope of a negation. However, this suggestion is not consistent with the results of MacDonald and Just (1989). Attention is normally interpreted as *facilitating* the activation level of an attended item's corresponding representation. Yet MacDonald and Just provide evidence that negations *inhibit* the representations of constituents in their scope. Using a sentence probe task in on-line sentence comprehension, MacDonald and Just (1989) found that participants were slower to read a probe word if it occurred in the scope of a negation in a sentence they had just read. MacDonald and Just interpret their results to indicate that a negation inhibits the activity levels of the representations of constituents in its scope and hence that negation typically directs attention *away* from a negated constituent. These discourse effects are not consistent with Evans' (1989) explanation of the *not*-heuristic.

However, the effects observed by MacDonald and Just are consistent with constructing contrast sets. It is simply not true that negations always deny presuppositions. For example, "the train is not late", said ironically on the platform to a fellow traveller may well focus attention on its normal late arrival. However, said anxiously to the ticket seller this utterance may focus attention on your urgent need for the train to be on time. The focusing effects of negations are simply not uniform. According to the contrast set account negations *normally* focus attention on the contrast set, i.e. consistent with MacDonald and Just, away from the negated constituent. Within the semantic and pragmatic literature this view of negation is known as the "otherness theory". This account goes back to Plato and has been espoused by Mabbott (1929) and Ryle (1929) and more recently by Apostel (1972). For example, "When I say 'Mrs. Smith's hat is not green' I can equivalently say '... but some *other* colour'" (Ryle, 1929, p. 85); or, similarly, "psychological negation means only the disjunction of a few [perhaps one] alternatives lying in some sense 'close' to the negated sentence" (Apostel, 1972, pp. 396–397). In sum, contrary to the *not*-heuristic, but consistent with the contrast set account, negations normally focus attention away from the negated constituent (C) and onto the relevant contrast set (C^c). In Oaksford, Chater, and Grainger's experiments it is the claim that, with respect to a reference class R, $P(C^c|R)$ is normally greater than $P(C|R)$ that determine their predictions.

Recently Evans, Clibbens, and Rood (1996) have argued that their findings using explicit negations in the selection task are consistent with the *not*-heuristic but not with the contrast set account. A negation is used explicitly when its referent includes a negation. So, for example, if I say "the card with not a 2 on it", an explicit use would be a card with "not 2" written on it. This contrasts with an implicit use where the card would have, say, "7" written on it. Evans, Clibbens, and Rood (1996) observed that explicit negations radically reduced participants' tendency to match in the selection task. Rather than select the cards that match, i.e. in our example the 2 card, participants would select the cards that are the verifying TA and TC cases, i.e. in our example the card with "not 2" written on it. A similar result, i.e. getting participants to select the TA and TC cards for all four rules, has been found using thematic material by Reich and Ruth (1982) and using binary material by Oaksford and Stenning (1992). Oaksford and Chater (1994a) argue that such materials allowed very constrained contrast sets to be identified such that $P(C^c|R) \approx P(C|R)$. Consequently the default rarity assumption held for all rules. However, such an account cannot explain the results of Evans et al.

We now argue that Evans, Clibbens, and Rood's (1996) experiments provide little support for Evans' heuristic account. When explicit negations are used a very simple strategy can explain people's behaviour. Evans (1972; Evans & Lynch, 1973) uses "matching" to describe ignoring the negation and simply matching the named item. However, there is more than one way to match. Oaksford (1989) suggested that when explicit negations are used on the instances, participants can match the whole antecedent or consequent clause *including the negation*. Let us call this the "matching$_2$" strategy. Evans et al. show that when using explicit negations participants predominantly select the TA and the TC cards for all rules. This selection is exactly what the matching$_2$ strategy predicts because these cards always represent the matching$_2$ cards for all rules. That participants resort to this strategy given such materials is of course of little theoretical interest to understanding people's normal everyday reasoning behaviour. In contrast, the similar results found by Oaksford and Stenning (1992) and Reich and Ruth (1982) without using explicit negations, cannot be explained away by such a trivial strategy and consequently remain of theoretical interest. It was these results that we showed in Chapter 11 could be explained by the optimal data selection model assuming the contrast set account of negations. In conclusion, results using explicit negations on the cards need not be taken to question the contrast set account.

Summary

There is a growing body of evidence supporting the optimal data selection model. These data confirm that people are indeed highly sensitive to probabilistic information and readily take it into account in their reasoning about data selection. This of course runs counter to the predictions of logical-based accounts of this task, like mental models or mental logic, that insist that people are attempting, but failing, to solve a logical task. This view lacks credibility in the light of these results and the fact that people's reasoning must have adapted to cope with the uncertainty of the real world.

Probabilistic Reasoning

The approach we have taken in this book might be characterised as arguing that although people are poor at logical reasoning they are nonetheless good at probabilisitic reasoning. We have shown how a probabilistic model of Wason's selection task can be used to provide a computational-level account that indicates that people's behaviour is rational, i.e. it seems to conform to the prescriptions of our model. However, this behaviour seems to be at odds with established results that appear to show that people are also very poor probabilistic reasoners (e.g. Tversky & Kahneman, 1974; Kahneman, Slovic, & Tversky, 1982). For example, people seem to be insensitive to base rates, i.e. in applying Bayes' theorem people often provide estimates of posterior probabilities that seem to reflect only the likelihoods and not the priors. People also seem to be over-confident in their probability judgements, i.e. they do not seem to be well calibrated to the actual frequencies of events in the world. Moreover, people also seem prone to the conjunction fallacy. That is, they violate the probabilistic law that the joint probability of any two events cannot be greater than either individual event, i.e. $P(A) \geq P(A, B) \leq P(B)$.

There are two points to make here. First, our account of optimal data selection is framed at the computational level, i.e. it characterises what is being computed not how. That people's behaviour well approximates the norm provided by optimal data selection, which is thereby descriptively adequate, does not necessarily mean that people are doing complex probabilistic computations in their heads. As we argued in Chapter 13, they could approximate the norm by a small set of hard-wired heuristics (Gigerenzer & Goldstein, 1996). To the extent that this is the case we would expect people to be relatively insensitive to probabilistic manipulations (see Oaksford, Chater, Grainger, & Larkin, 1997). However, we have seen in the last section that people are sensitive to a variety of probabilistic manipulations in the selection task. Consequently it would appear that people may be performing some form of rudimentary probabilistic calculations. Again, these may bear no direct relation to the explicit manipulation of probability values using the rules of probability theory represented in our model. For example, later we introduce recent interpretations of neural networks as mechanisms for Bayesian inference. However, if people are responding appropriately to probabilistic manipulations then this behaviour does seem inconsistent with their systematically falling into error on probabilisitic reasoning tasks.

Our second point then is that according to recent analyses many of the apparent errors and biases observed in probabilistic reasoning are a consequence of presenting the probabilistic information in an unnatural format (Gigerenzer & Hoffrage, 1995). Most often in experiments of this type people are given the probabilistic information in terms of explicit probability statements or percentages, e.g. 0.05 or 5%. However, Gigerenzer and Hoffrage (1995) argue that this is unnatural given the normal sampling situation where we build up frequency information as a result of multiple encounters with objects and events. What you discover by such a process is, for example, that something like 95 out of the 100 ravens you have examined are black. Mathematically this information can be expressed as 95% of ravens are black, or the probability of a bird being black given it is a raven is 0.95. However, this loses information about sample size (see our discussion of sequential sampling) and moreover, it seems unnecessary to make this conversion of the information format. Gigerenzer and Hoffrage suggest that if people naturally represent frequencies then presenting probabilistic information in this form should facilitate reasoning. We illustrate research showing that Gigerenzer and Hoffrage appear to be correct in the three areas where biases have been observed and which we introduced earlier.

Experiments revealing base rate neglect usually present the information as follows, using the mammogram problem:

> A 30-year-old woman discovers a lump in her breast and goes to her doctor. The doctor knows that only 5% of women of the patient's age and health have breast cancer (C). A mammogram (breast x-ray) is taken. It indicates cancer 80% of the time in women who have breast cancer but falsely indicates breast cancer in healthy patients 20% of the time. The mammogram (M) comes out positive. What is the probability that the patient has cancer?

Most participants in an experiment such as this give estimates that the woman has cancer given a positive mammogram of around 0.8, which appears to ignore the prior that most women of her age, i.e. 95% do not have breast cancer. However, a simple change in the instructions reverses this finding:

> A 30-year-old woman discovers a lump in her breast and goes to her doctor. The doctor knows that only 5 out of every 100 women of the patient's age and health have breast cancer (C). A mammogram (breast x-ray) is taken. For 80 out every 100 women who have breast cancer it gives a positive result. The mammogram (M) comes out positive. What is the probability that the patient has cancer?

Gigerenzer and Hoffrage argue that the frequency information also allows a simpler version of Bayes' theorem to be used, hence reducing cognitive load.

In discussing over-confidence, Gigerenzer points out that like is not being compared with like. People are typically asked a series of general knowledge questions and are asked to rate their confidence in each answer. To determine over-confidence, their average confidence rating is compared with the frequency of correct answers. That is, people are asked repeatedly about their beliefs in single events, and then their average performance on this task is compared with their relative frequency of correct answers. Gigerenzer observes that these can be independent judgements. To test whether over-confidence arises when like is compared with like, at the end of the task Gigerenzer also asked people to estimate their relative frequency of correct answers. Comparing their estimates with their actual frequency of correct answers revealed no evidence of over-confidence. That is, when like is compared with like, people seem well calibrated in judging their own like-lihood of success.

The conjunction fallacy seems also to emerge because of the unnatural presentation of probabilities. People are typically given information such as:

> Linda is 31 years old, single, outspoken, and very bright. She majored in philosophy. As a student, she was deeply concerned with issues of discrimination and social justice, and also participated in anti-nuclear demonstrations.

They are then asked to estimate the probability that (i) Linda is a bankteller, and (ii) Linda is a feminist bankteller. People typically estimate (ii) as more likely than (i), violating the conjunction rule. However, if people are asked this question using a frequency format such as: There are 100 people who fit the description; how many of them are: (i) bank tellers, (ii) bank tellers and active in the feminist movement, then they do not estimate (i) as less likely than (ii), conforming to the conjunction rule.

In summary, it would appear that people are not as bad at probabilistic reasoning as the evidence from the heuristics and biases programme had led us to believe. Moreover, as we have noted already, the theoretical accounts of reasoning we have discussed do not require that people possess quantitatively accurate probabilistic reasoning abilities. Thus, any apparent tension between the probabilistic approach to the rational analysis of reasoning that we advocate and experimental data on human probabilistic reasoning is illusory.

Extending the Probabilistic Approach

We are currently extending the probabilistic approach to a variety of other argument forms, e.g. syllogistic reasoning and conditional reasoning.

Syllogistic Reasoning

Syllogistic reasoning involves two quantified statements of the form, All X are Y (A), No X are Y (E), Some X are Y (I), or Some X are not Y (O). Some combinations of premises yield logically valid conclusions, e.g. All X are Y, All Y are Z (AA) yields the logically valid conclusion, All X are Z; others do not, for example, No Y are X, Some Y are not Z (EO), has no valid conclusion. If people were reasoning logically then they should be able to draw all and only the valid conclusions indicating that nothing necessarily follows from the invalid syllogisms. However, people have graded difficulty with drawing the valid syllogisms. Moreover, they make systematic errors on the invalid syllogisms, offering conclusions where none follows.

Chater and Oaksford (1997) adopt a probabilistic approach to syllogisms, arguing that people use their knowledge of the informational strength (probabilistically defined) of premises to guide conclusion construction. It turns out that the most informative conclusion that can follow from a syllogism is given by the least informative premise. Moreover, for most valid syllogisms the least informative premise also provides the form of the conclusion. Thus selecting the form of the least informative premise as the form of the conclusion will usually produce a valid conclusion if there is one. If this strategy is over-generalised it can also explain the systematic errors made on the invalid syllogisms. Consequently we can show that a very simple strategy can explain syllogistic reasoning performance. Moreover, this probabilistic account has the advantage that not only can it explain the data from the 64 syllogisms that use the standard logical quantifiers (as we have seen), it also extends naturally to the 144 syllogisms that result from combining these with the *generalised* quantifiers (Barwise & Cooper, 1981), Most and Few, which have no logical interpretation.

Conditional Inference

Conditional inferences, like the everyday examples with which we introduced this book in Chapter 1, involve two premises, one conditional, If A then B, and one categorical, either, A, not-A, B, or not-B. For example, given If A then B, and not-A, people are asked to say whether not-B follows. Endorsing this argument is to endorse the logical fallacy of denying the antecedent (DA). Interesting biases arise when negations are used in the conditional premise, e.g. If not-A, then not-B, and not-A, therefore not-B is an instance of the valid inference form modus ponens (MP). Evans observed a bias towards accepting conclusions containing a negation, like the MP inference just described (using a different rule an affirmative conclusion follows by MP, e.g. If not-A, then B, not-A, therefore B).

This effect, which Evans, Newstead, & Byrne (1993) call *negative conclusion bias*, may have a straightforward explanation, on the assumption that people endorse arguments to the extent that the conditional probability of the conclusion given the categorical premise is high (Oaksford, Chater, & Larkin, 1997). This will depend on the probabilities of A and of B and on the conditional probability relating the two. So if we look at DA the conditional probability that needs to be high is $P(not-B|not-A)$. The probability of a negated category is higher than an affirmative category (Oaksford & Chater, 1994a; Oaksford & Stenning, 1992), for example, the probability that you are not drinking whiskey as you read this chapter is higher than the probability that you are. To illustrate very simply how negative conclusion bias could arise, let us assume that you believe the rule is false. On the account of Wason's selection task outlined earlier, this means that you believe that A and B are independent. Consequently $P(not-B|not-A) = P(not-B)$, i.e. you should endorse the DA inference if the probability of the conclusion is high. And because negated conclusions have a higher probability than affirmative conclusions, the former should be endorsed more often.

So the probabilistic rational analysis that we developed for the selection task appears to carry over relatively directly to conditional reasoning. Moreover, we saw in the previous section that it provides a promising theoretical direction for research on syllogistic reasoning. This raises the apparently paradoxical possibility that explaining all of the key experimental paradigms for studying human deductive reasoning requires viewing people's performance as approximating to probabilistic rather than deductive inference. In short, people reason probabilistically even when faced with what the experimenter intends to be a deductive reasoning task. This possibility seems independently plausible in the light of the uncertainty of everyday reasoning that has been a theme of this book. Reasoning strategies are adapted to deal with uncertainty in everyday life—and therefore these strategies are likely to be carried over by people into laboratory settings. Thus, paying closer attention to everyday reasoning may provide the key to giving a detailed analysis of laboratory performance.

RATIONALITY RECONSIDERED

We have argued that apparently irrational behaviour on laboratory tasks, in particular on Wason's selection task, may, nonetheless, be given a rational analysis. In this way, we have argued that, on the right conception of rationality, people are rational both in everyday life and in the laboratory. This reaffirmation of human rationality is reassuring—because if our own rationality cannot be presupposed, then it seems inevitable that we must accept complete and devastating scepticism about the possibility of argument, interpretation of evidence, and consequently about our ability to have knowledge about the world or each other. But, although reassuring, this reaffirmation of rationality from the perspective of probability theory raises a number of difficult and controversial theoretical issues. Specifically, we reconsider the constraints of completeness* and tractability, which, we argued in Part I, logicist approaches are unable to meet. To what extent can probability theory capture the intuitions underlying everyday human inference? To what extent can probabilistic calculations be implemented in a tractable way? We then consider the possibility that rational norms may be dispensable in an account of reasoning—arguing that this viewpoint appears to leave the adaptiveness of human thought completely unexplained. Finally, we consider the possible origins of human rationality—what connections might there be between rationality, adaptation, and evolution?

Completeness*: Probability and Human Uncertain Inference

A complete* theory of inference would provide a full rational analysis of human inferential intuitions and judgements. Of course, this does not mean that it would precisely predict every piece of human reasoning—because such a rational analysis may only be approximately implemented in the cognitive system (we shall consider questions of implementation in the next section). But a complete* theory would provide a full explication of human *rationality*. Put in these terms, it is clear that completeness* is a very strong criterion indeed. Logic fails at the outset because it is a calculus of certainty, whereas almost all of human inference is uncertain; probability is at least a calculus of uncertainty. But how far does this take us to towards a complete* theory of reasoning?

There is a superficially plausible line of argument that probability theory, despite its remarkable simplicity, is complete*. In order to make sense of probability theory as a general theory of reasoning, we must adopt a *subjective* interpretation of probabilities—probabilities express *degrees of belief* about possible states of the world. According to the subjective interpretation, stating that the probability of a coin falling heads is 0.5 means that I have a 0.5 degree of belief that it will fall heads; similarly, with respect to the probability of it falling tails. Thus, $P(\text{Heads}) = P(\text{Tails}) = 0.5$ expresses the fact that I *believe* that the coin will fall heads and tails to an equal degree. In particular, the statement involves no assumption that the coin is "unbiased". Thus, if I am told that the coin *is* biased, but not in which direction, the probabilities expressing my degrees of belief in each outcome will remain unchanged. This example, of a coin with a known bias of an unknown type, nicely illustrates what is distinctive about the subjective interpretation of probability and why it is appropriate as a starting point for a rational analysis of reasoning. The subjective view captures the fact that a reasoner has no evidence to believe in one outcome more than the other, even once the fact of a bias is known. But according to non-subjective views of probability, the bias, although unknown, introduces an asymmetry between the probabilities of each outcome. Thus, according to the *frequentist* interpretation (e.g. Von Mises, 1939), where probabilities are viewed as limiting frequencies in an imaginary experiment in which the event of interest (here, the coin toss) is endlessly repeated, the side in favour of which the bias operates, has a higher probability—because it will, in the long run, occur more frequently in the imaginary experiment. Similarly, according to the propensity theory (e.g. Mellor, 1971), according to which probabilities are properties of coins and other objects in just the same way as mass and volume, a higher probability is assigned to the side on which the coin has a propensity to fall. Thus, non-subjective views allow differences in probability which are not known to the reasoner—and hence, such interpretations are not appropriate if the goal is to use probability theory as the basis for a theory of reasoning. By contrast, the subjective interpretation views the very meaning of probability in terms of the reasoner's beliefs. (Of course, non-subjective interpretations of probability may be most appropriate interpretations of probability theory in some contexts.)

Accepting the subjectivist view, we assume that beliefs are, in general, associated with probabilities that express the degree to which they are believed. There are, of course, constraints on what sets of beliefs are appropriate. For example, if I associate A with probability 0.5, then I should associate not-A with probability 0.5; and A and B with a probability between 0 and 0.5; and so on. These constraints can be turned into a theory of how people should reason with probabilities. Specifically, there has been a wide variety of arguments that purport to show that individual degrees of belief should obey the standard laws of the probability calculus that have been developed, based on betting quotients and "Dutch book" arguments (de Finetti, 1937; Ramsey, 1931), theories of preferences (Savage, 1954), scoring rules (Lindley, 1982), and derivation from minimal axioms (Cox, 1946, 1961; Good, 1950). Although each argument can be challenged individually, the fact that so many different lines of argument converge on the very same laws of probability has been taken as powerful evidence for the view that degrees of belief can be interpreted as probabilities (see e.g. Earman, 1992; Howson & Urbach, 1989; for discussion). The suggestion that probability theory can be viewed as a normative theory of uncertain reasoning sets the bounds of probability theory much wider than the confines in which it is frequently encountered in introductory textbooks. According to this view, probability theory is not just concerned with reasoning about coins, but is a general calculus for rational thought.

These arguments for the normative correctness of the laws of probability theory appear to imply that probability theory may, despite its simplicity, constitute a complete* theory of human uncertain inference. The story appears to be: assume that knowledge is encoded by a set of beliefs associated with probabilities; and assume that inference can proceed by the application of the laws of probability. This appears to give a general approach to uncertain inference—and thus, potentially, to meeting the completeness* criterion.

In reality, however, matters are not so simple for two reasons. First, it is not clear how to encode knowledge in terms of probabilities, as we shall see—particularly when there are infinitely many options to choose between, or where there are options that have simply not been considered at all. Second, from the perspective of successfully guiding the cognitive system, it is crucial that probabilities are not merely internally consistent (which is all that we have considered so far in describing the subjective interpretation), but also that these probabilities are somehow appropriately connected to the real world. With these issues in mind, we now briefly consider some ways in which probability is incomplete* as a theory of uncertain reasoning, and approaches to overcoming these limitations.

Probability Theory and Capturing Everyday Inference

Imagine you arrive home to find that the front door of your house has been broken open. Various possible explanations might spring to mind—perhaps you have been burgled; perhaps a relative has locked themselves out and had to break in; and so on. To apply a probabilistic analysis, we require prior probabilities for each possibility. But where are these to come from? Past experience can only be applied very indirectly, particularly if you have never been burgled before. But by using past experience, one is not really assigning prior probabilities at all—we are deriving probabilities from other knowledge (e.g. the prevalence of burglary in the area, whether any relatives are staying in the house). But this just pushes the problem of assigning priors back one step further—what probabilities are assigned to these beliefs, and how were they derived? An infinite regress threatens.

Now let us consider the evidence at the scene. Noticing that the television is missing from its usual location might appear to be evidence for the burglary hypothesis. Thus, making this observation might reasonably be expected to increase whatever prior probability is initially assigned to this possibility. But what prior specifies that missing televisions increase the probability of burglary? This knowledge, too, is presumably derived from more basic information—e.g. that burglars aim to steal things such as televisions, and (for that matter) that stolen televisions are no longer located in the house from which they are stolen. Notice that this knowledge must interact appropriately with other information that may be present—if it is recalled the television has been taken to the shop for repair, then noticing that it is missing gives no evidence whatever in favour of the supposition that a burglary has taken place. Appreciating that this is so requires further knowledge (e.g. that televisions are not returned by the shop, but await collection; even that televisions cannot be in two places at once, and so on). Thus, interpreting a piece of evidence requires a wealth of background knowledge; and each piece of background knowledge appears to presuppose a wealth of further background knowledge.

In short, where are the priors from which inference can begin? Each piece of information to which we would like to assign a prior appears to depend on other pieces of information—hence its probability must be calculated rather than specified a priori. This connects with what Fodor (1983) called the isotropy and Quineanness of world knowledge that we discussed in Part I. Isotropy is the property that all world knowledge is interconnected, however indirectly. Isotropy implies that attempting to assign a prior to any piece of world knowledge, we will instead be forced to view the probability associated with that knowledge itself—the search through the network of world knowledge for pieces of information for which genuine priors can be associated will never stop! But if the justification for (and hence the sub-jective probability of) each piece of knowledge depends on the others, then it seems that priors can never be assigned, and probabilistic inference can never begin. Quineanness merely compounds the problem. The Quineanness of world knowledge, in probabilistic terms, is that probabilities cannot be assigned to pieces of knowledge one by one—rather they can only be assigned to entire systems of belief, and only then to the individual pieces of knowledge of which those systems are made up. Thus, we cannot assign a probability to a burglary in isolation without considering entire accounts of the events that may have taken place and, in view of the connections between these accounts and the rest of world knowledge stemming from isotropy, entire systems of belief about the world.

The moral is that probability theory alone does not provide a theory of everyday reasoning—let alone a complete* theory of everyday reasoning. The deep problems faced by cognitive science and artificial intelligence in attempting to formalise everyday inference with logical methods still apply when probabilistic methods are used. Nonetheless, there are a number of interesting directions within a probabilistic framework, which may move towards developing probabilistic accounts of everyday inference.

One approach is simply to ignore these deep problems, and to use idealised small-scale models of reasoning about particular domains. In artificial intelligence, this is the approach adopted in developing probabilistic expert systems (e.g. Pearl, 1988), which we consider briefly later. The hope is that, in practice, we can simply assume certain background knowledge to be given, and to consider what follows from it using probabilistic methods. Indeed, this is the general approach of applied probability theory throughout science—idealisation assumptions are made about the world, and to the extent that these hold, and other factors can be ignored, such probabilistic analysis can be extremely valuable. In psychology, similarly, sweeping prior assumptions can be made and used to derive predictions according to the laws of probability—a great deal of work in the rational analysis paradigm (e.g. Anderson, 1990, 1991a) including our work on the selection task outlined in Part II of this book, takes this pragmatic strategy. Thus, the difficult questions of the origins of knowledge are evaded; but specific accounts of aspects of the knowledge in particular domains and the way it is used can be formulated.

In conjunction with this first pragmatic approach, there has been a great deal of research across a range of disciplines concerning how knowledge should be represented and used in probabilistic inference—this work may inform the development of rational analyses of human inference.

One important research area, for example, aims to address the fact that in almost all real-world inference problems, only very partial probabilistic information is available. To take a famous idealised example (e.g. Jaynes, 1989), suppose that we learn only that the average score when a die is thrown is abnormally high (e.g. 4.5, whereas a "fair" die would average 3.5), what probabilities should we estimate for the individual faces of the die? Intuitively, 5 and 6 would seem to receive an increased probability; 1 and 2 would seem to receive a decreased probability. But what is the justification for this inference; and how might it be justified? The most widely accepted solution to this problem is that we should assign the probabilities so as to make the minimal possible assumptions about the die—in the sense that the maximum uncertainty concerning how it will fall is maintained, consistent with the given average. This is known as the principle of maximum entropy (Jaynes, 1989) and has been widely applied in practical problems in science as well as used as a principle in artificial intelligence (Paris, 1992). Under specified problems of this kind are not merely mathematical curiosities—almost all everyday inference problems seem to be drastically under-specified in this way (Osherson, Shafir, & Smith, 1993; see also, Over & Jessop, 1998, who propose an application of maximum entropy in the selection task). Thus, in assessing the likely cause of the burglary, we may take account of the fact that crime is particularly high in the neighbourhood—but this is only relevant given that this general knowledge can be converted into a probability concerning the relevant sub-case: crime in which doors are broken open—i.e. only those that are consistent with the evidence. Specific information about this sort of crime is not available—only information about general prevalence; this is analogous to knowing only the average sum of the die, but needing to make inferences about a specific sub-case: e.g. the probability that it will show a "5". Moreover, of course, the specific sub-case is even more specific—this particular putative crime occurred at a particular type of house, with a certain degree of visibility to the neighbours, during a certain time period, and so on. General knowledge about the effects of these factors is not sufficient to specify the resultant probability that a crime has occurred, because it is not clear how these factors interact in the specific case. A principle such as maximum entropy is required to fill in the gaps between general knowledge and its specific application.

Another way in which knowledge is typically under-specified is in terms of prior probabilities. In scientific applications of probabilistic methods, estimating, for example, a physical magnitude such as the mass of a star requires specifying some prior distribution concerning what values this magnitude might have. Frequently, it is completely unclear how this prior should be set. Similarly, in cognitive contexts, it is equally unclear what priors should be assigned to alternative explanations—even given world knowledge. The principle of maximum entropy can also be applied in this context—the prior that is the least informative is chosen—although in the context of continuous distributions, there is the apparently paradoxical consequence that the recommendation of the maximum entropy principle (and many other criteria) depends on the choice of measuring unit. A range of other standard criteria for determining priors are also possible, such as "non-informative" priors (Box & Tiao, 1973) and minimum message length priors (Wallace & Boulton, 1968; Wallace & Freeman, 1987). Setting of priors of this kind is typically crucial if specifying a probabilistic account of cognition—thus, for example, Anderson's (1990, 1991a) rational analyses rely extensively on a particular kind of non-informative prior, the "Dirichlet" prior.

The problem of setting priors is more problematic when considering how to apportion prior probability between *entire classes of model*, rather than merely assigning priors to a particular magnitude or parameter in a single model. Most classical statistical methods familiar in the behavioural sciences (e.g. those based on the generalised linear model, such as the ANOVA, linear regression and so on) take a particular type of statistical model for granted, and do not deal with the question of how models can be compared (except in a relatively ad hoc way). In such methods, the class of models is presupposed (e.g. the relation between input and output variables is linear, quadratic or whatever)—the goal of inference is to decide, for example, what is the slope and intercept of the linear relationship. In the context of everyday reasoning, this framework is too restrictive, because everyday reasoning typically involves deciding between qualitatively different types of explanation of the data—that is, entirely different classes of model. But over the last 40 years, statistical methods have been generalised to the problem of comparing different classes of model, using concepts such as the VC-dimension (see e.g. Vapnik, 1995) and minimum description length (MDL) (Rissanen, 1987, 1989). Of these, the latter approach is perhaps the most straightforward to explain, as well as the most psychologically attractive. The principle is that alternative explanations should be compared with respect to the brevity with which they allow the data to be encoded in some description language. Thus, we define an "explanation" of the data to be a way of reconstructing that data—and we favour the shortest explanation. This principle is strongly reminiscent of the simplicity principle in perceptual organisation originated by the Gestalt psychologists, and it nicely captures the ubiquitous intuition in everyday and scientific reasoning that simple explanations are to be preferred (see Chater, 1997a, 1997b, for discussion). Moreover, the principle of favouring short description lengths can also be viewed as a principle of assigning highest probability to the simplest explanation—specifically, description lengths are associated with log-probabilities. Thus, a choice of description language can be viewed as automatically inducing a prior probability distribution over all hypotheses, explanations, and data that can be expressed in that language—they are assigned a prior probability dependent on the length of the shortest encoding that they have in that language. This remarkably simple approach to setting priors and to inference under uncertainty is also backed up by a rich mathematical theory, based on Kolmogorov complexity theory (Li & Vitányi, 1997).

The MDL principle also promises to help tackle, at least at a conceptual level, the deep problems raised by the isotropy and Quineanness of general knowledge. The principle can be applied to entire systems of belief, where the data to be explained are, in Quine's phrase, the entire tribunal of experience. The system of belief that provides the shortest description overall should be favoured. Quineanness is respected because the entire belief system is assessed together; and isotropy is respected because the inferential relations between different parts of the system of beliefs can be arbitrarily rich. Moreover, this avoids the problem of having to face the apparently endless search for propositions to which genuine priors can be assigned—because prior probabilities may be associated with entire belief systems at a stroke. But although theoretically attractive, the MDL principle is bedevilled by the fact that finding the shortest code length for a given set of data is provably not merely computationally intractable (like the logic-based approaches to uncertain inference that we discussed in Part I) but provably uncomputable—i.e. the shortest description length cannot be found even aside from restrictions of computing speed. Nonetheless, the

MDL principle may be a useful contribution to the rational analysis of human uncertain reasoning because it provides a simple objective that the cognitive system may follow: choose the simplest possible explanation of what is known that the cognitive system can find.

Independence and Relevance

In representing knowledge in probabilistic terms, whether in building rational analyses of thought or in any other application, perhaps the most crucial issue concerns the *structural* relationships between pieces of information. Does learning A raise or reduce the probability of B, or are A and B independent? How does the answer to this question change if C is known; or if D can be ruled out? What if E is also known? These questions are fundamentally qualitative in character—what is critical is the general form of the dependencies between pieces of information, rather than the actual numbers involved (Pearl, 1988). From the point of view of the cognitive system, this suggests that the structural relationships between propositions may be cognitively fundamental, rather than numerical calculations.

How can these structural relationships be expressed? One important recent development (e.g. Pearl, 1988) is the development of *graphical models* to express the dependencies between propositions. The idea is that pieces of information can be viewed as nodes in a graph, in which the edges of the graph represent dependencies. Thus, an entire system of knowledge can be viewed as a network of nodes and links capturing the relations between them. So, in this notation, if there is no path of edges connecting two pieces of information, A and B, then they are independent ($P(A) = P(A, B)$). If the only path between A and B is via C, then the two are conditionally independent, given C ($P(A|C) = P(A|B, C)$)—that is, if we know C, then learning A tells us nothing about B and vice versa. A rich range of dependencies can be expressed in these terms—which makes the structural relations between factors explicit. In particular, "hidden variables" may be introduced, to capture complex dependencies—these correspond to nodes concerning pieces of information about which no immediate knowledge is available, but which may be postulated to explain dependencies between pieces of information about which knowledge is available. Furthermore, these graphical structures may include a "direction" associated with each link, representing the direction of causality (see Glymour & Cheng, 1998, for an application of these ideas to causal inference); there are learning algorithms for such structures, which can be very directly related to neural network learning algorithms.

In short, a rich field of inquiry concerning the probabilistic representation of dependencies between knowledge is emerging. We may hope that future research in the psychology of reasoning and knowledge representation may be able to apply some of these ideas. Certainly existing research has recognised the fundamental importance for the cognitive system of finding dependencies and recognising independence—frequently under the heading of *relevance*. But, as we discussed in Chapters 4, 5, and 15, relevance is frequently taken as a given, or explained in circular terms; and in developing rational analyses, theorists are forced to makes sweeping assumptions about what depends on what, so that theorising can begin. We may hope that future research, using recent technical developments sketched here, may lead to a more fundamental understanding of this crucial aspect of cognition.

Summary

We hope in this section to have shown that although probability theory does *not* constitute a complete* theory of human everyday inference it offers a promising direction for future research. There is a wealth of profound issues that have not been addressed successfully in either the logical or the probabilistic framework, stemming from the incompleteness of the knowledge on which probabilistic inference must be based. Mere internal consistency in accordance with the probabilistic axioms is not, therefore, enough to give a rational analysis of human thought. But recent technical research, some of which we have briefly sketched here, does give rise to promising possible directions for future research. To provide an adequate rational analysis, of course, it must be possible to explain how the cognitive system deals with the incompleteness of the available knowledge in a way that is both normatively and descriptively adequate. On the normative side, whatever principles are used, whether drawing on maximum entropy, minimum description length, or applying graphical models, must be justifiable—it must be possible to explain *why* they lead to good inference. Here, the literature in statistics, computational learning theory, and philosophy of science, as well as the degree of success of practical applications based on these methods, may be drawn on to assess the justification for these methods. On the descriptive side, they must capture the empirical data. Here, we must rely first on qualitative fits between the behaviour of such models and common sense, which is the object of study; and the ability of specific rational analyses based on these principles to explain empirical data. This will require not only capturing existing cognitive psychological data, but also developing experimental paradigms for the systematic investigation of how people reason with incomplete information (Osherson, Shafir, & Smith, 1993). Developing rational analyses of everyday reasoning with incomplete information which can meet these criteria presents a major challenge for future research not just for the study of reasoning but for the cognitive sciences in general. The project is immensely difficult but of fundamental importance to understanding the nature of human rationality.

Tractability: Constraints on Rational Mechanisms

The move to rational analysis leaves open the possibility that people approximate the rational model using cheap, fast, and frugal heuristics rather than a full-scale, and possibly intractable implementations of a probabilistic account of knowledge representation and reasoning. This may give considerable scope to resolving some of the problems of intractability that we discussed in Part I. Moreover, it is in the spirit of recent approaches in psychology (Gigerenzer & Goldstein, 1996) and in artificial intelligence (e.g. Brooks, 1991) that much of human reasoning and decision making is achieved by crude tricks. Perhaps one problem with this approach is that the flexibility in response to probabilistic manipulations revealed in our experiments seems to argue for more general systems of knowledge representation and reasoning that are responsive to quite subtle changes in information. This of course leads to the problems we discussed in the last section. In reality it is likely that the cognitive system combines cheap heuristics with some limited general inferential capacity. Consequently it makes sense for us to consider the tractability of general models for probabilistic inference. Here we will see that issues of computational tractability are still a pressing concern.

In Part I of this book, we attacked logic-based approaches to cognition, and in particular non-monotonic logics, because of their computational intractability. But switching from logic to probability theory does not solve the problem of tractability. In the general case, probabilistic calculations are typically computationally intractable. Suppose that we have n binary variables—then there will be a probability that is associated with each of the 2^n combinations of these variables. So just listing these possibilities requires exponential memory, and calculating with them will require exponential time—i.e. such calculations will be computationally intractable. Thus the transition from logic to probability appears to have gained little regarding tractability, even though it may represent significant progress regarding completeness*.

But the general case is also the worst case; when strong independence assumptions can be made, so that, for example, the probability distribution over the n variables can be compactly represented in graphical form, as described earlier, then the number of pieces of information to be stored is radically reduced (to, essentially, probabilities associated with each node and each link between nodes), and much more efficient probabilistic calculations can be made over such networks. Moreover, such networks can, in principle, run on what may be a computationally plausible parallel, distributed "neural network" computational architecture (Feldman & Ballard, 1982; Rumelhart & McClelland, 1986), where nodes of the graph correspond to numerical processors, and the edges of the graph correspond to communication links between processors. Thus, as we noted earlier, probabilistic models can be mapped onto neural network methods. Moreover, the connection between probabilistic and neural network models can be run in reverse—broad classes of neural network model can be interpreted as specifying particular classes of probabilistic models (see, for example, Chater, 1995; MacKay, 1992b, 1992c; McClelland, 1998; Neal, 1993, for discussion of this connection). All this is reassuring—probabilistic methods, although generally intractable, may be more tractable in specific cases, and moreover can run naturally, and in parallel, in neurally plausible hardware. Moreover, the connection with neural networks is reassuring because neural networks are demonstrably implementable, and demonstrably successful in learning interesting classes of problems relevant to cognition.

We stress, however, that optimism regarding the tractability of probabilistic models of the mind must be cautious for two reasons. First, neural networks themselves face problems of tractability as they are scaled-up in size (Dagum & Luby, 1993). For example, the settling time (roughly, the time in which the probabilities of interest can be reliably "read off" the model) for a network corresponding to a graphical probabilistic model increases explosively with the number of nodes and training items. Moreover, learning the probabilities in such models from experience ("training" in neural network terminology) is also, in general, intractable. We have already noted that the general learning problem, at least according to the MDL principle is not merely intractable but uncomputable. Second, neural networks face a problem of scaling up along a different dimension—of the complexity of the knowledge represented. This is the notorious problem of implementing *structured representations* in neural networks, which we touched on in Chapter 2. Structured representations do not represent propositions as indivisible atoms, but display their internal structure—thus, in standard predicate logic, a representation of the statement *All artists are beekeepers*, $\forall x(\text{artist}(x) \rightarrow \text{beekeeper}(x))$, reveals the internal structure of the proposition in a way that representing it as an unanalysed state of a node in a neural network does not. Structured representations are required in order to store and use any reasonably rich body of knowledge; but despite a great deal of research, efficient implementations of structured representations in neural networks have yet to be developed. For example, one of the leading approaches, Smolensky's tensor product representation (Smolensky, 1990) requires explosively large numbers of nodes in the network as the number of propositions to be represented increases, and is also very slow for retrieving information. Moreover, in probability theory more generally, it has not been clear how to deal with inferences that depend on the structure of propositions, which are traditionally treated by logic. Indeed, representation of structure in a probabilistic framework is still relatively undeveloped, despite having been an important research goal since Carnap's attempt to develop a formal theory of inductive inference, based on logical representations and probabilistic inference (Carnap, 1950, 1952). In view of these issues, it remains as a challenge for future research to provide computationally tractable implementations of probabilistic inference which can scale up to deal with large amounts of structured representations. Nonetheless, the probabilistic approach to uncertain inference provides a range of promising directions for future work which aim to show how the cognitive system can implement (some approximation) to rational principles for uncertain reasoning.

Are Norms of Rationality Dispensable?

We have stressed the importance of norms of rationality in explaining cognition; we have suggested that it is by showing how reasoning conforms with such norms (to some approximation) that such inference is *successful*.

Recently, however, it has been proposed by a number of theorists that normative rationality may not be relevant to cognition; instead, a notion of *adaptive* rationality, which is defined in terms of success in dealing with real environments, *rather than* following norms, is required instead. Gigerenzer and Goldstein (1996) argue that human reasoning violates classical norms of rationality but nonetheless is adapted to the problems that it faces in the real world. Thus Gigerenzer and Goldstein (1996, p. 651) state that this approach implies that "the minds of living systems should be understood relative to the environment in which they evolved rather than to the tenets of classical rationality...." Evans and Over's (1996b) distinction between rationality$_1$ and rationality$_2$ points to the same distinction—they too argue that it is adaptive rationality, rather than normative rationality, that explains the success of human cognition.

The emphasis on the adaptive success of reasoning in the real world is, of course, entirely consistent with the rational analysis approach that we have been advancing; indeed, the idea of adaptive rationality was first broached by Anderson (1990) in introducing the notion of rational analysis. Moreover, Marr's (1982) account of cognitive explanation, on which Anderson's notion is built, was distinctive from previous work in computational vision precisely because it stressed studying the adaptive problem that the visual system faces in the natural environment. But rational analysis does not use adaptive rationality to *supplant* normative rationality—rather it explains the adaptive success of cognitive strategies in terms of their (approximate) adherence to rational norms, coupled with information about the nature of the environment (e.g. in the explanation of the abstract selection task outlined in Part II, the rational norms were given by the principles of Bayesian optimal data selection, and the key assumption concerning the environment was *rarity*). Thus, adaptive rationality is explained in terms of normative rationality, rather than being used instead of normative rationality.

Gigerenzer and Goldstein (1996) and Evans and Over (1996b) argue, from very different points of view, that cognitive algorithms may be adaptively successful in real-world problems without approximating *any* normative rational standard, and moreover that many algorithms used by the cognitive system may be of this type. One expression of this view is that "adaptive rationality", i.e. that which underlies successful performance in the real world, need not involve following the classical norms of rationality. The issue of whether adaptive rationality (success in the real world) requires normative rationality (approximation to some rational theory) is an important open problem. One viewpoint, with which we have sympathy, is that any adaptively successful algorithm must be approximating some rational standard, otherwise the success of the algorithm is rendered a matter of miraculous coincidence. An opposing viewpoint is that there are other modes of successful performance, which lie outside the scope of rational theories.

Perhaps the only way of addressing this issue is practical. Researchers in statistics, machine learning, neural networks, animal behaviour, and economics have typically assumed that adaptive rationality can be understood in terms of normative rationality. They have therefore pursued a research programme that attempts to explain the adaptive rationality of statistical methods, machine learning, or neural network algorithms, animal foraging strategies, or individual choices, by their approximation to rational standards. We suspect that only by pursuing this approach in cognitive science—by developing candidate rational analyses—will the question of whether adaptive rationality requires adherence to some normative rational standard be answered (see Kacelnik, 1998).

An interesting case study here is animal learning theory, which grew out of the behaviourist tradition. Animal learning theory provides a set of descriptive principles about how animals learn, under certain restrictive conditions. It provides no *justification* that following these rules will lead to successful behaviour. It has been suggested that learning theory provides an example of a psychological theory that concerns adaptive rationality, but for which no normative rational basis is available (Evans, 1993; Evans & Over, 1996b). But this appearance is misleading. First, in the absence of some normative justification for the principles of learning theory, it is currently not clear whether these principles are adaptively rational or not. These principles are derived under restrictive laboratory conditions, which are very different from the natural environments of the animals (typically rats and pigeons) that animal learning theorists have investigated, as ethologists have been keen to point out. This raises the concern that the principles of animal learning theory do not capture an aspect of adaptive rationality, but instead reflect a non-rational set of phenomena, which are side-effects of cognitive mechanisms that are unable to employ their genuinely adaptive functions because of the reduced character of the experimental set-up. Such concerns can, however, be put aside if some rational justification for these principles can be found. Second, rather than abandoning rational analysis, it is possible instead to attempt to understand how the environment must be for the principles of learning theory to be adaptive—that is, constructing a rational analysis, which has the principles of animal learning theory as an implementation.

This project has recently been carried out to some extent, and is an ongoing topic of research. At a qualitative level, Dickinson (1980) aims to explain why the various principles of animal learning have a rational basis; more formally, it has been noted that certain learning principles are rational, given certain environmental assumptions. Thus, for example, asymptotic results of learning according to the Rescorla–Wagner learning rule of classical conditioning (which serves as a simple and reasonably general summary of some of the most important learning phenomena) implements a kind of Bayesian inference. Specifically, this learning rule specifies how an animal learns the connection between a set of cues (e.g. a light or a tone) and some outcome (e.g. a mild shock or some food). The Bayesian analysis of Rescorla–Wagner assumes that the animal calculates (presumably some approximation to) the probability of the outcome, given the cues, using Bayes' theorem, with the environmental assumption that the cues are conditionally independent given the outcome (that is, if the outcome is known, then the value of any one cue carries no information about the values of any of the others). Moreover, recently Cheng (1997) and Shanks (1995) have argued that, under certain conditions, at asymptote the Rescorla–Wagner model computes the normative probabilistic contrast. These kinds of analysis explain why following the principles of animal learning theory is adaptive—and moreover gives evidence that the results of animal learning experiments are genuinely tapping adaptive learning processes that may be of importance in the natural environment. Thus, animal learning theory provides a good illustration of how adaptive rationality is usefully supplemented by a normative rational analysis, rather than displacing normative rationality.

We suggest that in any debate of this kind, there should be a methodological imperative to explore explanations based on normative rationality—only by doing so can the scope and limitations of this approach be assessed; and we caution that normative explanation cannot be abandoned wholesale, without losing the ability to explain why the cognitive system under study is adaptive. In the next section we address the recent distinction between rationality$_1$ and rationality$_2$ drawn by Evans and Over (1996b) which relates to our present concern with adaptive and normative rationality. We argue that this distinction, as it is drawn in the literature, is confused and unhelpful in understanding human reasoning.

Can Rationality₁ Exist Without Rationality₂?

Evans and Over (1997) distinguish between two notions of rationality:

> *Rationality₁:* Thinking, speaking, reasoning, making a decision, or acting in a way that is generally reliable and efficient for achieving one's goals.
> *Rationality₂:* Thinking, speaking, reasoning, making a decision, or acting when one has a reason for what one does sanctioned by a normative theory. (Evans & Over, 1997, p. 2)

They argue that "people are largely rational in the sense of achieving their goals (rationality₁) but have only a limited ability to reason or act for good reasons sanctioned by a normative theory (rationality₂)" (Evans & Over, 1997, p. 1). If this is right, then achieving one's goals can be done without following any normative theory—i.e. without there being a *justification* for the actions, decisions or thoughts that lead to success: rationality₁ does not require rationality₂. That is, Evans and Over are committed to the view that thoughts, actions, or decisions that cannot be normatively justified can, nonetheless, consistently lead to practical success. This claim appears to be both strong and far-reaching. However, we argue that the case that Evans and Over make for it is not compelling.

Specifically, we note (i) that the notion of rationality₂ has a range of interpretations, none of which is consistently adopted by Evans and Over. We then argue: (ii) that rationality₁ is in need of explanation in terms of rationality₂, according to what we take to be the most natural reading of rationality₂; (iii) that the goal of much functional explanation in the social and biological sciences is precisely to explain rationality₁ in terms of rationality₂, and that this is an appropriate goal for psychology—it underwrites the programme of the *rational analysis* of cognition (Anderson, 1990, 1991a; Oaksford & Chater, 1994a); (iv) that rationality₁ appears to be entirely mysterious unless tied to some rationality₂ explanation.

Evans and Over's definition of rationality₂, quoted earlier, depends on explaining what it is to have "a reason for what one does sanctioned by a normative theory". But in what this consists is not made clear. Possible interpretations, among many others, include:

A. Being able verbally to justify one's cognitive processes by reference to some explicit and publicly known normative theory (e.g. to be able to write down principles of, say, probability theory, decision theory or logic which reconstruct the reasons behind one's action).

B. Having the rules of a normative theory explicitly represented in some system of internal representation, and used to guide thought and action, whether or not these rules may be verbally reported. (The normative theory *guides* thought and behaviour just as a theory of grammar guides language production and understanding.)

C. Having one's cognitive processes operate according to rules of some calculus which can be viewed as normatively justified. These rules may or may not be explicitly represented by the cognitive system. (The normative theory *governs* thought and behaviour.)

D. Having one's cognitive processes approximate, to some degree, the dictates of some normative theory.

We shall see that the choice of interpretations A to D of rationality$_2$ is crucial in understanding the relation between rationality$_2$ and rationality$_1$ and that Evans and Over do not settle on a particular reading.

But note that in elaborating on rationality$_2$ in the context of deductive reasoning research, Evans and Over introduce further issues, not hinted at in their definition: "As we use the term, rationality$_2$ requires that participants respond to the instructions of the experiment, for example by suspending prior beliefs, assuming the premises and drawing only conclusions which necessarily follow" (p. 2). This claim does not follow from Evans and Over's definition—an experimental participant may be sanctioned by a normative theory (in any of sense A to D in our list) and entirely flout the intentions and expectations of the experimenter.

This suggests an orthogonal source of variation in the concept of rationality$_2$, that it requires either:

(i) Being sanctioned by *some* normative theory.

(ii) Being sanctioned by the normative standard that the experimenter has in mind, and following the experimental instructions, as interpreted by the experimenter.

This source of variation combines with all interpretations A to D and so we have at least eight very different ways of understanding rationality$_2$. Evans and Over appear to use different interpretations of rationality$_2$ at different points in their argument.

Regarding (i) and (ii), we have seen that Evans and Over appear committed to (ii). This is crucial in the psychology of reasoning. For example, experimenters who adopt a falsificationist view of theory testing will view people's performance in Wason's (1966, 1968) selection task as exhibiting a failure of rationality$_2$. Experimenters adopting a Bayesian optimal data selection account (Oaksford & Chater, 1994a, 1995c, 1996) may view people's performance as successfully conforming to this normative standard, and hence as rational$_2$.

But if Evans and Over intend (ii), then, prima facie, rationality$_2$ is a notion of very limited application. First, it appears to have no application outside the experimental context, and hence has no implications for everyday reasoning, for there will be no experimenter to interpret the task that the person has been set and what normative standard they should use to solve it. Second, and more importantly, general claims about people's rationality$_2$ cannot be made—because the status of such claims will depend on what normative standard the experimenter has in mind.

Each of senses A to C also appears to be in play in Evans and Over's discussion. Interpretation A is implicated in, for example, "Rationality$_2$ involves ... conscious explicit reasoning, providing good reasons for the actions we take" (Evans and Over, 1997, p. 27). On the other hand, senses B or C appear to be relevant in Evans and Over's discussion of what they call the "rational$_2$ agendum", which concerns "whether people solve reasoning problems ... by the application of inference rules embedded in a natural logic, or by manipulation of mental models" (Evans & Over, 1997, p. 4). On the mental logic approach people's behaviour is *guided* by logical rules embedded in the cognitive system, although they are not necessarily available to conscious access (sense B). In contrast, on the mental models approach, behaviour is *governed* by logical rules but they are not embedded in the cognitive system, which operates by different, semantic, principles (sense C) that nonetheless are capable, in theory, of perfectly capturing logical inference.

Each of these different readings has very different implications for the nature of the cognitive system. Consequently it is unclear what substantive claim Evans and Over wish to make by the introduction of this terminology. As far as the rational analysis approach is concerned it is sense D that is important. Conformity to a normative system simply means that we have a justification for why people behave as they do without making further assumptions about the mechanisms that achieve this. This is wholly familiar: throughout the biological and social sciences, a major goal is explaining *why* thought, action, and behaviour is efficient and successful (i.e. is rational$_1$). In the study of animal behaviour, the animal is assumed to forage, select a mate, or signal to other animals, in such a way as to approximate (often quite crudely) the dictates of a normative theory (i.e. their behaviour can be seen as rational$_2$). To the extent that the animal conforms to an appropriate normative theory (typically couched in a decision- or game-theoretic framework), the fact that its behaviour is successful can be explained. Conversely, if there is no normative theory to which behaviour approximates, then the success of behaviour is unexplained (Kacelnik, 1998). For example, as we have discussed, it has been a pressing concern in animal learning—Evans and Over's principal example of a pure rational$_1$ theory— to provide a normative justification for why the principles underlying learning are adaptively successful. As we pointed out, recently Cheng (1997) and Shanks (1995) have shown that, for example, the Rescorla–Wagner model (Rescorla & Wagner, 1972) computes the normative probabilistic contrast at asymptote. So rather than embracing Evans and Over's concept of rationality$_1$, animal learning theorists have been busy trying to relate descriptive and normative models. The whole point of rational analysis is that this is the only sensible way to proceed.

Evans and Over (1996b, 1997), on the other hand, reject this conventional wisdom—they claim that success can somehow be achieved without following normative principles. According to rational analysis, normative principles are important in explaining cognition, because they provide putative explanations of *why* cognitive processes work. But if cognitive processes do not follow or approximate *any* normative principles, then their success is entirely mysterious. Agents are simply held to do, to choose, or to think the right thing by non-rational means. What could such a means be? Evans and Over provide no answers to this question.

Rationality, Domain Specificity, and Evolution

Another line of attack on the role of norms of rationality in explaining human reasoning comes from the viewpoint that reasoning is not governed by general principles, but is instead governed by domain-specific strategies, which are innate, and have developed in response to evolutionary selectional pressures. This viewpoint has been recently widely advocated, although in a number of different varieties (e.g. Cosmides, 1989; Cosmides & Tooby, 1996; Cummins, 1996a, 1996b). A principal line of argument used by these theorists is based on Wason's selection task, which we have extensively considered in Part II. Specifically, they argue that the radically different patterns of performance in the abstract and thematic versions of the selection task can be explained by assuming that deontic tasks engage particular domain-specific reasoning strategies, which lead to a facilitation of reasoning. We briefly argue that claims made on this basis are not persuasive, in the light of the discussion of our rational analysis of the selection task.

First, we consider a possible argument based on levels of performance in the two tasks. According to early interpretations of the selection task, the "logical" response was assumed to be normatively correct for both tasks— but only to be "correctly" chosen in deontic contexts (Cheng & Holyoak, 1985). Thus, deontic contexts were viewed as "facilitating" reasoning—and hence it might seem appropriate to assume that reasoning is subserved by domain-specific knowledge, and that only when this knowledge can be applied is reasoning successful. For example, Cosmides (1989) assumes that knowledge of "social contracts" (concerning the making and breaking of agreements between individuals) underwrote "successful" performance in deontic tasks. The assumption is that people reason poorly in abstract tasks because they are floundering, unable to apply domain-specific knowledge. But our rational analysis treats abstract and deontic tasks as having different rational bases and hence different correct solutions. Moreover, according to each rational analysis, the modal response that people choose in both the abstract and deontic selection tasks is correct. Thus, there is no prima facie reason to assume that people reason "better" in deontic tasks. Of course, it might be possible to argue that, according to some more subtle measure of performance, people perform better in the deontic tasks (for example, perhaps a higher *percentage* of people make the "correct" selections; or perhaps correct deontic performance emerges earlier developmentally—see Harris & Nuñez, 1996; Cummins, 1996b). But this argument would still be invalid, because although deontic and indicative selection tasks may appear similar, the rational analysis reveals them to be profoundly different: their rational analyses are based on different underlying concepts (maximising expected information gain versus maximising expected utility), lead to different correct answers, and presumably have different levels of difficulty. Indeed, comparing deontic and indicative reasoning in *any* context appears to be a comparison between apples and oranges. Thus, it is not at all clear what criterion might be used to show that deontic reasoning is superior to indicative reasoning, let alone draw the conclusion that deontic reasoning must be subserved by innate domain-specific knowledge.

Second, the fact that rational analyses of deontic and indicative tasks have different solutions undermines the argument that the effect of domain-specific knowledge must cause the change in reasoning performance. Of course, to some degree knowledge must be involved in solving deontic reasoning tasks—in that knowledge determines the role (actor or enforcer) that it is appropriate to adopt when performing this task. Thus, for example, in the well-known deontic selection task context used by Cheng and Holyoak (1985), our knowledge of immigration procedure will tell us that immigration officers are likely to behave as enforcers (attempting to stop people who are not correctly immunised entering the country); and human rights activists are likely to behave as actors (trying to ensure that people who are correctly immunised *are* allowed to enter the country). But, in this sense, knowledge enters into any reasoning task—because knowledge is required to understand how the task should meaningfully be tackled. But there seems no reason to suppose that some particular body of domain-specific knowledge, concerning social contracts or anything else, is being drawn upon.

Third, even if the selection task did establish the importance of particular domain-specific knowledge in reasoning, this would in no way show that this knowledge was innately specified and the product of natural selection (Cosmides, 1989; Cosmides & Tooby, 1996; Cummins, 1996). Arguments for the role of natural selection in determining this domain-specific knowledge typically stress the fundamental role of this putative knowledge during evolutionary time—specifically, knowledge of social contracts or principles of social interaction more broadly are held to have been critical determinants of reproductive success.

But the mere prevalence, and importance, of deontic reasoning about social interactions offers no argument for its innateness. A vast range of knowledge and abilities are important in development, such as object permanence, the structure of space, natural language, perceptual and motor capacities, and so on—and these have been crucial to survival and hence reproductive success during evolutionary time. Indeed, these seem at least as fundamental to development as the aspect of human social behaviour concerned with deontic rules. Some theorists would argue that some of these capacities are underwritten by innate information (perhaps even innate "modules") (e.g. Fodor, 1983; Shallice, 1988). Others (e.g. behaviourists) would argue that none is underwritten by innate modules; and intermediate positions of many kinds are of course possible. Thus, simply noting the importance of an ability for human development either currently or during our evolutionary history, does not, in itself, count as evidence that this ability is innate.

Thus, claims concerning the importance of selectional pressures in shaping the special character of deontic reasoning are not convincing. It seems entirely likely that social reasoning poses problems that are of enormous importance from the point of view of natural selection. But it is clear that people can *solve* these problems. The question at issue is: to what degree are problems of social reasoning (and reasoning with deontic rules in particular) solved by innate structures and to what extent are they solved by learning? Let us use the two most extreme views for illustration. Suppose that social reasoning is underwritten by an innate module (e.g. Cummins, 1996b). It seems entirely plausible that evolutionary pressures will increase the adaptiveness of this module, just as for other innately specified structures, such as the hands or the lungs. Suppose, by contrast, that social reasoning is underwritten by learning. Then, evolutionary pressures will not act on an innate module, because there will be no innate module to act upon. Instead, these pressures might, for example, act upon the learning mechanism itself, to improve learning either in general, or learning about specifically social reasoning. The point is this: evolutionary considerations provide no *argument* that innate modules must have been produced by evolutionary pressures. Evolutionary pressures are pressures to solve problems *somehow*: they do not determine that a problem is solved by innate modules, by learning, or by some combination of the two.

We have argued that the selection task does not provide evidence that human reasoning is shaped by innate domain-specific knowledge. But we do suggest that, quite generally, reasoning is shaped by adaptation to the environment. Normative principles must typically be supplemented by assumptions about the nature of the environment in order to give a rational analysis of cognitive tasks. Thus, Marr's analysis of vision involved quite detailed specification of the constraints in the structure of the visual world, concerning the opacity and continuity of surfaces, the behaviour of light, and so on; on the other hand, the rational analysis of some aspects of memory may require only assumptions about the distribution of times at which pieces of information are re-used (Anderson & Schooler, 1991), and our rational analysis of the abstract selection task relies only on our rarity assumption—that natural language predicates typically refer to relatively small minorities of objects in the environment. But in all these cases the contribution of the environment is crucial, because only when the relevant environmental constraints are understood is it possible to determine what assumptions can be used in conjunction with normative principles to provide an explanation of how successful cognitive performance is possible.

CONCLUSION

In this book, we have argued that the cognitive science of human reasoning has mischaracterised the level and nature of human reasoning performance, because it has used logic as its normative standard. Almost all everyday inference is *uncertain*, and, thus, human reasoning should be assessed using probability theory, the calculus of uncertainty, rather than logic, the calculus of certainty.

In Part I, we argued against the logicist paradigm, in the psychology of reasoning, but also as a basis for computational models of knowledge representation in cognitive science and artificial intelligence. Such reasoning systems fail to capture everyday inferences—they are not complete*; and they are also typically computationally intractable. We also showed how these arguments bear on the psychology of reasoning and we responded to a variety of possible counter-arguments from within the mental logics and mental models approaches. Finally we showed that our account has implications for the philosophy of mind. In Part II, we argued that adopting a probabilistic viewpoint allows the development of rational analyses for human reasoning, rather than being forced to condemn much of people's reasoning performance as invalid when compared against logical norms. We showed how to construct a rational analysis of the task that has been taken to raise most questions about human rationality—Wason's selection task. We defended this view against objections, and showed how recent data from work by Sperber et al. (1995) could be interpreted as supporting the optimal data selection model. Finally in this chapter we have outlined further empirical work consistent with our probabilistic model, we have outlined areas of further research, and we have outlined the problems and prospects for probabilistic theories of knowledge representation and reasoning more generally.

In summary, the discussions in this book have argued for a profound shift in the cognitive science of human reasoning, from a logicist perspective to a perspective founded on the view that the fundamental goal of the cognitive system is to deal with the uncertainty of the everyday world. This shift leads to a radical reformulation of the theoretical foundations of reasoning research. This reformulation promises to provide rational explanations for what had previously seemed a confusing and irrational pattern of experimental reasoning performance. Consequently we hope to have gone some way to resolving the paradox between the apparent irrationality of human performance on laboratory reasoning tasks and the manifest success of human everyday inference.

References

Adams, E. (1966). Probability and the logic of conditionals. In J. Hintikka & P. Suppes (Eds.), *Aspects of inductive logic*. Amsterdam: North Holland.

Adams, E. (1975). *The logic of conditionals: An application of probability to deductive logic*. Dordrecht: Reidel.

Almeida, L. B. (1987). *A learning rule for asynchronous perceptrons with feedback in a combinatorial environment*. In IEEE First International Conference on Neural Networks Proceedings (pp. II/609–618). San Diego, CA: SOS Printing.

Almor, A. & Sloman, S. A. (1996). Is deontic reasoning special? *Psychological Review, 103*, 374–380.

Anderson, A. R. & Belnap, N. D. (1975). *Entailment: The logic of relevance and necessity* (Vol. 1). Princeton, NJ: Princeton University Press.

Anderson, J. R. (1983). *The architecture of cognition*. Cambridge, MA: Harvard University Press.

Anderson, J. R. (1990). *The adaptive character of thought*. Hillsdale, NJ: Lawrence Erlbaum Associates.

Anderson, J. R. (1991a). Is human cognition adaptive? *Behavioral and Brain Sciences, 14*, 471–517.

Anderson, J. R. (1991b). The adaptive nature of human categorization. *Psychological Review, 98*, 409–429.

Anderson, J. R. (1994). *Rules of the mind*. Hillsdale, NJ: Lawrence Erlbaum Associates.

Anderson, J. R. & Milson, R. (1989). Human memory: An adaptive perspective. *Psychological Review, 96*, 703–719.

Anderson, J. R. & Schooler, L. J. (1991). Reflections of the environment in memory. *Psychological Science, 2*, 396–408.

Apostel, L. (1972). The relation between negation in linguisitics, logic and psychology. *Logique et Analyse, 15*, 333–401.

Arrow, K. J., Colombatto, E., Perlman, M., & Schmidt, C. (Eds.) (1996). *The rational foundations of economic behavior*. Basingstoke: Macmillan.

Baars, B. J. (1986). *The cognitive revolution in psychology*. New York: Guilford Press.

Baddeley, A. D. (1976). *The psychology of memory*. New York: Basic Books.

Baddeley, A. D. (1986). *Working memory*. Oxford: Clarendon Press.

Baron, J. (1994). *Thinking and deciding*. Cambridge: Cambridge University Press.

Barsalou, L. W. (1987). The instability of graded structures: Implications for the nature of concepts. In U. Neisser (Ed.), *Concepts and conceptual development* (pp. 101–140). Cambridge: Cambridge University Press.

Bartlett, F. C. (1932). *Remembering: A study in experimental and social psychology*. Cambridge: Cambridge University Press.

Barwise, J. & Cooper, R. (1981). Generalized quantifiers and natural languages. *Linguistics and Philosophy, 4*, 159–219.

Barwise, J. & Perry, J. (1983). *Situations and attitudes*. Cambridge, MA: MIT Press.

Bayes, T. (1763). An essay towards solving a problem in the doctrine of chances. *Philosophical Transactions of the Royal Society, 53*, 370–418. (Reprinted in *Biometrika*, 1958, *45*, 293–315).

Beattie, J. & Baron, J. (1988). Confirmation and matching biases in hypothesis testing. *Quarterly Journal of Experimental Psychology, 40*A, 269–297.

Berger, J. O. (1995). *Statistical decision theory and Bayesian analysis*. New York: Springer-Verlag.

Bernoulli, J. (1713). *Ars conjectandi*. Basel.

Beth, E. W. (1955). Semantic entailment and formal derivability. *Mededelingen van de Koninklijke Nederlande Akadamie van Wetenschappen, Afd. Letterkunde, 18*, 309–342.

Birnbaum, M. H. (1983). Base rates in Bayesian inference: Signal detection analysis of the cab problem. *American Journal of Psychology, 96*, 85–94.

Block, N. (1986). Advertisement for a semantics for psychology. *Midwest Studies in Philosophy, 10*, 615–678.

Bobrow, D. G. &, Norman, D. A. (1975). Some principles of memory schemata. In D. G. Bobrow & A. M. Collins (Eds.), *Representation and understanding: Studies in cognitive science*. New York: Academic Press.

Boole, G. (1854/1951). *An investigation into the laws of thought*. New York: Dover.

Boolos, G. & Jeffrey, R. (1980). *Computability and logic* (2nd Edn). Cambridge: Cambridge University Press.

Bower, G. H. (1970). Analysis of a mnemonic device. *American Scientist, 58*, 496–510.

Bower, T. G. R. (1974). *Development in infancy*. San Francisco: Freeman.

Box, G. E. P. & Tiao, G. C. (1973). *Bayesian inference in statistical analysis*. Reading, MA: Addison-Wesley.

Brachman, R. J. & Levesque, H. (1985). *Readings in knowledge representation*. Los Altos, CA: Morgan Kaufman.

Braine, M. D. S. (1978). On the relationship between the natural logic of reasoning and standard logic. *Psychological Review, 85*, 1–21.

Braine, M. D. S. & O'Brien, D. P. (1991). A theory of if: Lexical entry, reasoning program, and pragmatic principles. *Psychological Review, 98*, 182–203.

Braine, M. D. S., Reiser, B. J., & Rumain, B. (1984). Some empirical justification for a theory of natural propositional logic. *The Psychology of Learning and Motivation, 18*. New York: Academic Press.

Bransford, J. D., Barclay, J. R., & Franks, J. J. (1972). Sentence memory: A constructive versus interpretive approach. *Cognitive Psychology, 3*, 193–209.

Bransford, J. D. & Johnson, M. (1972). Contextual prerequisites for understanding: Some investigations of comprehension and recall. *Journal of Verbal Learning and Verbal Behavior, 11*, 717–726.

Bransford, J. D. & Johnson, M. K. (1973). Considerations of some problems of comprehension. In W. G. Chase (Ed.), *Visual information processing* (pp. 389–392). New York: Academic Press.

Bransford, J. D. & McCarrell, N. S. (1975). A sketch of a cognitive approach to comprehension: Some thoughts on what it means to comprehend. In W. B. Weimer & D. S. Palermo (Eds.), *Cognition and symbolic processes* (pp. 189–229). Hillsdale, NJ: Lawrence Erlbaum Associates.

Bree, D. S. (1973). The interpretation of implication. In A. Elithorn & D. Jones (Eds.), *Artificial and human thinking*. Amsterdam: Elsevier Science Publishers.

Bree, D. S. & Coppens, G. (1976). The difficulty of an implication task. *British Journal of Psychology, 67*, 579–586.

Brooks, R. (1991). How to build complete creatures rather than isolated cognitive simulators. In K. van Lehn (Ed.), *Architectures for intelligence* (pp. 225–240). Hillsdale, NJ: Lawrence Erlbaum Associates.

Brown, H. I. (1988). *Rationality*. London: Routledge.

Bryant, P. E. & Trabasso, T. (1978). Transitive inferences and memory in young children. *Nature, 232*, 456–458.

Byrne, R. M. J. (1989). Suppressing valid inferences with conditionals. *Cognition, 31*, 1–21.

Byrne, R. M. J. (1991). Can valid inferences be suppressed? *Cognition, 39*, 71–78.

Carey, S. (1985). *Conceptual change in childhood*. Cambridge, MA: MIT Press.

Carey, S. (1986). Cognitive science and science education. *American Psychologist, 41*, 1123–1130.

Carey, S. (1988). Conceptual differences between children and adults. *Mind and Language, 3*, 167–181.

Carnap, R. (1923). Uber die Aufgabe der Physick und die Andewendung des Grundsatze der Einfachtsheit. *Kant-Studien, 28*, 90–107.

Carnap, R. (1950). *Logical foundations of probability*. Chicago, IL: University of Chicago Press.

Carnap, R. (1952). *The continuum of inductive methods*. Chicago, IL: University of Chicago Press.

Cartwright, N. (1983). *How the laws of physics lie*. Oxford: Oxford University Press.

Chaloner, K. & Verdinelli, I. (1994). *Bayesian experimental designs: A review (Tech. Rep. No. 599)*. Pittsburgh, PA: Department of Statistics, Carnegie Mellon University.

Charniak, E. & McDermott, D. (1985). *An introduction to artificial intelligence*. Reading, MA: Addison-Wesley.

Chater, N. (1986). *The present status of the innateness controversy: A reply to Fodor*. Unpublished manuscript, Department of Psychology, University of Cambridge.

Chater, N. (1989). *Learning to respond to structure in time*. Research Initiative in Pattern Recognition Technical Report, RSRE Malvern, September.

Chater, N. (1993). Mental models and non-monotonic reasoning. *Behavioural and Brain Sciences, 16*, 340–341.

Chater, N. (1995). Neural networks: The new statistical models of mind. In J. P. Levy, D. Bairaktaris, J. A. Bullinaria, & P. Cairns (Eds.), *Connectionist models of memory and language* (pp. 207–227). London: UCL Press.

Chater, N. (1997a). *The search for simplicity: A fundamental cognitive principle?* Unpublished manuscript, Department of Psychology, University of Warwick.

Chater, N. (1997b). Simplicity and the mind. *The Psychologist, 10*, 495–498.

Chater, N. & Oaksford, M. (1990). Autonomy, implementation and cognitive architecture: A reply to Fodor and Pylyshyn. *Cognition, 34*, 93–107.

Chater, N. & Oaksford, M. (1993). Logicism, mental models and everyday reasoning: Reply to Garnham. *Mind and Language, 8*, 72–89.

Chater, N. & Oaksford, M. (1997). *The probability heuristics model of syllogistic reasoning*. Unpublished manuscript, Department of Psychology, University of Warwick.

Cheng, P. W. (1997). From covariation to causation: A causal power theory. *Psychological Review, 104*, 367–405.

Cheng, P. W. & Holyoak, K. J. (1985). Pragmatic reasoning schemas. *Cognitive Psychology*, *17*, 391–416.

Cheng, P. W. & Holyoak, K. J. (1989). On the natural selection of reasoning theories. *Cognition*, *33*, 285–313.

Cheng, P. W., Holyoak, K. J., Nisbett, R. E., & Oliver, L. M. (1986). Pragmatic versus syntactic approaches in training deductive reasoning. *Cognitive Psychology*, *18*, 293–328.

Cheng, P. W. & Novick, L. R. (1990). A probabilistic contrast model of causal induction. *Journal of Personality and Social Psychology*, *58*, 545–567.

Cheng, P. W. & Novick, L. R. (1991). Causes versus enabling conditions. *Cognition*, *58*, 83–120.

Cheng, P. W. & Novick, L. R. (1992). Covariation in natural causal induction. *Psychological Review*, *99*, 365–382.

Cherniak, C. (1986). *Minimal rationality*. Cambridge, MA: MIT Press.

Chomsky, N. (1959). A review of B. F. Skinner's "Verbal Behavior". *Language*, *35*, 26–58.

Christiansen, M. & Chater, N. (1992). Connectionism, learning and meaning. *Connection Science*, *4*, 227–252.

Christiansen, M. & Chater, N. (1993). Symbol grounding—the emperor's new theory of meaning? In *Proceedings of the 15th Annual Conference of the Cognitive Science Society* (pp. 155–160). Hillsdale, NJ: Lawrence Erlbaum Associates.

Chrostowski, J. J. & Griggs, R. A. (1985). The effects of problem content, instructions and verbalisation procedure on Wason's selection task. *Current Psychological Reviews*, *4*, 99–107.

Churchland, P. M. & Churchland, P. S. (1983). Stalking the wild epistemic engine. *Nous*, *17*, 5–18.

Churchland, P. S. (1986). *Neurophilosophy*. Cambridge, MA: MIT Press.

Clark, H. H. (1977). Bridging. In P. N. Johnson-Laird & P. C. Wason (Eds.), *Thinking: Readings in cognitive science* (pp. 411–420). Cambridge: Cambridge University Press.

Clark, H. H., & Haviland, S. E. (1977). Comprehension and the given-new contract. In R. O. Freedle (Ed.), *Discourse production and comprehension* (Vol. 1, pp. 1–40). Norwood, NJ: Ablex.

Clark, K. L. (1978). Negation as failure. In *Logic and databases* (pp. 293–322). New York: Plenum Press.

Clocksin, W. F. & Mellish, C. S. (1984). *Programming in Prolog* (2nd Edn). Berlin: Springer-Verlag.

Cohen, L.J. (1981). Can human irrationality be experimentally demonstrated? *Behavioural and Brain Sciences*, *4*, 317–370.

Collins, A. M. and Quillian, M. R. (1969). Retrieval time from semantic memory. *Journal of Verbal Learning and Verbal Behavior*, *8*, 240–247.

Cook, S. (1971). The complexity of theorem proving procedures. In *The JACM third annual symposium on the theory of computing* (pp. 151–158). New York.

Cosmides, L. (1989). The logic of social exchange: Has natural selection shaped how humans reason? Studies with the Wason selection task. *Cognition*, *31*, 187–276.

Cosmides, L. & Tooby, J. (1996). Are humans good intuitive statisticians after all? Rethinking some conclusions from the literature on judgment under uncertainty. *Cognition*, *58*, 1–74.

Cover, T. M. & Thomas, J. A. (1991). *Elements of information theory*. New York: John Wiley & Sons.

Cox, R. T. (1946). Probability, frequency and reasonable expectation. *American Journal of Physics*, *14*, 1–13.

Cox, R. T. (1961). *The algebra of probable inference*. Baltimore, MD: Johns Hopkins University Press.

Craik, F. I. M. & Lockhart, R. S. (1972). Levels of processing: a framework for memory research. *Journal of Verbal Learning and Verbal Behavior*, *11*, 671–684.

Cummins, D. D. (1996a). Evidence for the innateness of deontic reasoning. *Mind and Language, 11,* 160–190.

Cummins, D. D. (1996b). Evidence of deontic reasoning in 3- and 4-year-old children. *Memory and Cognition, 24,* 823–840.

Cummins, D. D., Lubart, T., Alksnis, O., & Rist, R. (1991). Conditional reasoning and causation. *Memory and Cognition, 19,* 274–282.

Curry, H. B. & Feys, R. (Eds.) (1958). *Combinatory logic.* Amsterdam: North-Holland.

Dagum, P. & Luby, M. (1993). Approximately probabilistic inference in Bayesian belief networks is NP-hard. *Artificial Intelligence, 60,* 141–153.

Daston, L. (1988). *Classical probability in the enlightment.* Princeton, NJ: Princeton University Press.

Davidson, D. (1984). On the very idea of a conceptual scheme. In D. Davidson, *Inquiries into truth and interpretation* (pp. 183–198). Oxford: Oxford University Press.

Davies, M. (1992). Thinking persons and cognitive science. In A. Clark & R. Lutz (Eds.), *Connectionism in context* (pp. 111–122). Berlin: Springer-Verlag.

de Finetti, B. (1937). Foresight: Its logical laws, its subjective sources. La prévision: Ses lois logiques, ses sources subjectives. *Annales de l'Institute Henri Poincaré, 7,* 1–68. [Translated in H. E. Kyburg & H. E. Smokler (1964) (Eds.), *Studies in subjective probability.* Chichester: John Wiley.]

de Kleer, J. (1986). Extending the ATMS. *Artificial Intelligence, 28,* 163–196.

Dennett, D. C. (1987). Making sense of ourselves. In D. C. Dennett, *The intentional stance* (pp. 83–102). Cambridge, MA: MIT Press.

Derthick, M. (1987). *A connectionist architecture for representing and reasoning about structured knowledge.* Research Report No. CMU-BOLTZ-29, Department of Computer Science, Carnegie Mellon University, Pittsburgh.

Derthick, M. (1988). *Mundane reasoning by parallel constraint satisfaction.* Research Report No. CMU-CS-88-182, Department of Computer Science, Carnegie Mellon University, Pittsburgh.

Dickinson, A. (1980). *Contemporary animal learning theory.* Cambridge: Cambridge University Press.

Donaldson, M. (1978). *Children's minds.* Glasgow: Collins.

Dretske, F. (1981). *Knowledge and the flow of information.* Cambridge, MA: MIT Press.

Duhem, P. (1954). *The aim and structure of physical theory.* Princeton, NJ: Princeton University Press.

Earman, J. (1992). *Bayes or bust? A critical examination of Bayesian confirmation theory.* Cambridge, MA: MIT Press.

Elman, J. L. (1988). *Finding structure in time.* CRL Technical Report 8801, Centre for Research in Language, University of California, San Diego.

Elman, J. L. (1990). Finding structure in time. *Cognitive Science, 14,* 179–211.

Evans, J. St.B. T. (1972). Interpretation and "matching bias" in a reasoning task. *Quarterly Journal of Experimental Psychology, 24,* 193–199.

Evans, J. St.B. T. (1977). Toward a statistical theory of reasoning. *Quarterly Journal of Experimental Psychology, 29,* 621–635.

Evans, J. St.B. T. (1982). *The psychology of deductive reasoning.* London: Routledge and Kegan Paul.

Evans, J. St.B. T. (1983). *Thinking and reasoning: Psychological approaches.* London: Routledge and Kegan Paul.

Evans, J. St.B. T. (1983a). Selective processes in reasoning. In J. St.B. T. Evans (Ed.), *Thinking and reasoning: Psychological approaches.* London: Routledge and Kegan Paul.

Evans, J. St.B. T. (1983b). Linguistic determinants of bias in conditional reasoning. *Quarterly Journal of Experimental Psychology, 35A,* 635–644.

Evans, J. St.B. T. (1984). Heuristic and analytic processes in reasoning. *British Journal of Psychology, 75*, 451–468.

Evans, J. St.B. T. (1989). *Bias in human reasoning: Causes and consequences.* London: Lawrence Erlbaum Associates.

Evans, J. St.B. T. (1991). Theories of human reasoning: The fragmented state of the art. *Theory and Psychology, 1*, 83–105.

Evans, J. St.B. T. (1993). Bias and rationality. In K. I. Manktelow & D. E. Over (Eds.), *Rationality*, (pp. 6–30). London: Routledge.

Evans, J. St.B. T. (1995) Relevance and reasoning. In S. E. Newstead & J. St. B. T. Evans (Eds.), *Perspectives in the psychology of reasoning.* Hove, UK: Lawrence Erlbaum Associates.

Evans, J. St.B. T., Clibbens, J. & Rood, B. (1996). The role of implicit and explicit negation in conditional reasoning bias. *Journal of Memory and Language, 35*, 392–409.

Evans, J. St.B. T. & Lynch, J. S. (1973). Matching bias in the selection task. *British Journal of Psychology, 64*, 391–397.

Evans, J. St.B. T. & Newstead, J. S. (1977). Language and reasoning: A study of temporal factors. *Cognition, 8*, 265–283.

Evans, J. St.B. T., Newstead, S. E., & Byrne, R. M. J. (1993). *Human reasoning.* Hove, UK: Lawrence Erlbaum Associates.

Evans, J. St.B. T. & Over, D. E. (1996a). Rationality in the selection task: Epistemic utility versus uncertainty reduction. *Psychological Review, 103*, 356–363.

Evans, J. St.B. T. & Over, D. E. (1996b). *Rationality and reasoning.* Hove, UK: Psychology Press.

Evans, J. St.B. T. & Over, D. E. (1997). Rationality in reasoning: The problem of deductive competence. *Cahiers de Psychologie Cognitive, 16*, 1–35.

Evans, J. St.B. T., Over, D. E., & Manktelow, K. I. (1993). Reasoning, decision making and rationality. *Cognition, 49*, 165–187.

Fedorov, V. V. (1972). *Theory of optimal experiments.* London: Academic Press.

Feldman, J. & Ballard, D. (1982). Connectionist models and their properties. *Cognitive Science, 6*, 205–254.

Fine, K. (1985). *Reasoning with arbitrary objects.* Oxford: Basil Blackwell.

Fischhoff, B. & Beyth-Marom, R. (1983). Hypothesis evaluation from a Bayesian perspective. *Psychological Review, 90*, 239–260.

Fisher, R. A. (1922). On the mathematical foundations of theoretical statistics. *Philosophical Transactions of the Royal Society of London, A 222*, 309–368.

Fisher, R. A. (1956). *Statistical methods and statistical inference.* Edinburgh: Oliver and Boyd.

Fisher, R. A. (1970). *Statistical methods for research workers* (14th Edn). Edinburgh: Oliver and Boyd.

Fodor, J. A. (1968). *Psychological explanation.* New York: Random House.

Fodor, J. A. (1975). *The language of thought.* New York: Thomas Crowell.

Fodor, J. A. (1980). Methodological solipsism considered as a research strategy in cognitive psychology. *Behavioural and Brain Science, 3*, 63–109.

Fodor, J. A. (1981). The present status of the innateness controversy. In J. A. Fodor (Ed.), *Representations* (pp. 257–316). Cambridge, MA: MIT Press.

Fodor, J. A. (1983). *Modularity of mind.* Cambridge MA: MIT Press.

Fodor, J. A. (1987). *Psychosemantics: The problem of meaning in the philosophy of mind.* Cambridge, MA: MIT Press.

Fodor, J. A. (1990). *A theory of content and other essays.* Cambridge, MA: MIT Press.

Fodor, J. A. (1991). You can fool some of the people all of the time, everything else being equal: Hedged laws and psychological explanations. *Mind, 100*, 18–34.

Fodor, J. A., Bever, T. G., & Garrett, M. F. (1974). *The psychology of language.* York: McGraw Hill.

Fodor, J. A., Fodor, J. D., & Garrett, M. F. (1975). The psychological unreality of semantic representations. *Linguistic Inquiry, 6,* 515–531.

Fodor, J. A. & Pylyshyn, Z. W. (1981). How direct is visual perception? Some reflections on Gibson's "Ecological Approach". *Cognition, 9,* 139–196.

Fodor, J. A., & Pylyshyn, Z. W. (1988) Connectionism and cognitive architecture: A critical analysis. *Cognition, 28,* 3–71.

Frege, G. (1879). *Begriffschrift.* Halle, Germany: Nebert.

Frege, G. (1884/1950). *The foundations of arithmetic* [Translated by J. L. Austin]. Oxford: Basil Blackwell.

Furnham, A. (1987). *Lay theories: Everyday understanding of problems in the social sciences.* Oxford: Pergamon Press.

Galotti, K. M. (1989). Approaches to studying formal and everyday reasoning. *Psychological Bulletin, 105,* 331–351.

Garey, M. R. & Johnson, D. S. (1979). *Computers and intractability: A guide to the theory of NP-completeness.* San Francisco: W. H. Freeman.

Garfinkel, H. (1964). Studies in the routine grounds of everyday activities. *Social Problems, 11,* 225–250.

Garnham, A. (1993). Is logicist cognitive science possible? *Mind and Language, 8,* 49–71.

Gentner, D. & Stevens, A. (Eds.) (1983). *Mental models.* Hillsdale, NJ: Lawrence Erlbaum Associates.

Gentzen, G. (1934). Untersuchungen über das logische Schliessen. *Mathematische Zeitschrift, 39,* 176–210.

Gigerenzer, G. (1991). From tools to theories: A heuristic of discovery in cognitive psychology. *Psychological Review, 98,* 254–267.

Gigerenzer, G. (1993). The bounded rationality of probabilistic mental models. In K. I. Manktelow & D. Over (Eds.), *Rationality* (pp. 284–313). London: Routledge.

Gigerenzer, G. & Goldstein, D. G. (1996). Reasoning the fast and frugal way: Models of bounded rationality. *Psychological Review, 103,* 650–669.

Gigerenzer, G., Hell, W., & Blank, H. (1988). Presentation and content: The use of base rates as a continuous variable. *Journal of Experimental Psychology: Human Perception and Performance, 14,* 513–525.

Gigerenzer, G. & Hoffrage, U. (1995). How to improve Bayesian reasoning without instruction: Frequency formats. *Psychological Review, 102,* 684–704.

Gigerenzer, G., Hoffrage, U., & Kleinbölting, H. (1991). Probabilisitic mental models: A Brunswickian theory of confidence. *Psychological Review, 98,* 506–528.

Gigerenzer, G. & Hug, K. (1992). Domain-specific reasoning: social contracts, cheating, and perspective change. *Cognition, 43,* 127–171.

Gigerenzer, G. & Murray, D. J. (1987). *Cognition as intuitive statistics.* Hillsdale, NJ: Lawrence Erlbaum Associates.

Gigerenzer, G., Swijtink, Z., Porter, L., Daston, J., Beatty, J., & Kruger, L. (1989). *The empire of chance: How probability changed science and everyday life.* Cambridge: Cambridge University Press.

Ginsberg, M. L. (Ed.) (1987). *Readings in nonmonotonic reasoning.* Los Altos, CA: Morgan Kaufman.

Girotto, V. (1988). Pragmatic knowledge and deductive reasoning in children. *Giornale Italiano di Psicologia, 15,* 287–314.

Girotto, V., Blaye, A., & Farioli, F. (1989). A reason to reason: Pragmatic basis of children's search for counterexamples. *Cahiers de Psychologie Cognitive, 9,* 297–321.

Girotto, V., Light, P., & Colbourn, C. J. (1988). Pragmatic schemas and conditional reasoning in children. *Quarterly Journal of Experimental Psychology, 40A,* 469–482.

Girotto, V., Mazzocco, A., & Cherubine, P. (1992). Judgements of deontic relevance in reasoning: A reply to Jackson and Griggs. *Quarterly Journal of Experimental Psychology*, *45A*, 547–574.

Glass, G., McGaw, B., & Smith, M. L. (1981). *Meta-analysis in social research*. Beverly Hills, CA: Sage Publications.

Glymour, C. (1980). *Theory and evidence*. Princeton, NJ: Princeton University Press.

Glymour, C. (1987). Android epistemology and the frame problem: Comments on Dennett's "Cognitive Wheels". In Z. W. Pylyshyn (Ed.), *The robot's dilemma: The frame problem in artificial intelligence* (pp. 65–76). Norwood, NJ: Ablex.

Glymour, C. & Cheng, P. (1998). Causal mechanism and probability: A normative approach. In M. Oaksford & N. Chater (Eds.), *Rational models of cognition*. Oxford: Oxford University Press.

Good, I. J. (1950). *Probability and the weighting of evidence*. London: Griffin.

Good, I. J. (1960). Weight of evidence, corroboration, explanatory power, information, and the utility of experiments. *Journal of the Royal Statistical Society, Series B*, *22*, 319–331.

Good, I. J. (1966). A derivation of the probabilistic explication of information. *Journal of the Royal Statistical Society, Series B*, *28*, 578–581.

Goodman, N. (1951). *The structure of appearance*. Cambridge, MA: Harvard University Press.

Goodman, N. (1954/1983). *Fact, fiction and forecast* (4th Edn). Cambridge, MA: Harvard University Press.

Goodwin, R. Q. & Wason, P. C. (1972). Degrees of insight. *British Journal of Psychology*, *63*, 205–212.

Green, D. W. (1995). Externalisation, counter-examples and the abstract selection task. *Quarterly Journal of Experimental Psychology*, *48*, 424–446.

Green, D. W. & Larking, R. (1995). The locus of facilitation in the abstract selection task. *Thinking and Reasoning*, *1*, 183–199.

Green, D. W., Over, D. E., & Pyne, R. A. (1997). Probability and choice in the selection task. *Thinking and Reasoning*, *3*, 209–235.

Gregory, R. L. (1977). *Eye and brain* (3rd Edn). London: Weidenfeld & Nicolson.

Griggs, R. A. (1984). Memory cueing and instructional effects on Wason's selection task. *Current Psychological Research and Reviews*, *3*, 3–10.

Griggs, R. A. & Cox, J. R. (1982). The elusive thematic-materials effect in Wason's selection task. *British Journal of Psychology*, *73*, 407–420.

Griggs, R. A. & Cox, J. R. (1983). The effects of problem content and negation on Wason's selection task. *Quarterly Journal of Experimental Psychology*, *35A*, 519–533.

Haack, S. (1978). *Philosophy of logics*. Cambridge: Cambridge University Press.

Hacking, I. (1975). *The emergence of probability*. Cambridge: Cambridge University Press.

Hacking, I. (1983). *Representing and intervening*. Cambridge: Cambridge University Press.

Hacking, I. (1990). *The taming of chance*. Cambridge: Cambridge University Press.

Hampton, J. A. (1989). *Negating noun concepts*. Paper presented at the Edinburgh Round-Table on the Mental Lexicon: University of Edinburgh, Scotland, June.

Hanks, S. & McDermott, D. (1985). Default reasoning, nonmonotonic logics, and the frame problem. *Proceedings of the American Association for Artificial Intelligence*. Philadelphia, PA.

Hanks, S. & McDermott, D. (1986). *Temporal reasoning and default logics*. Yale University, Computer Science Technical Report, No. 430.

Harman, G. (1965). The inference to the best explanation. *Philosophical Review*, *74*, 88–95.

Harman, G. (1986). *Change in view*. Cambridge, MA: MIT Press.

Harris, P. L. (1975). Development of search and object permanence during infancy. *Psychological Bulletin*, *82*, 332–344.

Harris, P. L. & Nuñez, M. (1996). Understanding of permission rules by pre-school children. *Child Development*, *67*, 1572–1591.

Hayes, P. (1978). The naïve physics manifesto. In D. Michie (Ed.), *Expert systems in the microelectronic age*. Edinburgh, Scotland: Edinburgh University Press.

Hayes, P. (1979). The logic of frames. In D. Metzing (Ed.), *Frame conceptions and text understanding* (pp. 46–61). Berlin: Walter de Gruyter & Co.

Hayes, P. (1984a). The second naïve physics manifesto. In J. Hobbs (Ed.), *Formal theories of the commonsense world*, Hillsdale, NJ: Ablex.

Hayes, P. (1984b). Liquids. In J. Hobbs (Ed.), *Formal theories of the commonsense world*. Hillsdale, NJ: Ablex.

Hempel, C. (1952). *Fundamentals of concept formation in empirical science*. Chicago, IL: University of Chicago Press.

Hempel, C. (1965). *Aspects of scientific explanation and other essays in the philosophy of science*. New York: Free Press.

Henle, M. (1962). On the relation between logic and thinking. *Psychological Review, 69*, 366–378.

Hilbert, D. (1925). Über das unendliche. *Mathematische Annalen, 95*, 161–190.

Hill, B. M. & Hunter, W. G. (1969). A note on designs for model discrimination: Variance unknown case. *Technometrics, 11*, 396–400.

Hintikka, J. (1955). Form and content in quantification theory. *Acta Philosophica Fennica, 8*, 11–55.

Hintikka, J. (1985). *Mental models, semantical games, and varieties of intelligence*. Unpublished manuscript, Department of Philosophy, University of Florida.

Hinton, G. E. (1981). Implementing semantic networks in parallel hardware. In G. E. Hinton & J. A. Anderson (Eds.), *Parallel models of associative memory* (pp. 161–188). Hillsdale, NJ: Lawrence Erlbaum Associates.

Hinton, G. E. (1987). Learning distributed representations of concepts. In *Proceedings of the 8th Annual Conference of the Cognitive Science Society*. Hillsdale, NJ: Lawrence Erlbaum Associates Inc.

Hinton, G. E. (1989). Connectionist learning procedures. *Artificial Intelligence, 40*, 185–234.

Hinton, G. E., McClelland, J. L., & Rumelhart, D. E. (1986). Distributed representations. In D. E. Rumelhart & J. L. McClelland (Eds.), *Parallel distributed processing: Explorations in the microstructures of cognition* (Vol. 1: Foundations, pp. 77–109). Cambridge, MA: MIT Press.

Hinton, G. E. & Sejnowski, T. J. (1986). Learning and relearning in Boltzmann machines. In D. E. Rumelhart & J. L. McClelland (Eds.), *Parallel distributed processing: Explorations in the microstructures of cognition* (Vol. 1: Foundations, pp. 282–317). Cambridge, MA: MIT Press.

Hinton, G. E. & Shallice, T. (1991). Lesioning an attractor network: Investigations of acquired dyslexia. *Psychological Review, 98*, 74–95.

Hoch, S. J. & Tschirgi, J. E. (1985). Logical knowledge and cue redundancy in deductive reasoning. *Memory and Cognition, 13*, 453–462.

Hodges, W. (1975). *Logic*. Harmondsworth, UK: Penguin.

Hoenkamp, E. (1989). "Confirmation bias" in rule discovery and the principle of maximum entropy. In *Proceedings of the 11th Annual Conference of the Cognitive Science Society* (pp. 651–658). Hillsdale, NJ: Lawrence Erlbaum Associates.

Hogger, C. J. (1984). *An introduction to logic programming*. New York: Academic Press.

Holland, J. H., Holyoak, K. J., Nisbett, R. E., & Thagard, P. R. (1986). *Induction: Processes of inference, learning and discovery*. Cambridge, MA: MIT Press.

Holyoak, K. J. & Cheng, P. W. (1995). Pragmatic reasoning with a point of view. *Thinking and Reasoning, 1*, 289–314.

Holyoak, K. J. & Spellman, B. A. (1993). Thinking. *Annual Review of Psychology, 44*, 265–315.

Horowitz, E. & Sahni, S. (1978). *Fundamentals of computer algorithms*. Rockville, MD: Computer Science Press, Inc.

Horwich, P. (1982). *Probability and evidence*. Cambridge: Cambridge University Press.

Howson, C. & Urbach, P. (1989). *Scientific reasoning: The Bayesian approach*. La Salle, IL: Open Court.

Hughes, G. E. & Cresswell, M. J. (1968). *An introduction to modal logic*. London: Methuen & Co. Ltd.

Inhelder, B. & Piaget, J. (1958). *The growth of logical reasoning*. New York: Basic Books.

Israel, D. J. (1980). What's wrong with nonmonotonic logic? In *Proceedings of AAAI-80* (pp. 99–101).

Jackson, S. L. & Griggs, R. A. (1990). The elusive pragmatic reasoning schemas effect. *Quarterly Journal of Experimental Psychology, 42A*, 353–373.

James, W. (1890/1950). *The principles of psychology* (Vol. 1). New York: Dover.

Jaynes, E. T. (1978). Where do we stand on maximum entropy? In R. D. Levine & M. Tribus (Eds.), *The maximum entropy formalism*. Cambridge, MA: MIT Press.

Jaynes, E. T. (1989). *Papers on probability, statistics, and statistical physics* (2nd Edn). North Holland: Kluwer.

Johnson-Laird, P. N. (1975). Models of deduction. In R. J. Falmagne (Ed.), *Reasoning: Representation and process*. Hillsdale, NJ: Erlbaum.

Johnson-Laird, P. N. (1983). *Mental models: Towards a cognitive science of language, inference and consciousness*. Cambridge: Cambridge University Press.

Johnson-Laird, P. N. (1986). Reasoning without logic. In T. Myers, K. Brown, & B. McGonigle (Eds.), *Reasoning and discourse processes* (pp. 13–50). London: Academic Press.

Johnson-Laird, P. N. & Byrne, R. M. J. (1991). *Deduction*. Hove, UK: Lawrence Erlbaum Associates.

Johnson-Laird, P.N. & Byrne, R. M. J. (1992). Modal reasoning, models, and Manktelow and Over. *Cognition, 43*, 173–182.

Johnson-Laird, P. N., Legrenzi, P., & Legrenzi, M. S. (1972). Reasoning and a sense of reality. *British Journal of Psychology, 63*, 395–400.

Johnson-Laird, P. N. & Steedman, M. J. (1978). The psychology of syllogisms. *Cognitive Psychology, 10*, 64–99.

Johnson-Laird, P. N. & Tagart, J. (1969). How implication is understood. *American Journal of Psychology, 82*, 367–373.

Johnson-Laird, P. N. & Wason, P. C. (1970a). A theoretical analysis of insight into a reasoning task. *Cognitive Psychology, 1*, 134–148.

Johnson-Laird, P. N. & Wason, P. C. (1970b). Insight into a logical relation. *Quarterly Journal of Experimental Psychology, 22*, 49–61.

Jordan, M. I. (1986). *Serial order: A parallel distributed approach*. Institute for Cognitive Science Report 8604, University of California, San Diego.

Kacelnik, A. (1998). Normative and descriptive models of decision making: Time discounting and risk sensitivity. In M. Oaksford & N. Chater (Eds.), *Rational models of cognition*. Oxford: Oxford University Press.

Kahneman, D., Slovic, P., & Tversky, A. (Eds.) (1982). *Judgement under uncertainty: Heuristics and biases*. Cambridge: Cambridge University Press.

Kahneman, D. & Tversky, A. (1972). Subjective probability: A judgement of representativeness. *Cognitive Psychology, 3*, 430–454.

Kahneman, D. & Tversky, A. (1973). On the psychology of prediction. *Psychological Review, 80*, 237–251.

Kahneman, D. & Tversky, A. (1979). Prospect theory: An analysis of decision under risk. *Econometrica, 47*, 263–291.

Kaiser, M. K, McCloskey, M., & Proffitt, D. R. (1986). Development of intuitive theories of motion: Curvilinear motion in the absence of external forces. *Developmental Psychology, 22,* 67–71.

Karmiloff-Smith, A. (1988). The child is a theoretician, not an inductivist. *Mind and Language, 1,* 183–196.

Kelley, H. H. (1967). Attribution theory in social psychology. In D. Levine (Ed.), *Nebraska symposium on motivation* (Vol. 1, pp. 192–238). Lincoln: University of Nebraska Press.

Keynes, J. M. (1921). *A treatise on probability.* London: Macmillan.

Kirby, K. N. (1994a). Probabilities and utilities of fictional outcomes in Wason's four-card selection task. *Cognition, 51,* 1–28.

Kirby, K. N. (1994b). False alarm: A reply to Over and Evans. *Cognition, 52,* 245–250.

Kitcher, P. (1984). In defense of intentional psychology. *Journal of Philosophy, 81,* 89–106.

Klayman, J. & Ha, Y. (1987). Confirmation, disconfirmation and information in hypothesis testing. *Psychological Review, 94,* 211–228.

Klayman, J. & Ha, Y. (1989). Hypothesis testing in rule discovery: Strategy, structure, and content. *Journal of Experimental Psychology: Learning, Memory and Cognition, 15,* 596–604.

Kosslyn, S. M. & Hatfield, G. (1984). Representation without symbol systems. *Social Research, 51,* 1019–1054.

Kripke, S. (1963). Semantical considerations on modal logic. *Acta Philosophica Fennica, 16,* 83–94.

Kripke, S. (1972). *Naming and necessity.* Oxford: Basil Blackwell.

Kuhn, D. (1989). Children and adults as intuitive scientists. *Psychological Review, 96,* 674–689.

Kuhn, T. (1962). *The structure of scientific revolutions.* Chicago: University of Chicago Press.

Kuhn, T. (1970). *The structure of scientific revolutions* (2nd Edn). Chicago, IL: University of Chicago Press.

Kullback, S. & Liebler, R. A. (1951). Information and sufficiency. *Annals of Mathematical Statistics, 22,* 79–86.

Laird, J., Rosenbloom, P., & Newell, A. (1986). *Universal subgoaling and chunking: The automatic generation and learning of goal hierarchies.* Boston: Kluwer Academic Publisher.

Lakatos, I. (1970). Falsification and the methodology of scientific research programmes. In I. Lakatos & A. Musgrave (Eds.), *Criticism and the growth of knowledge* (pp. 91–196). Cambridge: Cambridge University Press.

Lakatos, I. (1976). *Proofs and refutations: The logic of mathematical discovery.* Cambridge: Cambridge University Press.

Lakatos, I. (1977a). *Philosophical Papers, Volume 1: The methodology of scientific research programmes.* Cambridge: Cambridge University Press.

Lakatos, I. (1977b). *Philosophical Papers, Volume 2: Mathematics, science and epistemology.* Cambridge: Cambridge University Press.

Laming, D. (1996). On the analysis of irrational data selection: A critique of Oaksford and Chater (1994). *Psychological Review, 103,* 364–373.

Leslie, A.M. (1987). Pretense and representation in infancy: The origins of "theory of mind." *Psychological Review, 94,* 412–426.

Levesque, H. J. & Brachman, R. J. (1985). A fundamental tradeoff in knowledge representation and reasoning (Revised version). In R. J. Brachman & H. J. Levesque (Eds.), *Readings in knowledge representation* (pp. 41–70). Los Altos, CA: Morgan Kaufman.

Levesque, H. J. (1988). Logic and the complexity of reasoning. *Journal of Philosophical Logic, 17,* 355–389.

Levinson, S. (1983). *Pragmatics.* Cambridge: Cambridge University Press.

Lewis, C. I. (1918). *A survery of symbolic logic.* Berkeley, CA: California University Press.

Lewis, D. (1973). *Counterfactuals.* Oxford, Oxford University Press.

Lewis, D. (1976). Probabilities of conditionals and conditional probabilities. *Philosophical Review, 85,* 297–315.

Li, M. & Vitányi, P. (1997). *An introduction to Kolmogorov complexity and its applications* (2nd Edn). New York: Springer-Verlag.

Light, P., Blaye, A., Gilly, M., & Girotto, V. (1989). Pragmatic schemas and logical reasoning in 6- to 8-year old children. *Cognitive Development, 4,* 49–64.

Lindley, D. V. (1956). On a measure of the information provided by an experiment. *Annals of Mathematical Statistics, 27,* 986–1005.

Lindley, D. V. (1971). *Bayesian statistics: A review.* Philadelphia, PA: Society for Industrial and Applied Mathematics.

Lindley, D. V. (1982). Scoring rules and the inevitability of probability. *International Statistical Review, 50,* 1–26.

Lindsay, P. H., & Norman, D. A. (1977). *Human Information Processing* (2nd Edn). New York: Academic Press.

Lloyd, D. E. (1989). *Simple Minds.* Cambridge, MA: MIT Press.

Lopes, L. L. (1981). Decision making in the short run. *Journal of Experimental Psychology: Human Learning and Memory, 8,* 1–26.

Lopes, L. L. (1991). The rhetoric of irrationality. *Theory and Psychology, 1,* 65–82.

Lopes, L. L. (1992). Three misleading assumptions in the customary rhetoric of the bias literature. *Theory and Psychology, 2,* 231–236.

Lorayne, H. & Lucas, J. (1974). *The memory book.* New York: Stein and Day.

Loui, R. P. (1986). *Defeat among arguments: A system of defeasible inference.* Technical Report No. 190, Department of Computer Science, Rochester University.

Loui, R. P. (1987). Response to Hanks and McDermott: Temporal evolution of beliefs and beliefs about temporal evolution. *Cognitive Science, 11,* 283–297.

Lucas, J. R. (1970). *The concept of probability.* Oxford: Oxford University Press.

Luttrell, S. P. (1985). The use of transformations in data sampling schemes for inverse problems. *Inverse Problems, 1,* 199–218.

Luttrell, S. P. (1989). Self-oganisation: a derivation from first principles of a class of learning algorithms. In *Proceedings of 3rd IEEE International Joint Conference on Neural Networks* (pp. 495–498). Piscatairay, NJ: IEEE Service Center.

Luttrell, S. P. (1990). Derivation of a class of training algorithms. *IEEE Transactions on Neural Networks, 1,* 229–32.

Luttrell, S. P. (1994). A Bayesian analysis of self-organising maps. *Neural Computation, 6,* 767–794.

Lyon, K. & Chater, N. (1990). Localist and globalist theories of concepts. In K. J. Gilhooly, M. Keane, R. Logie & G. Erdos (Eds.), *Lines of thought.* Chichester: Wiley.

Mabbott, J. D. (1929). Negation. *Proceedings of the Aristotelian Society* (Supplementary), *9,* 67–79.

MacDonald, M. C. & Just, M. A. (1989). Changes of activation levels with negation. *Journal of Experimental Psychology: Learning, Memory and Cognition, 15,* 633–642.

MacFarland, D. (1977). Decision making in animals. *Nature, 269,* 15–21.

MacFarland, D. & Houston, A. (1981). *Quantitative ethology: The state–space approach.* London: Pitman Books.

MacKay, D. J. C. (1992a). Information-based objective functions for active data selection. *Neural Computation, 4,* 590–604.

MacKay, D. J. C. (1992b). A practical Bayesian framework for backpropagation networks. *Neural Computation, 4,* 448–472.

MacKay, D. J. C. (1992c). The evidence framework applied to classification networks. *Neural Computation, 4,* 698–714.

Mackie, J. L. (1963). The paradox of confirmation. *British Journal for the Philosophy of Science, 38*, 265–277.

Manktelow, K. I. & Evans, J. St. B. T. (1979). Facilitation of reasoning by realism: Effect or non-effect. *British Journal of Psychology, 70*, 477–488.

Manktelow, K. I. & Over, D. E. (1987). Reasoning and rationality. *Mind and Language, 2*, 199–219.

Manktelow, K. I. & Over, D. E. (1990a). Deontic thought and the selection task. In K. J. Gilhooly, M. T. Keane, R. H. Logie, & G. Erdos (Eds.), *Lines of thinking* (Vol. 1). Chichester, UK: Wiley.

Manktelow, K. I. & Over, D. E. (1990b). *Inference and understanding.* London: Routledge.

Manktelow, K. I. & Over, D. E. (1991). Social roles and utilities in reasoning with deontic conditionals. *Cognition, 39*, 85–105.

Manktelow, K. I. & Over, D. E. (1992). Utility and deontic reasoning: Some comments on Johnson-Laird and Byrne. *Cognition, 43*, 183–188.

Manktelow, K. I. & Over, D. E. (1993). *Rationality: Psychological and philosophical perspectives.* London: Routledge.

Manktelow, K. I. & Over, D. E. (1995). Deontic Reasoning. In S. E. Newstead & J. St. B.T. Evans (Eds.), *Perspectives on thinking and reasoning.* Hillsdale, NJ: Lawrence Erlbaum Associates.

Markovits, H. (1984). Awareness of the "possible" as a mediator of formal thinking in conditional reasoning problems. *British Journal of Psychology, 75*, 367–376.

Markovits, H. (1985). Incorrect conditional reasoning among adults: Competence or performance. *British Journal of Psychology, 76*, 241–247.

Marr, D. (1982). *Vision.* San Francisco: W. H. Freeman & Co.

Masterman, M. (1970). The nature of a paradigm. In I. Lakatos & A. Musgrave (Eds.), *Criticism and the growth of knowledge* (pp. 59–90). Cambridge: Cambridge University Press.

McArthur, D. J. (1982). Computer vision and perceptual psychology. *Psychological Bulletin, 92*, 283–309.

McArthur, L. Z. (1972). The how and what of why: Some determinants and consequences of causal attribution. *Journal of Personality and Social Psychology, 22*, 171–193.

McCarthy, J. (1977). Epistemological problems in artificial intelligence. In *Proceedings of the International Joint Conference on Artificial Intelligence* (pp. 1038–1044), Cambridge, MA.

McCarthy, J. (1980). Circumscription: a form of non-monotonic reasoning. *Artificial Intelligence, 13*, 27–39.

McCarthy, J. M. & Hayes, P. (1969). Some philosophical problems from the standpoint of artificial intelligence. In B. Meltzer & D. Michie (Eds.), *Machine intelligence* (Vol. 4, pp. 463–502). Edinburgh: Edinburgh University Press.

McClelland, J. L. (1998). Connectionist models and Bayesian inference. In M. Oaksford & N. Chater (Eds.), *Rational models of cognition.* Oxford: Oxford University Press.

McClelland, J. & Elman, J. (1986). Interactive processes in speech perception: The TRACE model. In J. L. McClelland & D. E. Rumelhart (Eds.), *Parallel distributed processing: Explorations in the microstructures of cognition* (Vol. 2: Psychological and biological models, pp. 58–121). Cambridge, MA: MIT Press.

McClelland, J. L., & Rumelhart, D. E. (Eds.) (1986). *Parallel distributed processing: Explorations in the microstructures of cognition* (Vol. 2: Psychological and biological models). Cambridge, MA: MIT Press.

McClelland, J. L., Rumelhart, D. E., & Hinton, G. E. (1986). The appeal of parallel distributed processing. In D. E. Rumelhart & J. L. McClelland (Eds.), *Parallel distributed processing: Explorations in the microstructures of cognition* (Vol. 1: Foundations, pp. 3–44). Cambridge, MA: MIT Press.

McCloskey, M. (1983). Intuitive physics. *Scientific American, 24*, 122–130.

McDermott, D. (1982). Non-monotonic logic II: Non-monotonic modal theories. *JACM, 29*(1), 33–57.

McDermott, D. (1986). *A critique of pure reason*. Technical Report, Department of Computer science, Yale University, June 1986.

McDermott, D. (1987). A critique of pure reason. *Computational Intelligence, 3*, 151–160.

McDermott, D. & Doyle, J. (1980). Non-monotonic logic I. *Artificial Intelligence, 13*, 41–72.

Medin, D. L. & Schaffer, M. M. (1978). Context theory of classification learning. *Psychological Review, 85*, 207–238.

Medin, D. L. & Wattenmaker, W. D. (1987). Category cohesiveness, theories and cognitive archaelogy. In U. Neisser (Ed.), *Concepts and conceptual development: Ecological and intellectual factors in categorization* (pp. 25–62). Cambridge: Cambridge University Press.

Mellor, D. H. (1971). *The matter of chance*. Cambridge: Cambridge University Press.

Meulen, A. ter (1986). Generic information, conditional contexts and constraints. In E. C. Traugott, A. ter Meulen, J. Snitzer Reilly, & C. A. Ferguson (Eds.), *On conditionals* (pp. 123–146). Cambridge: Cambridge University Press.

Miller, G. A. (1956). The magical number seven plus or minus two, or, some limits on our capacity for processing information. *Psychological Review, 63*, 81–96.

Miller, G. A. & Selfridge, J. A. (1950). Verbal context and the recall of meaningful material. *American Journal of Psychology, 63*, 176–185.

Millikan, R. G. (1986). Thought without laws: Cognitive science without content. *Philosophical Review, 95*, 289–316.

Minsky, M. (1975/1977). Frame system theory. In P. N. Johnson-Laird & P. C. Wason (Eds.), *Thinking: Readings in cognitive science* (pp. 355–376). Cambridge: Cambridge University Press.

Minsky, M. & Papert, S. (1969). *Perceptrons: An introduction to computational geometry*. Cambridge, MA: MIT Press.

Minsky, M. & Papert, S. (1988). *Perceptrons: An introduction to computational geometry* (2nd Edn). Cambridge, MA: MIT Press.

Moshman, D. (1978). Some comments on Bree and Coppens' "The difficulty of an implication task." *British Journal of Psychology, 69*, 371–372.

Murphy, G.L. & Medin D.L. (1985). The role of theories in conceptual coherence. *Psychological Review, 92*, 289–316.

Mynatt, C. R., Doherty, M. E., & Tweney, R. D. (1977). Confirmation bias in a simulated research environment: An experimental study of scientific inference. *Quarterly Journal of Experimental Psychology, 29*, 85–95.

Neal, R. M. (1992). Asymmetric parallel Boltzmann machines are belief networks. *Neural Computation, 4*, 832–834.

Neal, R. M. (1992). *Bayesian training of backpropagation networks by the hybrid Monte Carlo method*. Department of Computer Science, University of Toronto, Technical Report CRG-TR-92-1.

Neal, R. M. (1993). Bayesian learning via stochastic dynamics. In S. J. Hanson, J. D. Cowan, & C. Lee Giles (Eds.), *Advances in neural information processing systems 5* (pp. 475–482). San Mateo, CA: Morgan Kaufman.

Newell, A. (1969). Heuristic programming: Ill-structured problems. In *Progress in operations research* (Vol. 3). New York: John Wiley and Sons.

Newell, A. (1990). *Unified theories of cognition*. Cambridge, MA: Harvard University Press.

Newell, A. & Simon, H.A. (1972). *Human problem solving*. Englewood Cliffs, NJ: Prentice-Hall.

Newell, A. & Simon, H. A. (1976). Computer science as empirical enquiry. *Communications of the ACM, 19*, 113–26. [Reprinted in M. Boden (Ed.), *The philosophy of artificial intelligence*. Oxford: Oxford University Press, 1990.]

Neyman, J. (1950). *Probability and statistics*. New York: Holt.

Neyman, J. & Pearson, E. S. (1928). On the use of interpretation of certain test criteria for purposes of statistical inference. *Biometrika*, *20*, 175–240 (Part I); 263–294 (Part II).

Nisbett, R.C. & Ross, L. (1980). *Human inference: Strategies and shortcomings of social judgement*. Englewood Cliffs, NJ: Prentice-Hall.

Norman, D. A. & Bobrow, D. G. (1975). On data-limited and resource limited processes. *Cognitive Psychology*, *7*, 44–64.

Norman, D. A. & Bobrow, D. G. (1976). On the role of active memory processes in perception and cognition. In C. N. Cofer (Ed.), *The structure of human memory*. San Francisco: Freeman.

Norman, D. A. & Bobrow, D. G. (1979). Descriptions: An intermediate stage in memory retrieval. *Cognitive Psychology*, *11*, 107–123.

Nosofsky, R. M. (1984). Choice, similarity and the context theory of classification. *Journal of Experimental Psychology: Learning, Memory and Cognition*, *10*, 104–114.

Nosofsky, R. M. (1986) Attention, similarity and the identification–categorisation relationship. *Journal of Experimental Psychology: General*, *115*, 39–57.

Nosofsky, R. M. (1990). Relations between exemplar-similarity and likelihood models of classification. *Journal of Mathematical Psychology*, *34*, 393–418.

Nute, D. (1985). *A non-monotonic logic based on conditional logic*. Working Paper, Advanced Computational Methods Centre, University of Georgia, Athens, GA.

Nute, D. (1986). *A logic for defeasible reasoning*. Research Report No. 01-0013, Advanced Computational Methods Centre, University of Georgia, Athens, GA.

Oaksford, M. (1989). *Cognition and inquiry: The pragmatics of conditional reasoning*. Unpublished PhD Thesis, Centre for Cognitive Science, University of Edinburgh, January, 1989.

Oaksford, M. (1993). Mental models and the tractability of everyday reasoning. *Behavioral and Brain Sciences*, *16*, 360–361.

Oaksford, M. (1997). Thinking and the rational analysis of human reasoning. *The Psychologist*, *10*, 257–260.

Oaksford, M. (1998). Task demands and revising probabilities in the selection task: A commentary on Green, Over and Pyne. *Thinking and Reasoning*.

Oaksford, M. & Brown, G. D. A. (Eds.) (1994). *Neurodynamics and psychology*. London: Academic Press.

Oaksford, M. & Chater, N. (1991). Against logicist cognitive science. *Mind and Language*, *6*, 1–38.

Oaksford, M. & Chater, N. (1992). Bounded rationality in taking risks and drawing inferences. *Theory and Psychology*, *2*, 225–230.

Oaksford, M. & Chater, N. (1993). Reasoning theories and bounded rationality. In K. I. Manktelow & D. E. Over (Eds.), *Rationality*, (pp. 31–60). London: Routledge.

Oaksford, M. & Chater, N. (1994a). A rational analysis of the selection task as optimal data selection. *Psychological Review*, *101*, 608–631.

Oaksford, M. & Chater, N. (1994b). Another look at eliminative and enumerative behaviour in a conceptual task. *European Journal of Cognitive Psychology*, *6*, 149–169.

Oaksford, M. & Chater, N. (1995a). Two and three stage models of deontic reasoning. *Thinking and Reasoning*, *1*, 350–356.

Oaksford, M. & Chater, N. (1995b). Theories of reasoning and the computational explanation of everyday inference. *Thinking and Reasoning*, *1*, 121–152.

Oaksford, M. & Chater, N. (1995c). Information gain explains relevance which explains the selection task. *Cognition*, *57*, 97–108.

Oaksford, M. & Chater, N. (1996). Rational explanation of the selection task. *Psychological Review*, *103*, 381–391.

Oaksford, M. & Chater, N. (Eds.) (1998a). *Rational models of cognition*. Oxford: Oxford University Press.

Oaksford, M. & Chater, N. (1998b). A revised rational analysis of the selection task: Exceptions and sequential sampling. In M. Oaksford & N. Chater (Eds.), *Rational models of cognition*. Oxford: Oxford University Press.

Oaksford, M., Chater, N., & Grainger, B. (1997). *Contrast sets and probability effects in the four card selection task*. Unpublished manuscript, School of Psychology, University of Wales, Cardiff.

Oaksford, M., Chater, N., Grainger, B., & Larkin, J. (1997). Optimal data selection in the reduced array selection task (RAST). *Journal of Experimental Psychology: Learning, Memory and Cognition, 23*, 441–458.

Oaksford, M., Chater, N., & Larkin, J. (1997). *Contrast sets and conditional inference: A probabilistic model*. Unpublished manuscript, School of Psychology, University of Wales, Cardiff.

Oaksford, M., Chater, N., & Stenning, K. (1990). Connectionism, classical cognitive science and experimental psychology. *AI and Society, 4*, 73–90. [Also in A. Clark & R. Lutz (Eds.) (1992), *Connectionism in context* (pp. 57–74). Berlin: Springer-Verlag.]

Oaksford, M. & Stenning, K. (1988). *Process and pragmatics in reasoning with conditionals containing negated constituents*. Paper presented at the International Conference on Thinking, University of Aberdeen, August.

Oaksford, M. & Stenning, K. (1992). Reasoning with conditionals containing negated constituents. *Journal of Experimental Psychology: Learning, Memory & Cognition, 18*, 835–854.

O'Brien, D. P. (1993). Mental logic and human irrationality. In K. I. Manktelow & D. E. Over (Eds.), *Rationality* (pp. 110–135). London: Routledge.

Ormerod, T. C., Manktelow, K. I., & Jones, G. V. (1993). Reasoning with three types of conditional: Biases and mental models. *Quarterly Journal of Experimental Psychology, 46A*, 653–677.

Osherson, D. (1975). Logic and models of logical thinking. In R. J. Falmagne, (Ed.), *Reasoning: Representation and process*. Hillsdale, NJ: Erlbaum.

Osherson, D., Shafir, E., & Smith, E. E. (1993). Ampliative inference: On choosing a probability distribution. *Cognition, 49*, 189–210.

Over, D. E., & Evans, J. St. B. T. (1994). Hits and misses: Kirby on the selection task. *Cognition, 52*, 235–243.

Over, D.E. & Jessop, A. (1998). Rational analysis of causal conditionals and the selection task. In M. Oaksford & N. Chater (Eds.), *Rational models of cognition*. Oxford: Oxford University Press.

Paris, J. (1992). *The uncertain reasoner's companion*. Cambridge: Cambridge University Press.

Pearl, J. (1988). *Probabilistic reasoning in intelligent systems: Networks of plausible inference*. San Mateo, CA: Morgan Kaufman.

Peirce, C. S. (1931–58). *Collected Papers*. 8 vols. C. Hartshorne, P. Weiss, & A. Burks (Eds.). Cambridge, MA: Harvard University Press.

Perner, J. (1991). *Understanding the representational mind*. Cambridge, MA: MIT Press.

Piaget, J. (1932). *The moral judgment of the child*. Glencoe, IL: Free Press.

Piaget, J. (1953). *Logic and psychology*. Manchester: University of Manchester Press.

Pineda, F. J. (1987). *Recurrent backpropagation*. Technical Report No. S1A-63-87, Applied Physics Laboratory, Johns Hopkins University, July 1987.

Pinker, S. (1984). *Language learnability and language development*. Cambridge, MA: Harvard University Press.

Pinker, S. (1984). *The language instinct*. Harmondsworth, UK: Penguin.

Pinker, S. & Prince, A. (1988). On language and connectionism: Analysis of a parallel distributed model of language acquisition. *Cognition, 28*, 73–193.

Place, U. T. (1992). The role of the ethnomethodological experiment in the empirical investigation of social norms and its application to conceptual anlaysis. *Philosophy of the Social Sciences, 22*, 461–474.

Plantinga, A. (1974). *The nature of necessity*. Oxford: Oxford University Press.

Platt, J. R. (1964). Strong inference. *Science, 146*, 347–353.

Platt, R. D. & Griggs, R. A. (1993). Facilitation in the abstract selection task: The effects of attentional and instructional factors. *Quarterly Journal of Experimental Psychology, 46*, 591–613.

Platt, R. D. & Griggs, R. A. (1995). Facilitation and matching bias in the abstract selection task. *Thinking and Reasoning, 1*, 55–70.

Politzer, G. & Braine, M. D. S. (1991). Responses to inconsistent premises cannot count as suppression of valid inferences. *Cognition, 38*, 103–108.

Pollard, P. (1985). Nonindependence of selections on the Wason selection task. *Bulletin of the Psychonomic Society, 23*, 317–320.

Pollard, P. & Evans, J. St. B. T. (1981). The effects of prior belief in reasoning; an associational interpretation. *British Journal of Psychology, 72*, 73–82.

Pollard, P. & Evans, J. St. B. T. (1983). The effect of experimentally contrived experience on reasoning performance. *Psychological Research, 45*, 287–301.

Poole, D. (1985). On the comparison of theories: Preferring the most specific explanation. In *Proceedings of the International Joint Conference on Artificial Intelligence*, Los Angeles, CA.

Popper, K. R. (1959). *The logic of scientific discovery*. London: Hutchinson.

Potter, J. & Wethrall, M. (1987). *Disourse and social psychology: Beyond attitudes and behaviour*. London: Sage.

Prince, A. & Pinker, S. (1988). On language and connectionism: Analysis of a parallel distributed processing model of language acquisition. *Cognition, 28*, 73–193.

Putnam, H. (1974). The "corrobation" of theories. In P. A. Schilpp (Ed.), *The philosophy of Karl Popper* (Vol. I, pp. 221–240). La Salle, IL: Open Court.

Putnam, H. (1962/1975). The analytic and the synthetic. In H. Putnam (Ed.), *Mind, language and reality* (Philosophical Papers, Vol. 2, pp. 33–69). Cambridge: Cambridge University Press.

Putnam, H. (1975). The meaning of "meaning." In H. Putnam (Ed.), *Mind, language and reality* (Philosophical Papers, Vol. 2, pp. 215–271). Cambridge: Cambridge University Press.

Putnam, H. (1981). *Reason, truth and history*. Cambridge: Cambridge University Press.

Pylyshyn, Z. W. (1973). What the mind's eye tells the mind's brain: A critique of mental imagery. *Psychological Bulletin, 80*, 1–24.

Pylyshyn, Z. W. (1980). Cognition and computation issues in the foundations of cognitive science. *Behavioral and Brain Sciences, 3*, 111–132.

Pylyshyn, Z. W. (1981). Complexity and the study of artificial and human intelligence. In J. Haugeland (Ed.), *Mind design* (pp. 67–94). Montgomery, VT: Bradford.

Pylyshyn, Z. W. (1984). *Computation and cognition: Toward a foundation for cognitive science*. Montgomery, VT: Bradford.

Pylyshyn, Z. W. (Ed.) (1987). *The robot's dilemma: The frame problem in artificial intelligence*. Norwood, NJ: Ablex.

Quine, W. V. O. (1953). Two dogmas of empiricism. In *From a logical point of view* (pp. 20–46). Cambridge, MA: Harvard University Press.

Quine, W. V. O. (1959). *Methods of logic*. New York: Holt, Rinehart & Winston.

Quine, W. V. O. (1960). *Word and object*. Cambridge, MA: MIT Press.

Quine, W. V. O. (1969). Epistemology naturalized. In *Ontological relativity and other essays* (pp. 69–90). New York: Columbia University Press.

Quine, W. V. O. (1990). *Pursuit of truth*. Cambridge, MA: MIT Press.

Ramsey, F. P. (1931a). *The foundations of mathematics and other logical essays*. London: Routledge and Kegan Paul.

Ramsey, F.P. (1931b). Truth and probability. In R. B. Braithwaite (Ed.), *Foundations of mathematics and other logical essays*. London: Routledge and Kegan Paul.

Reber, A. S. (1989). Implicit learning and tacit knowledge. *Journal of Experimental Psychology: General, 118*, 219–235.

Reich, S. S. & Ruth, P. (1982). Wason's selection task: Verification, falsification and matching. *British Journal of Psychology, 73*, 395–405.

Reiter, R. (1980). A logic for default reasoning. *Artificial Intelligence, 13*, 81–132.

Reiter, R. (1978/1985). On reasoning by default. In R. Brachman & H. Levesque (Eds.), *Readings in knowledge representation.* Los Altos, CA: Morgan Kaufman.

Rescorla, R. A. & Wagner, A. R. (1972). A theory of Pavlovian conditioning: Variations in the effectiveness of reinforcement and nonreinforcement. In A. H. Black & W. F. Prokasy (Eds.), *Classical conditioning II: Current theory and research* (pp. 64–99). New York: Appleton-Century-Crofts.

Rips, L. J. (1983). Cognitive processes in propositional reasoning. *Psychological Review, 90*, 38–71.

Rips, L. J. (1990). Reasoning. *Annual Review of Psychology, 41*, 321–353.

Rips. L. J. (1994). *The psychology of proof.* Cambridge, MA: MIT Press.

Rissanen, J. (1983). A universal prior for integers and estimation by minimal description length. *Annals of Statistics, 11*, 416–431.

Rissanen, J. (1987). Stochastic complexity. *Journal of the Royal Statistical Society, Series B, 49*, 223–239.

Rissanen, J. (1989). *Stochastic complexity in statistics inquiry.* Singapore: World Scientific.

Rohwer, R. (1990). The "moving targets" training algorithm. In L. B. Almeida & C. J. Wellekens (Eds.), *Lecture notes in computer science 412: Neural networks* (pp. 100–109). Berlin: Springer-Verlag.

Rosch, E. (1973). On the internal structure of perceptual and semantic categories. In T. Moore (Ed.), *Cognitive development and the acquisition of language.* New York: Academic Press.

Rosch, E. (1975). Cognitive representation of semantic categories. *Journal of Experimental Psychology: General, 104*, 192–233.

Rosenkrantz, R. D. (1981). *Foundations and applications of inductive probability.* Atascadero, CA: Ridgeview.

Rumain, B., Connell, J., & Braine, M. D. S. (1983). Conversational comprehension processes are responsible for reasoning fallacies in children as well as adults: IF is not the Biconditional. *Developmental Psychology, 19*, 471–481.

Rumelhart, D. E. (1980). Schemata: The building blocks of cognition. In R. J. Spiro, B. C. Bruce, & W. F. Brewer (Eds.), *Theoretical issues in reading comprehension,* Hillsdale, NJ: Lawrence Erlbaum Associates.

Rumelhart, D. E. (1989). Toward a microstructural account of human reasoning. In S. Vosnaidou & A. Ortony (Eds.), *Similarity and analogical reasoning* (pp. 298–312). Cambridge: Cambridge University Press.

Rumelhart, D. E., Hinton, G. E., & Williams, R. J. (1986). Learning internal representations by error propagation. In D. E. Rumelhart & J. L. McClelland (Eds.), *Parallel distributed processing: Explorations in the microstructures of cognition* (Vol. 1: Foundations, pp. 318–362). Cambridge, MA: MIT Press.

Rumelhart, D. E. & McClelland, J. L. (Eds.) (1986). *Parallel distributed processing: Explorations in the microstructures of cognition* (Vol. 1: Foundations). Cambridge, MA: MIT Press.

Rumelhart, D. E. & McClelland, J. L. (1986). PDP Models and general issues in cognitive science. In D. E. Rumelhart & J. L. McClelland (Eds.), *Parallel distributed processing: Explorations in the microstructures of cognition* (Vol. 1: Foundations, pp. 110–146). Cambridge, MA: MIT Press.

Rumelhart, D. E. & McClelland, J. L. (1986). On learning the past tenses of English verbs. In J. L. McClelland & D. E. Rumelhart (Eds.), *Parallel distributed processing: Explorations in the microstructures of cognition* (Vol. 2: Psychological and biological models, pp. 216–271). Cambridge, MA: MIT Press.

Rumelhart, D. E., Smolensky, P., McClelland, J. L., & Hinton, G. E. (1986). Schemata and sequential thought processes in PDP models. In J. L. McClelland & D. E. Rumelhart (Eds.), *Parallel distributed processing: Explorations in the microstructures of cognition* (Vol. 2: Psychological and biological models, pp. 7–57). Cambridge, MA: MIT Press.

Rumelhart, D. E. & Zipser, D. (1986). Feature discovery by competitive learning. In D. E. Rumelhart & J. L. McClelland (Eds.), *Parallel distributed processing: Explorations in the microstructures of cognition* (Vol. 1: Foundations, pp. 151–193). Cambridge, MA: MIT Press.

Russell, B. (1919). *Introduction to mathematical philosophy.* New York: Macmillan.

Russell, B. (1946). *History of western philosophy.* London: Macmillan.

Ryle, G. (1929). Negation. *Proceedings of the Aristotelian Society,* (Supplementary), *9,* 80–86.

Savage, L. J. (1954). *The foundations of statistics.* New York: John Wiley.

Schacter, D. L. (1987). Implicit memory: History and current status. *Journal of Experimental Psychology: Learning, Memory and Cognition, 13,* 501–518.

Schiffer, S. (1987). *Remnants of meaning.* Cambridge, MA: MIT Press.

Schiffer, S. (1991). Ceteris paribus laws. *Mind, 100,* 1–17.

Schustack, M.W. & Sternberg, R. J. (1981). Evaluation of evidence in causal inference. *Journal of Experimental Psychology: General, 110,* 101–120.

Scott, D. (1971). On engendering an illusion of understanding. *Journal of Philosophy, 68,* 787–807.

Shallice, T (1988). *From neuropsychology to mental structure.* Cambridge: Cambridge University Press.

Shanks, D. R. (1995). Is human learning rational? *Quarterly Journal of Experimental Psychology, 48A,* 257–279.

Shastri, L. & Ajjanagadde, V. (1993). From simple associations to systematic reasoning: A connectionist representation of rules, variables, and dynamics bindings using temporal synchrony, *Behavioural and Brain Sciences, 16,* 417–494.

Shastri, L. (1985). *Evidential reasoning in semantic networks: A formal theory and its parallel implementation.* TR166, Department of Computer Science, University of Rochester, September 1985.

Shepard, R. N. (1967). Recognition memory for words, sentences and pictures. *Journal of Verbal Learning and Verbal Behavior, 6,* 156–163.

Shoam, Y. (1986). Chronological ignorance: Time, non-monotonicity, necessity and causal theories. In *Proceedings of the Association of Artificial Intelligence,* Philadelphia, PA.

Shoam, Y. (1987). *Reasoning about change,* Boston, MA: MIT Press.

Shoam, Y. (1988). Efficient reasoning about rich temporal domains, *Journal of Philosophical Logic, 17,* 443–474.

Siegel, S. & Castellan Jr., N.J. (1988). *Non-parametric statistics for the behavioural sciences.* New York: McGraw Hill.

Simon, H. A. (1955). A behavioral model of rational choice. *Quarterly Journal of Economics, 69,* 99–118.

Simon, H. A. (1956). Rational choice and the structure of the environment. *Psychological Review, 63,* 129–138.

Simon, H. A. (1959). Theories of decision making in economics and behavioural science. *American Economic Review, 49,* 252–283.

Simon, H. A. (1969). *The sciences of the artificial.* Cambridge, MA: MIT Press.

Skilling, J. (Ed.) (1989). *Maximum entropy and Bayesian methods.* North Holland: Kluwer.

Skinner, B. F. (1957). *Verbal behavior.* New York: Appleton-Century-Crofts.

Skyrms, B. (1977). *Choice and chance.* Belmont: Wadsworth.

Smalley, N. S. (1974). Evaluating a rule against possible instances. *British Journal of Psychology*, *65*, 293–304.

Smedslund, J. (1970). On the circular relation between logic and understanding. *Scandinavian Journal of Psychology*, *11*, 217–19.

Smolensky, P. (1987). *On variable binding and the representation of symbolic structures in connectionist systems*. Department of Computer Science, University of Colorado at Boulder, Technical Report CU-CS-355-87.

Smolensky, P. (1990). Tensor product variable binding and the representation of symbolic structures in connectionist systems. *Artificial Intelligence*, *46*, 159–216.

Sperber, D., Cara, F., & Girotto, V. (1995). Relevance theory explains the selection task. *Cognition*, *57*, 31–95.

Sperber, D. & Wilson, D. (1986). *Relevance: Communication and cognition*. Oxford: Basil Blackwell.

Stalnaker, R. (1968). A theory of conditionals. In N. Rescher (Ed.), *Studies in logical theory*. Oxford: Oxford University Press.

Stampe, D. (1977). Toward a causal theory of linguistic representations. In P. French, T. Euling, & H. Wettstein (Eds.), *Midwest Studies in Philosophy* (Vol. 2). Minneapolis: University of Minnesota Press.

Staudenmayer, H. & Bourne, L. E. (1978). The nature of denied propositions in the conditional sentence reasoning task. In R. Revlin & R. E. Mayer (Eds.), *Human reasoning*. New York: John Wiley.

Stenning, K. & Levy, J. (1988). Knowledge-rich solutions to the binding problem: A simulation of some human computational mechanisms. *Knowledge Based Systems*, *1*, 143–152.

Stenning, K. & Oaksford, M. (1989). *Choosing computational architectures for text processing*. Technical Report No. EUCCS/RP—28, Centre for Cognitive Science, University of Edinburgh, April, 1989.

Stenning, K., Shepherd, M., & Levy, J. (1988). On the construction of representations for individuals from descriptions in text. *Language and Cognitive Processes*, *2*, 129–164.

Stich, S. (1983). *From folk psychology to cognitive science*. Cambridge, MA: MIT Press.

Stich, S. (1985). Could man be an irrational animal? *Synthese*, *64*, 115–135.

Stich, S. (1990). *The fragmentation of reason*. Cambridge, MA: MIT Press.

Strawson, P. F. (1950). On referring. *Mind*, *54*, 320–344.

Sutherland, S. (1992). *Irrationality: The enemy within*. London: Constable.

Taplin, J. E. (1971). Reasoning with conditional sentences. *Journal of Verbal Learning and Verbal Behavior*, *10*, 219–225.

Taplin, J. E. & Staudenmayer, H. (1973). Interpretation of abstract conditional sentences in deductive reasoning. *Journal of Verbal Learning and Verbal Behavior*, *12*, 530–542.

Thagard, P. (1988). *Computational philosophy of science*. Cambridge, MA: MIT Press.

Touretzky, D. S. (1986). *BoltzCONS: Reconciling connectionism with the recursive of stacks and trees*. Research Report No. CMU-BOLTZ-23, Department of Computer Science, Carnegie-Mellon University, Pittsburgh, 1986.

Touretzky, D. S. & Hinton, G. E. (1985). Symbols among the neurons: Details of a connectionist inference architecture. In *Proceedings of the Ninth International Conference on Artificial Intelligence*, University of California at Los Angeles (pp. 238–243), Los Angeles, CA, August 18–23, 1985.

Tsotsos, J. K. (1990). Analyzing vision at the complexity level. *Behavioral and Brain Sciences*, *13*, 423–469.

Tukey, D. D. (1986). A philosophical and empirical analysis of subject's modes of inquiry in Wason's 2–4–6 task. *Quarterly Journal of Experimental Psychology*, *38A*, 5–33.

Tversky, A. & Kahneman, D. (1971). Belief in the law of small numbers. *Psychological Bulletin*, *76*, 105–110.

Tversky, A. & Kahneman, D. (1973). Availability: A heuristic for judging frequency and probability. *Cognitive Psychology*, *5*, 207–232.

Tversky, A. & Kahneman, D. (1974). Judgement under uncertainty: Heuristics and biases. *Science*, *185*, 1124–1131.

Tversky, A. & Kahneman, D. (1980). Causal schemas in judgements under uncertainty. In M. Fishbein (Ed.), *Progress in social psychlogy*. Hillsdale, NJ: Lawrence Erlbaum Associates.

Tversky, A. & Kahneman, D. (1986). Rational choice and the framing of decisions. *Journal of Business*, *59*, 251–278.

Tweney, R. D. (1985). Faraday's discovery of induction: A cognitive approach. In D. Gooding & F. James (Eds.), *Faraday rediscovered* (pp. 159–209). London: Macmillan.

Vapnik, V. N. (1995). *The nature of statistical learning theory*. New York: Springer.

Veltman, F. (1985). *Logics for conditionals*. PhD Thesis, Faculteit der Wiskunde en Natuurwetenschappen, University of Amsterdam.

Valentine, E. R. (1985). The effect of instructions on performance in the Wason selection task. *Current Psychological Research and Reviews*, *4*, 214–223.

Von der Malsburg, C. & Bienenstock, E. (1986). Statistical coding and short-term synaptic plasticity: A scheme for knowledge representation in the brain. In *Disordered systems and biological organization* (Vol. F20). Berlin: Springer-Verlag.

Von Mises, R. (1939). *Probability, statistics and truth*. London: Allen and Unwin.

Wallace, C. S. & Boulton, D. M. (1968). An information measure for classification. *Computing Journal*, *11*, 185–195.

Wallace, C. S. & Freeman, P. R. (1987). Estimation and inference by compact coding. *Journal of the Royal Statistical Society, Series B*, *49*, 240–251.

Wason, P. C. (1960). On the failure to elminate hypotheses in a conceptual task. *Quarterly Journal of Experimental Psychology*, *12*, 129–140.

Wason, P. C. (1965). The contexts of plausible denial. *Journal of Verbal Learning and Verbal Behavior*, *4*, 7–11.

Wason, P. C. (1966). Reasoning. In B. Foss (Ed.), *New horizons in psychology*. Harmondsworth, UK: Penguin.

Wason, P. C. (1968). Reasoning about a rule. *Quarterly Journal of Experimental Psychology*, *20*, 273–281.

Wason, P. C. (1969). Regression in reasoning. *British Journal of Psychology*, *60*, 471–480.

Wason, P.C. & Golding, E. (1974). The language of inconsistency. *British Journal of Psychology*, *65*, 537–546.

Wason, P.C. & Green, D. W. (1984). Reasoning and mental representation. *Quarterly Journal of Experimental Psychology*, *36A*, 597–610.

Wason, P. C. & Johnson-Laird, P. N. (1970). A conflict between selecting and evaluating information in an inferential task. *British Journal of Psychology*, *61*, 509–515.

Wason, P. C. & Johnson-Laird, P. N. (1972). *The psychology of reasoning: Structure and content*. Cambridge, MA: Harvard University Press.

Wason, P. C. & Shapiro, D. (1971). Natural and contrived experience in a reasoning problem. *Quarterly Journal of Experimental Psychology*, *23*, 63–71.

Wellman, H. M. (1990). *The child's theory of mind*. Cambridge, MA: MIT Press.

West, L. & Pines, A. (Eds.) (1985). *Cognitive structure and conceptual change*. Orlando, FL: Academic Press.

Winograd, T. (1972). *Understanding natural language*. New York: Academic Press.

Winograd, T. & Flores, F. (1986). *Understanding computers and cognition*. Reading, MA: Addison-Wesley.

Winston, P. H. (1977). Learning to identify toy block structures. In P. N. Johnson-Laird & P. C. Wason (Eds.), *Thinking: Readings in cognitive science* (pp. 199–211). Cambridge: Cambridge University Press.

Wolf, F. M. (1986). *Meta-analysis: Quantitative methods for research synthesis.* London: Sage Publications.

Yachanin, S. A. (1986). Facilitation in Wason's selection task. *Current Psychological Research and Reviews, 5,* 20–29.

Young, M. N. & Gibson, W. B. (1962). *How to develop an exceptional memory.* Radnor, PA: Chilton.

Author index

Subject index